FG $5.00

THE RIFT

Off the Richter Scale and into history. . .

It was the U.S. Army Corps of Engineers who finally made the Swampeast habitable. Just south of Cape Girardeau the levee line began, to continue 2,200 miles to the Gulf of Mexico. The levees kept the floodwaters out. During the decades of prosperity, the farmers had forgotten the conditions under which they had prospered were artificial. Southeastern Missouri was as artificial as the Washington Monument, the St. Louis Gateway Arch, or the space shuttle, and like these, existed as a monument to the ingenuity of humankind. The land there had been *manufactured*.

But that which is artificial occupies a precarious position in the world of nature. Its existence depends upon the maintenance of the conditions under which it was designed. The Mississippi River's levee system was built with the understanding that two things would remain constant: The flood waters would not rise much higher than they had in the past, and the land on which the levees were built would not move of its own accord. The first of these constants was violated regularly. The result was a greater commitment to reinforced levees. The second constant, the requirement that the earth not move, had not been tested.

Though such a test, as history showed, was inevitable.

ALSO BY THE AUTHOR

THE RIFT

By
Walter J. Williams

HarperPrism

A Division of HarperCollins*Publishers*

HarperPrism
A Division of HarperCollins*Publishers*
10 East 53rd Street, New York, NY 10022-5299

This is a work of fiction. The characters, incidents, and
dialogues are products of the author's imagination and are not to
be construed as real. Any resemblance to actual events or
persons, living or dead, is entirely coincidental.

Visit HarperPrism on the World Wide Web at
http://www.harperprism.com

❖ 10 9 8 7 6 5 4 3 2 1

This work is dedicated to Willie Siros
without whose information on the geology of
the New Madrid Fault, given over lunch at a
truck stop in Bastrop, this book would not exist.

ACKNOWLEDGMENTS

The author would like to thank Joanna and Hamd Alkhayat for their information on shorting the Eurodollar; Fred Ragsdale; Michael Barrett, Dr. Stephen Howe, Dr. John Darby, PE, and John Metzger for their information on power plants; Pamela D. Clark at the U.S. Army Corps of Engineers' Mississippi Valley Division; Bob Norton for his treasure trove of publications concerning the 1811 New Madrid earthquake; Laura Mixon; Louise "not from Atlantis" Malone for proofreading, general good cheer, and a live wire to the zeitgeist; the Very Small Array (Sage Walker, Pati Nagle, Sally Gwylan, Pat McGraw, Joan Saberhagen, Gene Bostwick, Melinda Snodgrass) for their ruthless advice; "Nurse Nancy" Snyder for putting up with me during a lengthy trek through the historical and cultural sites of the Mississippi Delta; my wife Kathy Hedges for her proofreading and patience; and the commissioners of Kleberg County, Texas, who in a burst of other-worldly inspiration changed their county's official greeting to "heaven-o."

Lights of ships moved in the fairway—a great stir of lights going up and going down. And farther west on the upper reaches the place of the monstrous town was still marked ominously on the sky, a brooding gloom in sunshine, a lurid glare under the stars.

"And this also," said Marlow suddenly, "has been one of the dark places of the earth."

—Joseph Conrad, *Heart of Darkness*

PROLOGUE

LAST CHANT OF
THE SUN MAN

He was a god to his people. He lived high above the earth, in the realm of his brother the Sun, and his rule stretched from the world of life to the world of spirits. His word was absolute. Even the gods respected his desires.

So why did the dogs disturb his dreams? It seemed unfair that he could not order them to stop their howling.

The unearthly crying of dogs awakened the Sun Man before dawn. Leaving the slave Willow Girl asleep on the pallet beneath her buffalo robes, he dressed himself in the dark—a cape of bright bird feathers, a headdress of white swan feathers that ringed his head like the battlements of a tower, an apron of pierced whelk shells brought two thousand miles upriver from the Gulf of Mexico—and then he picked up his boots and made his way out of the long house and into the still, cool predawn air.

"How may I serve the Divine Sun, my husband?" said a voice.

The Sun Man was startled, then annoyed. His wife, the Great Priestess, had a habit of turning up when she was neither wanted nor expected. Now she lay before him, stretched full on the ground in a prostration of respect. He wondered how long she had been there.

The Sun Man dropped his boots before her. "You may lace up my boots, if it suits you," he said.

The Great Priestess rose to her knees. She held out one of his boots, and he stepped into it. Her tattooed face pursed with disapproval as she worked the hide laces.

"That lazy Willow Girl hasn't done the job?" she said. "She doesn't know enough to protect the feet of the Divine Sun against the dew?"

"She was asleep," the Sun Man said.

Her voice grew more severe at this weak excuse. "It is not her business to sleep when the Divine Sun is awake."

"I will speak to her."

"It is a whip of braided deerhide that will do the speaking," the Great Priestess said. "I will see to it myself."

The Sun Man kept his face still. "If you do not think such a matter beneath your notice," he suggested hopefully.

"Nothing that concerns the Divine Sun is beneath my notice," she replied.

The Sun Man restrained another sigh. His wife was the absolute ruler of the household, and he had no business disrupting her domestic arrangements. If she wanted to whip a slave, she could do so. He could only hope that she would do the whipping herself, frail and old as she was, and not order a burly male servant to do the job.

He would have to try to think of a way to make it up to Willow Girl later.

The problem, he reflected, was his wife's common birth. If she had been born into the privileged and sophisticated Sun Clan, the divine rulers of the People, she would have had a greater tolerance for his flings with the slave girls. She would have known that his liaisons meant nothing, that he was merely exercising one of the perquisites of his birth.

But the Sun Clan was very small, and the noble clans weren't very large, either, so both were required to marry outside of their caste, which meant marriages with commoners. The Sun Man's wife had brought her commoner's views into his household, and expected her husband to remain faithful to her bed as if he were merely a farmer or a stinking fisherman. Such behavior was proper to one of the lowborn, perhaps, but certainly not for an all-powerful autocrat whose rule had been ordained in heaven. The Great Priestess did not understand that his slave girls were not a threat to her own position, but were just a way of keeping his bed warm at night. They were an itch that he scratched, nothing more.

The Great Priestess finished tying the laces of his boot. She held out the other, and the Sun Man stepped into it.

"The funeral of your divine brother, the Fierce Badger, was very expensive," she said, her voice deliberately casual.

Here, he thought, was the real reason why he found her waiting here in the doorway.

"True," he said.

"And Eyes of Spring, your sister and the mother of your heir, is growing frail."

"Also true."

"It will be necessary to give her an expensive funeral as well. Should you not consider a war on the northern barbarians by way of acquiring spoils?"

"I will give the matter thought."

He *had* given it thought—these facts were obvious enough—but it was clear that he had not given it as much thought as the Great Priestess.

"The war chief is new to his post," she continued, "and we have a whole class of young warriors that require seasoning."

"Relations with the barbarians are good," the Sun Man said. "There hasn't been any trouble between us in years. I do not want my old age to be troubled by wars, and a war would disrupt our trade northward for copper and pipe clay."

"It is sad that Eyes of Spring is so weak," the Great Priestess reminded. "There will be great mourning soon, and disruptions one way or another."

She tied the bootlace with a little snap of finality, then turned her head to direct her stony face to the horizon. She had made her point, and now her husband was dismissed to go about his business.

Out in the town below, the dogs yowled.

"I will speak to my brother the Sun on this matter," the Sun Man said, and walked across the level, grassy field atop the mound until he gazed over the edge at his sleeping kingdom below.

The Sun Mound on which the Sun Man lived covered ten acres, its base larger than that of the pyramid of the Egyptian king Khafre. Across the plaza was another mound equally as large, the Temple Mound where the Sun Man worshipped his divine brother, the Sun. Each mound had been built over the last hundred years by the painstaking labor of thousands. The great mounds had been raised one basketful of earth at a time, each basketful dug by hand and carried to its destination by a dutiful citizen.

Twelve thousand people lived below the two great earthen mounds, half within the ditch and wooden stockade that surrounded its center. The City of the Sun was one of the great cities of the world, its population larger than that of barbaric Saxon London over four thousand miles to the northeast. Many more thousands of the Sun Man's subjects lived in large towns linked to the city by road and river, and thousands more in small villages or isolated farms. If the Sun Man ordered the new war chief, his nephew Horned Owl, to make war on the barbarians of the northwest prairies, he could bring over three thousand warriors into the field, more if the Sun Man called in the allies. It was the largest armed force on the North American continent, and assured the Sun People's domination of their world.

And the Sun People in turn were dominated by the Sun Man, the divine ruler who held the power of life or death over every single one of them, who spoke daily to his brother, the Sun, the great burning sphere that ruled the heavens and commanded all things on earth.

The Sun Man regulated everything within his empire. The time of planting, the time of harvest. He kept track of the calendar, scheduled all ceremonies, festivals, and initiations; ordered entire populations to report for duty to build mounds, repair the stockade, or maintain roads. He collected taxes in the form of corn, and traded it for precious objects or distributed it in times of famine. Though other chiefs acted as magistrates, the Sun Man was the court of final appeal—he gave justice, imposed fines, and ordered exile, punishment, or death. Although the war chief led the soldiers into battle, it was the Sun Man who declared the war and made the peace that followed.

His word was not only the law, it was the divine law. To defy him was no mere rebellion, it was blasphemy.

If only, he thought, he could command the dogs to be silent. What was bothering them?

The Sun Man began to descend the earthen ramp that led from his Dwelling Mound to the plaza below. Pain shot through his knees and back at the impact of each step. Walking downhill was always painful for him. His shoulders ached so dreadfully that he could barely raise his arms above shoulder height. He had lost half his teeth, and the rest were worn to nubs by grit in the stone-ground maize that made up most of his diet.

The Sun Man was very, very old.

He was forty-one years of age.

At the bottom of the grass ramp the Sun Man met his two chief attendants, his pipe-bearer He Who Leaps Ahead, and his new mace-bearer, Calls the Deer. Both had been about to chant their way up the Sun Mound in order to formally awaken him—approaching the Sun Man required a degree of ceremony—but the dogs had done their job for them. They prostrated themselves before the Sun Man, faces into the turf, outstretched arms offering the pipe and mace for his use. The carved and ornamented pipe and the simple, heavy stone mace symbolized the Sun Man's spiritual and temporal powers, the first able to summon spirits to the earth, the second capable of splitting a man's skull.

"Stand," the Sun Man said.

Calls the Deer, at twenty-five in the prime of life, sprang easily upright, then had to help He Who Leaps Ahead to his feet. The old pipe-bearer's name, the Sun Man thought, no longer reflected the man who stood before him, but instead the swift youth of memory, first in races and first in war, who had joined the Sun Man's official family back when they both, and in memory the world itself, were young. Now Leaps Ahead was ancient, crook-backed and white-haired, the tattoos on his face blurred with age, as if smudged by tears.

The Sun Man cast an admiring glance at Calls the Deer. The young man was a fine example of the noble caste: he was strong, a fine hunter, and his splendid memory gave him perfect recollection of the large number of chants and other religious ceremonies that were a part of his duties. He was deferent to his elders, but knew also how to maintain the dignity of his own high position.

A pity he will die soon, the Sun Man thought. For he knew that he, himself, would not last much longer. And when he died, much of his world would die with him.

> *He who dwells in the sky*
> *He who gives warmth and light to the world*
> *This is the one we come to praise*
> *This is the one whose greatness we come to exalt*

The Sun Man and his attendants wove left and right as they ascended the Temple Mound. It was not proper to face the god directly when approaching him.

> *Let all the world sing his praises*
> *Let the god rise into the sky*
> *Let him bring his blessings to the People.*

Through long practice, the words came easily to the Sun Man's lips. But his mind was occupied by thoughts of life and death.

Barring pains in his joints and in his teeth, the Sun Man remained healthy. He was still able to chant loudly at the ceremonies, participate in some of the slower dances, and pleasure himself with Willow Girl. His mind was clear. But at his age it only took a little thing to bring him down, a chest cold that wouldn't leave, a winter chill, a careless fall.

And when he passed from the world, Calls the Deer would die with him. As would He Who Leaps Ahead, and many others.

For the divine Sun Brother could not go unaccompanied to the spirit world. His two chief attendants would be strangled at the funeral by bowstrings, and so would his wife the Great Priestess, and Willow Girl, and all the slave girls who had borne him children. Members of the Sun Clan—including his sister Eyes of Spring, if she outlived him—would volunteer to be strangled, and so would prominent members of the noble and commoner castes. The cavernous long house atop the Sun Mound would be burned, the mound raised above its ashes, and a new long house constructed for the Sun Man's nephew, who would reign after him.

A new conical burial mound would be raised above the Sun Man, and at least thirty young girls would be laid to rest with him there, and an equal number of young warriors, all to serve the Sun Man in the afterworld. To provide these ghostly servants, any young person would do, including slaves. But if there was not a sufficient supply of slaves, then the People of the Sun would have to volunteer, or be persuaded to volunteer.

That was why the Great Priestess had chosen to speak of war this morning. The funeral of the Sun Man's younger brother, the war chief Fierce Badger, had reduced the number of suitable slaves, and his older sister, Eyes of Spring, was in frail health. If she died soon, a few dozen girls and warriors would be called upon to accompany her. If the supply of attractive, youthful slaves actually ran out, the Sun People themselves might be called upon to die before their time.

When this happened—and if there was an insufficient number of volunteers to make up the difference—there was sometimes an unseemly discord within the Sun People as the community's leaders chose those most suitable for strangulation, always the fittest warriors and the most beautiful and pleasing young women, people whose lives the selfish commoners sometimes wanted to preserve. In the past there had been loud protests and even violence, disharmony that could mar the funerals of the great. It was always good for the community's health if there were a supply of slaves on hand for sacrifice.

That was why the Great Priestess wanted war now, why she wanted the Sun Man to send the new war chief and three thousand warriors marching northeast onto the prairies.

She wanted to make certain that her husband's funeral, which would also be her own, would be suitably grand, and that the mound would be raised above them without disharmony among the People.

There was sense behind this plan, the Sun Man conceded.

But wars, also, lacked harmony. And the Sun Man, perhaps selfishly, did not want strife to mar his last years.

He would speak to his Brother Sun, he thought. And if the Sun was in favor of war, then the Sun Man would order his mace-bearer to carry the declaration of war to the war chief.

> *We obey the words of the Sun*
> *We follow him in all his ways*
> *We chant his praises to all the world*
> *It is our Brother Sun we exalt above all others*

The chant had carried them to the top of the mound. Before them was the big temple with its steeply pitched roof of prairie grasses. Fragrant pine smoke rose to scent the air. The three prostrated themselves before it once again, and then rose to approach the temple.

> *We walk in the ways of the Sun Brother*
> *He will bring us the corn and the deer*
> *He commands the wind and the rain*
> *Our hearts are filled with his essence*

Chanting voices answered from the temple where the night attendants waited. It was their duty to feed the eternal flame, to make sure that this little bit of the sun that glowed atop the altar was never extinguished. Horrid penalties waited for those who neglected this duty and permitted the fire to die, but these hideous tortures had never been inflicted in the Sun Man's lifetime.

The night attendants piled more pine boughs atop the altar. Flames crackled higher. The Sun Man stepped to salute the altar, arms raised high, blazing heat burning on his face and palms. Then he turned to face the East, where the first pearl light of dawn was spreading over the dark horizon.

> He who dwells in the sky
> He who gives warmth and light to the world
> This is the one we come to praise
> This is the one whose greatness we come to exalt

They chanted until the Sun Brother was high above the horizon, until Grandfather River to the east had turned first to gold, then to silver, and the fields and homes of the Sun People shone bright in the cloudless morning.

The Sun Man brought the chant to an end, and there was a moment of silence in which the Sun Man felt harmony radiating over the world like the beams of the sun. And then the dogs began to whine again, and the mood was spoiled.

"What is wrong with the dogs?" said Leaps Ahead. "Is there some kind of sickness among them?"

"Perhaps there is a cougar upwind," said Calls the Deer.

The Sun Man raised his face to the sky. He felt no wind on either cheek. The air was utterly still.

And still the dogs howled.

"If the Divine Sun wishes," Calls the Deer said, "I will order men out to look for a cougar."

"Yes," the Sun Man said. "That would be best. But come back after giving the order—I may have another errand for you." He might have to send the mace-bearer to the war chief with a declaration of war. He turned to He Who Leaps Ahead. "You may go to breakfast, old friend. I won't need you till my afternoon audience."

"As the Divine Sun wishes," Leaps Ahead said.

After the two chief attendants prostrated themselves before the Sun Man and then made their way down the mound, the Sun Man dismissed his other attendants as well. He wanted to be alone to consult the Sun concerning this weighty matter of war.

Beneath the sky's canopy of divine blue, the Sun Man could see the waking city spread out before him. Below the two giant mounds were lesser earthworks, peaked burial mounds and the ridged mounds where the nobles dwelt. Below these lived the commoners in mud-and-wicker buildings with peaked grass roofs. Round granaries were set on stilts to keep animals from plundering them. Smoke rose from breakfast fires, staining the air. Children played ball games in the plaza, women knelt in the open before their homes and ground corn for breakfast, craftsmen sat in the open working with flint or basketry. Fertile cornfields, the source of the Sun People's wealth, stretched out flat almost to the horizon, the young corn turning the red-brown soil to a sea of green.

To the west was the creek that supplied the town with its water. To the east was Grandfather River, the huge brown expanse, over a mile wide, that wound its serpentine way to the Gulf of Mexico far to the south. The City of the Sun was set a respectful distance from the Grandfather River, which usually overflowed its banks twice a year, and in fact sometimes flooded the city itself, forcing its population onto the mounds for protection.

Grandfather River was hidden along almost all its length by the tangle of cottonwood and cypress that lined its banks, but the Sun People had long ago cut all the nearby timber for building and for firewood, and now fields traveled down almost to the water's edge. Crops were planted there following the spring flood. On the water's edge were stacks of wood, lumber rafts that had been floated down Grandfather River and then broken up to provide the city's firewood.

The land, the crops, and the firewood were all owned by women, and descent and ownership traced through the female line—this was why the Sun Man's successor would not be a child of his body, but rather the eldest son of his eldest sister. The Sun Man could not but approve of this arrangement—freed from the distractions of property, economics, and agriculture, the men were able to concentrate on more important matters, like hunting, diplomacy, religion, and war.

War. It would be his decision, taken in consultation with his brother, the Sun. No mortal being had the right to interfere. What he planned to do now was to enter the temple alone, feed the temple's eternal fire with willow bark and tobacco to summon the god, and then explain the problem to his brother. Only then could harmony be achieved and the correct decision made.

But harmony was going to be difficult to achieve, even in the Sun Man's mind. The wailing dogs unsettled his thoughts. Their cries reached a kind of crescendo now, an eerie chorus that sent a shiver of fear up the Sun Man's back.

What is going on? he wondered. *What is happening?*

And then the Earth flung him off its back.

He landed on the turf with a cry, the wind going out of him. His swan-feather headdress fell from his head and rolled away. The mound throbbed beneath his belly, as if a giant was kicking the mound again and again. There was a crackling, snapping sound, and the Sun Man looked over his shoulder to see the great Sun Temple tumble and fall, the cypress posts that supported its roof snapped off clean.

My brother's home! he thought in anguish. The Earth, he thought, had committed a blasphemy against the Sun.

A sulfurous stench assailed his nostrils. The air was filled with a horrid growling noise, like a beast snarling through teeth it had planted in the throat of its prey. The Sun Man clawed at the turf and tried to rise, but the Earth threw him down again. He managed to get to his hands and knees and crawl to the edge of the mound.

A terrible incomprehension filled his mind. The scene before him was so unaccountably strange that he could not wrap his understanding around it.

The ground was heaving up in waves, rolling from east to west like a storm swell on a huge lake. Houses and people were being flung from the green wavetops like driftwood. The grass roofs waved in the weird, turbulent surf, or tumbled down as the lightly built houses collapsed. Great cracks split the earth, and here or there an entire house was swallowed, tumbled into dark chasms. Faint against the sound of the terrible growling, the Sun Man could hear screams and cries for help.

Everywhere, it seemed, the Earth was attacking the Sun People. Huge jets of water shot out of the land, dozens of them, taller than trees, their towering heads crowned with vapor. These fountains flung white sand into the air as well as water, and some had already built tall pale cones around their roots. Some of the water jets even spat big stones from the ground, black rocks large enough to crush houses.

Across the plaza, the Sun Man watched as the Sun Mound, his own home and that of his ancestors, came to pieces. An entire corner of the mound suddenly fell away, slumping onto the flat ground below as if it were nothing more than liquid mud instead of dry soil stabilized by turf. Tons of soil spilled like a wave onto the town below, sweeping away a half-dozen houses. Horror struck the Sun Man as he saw little human figures struggling in the moving flood of soil.

Above, atop the mound itself, the Sun Man's house had fallen as one corner of the foundation spilled down the mound into the town below. The grasses of the crumpled roof thrashed, and the Sun Man hoped that this was caused by survivors trying to dig their way out rather than by the motion of the earth.

The scent of smoke touched his nostrils. He turned, scuttling on hands and knees like an insect, and looked in horror as a tower of flame blazed up above the roof of the Sun Temple. It had fallen onto the roaring altar fire, just stoked with pine logs, and sacred flame had set the roof alight.

No! the Sun Man thought. There were sacred objects inside—ancient pottery and flint, a black stone that had fallen from the sky, figures of gods and animals, and these could not be sacrificed to the flame. The Sun Man tried to rise again, was once more flung to his knees. So he crawled, the Earth's terrible growling in his ears, toward the temple to rescue the holy things.

It was useless. The dry grass roof caught in an instant, and the old cypress log timbers and wickerwork walls were well seasoned. By the time the Sun Man could crawl more than a few paces, the entire structure was ablaze. Heat beat on the Sun Man's face. It was so intense that he had to turn and crawl back the way he had come. The strings holding together his whelk-shell apron had broken, and he trailed carved shells behind him as he crawled.

Still the Earth shook, still her horrid roar rumbled in his ears and in the very marrow of his bones.

It was beyond him. There was nothing he could do in this war of the Earth against the children of the Sun, nothing except finally to remember his chief role, that of intermediary between the people and the divine forces that controlled their world.

He crawled again to the edge of the mound, threw himself flat, and began to pray.

"Brother Sun, rescue us!" he cried. "Earth Woman, please do not punish your children! Cease the war between you!" And then he lost all sense and could only babble.

"My wife!" he said. "My children! Save them! Don't let them die! *Save my babies!*"

At his words, to his own great astonishment, the rumbling ceased. The Earth's violence faded, but the Sun Man could still feel smaller tremors shivering through the ground beneath him.

The Earth had ceased her attacks, and all at his divine command. He blinked in awe at his own power as he looked at the scene below. Thousands of buildings in his city had fallen, almost every one. Many, fallen onto breakfast fires, were now alight, columns of gray smoke rising in the still air. Most of the long wooden stockade that protected the central part of town had fallen. The fountains of water continued to gush from the ground, each now rising from a cone of white sand that had built up around its base. Some of the fountains were luckily placed so as to put out fires, but most just added to the confusion and terror of the people and animals below.

His poor people, he thought. Most that he could see were prone and helpless as himself. A few were on their feet, but they staggered helplessly, as if possessed by a fit. Howling dogs spun in circles or barked and snapped at everyone nearby. Hundreds of children were wailing. Many adults were screaming as well, injured or trapped in fallen houses.

The sky was very strange. A few minutes ago it had been blue and cloudless, but now low clouds were forming, black and threatening. He could see the clouds growing, expanding in the air like a black stain.

"Thank you, Earth Woman!" he said. "Thank you for sparing us!" He peered across the plaza—now torn in half by a rent twenty feet across—and tried to distinguish the few people he could see wandering around the Sun Mound. Had the Great Priestess survived? Eyes of Spring, his sister? His many children? Willow Girl?

The Sun Man tried to stand, but a horrid vertigo seized him, and he fell again. Why was the world so dark? he wondered.

"Praise to the Earth!" he continued automatically. "Praise to Brother Sun!"

He cast a look to the east, to where Brother Sun was rising above the riverbank, and he stared.

Grandfather River, he realized dumbly, was gone. *Gone*. Gone completely. Between the fields on the west side of the river, and the great thicket of oak and cottonwood on the far side—now mostly fallen, he saw—there was nothing but the muddy brown bed of the river, and here and there a long silver pond, all that was left behind when the river left its bed.

Grandfather River *fled*, the Sun Man realized. Horrified by the war between Sun and Earth, the river had turned its face from the world.

A moving cloud crossed the empty riverbed and poured itself across the Sun Man's vision, as if the river had inverted itself into the sky and was now in flood. Passenger pigeons, tens of thousands of them, risen in alarm from the wrecked forests on the far bank, headed west in search of a safe place to land.

"Praise to the Earth!" the Sun Man continued to chant, and turned again to the wrecked city below. He should try to stand again, he thought, and show himself to the people. Demonstrate to them that their divine ruler was unharmed, and ready to face the fearful emergency.

And then an actinic flash lit the dark sky, turning the world into light and shadow, and to the Sun Man's utter horror he saw the lightning strike his ruined house on the Sun Mound. The grass roof exploded, flinging burning thatch in all directions. At once the entire structure was alight. "My children," he moaned.

He had only a few seconds to absorb this dreadful sight before another firebolt lanced down, striking the burning temple behind him. The Sun Man clapped hands to his ears at the shattering sound, and cowered as flaming debris fell around him.

The Divine Sun, his brother, was fighting back, flinging his lightning bolts at the Earth. But his own people were caught in the middle.

"Spare us!" the Sun Man whimpered. "Turn your dreadful lightning away!"

His answer was another flash, another boom. He looked across the plaza to see people spilling down the slopes of the Sun Mound, fleeing from the dreadful thunder. "Don't run!" the Sun Man commanded. "Rescue my family!"

But they could not hear him. Another bolt smashed into a field not far away. The cloud of passenger pigeons overhead dispersed, each bird frantic to escape the blasts. Screams and wails were rising from the city.

"Save us," the Sun Man moaned. "Spare us your anger. Save my family."

But the shattering bolts continued to fall, one after another. The Sun Man felt the hairs on the back of his neck rise, and tried to burrow into the turf of the Temple Mound, clutching the soil with his fingers. The lightning bolt crashed to earth mere yards away. The Sun Man's head rang with the sound. The flash blazed through his closed eyelids. He could smell his own hair burning. Deafened, stunned by the blast and by the catastrophe that overwhelmed him, the Sun Man lay on the scorched grass, unable even to beg the gods for aid. He could hear the shiver and boom of lightning around him, but he kept his face pressed to the mound, cringing from the sound of each blast.

In time the blasts grew less. The Sun Man blinked, opened his eyes. The world was still dark, and low clouds still threatened overhead. Gray smoke rose into the heavens from dozens of fires. Tens of thousands of frantic birds circled madly in the air.

"My family," the Sun Man whimpered. He propped himself up on an elbow and gazed across the wrecked plaza to the Sun Mound.

The long house was still in flames. Nothing living could be seen on the mound, though a few sprawled, motionless figures testified to the deadly nature of the lightning blasts that had rained on the high platform.

The city below was half-concealed by smoke from burning lodges. Only a few stunned human forms moved in the murk. If they were wailing or calling for help, the Sun Man's deafened ears could not hear them. The tall fountains of water had subsided, though their white sand cones still covered the drenched corn fields.

The war between Sun and Earth seemed to have reached a truce.

The Sun Man rose to his knees. "Praise to the Sun Brother," he murmured, and held out his hands, palm upward, in a prayer position. "Save your people." His head whirled.

He looked around, and his mouth dropped open.

Grandfather River was coming back! But he was not returning to the old riverbed; he was pouring across the fields to the south, heading straight for the City of the Sun. *He was running backward, south to north!* And he was angry, foamy white teeth snarling as he rolled steadily toward the city, a wall of brown, churning water ten feet high.

Terror snatched the Sun Man and pulled him to his feet. His head spun. Madly he pointed and shouted at the stunned people below.

"Flood coming!" he cried. "Run to the mounds! Run now!"

A few people stopped and stared. "Run now!" the Sun Man screamed. "Run to the mounds! Grandfather River is flooding!"

The people seemed to be conferring. Only a few began to move toward the earthen mounds.

"Run! Run! Grandfather River is flooding!"

The river's foaming front poured into the southern reaches of the city, sweeping broken houses before it. The river was full of wreckage, entire uprooted trees standing in the flood like fangs. A few people looked south in alarm, but they were on the flat ground, lines of sight broken by mounds and wreckage and smoke, and they could see nothing.

"Run! Run!"

And then the river burst through the broken stockade, rolling the shattered logs of the wall before it like a row of pinecones. The people below stiffened in horror, and then, too late, began to run.

The Sun Man's words dried up on his tongue as the river ran through his city, sweeping away the shattered lodges, carrying the straw roofs and wicker walls along on the white-toothed tide. He saw dozens of people madly trying to swim, others clinging to wreckage and crying for help. Only a few dozen managed to stagger up the Temple Mound's earthen ramp, or climb its steep sides. Others scrambled up conical burial mounds, or clustered on the flat-topped mounds the nobles used for their lodges.

The Sun Man collapsed, wailing. Earth Woman had made war on him, and his divine brother the Sun had abandoned his people.

He would die, he thought. He would refuse food and

water, and he would perish along with his nation. He sat down on the Temple Mound, crossed his legs, and began to sing a song of death.

His people, cowed by the world's inexplicable fury, did not dare to approach him.

Within a few hours the river's level had dropped, and the survivors gazed down to a mass of wreckage that littered a steaming swamp.

Other than the rubbish that floated in the still water, and the mounds with their clusters of stunned, homeless refugees, nothing remained of the greatest city that had ever been raised on the continent of North America.

PART ONE

It is a remarkable fact, that there is a chain of low, level and marshy lands, commencing at the City of Cape Girardeau, in Missouri, and extending to the Gulf of Mexico; and between these two points there is not a rock landing except at the small town of Commerce, on the west side of the Mississippi River; there is, furthermore, only one ridge of high land from Commerce to be met with on the west side of said river, which is at Helena, in Arkansas.

Report on the Submerged Lands
of the State of Missouri (1845)

ONE

The horizon immediately after the undulation of the earth had ceased, presented a most gloomy and dreadful appearance; the black clouds, which had settled around it, were illuminated as if the whole country to the westward was in flames and for fifteen or twenty minutes, a continued roar of distant, but distinct thunder, added to the solemnity of the scene. A storm of wind and rain succeeded, which continued until about six o'clock, when a vivid flash of lightning was instantaneously followed by a loud peal of thunder; several gentlemen who were in the market at the time distinctly perceived a blaze of fire which fell between the centre and south range of the market.

Earthquake account, Feb 12, 1812

The sound of drumming and chanting rolled down from the old Indian mound as the school bus came to a halt. Jason Adams wanted to sink into his seat and die, but instead he stood, put his book bag on one shoulder, his skates on the other, and began his walk down the aisle. He could see the smirks on the faces of the other students as he headed for the door.

He swung out of the bus onto the dirt road. Heat blazed in his cheeks.

"Wooh!" one of the kids called out the window as the bus pulled away. "I can feel my chakras being actualized!"

"Your mama's going to Hell," another boy remarked with satisfaction.

Jason looked after the bus as it lurched down the dirt road, thick tires splashing in puddles left by last night's rain.

Another few weeks, he thought, and he wouldn't have to put up with them anymore.

Not for the length of the summer, anyway.

The drumming thudded down from the old overgrown mound. Jason winced. Aunt Lucy must have let his mother off work early. There wasn't going to be a lot of business at the greenhouse till Memorial Day.

It was bad enough that his mom was a loon. She had to drum and chant and *advertise* she was a loon.

Jason hitched the book bag to a more comfortable position on his shoulder and began the short walk home.

Green shoots poked from the cotton field to the north of the road. The furrows between the green rows were glassy with standing water. *Swampeast*, they called this part of Missouri, and the name was accurate.

The inline skates dangled uselessly off Jason's shoulder. Gravel crunched under his shoes. He could put up with the drumming, he thought, if only he were back in L.A. Drumming was even sort of normal there—well, not normal exactly, but there were other people who did it, and most other people didn't make a point of telling you that it qualified you for eternal damnation.

Jason passed by the Regan house, a new brick place on the lot next to where Jason lived with his mom. Mr. Regan was as usual puttering around *Retired and Gone Fishin'*, his bass boat parked inside his carport. So far as Jason could tell, Mr. Regan spent more time polishing and tinkering with his bass boat than he did actually fishing. The old man straightened and waved at Jason.

"Hi." Jason waved back.

"Found a place to skate yet?" Mr. Regan asked.

"No." Other than the outdoor basketball court at the high school, which was usually full of kids playing basketball.

Mr. Regan tilted his baseball cap back on his bald head. "Maybe you should take up fishin'," he said.

Jason could think of many things he'd rather do with his life than sit in a boat and wait for hours in hopes of hauling a wet, scaly, smelly, thrashing animal into the boat with him.

He really didn't even care for fish when they were cooked and on a plate.

"Maybe," he said.

"I could give you some lessons," Regan said, a bit hopefully.

Regan had made this offer before. Jason supposed that he sympathized with his neighbor's being retired and maybe a bit lonely, but that didn't mean he had to assist him in his rustic amusements.

"Maybe after school's out," Jason said.

After he finally went crazy from living in the Swampeast, he thought, sitting in a boat next to a stack of dead fish might not seem so bad.

The drum boomed down from the mound behind the houses. Jason waved to Mr. Regan again and cut across the soggy lawn to the old house where he and his mother lived. Batman, the dog that belonged to the Huntleys on the other side of his house, ran barking toward Jason in order to warn him off. Jason, as usual, ignored the dog as he walked toward his front porch.

Jason's house was very different from the four modern brick homes that shared its short dirt road. A dozen or so years ago, when the farmer who owned this area decided to retire, he sold the cotton fields to the north of the dirt road and created a small development south of it—two new brick homes built on either side of his own house, four altogether. When his widow died, Jason's mother had bought the old farmhouse, and when Jason first saw it, four months ago, he thought it looked like the house that Dorothy lived in before she went to Oz. It was a turn-of-the-century frame farmhouse, large and spacious, painted white. There were a lot of things that Jason liked about the house: the funky old light switches, which had pushbuttons instead of toggles. The crystal doorknobs and the old locks on all the bedroom doors, some of which still had their skeleton keys. He liked the sashes that made a rustling sound inside the windowframes when he lifted the windows, and he liked the screened-in front porch with its creaking floorboards. He liked the tall windows with the old, original window glass that had run slightly—he remembered his science teacher telling him that glass was really a liquid, just a *very slow* liquid—and which gave a slightly distorted, yellowish view of the world. He liked the extra room, because the house was intended for a much bigger family than the two people who lived in it now, and he liked having more space than he'd had in L.A., and having a room up on the second floor with a view.

But the view was of the wrong part of the world, and that was what spoiled everything.

Jason bounded across the porch, unlocked the front door with its fan-shaped window, and dumped his book bag on the table in the foyer. The house welcomed him with the smell of fresh-cut flowers that his mom brought home from Aunt Lucy's greenhouse. He passed through the dining room—Austrian crystals hung in the window, spreading rainbows on the wallpaper—and into the small, old kitchen that his mother was always complaining about. More crystals dangled in the windows there. Jason opened the refrigerator and poured himself a glass of water from the plastic jug, careful not to pour out the large quartz crystal that his mother had placed in the jug.

"The crystal expands the energy field of the water from one foot to ten feet," his mother had explained, "and then you can drink the energy."

He had never asked why he would want to drink energized water. The explanation would only have made his eyes glaze anyway.

He drank half the glass of water and refilled it, then returned the jug to the refrigerator. He took an orange from the refrigerator drawer, used a knife to cut it into quarters on the ancient zinc countertop, dropped the knife in the sink, and then—his stomach presumably radiating powerful metaphysical energy ten feet in all directions—he went up the narrow back stair from the kitchen to the second floor.

He went into the corner room he thought of as his study, with his computer, desk, and skating posters, and flicked the switch on his computer's power strip. The sound of his mother's drumming came faintly through the closed windows. Jason sucked the juice from a slice of orange while he looked out the side window.

To the east, the dirt road dead-ended against the green wall of the levee, the huge dike that kept the Mississippi from flooding into their front yard. The river was normally invisible, hidden by the cottonwood thicket that stretched almost a half-mile from the levee to the riverbed, but the river was unusually full right now, with the spring melt and a long series of rains, and had flooded partway up the levee. Through the tangled trees, Jason could glimpse an occasional patch of gray water.

He had thought, when told he would be living near the Mississippi, that he would at least be able to watch the boats go by, maybe even big white sternwheelers like on television, but the combination of the impenetrable underbrush and the levee's big green barricade had blocked any view from the flat ground. Even when he climbed onto the old Indian mound behind the house to see well over the levee, he could see water only here and there.

He turned his eyes to the north window, where the rain-soaked cotton field stretched on to a distant row of trees on the horizon. The cotton field was mostly brown earth marked by the wide rows of young green cotton, but here and there the soil was stained with circular pale blooms, as if God with a giant eyedropper had splashed white sand down onto the rich soil. Jason had sometimes wondered about those circular patches, but he hadn't thought to ask anyone.

The land was so flat that the trees at the end of the cotton field seemed to mark the edge of the world, hedging it to the north just as the levee did to the east. The only thing he could see past the trees was the tall water tower in Cabells Mound, the town where he went to school. The modern tower, all smooth curved metal, looked like a toilet plunger stuck handle-first into the ground.

He narrowed his eyes. He had plans for the water tower.

He wanted to climb the spiral metal stair that wound to the top, put on his skates, hop on the metal guard rail, and wheelbarrow down to the bottom: back skate in the royale position, crosswise on the rail, front skate cocked up so he was rolling only on its rear wheel.

He'd go down the spiral rail, *fast*, with centrifugal force, or whatever it was called, threatening to throw him off the tower at any second.

And then he wanted to do something cool and stylish on landing, like landing fakie, a 180-degree spin on the dismount to land moving backward; act as if zooming at high speed a couple hundred feet to the ground, right on the edge of wiping out the whole time, wasn't *anything*, was just something he did every day, and required a little flourish at the end to make it special.

That, he thought, was Edge Living. Edge Living was something to aspire to.

His mouth went dry at the thought of it.

The only question, of course, was whether he'd ever dare try it. He'd done the wheelbarrow on rails before, but the rails were all straight, not curved outward, and he'd never wheelbarrowed more than a single story.

Three metal-guitar chords thrummed from the computer. "I am at your service, master," it said.

Jason turned his attention to the screen. His friends in California, he thought, wouldn't be back from school for another couple hours.

He'd browse the Web, he thought, and check out all the chat lines devoted to skating.

For most of the eleven hundred years since the time of the Sun Man, the old Temple Mound had seen little change. The area remained a wilderness, low-lying and marshy and flooded every few years. The Mississippi flung itself left and right like a snake, carved a new course with every big flood. Every time it shifted course, it deposited enough silt over the next few years to raise the area through which it traveled. Then another flood would spread the river wide, and the river would find an area lower than that which it had built up, and carry its silty waters there.

Over the years the Mississippi had carried away the Sun Mound, the big mound where the Sun Man had built his long lodge and where he had lived with his family. Many of the smaller mounds had also been flooded away during inundations, and the rest had been plowed under by farmers, who saw no reason why some aboriginal structure should impede the size of their harvest.

Only the Temple Mound remained, the huge platform structure from which the Sun Man had witnessed the destruction of his people. The Mississippi had spared it, and the white men and their plows, daunted by its size, had spared it as well. The Cabell family, who had grown corn and wheat on the land for three generations, gamely holding on through deluge and drought and civil war, had built their home on one of the mound's terraces, safe from the floodwaters that regularly covered their corn fields. But even they had given up in the end, abandoning their home in the 1880s after too many floods had finally broken their spirit. The Swampeast had finally defeated them, just as it had defeated so many others. Nothing was left of the home now, nothing but some old foundation stones and a broken chimney covered with vines, and the mound was overgrown, covered with pumpkin oak and slippery elm and scrub.

It was the U.S. Army Corps of Engineers who finally made the Swampeast habitable. Just south of Cape Girardeau the levee line began, to continue 2,200 miles to the Gulf of Mexico. The long green walls, supported by a mammoth network of reservoirs, floodways, flood gates, flood walls, pumping stations, dikes, cutoffs, bendway weirs, and revetments, were unbroken save for where tributaries entered the Mississippi, and the tributaries were walled off as well, some for hundreds of miles. The levees kept the floodwaters out and finally permitted the farmers to clear the land and till their soil in peace. Cotton replaced wheat and corn in the 1920s, and the farmers grew wealthy on the rich alluvial soil.

During the decades of prosperity, the farmers had forgotten that the conditions under which they had prospered were artificial. The natural state of the land was a swampy, tangled hardwood forest, subject to periodic inundations. The People of the Sun, whom the whites later called "Mississippians" or "Mound Builders," had altered the land for a while, had changed its natural state from a nearly impenetrable hardwood thicket to corn fields dominated by huge earthen monuments, but the land reverted swiftly to its natural state once the Sun Man's time had passed. Now the cotton fields, graded to perfect flatness by laser-guided blades, stretched west from the levees, but they had been imposed on the land, and so had the titanic earthworks that protected them. The condition of southeastern Missouri was as artificial as that of the Washington Monument, the St. Louis Gateway Arch, or the space shuttle, and, like these, existed as a monument to the infinite ingenuity of humankind. The land, like the space shuttle, had been *manufactured*.

But that which is artifice occupies a precarious position in the world of nature. Artificial things, particularly those on the scale and complexity of the space shuttle, or of the levee system of the Mississippi, are manufactured at great cost, and must be maintained with great vigilance. Their existence is dependent on the continuation of the conditions under which they were designed. The space shuttle *Challenger* was destroyed when one of its systems was unable to react with sufficient flexibility to an unseasonable frost.

The levee system, on the other hand, was built with the understanding that two things would remain constant. It was understood that flood waters would not rise much higher than they had in the past, and that the land on which the levees were built would not move of its own accord. If either of these constants were removed, the levee system would not be able to prevent nature from returning to the highly artificial landscape which the levees were built to preserve.

The first of these constants was violated regularly. The epic flood of 1927 made obsolete the entire levee system, which was reengineered, the levees being built higher, wider, and with greater sophistication. The flood of 1993 again sent water to a record crest right at the juncture of the Mississippi and the Missouri, and briefly threatened to make St. Louis an island. The inevitable result was a greater commitment to reinforced levees.

The second constant, the requirement that the earth not move, had not been tested.

Though such a test, as history showed, was inevitable.

> INLYNE: I'm just bummin because I haven't got anyplace to sk8.

> DOOD S: Im almost the only aggressive sk8r here.

Where, Jason typed, is here?

He was almost holding his breath. Assuming that Dood S was female, which was likely if the online handle was intended to be pronounced "dudess," Jason might have found himself a potential girlfriend. So far Jason discovered that he and Dood S were the same age. They agreed on bands, on skate brands, and on the study of history ("sux"). They were both reasonably advanced skaters. They could royale and soyale, they could backside and backslide, they could miszou, they could phishbrain and Frank Sinatra. They were both working on perfecting various alley oop maneuvers, but Dood S was making more progress because she, or possibly he, had a place to skate.

The answer flashed on the screen.

> DOOD S: Shelby Montana.

> INLYNE: Bummer.

Jason's answer was heartfelt.

> DOOD S: Where RU?

INLYNE: Cabells Mound, Missouri.

DOOD S: Where is that?

Good question, Jason thought.

Between Sikeston and Osceola, he typed, feeling sorry for himself. If he were feeling better about living here, he might have mentioned St. Louis and Memphis.

DOOD S: hahahahaha Im sorry.

INLYNE: Me too.

Jason heard the door slam downstairs. His mom must be home.

RU a girl? he typed. Flirtation was fairly useless if they lived a thousand miles away from each other, but what the hell. He was lonely. It never hurt to stay in practice.

DOOD S: Cant U tell?

Your pixels look female to me is what Jason wanted to type, but he couldn't quite remember how to spell "pixel," so he typed, I think you are a girl.

DOOD S: Im 85 and Im a peddofile hahahahahaha. Want to meet me in the park little boy?

INLYNE: Very funny.

This was not lightening Jason's mood. He heard his mother's footsteps on the front stair, and turned as she passed by the door. She was wearing jeans and a tank top. Her cheeks glowed, and there was a sheen of sweat on her chest and throat.

"Hi," Jason said. "Have fun?"

"It was exhilarating!" she said. "I really felt actualized this time! I could feel the energies rising from the mound!"

"Great," Jason said.

Catherine Adams was tall and trim and blonde. One of Jason's friends had once described her as a babe, which had startled him. He hadn't thought of his mother in those terms. But once it was pointed out to him, he had realized to his surprise that she was, indeed, an attractive woman. At least compared to the mothers of most of his friends.

Catherine walked into the room, her drum balanced on her hip. "Talking to your friends?" Her voice was husky from chanting.

"Yes." He turned and saw Dood S's last statement.

> Dont mind my jokes hahahahaha Im toking as Im typing.

Jason looked at the screen and concluded that this really wasn't his day. Catherine looked over his shoulder at the screen and he could hear a frown enter her voice. "Is this anyone *I* know?"

"No," Jason said. He was tempted to say, *He's a pedophile in Montana,* but instead said, "Someone I just met. Some little town in Montana. Don't worry, she's not going to sell me any grass."

"We'll talk about this later," Catherine said. There was an ominous degree of chill finality in her tone.

"Right," Jason said.

About 8 o'clock, a fifth shock was felt; this was almost as violent as the first, accompanied with the usual noise, it lasted about half a minute: this morning was very hazy and unusually warm for the season, the houses and fences appeared covered with a white frost, but on examination it was found to be vapour, not possessing the chilling cold of frost: indeed the moon was enshrouded in awful gloom.

Louisiana Gazette *(St. Louis)*
Saturday, December 21, 1811

Supper was *not* a good experience. Jason ate chicken soup left over from the weekend and day-old homemade bread while his mother quizzed him on the temptations of the Internet. "You spend too much time online," she said.

"My *friends* are online," Jason said. "It's cheaper than calling them long distance."

"You need to make new friends here," Catherine said. "Not hang out with druggies on your computer."

"I can't get high online," Jason pointed out. He could feel anger biting off his words. "I was just waiting in the chat room for Abie and Colin. I can't ask everyone in the chat room whether they do drugs before I talk to them."

"Drugs are a black hole of negativity," Catherine said. "I don't want you around that scene."

"I'm not into drugs!" Jason found himself nearly shouting. "I couldn't skate if I took drugs, and all I want to do is skate!"

"What's on the Web that's so wonderful?" Catherine demanded, her own anger flaring. "Drugs and porn and *advertising*. Nothing but commercialism and materialism—"

"Talk!" Jason waved his hands. "Conversation! Information! My *friends* are online!"

"You need to make friends here," she said. "We live in Missouri now."

"I don't *need* to make friends here! I've already *got* friends! And the second I can get back to them, I will!"

She looked at him from across the table. The anger faded from her expression. She looked at him sadly.

"You can't go back to California," she said. "You know why."

"I know, all right," Jason said.

Concern filled her eyes. "If you go back to California," she said, "you'll die."

Jason looked at the framed photograph of Queen Nepher-Ankh-Hotep that sat on the side table between two sprays of Aunt Lucy's irises. The Egyptian queen looked back at him with serene kohl-rimmed eyes.

"So I hear," he said.

* * *

Back in 1975, an Oregon housewife named Jennifer McCullum was informed by a vision that in a previous life she had been Queen of Egypt. So benevolent and spiritual had been her reign that she had since been incarnated many times, always with her consciousness located on a higher celestial plane than most of the other people stuck on this metaphysical backwater, the earth. Subsequent visions instructed the reincarnated monarch in spiritual techniques which she subsequently taught to her disciples. According to her own account, around the same time as the "Nepher-Ankh-Hotep Revelations," as they were subsequently called, McCullum also began to experience another series of visions terrifying in their violence and destruction: communities ravaged by earthquake and fire, flood and tidal wave. These visions were first experienced in black-and-white, like an old newsreel, but by 1989 McCullum was receiving in full color. Eventually, with the aid of a disembodied Atlantean spirit guide named Louise, McCullum was able to piece together the narrative thread of her visions.

In the near future, McCullum reported, a series of natural disasters would strike North America. California would be leveled by earthquakes and would then drop into the sea. Other bits of the American continent were also doomed, either by quake, submergence, tornadoes, volcanoes, or "poisonous vibrations." Atlantis would rise from the Atlantic, and Lemuria from the Pacific, causing tidal waves that would wash most coastal cities out to sea.

Few places on earth would be safe from this apocalypse.

Among them, the former Queen of Egypt asserted, were several states in the American heartland, among them Missouri. Positive vibrations emanating from the Memphis Pyramid would exert a spiritually calming influence on the surrounding countryside.

Which was why Catherine Adams moved herself and her son Jason to Cabells Mound, where her Aunt Lucy, recently widowed, needed someone to help out in her greenhouse business.

And which was why city boy Jason, skilled at urban pastimes like inline skating and speeding packets of data along the Information Superhighway, found himself among the watery cotton fields of the Swampeast.

"Have you ever thought," Jason said, "that Queen Pharaoh Nepher-Whatsis is just plain *crazy*?"

"How can you say that?" Catherine asked. "She's only trying to help people. She wants to save our lives. Nepher-Ankh-Hotep means 'Gift of a Beautiful Life.' She is the most actualized being I have ever met."

Actualized. There was that word again. Every time he listened to his mother talk about metaphysics, she'd use a term like *actualized* or *negative thoughtform* or *color vibration*, and Jason's brain would simply shut down. It was as if his understanding had run smack into a linguistic wall. What did these words mean, anyway?

They meant whatever his mother wanted them to mean. They all meant, *You have to stay here and like it.*

"And it's not just Nepher-Ankh-Hotep," Catherine said. "*Lots* of people have received catastrophe revelations. They *all* agree that California is going to be destroyed."

"So Colin's going to be killed? And Aunt Charmian. And Abie?" He looked at her. "*Dad* is going to be killed?"

His mother gazed at him sadly. "It's not up to me. It's karma. California has so much negative karma that it can't survive, and it's going to be wiped out for the same reason Atlantis was destroyed. But we can always hope that our friends will survive, the way the people from Atlantis survived and went to Mexico and Egypt. But if they *do* die, it's because they *chose* it, they chose this incarnation in order to experience California's destruction."

Jason could feel his brain de-focusing under this onslaught—he couldn't understand why people, or even disembodied spirits, would choose to experience mass destruction, why they'd line up to get annihilated like people paying for the earthquake ride at Universal Studios—but he gathered his energies and made the attempt.

"What's wrong with California's karma, anyhow?" he asked. "And how can a whole state have karma anyway? And why," warming to the subject, "is Missouri's karma supposed to be all that great? They had *slavery* here. And all those Cherokee died just north of here on the Trail of Tears."

The Trail of Tears had been the subject of a field trip the previous month.

It had rained.

Jason, stuck in an alien land, in lousy weather, and far from his spiritual home, had taken the Cherokee experience very much to heart.

"I am trying to save your life," Catherine said.

"I'll take my chances in L.A.! My karma can't suck that badly!"

"We were talking," Catherine said, narrowing her eyes, "about the Internet. I don't want you spending all your time online—I want you to restrict yourself to an hour a day."

Jason was aghast. "An hour!"

"One hour per day. That's all." There was a grim finality in Catherine's tone. "And I want you to make some effort to make friends here."

"I don't *want* to know anyone here!"

"There are good people here. You shouldn't look down at them just because they don't live in the city. You should get to know them."

"How?" Jason waved his hands. "How do I meet these good people?"

"You can stop radiating hostility all the time, for one thing."

"I don't radiate hostility!" Jason shouted.

"You certainly do. You glare at everyone as if they were going to attack you. If you met them halfway—"

"I am *not interested*! I am *not interested at all*! One minute after I'm eighteen, I'm out of here!" Jason bolted from the dinner table, stormed up the stairs to his study, slammed the door, and turned the skeleton key that locked it.

His mother's voice came up from below. "You better not be online!"

Jason paced the room, feeling like a trapped animal. His life was one prison after another. He was a minor, completely dependent on other people. He was in an alien country, walled off by the levee, with nothing but soaked cotton fields to look at. His school, with its red brick, concrete, and windows protected by steel mesh, even *looked* like a prison.

And now he was in a prison cell, on the second floor of his house.

And the worse thing about *this* cell, he realized, was that he had turned the key on himself. He had to get out of here somehow.

As he paced, his eye lighted on the telephone, and he stopped in his tracks.

Ah, he thought. *Dad.*

"Well," Jason said, "I'm bummed. I sort of had a fight with Mom."

"Have you apologized?" said Frank Adams.

This was not the initial response that Jason had hoped for. "Let me tell you what it was about," he said.

"Okay." Frank sounded agreeable enough, but over the phone connection Jason could hear his father's pen scratching. The pen was a Mont Blanc, and had a very distinctive sound, one loud enough to hear over a good phone connection. Frank was working late at the office, which was normal, and Jason had called him there.

"Mom says I have to restrict my Internet access to one hour per day. But the Internet is where all my friends hang out."

"Okay."

"Well," Jason said, "that's *it.*"

"That's what the whole fight was about?"

"There was a lot more about karma, and how yours sucks so bad you're going to get washed out to sea along with my friends, but keeping me offline is what it all came down to."

"Uh-huh." There was a pause while the pen scratched some more. Then the pen stopped, and Frank Adams's voice brightened, as if he decided he may as well pay attention, "It wasn't about your grades or anything?" he asked.

"No. My grades are up." The Cabells Mound school was less demanding than the academy he'd been attending in California. Also far more boring—but that, he'd discovered, applied to the Swampeast generally and not just to school.

"So if it's not interfering with your schoolwork, why is she restricting your Internet access?"

Jason's dad was very concerned with grades and education, not for themselves exactly, but because they led to success later on. Frank was big on hard work, dedication, and the rewards the two would bring. Jason's mom, by contrast, thought of this goal-oriented behavior as "worshiping false, nonintegrative values."

"She wants me to spend more time doing stuff here. But there's nothing to do here, so—"

"She wants you to try to make friends in Missouri."

Jason could not understand how his parents knew these things about each other. Were they telepathic or something?

"Well, yeah," Jason said. "But there's, like, no point to it. Because the second I'm eighteen, I'm checking out of this burg."

"You've got a few years till then," his father pointed out.

"But I'm going to be spending as much time in L.A. as I can between now and then."

"Jason." His father's voice was weary. "Where are you going to be spending most of your time between now and your graduation?"

Jason glared out the window and realized he was trapped. "Here," he said. "In Missouri."

"So isn't it, therefore, a good idea to get to know some people where you live? Maybe date a few girls, even?"

Jason never liked it when his father started using words like *therefore*. It meant he was doing his whole lawyer thing, like he was talking to a witness or something. It was as bad as when his mother talked about negative thoughtforms.

"I don't *mind* making new friends," he said. "But I want to keep the ones I've got, too, and I can't do that unless I stay in touch with them."

"I will speak to your mother about your Internet privileges, then. But I won't do it for another week or ten days, because I want you to soften her up between now and then, okay? Try to make an effort? Take someone home? Play a game of baseball? Something?"

Jason glared at his reflection in the blank computer screen. "I'll see what I can do," he said.

"Good."

Jason made a grotesque face into the computer screen. Snarled, bared his canines, made his eyes wide. His distorted reflection grimaced back at him like a creature out of a horror film. "I was wondering," Jason began, "if I could come and stay with you after you and Una get back from China."

Jason heard a page turn over the phone, and then heard his father's pen scratching again. "I don't think that's such a good idea," Frank said. "I'm going to be working sixteen-hour days to catch up on the work I've missed. I wouldn't really have a chance to spend time with you. It wouldn't be fair to Una to have to spend all her time looking after you."

"I wouldn't bother her. I can just hang with my friends."

"You'll still be able to visit in August, like we planned."

"I could house-sit for you, while you're gone."

Frank's pen went *scratch, scratch.* "I don't think so," he said. "I don't want to leave you alone in the city all that time. What if you got into trouble?"

What if I didn't? Jason wanted to respond.

"Or I could fly to China and join you there," he said instead.

His father gave a sigh. Jason could hear the pen clatter on the desktop. "This is my first vacation in almost ten years," Frank said. "I'm a partner now. It used to be that partners took it easy and waited for retirement, but that's not how it works anymore. Partners work harder than anyone else."

"I know," Jason said. He remembered the last vacation, ten years ago in Yosemite. He didn't remember much about the park, he could only remember being sick to his stomach and throwing up a lot.

"Una and I have never had much time alone together,"

Frank said. "We're going to be meeting her family, and that's important."

And a step-kid, Jason thought, *would just get in the way.*

Una, whom Frank had finally married a few months ago, was half Chinese. The Chinese part of the family was scattered all through Asia, and Frank and his new bride were going to travel to Shanghai, Guangzhong, Hong Kong, Singapore, Bangkok, and Kuala Lumpur, seeing the sights and meeting the relatives.

Jason made another grotesque face into the computer screen.

He did not dislike Una, who had made a determined effort to become his friend. But she troubled him. For one thing, she was young enough, and pretty enough, for him to view as desirable. That she sometimes figured in his fantasies made him uncomfortable. For another, her moving in with his dad made it that much less likely that Jason would himself be able to move in with Frank.

And thirdly, she was monopolizing Frank's first real vacation in a decade, and going to places Jason very much wanted to see.

"I wouldn't get in your way," Jason said. "I'd just go off and, like, see stuff."

Frank's pen kept skritching on. "You don't *do* that in Asia," he said. "Besides, we're going to be spending most of our time with a lot of old people who don't speak English, and you'd be bored."

"No way."

Frank sighed again. "Look," he said. "We *need* this trip, okay? But we'll go to Asia another time, and maybe you can come along then."

In another ten years maybe, Jason thought. He made a screaming face into the video monitor, mouth open in a hideous mask of anguish.

"Okay," he said. "But you'll talk to Mom about the Internet, okay? Because if I can't visit China, I want at least to visit their homepage."

"I'll do that," Frank said. His tone lightened. "By the way,

I bought your birthday present today. It's sitting right here in the office. I think you're going to like it."

"I'll look forward to seeing it," Jason said. Perhaps the only benefit of the divorce had been that, in the years since, the size and expense of Jason's presents had increased. "I don't suppose you're going to tell me what it is."

"That would spoil the surprise."

Jason could hear his father's pen scratching again, so he figured he might as well bring the conversation to an end. After he hung up, he sat in his chair and stared across the sodden cotton field to the line of trees on the distant northern horizon.

No Shanghai, no Hong Kong, no Internet. No California till August.

The Cabells Mound water tower stood beyond the line of trees, the setting sun gleaming red from its metal skin.

Jason looked at the tower for a moment, then at the Edge Living poster on the wall, the extreme skater, armored like a medieval knight, poised on the edge of a gleaming brushed aluminum rail. He turned his eyes back to the water tower.

Yes, he thought.

If he couldn't escape his fate, he could at least make a name for himself here.

TWO

By a gentleman just from Arkansas, by way of White river, we learn that the earthquake was violent in that quarter that in upwards of 500 places he observed coal and sand thrown up from fissures in the earth, that the waters raised in a swamp near the Cherokee village, so as to drown a Mr. Carrin who was travelling with his brother, the latter saved himself on a log. —In other places the water fell, and in one instant it rose in a swamp near the St. Francis 25 or 30 feet; Strawberry a branch of Black river, an eminence about 1–1/2 acres sunk down and formed a pond.

St. Louis, February 22, 1812

The ringing signal purred in Nick Ruford's ear. He felt adrenaline shimmer through his body, kick his heart into a higher gear. He felt like a teenager calling a girl for the first time.

It was Manon who answered. His nerves gave a little leap at the sound of her voice.

Stupid, he thought. The divorce was two years ago.

But he couldn't help it. She still did that to him.

"Hey," he said. "It's me."

"Hey, yourself," she said. There was always that sly smile in her contralto voice, and he could tell from her intonation, the warmth in her tone, exactly the expression on her face, the little crinkles at the corners of her eyes, the broad smile that exposed her white teeth and a little bit of pink upper gum. With the gum exposed like that it should not be an attractive smile, but somehow it was.

"You finished with the move?" Manon asked.

Nick looked around the room with its neatly stacked boxes under the eye of Nick's father, who gazed in steely splendor from his portrait on the wall, and for whose spirit no stack of boxes would ever be neat enough. "Oh yeah," he said. "I'm moved in. I just don't have a place for everything yet."

Don't have a place for myself *yet*, he thought. That's the trouble.

"Is it a nice apartment?"

Nick looked out the window at the crowded sidewalk, the people hanging out on the streets. The windows were closed, and the air-conditioning unit in the window turned up high, so that Manon couldn't hear the boom box rattling away from the front porch. "Well," he said, "it's *urban*, you know, but it isn't squalid. And my building is nice."

And would be nicer. Once he finished wallpapering Arlette's room, he could move her furniture in there, the mattress and frame that were now occupying most of the living room.

"It was Viondi found it, right?"

"Uh, yeah."

"I can just imagine."

Sudden resentment sizzled along Nick's nerves. Manon always knew how to get to him. *I can just imagine*. His friends weren't good enough, his apartment wasn't good enough, his job wasn't good enough. *He* wasn't good enough.

And it wasn't like she even meant to put him down, not really. Her damn spooky family had been royalty so long in their little part of Arkansas that it was natural for her to judge other people, judge them without even thinking about it. There wasn't any malice in it, not really.

"Can I talk to Arlette?" he asked.

"She's in her room. I'll get her."

Over the phone he heard Manon's heels clacking on the polished cypress floor of their old house. Nick paced up and down next to the dinette set, working off his aggravation. Was it his fault he'd been laid off at McDonnell? Or that a weapons systems engineer was a useless occupation in the aftermath of the Cold War?

He looked at the portrait of his father: Brigadier General

Jon C. Ruford, U.S. Army, winner of the Distinguished Service Cross for service in Vietnam and the Soldier's Medal for service out of it. Author of *Sun Tzu and the Military Mind* (1985), and one of the first dozen or so black men to rise in the Army to the rank of general officer, clearly destined for higher rank until forced to resign by the multiple sclerosis that finally killed him, four years later, in the V.A. hospital here in St. Louis.

You didn't tell me, Nick silently told the portrait, that I was going to be made obsolete. That I was going to be as much a dinosaur as you are.

Arlette's young voice brightened his thoughts. *"Allô, papa! J'ai des nouvelles merveilleux! Une situation vai a devenu libre!"*

Nick tried to find his way through this torrent of half-understood words. His last real exposure to French had been years ago, when his father was stationed at NATO headquarters in Brussels. "Good news?" he said. "Uhhh . . . *bien.*"

"Je vais à l'école d'été après tout! Je vais passer l'été à Toulouse!"

Nick's heart sank as he deciphered Arlette's phrases. He glanced into the room he was preparing for her, at the stack of wallpaper and the gilt-edged mirror . . . his hand automatically touched the pocket where he carried the gift he'd bought her today, and which he really couldn't afford. A gold necklace in the shape of a lily, sprinkled with diamonds and rubies, and matching earrings. A real grown-up gift.

He had imagined her eyes lighting up as she opened the gift-wrapped box. He had imagined the way she'd gasp in delight and wrap her arms around his neck and breathe her warm thanks against his neck.

And now he'd never see it. Now he'd just have to give the package to Federal Express and experience his daughter's joy only in his imagination.

"That's great, baby," Nick said. "That's wonderful." He tried hard to keep the disappointment from his voice. "When does summer school start?"

"Right after school ends here," Arlette said, switching—Nick was grateful—to English. "The school in Toulouse doesn't open right away, but Mrs. Rigby said she'd take some of us to France for ten days of travel beforehand."

"That's wonderful, honey," Nick said. His hand clenched into a fist, and he wanted to drive it through the newly papered wall.

It wasn't that he didn't think his daughter shouldn't spend the summer in France. It was a wonderful opportunity, and she would be staying with a French family and getting a lot of exposure to a world she hadn't seen, which could only do her good after Manon decided their daughter was going to grow up as African-American royalty in some little half-assed village in Arkansas.

Manon's family, the Davids, had been royalty for generations. Back before the Civil War they'd been Free Men of Color in New Orleans, and they'd spoken French at home, pronounced their name "Dah-veed," and sent their sons to France to be educated. After the war the Freedmans' Bureau had created a utopian colony of freed slaves in Arkansas, and the Davids had condescended to be put in charge of it.

Unlike most of the colonies the Freedmans' Bureau planted, the one in Toussaint, Arkansas, had prospered. Partly because of its isolation—none of their white neighbors really *wanted* the land—and partly because of the Davids. In Toussaint the Davids owned the hardware store, and the grocery, and the pharmacy. And the lumber yard, the feed store, and the town's one office building. And probably the traffic light, too.

And they still gave their kids French names, and sometimes sent their kids to France for an education. Even if, as in Arlette's case, it was summer school in Toulouse.

But Nick wanted her *here*. He craved her presence. He yearned for her. He needed his daughter in his life, not as just a tantalizing, infuriating ghost he could only hear on the telephone.

And besides, he didn't have a job now. He could spend time with her, not like before, when he was working and barely saw his family at all.

He had rented a two-bedroom apartment, more than he could afford, so that she could have a nice room when she spent the summer with him. Along with the bed with the graceful rococo scalloped headboard, the chest of drawers, the gilt-edged mirror with the decals of roses along the borders.

All money he could not afford to spend. And now he would be expected to pay for half of the cost of Arlette's trip to France.

"How did things go with Lockheed-Martin?" Arlette asked, almost as if she was reading his mind.

"Same story in Colorado as everywhere else." Nick tried to keep his voice cheerful. "Over two hundred applicants for the same job, and the ones already laid off from Lockheed get priority over the ones that got laid off from Boeing-McDonnell and Hughes."

If only, he thought, *we could get a nice juicy war started. Not a bad war,* he immediately corrected, *not with a lot of casualties or anything. Just some murdering old dictator that needs removing.* It wasn't like there weren't plenty to go around. One lousy dictator, and the defense dollars would start flowing again.

"You'll find a place, Daddy," Arlette said.

"Oh yeah," Nick said. "Sooner or later, baby, somebody's gonna want an engineer."

I hear Burger King is hiring, he thought.

And with unemployment running out along with his bank account, it would probably come to that soon.

Omar Paxton chose to take the oath under the statue of the Mourning Confederate in front of the courthouse. It was just as well he did it outdoors: there were so many reporters clustered around that they would never have fit inside Judge Moseley's office. Some of the boys turned up with rebel flags to provide a colorful and ideologically significant background, and Wilona was there to stand beside him, wearing white gloves, a corsage, and the pearls that her great-aunt Clover had left her in her will.

Trying to ignore the constant whirring and buzzing of the cameras, which sounded louder than the cicadas in the surrounding blackjack oaks, Omar put his hand on the judge's well-worn Bible and swore to uphold the laws of the State of Louisiana and Spottswood Parish, and added a "So help me God!" for the benefit of his friends and of the media. Rebel yells rang out from the crowd. Confederate flags waved in the air, the sunshine turning their color a brilliant red. Judge Moseley held out his hand.

"Good luck there, Omar," he said.

Omar shook the hand. "Thank you kindly, Mo," he said. Moseley's little waxed white mustache gave a twitch. Only certain people in the parish were high enough in caste to call the judge by his nickname, and Omar had just announced that he considered himself among them.

Omar put on his hat and turned to face the crowd of people. He waved to Hutch and Jedthus and a few of the others, and then turned to kiss Wilona on the cheek. People in the crowd cheered. He beamed down at the crowd, and waved some more, and encouraged Wilona to wave with a white-gloved hand. He looked into the lens of a network cameraman.

Got you all, you bastards, he thought.

After the media storm and the court challenge and the recount, after the governor had called him a reptile and the Party had disavowed his very existence, Omar Bradley Paxton had finally taken the oath of office and was ready to begin his term as sheriff of Spottswood Parish.

"Do you plan to make any changes in the department?" a reporter shouted up.

Omar smiled down at him. *Little weevil,* he thought. "I don't anticipate any major changes," he said. "Maybe we'll save the people some tax dollars by putting regular gas in the patrol cars, 'stead of premium."

The locals laughed at this. Omar's predecessor had been prosecuted, though not convicted, for taking kickbacks for keeping Pure Premium in all the county's cars.

The next question was shouted up by a little red-haired lady reporter with a voice like a trumpet. "Will there be any change in the style of law enforcement here in Spottswood Parish?"

"Well, ma'am," tipping his hat to the lady, "we *do* plan to continue giving tickets to speeders and arresting drunks."

More laughter. "What I meant," the woman shouted up, "was whether the department will change its racial policy?" Omar's ears rang with her shrill tones.

"Ma'am," Omar said, and tried not to clench his teeth, "the racial policies of the department and the parish are determined by law. You have just heard me swear to uphold and enforce that law. I would be in violation of my oath were I to make any changes upholding illegal discrimination."

Take that, you little red-haired dyke, he thought.

"Do you plan," shouted a foreign-accented voice, "to resign your position as King Kleagle of Louisiana?"

Omar recognized a German reporter, one of the many foreigners who were putting their pfennigs into the local economy as they covered his story. He couldn't help but smile.

"The voters of Spottswood Parish knew I belonged to the Klan when they elected me," he said. "Obviously they decided that my membership in the world's oldest civil rights organization was not an important issue. I can think of no reason why I should resign at this point, not after the voters and the courts have validated my candidacy. My family has lived in this parish for seven generations, and people knew what they were getting when they elected me."

Rebel yells whooped up from the crowd. Confederate flags waved at the election of the first admitted Klan leader of modern times.

Up your ass, you kraut-eating Dutchman, Omar thought, and smiled.

"God damn," Judge Chivington muttered. "Where did all these good-looking Klansmen come from? Back when I grew up in Texas, none of 'em had chins, and they all had puzzel-guts and weighed three hunnerd pounds. And that was just the *women*."

The President cast a professional eye over Omar Paxton's chiseled features.

"David Duke's good looks came from a plastic surgeon," he said. "He looked like a little weasel before Dr. Scalpel and Mr. Bleach made him a blond Aryan god. But this gent," nodding at the evening news, "I believe he just has good genes."

"The man was made for television," sighed Stan Burdett, the President's press secretary, who, with his bald head, thin lips, and thick spectacles, was not.

"He was made for givin' us *shit*," the judge proclaimed. "That fucking weevil could cost us Louisiana in the next election."

"We kicked him out of the Party," the President offered.

"We'll be lucky if he don't take half the Party with 'im."

The President sat with his two closest friends in one of the private drawing rooms in the second floor of the White House. He had never been comfortable with the formal displays of antiques and old paintings so carefully arranged in much of the public White House—he felt uneasy living in a museum, and privately cursed Jacqueline Kennedy, who had found most of the antiques and furniture in storage and spread them throughout the house, so that every time he turned around he was in danger of knocking over a vase once owned by Mrs. Rutherford B. Hayes, or a pot that James Monroe might have pissed in.

So he had filled his own apartments with far less distinguished furniture, comfortable pieces which, even if they might date from the Eisenhower Administration, were scarcely refined. Even Jacqueline Kennedy couldn't reproach him for putting his feet up on *this* couch.

The President settled comfortably into his sofa and reached for his Pilsner Urquell. "So," he said, "how do you stop Party members from bolting to Omar Paxton?"

"Discredit him," Stan said.

The judge cocked an eye at the younger man. "Son," he said, "we're talkin' 'bout *Louisiana*. Nothing makes the Louisiana voter happier than casting a ballot for someone he *knows* is a felon. If Jack the Ripper had been born in Plaquemines Parish, they'd have a statue to the son of a bitch in the statehouse in Baton Rouge."

Stan was insistent. "There's got to be *something* that'll turn his people against him."

"Maybe if you get a photo of Omar there in bed with Michael Jackson," the judge said, then winked. "But I don't guess he's Michael's type."

"What part of Louisiana is he from, anyway?" Stan asked.

The President smiled. "The part where they name their children 'Omar,'" he said.

It was one of the President's rare free nights. Congress was in recess. Nobody in the world seemed to be dropping bombs on anybody else. There was little on the President's schedule for the rest of the week other than a visit to an arts festival at the Kennedy Center. The First Lady was in Indiana making speeches against drunk drivers, a cause with which she had become identified—and a politically safe issue, as Stan had remarked, as there were very few voters who were actually in *favor* of drunk driving, and most of those were too inebriated to find a polling place on election day.

Since everything could change in an instant, the President reckoned he should take advantage of the opportunity to relax while it was offered.

It was characteristic of him, though, that his idea of relaxation consisted of spending an evening watching CNN, drinking Bohemian beer, and talking politics with two of his cronies.

The President removed a briefing book on economics that sat on his couch—the G8 economic summit in London was coming up in a few weeks—and then he put his feet up and raised his beer to his lips. "We can hope that Omar over there is just a fifteen-minute wonder," he said. "He's just some deputy lawman from the sticks, you know—he's not used to this kind of scrutiny. He could self-destruct all on his own."

Stan's spectacles glittered. "So I suppose you won't be discussing Sheriff Paxton when you have that meeting at Justice next week."

"I don't believe I said that." The President smiled.

"Oh God, you're not gonna *investigate* the boy, are you?" the judge interrupted. "You've already halfway made him a martyr." He waved one arm. "What you want to do, hoss, is buy the next election for his opponent, even if the man belongs to the other party. Then Omar there will be a *loser*. That'll tarnish his damn badge for him."

The President looked at the Judge and smiled. Chivington was one of his oldest allies, the heir to an old Texas political family that had once controlled fifty thousand votes in the lower Rio Grande Valley—a hundred thousand, if you counted the voters in the cemeteries. He had spent ten terms in the House of Representatives, and then, having lost his seat in one of those vast political sea-changes that swept the country every dozen years or so—that in his case swept even the graveyards—he'd been a federal judge known for outspokenness on the bench, extravagant behavior off it, and the highest number of calls for impeachment since the glory days of Earl Warren. Since his retirement he'd joined a law firm in D.C. and become an advisor to the powerful—including the young telegenic fellow he'd helped to win the White House.

"I am keeping all my options open in regard to Sheriff Paxton," the President said.

"That's fine for now." The judge nodded. "But you've got to take care of that problem before the next election. Trust me."

The President nodded. "He's on the agenda."

Stan looked at the television again, at the picture of Omar Paxton taking the oath. "*Made* for television," he said, and his voice was wistful.

"There's a thousand reporters here," Omar said later, addressing his deputies in the little high-ceilinged lounge the parish pretended was something called a "squad room." "Most of them are going to go home before long, but there's still going to be a lot of attention placed on this parish."

"So," Merle said as he stood by the machine and poured himself coffee. "No incidents."

"Particularly no incidents that could be described as racially motivated," Omar said.

"We don't get to have no fun at all?" Jedthus asked. He had to raise his voice to be heard over the air conditioner that rattled in the window. "We don't even get to knock the heads of the niggers we're *used* to knocking?"

"We live in a video world," Omar said. "Let's remember that half the people in this state have camcorders, and they'd just *love* a chance to earn ten grand selling the tabloids pictures of one of us whacking some coon upside the head. And then you'd be on network news, and we'd all be so surrounded by federal agents and judges and lawsuits we wouldn't be able to do *anything*."

"Damn." Merle grinned. "For ten grand, *I'd* sell pictures of y'all."

Merle settled with his coffee onto the cheap sofa. Cracks in its orange plastic had been repaired with duct tape.

"Just take it easy for now," Omar said.

"By the way," said Merle, "I heard from D.R. at the Commissary. He was afraid that the election might scare all the little niggers away from the camp meetings this summer."

"Awww." Jedthus moaned with mock sympathy.

"Well," Merle said defensively, "they bring a lot of money into this parish. And a lot of it gets spent at the Commissary. It ain't like D.R.'s got that much money to spare."

The Commissary was the general store in Shelburne City, and had retained its name from the time when it was the company store of the Shelburne Plantation, which had once occupied much of the parish. Now it was owned and run by D.R. Thompson, who had married Merle's sister Cordelia. D.R. was all right, Omar figured. He had slipped Omar some under-the-table contributions during Omar's campaign and was a prominent business leader, for all that his business was just a general store. So he deserved some reassurance.

Omar nodded. "Tell D.R. we're not fixing to do anything to the tourists. In fact," he added, "I'll talk to him myself."

"But Omar." Jedthus looked pained. "When *are* we going to get to do something, you know, special?"

Omar fixed Jedthus with a steely eye. "Wait for the word,"

he said. "We've got to get these bloodsucking reporters out of here first."

"Churches and meeting halls burn up real nice," Jedthus said.

"One damn church," Omar scowled, "and we'd have the FBI moving in with us for the next five years." It was one of his nightmares that someone—possibly someone he hardly knew—was going to get overenthusiastic and create what would literally be a federal case.

The whole point of the Klan, he knew, was violence. The Klan often gave itself the airs of a civic organization, interested in charities and betterment—but the truth was that if people wanted civic betterment, they'd join the Rotary.

You joined the Klan because you wanted to be a part of an organization that stomped its enemies into the black alluvial soil of the Mississippi Delta. And what Omar had to do now was restrain his followers from doing just that.

"Concentrate on lawbreakers," Merle advised. "Just do your regular job."

Jedthus scowled. Omar looked at his deputy and sucked his teeth in thought.

The problem was, he had been elected by people looking for *change*. And change wasn't exactly in his power. He couldn't change the last fifty years of history, he couldn't repair the local economy, he couldn't alter the power of the liberal media or the Jews or the federal government. He couldn't change Supreme Court rulings, he couldn't deny black people the welfare that guaranteed their independence from white control. Least of all, he couldn't alter the situation by cracking heads. Cracking heads would only make the situation worse. Getting himself or one of his deputies thrown in jail wasn't going to help anybody.

"Jedthus," Omar said, "don't do anything you don't want to see on the six o'clock news. Remember Rodney King, for God's sake. That's all I'm saying." He winked. "Things'll change. Our time will come. You know that."

"Reckon I do," said Jedthus, still scowling. He cracked his big knuckles.

Omar looked at Merle with a look that said *You'll speak to Jedthus about this little matter, won't you?*, and Merle gave an assuring nod.

"I've got an interview with somebody from the *Los Angeles Times*," Omar said. "Guess I've kept the little prick waiting long enough."

He left the squad room with a wave. "See you-all at the shrimp boil," he said.

Omar lived in Hardee, twelve miles from Shelburne City, just north of the Bayou Bridge. The house he shared with Wilona was of the type called a "double shotgun," two long, narrow shiplap homes that shared a single peaked roof. Early in his marriage, when Wilona had first got pregnant, he'd borrowed some money from his father and his in-laws, bought both halves of the house, knocked down some of the walls separating the two units, and created a spacious family home. They'd raised their son David here, and saved enough money to send him to LSU.

Though he and Wilona—chiefly Wilona—had created a pleasant little oasis on their property, with a lawn and garden and a pair of huge magnolias to shade it all in summertime, the rest of the neighborhood was less impressive. The asphalt roads were pitted and badly patched, with grass and weeds springing up here and there. The houses were a mixture of old shotgun homes and newer house trailers, with an occasional clapboard church. Cars and trucks stood on blocks in front yards. Some of the vehicles had been there so long they were covered by vines, and fire ants had piled conical mounds around the deflated tires. Cur dogs lolled in the shade, dozens of them. Laundry hung slack on lines. Old signs were still pegged on front lawns: *Omar Paxton for Law and Decency.* Confederate flags hung limp in the still air.

Omar waved to everyone as he drove slowly through the neighborhood in his chief's cruiser. People waved back, shouted out congratulations.

These were the people who had turned out in droves to see

him elected, who had overturned the local establishment and put him in office.

Maybe now, he thought, *we can get the roads resurfaced.*

He pulled into his carport and stepped from its air-conditioned interior into the Louisiana heat. The air was so sultry, and hung so listlessly in the still afternoon, that Omar thought he could absolutely feel the creases wilt on his uniform. He sagged.

People used to work in this heat, he thought. He himself had spent one whole day chopping cotton when he was a teenager, and by the end of the day, when he'd quit, he knew he'd better finish high school and get a job fit for a white man.

Sweat prickled his forehead as he walked the few paces from the carport to his front door. Inside, chill refrigerated air enveloped him, smelling of chopped onion and green pepper. He stopped inside the door and breathed it in.

"Is that potato salad I smell?" he said cheerfully. He took off his gun belt—damned heavy thing—and crossed the room to hang it from the rack that held his .30-'06, his shotgun, his Kalashnikov, and the Enfield his multi-great grandfather had carried in the War Between the States.

Wilona—who pronounced her name "Why-lona"—came from the kitchen, an apron over her housecoat. "Enough potato salad for twenty people," she said. "There aren't going to be more, are they?"

"I don't know. I didn't do the invitations." He kissed her.

Wilona's expression brightened. "Look!" She almost danced to the coffee table, where she picked up a cream-colored envelope. "Look what else we got!"

Omar saw the address engraved on the envelope and smiled. "I was wondering when this was going to come."

"Mrs. Ashenden invited me to tea on Wednesday!" Wilona's eyes sparkled. She was happy as a child at Christmas.

Omar took the envelope from her, slipped the card out of the envelope, opened it. Looked at the elegant handwriting. "Very nice," he said. "Guess we're among the quality now."

"It's so exciting!" Wilona said. "We finally got an invitation to Miz LaGrande's! It's just what we've wanted!"

What Omar wanted, actually, was for Mrs. LaGrande Davis Rildia Shelburne Ashenden to die, choke on one of her little color-coordinated petit fours maybe, and for her big white house, Clarendon, to burn to the ground. She was the last of the Shelburne family, and they'd been in charge of Spottswood Parish for too long.

"I'll have to find a new frock," Wilona said. "Thank God I have Aunt Clover's pearls."

"Your frocks are fine." Omar put the invitation back into its envelope and frowned. "You'll buy a new frock for old Miz LaGrande and you didn't buy one for my swearing-in?"

She snatched the invitation from his hand. "But I'll be going to Clarendon! Clarendon is different!"

"I wouldn't buy a new frock for some old biddy who will never give us the vote," Omar said. "Is there beer in the ice-box?"

"I bought a case yesterday. There was a sale at the Super-B."

Omar found some Coors Light in the icebox, twisted off the tops of two bottles, and returned to the living room to hand one to Wilona. She was sitting on the couch, paging through a copy of *Southern Accents* that she'd probably bought the second she'd received Miz LaGrande's invitation.

Wilona took the beer she handed him and sighed. He had neglected to bring her a glass.

Wilona had always harbored ambitions above her station, probably inherited from her mother, who was a Windridge but who had done something disgraceful at LSU and ended up living with her shirttail relatives in Shelburne and had to marry a filling station owner.

Wilona longed for the lost world of mythic Windridge privilege. She longed to have tea at Clarendon and join the Junior League and wear crinolines at Garden Club functions. She wanted to be Queen of the Cotton Carnival and every so often invite a select group of friends to a pink tea, where everything, including the food, was color-coordinated, and even the waiter wore a pink tie.

Omar knew that none of this was ever going to happen.

Even Windridge pretensions had never extended that far. Instead of the pink teas, there would be shrimp boils, and fish fries, attendance at Caesarea Baptist, and meetings where people wore hoods of white satin and burned crosses. This was Wilona's destiny, and his. This was the fate to which their birth had condemned them.

And it was the quality, the people like Miz LaGrande, who did the condemning. Whose gracious lives were made possible by the sweat of others, and who somehow, along with their white houses and cotton fields, had inherited the right to tell everyone else how to run their lives.

It was traditional, in Spottswood Parish, for anyone running for office to have tea at Clarendon, explain what they hoped to accomplish, and ask for Miz LaGrande's blessing on their candidacy.

Omar had not gone to tea at Clarendon. He had just announced he was running, and then he ran hard. He beat the Party, and then the official candidate, and then the courts. And all the opposition ever managed to do was make him more popular and more famous.

And he did it all without asking Miz LaGrande for anything. And he never *would* ask her for anything. Not a damn thing. Not ever.

But now Miz LaGrande was fixing to have that tea, after all. And not with Omar, but with his wife.

The old lady still had a few brain cells left, that was clear.

"Miz LaGrande has never been interviewed by the *Los Angeles Times*," Omar said. "No Yankee reporter is ever going to ask her for *her* opinion, I bet. I reckon German television isn't gonna send a camera crew to Clarendon."

"Of course not." Wilona paged through her magazine, sipped on her beer.

"What's so great about the Shelburnes?" Omar asked. "They come out here from Virginia, they ship in a couple hundred niggers from Africa to do their work for them, and they build a Greek temple to live in. Would you call that normal?"

Wilona looked up from her magazine, her eyebrows

tucked in a frown. "Don't be tacky," she said.

"She's trying to get at you because she can't get at me. She's trying to get you on her side."

"Oh, darlin', it's just tea. And I'm always on your side, you know that." She turned the page, and then showed Omar a picture. "Look at that kitchen! Isn't that precious?"

Omar looked at the polished cabinets and the cooking implements, some of them pretty strange-looking, hanging from brass hooks. "It's nice," he said.

"It's precious," She looked wistfully at the picture, then looked up at Omar. "Can't we have a kitchen like this? Can't we have a new house?"

"Nothing wrong with the house we live in now," Omar said.

"Of course there's nothing wrong with it," Wilona said. "I just think we deserve something better after all these years. You've got a much better salary now, and—"

"People voted the way they did for a reason," Omar said. "They voted for us because they thought we were just like them. Because we lived in their neighborhood, because they saw us in their church, because they knew we were born here, because we didn't pretend to be anything we weren't. Because we live in a double shotgun that we fixed up, okay?"

Wilona cast a wistful look at her copy of *Southern Accents*. "I just want some things in my life to be lovely," she said.

He fixed her with a look. "Wilona," he said, "it's too late to pledge Chi Omega now."

She looked away. "That was a mean thing to say, Omar."

"It's true, ain't it?"

"You should shower and change your clothes. We'll be late for the shrimp boil."

The phone rang. Omar took a pull from his long-neck, then rose from the couch to answer. It was his son David.

"Congratulations, Dad!" he said. "I'm popping a few brews to celebrate!"

"Thanks." Omar felt a glow kindle in his heart. David was finishing his junior year at LSU and would be the first Paxton ever to graduate from college. Omar had got David through some rocky years in his teens—the boy was hot-tempered and had traveled with a rough crowd—but now David was safe in Baton Rouge and well on his way to escaping the shabby, tiny world of Spottswood Parish.

A place that Omar himself planned to escape, rising from his double shotgun home on the wings of a Kleagle. Once you get the people behind you, he thought, who knew how far you could go?

The concussions of the earthquake still continue, the shock on the 23rd ult. was more severe and larger than that of the 16th Dec. and the shock of the 7th inst. was still more violent than any preceding, and lasted longer than perhaps any on record, (from 10 to 15 minutes, the earth was not at rest for one hour.) the ravages of this dreadful convulsion have nearly depopulated the district of New Madrid, but few remain to tell the sad tale, the inhabitants have fled in every direction . . . Some have been driven from their houses, and a number are yet in tents. No doubt volcanoes in the mountains of the west, which have been extinguished for ages, are now opened.

Cape Girardeau, Feb. 15th, 1812

"This is delicious, Rhoda," Omar said. He had some more of the casserole, then held up his plastic fork. "What's in it?"

Rhoda, a plump woman whose shoulders, toughened to leather by the sun, were revealed by an incongruous, frilly fiesta dress, simpered and smiled.

"Oh, it's easy," she said. "Green beans with cream of mushroom soup, fried onion rings, and Velveeta."

"It's *delicious*," Omar repeated. He leaned a little closer to speak above the sound of the band. "You wouldn't mind sending the recipe to Wilona, would you?"

"Oh no, not at all."

"This casserole is purely wonderful. I'd love it if Wilona knew how to make it."

Another vote guaranteed for yours truly, he thought as he left a pleased-looking constituent in his wake.

He wasn't planning on staying sheriff forever. He had his machine together. He had his people. The state house beckoned. Maybe even Congress.

How long had it been since a Klan leader was in Congress? A *real* Klan leader, too, not someone like that wimp David Duke, who claimed he wasn't Klan anymore.

Omar waved at D.R. Thompson, the owner of the Commissary, who was talking earnestly with Merle in the corner by the door to the men's room. D.R. nodded back at him.

Ozie's was jammed. The tin-roofed, clapboard bar past the Shelburne City corp limit had been hired for Omar's victory party, and it looked as if half the parish had turned out for the shrimp boil and dance.

The white half, Omar thought.

Omar sidled up to the bar. Ozie Welks, the owner, passed him a fresh beer without even pausing in his conversation with Sorrel Ellen, who was the editor and publisher of the *Spottswood Chronicle,* the local weekly newspaper.

"So this Yankee reporter started asking me about all this race stuff," Ozie said. "I mean it was Klan this and militia that and slavery this other thing. And I told him straight out, listen, you've got it wrong, the South isn't about race. The South has its own culture, its own way of life. All everybody outside the South knows is the race issue, and the South is about a lot more than that."

"Like what, for instance?" Sorrel asked.

"Well," Ozie said, a bit defensive now that he had to think about it. "There's football."

Sorrel giggled. For a grown man, he had a strange, high-pitched giggle, a sound that cut the air like a knife. Being too close to Sorrel Ellen when he giggled could make your ears hurt.

"That's right," he said. "You got it right there, Ozie." He turned to gaze at Omar with his watery blue eyes. "I think Ozie has a point, don't you?"

"I think so," Omar agreed. He turned to Ozie and said, "Hey, I just wanted to say thanks. This is a great party, and I just wanted to thank you for your help, and for your support during the election. Everybody around here knows that there's nothing like an Ozie Welks shrimp boil."

"I just want you to do right by us now you've got yourself elected," Ozie said. He was a powerful man, with a lumberjack's arms and shoulders, and the USMC eagle-and-globe tattooed on one bicep and "Semper Fidelis" on the other. His customers cut up rough sometimes—pretty often, to tell the truth—but he never needed to employ a man at the door. He could fling a man out of his bar so efficiently that the drunk was usually bouncing in the parking lot before the other customers even had time to blink.

"I'll do as much as I can," Omar said. "But you know, with all these damn Jew reporters in town, it's going to be hard."

"I hear you," Ozie said.

Sorrel touched Omar's arm. "I'm going to be running an editorial this Saturday on welfare dependency," he said. "It should please you."

Omar looked at the newspaperman. "Welfare dependency, huh?" he said.

"Yeah. You know, how we've been subsidizing bad behaviors all these years."

"Uh-huh." Omar nodded. "You mean like if we stop giving money to niggers, they'll go someplace else? Something like that?"

"Well, not in so many words." Sorrel winked as if he were confiding a state secret. "You're going to like it."

"So I'm going to like it, as opposed to all the editorials you've been running which I *didn't* like."

Sorrel made a face. "Sorry, Omar. But you know a paper's gotta please its advertisers. And the folks who pay my bills weren't betting on you winning the election."

Omar looked at the publisher. "You betting on me now, Sorrel?"

Sorrel gave his high-pitched giggle. "I reckon I know a winner when I see one," he said.

"Well," Omar said. "God bless the press."

He tipped his beer toward Ozie in salute, then made his

way toward the back of the crowded bar. Sorrel, he had discovered, was not untypical. People who had despised him, or spoken against him, were now clustering around pretending they'd been his secret friends all along. A couple of the sheriff's deputies, and one of the jailers, standoffish till now, had asked him for information about joining the Klan. Miz LaGrande was more discreet about it, with her hand-written invitation on her special stationery, but Omar could tell what she was up to. People were beginning to realize that the old centers of power in the parish were just about played out, and that there was a new force in the parish. They were beginning to cluster around the new power, partly because they smelled advantage, partly because everyone liked a winner.

Omar was perfectly willing to use these people, but he figured he knew just how far to trust them.

He stepped out the back door into the dusk. People had spilled out of the crowded bar and onto the grass behind, clustered into the circle of light cast by a yard light set high on a power pole. Wild shadows flickered over the crowd as bats dove again and again at the insects clustered around the light. The day's heat was still powerful, but with the setting of the sun it had lost its anger.

Omar paused on the grass to sip his beer, and Merle caught up to him. "I spoke to D.R. about that camp meeting matter," he said. "I squared it."

"Thanks," Omar said. "I don't want people scared of losing their incomes just 'cause I got elected."

"Not *our* people, anyway."

"No."

"And I think I calmed Jedthus down. Though it's hard to tell with Jedthus."

Omar frowned. "I know."

Merle grinned. "Hey, wasn't it nice of the Grand Wizard to turn up?"

"Yep." Omar tipped his beer back, let the cool drink slide down his throat.

"He said he wanted to speak with you privately, if you can

get away."

"Yeah, sure." Omar wiped his mouth. "Do you know where he is?"

"Talking to some folks over in the parking lot."

"Right." He put a hand on Merle's shoulder and grinned. "We're doin' good, ain't we?"

Merle grinned back. "You bet, boss."

Omar crossed to the gravel parking lot and found the Grand Wizard perched on the tailgate of his camper pickup, talking to some of the locals. He was a small man, balding, who dressed neatly and wore rimless spectacles. He was not much of a public speaker, and even the white satins he wore on formal occasions did little more than make him look like a grocery clerk decked out for Halloween. He had risen to his position as head of the Klan—this particular Klan anyhow—by virtue of being a tireless organizer. He ran things because it was clear that nobody else would do it as well, or as energetically. In his civilian life, he ran a bail bond agency in Meridian, Mississippi.

"Hi, Earl," Omar said.

The Grand Wizard looked up and smiled. "Damn if it ain't a fine day," he said. "I was tellin' the boys here how good you looked on television."

"Knowing how to use the media," Omar said, "that's half the battle right there."

"That's right." The Grand Wizard looked down at the ice in his plastic go-cup and gave it a meditative shake. "That's where the Klan's always been strong, you know. The uniforms. The burning crosses. The flags. They strike the eye and the heart. They makes you *feel* something."

"That's why I took the oath in front of the statue," Omar said.

The Grand Wizard gave a sage nod. "That's right," he said. "Give everyone something to see and think about. The Mourning Confederate. The Cause that our people fought and died for. The Cause that still lives in our hearts. It speaks to everyone here."

"Amen," one of the boys said.

"We send signals to *our* people," Omar said. "The media and the others read it however they like, but *our* people know the message we're sending."

"That's right." The Grand Wizard nodded.

"Merle said you wanted to talk to me or something?" Omar said.

"Oh, yeah." The Grand Wizard slid off his tailgate to the ground. "Now if you gentlemen will excuse us . . ."

Omar and the Grand Wizard walked off to the side of the parking lot, where rusty barb wire drooped under the glossy weight of Virginia creeper. The sound of "Diggy Diggy Low" grated up from Ozie's, where the fiddler was kicking up a storm.

"I was wondering if you could address our big Klanvention on Labor Day," the Grand Wizard began.

"Sure," Omar said.

For years, white supremacists had a big Labor Day meeting in Stone Mountain, Georgia. But the Grand Wizard had quarreled with the Stone Mountain organizers, and he'd started his own Labor Day meeting in Mississippi. He was always working hard to get more of the troops to turn out to his Klanvention than to the other meeting.

The Grand Wizard did not march to anyone else's drum. He was the leader, and that was that. And if other people didn't like it, they could just go to Stone Mountain.

Which brought to mind another problem, Omar thought. Whenever anyone in the Klan had challenged the Grand Wizard's authority, the Grand Wizard had succeeded in cutting them off or driving them out of the organization.

Omar was now a good deal more famous than the Grand Wizard would ever be. If he wanted to take control of the entire Klan, Omar could probably do it.

But he didn't *want* to become the new Grand Wizard. King Kleagle of Louisiana, as far as Omar was concerned, was quite enough work. Earl could stay in his office in Meridian and organize and speechify and push papers forever, and with Omar's blessing.

Omar wondered if the Grand Wizard understood this. He

should find the moment, he told himself, and reassure the man.

"You come to the Klanvention," the Grand Wizard was saying, "we'll get our message on TV. And every time we get media attention, we get more members." The Grand Wizard grinned out into the night. His teeth were small, like a child's, and perfectly formed. "The liberal media do us a favor every time they run a story on us. It's only when they ignore us that people lose interest."

Omar nodded. "I noticed that there were a lot of people in this parish that didn't care to know me till I got on television. It's like being on TV makes you more real somehow."

"It's that symbol thing, like I said earlier. They see you standing up for something."

Omar suspected there was more to it than that, that maybe television had changed people's ideas of what was real, but he was more interested in what the Grand Wizard was getting to. There wasn't any reason to take Omar aside just to be talking about speaking engagements.

"I've got some other requests for you to speak, but they're not from *our* people, so I can't judge."

"Just forward 'em to me," Omar said.

"I'll do that."

The Grand Wizard paused, hands in his pockets, and glanced around.

"I met a fella the other day you might want to talk to," he said. "His name's Knox. Micah Knox. You ever heard of him?"

"Can't say as I have."

The Grand Wizard's foot toyed with the butt-end of an old brown beer bottle half hidden in the creeper. "He belongs to a group called the Crusaders National of the Tabernacle of Christ. He's got some interesting views about, you know, the situation. Very well informed. He's on a sort of tour of the country, and you might want to have him give a talk to your boys here."

Omar vaguely remembered hearing about the Tabernacle of Christ—they were some kind of Western group, he thought—but there were so many little groups on his end of the political spectrum that he had trouble sorting one out from another. It was hard enough just keeping track of the sixty-odd groups that called themselves the Klan.

"He doesn't charge or anything," the Grand Wizard added, misinterpreting Omar's hesitation. "He's just trying to make contacts."

"He can come by if he wants, I guess," Omar said.

"This isn't a matter for an open meeting or anything," the Grand Wizard said. "No cameras, no reporters. Just you and Knox and Merle and a few of the boys you best trust."

Omar gave him a sharp look. "Earl, is there a *reason* this Knox is under cover?"

The Grand Wizard gave a little shake of his head as he rolled the old beer bottle under his sole. "No, no. What I'm saying is that this boy is *radical*. People who haven't already given their lives completely to the Cause might misunderstand his message. We wouldn't want that. That's all."

"Okay, then," Omar said. "He can say whatever he likes, as long as he's not planning on doing anything radical while he's here."

The Grand Wizard kicked the beer bottle. Restrained by the creeper, it hopped about three inches, then came to a stop, edge-side up. The Grand Wizard sighed, then began to amble back toward Ozie's. "I'll be in touch about him," he said. "I don't know what his schedule is, exactly."

"Fine."

"By the way," the Grand Wizard said, "I saw that new sign—Hess-Meier Plantation Farm."

"Inc.," Omar added. Then, "Jews. Swiss Jews."

"They buy the gin, too?"

"Of course," Omar said. "If they took their cotton to someone else's gin, they wouldn't make so many sheckels." Omar shrugged. "Well, at least there's another gin in the parish, down to Hardee, and *that* one's American."

The Grand Wizard shook his head. "Wrightson couldn't at least sell out to Americans?"

"Hess-Meier was top bidder. Now half the agricultural

land in the parish is owned by the fuckin' Swiss."

"It isn't our country anymore." The Grand Wizard sighed.

It never was, Omar wanted to tell him. It's always been owned by the wrong people, who traded land and money back and forth within their circle, and the people who lived on the land and worked it never figured in their calculations.

Omar and the Grand Wizard walked up to Ozie's back door. Wilona was there, a plate in her hand. She was talking to Deb Drury, whose husband ran the towing service. "This fruit salad is so *special*," she said. "I can taste something different in it."

"Black cherry Jell-O," Deb said. "Fruit and pecans, and Co-Cola."

Wilona leaned close to Deb and lowered her voice. "I don't want to impose," she said, "but could you send me the recipe?"

Omar looked at his wife and gave her a wink.

Just treat the people like they exist, he thought, *and next thing you know, they put you in charge.*

THREE

We are informed from a respectable source that the old road to the post of Arkansas, by Spring river, is entirely destroyed by the last violent shocks of earthquake. Chasms of great depth and considerable length cross the country in various directions, some swamps have become dry, others deep lakes, and in some places hills have disappeared.

Charlestown, March 21, 1812

Jason craned his neck up at the water tower and pushed his helmet back to give himself a better view. It looked much bigger now that he stood at its base, a metal mushroom that bulged out over Jason's head, blocking out a sky filled with low dark clouds. Its surface was painted a glossy shade of vegetable green that Jason had never seen on any object not owned by the government. It was as if Cabells Mound had tried to disguise their water tower as something natural, as a peculiarly shaped tree, and failed miserably.

The tower stood in a soggy little park planted with overgrown hibiscus. Pumps whined from the cinderblock wellhouse next to the tower. There didn't seem to be any human beings in the vicinity.

Jason hopped off his bike and examined the metal stair that spiraled to the top of the tower. A tall metal pipe gateway stood at the bottom of the stair, with a gate made of chain link secured by a padlock. There was a half-hearted coil of barbed wire on the top, and more chain link on the side, obviously to keep someone from climbing over the lower part of the stair.

Nothing that would stop a determined, reasonably agile young person. Jason had always thought of chain link as a ladder. The barbed wire had not been extended along the side of the stair, in itself almost an invitation. And from the state of the chain link, it was obvious that he was not the first person to think of climbing the tower.

That gate and the barbed wire, though, would complicate the dismount at the end of his ride. He couldn't do a fakie or anything fancy at the bottom, he'd just have to jump off the rail. And he'd have to jump off onto the stair, because if he jumped off onto the soft turf under the tower, he might get hung up on the fence that was draped over the side of the stair.

Jumping off onto the stair might be a good thing, he finally decided. He could use the mesh of the gate to brake his remaining momentum. It would be like running into a net.

Jason parked his bike under the stair, hooked his skates around his neck by the laces, and then swarmed up the chain link and dropped onto the metal stair. He ran a hand along the pipe of the guard rail: smooth, round, painted metal, a little scarred by rust. Nothing he hadn't coped with before. He hiked up the first fifty feet or so, took the rail in his hands, and shook it, tried to find out if it was loose. It was solid. It would make good skating.

Jason's heart was racing as if he'd run five miles instead of climbed fifty feet. A delicate sensation of vertigo shimmered through his inner ear.

He took a breath and looked out over the town, laid out in perfect, regular rectangles that marched down to the levee. On this dark, cloudy morning, Cabells Mound looked drab. The older buildings were frame and often set on little brick piers, and the newer homes tended to be brick and set on slabs or conventional foundations. There was a little trace of the South in the white porticoes with their little pillars that were grafted onto the front of otherwise unremarkable buildings. Elms and oaks stood in yards. The river ran right up to the levee here because there was a landing, and because a little to the north there was a lumber mill that loaded its product onto barges. The river was an uneasy wide gray mass, very full, at least halfway up the side of the levee. Jason realized with a touch of unease that Cabells Mound, were it not protected by the levee, would be under water.

Because the river was so high it was carrying a lot of junk with it, and Jason could see an entire cypress tree floating past, a splayed clump of roots at one end and still-living foliage at the other. Three crows sat in the green branches and watched the world with curiosity as it moved by. Black against the opalescent surface of the water, a tow of sixteen barges made its way in the opposite direction, heading for St. Louis.

There were very few people to be seen. It was Saturday morning, and many, perhaps most, of the residents were off at the shopping malls of Memphis or Sikeston.

He turned south, saw the green of the old Indian mound beneath its tangle of timber, the peak of his house above the line of trees that marked the end of the cotton field.

Jason was above it all. His heart was racing in his chest like a turbine. He looked down at the ground below, and though he wasn't even halfway up the tower, the green turf seemed a long distance away.

Maybe, he thought, the very *first* time he went down the rail he shouldn't start at the very top. He could start partway down, just to get his reflexes back and make sure he could handle the curve that would tend to throw him off the rail as he gathered speed.

He went down a few stairs, until the distance to the ground did not look quite so intimidating, and then sat on one of the metal steps and took off his sneaks. He leaned around the metal center post of the tower and threw his shoes to the bottom of the stairway. They hit the mesh door at the bottom in a ringing splash of metal. Jason checked his skates, make sure the wheels spun freely and the brakes worked, then laced them on. Stood, adjusted his knee, elbow, and wrist armor, put a hand on the rail so that he'd know where it was.

Usually, when he was going to ride a rail, Jason would start on the flat, get some speed and momentum, and then jump onto the rail for his grind to the bottom. But now, on the tower, he was going to have to jump straight up onto the rail from a standing start, which meant that his balance was going to have to be perfect right from the beginning.

His pulse crashed in his ears. His vision had narrowed to the length of that metal rail that spiraled down out of sight to the bottom.

A gull sailed overhead, cawing.

Jason bent, jumped up, kicked. Landed on the rail—*yes!*— clicked in!—back foot athwart the rail in the royale position, front foot bang on the center of the rail, arms out for balance.

And began to move. Down—*yes!*—arms flailing at first, then steadying. Rear skate grinding down the rail, checking his speed. He leaned opposite to the direction of the curve, enough to counter for centrifugal force that threatened to throw him off—*yes!*—he needed only a slight lean, he wasn't going very fast.

The ride was over in mere seconds. *Yes!* He threw himself off the rail, spun neatly in air, landed fakie—a cool landing after all, even if it was only a few feet—he spread his arms and let himself fall backward into the chain link. It received him with a metallic bang.

"*Yes!*" he yelled as he bounced off the mesh. He readied himself to spring back to the top.

"Reckon not," said a very grownup voice.

He told himself afterward that he should have just sprinted for the top, skates and all, hopped on the rail, and wheel-barrowed to the bottom. *That* would have been Edge Living. That would have been the way to go. Then the experience that followed would have been worth it.

But instead he turned around and caught sight of the policeman, and then he froze.

"Get your ass off public property," said the cop.

His name was Eubanks, a skinny little bald guy with a big voice, and he seemed to specialize in following Jason around and telling him not to do things. It was Eubanks who told him he couldn't skate in the courthouse parking lot, or on the streets—old and potholed though they were—

or on the sidewalks, which were even more beat up.
Eubanks had even chased him off the parking lot at the
Piggly Wiggly, and the city didn't even *own* the Piggly
Wiggly.

"Get your ass over here!" Eubanks yelled.

Jason turned, trudged up a few steps to get clear of the
chain mesh, and prepared to hop over the rail to the ground
below.

"Get your damn shoes," said Eubanks.

Jason turned, trudged down the stairs, picked up his
sneaks, and headed up the stairs again. He vaulted over the
chain link to the ground, and stood waiting for instructions.

"Get into my car."

Jason walked as directed, went behind some hibiscus, and
saw Eubanks's prowl car just sitting there, in a position to
spring out at any speeders racing down Samuel Clemens
Street. The car had probably been there all along.

Bastard was probably taking a nap, Jason thought.

"Into the back," Eubanks said.

"I've got my bike over there," Jason said.

"It can stay there."

"It's not locked or anything."

"Not my problem," said Eubanks.

Jason got in the back of the prowl car, behind the mesh par-
tition where the real criminals rode. Eubanks got in the front
and started the car.

"You'd of broke your neck if you'd fallen off," Eubanks
said. "And your mama would have sued the town."

"She would've said it was karma," Jason said.

"Oh yeah, I forgot," Eubanks said, and gave a little dis-
paraging laugh. "Your mama's the New Age Lady."

My mom's the New Age Lady, Jason thought in despair.
That's probably what the whole town calls her.

Eubanks pulled out onto Samuel Clemens, then followed
it to the highway. Jason recognized some kids from the
school at the corner, in the gravel parking lot of the Epps
Feed Store. Among them was the boy who, the other day, had
taken such pleasure in announcing that Jason's mom was

going to Hell. He spotted Jason in the back of the prowl car, nudged his friends, and pointed.

The kids silently watched as Eubanks waited to make his left turn onto the highway. Jason stared back.

Then he raised a gloved hand and waved. Gave a little smile.

Might as well get whatever mileage he could out of the situation.

He wasn't arrested or anything. Eubanks took him home, past where Mr. Regan was buffing his bass boat, then pulled to a stop in front of Jason's house. Mr. Regan watched while Jason, still in his helmet, skates, and pads, marched across the lawn to the front porch with Eubanks as his escort. Batman the boxer barked loud enough to call the attention of the entire Huntley family to the spectacle.

Jason's mom met Jason and Eubanks at the door.

Eubanks explained the situation. Violation of public property, he said. Town ordinance against skating in the town, he said. Upsets the elderly residents, he said.

Could of broke his neck, Eubanks said. You'd of sued the town.

After the police officer left, Catherine Adams confiscated Jason's skates and armor, and locked them in the trunk of her car. On Monday, she said, she would take them to work and leave them there, at the greenhouse, until Jason "demonstrated a more responsible behavioral system."

Then she went up to his room, took down all his skating posters, and threw them in the trash.

After which she paused for a moment, trying to think of another privilege she could revoke. It was difficult, because Jason didn't drive, had no friends here, and never went out.

"No Internet till the end of the month," she decided. A satisfied smile touched her lips when she saw his stricken look.

"I need to get my bike," he said.

"Walk," she said, and left his room in triumph, closing the door behind her, so that he couldn't even have the satisfaction of slamming it.

* * *

Major General J.C. Frazetta rose at dawn to the sound of mockingbirds chattering outside the window and had a hard time resisting the impulse to head for work early. It was the general's first day on the job, not counting the ceremony the day before, in which command was officially transferred by the outgoing commander. Frazetta was too full of nervous energy to go back to sleep.

So Frazetta prepared herbal tea, fried some boudin that had been purchased while driving through Louisiana to Vicksburg a couple days earlier, and prepared a soufflé cockaigne, with Parmesan and Gruyère cheese. It was too aggravating simply waiting for the soufflé to rise, so the general sauteed some Italian squash, fried some leftover boiled potatoes with onions and green pepper, and threw some popovers in the oven along with the soufflé. Made coffee for Pat, the spouse, and sniffed at it longingly as it bubbled from the Braun coffeemaker. And thought about making coffee bread, because excess energy could be usefully employed in punching down the dough as it rose.

The general looked at the clock. No, not enough time.

Pat, who was not a morning person and who generally ate nothing before 11:00 A.M., was nevertheless sensitive to Frazetta's moods and ate a full share of the preposterous meal.

The only comment offered by Pat on all this activity was to retire to the workshop and pluck out "I am the Very Model of a Modern Major General" on his fiddle.

Which was all, General Jessica Costanza Frazetta had to conclude, that she deserved.

Exactly on time, to the minute, 0900 hours exactly, General Frazetta greeted her secretary. Her driver, the experienced Sergeant Zook, seemed to know to the second how long it would take to deliver her to her new headquarters.

"Good morning."

"Good morning, General Frazetta."

The secretary smiled. "Can I get you some coffee?"

"Not exactly." The general opened her briefcase, produced a box of tea bags, Celestial Seasonings Caribbean Kiwi Peach. She handed the box to her secretary. "Would you mind bringing me a cup of this?"

"Not at all, General."

Major General Jessica C. Frazetta, U.S. Army, closed her briefcase, thanked her secretary, and walked into her office. Closed the door behind her.

And grinned like a chipmunk. She walked to the map of the Mississippi Valley that hung on one wall.

Her domain. She had just been appointed to command of the Mississippi Valley Division, U.S. Army Corps of Engineers. The President had appointed her to the presidency of the Mississippi River Commission, the outfit that with the MVD ran all federal projects on the river, but that would wait on the approval of Congress.

It was a great job. She was, for all intents and purposes, in charge of the entire Mississippi River and its 250 tributaries. The drainage basin included all or part of thirty-one of the lower forty-eight states—and also a part of Canada, which was a bit outside of her jurisdiction. All of the federal works on the river—the cutoffs, levees, dikes, revetments, spillways, and reservoirs were in her charge. All the dredges, the dams, the floodwalls, and locks.

All the responsibility. Which didn't bother her at all—she *liked* being in charge.

Where she told the water to go, it would go, or she would know the reason why.

She turned to the photograph of the President on the wall behind her desk and gave it a wave.

"Thanks, boss," she said. And tossed her hat across her desk and onto the brass hat stand behind.

By the time her secretary came with the tea, Jessica was seated behind the desk and was halfway through the stack of congratulatory messages and faxes that had arrived from all over the world: from Bob in Sarajevo, from Janice in Korea, from Fred in some place called Corrales, New Mexico.

"Thanks, Nelda," she said, and sipped at the tea.

"Does it taste okay?"

"Tastes fine. It's only weeds and water, after all."

Nelda smiled. "We're mostly java drinkers around here."

"Never cared for it myself." Jessica preferred not to explain that she avoided caffeine on the theory that it might exaggerate her hyperkinetic manner, which she had been told, occasionally at length, was not her most attractive characteristic.

"Anything else I can do?"

"Can you get me Colonel Davidovich?"

"He's out at the Riprap Test Facility at the moment, but I can page him if you like."

Jessica considered. She wanted private meetings with all her senior staff, as well as the officers who commanded the six districts that made up the division. Davidovich was her second-in-command, and she wanted a meeting with him first.

"No—don't bother. You wouldn't happen to know when he'll be in his office?"

"By eleven-thirty, General."

"I'll call him then."

"Is that all?"

"Yes. Thank you."

She returned to the congratulatory notes. Then, because it was hard to sit still, she opened her briefcase, took out the photograph of her husband Pat Webster, and put it on her desk. In the photo Pat was leaning back in an old armchair, sleeves rolled up, boots up on a table, playing a banjo.

Next to Pat, she placed the photo of her parents, taken on their fiftieth wedding anniversary, and the photo of her sister with her husband and children.

There were empty picture hangers on the wall where her predecessor had hung various photos and certificates, and she was able to fill the blank spaces with her own. Jessica had an impressive number of credentials to display, even considering her rank and number of years in the service.

One reason for the large number of degrees was the Army's uncertainty, when she graduated from Engineer Officer Candidate School, as to exactly what to do with a female military engineer. There weren't very many precedents. Her arrival at her first assignment—in Bangkok, of all places, scarcely then or now a bastion of progressive feminist thought—had been greeted by jeers and catcalls from the enlisted men. But her fellow officers, who appreciated the presence of a round-eyed woman, were supportive enough, though perhaps a little uncertain as to the social niceties.

That uncertainty—what *was* her place, assuming she had one at all?—resulted in the Army's apparent decision to keep Jessica in school as much as possible. Which resulted in her getting a master's degree in civil engineering from the University of Virginia and another master's degree in contract management and procurement from the Florida Institute of Technology. She had graduated from the U.S. Army War College, the U.S. Army Engineer Basic, Construction, and Advanced Courses, Army Command and General Staff College, the Medical Service Corps Advanced course, and even the Naval War College. She belonged to the National Society of Professional Engineers, the American Society of Civil Engineers, the Army Engineer Association, and the Society of American Military Engineers.

The end result of all this education, the overwhelming weight of her credentials, was that it had become very difficult to refuse her any job that she really wanted.

She really wanted the Mississippi Valley Division. And now she had it.

And she was only forty-one years old.

She paused, a framed certificate still in her hand. She had run out of picture hooks. Apparently she had a few more credentials than her predecessor.

She laughed. This was probably a good sign.

Cellphone plastered to her ear, Jessica nodded good-bye to her driver, Sergeant Zook, and walked past Pat's red Jeep Cherokee to the new house, the one with the rustic wooden sign marking it as the dwelling of the Commander, MVD. She could hear Pat playing "Hail to the Chief" on his fiddle. She opened the door, and the fiddle fell silent when Pat saw she was on the phone. "If you're sure," she said, "that water at the levee toe is from the rain, and not—" she said as she marched across the polished wood floor of their new house, dropped her heavy briefcase onto the couch, then spun and tossed her hat at the wooden rack by the front door.

Missed. Damn.

Pat already had the place smelling like home, which meant wood shavings and glue. She finished her conversation and snapped the phone shut. A mental image of Captain Kirk folding his subspace communicator came to her, and she grinned. Then she bounded across the room and let Pat fold her in his arms.

"I take it that things went well," he said.

"Mm-hmm."

"Careful of the fiddle."

Pat Webster was a tall, bearlike Virginian, and Jessica's second husband. Her first marriage, in her early twenties, had been a catastrophe—a pair of obsessive, overachieving bipolar maniacs was not a recipe for success in a relationship— and by the time she'd met Pat, she'd pretty much given up on anything but transitory romance with colleagues temporarily stationed at the same base.

It was her friend Janice, when they were both stationed at Army Material Command in Alexandria, who talked her into going to a contra and square dance, overcoming her expectation that she would be encountering women in Big Hair and crinolines. Instead Jessica found herself quickly defeated by the fast-moving patterns, the allemandes and honors and courtesy turns and chains, and she ended up at the head of the dance hall, talking to the members of the band in between numbers.

And there, with his fiddle and mandolin, in his jeans and boots and checked shirt, was Pat Webster, laconic and smiling. She watched his hands as he played, the long expert hands that made light of the intricate music that he coaxed so effortlessly from his instruments.

She fantasized about those hands all the way home. And, a week or so later, when they finally touched her, she was not disappointed.

She found that Pat had a career, but to her utter relief, it was one that could stand uprooting every couple years as one assignment followed another. He was a maker of fiddles, guitars, dulcimers, and mandolins—in fact, a genuine hand-made Webster guitar sold for up to a couple thousand dollars, depending on the model, and until Jessica got her general's star he brought more money into their marriage than she. He brought with him the pleasant scent of seasoned wood, of varnish, of glue. He brought her his calm, measured presence, a balance to her own unbridled energy.

He brought her the eternal gift of music.

Inspired, she had even learned to dance squares and contras.

"So how are the levees up in Iowa?" Pat asked.

"Holding. It was the private levees that broke."

It had been all Jessica could do to keep from flying north to check the situation personally. But her deputy at Rock Island assured her that there was no significant danger to Corps structures, and she concluded that she would be better employed in Vicksburg, getting her teams up to speed for when the flood waters headed south.

"Private levees," Pat mused. "Funny we've still got so many of 'em."

"The Corps budget will only do so much," Jessica said. Corps levees were built to a standard height and width, faced with durable Bermuda grass, and protected by revetments from the river's tendency to undermine them. But much of the Mississippi's flood plain was still guarded by levees privately built by local cities, towns, and corporations, and they built what they could afford—to Corps standards when it was possible, but often not.

In the catastrophic floods of 1993, when ten million acres had gone under water, it had been the private levees that had broken, and the Corps levees that stood. When the city of Grand Forks had been submerged by the Red River in the spring of '97, it had been because the city's politicians had been reluctant to raise tax rates in order to provide proper flood protection. Upstream, Fargo, with its more realistic government and higher rate of taxation, stayed dry.

Jessica loosened her collar and jacket, headed for her room to change. "What's for dinner?" she asked.

"There seem to be a lot of breakfast leftovers," Pat said, following.

Jessica felt her cheeks grow hot. "Sorry," she said. "I was nervous."

"I could tell."

"What *else* is for dinner?"

"I could make some tuna fish sandwiches. You used up practically everything else in the refrigerator."

"Tuna is fine."

Pat was actually a perfectly adequate cook whose capabilities extended well past tuna sandwiches. But he didn't *care* about cooking, he didn't throw his whole being into it, the way Jessica did, to leave the palate delirious and the kitchen a litter of dirty pots and pans.

Pat saved all that for music.

And, strangely enough, for Jessica.

"We could go out, maybe," Pat said. "And celebrate your ascension."

Jessica shook her head. "Too much homework," she said, and looked at the heavy briefcase she'd brought home.

"Okay. Tuna fish it is."

Jessica followed him into the kitchen. "Why do people say tuna *fish*?" she asked.

He looked at her over his shoulder as he opened the pantry door. "Maybe because a tuna is a fish?" he suggested.

"But people don't call a salmon a salmon *fish*, or a grouper a grouper *fish*, or a bass a bass *fish*."

"You've got a point there." He took the can of tuna from the shelf, glanced over the unfamiliar kitchen for an opener. He cocked an eye at her. "Didn't you say you've got some homework?"

He hated it when she hovered over him in the kitchen.
"You bet," she said, and headed for her briefcase.

We have the following description of the Earthquake from gentlemen who were on board a large barge, and lay at anchor in the Mississippi a few leagues below New Madrid, on the night of the 15th of December. About 2 o'clock all hands were awakened by the first shock; the impression was, that the barge had dragged her anchor and was grounding on gravel; such were the feelings for 60 or 80 seconds, when the shock subsided. The crew were so fully persuaded of the fact of their being aground, that they put out their sounding poles, but found water enough. "At seven next morning a second and very severe shock took place. The barge was under way—the river rose several feet; the trees on the shore shook; the banks in large columns tumbled in; hundreds of old trees that had lain perhaps half a century at the bottom of the river, appeared on the surface of the water; the feathered race took to the wing; the canopy was covered with geese and ducks and various other kinds of wild fowl; very little wind; the air was tainted with a nitrous and sulphureous smell; and every thing was truly alarming for several minutes. The shocks continued to the 21st Dec. during that time perhaps one hundred were distinctly felt. From the river St. Francis to the Chickasaw bluffs visible marks of the earthquake were discovered; from that place down, the banks did not appear to have been disturbed.
There is one part of this description which we cannot reconcile with philosophic principles, (although we believe the narrative to be true,) that is, the trees which were settled at the bottom of the river appearing on the surface. It must be obvious to every person that those trees must have become specifically heavier than the water before they sunk, and of course after being immersed in the mud must have increased in weight. —We therefore submit the question to the Philosophical Society.

Natchez Weekly Chronicle, January 20, 1812

Cover your six o'clock, as the chopper pilots said. Or, in the language of the marketplace, *cover your ass.*

Jessica Frazetta knew that there were two natural forces that could sneak up on her and wreck the Mississippi Valley, and her career along with it.

The first was flood. The second was earthquake.

Flood and the Corps of Engineers were old acquaintances. The Corps had been fighting the river since well before Colonel of Engineers Robert E. Lee, in the 1850s, had been sent to Missouri to prevent the Mississippi from crabbing sideways into Illinois and stranding St. Louis inland, a mission he had performed with his usual efficiency.

Practically all of the Corps' efforts in the Mississippi went into controlling the water and keeping river navigation safe. It was to secure these goals that all the levees had been built, the dams, the locks, the revetments, the spillways. For these reasons the Corps had planted lights and buoys, dredged the harbors, charted the depths, pulled snags by the thousands from the bed of the river.

But the second, far more dangerous threat was that of earthquake. Jessica knew that an earthquake of sufficient force could undo hundreds of years of the Corps' efforts in an instant. The levees, the revetments, the dams, the spillways . . . all gone at once.

The Mississippi Valley's last big earthquakes had occurred from 1811–12, when there were less than three thousand people of European descent living west of the Mississippi.

The world of those three thousand, and the thousands more Indians who lived in the area, was torn asunder by three major earthquakes and thousands of aftershocks. The first of the quakes had been estimated as 8.7 on the Richter scale, the second-largest quake in all human history. Fifty thousand square miles were devastated, and millions more suffered damage. Fissures tore open every single acre of farmland. The Mississippi ran backward for a day. Islands vanished, while other islands were formed. Dry land submerged, and the bottoms of lakes and rivers rose dry into the sunlight. The Missouri town of New Madrid, where the quakes had been centered, had been destroyed, and the Mississippi rolled over the remains. The quakes were so powerful that they smashed crockery in Boston, caused panicked people to run into the streets in Charleston, rang church bells in Baltimore, and woke Thomas Jefferson from sleep at Monticello.

The New Madrid fault had remained active through much of the nineteenth century, providing the country an occasional jolt, but it had fallen quiet during the twentieth. And it was during the twentieth century, when memories of the quake had faded, that the Corps built most of its structures in the Mississippi Valley.

In the years since the New Madrid quakes of 1811–12, millions of people moved into the danger zone. Major cities, like St. Louis and Memphis, were built close to the fault, supported by a complex infrastructure of bridges, dams, reservoirs, power stations, highways, and airstrips, few of which had been built with earthquake in mind. Industries flourished: factories, chemical plants, and refineries had been built on the yielding soil of the Mississippi Delta. Billions of dollars in commerce moved up and down the river every year. Millions of acres of farmland, fertile as any in the world, stretched from the rivers, protected by manmade levees.

It had only been in recent decades, when geologists began to study the mid-continental faults, that the true scope of the danger was known. The New Madrid fault, and other faults beneath the Mississippi, were still seismically active, although the vast majority of its quakes were so small as to be undetectable by humans. To judge by historical precedent, a much larger and more destructive earthquake was inevitable.

If the faults should snap again, Jessica knew, millions of lives, and billions of dollars in property, were in jeopardy. The Corps had been striving to reengineer its public works so as to make them resistant to earthquake damage, but the procedure was far from complete.

In her briefcase, Jessica had the Corps' earthquake plan, released in February 1998, as well as reports concerning the regular inspections of Corps facilities and reports relating to the floods in Iowa.

The floodwaters would inevitably channel into the Mississippi from Iowa, and would inevitably test Corps structures farther south as they progressed to the Gulf.

Jessica looked at the stack of papers, at the heavy report.

The earthquake, she thought, was in the indefinite future. The floods were *now*.

She put the earthquake plan back in her case.

She would deal with it when she had the time.

"I've got a proposition for you, Vince," Charlie said, "and— I warn you—I am talking risk here."

Vincent Dearborne steepled his fingertips and looked at him with a little frown. His eyes, however, were not frowning, not frowning at all . . . Charlie could see a glimmer of interest, and the little lines around the eyes were smiling. Vincent Dearborne, Charlie knew, had been hoping that this moment would come.

"Tennessee Planters and Trust," Dearborne said in his cultured Southern voice, "is, generally speaking, risk-averse."

"I know, Vince," said Charlie, and smiled with his white, dazzling, even, capped teeth. "But you're not averse to taking a little flyer now and again. When I told you about those straddles two years ago, you backed my play."

"Yes. And I wondered if doubling the bet was sound. But . . ." The glimmer in Dearborne's eyes increased in candlepower. "You made us twenty-four million dollars."

"Twenty-four million dollars in *three days*," Charlie reminded.

"And almost gave me an ulcer."

Charlie laughed. "You can't fool me, guvnor. You can't get an ulcer in three days."

Dearborne grinned and tilted his noble graying head quizzically, the way he always did when Charlie let his East London origins show. It was as if he were amused and puzzled both at the same time. Here was this strange Englishman who talked like a movie character, and who could make tens of millions in a matter of days, and who amounted to . . . what?

It was as if Dearborne couldn't figure Charlie Johns out. Charlie came from . . . *some other place.*

Whereas Dearborne's place in the world was not only clear, it was on display. His office was a monument to mahogany and soft brown leather, subdued lighting and brass accents. Golf trophies stood on display in the corner—golf was a *safe* sport. Certificates and awards were ranked elsewhere on the walls. Chamber of Commerce, Lions, United Way—*safe* organizations. There were pictures of ancestors on the walls: judges, legislators, bankers. *Safe* ancestors. His pretty wife, displayed in photographs, wasn't *too* pretty, and his well-scrubbed children, pink-cheeked in school uniforms, looked—well—*risk-averse.*

Tennessee Planters & Trust was a *safe* place to put your money, and Dearborne was a *safe* director for a bank to employ. That was the message sent by the office decor, by the Memphis skyline visible through the office windows, by the ten-story Planters Trust building of white Tennessee field-stone, even by a bright turquoise pattern in Dearborne's tie, which was laid to rest next to another, more tranquil shade of blue, like a moment's bright, shining thought being smothered beneath a reflex of conformity.

But Charlie, who prided himself on his discernment, knew that Vincent Dearborne was not quite as sound as his calculated environs made him out to be. A little over three years ago, when Charlie was working in New York for Salomon Brothers and Tennessee Planters Securities flew him out for a secret weekend meeting with the directors, Dearborne had taken Charlie not to the office but to the country club, and made him part of a foursome with two of the other directors.

It had been Dearborne who suggested the wager, "to make it interesting."

Charlie was hopeless at golf. He'd always thought it a sport for wankers, and he'd never really learned to play; but he knew this was a test, so he flailed his clubs with a will until at last the horrible afternoon was over and he could relax in the clubhouse with Boodles and tonic.

And he could whip out his pen and write Dearborne a check for four hundred and thirty-two dollars, and hand it over with a smile.

Dearborne's eyes had gleamed, then. Just as they were gleaming now.

The conclusion that Charlie had drawn was that Dearborne liked a fling, but was only happy with a sure thing. Before Charlie's arrival on the scene, Dearborne's idea of a fling had been to spread some money on the Cotton Exchange.

Charlie played golf with Dearborne on a regular basis now. And regularly wrote him checks afterward. He considered it a form of investment.

An investment that he hoped was about to pay off.

"Since those straddles," Charlie said, "you know I've played it safe, no flyers. Too many conflicting signals, mate. Too much vega in the market, right?"

"Vega." Dearborne repeated, the gleam in his eyes fading, going a little abstract. "You mean volatility."

"Almost. Vega is the impact of *changes* in volatility," Charlie said. Too much jargon only confused the man. "I've made a nice profit for you, but it was nickel-and-diming, a little bit here, a little bit there. I wasn't taking any flyers—I was, as you say, risk-averse."

Dearborne nodded.

"I was waiting for a clear signal." Charlie grinned, twisted the diamond ring on his finger. "This morning, just as the markets opened, Carpe Diem gave me the signal."

"Ah." The gleam returned to Dearborne's eyes. "Your new program," he said.

The convoluted business of trading options required a lot of calculations, and traders depended on sophisticated computer programs to mash the numbers and spew out the complex answers they needed to make their trades. The programs had names like Iron Butterfly and Jellyroll, and they could assemble raw data at lightning speed and configure awesomely complex combinations of options.

Carpe Diem was of the next generation of trading programs. A trading whiz Charlie knew from his days at Salomon's had slipped Charlie a beta test version of the program. His program was ahead of the market. And he planned for his purchasing to be ahead as well.

"What's Carpe Diem telling us?" Dearborne asked.

"The economy's going to tilt into recession," Charlie said.

"People have predicted that for years."

"Everyone knew it would happen sooner or later," Charlie said. "The question is *when*. Carpe Diem says it's going to happen *now*.

"And because this last boom has lasted so long, I think the recession's going to be a big one." He raised a stub-fingered hand and ticked off the points on his fingers. "Unemployment is down and wages are up, which means a season of inflation unless the Fed acts to cool the economy. Consumer price rises were only point-one percent in April, but that comes off a big rise over the holidays. The visible trade deficit went up over the holiday season, like always, but it hasn't dropped much in the months since."

"The Dow is up," Dearborne offered.

Charlie flashed his grin again. "Those blokes are always the last to know," he said. "Here's the two factors that Carpe Diem thought were significant." He ticked off numbers on his fingers again. "There's a debt bomb about to go off in Europe. Public debt is out of control in the old East Bloc—well, that's normal—and it's normal for Belgium and Italy, too. But in *Germany*? Public debt is over sixty-five percent of GDP. Britain's at over fifty percent. And even the Dutch, for God's sake, have been on a spending spree." Charlie dropped his hands, leaned forward, gave Dearborne a look from his baby blues. "It can't last, and when the European economy slows, the effects are going to be worldwide.

"Secondly," Charlie said, "Carpe Diem noticed a lot of action on certain commodities—copper and other strategic minerals, because China is sucking up titanic amounts of raw materials as they modernize. And there's a lot of volatility on foodstuffs, because those floods in Iowa are making people nervous. But what Carpe Diem is really interested in is this weird speculative trend on certain fringy areas of the commodities market. Coffee—why speculate in coffee when there's stable supply and demand? Also natural gas, foodstuffs, certain petroleum products. Which means the money is moving out of the market's center, as it were, possibly because people are getting uneasy about it."

Dearborne looked worried. "You're not suggesting that we speculate in these commodities ourselves, are you?"

"No way, guv," Charlie said.

He knew Dearborne liked it when he called him "guv."

"If I studied the way those commodities were moving," Charlie said, "I reckon I could make you some money, but it wouldn't be worth the aggravation. Those trades are powered by insecurity and ignorance, which means that you can't predict them, and if you can't predict what's going to happen, that's not investment, that's *gambling*." Charlie flashed his brilliant capped teeth again. "That's why we've got tools like Carpe Diem—to help reduce the risk."

Dearborne was reassured. "Does Carpe Diem have any other points to make?"

"The Chinese have the world's largest supply of foreign currency reserves, but they're going to have to sell in order to pay for their economic expansion. So will the Taiwanese, because their economies are linked to the Chinese. I expect that the Japanese will begin to sell as well, to finance the amount of debt they've acquired as a result of the bailouts they've indulged in."

"Dollar down." Dearborne nodded, absorbing this lesson.

"Which would normally be good for exports, except that due to the other problems I've mentioned, the world won't be able to *afford* so very many of our exports in the next few years."

Leather creaked as Dearborne leaned back in his chair. The gleam in his eyes burned with a new intensity. "So what are you planning to do?"

"I'm positioned nicely in T-bonds, which I expect to rise soon and make us a packet. But that's the short run."

"Long-term?"

"Well." Charlie grinned. "There's that risk I was telling you about."

"Ahh," Dearborne said.

"Once the rest of the world catches up to Carpe Diem—and that won't be long, perhaps even hours—I expect the markets are going to take a tumble. Which is fine as far as we're concerned—we can make some nice profits right then. But the best course, the way interest rates are running right now, is to sell the market short, and not lose our nerve."

Dearborne looked thoughtful. If he was *sure* the market was going to fall, it would be cheaper to let Charlie, right now, sell a fistful of short positions that reflected that belief.

Dearborne's face turned sulky as a new factor entered his thoughts. "Vega," he said, remembering the jargon for once.

"Vega's the fly in the ointment, all right," Charlie said. "When the market starts to slide, volatility's going to go up. Which will mean an increased chance for profit, but it also means the administrators at the various exchanges are going to get nervous and start calling on us to meet our margins."

Margin calls were the bane of the trader's life, particularly if he traded on the Mercantile Exchange in Chicago, which had a system called SPAN that continually calculated margins and could call for margins right in the middle of the trading day, meaning that the trader would have to find money for the margin call right then, instead of having overnight to make the arrangements.

"How many short futures are we talking about?"

"Well, guv . . ." Charlie took a deep, theatrical breath. "For the plan that Carpe Diem and I suspect will maximize our profit, we'll need a fund of between forty and fifty million."

Involuntarily, and without Charlie's theatricality, Dearborne echoed Charlie's intake of breath. "Jesus God," he said.

Charlie threw up his hands. "Understand that there are ways of making this less risky," he said. "Every time the market moves, I'm going to be hedging our position. Every minute, practically. And in a volatile market, I'm going to be able to make a lot of short trades that should keep our cash flow positive."

"Jesus God," Dearborne said again. He gave a glance at his bowling trophies, as if for reassurance. "What if the Fed acts?" he said. "What if the Federal Reserve decides to lower interest rates?"

"I don't think it'll happen," Charlie said. "The chairman's too bloody conservative. But just in case, I'll hedge by shorting Eurodollar puts. If the Fed cuts interest rates, then Eurodollars will rise and I'll make a packet when the puts fall in price."

"Mmm," Dearborne said as he steepled his fingertips and sought communion with his trophies.

"Vince," Charlie said as he leaned forward and sought Dearborne's uneasy eyes with his own eyes of brilliant blue. "I've been a good lad these two years—I've been risk-averse—haven't yet steered you wrong."

"True," Dearborne admitted. But the acquisitive glimmer in his eyes was dull, uncertain.

"You know what *Carpe Diem* means in Latin, Vince?" Charlie asked. "Seize the Day. This day *must* be seized, and soon. Because if we seize it now, I can give you profits that would make those twenty-four millions look like your kids' milk money."

Dearborne bit his lip, fiddled with something on his desk. Looked anywhere but at Charlie. *Move, you bastard!* Charlie thought. *You think I spent all those hours playing golf just for the fun of it?*

Slowly, a calculating gleam returned to Dearborne's gaze.

"Well," he said, "I'll make some calls."

Before Charlie even left Dearborne's floor at the Tennessee Planters & Trust, he used his cellphone to call Deborah, his assistant at Tennessee Planters Securities, and had her begin to place his trades. Then, from the old Otis elevator as it creaked its way to the ground floor, he called Megan Clifton, who ran the "back room"—the settlements office—at TPS.

"Megan Clifton." Her low, cool Southern voice sent a little tremor up Charlie's spine.

"It's on, love," Charlie said.

The low, cool voice dissolved at once into high-pitched excitement. "*Oh, yeah!* Whoa, Charlie, you're a *genius*!"

"Better get ready for a long, busy day," Charlie said. "But for later, I suggest that we call the caterers now and have them deliver dinner for two to my place. There's some Bollinger in the fridge, and I can warm up the spa."

"I will make the call as you suggest, sir." Megan's cool professional voice was back.

The elevator moved uneasily back and forth as it adjusted itself to the ground floor, overshooting a little bit each time. The doors opened and revealed that the elevator was at least a half-inch too high.

"I'll see you in a few minutes," Charlie said, and snapped the phone shut as he stepped into the lobby.

He didn't work in the same building as the bank. His own office, and that of TPS, was in a different building, a modern steel-and-glass office building two blocks away. The Glass-Steagal Act prevented banks from dealing in securities, and Tennessee Planters & Trust was nothing if not law-abiding. Tennessee Planters Securities—originally Bendrell Traders— was a separate firm which the bank just happened to control, having picked it up for the cost of its office furniture after Bendrell went smash in the wake of Black Friday in 1987. The bank also just happened to provide TPS with most of its operating capital, including that which TPS used for proprietary trading and for meeting its margins.

The separation between the bank and TPS was more than just physical. There was a difference in culture as well, between the cautious, conservative bankers in their mahogany offices, and the traders with their glass-walled cubicles and blinking computer monitors. The bankers were wedded to prudence, to circumspect accumulation of capital, to *safety*. The traders were after the money, and knew that big profits occasionally required big risks. The bankers dealt with long-term loans, with gilt-edged stocks, with thirty- or twenty-year mortgages. The traders' deals sometimes were constructed so as to last for mere *hours*. Successful bankers drove Lincoln Towne Cars and belonged to the country club. Successful traders drove Ferraris and spent every night at the disco.

Successful traders also made a *lot* more money than successful bankers.

Charlie Johns had done his best to bridge the gap between the two cultures. He knew that traders could offend their conservative bosses with their flash and their style—not to mention their profits—and so he took care to present a façade that was more in harmony with Tennessee Planters & Trust than with TPS. He bought his suits from the same tailor that Dearborne used, though his natural style ran more toward Armani. His Mercedes E320 was a calculated degree less ostentatious than Dearborne's S500. Ferraris and Lamborghinis were too flash, even if he didn't drive them to work. He joined Dearborne's country club, and he lost regularly to Dearborne at golf. He had lunch with Dearborne once a week, and consulted Dearborne on trades that he had the authority to make on his own, just to make Dearborne feel his opinion mattered.

And he made Dearborne money. Which was probably better than anything at cementing their relationship.

And, if Carpe Diem and Charlie's own instincts were anything to go by, he was about to make Tennessee Planters enough money to gold-plate their office building.

By the time Charlie swept into the TPS offices, he had called his three largest clients and convinced them it was time to commit to some major action.

He grinned as he boomed through the big glass doors and gave a jaunty wave to the salesmen and traders sitting behind their desks. Once he was at his desk, he shorted nearly forty million dollars of S&P contracts. As a hedge, he shorted ten million dollars' worth of Eurodollar puts, just as he'd promised Dearborne he would.

It was a *great* way to make a living.

FOUR

This morning at eight o'clock, another pretty severe shock of an earthquake was felt. Those on the 16th ult. and since done much damage on the Mississippi river, from the mouth of the Ohio to Little Prairie particularly. Many boats have been lost, and much property sunk. The banks of the river, in many places, sunk hundreds of acres together, leaving the tops of the trees to be seen above the water. The earth opened in many places from one to three feet wide, through whose fissures stone coal was thrown up in pieces as large as a man's hand. The earth rocked—trees lashed their tops together. The whole seemed in convulsions, throwing up sand bars here, there sinking others, trees jumping from the bed of the river, roots uppermost, forming a most serious impediment to navigation, where before there was no obstruction—boats rocked like cradles—men, women and children confused, running to and fro and hallooing for safety—those on land pleading to get into the boats—those in boats willing almost to be on land. This damning and distressing scene continued for several days, particularly at and above Flour island. The long reach now, though formerly the best part of the river is said to be the worst being filled with innumerable planters and sawyers which have been thrown up from the bed by the extraordinary convulsions of the river. Little Prairie, and the country about it, suffered much—new lakes having been formed, and the bed of old ones raised to the elevation of the surface of the adjacent country. All accounts of those who have descended the river since the shocks give the most alarming and terrific picture of the desolating and horrible scene.

Account of Zadock Cramer

"Hey," the kid said. "Heard you got arrested." He slid into the seat opposite Jason at the cafeteria, plopped down his plastic tray with his plastic-looking sloppy joe.

"Not arrested," Jason said. "Not exactly." He was trying to remember the kid's name. All he could think of, for some reason, was "Muppet," which did not seem likely. Could it be Buffett? Moffett? He had curly dark hair and a compact, strong body, and wore a striped shirt, boots, and jeans.

The cafeteria juke box, which had been playing something by Nirvana, switched to Garth Brooks. One of the little cultural contrasts that came with the neighborhood.

"What did you do to get Eubanks after you?" Muppet asked. His two friends, one of whom was the son of the Epps who ran the feed store, plunked their sloppy joes down on either side of him.

"Took a ride down the water tower on my skates. Down the rail, I mean."

"Cool," said Muppet. "I'd like to do that."

Young Epps grinned at him. "If you did that, Muppet, you'd break your neck."

His name actually *was* Muppet, Jason thought. How about that?

"You would have died," Jason confirmed. "I've been skating for years, and it was a rough ride."

The others looked at him with a degree of admiration. Jason realized that they thought he had ridden the whole tower, all the way from the top.

He thought about telling them the truth, then immediately dismissed the idea. After all, he *would* have ridden the entire rail if he had the chance.

"What did Eubanks do to you?" asked Epps.

"Yelled at me some. Took me home so my mother would yell at me, too."

"That bastard," said Muppet. "He's so wack."

"Wack," Epps agreed. "He spends his day following teenagers around hoping to catch us at something. If he followed grownups around that way, he'd get his ass kicked off the force."

Jason looked at the dark-haired kid sitting across from him. "Is your name really Muppet?" he asked.

Muppet gave an embarrassed grin. "That's what everyone's been calling me all my life," he said. "But my name's really Moffett. Robin Moffett."

"Robin?" His other friend, the one who wasn't Epps, seemed surprised. "Your name is really Robin?"

"Yeah."

"Robin Hood? Robin Redbreast?"

"Robin Lawrence," Muppet said.

"Pleased to meet you," said Jason.

Muppet looked at Jason. "What did your mom do?" Muppet asked. "Did she ground you or anything?"

"No. She took away my skates, and she said I couldn't use the Internet for the rest of the month."

"That's tough. 'Course, there's no place to skate anyway."

"I know. And I can sneak some online time when my mom is at work, at least for email, but I can't stay online too long, because if she calls there'll be a busy signal, and if the busy signal goes on too long, she'll know what I'm doing."

"You and me can come over to the store," said Epps, "and use the computer there. It would have to be after hours, though."

Jason looked at him. "You've got an Internet connection?"

"Oh, yeah."

Jason smiled. "Thank you," he said.

His future, suddenly, did not seem quite so bleak.

And all he had to do to secure a place in the community was to take a little ride in a police car.

Seven Indians were swallowed up; one of them escaped; he says he was taken into the ground the depth of 100 trees in length; that the water came under him and threw him out again—he had to wade and swim four miles before he reached dry land. The Indian says the Shawnee Prophet has caused the earthquake to destroy the whites.

Lexington Reporter

"Verily I say unto you," said Noble Frankland, "There shall not be left here one stone upon another, that shall not be thrown down." He nodded into the microphone as if it were a member of an audience. "That's Matthew 24:2. What could be plainer than that?"

He leaned closer to the microphone, raised his voice. "*Not be left one stone upon another! That* is the voice of our Lord! And what he said came to pass, for in the Year 70 A.D. the Temple was thrown down!"

Frankland scanned the rows of dials and potentiometers before him. His station, steel-walled, bolted down to a concrete foundation he had poured himself in Rails Bluff, had been designed so as to be operated by only one person. He and his wife Sheryl were the owners, the chairmen, the programming directors, the disk jockeys, the talk show hosts, the advertising managers, the engineers, the electricians, and usually the janitors as well. They did it all, together with a little volunteer labor from Frankland's parishioners.

Money rolled in, from the syndication of his daily Radio Hour of Prophecy program, and from the Tribulation Club members across North America. But it was all spent as soon as it arrived, on maintaining the station and his small church, on the supplies necessary to survive till the arrival of God's Kingdom, and on the weather-proof, disaster-proof bunkers he'd dug on his ten Arkansas acres in which to house the supplies till the Tribulation Club members needed them.

Frankland leaned closer to the mic again.

"And what else did our Lord tell us that came to pass?" he asked. "Wars and rumors of wars!—verse six. Famines, pestilence, and earthquake!—verse seven. Betrayal!—verse ten. False christs and false prophets!—verse twenty-four. And that's only the Book of Matthew! You want more? Let's look at Luke 21:10!"

His stubby, powerful fingers ran down his notes, ticking off the quotations one by one. Citations spilled from his lips in a cascade of verses, interpretations, commands. The Spirit was rising in his heart.

It usually took him a while to get warmed up. It was harder when he was talking on the radio, because he didn't have the feedback from a live congregation before him. Alone in the steel-walled studio, Frankland had to *imagine* the audience before him, imagine their responses to his calls, the love they sent him, a love hot as a flame, that he used to kindle the Spirit.

"The Word of God isn't hard to understand!" he said. At his sudden burst of volume the needles jumped on the peak level meters, but this was no time to drop his voice. "It's in plain language. Just *read* it, Mr. Liberal God-just-wants-us-all-to-get-along! I've got news for you—God *doesn't* want us to just get along! God doesn't want us to be *nice*! God doesn't think that obedience to the Antichrist is *just another lifestyle choice*! God wants us to *obey his word*!"

The needles on the level meters had just about maxed out, and Frankland, concerned that some of his listeners' speakers, if not their eardrums, might be about to explode, decided it was time to attempt sweet reason. He lowered his voice.

"But let's just look at the evidence," he suggested. "Let's look at Matthew 24:29. 'Immediately after the tribulation of those days shall the sun be darkened, and the moon shall not give her light . . .' And then *afterward*, in verse 30, the Son of Man appears in the heavens, in clouds of glory, to bring His Kingdom!

"What do you think of *that*, Mr. Pre-Tribulationist Rapture Wimp!" Frankland realized he was shouting again. "The Tribulation happens *first*! It's right there in plain English! And if you don't believe *that*, if St. Matthew isn't *good enough* for you, let's look at the *Book of Revelation*!"

The hell with his listeners' eardrums! What was more important, eardrums or God's Word?

The Spirit had taken command, as the Spirit so often did. And as the Spirit rolled on, the words flowing from his mouth without his conscious thought, he wondered if his colleague, Dr. Lucius Calhoun of the Pentecostal Church of Rails Bluff, was by any chance listening and resented the characterization of "rapture wimp." He hadn't meant to offend Dr. Calhoun, to whom he sold air time at a bargain rate and with whom he agreed on just about everything but the timing of the Rapture in relationship to the Tribulation, but when the Spirit took hold, Frankland just couldn't hold back. It was all so *obvious*.

"The arm of prophecy smiteth the wicked," he said, "and exalted shall be the prophet among his kind."

In the back of his mind, Frankland wondered if that last phrase was actually in the Bible. The unfortunate truth was that he was not very good at memorization, a fact that put him at a serious disadvantage as a preacher. The stock of biblical quotes he could summon from memory, without the notes he usually kept handy, was not very large.

Perhaps that is why he had not made it to the big time. His Radio Hour of Prophecy did well enough, and he was thankful that he had been allowed to bring people to God in this way, but he had always hoped to graduate to television, to gain the huge audience that worldwide syndication could bring. Yet despite several attempts to make the leap to video, he'd never quite managed it. He looked all right—he was a big sandy-haired man, and his overbite wasn't *too* large a problem, even though it did have the tendency to make him look like a chipmunk—but the sad fact was that he and television had somehow never connected.

The closest he'd come had been a three-month stint as a TV preacher in El Dorado, Arkansas, before his move to Rails Bluff. First, the program director had asked him to vary his message a little, to talk about something other than the end of the world. Frankland had tried to comply, but somehow when the Spirit seized him, the Spirit swerved right back to the Apocalypse.

And the other problem was the biblical quotes. "You can't go on making this stuff up," the program manager had told him. "People in Arkansas know their Bible."

It had been useless to explain that it had been the Spirit talking, not Frankland. Who was the program manager to question the words of the Spirit? But Frankland's Video Half-Hour of Prophecy was canceled anyway.

"The seals produce the trumpets and the trumpets produce the bowls!" he proclaimed. "What could be clearer? What do you have to say to *that*," he demanded, "Mr. Roman go-to-confession-once-a-week-and-everything-will-be-fine Catholic?"

People needed to wake up, that was for sure. The signs were all around. The world was going to come to an *end*, practically any second, and the people were going to need instruction as to what to do, how to behave.

He didn't know how long he would be permitted to continue. Once the Tribulation started, the servants of Satan were bound to try to silence him.

"And who is this prince?" he asked. "The prince is the little horn of Daniel! It's all so *clear*!"

Frankland was ready for the servants of Satan when they came. He had a sawed-off, double-barreled shotgun clipped under the desk in the front office. There was a pistol in a drawer here in the studio, and another in his truck.

And, in the concrete bunkers he'd poured for the members of the Tribulation Club on the back of his property, there were a lot *more* surprises for Satan.

Cases and cases of them.

He brought his hand down on the control panel in front of him, thumping it with his fist as if he were banging a pulpit. Needles leaped on the displays.

"What more do you people need to *know*?" he demanded.

Charlie sipped at his Cohiba, letting the smoke of the Cuban cigar roll over his tongue. He let the taste soak into his palate for a moment, then tilted his head back and exhaled.

"And the hell of it is," he said, "we're going to make a fortune while the economy of the entire world goes straight down the tubes. Firms will go bankrupt. Careers will be wrecked. Millions of people will lose their jobs. We may even see a war or two when economies crash in the Third World."

"You mean like in Arkansas?" Megan said.

Charlie grinned and sipped his Remy Martin. Under the water of his spa, he slid the bottom of his foot along her smooth bare thigh. She smiled back, then took a taste of her own cigar.

They were sitting opposite one another in the spa on Charlie's second-floor deck, overlooking his yard and pool. Pulsing jets of water massaged their backs, feet, and legs. Wind chimes rang distantly over the throb of the spa's pumps.

Charlie tilted his head back against the plastic headrest, looked at the few stars visible through high banks of cloud. "There's a market in everything nowadays," he said. "Currency, commodities, metals, bonds. There's a market in markets." He tilted his head down and looked at her. "With all our short positions, we've just placed our bets on the market in catastrophe."

Megan gave a low laugh. She leaned forward, held out her crystal glass. "Here's to catastrophe," she said.

He bent toward her, touched his glass to hers. A crystal chime sang out, hung for several seconds in the air.

Charlie leaned further, pressed his lips to hers. Her lips were moist, tasted of smoke and desire.

A throb of pure lust pulsed through his nerves. For a half-second he considered flinging his drink and cigar off the edge of his patio and throwing himself on Megan, but on reflection he decided to wait.

Timing, he found, was everything.

He leaned back, let the water jets pulse against his back, sipped again at his drink. Megan rescued a strand of her pinned-up auburn hair that had trailed into the water, then looked back at him with dark eyes.

Charlie adored Megan, and it was because he could look into her and see a reflection of himself. Someone who had come from nowhere—from *worse* than nowhere—and turned herself into someone else by talent, by energy, and by pure force of will. And the process wasn't over. Megan was improving her vision of herself all the time.

Charlie loved Megan not for herself, but for her *potential*.

Megan was born in the Ozarks—Charlie didn't know just where. Her father was a *trapper*, for God's sake, someone who spent most of his life in the woods and mountains looking for animals to skin. Her mother was an alcoholic, abusive when she wasn't drinking herself unconscious. Megan had clawed her way out of that environment through pure courage and determination, got her college degree, worked her way up in the TPS back room to the point where she was in charge of the whole settlements office. Changed her hick accent to the smooth tones of a Southern beauty queen—now he could only hear the Ozarks in her voice when she got excited. Megan had remade herself.

And so had Charlie. The son of an East London machinist, the product of the local Mixed Junior School, he had ridden a talent for maths to London University, to a first-class degree in mathematics, to jobs at Morgan Stanley in London and Salomon in New York—both American firms where his lowly origins and Cockney accent were not a liability—and now to head of the front room at Tennessee Planters Securities. Along the way he'd had his teeth capped, his jawline reshaped, and his straight, mousy brown hair had gone blond and curly.

He hadn't managed to lose his Cockney accent the way Megan had lost the tones of the Ozarks, but he'd worked out ways of turning the accent to his advantage.

In Megan he had found a kindred soul, someone who understood that sometimes a person just needed to be *someone else*, could *decide* who that person was to be, and then *become* that person.

The way Charlie figured it, there was a kind of empty space, a virtual space in the world where a successful person was destined to be. He planned to occupy that space.

So far, it was working very well.

Charlie adjusted his body to the massaging jets that throbbed behind his back. He tasted his cigar again and looked at Megan over the smoke that curled from his mouth. "Life is good, innit?" he said.

Megan blew a kiss at him over the rim of her brandy snifter, and gave voice to the two words that were her motto. "No guilt," she said.

"Why be guilty?" Charlie sipped his cognac. "We're not going to *cause* the recession."

"For every winner in the market," Megan said reasonably, "there is a loser. For every fortune we make, a fortune is lost somewhere else. People who aren't as smart, or as quick, or are just unlucky."

Charlie smiled. This was the settlements officer talking. In the end, for Megan everything had to balance.

It was her job to catch his mistakes. Trading was fast and manic, and sometimes in the heat of action traders placed the wrong orders or entered the wrong figures. It was not unknown for traders to attempt fraud and deception. It was the task of the settlements office to catch those mistakes on the fly, to make sure that all the accounts were balanced at the end of the day. The job required skill, intelligence, instinct, and tact.

All skills that Megan possessed in abundance. But her instinct to bring columns of figures into balance did not necessarily encompass all financial reality.

"That's not exactly true, is it?" Charlie said. He leaned back and waved his cigar at the sky. "The market isn't a zero-sum game," he said. "Because wealth isn't limited. The market can be used to *make more wealth*. And then everyone benefits. A rising tide lifts all boats, as that great statesman John F. Kennedy used to say."

Megan examined her cigar. "That's not what's going to happen in this case, Charlie. We're fast and smart, and we're going to take money from the people who are slow and stupid."

Charlie shrugged. "They can afford to lose," he said, "or they wouldn't be betting at all."

"No guilt," she said.

He rolled the firm gray ash off the end of his Cohiba. He and Megan had formed their—they called it a "partnership"—about three months before, after dancing around their mutual attraction for the better part of a year. They kept their relationship a secret from the others at Tennessee Planters, not because there was a company policy against it, but because people might begin to wonder what an overly intimate relationship between the front and back offices of TPS might *mean* in terms of what Megan actually reported to their superiors about Charlie's trades. She had, theoretically, the power to suppress information about his activities. If he was in hot water, she could cover for him.

She hadn't ever done any such thing, of course. But Charlie liked to think that, if he ever really needed it, he could count on her to do just that.

He knew that she trusted him. He was managing her portfolio for her, had made her some money. Was about to make her enough money so that she could retire on her capital now, at the age of twenty-eight.

"I keep thinking of my dad," he said. "What he'd make of all this." He made a gesture that took in his house, the spa bubbling on the deck, the swimming pool glowing on the lawn below, the cigar and the cognac and the money in the bank.

"We lived in a little semidetached, you know?" he continued. "Recessions always hit us hard. When I was growing up my dad was laid off half the time. And even when he was working, my mum would meet him at the factory gate at five P.M. on Fridays, so she could get her week's allowance before he could spend it at the boozer. All the wives did that. Imagine what it was like for the men—walk out of your place of work into this mob of women, all waiting for the money you've had in your hand for only a few minutes. He got to see his money for the length of time it took him to walk to the gate, and then it was gone. Year after year."

"At least your dad had a paycheck," Megan said. She shifted in her seat so that her foot could slide along his inner thigh. Pleasure sang along his nerves, and he caught his breath. He could see a wicked little smile touching the corners of Megan's lips.

She wasn't interested in his family history, in fact thought his affection for his family improbable. She hated *her* family and saw no reason why anyone else should like his. And so, to avoid the topic altogether, she was playing a game of distraction.

But Charlie preferred to demonstrate that he could not be distracted so easily. Other men might be led by their dicks, but Charlie's moves were more calculated.

Despite the fire that quickened his blood, he leaned back and kept his voice deliberately casual.

"My dad's a union man," Charlie said. "Always votes Labour. Gets tears in his eyes whenever he hears the 'Internationale.'" Charlie shook his head. "I'd buy 'em a nice place in the suburbs, but what would my dad do? He's still at the factory, still doing his job—doesn't want to commute to work. I'd buy them a car, but they don't drive."

Megan's foot slid up one thigh, crossed his abdomen— Charlie's belly muscles fluttered at the touch—and then her foot descended the other thigh. Charlie felt heat flowing into his cock. By a pure act of will he kept his voice from breaking.

"So," he said, "I got my family some nice furniture, and in case I stroke out on the trading floor, I'm leaving them a packet in my will. God knows what they'll do with the money. Buy a new telly, maybe. Take a trip to Disney World."

Megan's foot rested lightly on Charlie's thigh. "My will leaves everything to my buddy Maureen," she said. "My family can go fuck themselves."

"What?" Charlie grinned at her over the rim of his glass. "You're not leaving anything to *me*?"

Megan's foot slid up his thigh again. Fire sang along his nerves. Deliberately he caressed her own inner thigh with his instep.

"If this works," Megan said with a little gasp, "you're not going to need *my* money."

"What do you mean *if*?" Charlie said. She had reacted to his underwater caress: that meant he had won. He rested his cigar and drink on the edge of the spa, then moved forward, slid weightlessly between Megan's legs as a wave foamed over his shoulders. He kissed her smoky lips. A smile tilted Megan's mouth as she arched lazily against him. Water spilled from her breasts. She cocked up one leg and ran her heel up his lower spine.

"Why, Mistah Johns," she said, in her best Southern-deb voice, "ah am so totally astonished by such gallant attention directed toward li'l old me."

She tipped her head back and finished her cognac in one swallow. A tiny rivulet of brandy coursed from the corner of her mouth and ran down her left breast. Charlie licked it off, felt the fire on his tongue. He licked up to her neck, tasting sweat and chlorine, and feasted for a moment on her throat. Megan laid her cigar carefully on the edge of the spa, then gave her brandy glass a careless toss over her shoulder, off the deck. Charlie heard the little splash as the glass hit the swimming pool below.

He kissed her again, and she drove her lips up into his. Her long fingernails combed his hair. He was already fully erect, and could feel her coarse pubic hair grating against the underside of his cock. He cupped her breasts, held them up out of the water. Foam sluiced down her flesh as he kissed her breasts, tongued the nipples. Her fingernails expertly slid up his back, bringing a shiver of sensation along his spine.

"Mistah Johns." Still in her Southern belle voice. "Ah do believe that you are growing ovah-excited by the thought of all those Yankee dollahs."

She took his head in her hands and pressed him to her breast. Her nipple was swollen with pleasure, and he drew it into his mouth, flicked the rubbery bud with his tongue. She gave a tremulous sigh, a bit theatrical—still playing Scarlett O'Hara. "Oh my," she said in a lazy voice, "it is certainly my impression that you are taking advantage of mah generous and yieldin' nature."

"Sorry, love," he paused to say. "But I can't do Rhett Butler."

"You could try Leslie Howard," she suggested.

Charlie couldn't remember who Leslie Howard was, a film star or a character in *Gone with the Wind* or some other bloke entirely, and he really wasn't in the mood to do imitations anyway. He kissed her again, teasing her breasts under water, stroking them from the armpits to the nipples. He could taste the tang of salt on her lips. She encouraged him with a little sigh.

At least she'd dropped the Scarlett O'Hara routine.

He stroked her ribs, her thighs. Megan nipped his lower lip with her sharp front teeth. He slipped his hand between their two bodies, between her legs. Her lips had a different texture—normally velvet-soft, under water they were more rubbery. She shifted her hips to give him room to stroke her. One of her hands dipped under water, and Charlie felt her long fingernails scratching up the underside of his cock. He arched his back, gasped. She gave a demonic little giggle and enclosed him in her fist. He slid the tip of his middle finger between her lips, felt warmth and readiness. Megan gave a little moan, close to his ear.

"I don't think you're exactly immune to the lure of those dollars yourself," Charlie said. He slid his finger up to her clitoris, heard her sudden gasp, saw her bite her lip. He couldn't tell if the reaction was pain or pleasure—the problem with sex under water was that the natural lubricant tended to get washed away.

"Are you all right?" he asked.

Her dark eyes challenged him from under her brows. "I'm all right for anything you care to try, Mr. Johns," she said. The Southern-deb voice was gone, and the Ozarks twang had slipped back into her voice.

He positioned her on the molded fiberglass seat—she was near-weightless under water—and slid himself into her. Her softness folded around him, a half-degree warmer than the spa-water. She gave her demonic little giggle again, and her knees clamped hard on his ribs. He adjusted his position with little thrusts.

Megan drove her pelvis into him with a sudden urgent thrust that almost sent him floating away. The water made him so buoyant that he'd bob away like a cork if he wasn't careful. Charlie clamped his hands on the sides of the spa and met her thrusts. Her ankles crossed behind his back and locked him to her.

She drove herself into him, hips pumping, breath hissing

past her teeth, her eyes closed to slits. She could usually trigger her first orgasm right away. Water splashed up, fountained over the edge of the spa. Megan gave a series of low, guttural cries as she came, her strong thighs clamping down hard on his ribs. Charlie scarcely had to move at all.

Megan's orgasm passed, and she lay back against the spa's side and let her breath sigh out as she tried to relax. The grip of her thighs eased. Charlie looked down at her and smiled at the way her breasts, more buoyant than the rest of her, bobbed in the surging water. She looked up at him with a ragged grin, then reached for her cigar with shaking fingers. She inhaled luxuriously, held the smoke for a moment, and then formed her mouth into an O and blew out into the space between them. The blue smoke mushroomed off his chest, floated up past the chest hairs that were plastered to Charlie's skin. He inhaled deeply through his mouth, bringing the tart flavor of the Cohiba across his tingling palate.

He thrust gently, making certain she was comfortable, then increased his movement. Megan gave a little cry of surprise at the post-orgasmic intensity of her pleasure. She set the cigar on the edge of the spa again. Charlie lengthened his thrust. The intense look came back to Megan's face; her breath began to hiss again. Charlie grabbed ahold of her hips and lunged into her. She met him with a grin and a gleeful half-shout, a kind of sexual battle cry. He drove furiously into her, his fingers slipping beneath her to cup her buttocks, lifting her off the formed fiberglass seat. She clasped her arms around his neck. Charlie lifted her just above the lowest of the several water jets set into the back of her seat. Both gasped as a jet of water pulsed over their genitals. Her breath hissed in his ear. Frantically he licked her neck and shoulder. Her hips began the sequence of furious lunges that signaled the approach of orgasm, and Charlie increased the fury of his thrusts. The spa poured a jet of bubbling pleasure along the underside of his cock. A river of sweat ran down his face. Water leaped out of the tub, poured onto the deck around them. His orgasm triggered first, and hers a half-second later.

Afterward he ducked his head under water to wash away

the sweat and clear his head. He rose, shaking water from his bleached locks. Megan was perched half out of the water, letting the night air cool the glistening water drops on her shoulders and breasts. Strands of her pinned-up hair had straggled into the water, and wet hanks of hair curled about her shoulders like dark serpents.

"We'll do it slow next," Charlie said.

"If I'm not too sore," she said.

He grinned at her. "I'll kiss and make better."

"Ha ha," she mocked. She looked around for her cigar, then bent to peer over the edge of the spa. "Shit," she said. "I dropped my smoke."

"I'll get it."

He vaulted out of the spa, water pouring off his body, and found her Cohiba where it had rolled next to a potted ficus. The night air was wonderfully cool on his overheated body. He sipped at the cigar, found it had gone out. He reached for his lighter, puffed it into life, and handed it to her.

He clamped his hands on the deck rail and looked at the glowing pool below. Well-being sang through his blood. "I feel like Tarzan, Lord of the Jungle," he said.

"If you do that yell," Megan said, "I'm leaving."

"Maybe I'll just go find an alligator and fight him hand-to-hand." On sudden impulse he jumped up on the rail, swayed back and forth on his bare feet. Megan's eyes widened in surprise.

"Get down from there!" she said.

"We're going to make money!" Charlie shouted into the night. He pounded his chest with one hand while the other arm, extended, helped him balance. "Tarzan make big bucks!" he shouted in Weissmuller-inspired pidgin English.

"You're crazy!" Megan said. The Ozarks rang in her voice. "Your neighbors are going to—"

"Tarzan is Lord of Jungle!" Charlie yelled. "Tarzan swing big dick in world of finance!"

"You're out of your mind, Charlie!" Megan yelled back.

He bent at the knees. He could feel a wide grin spreading across his face at the thought of what he was about to do.

"You'll kill yourself!" Megan shouted, guessing what was on his mind.

"Tarzan live forever!" Charlie shouted, and leaned forward, toes digging into the wooden rail for one last push as his body sailed out into the night.

"Charlieeee . . . !" Megan called.

The wind flowed through Charlie's hair as he flew, straight as an arrow, downward to the pool.

The cool waters received him as their lord.

FIVE

Arrived in this place on Friday morning last. Mr. John Vettner and crew, from New Madrid, from whom we learn, that they were on shore five miles below the place on Friday morning the 7th instant, at the time of the hard shock, and that the water filled their barge and sunk it, with the whole of its contents, losing every thing but the clothes they had on. They offered, at New Madrid, half their loading for a boat to save it, but no price was sufficient for the hire of a boat. Mrs. Walker offered a likely negro fellow for the use of a boat a few hours, but could not get it.

The town of New Madrid has sunk 12 feet below its former standing, but is not covered with water; the houses are all thrown down, and the inhabitants moved off, except the French, who live in camps close to the river side, and have their boats tied near them, in order to sail off, in case the earth should sink. It is said that a fall equal to that of the Ohio is near above New Madrid, and that several whirls are in the Mississippi river, some so strong as to sink every boat that comes within its suck; one boat was sunk with a family in it. The country from New Madrid to the Grand Prairie is very much torn to pieces, and the Little Prairie almost entirely deluged. It was reported when our informants left it, that some Indians who had been out in search of some other Indians that were lost had returned, and stated that they had discovered a volcano at the head of the Arkansas, by the light of which they traveled three days and nights. A vast number of sawyers have risen in the Mississippi river.

Russelville, Kentucky, Feb. 26

"Damn. Look at that. River's sure high." Viondi paused at the top of the crumbling concrete ramp.

Nick Ruford passed him and kept walking down the ramp. "There's floods up north, you know."

"Hadn't heard," Viondi said.

"Haven't been watching the news, huh?"

"Been workin' double shifts remodeling those old buildings down on Chouteau. Ain't had time to watch the news."

Nick paused at the water's edge. The swift river rippled purposefully across the boat ramp, as if it resented the presence of the concrete. There was a splash as the wake of a towboat raised a wave that splattered Nick's shoes. He stepped back.

Viondi Crowley walked down the worn ramp in his sandals, paused to put down his creel, then stepped into the water, washing the dust from his big, square toes.

"River's a cold motherfucker today," he said.

"Careful. Or you'll fall on your ass."

The towboat's wake slopped water over Viondi's ankles. He backed out of the river, shook the Mississippi off his feet.

"Hand me the soap," he said.

The Mississippi ran blue here—thirty miles above where, at St. Louis, the Missouri dumped half the mud of the Midwest into the Father of Waters. Long wooded islands stretched down the river, though at the moment most of them were half submerged, willow branches trailing listless in the flood. Two towboats were in sight, both pushing long tows against the current. The sound of their powerful turbines whined distantly off the water.

Nick looked out at the sparkling waters, felt the sun on his face. A mild wind stirred the hairs on his neck. He took a breath, tried to relax. Tried to *make* himself relax. And then wondered why it was so hard.

It's not like he had a job to worry about. Or a home. Or a family.

Hell, relaxing should be *easy*. So why wasn't it?

He looked down as Viondi held the bar of soap in one big hand and carved it into chunks with his pocket knife. He retained two of the soap chunks, put the rest in their original wrapper, then put the wrapper in his pocket.

He reached out a hand, and Nick mutely handed him the fishing rods. Viondi baited them both with chunks of soap, then handed one to Nick.

"Better cast off the ramp," he said. "With the river this high, there's bound to be snags everywhere else."

Viondi stepped away to give himself some casting room, then brought the rod back over his shoulder and let it fly out. The reel sang as the baited line flew out over the river. There was a splash as it struck the water.

Relax, Nick told himself. *You should relax. Fishing is the most relaxing thing in the world.*

He cast into the water, his movement more awkward than Viondi's. The hook and its chunk of soap landed about twenty feet from where Nick intended. He had come to fishing late in life—his father, as he was growing up, had always thought the son of a general had more important things to do. Nick's sports had been wrestling and track, and he'd been expected to stay on the honor roll for academics as well. There'd been Scouting—if a general's son couldn't make Eagle Scout, there was obviously something wrong with them both. And afterward there had been more school, and family, and his job with McDonnell.

Where did fishing fit into all that?

He hadn't gone fishing in his life until he met Viondi.

"Hey, Nick," Viondi said, as he reeled in. "What do you call a woman who can suck a golf ball through a garden hose?"

Nick looked at Viondi's grin. "What?" he said.

"'Darling.'"

A reluctant laugh pushed itself up from Nick's diaphragm. "Where you hear these?" he asked.

Viondi retrieved his lure, cast again. "There's this rich white lady, see, goes to the doctor. And the doctor sits her down and says, 'You're in good health. And in fact I want to compliment you on the fact that your pussy is the cleanest I've ever seen.'

"And the lady says, 'It better be, I got this colored man comes in twice a week.'"

Nick's laugh bubbled up like a spring.

"Made you laugh twice in a row," Viondi said. "Gold star for me."

Nick wished he knew some good jokes he could use to answer Viondi's. But Viondi was the only person who ever told Nick jokes.

"Where do you get these from?" Nick asked weakly.

"Work. Niggas gotta keep themselves amused working eighteen hours a day." Viondi's eyes narrowed as he looked at the water. "Strike," he advised.

Nick had reeled his lure close to the shore; he looked down to see a dark shadow in the clear water, an engulfing mouth that opened startlingly wide before closing on the slice of soap and darting away. Nick jerked the rod to set the hook, felt the fish resist, heard the whine of the reel as the fish took the line out. Viondi cranked his reel to get his own line out of the way.

"Big ol' catfish," Viondi said, after they landed the fish. He laid the gasping fish on the fresh-cut grass he'd put in his creel, then smiled up at Nick. "Soap gets 'em every time."

Viondi was a plumber. He ran his own plumbing company with about a dozen employees, and Nick had made his acquaintance when he'd hired Viondi to replumb his old house back in Pine Lawn. He and Viondi had hit it off. Manon hadn't liked Viondi as much as Nick had. She thought Viondi was crude and irresponsible. "How can he be irresponsible," Nick had pointed out, "when he's running a successful company?"

"He's irresponsible in his personal life," Manon said.

Nick had to admit that this was true. Viondi was either working or playing, either pulling double shifts with his crew, or at a party that could last for days. Nick wasn't quite certain how often Viondi had been married, but he'd heard reference to at least three wives, and he'd had children by at least three women, not necessarily the same women as his wives.

And Viondi *looked* like such a roughneck. He was big, with wide shoulders and big biceps and a short-cropped beard.

He looked as if he could tear apart a human being with his large bare hands. Just Viondi's looks made Manon nervous.

For weeks Nick would leave messages on Viondi's answering machine without a reply, and then he'd know Viondi was working. But then he'd get a call, and Viondi would want Nick to pile with a few other friends into Viondi's Buick and drive off for a weekend's debauch in Memphis, or a road trip to Chicago, or to spend some time at the Greenville Blues Festival.

Or sometimes the call was just to go fishing on a Wednesday morning. A Wednesday like today.

Whatever the call, it had been easier for Nick to say yes once Manon had gone home to Toussaint.

A pair of freshwater gulls wheeled overhead in hopes that someone would clean a fish and give them the remains. Viondi rebaited Nick's hook with another piece of soap. "You heard from Arlette?"

Nick's heart sank. Just when he'd started feeling good.

"Yeah," he said. "She's going to France in a couple weeks." Nick frowned at the river. "I'm not going to get to see her till, maybe, Christmas."

"Shit. That's tough. Your old lady ain't cutting you no slack at all."

Nick found himself wanting to defend Manon. "Well," he said, "it's an opportunity, you know. Going to France."

"Arlette needs a daddy more than she needs a trip to France," Viondi said. "I've kept all my kids in my life, no matter what else happened." He finished baiting the hook and let it fall. Nick cast, heard the splash, saw the pale chunk of soap sink into the rippling water. Viondi cast, dropped his hook precisely. One of the gulls dipped toward the splash, then decided it didn't want to eat soap. Viondi began reeling in.

"Why don't you go down to Arkansas," he asked, "see your girl?"

Nick's heart gave a little jump at the thought. "My old car wouldn't make it," he said automatically. It needed new engine and transmission seals that he couldn't afford. When he drove it, even the *driver's* compartment filled with blue smoke.

"Take the bus." Viondi gave him a severe look. "It's not like you've got anything critical to do in St. Louis."

Nick thought about it for a long, hopeful moment, calculating how much it would cost, how long he could afford to be away. As Viondi said, it wasn't as if he had anything important here, a job or anything.

There wasn't a hotel in Toussaint, he'd have to stay at the boarding house run by Manon's aunt.

Man, Nick thought, Manon would be pissed.

He thought about Arlette's eyes lighting at the sight of the diamond necklace.

"Tell you what," Viondi said. "I could use a little R and R down in N'awlins. I'll drop you off in Toussaint on the way."

Nick looked at him. "What about those buildings on Chouteau?"

"Nearly done. I'll let Darrell finish the job." Darrell was Viondi's eldest son. "Do him good to have a little responsibility for a change." Viondi smiled. "I've got a weekend's worth of work first, though, that can't do without me. How about I pick you up on Monday?"

Hope rose in Nick, but he found that he was wary of hope these days. He didn't want this to disappear.

"You sure about this?" he asked. "I mean, this is pretty sudden."

Viondi shrugged. "It's like I'm always telling you, man, you want a flexible schedule, you get a job like mine. Work hard, play hard, die with your boots on." He looked at Nick. "It's not too late for you, you know. I'm bidding up a big contract, could use a new apprentice."

"Well," Nick said "it may come to that."

Viondi grinned. "Hey," he said. "You know why God invented golf?"

Nick shook his head. "No idea," he said.

"So that white folks could dress up like black people."

A few more hours of this, Nick thought, and he might even start to relax.

*   *   *

As he drove around the bend and the plant came in sight around the pine thicket, Larry Hallock lifted his eyes automatically to the huge cooling tower and found something wrong. His eyes checked in their movement and returned to the tower, the elegant concrete hyperboloid curves whitened by the morning sun.

Something was missing. The plume of steam that normally floated above the tower.

Larry was annoyed with himself. He *knew* that. He knew that the reactor had been shut down for refueling, something that happened every eighteen months or so. He knew that there would be no plume of steam when the reactor wasn't in operation.

But he'd got used to the steam plume being there, perched above the tower. Eighteen months was just long enough for him to forget how the plant looked when the reactor was shut down.

He passed by the old Indian mound that archaeologists, somewhat to the inconvenience of the facility's designers, had insisted remain on the property. The front parking lot looked full. One of the concessions the power company had made to the locals when they'd acquired the site was that one-third of the plant workers had to come from the immediate area. As there are relatively few nuclear engineers and qualified power plant managers in rural Mississippi, the Poinsett Landing plant was blessed with a large and splendidly equipped janitorial, maintenance, and machine-shop force.

The parking lot was unusually full as workers busied themselves with maintenance and preventative maintenance while the reactor was cold, so Larry turned the Taurus down the fork in the road that led behind the plant, toward the river hidden behind the long green wall of the levee. The long morning shadow of the cooling tower reached across the grass and fell on him as he drove, and in the air-conditioned silence of the car, he felt a chill.

*   *   *

Larry's feet rang on metal as he climbed the ladder that led up the maintenance truss that ran up the curved roof of the primary containment building. He tilted his head back in the bright yellow hood of the clean suit he wore and kept on climbing. The structure smelled of emptiness and wet concrete. Masses of concrete and steel loomed around him. Below, in addition to the water-filled chamber and the crane, the building was filled with a chaos of tanks, pipes, valves, conduit, ductwork, electric motors, girders, accumulators, and bundles of cable. All of it on a massive scale, dwarfing the suited figures of the crane operators.

Jameel, the foreman who was supervising operating the refueling machine, looked up as Larry passed overhead, then gave a wave. Larry waved back.

"How 'bout the Cubbies?" Larry called down. Jameel was from Chicago and maintained a dogged loyalty to the National League's perennial losers.

"Two in a row!" Jameel shouted. He gave the thumb's-up sign.

"Guess they didn't need Gutierrez after all!"

Jameel made a face. He had complained long and hard about the Cubs' preseason trade.

The refueling was relatively simple, but the scale of it was always impressive. Larry enjoyed his visits to the containment structure, and since the reactor was shut down, and everyone else going through routine maintenance checklists, he had nothing more urgent at the moment than to suit up, enter the containment building, and play tourist.

The bright yellow clean suit he wore, complete with boots and gloves and a hood over his head, had nothing to do with protecting himself from radiation—the water flooding the space above the reactor would do that. The suit was to keep him from contaminating the water with one of his accidental byproducts, such as, for example, a hair. The demineralized water that was used to cool the reactor and its fuel was carefully maintained in order to make certain that it gave no chemical or mechanical problems.

The refueling machine began to hum as chains rattled in. Larry put his hands on the rail, looked down. The machine was large and moved back and forth on tracks placed over the water-filled refueling cavity. Its operators sat atop it, peering into the watery depths below.

Glimmering in the glow of floodlights, the squat silver-metal form of a fuel assembly began its descent into the reactor. Its glittering image was broken by the refraction of the little wavelets in the pool. The chains ceased to rattle, and the sound of the engine died. Electric motors gave brief whines. Jameel signaled to another of his crew. There was a subdued metallic clang, and then chains began to rattle again as the hook that had lowered the fuel assembly into the reactor withdrew.

The refueling process was nearing its end. Over eight hundred fuel assemblies needed to be moved—most were just moved within the reactor, but a third had to be replaced completely, the old assemblies moved through an underwater channel to the Auxiliary Building for storage, while new assemblies were carried the other way.

With an urgent hum of electric motors, the refueling machine began to move, sliding on its tracks toward the fuel channel, where it would pick up another fresh fuel assembly for movement into the reactor.

Larry smiled down at the operation and thought of horses.

Even with his fifty-five years and his degree in nuclear engineering, Larry Hallock still considered himself a cowpuncher. He had been raised on a ranch near Las Vegas, New Mexico, a long, rambling adobe building, built over generations, with a tin roof and a homemade water tower. Every summer afternoon, as the thermals rose from the valley floor, cool air would flow down from the Sangre de Cristo Mountains and bring with it the scent of the high meadows, the star flowers, white mountain daisies, and purple asters, the flowers that flourished in the brief growing season at ten thousand feet.

For Larry, this was the perfume of paradise. Sometimes, even now, he woke from a dream with the scent in his nostrils.

When he was fourteen, his father had called him, his brother, and his sister into the little office from which he ran the ranch business, the mud-walled room with its old rolltop desk, well-thumbed ledger books, and Navajo rugs. His blue eyes gazed at them all from his leathery face.

"Do you love this business?" he asked. "Do you want to ranch for the rest of your lives?"

All three siblings nodded.

"Well, then," their father said, "you better all go to college and become professionals, because it's the only way you're going to be able to afford to keep this place alive."

They had taken their father's advice to heart. Larry's younger brother Robert was a doctor in Santa Fe. Larry had become a nuclear engineer. Both considered themselves cowboys at heart, and spent as much time as possible in New Mexico doing ranch work. And their older sister Mimi, who still lived on the ranch, commuted in her Chevy pickup truck to her law practice in Las Vegas. She had raised her children to carry on after her, which was more than Larry had managed— his daughter worked in biostatistics, whatever those were, in North Carolina's Research Triangle, and his son studied Chinese literature at the University of Chicago. Both places were a long way from New Mexico, and when Larry thought about it he felt a breath of sadness waft through his heart.

He was remembering a grulla mare named Low Die that he had ridden when he was maybe twelve. She would set down wonderfully on her hocks, but for some reason she would not fall off to the right as well as she fell off to the left. When she spun to the left it was a thing of beauty, but when he wanted her to cut right, for some reason her coordination fell apart, and there were strange, unpredictable hesitations in her movement. It was almost as if she were *afraid* to turn right.

Experience suggested that such a fault might be the result of a spinal injury or deformity. But after a thorough examination it was concluded that Low Die's spine was in perfectly fine shape.

So Larry had worked that strange horse patiently for weeks. He would work her first on moves that she could do well, moves in which she had confidence. He would praise her lavishly for every successful maneuver. Then he would run her for a while, so that she'd get tired and not think so much, just respond to the touch of his feet and hands.

And then he'd start turning Low Die in wide circles to the right. And the circles would get smaller and smaller until, eventually, she was falling off to the right just as he wanted.

That was how you solved a problem. You broke it down into pieces, and you solved the pieces one at a time. With patience, you could get anywhere, even into the dimwitted brain of a horse.

Low Die. A beautiful cutting horse. He'd ridden her for years.

"You see that homer in the Red Sox game?" Jameel called up from his post on the refueling machine.

"Oh yeah," Larry said. "A thing of beauty."

In Larry Hallock's estimation, the problems involved in managing nuclear power were not dissimilar to those involved in training a horse. The universe operated by certain principles, and these principles could be applied anywhere, by anyone of sufficient skill and intelligence. The statement of a problem contained within itself the elements of its own solution. You needed to break the problem into its parts, to work on each in its turn. You needed patience and a sense of perspective. Humor didn't hurt, either. Sometimes you found yourself turning circles, as Larry had when he was training Low Die, but you needed to realize that even when you were turning in circles, you were still getting somewhere.

Poinsett Landing was a complex system, and its complexities were increased by its massive scale. The statistics themselves were vast enough to strain the imagination. The power station required a dozen years to build, 1,800 miles of electrical wire, 100 miles of pipe, 125 miles of conduit, 16,000 tons of steel, 29,000 tons of rebar, and nearly 150,000 cubic yards of concrete. The reactor vessel, the steel pressure cooker in which nuclear fission took place, stood eighty feet high, its sides were over eight inches thick, and it weighed two million pounds. It sat in a steel-and-concrete containment structure twice as high as the reactor vessel, three and a half feet thick and sheathed with stainless steel, built so strongly that it could withstand the 300-mile-per-hour winds of a tornado, or even the impact of a Boeing 747 being deliberately crashed, by suicidal terrorists, into the building from above.

But when you got right down to it, a nuclear power station, with all its vastness, was a very simple system compared to a biological organism such as a horse. Its size was a measure of its relative inefficiency—it was enormous because people hadn't worked out how to generate power with the compact efficiency of a biological organism. Animals, with their complex organization and chemistry, their mobility and intelligence, were marvels of concentrated efficiency. They were brilliant engineering. By comparison, Poinsett Landing Power Station, complex as it was in certain ways, was simplicity itself.

Which was good, as far as Larry Hallock was concerned. An animal, be it a human being or a horse, was intricate enough so that when something went wrong with it—a broken leg, cancer, mental illness—it was difficult to fix. The problems at Poinsett Landing were, by comparison, simple.

Take the problem of Poinsett Landing's site, for example.

The massive containment building, with its huge steel nuclear reactor, its three-foot-thick concrete walls sheathed with steel, had presented a particular problem to the plant's designers. A large, heavy building requires a large, stable foundation. The best foundation of all is solid bedrock.

But bedrock is at a premium in the Mississippi Delta. The land consists of layers on endless layers of mud laid down by repeated floodings of the great river. The mud can extend thousands of feet below the level of the land. There *is* no bedrock on which to safely build large structures and anchor them against the dangers of their own weight.

But the Delta land was cheap, much cheaper than elsewhere. With the plant requiring two thousand acres of land, the price of the land was a prime consideration in the plant's cost. The plant's designers were asked to solve the problem of building the huge, heavy structure on land that would not support it.

The engineers simply built their own bedrock beneath the containment structure, a huge mat of concrete laced with a webwork of steel. This pad was twelve feet thick and sat in the rich Delta land like a paving stone, and it supported the vast two-million-pound weight of the reactor vessel, the steel-and-concrete containment structure, and the control facility, which leaned against the featureless containment building like a child clinging to his mother's hip.

It was a tried and true technique, Larry knew, often used in areas like Miami Beach, where large buildings had to be constructed on shifting sand. It had the advantage of simplicity. The huge pad would be there forever: after it had been set in the Delta soil, no one would ever have to think about it again.

"Waaal," Larry Hallock said, "let's get this sucker warmed up." He stood behind his metal desk, perched on its platform above the rest of the control room. The lights and indicators, which were on panels above the operators' heads, were at eye level for Larry. He scanned them, noted the orderly rows of green and red lights, nothing amiss.

The room looked like the headquarters of a James Bond villain. Metal surfaces, control panels, thousands of buttons, displays with blinking lights. All painted in avocado green and harvest gold, the signature colors of the 1970s, the decade in which the room was designed and built.

Larry wondered if a more recent control room would be painted different colors. Would a nineties control room be Hunter Green?

A box from Dunkin' Donuts on one of the computer monitors near the door spoiled the illusion of a supervillain's retreat. Larry helped himself to a chocolate doughnut.

"We're set," Wilbur said, having, from his lower perspective, just scanned the displays himself.

"Let's give 'er the spur," Larry said.

You didn't want to start up a nuclear reactor with a bang. It would take almost a full day to get the reactor on line, to first increase temperature within the reactor, then start pushing steam through the turbine to generate enough power to put on the grid.

It was like handling a big horse, one that could stomp you flat just by accident, just because you weren't paying attention. You just wanted to give it a little kick with your heels, get it moving without startling anyone, least of all yourself.

It was tricky enough so that Larry wanted to be in the control room for the procedure, just in case Wilbur, who was the control room operator and would be giving the orders, needed some backup. Larry was the shift supervisor, in charge of everything going on at the plant during his shift. Wilbur was in charge of the reactor under Larry's supervision.

Larry and Wilbur watched the displays as boron carbide control rods were partially withdrawn from the reactor, as neutrons began to multiply and the chain reaction began. The scent of roses floated through the control room: Larry had bought a massive vase of yellow roses for his wife, who had a birthday today. He moved the roses out of his line of sight, sat in his wheeled metal chair, and thought about putting his boots up on his desk, but decided not to.

Larry put a hand on the scarred metal surface of his desk and felt a little tremor through his fingertips. Pumps, distant but powerful, steam moving through massive pipe. Valves tripped open as pressure built.

Words floated to Larry as he watched the displays. Something about Ole Miss and the Rose Bowl.

No day was complete without talk of football. Not in Mississippi.

One of the operators interrupted the talk of the gridiron in order to make a report. "Holding at ten percent."

Ten percent was one of the check points, where all concerned would be checking their instruments, making certain that everything was operating normally.

Larry scanned the displays over the operators' heads. Everything looked fine.

"You going to do anything special for your wife's birthday, Mr. Hallock?" Wilbur asked.

"Tonight we've got reservations at the Garden Court in Vicksburg."

"Getting some of that creole food, huh? It's too hot for me."

Larry grinned. "You best not try any New Mexico chile, then."

"I don't even put pepper on my grits in the morning."

Larry looked at the displays, at the lights shifting, red and green.

"Bland is boring," he said. "Me, I like a little spice in my life."

"Everything checks, Larry," Wilbur said. "Still holding at ten percent."

"Waaal," Larry said, "let's goose her a little."

Boron carbide rods slid smoothly out of the reactor. Neutrons turned water to steam. Steam shot under unimaginable pressure through massive thirty-six-inch pipes.

Larry put his boots on the desk and thought about horses.

Four shocks of an Earthquake have been sustained by our town, and its neighborhood, within the last two days. The first commenced yesterday morning between two and three, preceded by a meteoric flash of light and accompanied with a rattling noise, resembling that of a carriage passing over a paved pathway, and lasted almost a minute. A second succeeded, almost immediately after, but its continuance was of much shorter duration. A third shock was experienced about eight o'clock in the morning, and another today about one.

Savannah, Dec. 17

Perfume floated into the Oval Office from the Rose Garden. The economics briefing book, with its tasteful white plastic cover and presidential seal, had migrated from the President's footstool to the top of his desk in the West Wing. The London meeting of the G8 countries was only a week away. The President was now immersing himself in figures concerning gross domestic product, financial markets, foreign direct investment, prices and wages, output, demand, jobs, commodities, exchanges, and reserves.

Fortunately the President liked this kind of detail work. Facts and statistics were easy compared to trying to manage Congress, foreign leaders, or for that matter the arrogant turf warriors of his own party.

He had a number of proposals he wanted to make at the G8 conference. Proposals having to do with the removal of trade barriers, pollution control, expansion of the information infrastructure, practical assistance to Third World countries. Proposals that only the leader of the world's primary superpower could make.

If only, he thought, goddam Wall Street didn't stab him in the back while he was off in London trying to get things done.

The President's phone buzzed, and he reached for it while trying to absorb a graph on current-account balances. Oil-producing states, he saw, were benefitting from a slight rise in the cost of fossil fuels.

"Judge Chivington for you, sir," said his secretary.

"Thank you. Put him on, please."

"Mr. President! Rosalie told me you called!" the judge bellowed. He was not the sort to moderate his voice merely for the telephone.

The President switched to the speaker phone and put the handset in its cradle. "I'm cramming for the G8 conference," he said.

"*That* will relieve the voters, sir," the judge said. "People worrying about employment and meetin' the mortgage are going to be encouraged as all hell when they turn on their televisions and see the President talking to the French economic minister about the price of brie."

The President smiled, leaned back in his chair, and was about to put one foot up on the corner of his desk when he remembered that this massive and colossally ugly item was made from the timbers of the HMS *Resolute*, God alone knew why, and had been a gift of Queen Victoria, the reasons for which seemed pretty damned obscure, too, but that this meant the desk was therefore a valuable antique that did not deserve to have his heel marks on it. He reluctantly put his shoe back on the floor.

I am a prisoner of history, he thought. *Damn Jackie Kennedy anyway.* He spun his chair about to face the tall windows and the Rose Garden.

"My views on the price of brie," he said, "are going to be taken more seriously if they come from the representative of the strongest economy in the world."

"Ah," the judge said. "So you reckon this is an inconvenient time for Wall Street to have the jitters."

"That is correct."

"And your economic advisors tell you that they can't be absolutely positive about it, but it looks as if the market has entered an uncertain period."

"Correct . . ."

"And that while they can't be definite about it, because the indicators are as yet unclear, it may be possible that the bull market is due for a correction."

"Something like that."

"And that the *last* thing you want, hoss, is for Dow Jones to drop four or five hundred points when you are talking to the French economic minister about the price of brie, because that would blow your credibility to hell and gone."

"I think that is about the gist." The President nodded. "Judge, you have a remarkable ability for summing up."

"And therefore, sir, you want me to talk to Sam."

"If you could. He is your friend."

"Lots of people are my friends, Mr. President," the judge said.

The President smiled his brilliant telegenic smile—even though there was no one to see it, the smile was still an essential part of his repertoire—and put the tiniest trace of syrup into his voice. "If the chairman of the Federal Reserve Board could be said to *have* a friend," he said, "that friend is you."

There was a moment's hesitation, and then the judge spoke. "Have you talked to him yourself, Mr. President?"

"I have."

"And what has he told you?"

"He said that the bull market might be due for a correction, and that he was monitoring the situation and would act, if necessary, at the appropriate time. But that a mere downturn in stock prices was not a case, strictly speaking, for intervention."

"I take it, sir, that you pointed out the importance of the economic summit?"

"I did my best. He suggested, first, that this unsettled period in the markets might end before the conference begins, and might in fact end in a big upswing. Also, he said that it would be better for the conference if plans were made on a basis of actual conditions and not, as he put it, false optimism."

"Damn," the judge said. "Sam's really being a hardass, isn't he?"

The problem was, the President knew, that there was little for a president to shine at anymore. The Cold War was over and foreign policy had come down to mediating agreements between various competing ethnic groups that the electorate hadn't heard of and didn't care about. The arrogant blowndry busybodies in Congress had ignored, watered down, or eviscerated every domestic policy initiative undertaken by the Executive Branch. For over twenty years, in every administration, every budget sent by the President to Congress had been declared dead on arrival. They couldn't decide on their own what to do, jerked this way and that by lobbyists and opinion polls, but they were certain they didn't want the President doing anything, either.

So like it or not, the President's job now came down to two things: he had to be seen to make money for people, and he had to be seen to be caring. He had to go to meetings like the G8 summit and return with promises of jobs and increased prosperity. And he had to be able to listen to people who were in the midst of hard times, and he had to look concerned. The people wanted a president who Cared, and so the President spent a lot of time, in day care centers or drug rehabilitation clinics or veterans' hospitals, doing his job of Caring. There were no more *issues*, there were no more real conflicts in politics, it had all become soap opera. The President had to pretend to everyone that the soap opera mattered.

And, as his press secretary Stan Burdett always remarked, it was no good Caring if he weren't *seen* to be Caring, and no good making money for people if he weren't making money for *everyone*, and furthermore seen to be doing it.

The President just wished he could appoint a Cabinet Secretary for Caring and have done with it.

"I'm not asking for much," the President said. "What's wrong with boosting investor confidence?"

The judge thought silently for a long moment. "Mr. President," he said, "I'll talk to Sam about it."

"He's always been a loyal Party man," the President said. Until, he did not need to add, Sam had been made the nation's chief banker, at which point he had given up politics for a Higher Calling, rolling the bones and gazing at chicken entrails in the name of the High God of Interest Rates.

"True," the judge said. "Very true." His voice boomed out. "Sir, I'll do as you ask."

"Thank you, Judge."

"You're very welcome, Mr. President."

"How about some golf next week?"

"You're very kind, sir. I would like that very much."

The President smiled. "I'll have my flunky call your flunky."

The President snapped off the speaker phone, picked up the briefing book, and leaned back in his chair.

He had been raised on the history of presidential greatness. Franklin Roosevelt fighting the Depression and Hitler, Lincoln freeing the slaves and seeing the country through its greatest crisis, Jack Kennedy staring down the Soviets over Cuba, Lyndon Johnson creating programs to eradicate poverty and establish civil rights.

And now the President couldn't even ask the chairman of the Federal for a favor, but had to get a friend to ask it for him.

A prisoner of history, he thought again.

He considered putting his feet up on the desk, but refrained.

Once the slide began, the market fell faster than even Charlie had anticipated. Charlie and TPS, even with all their money committed to Charlie's positions, weren't big enough to shift market prices very far, but once big traders like Salomon and Morgan Stanley started moving into short positions, the balance changed. Once the smart money moved, the stupid money trotted after—too late, as usual—and the *really* smart money tried to make profit out of both.

Charlie began to wonder how many beta-test versions of Carpe Diem were out there.

He stayed at his desk for the entire trading day, fueled by pots of coffee and takeout food brought in by his secretary. He traded constantly, making hedges, shoring up his position. He was afraid to take a pee break for fear that he'd miss something and lose money.

After each trading day was over he went to the back room to help Megan with the long task of reconciliation. The TPS back room wasn't really set up for trading at this volume, and Charlie's trades were so many, and so frantic, that toting up the figures sometimes took them late into the night.

And Dearborne was on Charlie's neck every minute. Charlie hadn't thought that Dearborne was going to be this involved, but apparently the banker had figured out that it was his future at stake as well as Charlie's, and every night he waited in his office for the reconciliation figures to be transmitted to him. If they were late, he called Megan's office to ask when they could be expected.

Go home, Charlie urged him mentally as he heard the jangle of the phone. *Go to the country club. Go* anywhere!

But Dearborne hung on. "You're going to give me that ulcer yet," he told Charlie.

Charlie figured that if anyone was going to get an ulcer, it would be Charlie, and it would be Dearborne who gave it to him.

The market fell far enough so that Charlie was able to liquidate his position in treasury bonds, which gave him a great lump of profit that made him itchy. He could add it to the margin account, because he knew big margin calls would be inevitable as soon as the regulators noticed how exposed his positions were growing. He could use the money to further hedge his positions, which would lessen the risk of the big margin calls. Or he could buy more short positions, which, because it would make a lot more money in the long run, is what he really wanted to do.

But the smart traders don't take those kind of risks on their own, Charlie thought. Not without covering their asses.

So he called Dearborne. "I just made you pots of money, guv," he said.

"How big are the pots?" Dearborne asked.

Charlie told him.

"Nice pots," Dearborne said, impressed.

It was a clumsy metaphor, Charlie thought, but he could run with it. "I can get you newer and nicer pots," he said, "but there's a risk."

"Oh God," Dearborne whimpered. "My ulcer's really kicking up."

"You don't *have* an ulcer yet," Charlie pointed out, and then explained his point of view.

"But if we buy all those unhedged positions," Dearborne said, "what do we use to cover the margin calls?"

"That's *your* department, guv," Charlie said.

Dearborne groaned.

"In the words," Charlie said, "of that great statesman, Ronald Wilson Reagan, *stay the course.*"

"You're going to kill me," Dearborne said.

"Trust me," Charlie said. "I know what I'm doing."

Charlie got his way. But as soon as he started putting the money on the market, the regulators noticed his vulnerability and began calling in margins, and he had to call Dearborne for money. Which led to even more anxiety on Dearborne's part, and more phone calls.

"The margin calls are signs of *success*," Charlie kept telling him. "It means the market is moving our way."

But it wasn't moving Charlie's way all the time: it jittered up and down on an almost hourly basis. Charlie took advantage of the upswings to sell as many of his hedges at a profit as he could, then buy more short options. Which led to more margin calls, more aggravation. More phone calls from Dearborne.

On Thursday night Charlie drove home after reconciliation, planning on nothing more exciting than eating some Chinese takeout and having a long soak in the spa, only to find an urgent message from Dearborne on his answering machine.

"Turn on your TV!" Dearborne shouted from the tinny speaker. "The chairman of the Fed is on!"

The chairman wasn't there when Charlie looked, so he switched to CNN and ate orange peel beef from the cardboard container while he waited for the financial report. Right at the top of the report was the chairman of the Federal Reserve, with a strange gnomic smile pasted to his face, announcing that the Fed was cutting interest rates a full point. Announcers were treating it as if the chairman had just turned water into wine.

Fuck, Charlie thought. *Fuck I am so screwed . . .*

And then, as if on cue, the phone rang. Charlie didn't answer. He just waited for Dearborne's voice to come out of the answering machine.

It didn't say anything that Charlie hadn't already imagined.

The President choked on laughter at the sight of the chairman of the Federal Reserve making his announcement. The unnatural grin, on Sam's reserved and owlish face, looked more like the product of a jolt of electricity than a result of fiscal confidence.

"I love it!" he whooped. "Damn, I am some kind of slick son of a bitch!"

The First Lady gave him an indulgent look from over her reading glasses. She sat in a lounge chair in their drawing room, a glass of sherry by one hand, briefing books in her lap. Her husband was not the only person doing homework for the economic summit.

"Sam's peculiar behavior is not unanticipated, I gather?" she said.

"Judge Chivington gave him a little phone call. But I didn't think it would work so soon, or so fast. And I sure as hell didn't think it would work by a whole interest point."

The First Lady looked down at her briefing book and with a marking pen drew a thick pink line along a critical factoid. "You think we can sustain this rally?" she said.

"Barring some unforseen disaster." He grinned at the television analyst who was urging fiduciary caution upon his audience. "I won't have egg on my face at the economic summit, anyway."

"Let's just hope," the First Lady said, returning her gaze to her briefing book, "there isn't a market adjustment while we're in London."

"We'll have to hope," said the President, "that we've put it off."

All day Friday, Charlie felt as if he'd fallen during the running of the bulls at Pamplona. Except that it was the bulls of Wall Street that were stomping him into the pavement, one sledgehammer hoof after another. Every kick to the kidney, every hoof to the spleen, and he was bleeding dollars. Buoyed by the Fed chairman's apparent optimism, the market was on a big upswing, regaining practically all the ground it had lost over the last week.

Dearborne didn't help, not with his panicky phone calls. "It's false optimism," Charlie said. *"Stay the course."*

"Over thirty percent of Tennessee Planters' capital is committed to backing your positions," Dearborne said. "We are a risk-averse institution. You told me you'd be hedging every single minute."

"I *have* hedged. I just cashed in ten million dollars' worth of Eurodollar futures. *I made you money!"*

"You haven't hedged *enough.* That's what I'm saying."

"Stay the course," Charlie said. "It's not as bad as you think."

It's going to be worse, he thought. Even though prices fell at the end of the day, as people started taking their profits, the S&P had gone up five whole percentage points.

After the markets closed, Charlie helped Megan with the process of reconciliation. Before they were completely finished, Megan sent her other employees home, then took Charlie into her office and closed the door. She looked at her monitor, and Charlie could see the green columns of figures reflected in her eyes.

"If you liquidate now," she said, "your S&P futures will have lost sixty-two point five million dollars." Charlie's heart gave a lurch. "Sixty-two and a half," she repeated. "Now you've purchased these options for forty million, and your Eurodollar hedges gives you another ten, but what's going to happen to you first thing Monday morning is a twelve-and-a-half-million-dollar margin call. I'm amazed you haven't got it already—probably the computers haven't caught up to the day's trading." The strain of maintaining her low, cultured tones turned her voice husky. "If you *don't* liquidate, my dear, your losses are unlimited."

Charlie licked his lips. He could feel sweat breaking out on his forehead. "You've got to help me hide it," he said.

She stared at him. "Hide twelve and a half *million*? Are you out of your mind?"

Charlie spoke out loud as calculations rattled frantically in his skull. "Not that much. Just eight or nine. We can't hide *all* of it, they'll be expecting *some* loss. So we give them a loss, okay? Just help me make it an *acceptable* loss—three or four million, something like that. And put the rest of it—where?" His mind spun through a mental list of his clients.

Megan stared at him. "Charlie, that's fifteen ways illegal."

"What drives markets?" Charlie asked. "FIG. Fear, Ignorance, Greed. The directors at Tennessee Planters are ignorant of the securities marketplace. They really don't understand what I'm doing. I have to stroke Dearborne every second to get him into line, and I can't stroke all of the directors all of the time. Once they see our current position, fear will take control of their minds. They're going to try to take charge of TPS, and ignorance and fear will have them doing the wrong thing. We don't dare panic them. If they panic, they could *order* me to liquidate, and those millions of losing *positions* will turn into millions of *real losses*."

Charlie could tell from the look on Megan's face that she understood all too well what might happen.

"What have we got in the error account," Charlie said, "a couple hundred thousand dollars? Just put the losses there instead of the real account. Who's going to check the error account?"

"The figures in the error account get reported just like everything else," Megan said. "All Dearborne or anyone else has to do is just call it up on the screen."

Good, Charlie thought. She was responding to the problem. She was starting to think of ways to do what he needed.

"We can't put it in *my* account. My profile is too high." He looked at Megan. "*Your* account?"

Megan's answer was a flat stare.

"Right," Charlie said. "So we put the loss in one of my client accounts. Sanderson—no, he'll smell something wrong. Caldwell." He grinned. "Caldwell. Caldwell's on vacation. He won't even notice. And he has sufficient collateral to cover any margin calls."

"He's not going to notice millions of losses? This won't attract his attention?"

"Issue a correction once we're in the black. I'll call Caldwell and tell him it was a computer error."

"Charlie," Megan said, "I dassant do this for you." The Ozarks was beginning to seep into her voice.

"These sorts of mistakes happen every day. You know they do."

"Not for this much money. And it's my *job* to catch just this sort of error."

"Just till Monday," Charlie said. "Dearborne plays golf every Monday at one o'clock."

Megan's eyes flashed. "How's Monday going to make a difference?" she demanded.

"The rally was over, I could tell," Charlie said. "The momentum was gone. People are going to have the whole weekend to reevaluate their positions. Prices are going to fall on Monday."

He hoped.

He leaned forward over Megan's desk, fixed her with his blue eyes. "Just till tee time, that's all I ask. Then you can issue a correction. Dearborne won't even look at it, he'll just see Monday's totals after the markets close."

Megan bit her lip. "This is how Nick Leeson lost Baring's," she said.

"No!" Charlie shouted. Anger seemed to flash his blood to steam. He pounded a fist on the desk. "Nick Leeson lost Baring's *because he was a fucking incompetent trader!*" He thumped his own chest. "I am a *fucking great trader!* I am the lord of the fucking trading jungle!"

He realized Megan was leaning back, away from his anger. What he saw in her eyes wasn't fear, it was distaste. She hated weakness, he reminded himself. Hated fear, hated panic.

Charlie lowered his voice, tried to catch his breath. He had to make it all logical, all reasonable.

He reminded himself that he was asking her to go clean against her training and instincts. Not to mention the law. It was her job to balance the books. It was something she took pride in. Now he was telling her *not* to balance them, to shove a colossal loss under the rug. He had to keep talking, to keep Megan working on the problem, see it from his point of view.

"I just need to get over this little bad patch, that's all," he said. "Just help me with this." He felt sweat running down his face. "After this is done, we can relax. Call the caterers, get some duck, some veal. Call a masseuse over to the house, make sure we're good and relaxed. Open a bottle of Bolly. We can have a quiet weekend together." He looked at her. "It's your money, too, sweetheart."

She looked at the screen. Gnawed a nail. Then bent over her keyboard, her lacquered nails rattling on the keys.

"Caldwell *better* be on vacation," she said.

"You're brilliant!" Charlie cheered.

"No, I'm not," she said. "I'm just crazy." She looked at him darkly. "But not as crazy as you."

SIX

At the little Prairie, thirty miles lower down, [the steam-boatmen] were bro't to by the cries of some of the people, who thought the earth was gradually sinking but declined to take refuge on board without their friends, whom they wished to collect. Some distance below the little Prairie the bank of the river had caved in to a considerable extent, and two islands had almost disappeared.

Natchez, January 2, 1812

The Reverend Noble Frankland looked into his wife's sitting room. "Time to go, sweetie pie," he said.

Sheryl looked up from her work. "Just a second, teddy bear," she said.

Sheryl used tweezers to pick up a tiny piece of paper, no larger than the head of a pin, dip it carefully in glue, and then place it carefully in the eye of an angel.

She was doing her art. Sheryl had been working at this project for longer than the twelve years of her marriage to Frankland.

Her chosen medium was postage stamps. Sheryl bought them by the thousands, the more colorful the better, and cut them up into tiny pieces each the size of a snowflake. These she glued onto bolts of black-dyed linen in designs representing scenes from the Book of Revelation. The pictures were amazingly intricate, like those miniature paintings drawn with three-hair brushes, but the scale of the work was enormous. The entire work was over fifty feet long, and Frankland had never been permitted to see all of it, though occasionally he'd caught glimpses of it over Sheryl's shoulder as she worked. Just the bits he'd seen took his breath away. Horsemen and angels, the saved and the damned, the Whore of Babylon and the City of God, all blazing in the brightest of colors, all shown in the most exacting detail. When Sheryl depicted a demon, she showed it to the pockmarks on its skin and the gleam of wickedness in its eyes. You could practically smell the garlic on its breath.

No commercial artist could ever produce work like this. The labyrinthine detail combined with the huge scale would have defeated any attempt to profit from such a work. Only a person inspired to devote her life to the work could possibly assemble such a thing.

Frankland stood by and waited for Sheryl to finish. She had always wanted to be a pastor's wife, and she hadn't shrank from any of her duties, but when they married she had demanded one promise from him. "I want you to let me have an hour a day to work on my Apocalypse," she'd said. "And the rest of the time is for you and the Lord."

He hadn't minded. Frankland had projects of his own. They'd spent many hours in pleasant silence, Sheryl working on her art, Frankland working on his plans—perhaps equally detailed—for the End Times, the plans that he kept in fireproof safes in the guest bedroom closet.

Sheryl finished the angel's eye—it glowed a beautiful aquamarine blue, with a little wink of postage-stamp light in a corner of the pupil—then blew on the glue to dry it and rolled up the linen scroll. "I'm ready, sugar bear," she said.

The picket signs were thrown in the back of the pickup truck, and Sheryl climbed into the driver's seat. Sheryl put the truck in gear and wrestled the wheel around to point it toward Rails Bluff.

The pickup was a full-size Ford, and Sheryl had to work hard to make the turn, but Frankland did not want power steering on his vehicles. Or air-conditioning, power brakes, power windows, or power *anything*.

It wasn't that he objected to these conveniences as such. It was just that he figured that during the Tribulation, spare parts for power steering mechanisms and other conveniences might be hard to come by, and he didn't want his ministry to be immobilized by the failure of something he didn't actually need.

He wiped sweat from his brow with his handkerchief. Maybe, he thought, he should have relaxed his principles in regard to air-conditioning.

At least the sun was beginning to sink toward the west. The heat would soon begin to fade.

The truck jounced out of the driveway and onto the asphalt. Frankland rolled his window all the way down, and inclined his head toward the air that blasted into the cab as the truck picked up speed. He waved at Joe Johnson, one of his parishioners, who was pacing along the edge of one of his catfish ponds. Johnson looked up from beneath the brim of his Osgold feed cap and gave a wave.

The pickup drove on. Cotton fields broadened on either side of the road.

"Robitaille," Sheryl said flatly. She slowed, swinging the big truck toward the shoulder. A large, elderly Lincoln zoomed past, heading in the opposite direction, its driver a dark silhouette behind its darkened windshield. Frankland looked over his shoulder at the Lincoln as it roared away. He could feel distaste tug at his features.

"Driving like a maniac, as usual," he said.

"Driving like a drunk," said Sheryl.

The Roman Enemy, Frankland thought, and turned to face the foe.

The Rails Bluff area had so few Catholics that there was no full-time priest in the community. The little clapboard Catholic church shared its priest with a number of other small churches in the area, and Father Robitaille drove from one to the other on a regular circuit. In Rails Bluff he heard confession and said mass on Monday nights, then roared off in his rattletrap Lincoln to be in another town by Tuesday morning.

Robitaille did not show the Church of Rome to very good advantage. He was from Louisiana originally, but alcoholism had exiled him to rural Arkansas. And he drove like a crazy man even when sober, so sensible people slowed down and gave him plenty of room when they saw him coming.

"I don't know how he's avoided killing himself," Sheryl said.

"The Devil protects his own," said Frankland.

A cotton gin shambled up on the right, corrugated metal rusting behind chain link. 750 FRIENDLY PEOPLE WELCOME YOU, a road sign said.

The population estimate was an optimistic overestimate. Both in terms of number, and perhaps even in friendliness.

The Arkansas Delta, below the bluff, featured some of the richest agricultural soil in the world combined with the nation's poorest people. The mechanization of the cotton industry had taken the field workers off the land without providing them any other occupation. The owners had money—plenty of it—but everyone else was dirt-poor.

Rails Bluff, however, envied even the folks in the Delta, and sat on its ridge above the Delta like a jealous stepsister gazing down at a favored natural child. The county line ran just below the town on its bluff, and all the tax revenue from the rich bottom land went elsewhere. It was as if God, while showering riches on everyone in the Delta, had waved a hand at everyone above the bluff and said, "Thou shalt want."

In the Delta, many people were poor, and a few were rich. In Rails Bluff, *nobody* was rich.

Now that a Wal-Mart superstore had opened in the next county, things in Rails Bluff had grown worse. The hardware store had just gone under, and the clothing store was hanging on by its fingernails.

If the world did not end soon, Frankland thought, Rails Bluff might well anticipate the Apocalypse and vanish all on its own.

The truck drove past an old drive-in theater, grass growing thick between the speaker stanchions, and then passed into town. Sheryl pulled into the parking lot of the Piggly Wiggly, and Frankland saw that Reverend Garb was already waiting, standing with one of his deacons, a man named Harvey, and a smiling, excited crowd of young people, members of his youth association.

Garb was a vigorous man in gold-rimmed spectacles, pastor of Jesus Word True Gospel, the largest local black church. The kids—all boys between the ages of twelve and eighteen—were all neatly dressed in dark slacks and crisp white shirts. Garb and Harvey added ties to the uniform. All wore white armbands.

Frankland hopped out of the pickup and shook Garb's hand. "Glad you could make it, Brother Garb." He looked at Garb's youth brigade. "I hope *my* parishioners give us such a good turnout."

"I'm sure they will, Brother Frankland. Some are here already."

Frankland looked at the rows of cars and trucks parked at the Piggly Wiggly, saw familiar faces emerging. He greeted his parishioners as they approached, heartened by their numbers.

As he was talking to one of his deacons, a battered old 1957 Chevy pickup, rust red and primer gray, rolled off Main Street into the parking lot, a big man at the wheel. There was a gun rack in the truck's rear window with an old lever-action Winchester resting in it. Frankland walked toward the pickup truck to greet its driver. Pasted on the back window was a sticker that read TRUST IN GOD AND THE SECOND AMENDMENT.

"Hey, Hilkiah," said Frankland.

"Hey, pastor," Hilkiah said cheerfully.

Hilkiah Evans stepped out of the truck. He was a tall man with broad shoulders, powerful arms, and a pendulous gut. His prominent nose had been broken over most of his face, and his arms were covered with tattoos. The old ones, the skulls and daggers and the Zig-Zag man that dated from his time in prison, were getting blurry with age as the ink began to run—a contrast to the later tattoos, the face of Jesus and the words "Jesus is Lord," which were sharp and clear. A naked woman, prominent on his left bicep, had been transformed into an angel through the addition of a pair of wings and a halo.

Hilkiah was one of Frankland's success stories. After his

second stretch for armed robbery, Arthur Evans had been introduced to Frankland by a member of his church, Eliza Tomkins, who was also his parole officer. Though Arthur had at first resisted Frankland's efforts to get his mind straight, it was clear that Eliza had detected a void in the man, a void that needed to be filled with belief and with the Light.

And, by and by, Arthur had listened, and as a mark of his conversion had changed his name to Hilkiah. Now he was one of Frankland's stalwarts, a deacon and a tireless organizer. He had joined the Apocalypse Club and purchased a two years' supply of food, although he'd had to do it on credit. Though he always had to scrape to make ends meet and was always working at least two jobs in the community, Hilkiah nevertheless donated much of his time to work at the radio station, to helping with church projects, with the youth and outreach programs.

And of course with the Christian Gun Club. He had given a great many young parishioners their first lessons in the use of a firearm.

His involvement with the Gun Club was, technically, illegal and a violation of his parole. But since his parole officer was also a member of Frankland's congregation, she had decided to ignore the technicalities.

Besides, it was ridiculous to tell someone in a place like Rails Bluff that he couldn't own a gun, even if he was a convicted armed robber. Sometimes the law was just silly.

"Hope I'm not late," Hilkiah said.

"Not at all. I've barely got here myself."

Hilkiah reached into the bed of his truck and lifted up a large Coleman cooler. "I brought some Gatorade. Thought people might get thirsty in this heat."

"Bless you, Brother Hilkiah," Frankland said. He should have thought of that himself.

Hilkiah set up the cooler on the tailgate of his truck along with some plastic cups. Reverend Garb came over to shake hands with Hilkiah, and then he turned to Frankland.

"Shall we get started?" he asked. "Or are we waiting for someone?"

Frankland glanced along the road. "I was expecting Dr. Calhoun," he said. "Maybe we should wait a few more minutes."

Garb glanced toward Bear State Videoramics. "There's Magnusson standing in the door," he said. "He doesn't look so happy to see us."

"He that seeketh mischief," Hilkiah said, "it shall come unto him."

"The way of transgressors is hard," said Garb, skipping a little further in the Book of Proverbs.

There was a silence while the others waited for Frankland to produce a quote, but Frankland's mind spun its gears while it groped through its limited stock of citations, and it was Hilkiah who finally filled the silence with "A wicked man is loathsome, and committed to shame."

"'Scuse me, teddy bear," said Sheryl. "You forgot something."

Sheryl approached and tied a white band around his arm. "Thanks, honey love," said Frankland.

"I'm going to go back to the studio and check up on Roger," Sheryl said. "I'll be back at ten o'clock to pick you up, okay?"

"Okay," Frankland said. They kissed, and she walked to the truck. Roger was the boy volunteer they had minding the radio station—not a big job, because all he had to do was load the tapes of prerecorded programs—but Roger was fourteen, and Sheryl didn't want to leave him alone with complicated equipment for too long a stretch of time.

"The Lord gave you a good woman, there," Garb said with a smile.

"Don't I know it," said Frankland.

The rear wheels of the Ford spat gravel as it wheeled out of the parking lot, horn tooting. Another auto horn answered, and Frankland saw Dr. Lucius Calhoun boom into the parking lot in his Oldsmobile, waving from the window with his left arm as he spun the wheel with his right. He was followed by a regular convoy of vehicles, and as they drove into the parking lot they all began to sound their horns, a joyous noise unto the Lord.

"Sorry to be late," Calhoun said as he popped out of his car. He was a young man, short and vigorous, barely thirty though already bald on top, with a ginger mustache and a broad grin. He shook Frankland's hand and Garb's.

"We were planning on coming in the bus," he said. "We had bus-sized banners and everything. But that ol' fuel pump started kicking up again, so we had to convoy down."

Dr. Calhoun seemed to spend as much time waging war with his church bus as he did fighting the Devil. Frankland had always enjoyed the stories of Calhoun's travails.

On the other hand, the Pentecostal Church could at least *afford* a bus. At Frankland's outfit, all the money went into the radio station and the bunkers of survival supplies.

"Shall we get started?" Frankland said.

Each pastor organized his own flock, handing out signs that said PORNOGRAPHY ATTACKS THE FAMILY or RAILS BLUFF FAMILY VALUES CAMPAIGN or FIRST AMENDMENT DOES NOT PROTECT FILTH. Some of the children had signs that said PROTECT ME FROM SMUT.

Bear State Videoramics, to its disgrace, had been renting pornographic videos out of its back room. And, to the disgrace of the community, this had apparently been going on for some time.

Action was clearly required. The world would end soon, and Frankland did not wish Rails Bluff to acquire more than its necessary share of the divine wrath.

Frankland had an idea about how to deal with these sorts of situations. He could, of course, gather signatures on a petition, and lobby and persuade the county council to pass an ordinance against pornography, but then the ordinance would immediately become the subject of legal contention—the Civil Liberties Union, or other secular satanist busybodies, might intervene, and lawyers would cost the county money, and the thing could drag on for years without resolution, and in the meantime Eric Magnusson would still be peddling porn.

So quicker action was called for. A stern warning from the guardians of the community. A picket line, a public protest, and a call for a boycott.

Hit him where it hurts, Frankland thought. Right in the pocketbook. Magnusson couldn't be making *that* much money as it was—*nobody* in Rails Bluff was making money. Magnusson couldn't afford to lose much business.

And the best part was, even the Civil Liberties Union agreed that picket lines and civil protest were just fine. Just citizens exercising their rights to state their opinion.

"Don't reckon you're going to give up this foolishness any-time soon, huh?" said Magnusson.

Frankland looked up from tying a white band on the arm of one of his Sunday School class. The owner of Bear State Videoramics stood above him, red-gold hair gleaming in the setting sun, a scowl on his long Swedish face.

"I reckon not," Frankland said.

"What's the problem?" Magnusson said. "I've got a right to earn a living."

"You're not allowed to earn a living by poisoning the community," Frankland said. "Somebody might pay you to put cyanide in the water, but that doesn't mean you should take the money."

Magnusson scowled. "I don't sell to no kids," he said, "so I don't know why you got kids here. They'll find out more about porn from you than from me."

"They'll know to avoid it," Garb said. He had walked over from where he had been organizing his youth association members.

"I won't stay in business without the back room," Magnusson insisted. "You want another business to close in this town? What about *my* family?"

"The righteous," said Garb, "eat to the satisfaction of their soul; but the belly of the wicked shall want."

"Vileness shall meet with requital, and loud shall be the lamentations thereof," Frankland said, his mind spitting out the quote before his tongue could put a stop to it. He had to admit he had no idea whether the verse was actually in the Bible or not, and out of the corner of his eye he saw Garb's eyes flicker as he tried to identify the quote.

Magnusson only looked grim. He glanced over the assembling parishioners and nodded to himself. "I see some of my best customers here," he said. "People who rent from the back room a *lot*. You want their names?" He looked at Frankland. "What's that quote, from the Bible? About the beam in the eye messing up your view, or something?"

Garb seemed troubled by this revelation, but Frankland knew the answer. "They would not have sinned," he said, "if you had not provided the means."

"Oh yeah. It's all my fault. Blame the lusts of the world on me." He waved his arms. "If they don't get the stuff from me, they'll get it on mail order."

He stalked back to his store. Frankland watched him go in satisfaction.

"It's working," he said, and smiled.

Calhoun approached, a broad grin on his face. "Shall we start with a prayer?" he said.

The demonstration went well. A number of people, heading into the parking lot with the obvious intention of renting a video from Bear State Videoramics, saw the demonstrators, their friends and neighbors, circling in front of the store with their signs, sometimes chanting slogans and sometimes singing hymns. The customers would usually hesitate, then shy away.

There were a few exceptions. A couple young men, obviously drunk, made an elaborate show of renting some pornographic videos, which they waved at Frankland as they got back in their Jeep and sped away. A few other adults came into the store to return videos, and a couple stayed to make other rentals, conspicuously from the family section.

But for a Friday night, Frankland figured, Magnusson's business was lousy. The protest was really hitting him in the pocketbook.

"It's working," he told Dr. Calhoun as they fell into step.

"For one night, anyway," Calhoun said. Calhoun grinned up at him and wiped sweat from his bald head. "By the way, Reverend," he said, "I've been meaning to ask you about your radio address the other day. What was that term you used? 'Rapture wimp,' was it?"

Frankland felt heat rise to his face. "I do apologize, Dr. Calhoun," he said. "The Spirit was in me pretty strong at the time—but I should have chosen more appropriate language."

Calhoun gave a chuckle. "Well, I'd *like* to think I'm not a wimp. I just happen to believe that there isn't necessarily an interval between the Rapture and the Second Coming."

"I believe I explained my reasoning in that radio speech," Frankland said.

"But what about the Bema Judgment?" Calhoun said.

And Calhoun and Frankland then had a pleasant time, for the next hour or so, arguing back and forth about the Tribulation, the Bema Judgment as opposed to the Krinô Judgment, the Twenty-Four Elders, Christ's Bride in Heaven, the Judgment of the Gentiles, the role of the 144,000 Jews, and other significant matters pertaining to the end of the world.

They were interrupted by the publisher of the local weekly paper, who interviewed the leaders of the protest as well as Magnusson. Frankland had a feeling the coverage would be favorable, as the publisher was a member of Dr. Calhoun's congregation.

The only real sour note came later, when the pastor of the Lutheran Church of the Good Shepherd, Pete Swenson, turned up to rent a video. He crossed the parking lot slowly, a thoughtful frown on his beefy Swedish face, hands in the pockets of his chinos. He nodded at Frankland and Garb, walked into Bear State Videoramics, and could be seen having a long conversation with Magnusson.

Hilkiah approached, clenching his tattooed fists.

"G—" he began, then corrected himself. "Dad-blame that squarehead, anyway."

"I can't figure him out," said Calhoun.

A good third of the inhabitants of the community were the descendants of a colony of Swedish and Norwegian immigrants that had been planted here in the 1880s. A great many of the members of the commercial class, such as it was, bore

Swedish names. The lofty red brick Church of the Good Shepherd, sitting next to the immaculate green lawn of the immigrant cemetery, was the largest of the area's churches, and the oldest.

And the Swedes' attitude was *different*. It just was, and Frankland didn't understand it. Why Swenson wouldn't stand with the community against pornography, why he didn't participate in the Love Offering Picnic, why he didn't urge his flock to join the Christian Gun Club with their children—why wouldn't a minister do these obvious things, which were so clearly a part of his duty?

Swenson left the video store and nodded at Frankland again as he shambled toward his car. There was a tape of *Spartacus* in his hand.

"Well," Frankland said finally, as Swenson drove away. "Those Lutherans, they're pretty close to being Catholics, you know."

Calhoun and Hilkiah looked at him and nodded.

That probably explained it.

The stock market was going mad, the President thought, and all because Sam made a weird face on television. Some days he just loved his job.

"We need a full-court press on this issue," he said. "Point out that the market is bearing out what the Administration has said all along."

"Yes, sir," said Stan Burdett. His spectacles glittered. He knew just how to handle something like this.

"Maybe the First Lady can say something in her speech in Atlanta tonight."

"I'll talk to Mrs. Grayson about it."

There was the sound of a door opening. "Mr. President." The President's secretary entered the Oval Office—without knocking, the first time ever. "Something's just happened." There was a stricken look on her face.

The President saw the look and felt his heart turn over. For a moment he pictured the First Lady in a plane crash, his children in the sights of assassins . . .

"What happened?" he said, and tried to control the tremor that had risen in his voice.

"I called Judge Chivington's office to make your golf appointment for next week." His secretary's lip trembled. "The judge is dead, sir. He passed away in his office about ten minutes ago. The paramedics are still there, but they say they can't revive him."

The President began to breathe again. Relief warred with sorrow in his mind, and then with shame at his being glad it was the judge and not his family.

"I thought the judge would bury us all," he said, and then his voice tripped over the sudden ache in his throat.

Judge Chivington gone. The judge had been such a constant in the President's life, from the very beginning of his career to the present, that he had truly never pictured his life without the man.

He looked at his secretary, then at Stan. "Could you leave me alone for a while, please?" he managed.

"Yes, sir," Stan said.

The others left in silence. The President turned his chair to the tall windows behind him, to the roses ranked in the garden beyond.

It was like losing a father, he thought.

Judge Chivington had been one of the greats. Legislator, jurist, advisor to the powerful. One of the few things that the President could absolutely rely on throughout his life.

The President would see that the judge was properly recognized as he began his trip to the beyond. A funeral in the National Cathedral, a procession of Washington's great orators from the pulpit, a choir that spat holy fire.

The judge's wife had died about five years ago. The President would have to call the judge's daughter, who was a high-powered lawyer on the West Coast.

Do this right, he thought. *If you ever do anything right in your life, do this.*

He turned and reached for the phone.

SEVEN

The two last being mechanics, and up late, mentioned that they were much alarmed at about 11 o'clock last night, by a great rumbling, as they thought, in the earth, attended with several flashes of lightning, which so lighted the house, that they could have picked up the smallest pin—one mentioned, that the rumbling and the light was accompanied by a noise like that produced by throwing a hot iron into snow, only very loud and terrific, so much so, that he was fearful to go out to look what it was, for he never once thought of an earthquake. I have thrown together the above particulars, supposing an extract may meet with corroborating accounts, and afford some satisfaction to your readers.

Extract of a letter dated West River, January 23, 1812

Omar gave himself Monday off and drove to Vicksburg to pick up Micah Knox, the speaker from the Crusaders National of the Tabernacle of Christ, who was supposed to meet him at the bus station. There was only one white man in the station when Omar arrived, a skinny kid slumped in a plastic waiting room chair with his feet propped on an army surplus duffel bag, and he seemed so unlikely to be a Crusader that Omar's gaze passed over him twice before the kid stood up, hitched the duffel onto his shoulder, and walked straight up to him.

"Sheriff Paxton."

His voice was nasal and unpleasantly Yankee. He was thin and very small, coming maybe up to Omar's clavicle, and thin, with red hair cut short enough to show the odd contours of his skull. He wore a long-sleeved flannel shirt, black jeans, and worn work boots. He looked maybe all of seventeen years old.

"Micah Knox?" Omar shook the kid's hand. With the

duffel and the short haircut, he looked like a teenage soldier on leave.

"Thanks for coming to meet me," Knox said. His eyes were eerie, with bayou-green pupils entirely surrounded by eye-white.

"Can I help you with that?" indicating the duffel.

"No, I got it. Thanks."

They walked out of the waiting room into the blazing heat. Omar opened the trunk of his car and let Knox put his duffel inside. The duffel seemed surprisingly heavy. Sweat was already popping out on Knox's forehead.

"Damn, it's hot down here," he said.

"You're not exactly dressed for the South," Omar said. Knox looked self-consciously at his long-sleeved flannel shirt.

"I got Aryan tattoos," Knox said. "I don't want the niggers to see them. Nothing but niggers on that bus." Omar unlocked his car doors and he and Knox got inside.

Omar started the car, and for Knox's benefit turned on the air conditioner full blast. Two young black men, leaning against the shaded wall of the station, looked at them both with expressionless faces. Probably they recognized Omar from television. Knox glared sullenly back at them.

"I hate the way they stare," he said.

"You had a chance to eat? You want to stop somewhere?"

Knox shifted uneasily in his seat. "I don't eat much."

It occurred to Omar that maybe Knox didn't have any money. "I'm buying," he said.

"I'm not hungry," Knox said. "But you go ahead and eat if you want."

Omar drove in silence over the crumbling Vicksburg streets until he got onto I-20 heading west. The freeway vaulted off the Vicksburg bluff and was suddenly over water. Omar looked down at a huge gambling casino dressed up as a nineteenth-century riverboat, with huge flowering stacks and gingerbread balconies, then saw Knox sitting with his hands clamped on the passenger seat, his eyes closed and his face gone pale.

"Something the matter?" Omar asked.

"I hate heights," Knox said in a strained voice. "Can't stand bridges."

Omar was amused. When he'd got to the end of the bridge, he told Knox it was safe and Knox opened his eyes and began to breathe again.

"So you're on a speaking tour or something?" Omar said. "The Grand Wizard didn't make that clear."

"Speaking. Recruiting." He gave Omar a look with his strange eyes. "Fund-raising."

"Can't have raised too many funds if you're traveling by bus."

Knox shrugged. "I raised money here and there, but I didn't keep it. I sent it to other Crusader groups."

"That's good."

Knox shifted uneasily in his seat. "You got a bank in Shelltown, or whatever it's called?"

"Shelburne City. And we've got two."

"I might need to get some more money." He scratched his head. "Either of the banks owned by Jews?"

"Nope. You can do business in either of 'em."

"Mm." Knox pulled his feet up into the seat and crossed his arms on his knees, resting his chin on his forearms. His fingers tapped out strange little rhythms on his flannel-covered biceps.

"I got a good feeling about Shelburne City," he said. "I think we're gonna give people something to think about."

Omar and Knox didn't talk much on the way to Spottswood Parish. Knox clamped his eyes shut when they crossed the Bayou Bridge, then sat up and grinned. "We're in Liberated America now!" he said.

"As liberated as it gets," Omar said.

"This is the only county in America not run by ZOG. You chased ZOG out of Spottswood County."

"Parish," Omar corrected automatically. ZOG was Zionist Occupation Government, a term that some of the people used.

They passed a sign with a blue spiral design and the words EVACUATION ROUTE. Knox narrowed his eyes as the sign passed.

"What *is* that? Is that some kind of nuclear war thing?"

"It's in case of a big hurricane," Omar said. "This state is so flat that a big enough storm could put half of us under the Gulf of Mexico."

Knox looked around. "It's flat all right."

"It looks flatter'n it is," Omar said. "You can't really tell from looking, but most of the parish is actually higher than the country around. In the big flood of '27, thousands of people saved their lives by evacuating here."

"Jesus H. Christ," Knox said. He peered at a strange figure that strolled up the road toward Hardee. He was an elderly black man dressed in worn overalls, with a ragged wide-brimmed hat on his head. He carried a wicker bag over one shoulder, and a stick over the other shoulder with a half-dozen dead birds hanging from it.

"What the hell is that?" Knox demanded.

Omar grinned. "That's ol' Cudgel," Omar said. "He's from down south in coonass country somewhere, came up here fifteen or eighteen years ago. Lives in a shack up in Wilson's Woods, has a skiff on the bayou. Lives off what he can catch or trap, fish or birds or animals."

Knox turned around in his seat, looking at the strange figure loping along the road in his homemade sandals. "Looks like he just came down from the trees," he said. "He looks like the original Mud Person."

"Mud people" was a term that some of the groups used for inferior races. The theory was that they weren't created by God like white folks, they were spawned out of the mud.

"Cudgel's all right," Omar said. "Cudgel's never been any trouble."

Knox gave Omar an intent look. "Ain't none of 'em *all right*. I'm from Detroit and I know. They chased us out of Madison Heights, they chased us out of Royal Oak. They're animals, every one of 'em." He flung himself back into his seat with a thump. "They should be put to sleep," he said. "I get upset just thinking about it."

"Well," Omar said, "you're in liberated country now. You can take it easy."

"Hurricanes," Knox muttered. "Swamp-niggers. Floods. Jesus H. Shit."

Omar figured that the rest of the day was going to be very long. He was looking forward to getting his guest to the bus station in Monroe next morning. The kid was just too twitchy, too moody. He doubted that Knox had anything new to say about the situation. He wondered why the Grand Wizard had arranged to send him here.

Knox was pleased by the election signs and flags that were still visible in Hardee, and by the way some of Omar's neighbors waved at him as he drove by. "You got some real support here!" he said, slapping his thighs. "That's great! It's great to see this stuff!"

Omar slowed as he approached his house. "I want to check if there's reporters around," he said. "I don't want them following us to the meeting."

"Jesus, no," Knox muttered. He slumped low in his seat, just letting his eyes peer above the level of the door.

"I think most of them went home," Omar said. "They got a short attention span, you know, Madonna farts in Hollywood and they've got to go cover it."

The road was empty of any living thing except for a couple of cur dogs panting in the shade of some forsythia. Omar parked in his carport. Knox seemed spooked by the idea that reporters might be lurking around, and he continued to slump in the passenger seat until he got out, and then kept his head down as he left the car and collected his duffel from the trunk.

Wilona wasn't home, and Omar remembered that this was the date for her afternoon tea with Ms. LaGrande. Omar showed Knox through Wilona's sewing room to the bedroom that Omar's son David had occupied until he left for LSU. "Thanks, Sheriff," he said. "This'll do fine."

"Would you like a beer?" Omar asked. "Co-Cola? Lemonade?"

"Coke would be good," Knox said. He stowed his duffel under David's narrow bed.

Omar got Knox a Coke and himself a beer. He sat on the sofa in the living room, and Knox sat crosslegged on the floor in front of him. He looked down the length of the building, through Wilona's sewing room to his own bedroom.

"Why do they build 'em like this?" he asked. "Long and narrow, all the rooms in a row?"

"Ventilation," Omar said. "A shotgun home was built so that any breeze would blow through all the rooms."

"But now you've got air-conditioning."

"Yep." Omar sipped his Silver Bullet. Knox fidgeted with his Coke, making a continuous ring of ice against the glass.

"I'm curious," Omar said. "The Grand Wizard didn't really have a chance to tell me where your outfit is based."

Knox turned his staring green eyes on Omar. "My action group formed in Detroit," Knox said. "Most of us are in the West, I guess. Montana, Oregon, Washington State. But there's no particular place we meet—we all travel a lot, and we only get together on special occasions."

"A traveling Klan?" Omar smiled thinly to cover his unease.

He was beginning to feel a degree of anxiety about his guest. "You all salesmen or something?" he asked.

Knox shook his head. "Not like you mean. I mean we all recruit, yeah, but we travel because we're all warriors in the cause. See, I don't *know* many other Crusaders—I've only met a handful. I only know the ones in my action group—that's my cell. That way if one of us is an informer, he can only betray so many."

"Uh-huh," Omar said. He sipped his beer while alarms clattered through his mind. He didn't like what he was hearing.

"You're a police officer, right?" Knox said. "So you know how it is that serial killers get away with what they do."

Omar thought about it. "You mean that there's no connection—" he began.

"Right. They kill *perfect strangers*. There's nothing to link the killers and their victims."

"Uh-huh," Omar said again. He narrowed his eyes, tried to think his way out of this. *Cocksucker set me up,* he thought.

"Just apply that principle to the revolution," Knox said. "That's all the Crusaders National are doing. You don't do *anything* in your own area, or to anyone who knows you." He looked up. "Say, did you ever read *Hunter*?" Knox said.

"Heard about it," Omar said, still thinking. He carefully put his beer down on the side table.

"*Hunter*'s a great book. Tells exactly how to do it," Knox said. "Exactly how to overthrow ZOG and put Aryans back in charge again. It's just about this *one guy* . . . and all he does is travel around, and he kills nigger leaders and kike politicians and queers and black men who fuck white women. And he's *so inspirational*, see, that soon other people follow his example."

Set me up, Omar thought. *That fucking bondsman bastard.*

Knox's face glowed with enthusiasm. "ZOG doesn't know how to fight them. Because they're *not organized,* they're just people doing what's right. If they catch one, he can't help them, 'cause he doesn't know the others. Now the Crusaders National are a little more organized than that, but not much. We use codes to communicate, and the Internet. And we meet only to plan our actions and carry them out, see . . . you know, find a bank in some little town—"

Omar moved. He lunged off the couch and slammed Knox in the breastbone with the palm of his hand. Knox's eyes widened in shock as he went over on his back. Coke splashed over the floor.

"*Down!*" Omar shouted. "*Down on your face!*"

Ice skiddered across the wooden floor. Knox was on his back with his legs still half-locked in the crosslegged position. Fabric tore as Omar grabbed his shirt and rolled him over onto his face.

"*Arms straight out!*" Omar said. He could feel sweat popping out on his face. He straddled Knox and slammed him in between the shoulder blades to keep him on the floor.

"What—?" Knox began.

"Just shut up!" Omar said. "Put your arms straight out!"

Knox obeyed. "I didn't do nothing, man," he said. Omar began patting him down. He found a knife in a sheath inside Knox's jeans on the right side, so that it would be invisible till he drew it, and a little snubnosed .38 special in an ankle holster. Omar stood up, looked at the five bullets in the cylinder. Knox was carrying it loaded. Omar cocked the pistol and pointed it at the back of Knox's head.

"Take your pants off," he said.

Knox twisted his head to stare at Omar in alarm. "Hey!" he said. "You think I'm queer or something?" Fear made his voice crack. "I'm not a queer! I *hate* queers!"

"I want to find out if you're wearing a wire," Omar said. "Do it or I blow your fucking head off." Knox put his hands on his belt, then hesitated.

Sweat slid off Omar's nose, pattered on the floor. "This is my parish," he reminded, "and you can disappear into the bayou real easy."

Knox squirmed on the floor as he drew his jeans as far down as his boots would permit. Beneath the jeans were worn boxer shorts. Omar knelt and carefully felt Knox's crotch. Knox straightened and gave a little gasp at the touch, but did not protest. Omar could detect no electronics.

"Right," he said, stepping back and raising the pistol again. "Now I want you to crawl toward the bedroom."

"I'm not an informer," Knox gasped. "I'm not a race-traitor. I don't know who told you different, but—"

Omar swiped with his sleeve at the sweat that poured down his face. "Shut up and do as I say," he said.

Still aiming the pistol, he walked behind Knox as Knox crawled into David's room. The boy's jeans were still down around his knees. Omar had Knox lie facedown in the corner while he dumped out Knox's duffel on the bed. He found some clothing, a zipped case of toiletries, a laptop computer in its original foam packing held together by duct tape, some books and magazines, including well-worn copies of *Hunter*, *Protocols of the Elders of Zion*, and *The Turner Diaries*, ammunition, a 9mm Beretta, and a pump shotgun with a folding stock and pistol grip—

disassembled, but it could have been put in working order in seconds.

"I can explain, you know?" Knox said.

Omar sat on the bed and contemplated the weapons laid out before him. The Grand Wizard, he thought, had set him up. He'd got jealous of Omar's prominence in the organization, was afraid that Omar might set up his own Klan. It had been the Grand Wizard who had sent this kid to Spottswood Parish to talk about bank robbery and sedition. Maybe even rob the bank and claim Omar as an accomplice.

Well, Omar thought. *The Grand Wizard's plan just got derailed.*

Omar looked up at Knox. The redheaded man had turned partly onto his side and was watching Omar with those strange eyes.

"Let me tell you how it's going to be," Omar said. "So far as I know, these weapons belong to you and have not been used in the commission of any crime."

"That's true," Knox said. "They're clean. I bought 'em at a gun show. You can—"

"Shut the fuck up," Omar said. Knox closed his mouth with an audible snap.

"Just listen," Omar said. "Now—you're a colleague, and you're here in Spottswood Parish to talk to my people, and you can do that. *But*—" He pointed the pistol. "I've worked hard to get where I am, and I am not going to let you fuck up my work by preaching anything illegal. There are going to be people at the meeting tonight who are peace officers, and who are sworn to uphold the law. You are *not* going to compromise us in any way. You are *not* going to advocate killing people, or robbing banks, or committing crimes."

"I won't," Knox said quickly. "You can trust me. I didn't understand your situation, that's all."

"Because," Omar said, continuing as if he hadn't heard, "if you *do* that, if you advocate illegalities, you are just going to *disappear*. And don't think I can't make that happen, because everybody you're going to meet tonight are people I grew up with, and I know them all very well, and I can trust every single one of them to do what's necessary." He wiped sweat from his face. "You understand what I'm saying, podna?"

"Yes." Knox nodded. "I understand."

"I'm going to tape-record the meeting tonight," Omar said, "so there's a record of what you say. Just in case someone later alleges that you came here preaching sedition or something."

Just in case the Grand Wizard sics the fucking FBI on me, he thought.

Knox nodded again. "Fine," he said. "Whatever you say."

They both froze at the sound of the front door opening, at the sound of heels on the wood flooring.

"Oh, my God in this world!" Wilona's voice. "What happened here?"

"Just a little accident," Omar called. He was surprised to find that his voice was steady. "I'll help you clean it up in just a second."

Omar stood and opened the gun and dropped the bullets out of the cylinder. He tossed the pistol back on the bed. He unzipped the bag of toiletries, dumped its contents on the bed—shaving cream, bag of disposable razors, and a huge economy-sized bottle of aspirin—and then Omar gathered up all of Knox's ammunition and zipped it into the toiletries case. Knox watched in silence from the floor.

Omar paused in the door, looked down at Knox for a long second, then closed the door behind him as he left the room. He walked through Wilona's sewing room into the living room and found Wilona cleaning up the spilled Coke with a roll of paper towels. She wore heels, her new frock, and Aunt Clover's pearls.

"Don't do that, darlin'," Omar said. He tossed the bag of ammunition on the sofa and bent to help her clean up. "You'll make a mess of your nice clothes."

Wilona straightened. "What is going on?" she said. "It looks like you just threw your drink halfway across the room. And you're all sweaty like you've been working."

"Mr. Knox had a little fall," Omar said. "I wanted to make sure he was all right before I cleaned up."

"My goodness." Wilona looked alarmed. "I forgot he was coming. Is he all right?"

"He's fine." Omar swabbed at the floor and noticed idly that termites were digging a tunnel across one of the floor-boards. Time to call the exterminator. "He's changing clothes right now." He looked up. "How was your after-noon?"

"Oh, it was lovely!" He picked up the gloves she had left on the little table by the door. "Ms. LaGrande was so gra-cious—she met me right on the front portico. The portico is a special design, she told me—it has a special name and every-thing. Did you ever hear what it's called?"

Omar ripped another towel off the roll. "A front porch?" he asked.

Wilona laughed. "It's called 'distyle-in-antis.'" She pro-nounced the unfamiliar words carefully. "That's with the two round columns between the two square columns. Ms. LaGrande's great-grandfather modeled it after the Tower of the Winds in Athens, Greece."

Omar straightened, looked down at the floor.

"That's going to have to be mopped," Wilona said. "Otherwise it'll get sticky."

"I'll get the mop," he said.

They both turned at the sound of a door opening. Knox appeared at the door to his room. He was wearing a fresh flannel shirt and the same black jeans. He walked uneasily through the sewing room to the living room door.

"Micah Knox," Omar said, "this is my wife Wilona."

"Pleased to meet you," Knox said slowly.

"Mr. Knox, are you all right?" Wilona walked toward him to shake his hand. "I heard you had a fall."

Knox leaned on the door frame and gave an apologetic grin as he took Wilona's hand. "I'm just fine, ma'am. Sorry about your floor."

"I'll mop that up," Wilona said. "That's not a problem. I'm just glad you're feeling all right."

Knox looked over Wilona's shoulder at Omar. Omar looked back into Knox's staring green eyes.

"I think everything's fine now," Knox said. "We had a little accident, but everything's going to be okay."

On Monday, the market dropped off a precipice and didn't find bottom. A large Dutch bank failed. The Chinese chose this moment to dump billions of dollars of currency reserves, and in every market from Singapore to London the bears contemplated the chaos and sharpened their claws.

At twelve-thirty, Charlie called Dearborne's office and found he'd left for the country club. He looked at Megan through the glass wall of her office and gave her a nod. She typed in the correction, and millions of dollars of losing positions pulsed into the TPS computers on a silent electronic wave.

Not that it mattered. What had been catastrophic positions on Friday were turning into mountains of solid gold on Monday. By three o'clock, when the exchange closed, the S&Ps had dropped sixteen percent, Charlie was in the black, and he was standing on his desk, beating his chest and giving a Tarzan yell.

Selling short the S&Ps had made him a profit of $137,500,000, give or take a few hundred thousand. Added to this was the forty million he'd started with, and the ten million he'd made on the Eurodollar puts. This was a 370 percent profit in less than a week.

And on any large gain made for TPS, Charlie's contract called for him to collect a bonus of seventeen percent. Seventeen percent of $147,500,000 . . .

"I'm lord of the fucking jungle!" he shouted. "We're all going to die rich!"

His people, the traders and salesmen, looked up from their screens, hesitated a moment, then began to applaud. As cheers began to ring out, Charlie looked up to Megan's office, and he could see her eyes gazing levelly at him over the top of her monitor. He couldn't tell whether the eyes were smiling or not.

By four o'clock, when the Merc closed in Chicago, Tarzan yells seemed inadequate to the situation. Instead he put on his phone headset and punched Megan's number.

"Sod the proles," he said when she answered. "Let your staff do the reconciliation. Come home with me tonight."

"*No guilt*," she whispered. The words sent a surge of desire up his spine.

"I'll call the caterer," he said.

"Welcome to the observation deck of the Gateway Arch of the Jefferson National Expansion Memorial," said Marcy Douglas. "On exiting, please step to your left and make your way up the stairs. If you are waiting for a tram, please wait for everyone to exit before taking your place."

The latest group of tourists climbed from the south tram to the observation platform. Marcy noticed, among the usual ambling tourists, the parents and children and people with cameras, an elderly lady on the arm of a younger woman, a young Japanese couple in baseball caps, and a cluster of middle-aged people talking to one another in French.

The usual. Marcy evaded an impulse to look at her watch. She was on duty till ten o'clock and had many hours to go.

"Please stay on the yellow stairs," she told the tourists.

Marcy was twenty-two years old and had worked for the Park Service for two years, since she'd given up on college. She was tall and thin and black, and kept her hair cut short and businesslike under her Smokey Bear hat. She was from rural Florida and loved the out-of-doors, and had hoped to work in one of the big national forests. Failing that perhaps in Jean Lafitte National Park—better known as the French Quarter of New Orleans—but those with seniority were lined up for those jobs, so she found herself working 630 feet above the St. Louis waterfront, shepherding tourists through the largest stainless steel sculpture in the world, the silver catenary curve of the Gateway Arch. The giant wedding ring that St. Louis had built to the scale of God's finger.

The elderly woman put her hand on Marcy's arm. "That was the most unpleasant elevator ride I've had in my life," she said.

"I'm sorry, ma'am," Marcy said. "I know they're crowded."

The huge arch couldn't use regular elevators: it had special trams, trains of little cars, built to ride up the inside of the curve. Each car seated five, if the five were close friends, weren't too large, and if none of them smelled bad.

"And the *swaying*," the lady said. "I felt like I was going to get sick to my stomach."

Marcy patted her hand. "You take as long as you need to catch your breath before going down."

"Is there another way down?"

"You can take the stairs, ma'am, but there are over a thousand of them." Marcy tried to look sympathetic. "I think the tram ride would be better for you."

"Come along, Mother." The old lady's companion tugged gently at her arm. "The young lady has work to do."

Marcy shuffled the line of waiting tourists into the trams and sent them to ground level. She could be in *nature*, she thought. She could be in *Yosemite*.

Or she could be in the French Quarter, sipping a planter's punch in the Old Absinthe House.

"Why are the windows so small?" a little girl asked.

"A lot of people ask that question," Marcy said. She didn't know the answer.

Marcy stood with a couple of tourists for a photograph. She didn't know why so many people wanted to take her picture, but many of them did.

The French people went from one window to the next in a group, comparing the view with a map they'd brought with them. She heard "Busch Stadium" and "*Cathédrale de St. Louis.*"

A lot of French people came to St. Louis, figuring that since the French had once owned the place, they'd find French culture here. Marcy figured they were usually disappointed.

The French men, she noticed, were casually dressed, but the women looked as if they were on a modeling assignment.

"My goodness!" The old lady clutched at her heart. "Is it *swaying* up here?"

Marcy smiled. She spent a lot of her shift smiling. *It adds to your face value*, her mother used to tell her.

"We sway a little bit when the wind picks up, yes," she said. "But don't worry—the Gateway Arch is built to withstand a tornado."

"Pardon, please," said one of the Japanese. "How do you get to the Botanikkogoden?"

It took two tries before Marcy realized that she was asking for guidance to the Botanical Gardens. She gave directions. Her colleague, Evan, had just brought another load of tourists up on the north tram and was urging people to stay on the yellow stairs.

One of the tourists was tilting his camera, trying to get a picture of the *Casino Queen*, the big gambling boat just pulling into its mooring across the river in East St. Louis. Revenues from the *Casino Queen*, Marcy knew, had rescued East St. Louis from being the poorest city in the United States, a position it had held for decades.

"How do you pronounce the name of the architect?" an anxious woman asked.

"I'm not very good at Finnish," Marcy said, and then did her best to pronounce Eero Saarinen's name.

"Why didn't they get an *American* architect?" the woman demanded.

EIGHT

*At 8 o'clock a noise resembling distant thunder was heard,
and was soon after followed by a shock which appeared to
operate vertically, that is to say, by a heaving of the ground
upwards—but was not sufficiently severe to injure either
furniture or glasses. This shock was succeeded by a thick
haze, and many people were affected by giddiness and nausea. Another shock was experienced about 9 o'clock at night,
but so light as not to be generally felt—and at half past 12
the next day (the 17th) another shock was felt, which lasted
only a few seconds and was succeeded by a tremor which
was occasionally observed throughout the day effecting
many with giddiness. At half past 8 o'clock a very thick haze
came on, and for a few minutes a sulphurous smell was
emitted. At nine o'clock last night, another was felt, which
continued four or five seconds, but so slight as to have
escaped the observation of many who had not thought of
attending particularly to the operations of this phenomenon.
At one o'clock this morning (23d) another shock took place
of nearly equal severity with the first of the 16th. Buried in
sleep, I was not sensible of this, but I have derived such correct information on the fact that I have no reason to doubt
it; but I have observed since 11 o'clock this morning frequent tremors of the earth, such as usually precede severe
shocks in other parts of the world.*

Evening Ledger, *December 23, 1811*

It was the first sunny day in weeks. Jason sped along the
top of the levee, listening to his tires grind on the gravel
road that capped its top. The ATV's exhaust rattled off the
tangle of trees between the levee and the river. The river
was very high now, only ten feet below the top of the levee,

and the cottonwood and cypress stood in the gray water, leafy branches trailing in the current. The mass of water, the evident *weight* of it, all moving so relentlessly under Missouri's skies . . . it made him uneasy. What if it got higher? What if it went over the top of the levee and flooded out his house? Somewhere to the north, up in Iowa, there was supposed to be flooding. What if the floodwaters came south?

But no one else here seemed concerned. "The river gets high twice a year," Muppet had told him. He figured Muppet should know, and Muppet wasn't packing survival supplies into a boat, so he supposed it was all right.

Jason was driving Muppet's Yamaha ATV, speeding along the top of the levee with the throttle maxed out. Muppet sat behind, his butt above the rear wheels, bouncing along with his feet splayed out to each side, the heels of his sneakers just above the roadbed.

The little vehicles—essentially motorcycles with four wheels—were the passion of Muppet's crowd, and indeed half the kids at school. No drivers' licenses were required to run the vehicles as long as they stayed off the road. The ripping sound of the ATVs' engines was heard over the entire district on weekends. On the far side of the levee, on the river's muddy sandbanks, on islands made accessible by low water, and on trails beaten into the hardwood tangle, the brightly colored vehicles sped along like ants on the trail of honey.

But now, with the river high, a few rural roads and the crest of the levee were the only places to drive. Jason was determined, though, to make the most of it. At least on the top of the levee he could go *fast*.

It wasn't as good as skating, Jason thought. Nothing was. But it was better than staring at the walls and waiting for his parents to change their minds and bring him back to California.

He wondered how he was going to get his father to buy him an ATV. It was too late for his birthday—his dad had already bought the present, or so he said. And Christmas was far away.

Maybe, he thought, if he did *really well* on his finals . . .

The Indian mound loomed up on the right, and below it, the row of five houses with Jason's in the middle. Jason decelerated, clutched, shifted into a lower gear, then steered off the top of the levee and onto the steep grassy grade. Muppet's feet flew high as the ATV pitched over the brink and accelerated, engine buzzing like an angry beehive. Jason heard Muppet give a whoop.

Jason gave the machine more throttle.

The ATV hit the flat with a bump, bouncing high and throwing Muppet forward into Jason. Jason laughed. He upshifted and felt the wheels spin on gravel, and then the cart took off, throwing Muppet back on the seat and bringing a fierce grin to Jason's face. The ATV lurched as he corrected his course, and then he accelerated down the lane. His house came up faster than he expected and he overshot the driveway, coming to a stop on the front lawn.

"You're getting the feel of it, all right," Muppet said.

"Thanks for letting me drive." Jason put the vehicle into neutral, then dismounted. "Want to come in?"

Muppet shook his head. "No thanks. My mom is having her piano lesson now, and I've got to get dinner ready for my baby sister."

"Okay." Backing toward the porch. "I'll see you tomorrow, then."

"See you then."

"Thanks!"

Muppet revved the engine and took off, making a U-turn on the front lawn and heading back to the levee. As the buzzing engine receded, Jason could hear the Huntley dog, Batman, barking like fury from his confined yard.

Jason took off his helmet—his mother had relented to the extent of giving his armor back, if not his skates—and then he turned and bounced up the porch steps before noticing the large UPS package that sat before the screen door. His nerves gave a little joyous leap. His birthday present from Dad!

He picked it up, and it had quite a respectable weight. At least it wasn't clothing.

He unlocked the door and took the package upstairs to his study. His birthday wasn't until Friday, but he saw no reason not to open it now, so he took out his pocket knife and slit open the strapping tape that held the box together. When he'd finally placed the contents of the box on top of his desk, he looked at it in puzzlement.

Astroscan, it said. Reflector telescope. And there was a book with it, explaining how to find and view astronomical objects.

The telescope made sense as a gift, Jason supposed, though he couldn't remember expressing any interest in astronomy to his father, or his father to him. Here in rural Missouri, with only the minimal glow of Cabells Mound on the north horizon, the night starscapes were spectacular.

On those nights when the sky wasn't covered with cloud, anyway. There hadn't been many clear nights this rainy spring.

He suspected that his father hadn't thought of the gift, though. It seemed more like something that Una might pick.

The thing was, the Astroscan didn't look like a telescope. Telescopes were supposed to be long tubes, Jason knew, with a piece of glass at one end and someplace to put your eye at the other. This thing looked, if anything, like a giant red plastic cherry.

There was a round, red hard plastic body, maybe ten inches across. It was round on the bottom, and wouldn't stand by itself, but there was a stand provided in which it could sit and rotate freely. And then there was a thick stem, six or seven inches long, that stuck out from the body. Removing the plastic cap on the end of this revealed a piece of glass that Jason assumed was a lens. There was another lens, an eyepiece, in a foam-padded box, but it seemed to go in the stem, not on the end away from the front lens.

It seemed very strange.

Jason wondered for a while if this was some kind of kiddie scope, if his father had got him something intended for a six-year-old.

The Huntleys' dog Batman was still barking, barking as if

it were deranged. Jason looked out the window to see if the dog was barking at an intruder, but Batman was sitting in the backyard next to the little Huntley girl's inflatable wading pool, with its muzzle pointed to the sky, barking into the air.

Maybe, Jason thought, it had a bad case of indigestion or something. He returned his attention to the telescope.

He shoved his computer monitor out of the way, put the scope on his desk, put the eyepiece into the aperture, then pointed the Astroscan out the window and put his eye to it. He could see nothing but a blur. He spun the focusing knob.

And the world leaped into focus. There, amazingly close, was the line of trees at the far end of the cotton field. And beyond that, the water tower of Cabells Mound with its winding stair, its metal skin painted its strange unnatural green. Birds flew past, sun glowing on their feathers.

But it was upside-down. The water tower and the trees were planted in the sky and pointed down to the earth. Weird.

Jason rolled the telescope over in its cradle, then walked around the desk and looked through the eyepiece from the other side. The picture was *still* upside-down.

He guessed he would have to get used to it.

At least it wasn't a kiddie scope. He could see *miles* with this thing.

He wished Batman would stop barking.

He scanned the horizon, but the view to the north was too flat to see very much, just the tower and the line of trees. He cleared the other end of the desk, shifted the scope, and looked east toward the river, twisting the focus knob until the flooded cottonwoods leaped out in bright detail. The inverted image revealed a big hawk sitting atop one of the trees, its back turned to him. Its dull red tail was clearly visible, as was the mottled pattern of feathers on its back.

And then something big moved behind the hawk, and Jason turned the focusing knob until he saw a tow boat churning upstream, the hot exhaust that poured from its stacks blurring Jason's view of the river's far bank. The tow consisted of fifteen barges lashed together by steel wire, and Jason could see the ribbed capstans that held the wire taut, the rust that streaked the sides of the barges, the white bow wave that marked the tow's speed. He could see the radar spinning on top of the tow boat, and see the red flannel shirt and heavy boots of one of the crewmen as he busied himself on the afterdeck.

He tried to follow the tow boat with the scope as it moved upstream, but it was difficult because he kept forgetting the image was inverted—he'd push the scope in the wrong direction, and the image would leap out of sight as if the host of a slide show had clicked from one slide to the next. Jason then spent too much time finding the tow boat again—crazy views of sky and field flashed through the eyepiece—and then, once Jason found the tow boat, he had to refocus the scope. The boat was now stern-on, and above the huge double swell of its wake he could read its name in black letters on the white stern counter: *Ruth Caldwell.*

"Cool," Jason said.

He needed to go someplace higher and get a better view. For a moment he considered trying to get up on the roof, and then he remembered that there was a vantage place just behind his yard.

The old Indian mound that towered over the property in back. Between the height of the mound and the reach of the scope, Jason could probably see Memphis.

There was a shoulder strap that had come with the scope, which would make it easy to carry—now Jason saw the value of the Astroscan's compact design. He clipped the strap to the scope, put the big plastic lens cap over the objective lens, and put the eyepiece back in its padded box, then put the box in his pocket. He swung the shoulder strap experimentally over his shoulder and found that he could hold the Astroscan reasonably secure under one arm.

Then he bounced down the back stairs, paused by the fridge for an apple and some supernaturally charged water, went out the door. The huge mound loomed above him. A gust of wind rustled the oaks and elms that crowned its massive height.

The Huntley dog had given up barking and was whining now, whining as if it were in pain. Jason looked over the fence, but he couldn't see anything wrong, and he couldn't think of anything that he could do, so he passed by the propane tank, crossed the soggy backyard, and began walking briskly toward the mound.

There was a kind of steep earthen ramp that led to the top, with a path that zigzagged through the brush and trees. Jason began to climb. Within moments he was breathing hard, and his thighs were aching with the strain. The Indian mound was bigger and steeper than it looked.

On another side of the mound, by the highway, was a little plaque that the town of Cabells Mound had put up. It explained that it was this mound that had given the town of Cabells Mound its name, and that the mound had been built approximately 800–900 A.D. by the Mississippian Culture, and was once surrounded by a large town. About the year 900 the site had been abandoned for reasons unknown.

Jason's mother, on the other hand, held to the opinion that the mound had been built thirty thousand years ago by refugees from Atlantis, a theory that Jason had once dared to doubt out loud. "Who are you going to believe?" Catherine retorted. "A bunch of know-nothing archaeologists, or people who are *in touch with the Atlantean survivors today*?"

Jason's mother had a knack for bringing conversations to a screeching halt with statements like that.

Fortunately Muppet and his friends didn't seem to mind hanging around with the son of the New Age Lady. They thought her beliefs were sort of interesting—when Jason had them over and showed them the house, they asked what the crystal in the water jug was for, who the Egyptian person in the photo was, and for details concerning the expected demise of California. When they met Catherine, a few hours later, they looked at her with a curious expectancy, as if she might begin chanting or channeling Elvis at any moment.

Jason figured he'd made some real friends here. Friends

would stick by you no matter how crazy your mom happened to be.

Jason paused halfway up the mound, panting for breath. He turned and gazed out at the world below, the flat country that stretched forever to the north and west, eastward the gray-brown river spotted with silver flecks of reflected sunlight, the *Ruth Caldwell* disappearing around a distant island. The strange white splotches on the brown, level fields were more distinct from this height than from the second floor of his home. Mr. Regan, he saw, was in his carport, bent over his boat. Birds chattered at Jason from the trees, but louder still was the howling of dogs. It sounded as if every dog for miles around had gone berserk.

His mom's car, he saw, was just turning off the highway on its way to their house.

He turned again and climbed steadily to the top of the mound. An old pumpkin oak stood on the mound's verge. It had been struck by lightning, Jason observed. Part of the trunk was scorched black, limbs were splintered and bare of leaves, and much of the crown had burned away, but the oak had somehow survived the sky's onslaught. New shoots were sprouting out of the burned part, looking frail in the sunlight, but waving their leaves proudly.

There were some bundles of dried flowers laid before the tree, Jason observed, among the tangled roots, and the remains of incense cones. His mother had made offerings here, though he could not say whether they had been to the tree's burgeoning life or to the spirits of dead Atlanteans.

The mound was thoroughly forested, and the view was largely blocked by the crowns of trees that grew on the steep slopes. Jason made his way to a little cleared space, where he found trampled grass and a used condom. Courting couples, he guessed, came up here to watch the sunset. He felt a sudden flush of distaste for the latex object, and he kicked it away, then reached into his pocket for the eyepiece to the scope.

There was nothing to rest the Astroscan on, so Jason just let it hang from the shoulder strap while he put his eye to the rubber eyepiece. He turned the scope on his own home, and through the back window he could clearly see his mother in the light of the kitchen, drinking a glass of energized water while frowning and contemplating something beyond the edge of the windowframe—Jason realized after a few seconds that she was looking into the open refrigerator, presumably trying to make up her mind what to have for dinner.

And then Jason realized that the image was, for a change, rightside-up. He wondered about that, until he realized that he was standing with the telescope under one arm and he was bending over it, head hanging down, to put his eye to the eyepiece. The image seemed rightside-up because his *head* was upside-down.

The ripping engine noise of an ATV sounded in the distance. Jason took his eye from the scope, and saw Muppet's little green vehicle racing down the levee with Muppet bent over the handlebars. Behind, throwing up dust, was a Cabells Mound police car, lights flashing. Though Muppet had cranked the ATV's throttle as far as it would go, the car, following behind, seemed only to be loitering.

"Asshole Eubanks," Jason said. "You're not even in your jurisdiction, damn it!"

He bent his head and tried to focus the scope on the top of the levee. With more luck than skill he managed to catch Muppet in the scope's image. He saw the green helmet turn, look over his shoulder at the car following so easily behind, and then glance down the slope of the levee, toward the cotton field below.

Yeah, Jason thought. He could almost read his friend's mind. *Go for it.*

He saw Muppet's gloved hand twist the throttle, heard the change in engine pitch that came with the shift in gears. And then the ATV rolled off the top of the levee, accelerating for the field below, where the car might not follow.

"Go!" Jason shouted. "Run for it!"

The ATV raced down the levee's flank. The police car slowed, hesitated. Above the chainsaw rip of the ATV's

NINE

A report prevailed in town yesterday, that a part of the town of Natchez had been sunk by an Earthquake, and that four thousand persons perished. —We trust that this report will prove to be unfounded; but if such a deplorable circumstance has taken place, it could not have been on the morning of the 16th December, as a letter dated on that date at Natchez, and published some time since at the city of Washington, says "A considerable shock of an Earthquake was felt here last night," without adding anything further . . .

Charleston, Jan. 24, 1812

They were late in getting started because Viondi needed to pick up something to deliver to one of his relatives in Mississippi. What the object turned out to be was a large silver samovar, over two feet tall, tossed casually in a cardboard box in Viondi's trunk, next to another cardboard box that held Viondi's clothes and toilet articles. Nick put his soft-sided suitcase and his satchel in the trunk next to the boxes.

"A samovar?" Nick said. "What's your family doing with a samovar?"

"Is that what it's called?" Viondi shrugged. "No idea how we got it, brother. You can ask Aunt Loretta when you meet her. We use it to make tea and shit."

"And what happened to your suitcase? Why's your stuff in a box?"

"I loaned my suitcase to Dion." Dion was one of Viondi's sons. "But he was living with his girlfriend, and when she moved out, she packed her stuff into the suitcase and never gave it back. And she and Dion don't talk to each other no more, so odds are I won't ever see it again."

Nick looked at Viondi. "It's a complicated family you've got, Viondi."

Viondi grinned at him through his bushy beard. "*All* families are complicated."

He slammed the trunk with his big hands, mashing the cardboard box of clothes. "You want to drive?"

Nick shrugged. "Might as well."

"She won't bother." The loud voice of a well-dressed white businessman cut across from the sidewalk, talking to another businessman. "The nigger who's right? No way."

Nick hunched for a moment, anger kindling in his soul at the slur that just flew in from nowhere, and then he realized that what the man had actually said was, "She won't bother to figure who's right." And he tried to relax, but the carefree moment was gone.

He looked at Viondi, and could tell from his expression that he had processed the random words the same way Nick had, and had then made the same correction.

Shit, Nick thought. You were always ready for it. Always braced for bigotry until sometimes you heard it where it didn't exist. No wonder so many black people die of hypertension.

"Give me the keys," Nick said.

The keys to the Buick spun glittering through the air. Nick caught them on his palm, opened the door, slid into the leather seat.

The car still smelled new.

Viondi jumped into the shotgun seat and picked up a satchel of tapes. "What you want to listen to?"

Nick narrowed his eyes as he gazed over the wheel at the busy street in front of him. "The blues," he said.

Viondi looked at him. "You got some more bad news?" he asked.

"Heard from Lockheed on Friday," he said. "I didn't get the job."

"Sorry, man. That's bad."

Nick started the car.

"You got any more places to apply?"

Nick shook his head. "Not for the kind of work that I do."

"There's all sorts of engineers, though, right? I mean, you can get a job in another field?"

"Yeah. Maybe. But I'm about fifteen years out of date for anything but what I've been doing."

Viondi thought for a moment. "You get back from seeing your girl," he said, "we'll talk. I'll get you some work."

"I don't know anything about plumbing."

Viondi's laugh boomed out in the car. "Nick, you an *engineer*! You don't think you can learn *plumbing*? Only two things you got to know about plumbing. The first is that shit runs downhill, and the second is that payday's on Friday."

A reluctant laugh rolled up out of Nick. "Yeah, okay," he said.

"A man sends his daughter to France, that man needs a job."

Nick sighed. "I know," he said.

"Professor Longhair's what you need," Viondi said. He slotted in a tape. "Let's hear a little of that N'Yawlins music, get that Louisiana sound in your soul."

So they listened to Professor Longhair on their way out of St. Louis, and as they headed south on I-55 they followed it with Little Charlie and the Nightcats, Koko Taylor, and Big Twist and the Mellow Fellows. They avoided the Swampeast by crossing into Illinois at Cape Girardeau, the silver bridge vaulting them over a brown, swollen Mississippi that was packed high between the levees and walls. Even from high above, on the bridge, the slick, glittering river looked fast, deep, and dangerous.

The old town of Cairo was decaying gently behind its tall concrete river walls. Viondi took over the driving because he wanted to stop at a barbecue place he remembered, and he drove around the shabby downtown area for twenty minutes, but the restaurant had closed or he couldn't find it, so they got some burgers and crossed the Ohio into Kentucky. They followed Highway 51 through Fulton into Tennessee, and then south through Dyersburg and Covington. And as they approached the homeland of the blues, Viondi's music drifted back in time, a connection to the heat and toil and sadness of the Delta, all the horrible old history, shackles and cotton fields, mob violence and the lash. Lonnie Johnson. Son Seals. Victoria Spivey. Robert Johnson.

"My granddad came north up this road," Viondi said. "Highway 61 out of the Mississippi Delta to Memphis, then 51 north on his way to Chicago."

"That's the way a lot of people went," Nick said. "My mother's people came north that way."

"North to the Promised Land. Get away from the Bilbos and the coneheads. And what they got was South Chicago." Viondi shook his head. "I remember driving down with my family during the summers to see all the relatives we left behind. All the old folks, still in Friars Point. The backseat all packed with kids and packages and the smell of food."

They carried their food, Nick knew, because black people could never be sure if restaurants would serve them. And even after segregation ended, the habit of carrying food along continued.

Nick's stomach rumbled. He found himself wishing there was a full hamper on the backseat.

"You still got people there?" Nick asked.

"A few. All working for Catfish Pride."

"And one of them owns a samovar."

"Aunt Loretta isn't a relative, she's a used-to-be in-law. She's kin to Darrell's momma." Viondi smiled. "She'll put us up tonight. You'll see." He lifted his sunglasses, looked at Nick out of the corner of one eye. "You getting hungry?"

"Yeah. That burger didn't last. Maybe we can get something in Memphis."

"I know a place that's closer."

Nick sighed. "Sure we can find it?"

Viondi dropped his sunglasses back on his nose and laughed. "Let's check it out. You don't want to eat now, we'll get some takeout."

The restaurant was open, an old ramshackle seafood place that loomed above the Hatchie north of Garland, gray weathered clapboards and mossy shakes on the roof. Nick and Viondi ate fish, cole slaw, greens, a bottle of Bud apiece, then stepped out onto the dense heat of the late afternoon and looked down at the thick, slow river, swollen by the backwash of the Mississippi. Nick felt an unaccustomed contentment easing his strung-wire muscles, and he touched the little box in his shirt pocket, the diamond necklace he had bought for Arlette.

Tomorrow he'd give it to her. He imagined her eyes shining.

Shadows were starting to lengthen. Nick got behind the wheel and crunched away down the gravel drive. "I can get us to Memphis from here," Viondi said. "We don't have to backtrack. Just turn right." He slotted a Lonnie Mack tape as Nick made the turn. "My token white guy," he said.

They drove down a winding two-lane blacktop. There were few buildings, and no people. Pines clustered thick on all sides.

Lonnie Mack's voice grated from the car's speakers.

Viondi adjusted the seat to recline more, leaned back with his hands pillowed on his stomach. The bottle of beer had made him drowsy. "So," he said, "what do you call a whore with a runny nose?"

Nick looked at him suspiciously. "What?"

"Full."

Viondi's laugh boomed out in the car. Nick shook his head. "That's the third most disgusting joke you've told today," he said. Lonnie Mack's guitar stung the air.

The car took a leap, left the road for a second, and Nick's eyes shot to the road, his hands clenching on the wheel. Had they just blown a tire? Hit something?

Nick looked into the rearview mirror to see if there was a dead animal in their wake, but there was nothing.

The Olds made a sudden lurch to the left, then to the right. Blown tire, then. Nick's foot left the accelerator.

"What happened?" Viondi said, sitting bolt upright.

Nick looked up in surprise as he saw that the pines on either side of the road were leaping, branches waving madly as if in a high wind. Then one of the trees ahead on the right *exploded*—there was a puff of bark and splinters partway up, as if it had been hit with an artillery shell, and the top half of the tree tipped, began to fall toward the road.

"*Look out!*" Viondi shouted, one big hand reaching for the wheel.

Nick flung the Olds to the left and stomped the accelerator. He felt himself punched back in his seat as the car took off. Splinters spattered off the windshield. Viondi gave a yell and leaned toward Nick as he tried to get away from the tree that was about to crash through his window. Nick's heart pounded in his ears.

Boughs banged on the trunk as the tree crashed to the ground just behind the car. "*She's a natural disaster!*" sang Lonnie Mack.

"What's going on?" Viondi shouted.

Nick tried to get the car into the middle of the road. Trees shot by on either side, and suddenly they were in a clear space, green soybeans in rows on either side of the road. Nick took his foot off the accelerator. Nothing could fall on them here.

And then the earth cracked across, right in front of them, a crevasse ten feet across. Nick yelled and slammed on the brake.

The last words he heard were *natural disaster*, and then the Olds pitched into the crack.

The choir mourned softly in the great space of the National Cathedral. Judge Chivington lay in state in his great mahogany coffin, and around him was a golden pool of light cast by floodlights overhead. Television cameras hunched inconspicuously in the cathedral's darker recesses. The President sat in the front pew, with the First Lady on one side and the judge's daughter, her husband and children, on the other.

The stock market, he was given to understand, was going to hell in a handcart. The Fed chairman's bizarre smile of the previous week had been analyzed and, probably, laid down to indigestion. The G8 summit was going to fall flat, all the President's initiatives going the way of *all* the President's initiatives, and his mark on history would be that of a caretaker, a Grover Cleveland or a Gerald Ford, someone fated to occupy the President's Office in between the crises that made or tested greatness.

Damn it, Chivington, he mentally addressed the coffin, *why did you have to leave? Why now?*

A shudder ran through the pew beneath him, and the President looked up, wondering if a big truck had just passed. He felt an unease in his inner ear.

The voice of the choir dimmed—the President saw chorister eyes glancing around—and then the choral director gestured emphatically, getting his crew back in hand, and the massed harmonies strengthened. The President felt a strange vibration in the palm of his hand where it was gripping the pew.

From overhead there was a chime. It hung in the air for a long moment, producing a discord in the choral sound below. Another chime rang out, a deep metallic bellow.

The President felt the First Lady's gloved hand close on his arm, and he heard her whisper in his ear. "What's going on?"

He shook his head. Another peal sounded. The choir's voice faltered again.

The President looked up in surprise. The cathedral bells were ringing, softly at first, then with greater and greater insistence.

"Can they turn those off?" the First Lady hissed.

The President shook his head again. This wasn't a regular bell peal, the sounds were too random. Something else was happening.

Another shudder ran through the building. Near the catafalque, a stand of media lights tottered and then fell with a crash. The choristers were singing as loud as they could to cover the growing chaos.

In wonder the President gazed upward as the bells sounded, ringing as if they were mourning the end of a world.

The fairest opportunity that was presented (to our knowledge) of judging of its force and direction, was from an ostrich egg which was suspended by a string of about a foot in length from a first floor ceiling, which was caused to oscillate at least four inches from point to point. We are informed that the steeple of the State House, which is supposed to be 250 feet in height, vibrated at least 6 or 8 feet at the top, and the motion was perceptible for 8 or 10 minutes. A number of clocks were stopped, and the ice in the river and bay cracked considerably. Some persons, who were skaiting, were very much terrified, and immediately made for the shore. In the lower part of the city it appears to have been most forcible, some people abandoning their homes, for the purpose of seeking safety in the open air.

Annapolis, Jan. 23, 1812

Marcy, in response to the tourist's question, was about to explain that the Westward Expansion Memorial was an international competition open to everybody, but at that moment she heard a strange roaring sound, like all the cattle in the stockyards had broken loose and were climbing the monument's stairs. She gave a look to Evan, her colleague, to see if there was something wrong with the north tram. No, the sound wasn't coming from there.

The entire Gateway Arch jumped about ten feet to one side.

Marcy went down, tangling her legs with those of the tourist. There was a sound like a freight train inexplicably roaring through the tram stop. A painful series of throbs went up Marcy's spine, as if someone was kicking her repeatedly on the tailbone. Each kick lifted her a couple inches from the floor, then dropped her again.

"Everyone keep calm!" she shouted through sudden terror.

About a third of the tourists had fallen. The rest were shrieking, swaying, staring—all except the two Japanese, who had thrown themselves to the ground at the first impact, and were lying curled into little fetal balls, hands over their heads. Some of the people that had fallen were trying to rise. Marcy made flattening motions with her palm. "Everyone get on the floor!"

Her ears ached with the volume of the roaring. One of the windows shattered, fragments spilling outward into space, and a group of tourists screamed.

"Get down!" Marcy yelled.

Nobody could hear her, but the tourists were looking around for instruction, and enough of them saw her gestures so that they began to drop to the ground. Marcy put her hands atop her hat to show they should protect their heads, and they understood and began to cover up.

Marcy wanted to reassure them. "You're safe! You're safe!" she shouted, and then, because she could think of no other words, she added, "This place is built like a brick shithouse!"

She hoped.

The whole Gateway Arch kept kicking her in the butt, hard.

Marcy had all the statistics memorized, all the tons of concrete and steel that had gone into the Arch's construction. Eero Saarinen's modest intention had been to create a monument that would last 8000 years, and he had built it proof against the winds of a tornado, against the shattering force of an earthquake.

She hoped his calculations had been on the money.

"A brick shithouse!" she repeated.

Another window blew out, letting in the hot, moist Missouri air, and Marcy began to pray.

Jason lay stunned on the grass with the telescope partly under him. There was a horrific noise and vibration as if a thousand semi trucks were thundering past at once, all blowing their horns. He could feel the vibrations on his insides, as if his internal organs were shaking themselves apart.

Earthquake, he thought. He was a California boy and he knew.

And he knew it was a bad one.

Cracking noises split the air like gunshots as tree limbs snapped. There was a tremendous crashing overhead as a huge elm branch snapped off high up, bouncing off other branches as it fell, and Jason hunched into his shoulders as it smashed to the ground just a few feet away, its jagged butt-end driving into the turf like a spear, the leafy end still tangled in the tree above.

Jason tried to stand and was thrown down before he could even rise to one knee. He gulped in the air and found that it tasted of sulfur—he had been so astounded by the force of the quake that he had forgotten to breathe—and then he belly-crawled the few feet, through a rain of fallen branches, to the brink of the mound. Below, the earth was heaving up in long rollers like the Pacific rolling onto the shore at Malibu. Here and there deep cracks gouged their way across the fields as if a savage giant were slashing at the soil with a knife. The earth moaned aloud as the giant struck again and again.

But it was at the row of five houses that Jason stared. He couldn't see his mother, but was relieved to see that the house was still intact. The windows were broken out and the old brick chimney had sprawled across the roof like a fallen prizefighter, but the building was still standing.

Which was more than could be said for the other neighbors. Their houses were brick, and any Californian knew that masonry was death in an earthquake. Two of the houses, including the Huntleys', were already piles of broken brick lying beneath shattered roofs. And as he watched the Regans' house swayed and fell, collapsing into its basement, tearing away the metal roof of the carport from its supports and dragging it into the pit with a screech of metal. Jason couldn't see Mr. Regan, though the old man had been in the carport just moments ago.

There was an explosion a scant hundred feet from his mother's house, the sound buried beneath the roaring and moaning of the earth, and then water and white sand were blasted into the air, followed by a plume of water higher than the roof of the house. Jason wondered dazedly if the geyser came from a broken water main—but no, this was the *country*, there were no water mains here. There was a horrific noise as a slippery elm, fifteen feet away on the right and sixty feet tall, pitched over the edge of the mound and flung itself downward like a javelin.

And then Jason cried out in fear as his own house gave a lurch and fell, dropping with an audible crack onto one corner. A rain of chimney bricks spilled from the roof. The old frame house had been built on little brick piers, and the heave of the earth had walked the house right off its foundation.

Another geyser burst out of the cotton field, and then another. And then another geyser burst up from the Huntley house—but this wasn't water, it was a bubble of fire, blasting up from beneath the broken roof. The Huntley's propane tank, couplings shattered, had ignited. Jason's heart leaped into his throat. He tried to shout a warning, but it was lost in the groaning of the earth.

The last of the five houses shattered as the earth gave another wrench. Cracks tore across the surface of the ground. Sulfur tainted the air. Jason's stomach turned over as he felt a new element enter the earth's motion—he felt as if two strong men were kicking him at once, and in different directions.

It was this that brought the Adams house down. The old farmhouse swayed back and forth, as if to blows, and then there was a rending and cracking of timber, and the roof spilled into the backyard, taking most of the house with it. Terror roared through Jason like a flame. He screamed and again tried to stand. The earth flung him down, pitched him down the slope. For a whirlwind moment he felt himself falling free. He screamed again and came to an abrupt stop, brought up short as he fell into the limbs of a scrub oak. Branches slashed at his face. He clawed his way through the branches, slid another ten feet down the slope, was caught by more brush.

And suddenly the earth fell silent. Jason's inner ear spun in a giddy circle and he bit back nausea. He shouted, was surprised to find he could hear himself. *"Mom!"* he yelled. *"Are you okay?"* There was no answer. He looked wildly for the path he'd ascended by, but it was buried in broken timber, so instead he ran straight off the edge of the mound. He clung madly to branches to steady himself as he tried to scramble directly down the sides, but the mound was too steep, and there were too many uprooted trees, fallen limbs, and tangled brush for him to make any kind of swift progress.

He heard someone shout below—a male voice calling for help. He shouted in answer as he dove through the trees. And then he came to a clear area, where he could get a good view of what was going below, and stopped to orient himself.

His heart almost failed him, and his knees threatened to give way. He had to clutch at a tree limb to keep from falling.

The broken houses were plain to see. The Huntley place had turned into a torch as a jet of propane consumed the entire property. The dog Batman wailed from amid a cloud of black smoke that roiled into the sky. Another fire was rapidly building in the ruins of another house, the one at the west end of the row. The tumbled, broken mass of his own home had partly fallen toward the Huntley ruin, and was dangerously close to the flames. It was clear that Jason had to get his mother clear of the wreckage before fire consumed the whole street.

In the field beyond the house, a dozen geysers spat water and white sand into the sky. Some had built up cones of sand around their bases. But it wasn't the geysers, or even his wrecked home, that held Jason's gaze.

It was the levee to the east.

The long green wall had been breached in at least two places. The water that poured through was not coming gently—it didn't *run* through, it wasn't as if a jug of water had been spilled in the kitchen and was gently emptying itself on the floor. The water *jetted* through, with the entire great weight of the river behind it. It was as if a thousand high-pressure hoses had been turned on behind each breach. Mist boiled upward from the two breaches as the brown water poured onto the laser-level fields below.

In the midst of all this, between the two breaches, was Eubanks's cop car, which sat motionless atop the levee as if trying to make up its mind what to do. And below, a tiny figure amid the giant water plumes, Muppet was struggling to right his overturned ATV.

"Run!" Jason screamed. *"Run for it!"* He didn't know who he was shouting at—Muppet, his mother, Mr. Regan, maybe even Batman the dog.

Everyone. Everyone run.

Terror launched him down the mound. Branches lashed his face as he fell as much as ran down the mound's steep face. As he ran he caught brief glimpses of the catastrophe from between the trees . . . Muppet getting on his ATV and beginning his race with the advancing water . . . a huge chunk of the levee, tons of stone and concrete, breaking away in the torrent, carried into the field by the powerful flood . . . Eubanks hesitantly backing his car away from the widening breach . . .

And then Jason ran head-on into a tree limb and knocked himself sprawling, the air knocked out of his lungs. *"Run,"* he urged weakly, though he knew no one could hear him.

Over the Niagara roar of the breached levee he could still hear the faint hornet buzz of Muppet's ATV. He sat up, breath rasping in his throat, and felt his heart sink as the sound of the ATV faltered. His head spun. He batted aside leaves, peered between the wrecked trees, and saw that the little vehicle had run as far as it could, that it was stopped at the edge of a crevasse that lay across its path and was too wide to drive across. Muppet's green helmet turned to gauge the approaching water, and then he dismounted the vehicle and took a few steps back so as to run at the breach and leap across. His sneakers splashed in water that was already ankle-deep.

"Run," Jason urged. There was a huge pain in his chest, as if something inside had ripped away.

There was a grating roar as another piece of the levee tore

away, and then Muppet ran and launched himself across the fissure. He reached the other side, falling to hands and knees, then picked himself up and began to run. *"Run,"* Jason advised. He clutched at branches and tried to stand. His head spun. He was whooping for breath. The breach in the levee widened again, the river shifting ten tons of stone as if it were foam packing. The flood burst through, a wall of water twenty feet high, six-foot wavecrests foaming at its top.

Muppet looked over his shoulder at the oncoming wall, and his stride increased.

And then the foaming wall overtook him—Jason caught a brief glimpse of tumbling puppet limbs, a green helmet flashing in the brown water—and then his friend was gone.

Jason reeled down the face of the mound, but he knew it was too late to save Muppet—to save anyone. The flood waters raced on, a mass almost solid in the weight of its onslaught ... the wave front gave a glancing blow to the shattered house on the end of the row, and the roof came apart under the impact, the pieces floating onward, piling into the flaming wreck of the Huntley house. Batman the dog gave a last wail, and was silent. The Huntley house came apart as well, turning into a wall of burning wreckage that surged up against Jason's house.

"No," Jason said. His Nikes splashed into water and he kept going, wading out into the rising flood. He watched his house dissolve, mingle with the flaming wreckage carried in by the flood. There was a bang as something exploded, and the fires spread. Jason paused as a surge of water lapped to his waist and almost took him off his feet. Tears spilled down his face, blurred his vision. Water tugged at his knees, and more waters were clearly coming.

Jason turned and began to claw his way back up the mound, grabbing handfuls of turf and hauling himself by the branches. The flood surged up to his waist, lifted him upward, toward a fallen elm that lay athwart his path. Jason reached for it, pulled, got a foot over the bole of the tree, and rolled over the tree onto dry ground.

He wiped tears from his eyes, sat up, and turned to see a clump of burning wreckage, all that remained of the five houses on his road, being carried on the flood toward the highway. Very little of the wreckage was even recognizable as belonging to the house that Jason had lived in.

His mind whirled. It had only been a few brief minutes since he had been standing atop the mound, watching his mother in the kitchen through the telescope. Now the kitchen was gone, and the house, even the field in which the house had stood.

There was a weird singing in his heart, a wail of loss and grief and shock. He couldn't think what to do. He didn't know whether to allow himself the hope that his mother might be alive. Alive and where? In the burning ruins?

The elm tree below his feet shifted in the current. Jason looked at the breaches in the levee, saw them wider than ever before. The Mississippi didn't seem to be an inch lower than it had been: there were six-foot waves in both the breaches, and flying white scud. Eubanks's cop car was perched on an island that was getting smaller by the second.

Jason needed to move to higher ground. Wearily he turned and began to climb.

A shadow fell on him and he looked up. Though only moments ago the day had been perfectly sunny, now a low dark cloud nearly covered the sky.

Jason viewed this phenomenon with the same dull acceptance with which he accepted the need to climb. He was beyond thinking about things. He could only react.

He began to claw his way up the mound, bracing his feet against trees or broken stumps, digging in the turf for handholds or pulling himself up with branches. Twice, powerful aftershocks knocked him flat, belly to the damp earth, sent him clutching for anchors to keep from falling off the mound's steep flank. Finally he dragged himself to the topmost level, the little clear area from which, a few moments ago, he'd viewed his world. The telescope sat there waiting for him, unbroken. Apparently its hard red plastic case was adequate for an earthquake. The lens cap lay where he left it.

Without thought he put the cap on the objective lens, then turned and gazed at the scene below him.

The burning wreckage that once was his home had dispersed a bit, though it was still heading west with the flood. To the north, a dark, lowering cloud of smoke, its bottom marked by scarlet flame, hung above Cabells Mound. It seemed as if the whole town was burning. He could not see the water tower and assumed it had fallen. With no water pressure, he knew there was no way that Cabells Mound could fight the fires.

Not until the river water smothered them, anyway.

To the east, the two gaps in the levee were growing toward each other. As chunks of the levee tore away, Eubanks kept shuttling his police car back and forth, trying to remain in the exact center of his diminishing island. His car's rack lights continued their mute flashing: *Emergency! Emergency!*

Within a few minutes, however, the island was not much bigger than the car, and Eubanks had nowhere to go.

Jason could see his dark silhouette moving inside the car. At first he wondered what Eubanks was trying to do, and then he realized that he was closing all the car's windows, making it as watertight as possible.

He was planning on floating away, then, as far as he could. Jason supposed it was as sensible a plan as any.

But Eubanks's plan never had a chance. The levee did not tear away beneath his car, it *was torn*—a mass of laden metal rammed through the breach, trailing a nest of cables, a barge that had broken free from its tow. Perhaps it was one of the barges that Jason had just watched the *Ruth Caldwell* push upstream. It smashed the levee beneath the front half of Eubanks's car, and as the barge swept past, the car pitched down nose-first into the gap, then toppled over onto its roof. Jason could hear the thud from where he sat, along with the sound of shattering glass. The car spun madly in the current for a few seconds, water pouring into the broken windows, and then the river swallowed it with the same fantastic speed with which it had swallowed everything else.

Jason watched with the same dull, mute acceptance with

which he had viewed the rising waters, the burning of Cabells Mound. It was as if he'd already used up all his stock of emotion and there was nothing left.

A gust of cool wind blew across the mound, and Jason shivered in his wet clothes. He looked up into the dark, threatening sky.

And then, out of nowhere, the first lightning bolt rained down.

SIGNS OF THE TIMES

Has such a succession of Earthquakes as have happened within a few weeks been experienced in this country five years ago, they would have excited universal terror. The extent of territory which has been shaken, nearly at the same time, is astonishing—reaching on the Atlantic coast from Connecticut to Georgia and from the shores of the ocean inland to the State of Ohio. What power short of Omnipotence, could raise and shake such a vast portion of this globe? The period is portentous and alarming. We have within a few years seen the most wonderful eclipses, the year past has produced a magnificent comet, the earthquakes within the past two months have been almost without number—and in addition to the whole, we constantly 'hear of wars and summons of wars.' May not the same enquiry be made of us that was made by the hypocrites of old—"Can ye not discern the signs of the times."

Connecticut Mirror

"Is this the day?" Frankland demanded. "Is this the day? Is this the Day of the Lord?"

The station was vibrating to pieces around him as he shouted into the microphone. Things tumbled off shelves: a stack of tapes slid off their metal trolley and spilled on the floor with a clang. Frankland's chair was moving in wild circles across the tile floor, anchored only by his hand on the mike. He ducked into his collar as a fluorescent light exploded overhead.

"And I looked when He broke the sixth seal," Frankland shouted, "and there was a great earthquake—*are you ready for judgment?*—and the sun became black as sackcloth made of hair—*are you ready for Jesus?*—and the whole moon became like blood—*are you ready for God's Tribulation?*"

Frankland, trying to hold on, was wringing the microphone as though it were the neck of the Devil himself. "*Are you ready?*" he howled as something in the outer office crashed to the floor.

And then the lights went out. Frankland waited, in the rumbling darkness, for the emergency generator to kick on, but nothing happened.

Darn that diesel anyway. Frankland tried to stand, but he put a foot on something that had tumbled from a shelf and fell clumsily to his knees. Crawling, he made his way to the door, tugged it open, and then crawled through the office— all the shelves had fallen, all the furniture had moved—to the exterior door.

Suddenly the shaking ceased, and the rumbling receded, like a train passing on to somewhere else. Frankland hauled himself upright by the doorknob. Vertigo swam through him. He needed to use his shoulder to drive the metal door from its bent frame.

As he burst open the door, sunlight and the smell of sulfur hit him in the face. *Brimstone!* he thought delightedly. The dirt parking space in front of the studio was torn clean across by a rent four feet across. He made his way around the building, one hand on the wall to keep him steady. The church, he saw, was still standing, though its windows were gone. He felt a grim satisfaction: he had built his station, and his church, to survive this and more.

His hands were trembling, and it took him a while to get the padlock on the generator room open. Once there, it only took a moment to start the piggyback electric motor on the diesel.

The diesel coughed into life. The light in the shed winked on. Frankland staggered out of the shed and waved his arms at the heavens. "The voice of the Lord is back on the air!" he shouted.

And the heavens answered. Frankland's hair sizzled as it stood on end. There was a flash, a boom, the smell of ozone. Frankland tottered and fell to his knees, his mind swimming.

A lightning bolt, he thought, from a clear blue sky. What more sign did a man of God need?

He stayed on his knees, clasped his hands, began to pray.

"Thank you, Lord, for letting me see this day," he said. "Thank you for this destruction out of which Your kingdom will be born. Thank you for giving me my mission."

Heaven's lightning rained down around him. He raised his hands in praise.

It was a new world, he thought, and he knew exactly what to do.

The Reverend Noble Frankland had come into his own.

TEN

We entered the Mississippi on the morning of the 14th, and on the night of the 15th came to anchor on a sand bar, about ten miles above the Little Prairie—half past 2 o'clock in the morning of the 16th, we were aroused from our slumber by a violent shaking of the boat—there were three barges and two keels in company, all affected the same way. The alarm was considerable and various opinions as to the cause were suggested, all found to be erroneous; but after the second shock, which occurred in 15 minutes after the first, it was unanimously admitted to be an earthquake. With most awful feelings we watched till morning in trembling anxiety, supposing all was over with us. We weighed anchor early in the morning, and in a few minutes after we started there came on in quick successions, two other shocks, more violent than the former. It was then daylight, and we could plainly perceive the effect it had on shore. The bank of the river gave way in all directions, and came tumbling into the water; the trees were more agitated than I ever before saw them in the severest storms, and many of them from the shock they received broke off near the ground, as well as many more torn up by the roots. We considered ourselves more secure on the water, than we should be on land, of course we proceeded down the river. As we progressed the effects of the shock as before described, were observed in every part of the banks of the Mississippi. In some places five, ten and fifteen acres have sunk down in a body, even the Chickasaw Bluffs, which we have passed, did not escape; one or two of them have fallen in considerably.

Extract of a letter from a gentleman on his way to New Orleans, dated 20th December, 1811

Father Guillaume Robitaille rolled over the Arkansas blacktop at 85 miles per hour, his radar detector alert to the presence of the state police. Traveling throughout his parish, if such it could be called, put at least 800 miles on his old Lincoln every week, and his policy was to spend as little time in the car as possible, which meant getting from one place to another as fast as the machinery permitted.

The words to the old song "Hot Rod Lincoln" tracked through his mind as he squinted through the windshield. Commander Cody, he remembered, and His Lost Planet Airmen. It had been a hit when he was young.

Tonight he would say mass for his tiny congregation in Rails Bluff, all six of them—maybe seven, if Studs Morris had succeeded in raising his bond money.

He raised his 64-ounce Big Gulp and sucked on the plastic straw. The motivation with which he had spiked his Sprite warmed his insides.

Though whisky was his preferred drink, he used vodka when he was on the road. It wouldn't fill the confessional with telltale fumes.

> It's got a Lincoln motor and it's really souped up.
> That Model A Vitimix makes it look like a pup.
> It's got eight cylinders; uses them all.
> It's got overdrive, just won't stall.

A cotton wagon blocked the lane ahead, drawn by a rusty old tractor and moving at ten miles an hour. The Lincoln swooped around it as if it were standing still. Father Robitaille drove one-handed, his Big Gulp in the other. He overcorrected, had to straighten out, felt the Lincoln fishtail.

Only one way to fix that. Hit the accelerator.

The big car responded. Robitaille smiled.

> Now the fellas was ribbin' me for bein' behind,
> So I thought I'd make the Lincoln unwind.
> Took my foot off the gas and man alive,
> I shoved it on down into overdrive.

At first Robitaille thought he'd blown a tire—maybe more than one. The car leaped as if each wheel was trying to go in a different direction, some of them no longer horizontal.

Robitaille lifted his foot from the accelerator, put his Big Gulp between his thighs, grabbed the wheel with both hands. Now he could see it wasn't just the car—power poles and fence posts were dancing, and branches waved in the air. The cotton fields on either side of the road heaved up in waves.

Robitaille fought to keep the car on the road. At times it seemed it was jumping out sideways from beneath him.

He looked in the rearview mirror, and his heart leaped into his throat as he saw it coming at him from behind.

Behind him, the ground was collapsing. A line was crossing the land, and behind the line it looked as if the ground was dropping ten or fifteen feet, like a stage set with the props knocked out.

The line reached the cotton wagon and its tractor. They both fell—Robitaille saw the arms of the driver rise, an expression of dismay on his face, as the tractor dropped out beneath him, its nose kicking up as it threatened to roll over on him. Behind the moving line, where the land had fallen, was nothing but wreckage. The line was rolling up on the Lincoln's rear bumper.

A cocktail of adrenaline and vodka surged through Robitaille's veins. There was only one response. *Accelerate!*

Robitaille punched the accelerator and felt the big car leap in answer. Duct-taped upholstery absorbed his weight as he was pressed back into the seat. He clutched the wheel with white-knuckled hands, tried to keep the car on the pavement as his speed increased.

He wasn't getting the smooth acceleration he was used to—the car was jumping so much that the drive wheels weren't in contact with the pavement half the time, they were just spinning in air. But the speed built nonetheless. Robitaille's glances at the mirror assured him that though the line was still overtaking him, it was doing so more slowly.

Faster. He mashed the accelerator to the floor. Sooner or

later, he hoped, the geology might change, the land wouldn't be so susceptible to quake.

The Lincoln vibrated like a mad thing under his touch. The engine roared. Robitaille felt it trying to leave the road, become airborne.

He rocketed around a parked pickup, saw the open-mouthed woman behind the wheel staring at oncoming ruin. *Faster.* The car landed heavily—or perhaps the ground had leaped up to meet it—and the suspension crashed. He felt the oil pan scrape on asphalt. The drive wheels screeched as they dug in and flung the car forward. He saw his muffler and tail pipe assembly bounce free in the road behind him before being swallowed by the encroaching abyss.

Faster. He saw the road arching up ahead of him, the bridge over the Rails River. Exultation sang through his mind. Surely the wave that was collapsing the country behind him wouldn't cross the river?

Behind he saw the line of ruin recede. He was gaining on it.

The bridge was just ahead. The unmuffled engine thundered like an artillery barrage. Robitaille began to laugh. The Lincoln bottomed again at the bridge approach, then flung itself up the arching roadbed. The laugh froze in Robitaille's throat.

The far half of the Rails River Bridge was gone, just a fallen rubble of steel and asphalt.

The Lincoln's wheels spun in air as it launched itself into space. The engine roared.

Robitaille felt the car's nose tip downward, saw the water below.

Wished he had time for another drink.

> *My pappy said, "Son, you're gonna' drive me to drinkin'*
> *If you don't stop drivin' that Hot ... Rod ... Lincoln."*

* * *

"Hey, darlin'," Larry said to the phone. As he spoke his greeting, he raised his voice slightly to let everyone in the control room know that it was his wife Helen who had interrupted the day's desultory football analysis.

"Are you busy?" Helen asked.

"We are analyzing the Cowboys' jackhammer offensive," Larry said.

"I'll take that as a no, then."

After a lot of work during refueling, and stacks of related paperwork afterward, Larry and the Poinsett Landing Station were in a fairly relaxed period. The plume of steam floated above the cooling tower, a finger of white that pointed toward Louisiana. The facility was running at eighty percent capacity, and the operators had little to do but watch the controls. Sometimes Larry wondered how long Poinsett Landing would continue to run if he, and everyone else in the control room, simply left, locked the door behind them, and never came back.

Months, probably. Possibly even years, until the enriched U-235 in the fuel assemblies finally spent itself, until the fuel finally lacked the ability to heat the demineralized water in the reactor vessel to anything greater than the temperature of hot tea, and the huge steam generator, rotating on its 160-foot shaft, finally cooled and cycled to a stop.

Larry stole the last glazed doughnut from the box parked atop the computer monitor, then settled into his chair with the phone at his ear. Below, the football discussion continued uninterrupted.

"I thought I'd call about Mimi's birthday," Helen said.

"It's not for another month," Larry said. He bit his doughnut, felt sugar melt on his tongue.

"Yes, but I saw something this morning that was just perfect for her. Do you know that old antique store up by the courthouse?"

"Uhh—guess not."

"Well, I saw this amazing lamp. It's a bronze horse, a kind of Frederick Remington thing . . ."

Larry sat up in his chair as something jolted up his spine. "Just a minute," he said.

It felt as if someone had just kicked the bottom of his chair seat. His eyes darted to his metal-topped desk, where pens and pencils were suddenly jiggling. He lowered the hand holding the doughnut to his desktop.

"Hey," he called out, trying to get the attention of the operators below. Larry's eyes were already scanning the displays. *Pump malfunction?* he wondered. *Something with the turbine?*

He heard a kind of percussion in his ear, like a shelf had fallen on the other end of the phone. "What was *that*?" Helen called in his ear, alarm in her voice. And then, a second or two later, Larry felt it himself, a lurch as if something large had fallen sideways against the control building.

"What was *that*?" Wilbur echoed.

The lurch came again, then again, a thudding, *wham-wham-wham-wham*, a steady pounding triphammer. Everything on Larry's desk was shivering over to the right. He stood, phone in one hand, doughnut in the other. His eyes frantically scanned the control room displays. A folder of documents spilled from his desk, splashed unnoticed to the floor.

"Power spike on station transformers!" one operator shouted.

"Turbine feedwater pump's offline!" shouted someone else. Books pitched off shelves.

And then Larry heard it coming, a chuffing noise like an express train hurtling forward on its tracks, *choom choom choom choom choom CHOOM*, coming closer at terrifying speed. Larry had a moment to wonder if it was a tornado; he'd heard that tornados could sound like trains . . .

Then the express train hit the building. Larry felt a shocking blow to his right shoulder as he pitched sideways into the wall. The computer monitor flung itself into his lap, making him cry out. Fluorescent light shattered overhead, glass raining down on the room.

"Fuuuuuck!" Wilbur yelled.

Larry rolled the monitor off his lap and attempted to

stand, one hand groping at his desk, trying to lever himself upright. His boots went out from under him and he shouted as he fell and received another slam to his shoulder.

"Turbine trip! Turbine trip!" The voice was so distorted by fear and shock that Larry did not recognize it. Larry could barely hear the voice over the express-train sound of the catastrophe.

He felt the teeth rattling in his head. Glass shattered throughout the control room. Panels spilled from the ceiling, revealing ducts and bundles of cable. There was an actinic arc of electricity, a chaotic series of shouts from the operators. Larry rolled over on his stomach and tried to crawl toward the door. The floor kept trying to kick him in the belly.

Think, he urged himself. But he couldn't think at all, couldn't put one thought in front of another. The express train seemed to have run off with his mind.

The remaining lights faded to a dull amber. Dismayed cries filled the air. Electricity arced somewhere in the room.

Emergency lighting, Larry thought. *Wait for the emergency lighting.*

The lights brightened for a moment, and Larry felt relief flood into him. Then all light faded.

There were shouts in the darkness, crashes as things fell. The whole building seemed to take a massive lurch to one side. Larry felt himself pitch forward. His hands scrabbled for support. He could smell burnt plastic. And then there was a roaring as the electric arcs triggered the control room's gas extinguishing system, as pressurized cylinders of Halon 1301 began to flood the room with gas in order to suppress electric fires.

"Out!" Larry shouted. "Everyone out!"

Halon gas wasn't poisonous, not exactly. You could breathe it and it wouldn't kill you. But it drove the oxygen out of the room, and that *would* put you six feet under.

There was so much noise that he couldn't tell if anyone heard him.

Earthquake, he thought. No other explanation.

Vertigo eddied through his brain. The floor didn't seem to

be strictly horizontal anymore. Larry groped his way to the door, felt the metal frame under his hand, tried to haul himself upright. A bolt of pain shot through his injured right shoulder.

CHOOM CHOOM Choom choom choom choom . . .

The express train sound faded. Larry found himself standing in the door to the control room. Over the hiss of the Halon cylinders he could hear a babble of confused voices both within and without the control room. A shrill call for help echoed down the corridor. He moved instinctively toward the sound, groping his way down the corridor. Broken glass crunched under his boots. The only light he could see was an exit sign that glowed a ghostly red in the middle distance.

Someone slammed into him from behind, and pain shot through his shoulder. "Careful!" he snapped.

"Did the reactor trip?" Wilbur's voice shouted in his ear. "Did we have reactor trip?"

"Must have," Larry said. "Power loss this bad. Whole grid must be down." He rubbed his shoulder, tried to make himself think. In event of electric power failure to the reactor, control rods would slide into the reactor to stop nuclear fission. It wasn't something he had to order, it was something that happened automatically.

"Help!" a man screamed.

So the reactor, Larry forced himself to think over the noise, was shut down. The problem now was getting rid of the waste heat already in the core. Which should be happening automatically; there were systems that would do that.

There were also supposed to be backup electrical systems for the control room. And *those* had failed.

"Did the reactor trip?" Wilbur was shouting at the people shuffling out of the control room. *"Did the reactor trip?"*

"I don't know," came the answer from the dark. "I didn't get a light or a warning. But things went to hell so fast."

"Help!" someone shrieked. *"Jesus Christ I'm trapped!"*

Larry kept trying to put his thoughts together. *One thing after another*, he reminded himself. *Just keep turning that horse in circles*. If the reactor's primary cooling system suffered a LOCA—Loss-Of-Cooling Accident—gas-pressurized accumulator tanks within the containment building would dump a boric acid solution into the reactor core. This would serve very well for cooling, at least for a time, but in the event of a continued loss of pressure, auxiliary diesel generators belonging to the Emergency Core Cooling System, the ECCS, would automatically switch on and dump cooling water from accumulator tanks into the reactor, then keep the water circulating until the interior of the reactor cooled. If the diesels failed, the accumulator tanks would dump anyway, but the water would have no way to circulate.

"Help!" the man shrieked. Larry reached out into the darkness toward the huddle of men and grabbed Wilbur's shoulder. He was alarmed to find the shoulder was covered with something warm and wet that felt like blood.

"Listen," he said. "We've probably suffered a LOCA. We've got to make sure the ECCS is doing its job. We've got to get people down the stairs and out to the diesels." Suddenly the building shuddered as if to a blow. Glass shattered somewhere nearby. Larry lurched and reached protectively for his shoulder, but did not fall. Panic whirled through his thoughts. *I could die here*, he thought.

"Heeeelp!" the man screamed.

The building ceased to move. Even the trapped man was silent in the next few hushed seconds as everyone waited for the whole building to tumble down.

The silence held. So did the building.

"Listen," Larry said. "Who've we got here? Wilbur, can you check generator three down by the machine plant?"

"Right," Wilbur said.

"Bill—you there?"

"Ayuh."

"I'm trapped!" called the voice again.

"Bill," Larry said, "I need you to check number two, by Reactor Services."

"Right."

"I'll check number one myself." The man kept screaming down the corridor, but Larry's mind had started working again, was putting one thought atop the next. "Marky? You there?"

"Yeah."

"Can you go to the secondary shutdown room?"

The secondary shutdown room, at the very base of the containment structure, contained all the duplicate controls necessary to bring the reactor to a safe shutdown. Maybe the emergency power was working *there*.

"I don't reckon I can get there," Marky said. "I think I busted my leg. Somebody's going to have to carry me out."

"I'll go instead," said someone else.

"Good. You do that."

"Somebody help meeee . . ."

"Okay," Larry said. "The rest of you help Marky and that other poor soul. Check every office and make sure there aren't people trapped up here. And take them down by the stairs—don't use the elevators even if you can find one that seems to be working."

Larry groped his way toward the illuminated exit sign. He found the steel push bar on the stair, put his weight on the door, and failed to budge it. The doorframe was bent, he realized. He put his unwounded shoulder against it, shoved. Nothing.

"Door's jammed," he said. "Can somebody help me here?"

Three of them, with effort, finally bashed the door open. The stairwell was dimly lit from the few battery-powered emergency lights that hadn't been completely shattered. A strange bellowing sound echoed up the stair, like lions roaring in the African bush. Larry paused for a moment, sniffing for scent of fire and detecting none. Then he reached for the metal stair rail and began to descend.

The stair was tilted at crazy angles, as if it were trying to pitch him off. His inner ear swam with vertigo as he groped his way down the stair, one slow step after another. He worried that the metal stair might have been structurally damaged, that his weight might prove too much and that it might fall away with him on it.

The roaring sound got louder as he descended. He began to feel a vibration through the metal rail. The roaring was terrifyingly close. Larry couldn't imagine what might be causing it. Perhaps, he thought, a fire was raging somewhere nearby.

He reached the bottom of the stair, put his palm against the metal door to see if fire had turned it hot. The door was cool, but it vibrated in sympathy to the roaring sound. For a moment Larry hesitated, wondering if opening the door was at all wise. Then, when he tried to push the door open, he found again that the door was jammed.

It took them longer this time to get the door open. The concerted efforts of four grown men were necessary to bash the door open. When it finally moved, it flung open about two feet, then stuck fast on broken concrete. A cold mist drifted in through the opening, and along with it the stench of sulfur.

Larry stepped out onto the east side of the control building and looked in astonishment at a series of fountains, a line of them forty feet away, that jetted water a good hundred feet into the air. Mist plumed high in the air, and water rained down on a level field thick with debris.

Water from the *reactor*? he thought, thunderstruck. But no. Reactor water would be boiling hot, not cool. Besides, there wasn't enough buried pipe in this area to account for the volume.

Somehow, Larry decided, the geysers had to be natural. And therefore they were not his problem. He would think about them later.

Larry wiped mist from his spectacles and shuffled to one side to let the others emerge from the structure. They gazed in consternation at the devastation around them.

The control building they'd just left was a wreck. It was tilted on its foundation and loomed over Larry's head like a concrete cliff. Larry felt a strong urge to slip away before it fell on him.

The control structure leaned against the containment building like a drunken prizefighter hanging on the ropes. Larry's head whirled as he realized that even the *containment structure*, with its tons of concrete and steel, was leaning at an unnatural angle. Water fountained from beneath its foundation, from beneath the twelve-foot-thick pad of concrete and steel on which the structure rested. Occasionally the geysers would spit out a rain of sand or a rock, twenty- or thirty-pound stones lofting through the air to thud onto the debris field. Larry was relieved that the fountains seemed generally to be tilted away from the building.

No time to be a tourist, Larry thought. He blinked in the mist.

"Are we ready?" he said. The others turned to him. Wilbur swiped with his sleeve at the blood that was running down his face from a scalp wound.

"You all right, there?" Larry asked.

Wilbur looked at his bloody sleeve in dull surprise. "Guess so," he said.

"Let's do it."

"Right," Bill said. He headed north toward the containment building, to get to the diesel by Reactor Services on the other side of the reactor.

Larry turned and loped the other way, down the length of the control building, keeping between the wall and the geysers that were roaring up from beneath the building's foundation. He tried not to trip on the stones and chunks of broken concrete that slid under his bootsoles. He could hear Wilbur stumbling after. Larry turned the corner, now heading west, then slowed and came to a halt as he saw the turbine house.

Through fountaining water Larry could see that the long building that housed the 160-foot Allis-Chalmers tandem-compound turbine no longer existed. The entire central section of the building seemed simply to have been blown to confetti. The rest had collapsed, chunks of aluminum roof or concrete wall tumbled down on the hulking forms of wrecked transformers, pumps, and condensers. Twisted rebar had been sculpted into weird shapes.

Larry could see no human beings in or near the colossal wreck.

Wilbur's footsteps, behind Larry, slowed to a halt. "Good God," said Wilbur's voice. "What the hell happened? A tornado?"

"Earthquake, I think."

Wilbur looked wild, wide eyes staring from the coating of blood that rained down his face. "There must've been a hundred people in there. We've got to help them."

Larry shook his head. "One thing at a time," he said. "The reactor comes first. We've got to make sure we have an SSE. Deal with the diesels before anything else."

Wilbur blinked blood from his eyes. SSE was Safe Shutdown, Earthquake. There were supposed to be contingencies already worked out. "Yeah," Wilbur said. "Guess you're right."

"Let's go."

The ground was covered with broken concrete and bright sharp metal. The metal was strangely twisted, torqued and strained and drawn, as if by steel hands, into bizarre shapes. Chunks sharp as guillotine blades were embedded in the wall of the control building, as if they'd been hurled there by a hundred-handed giant. The building wall, with its shining embedded blades, looked like some weird modernist sculpture.

The turbine's main shaft, Larry thought, had been rotating thirty times *per second* when the earthquake struck. If the quake had bent the turbine shaft, or if something massive had fallen on it and stopped its rotation . . .

Good Lord, he thought. *Tons* of swiftly rotating metal had slammed to a sudden halt. Turbine blades, even big ones, were notoriously delicate. Bringing the Allis-Chalmers to a sudden stop would have been like throwing a huge boulder into a 160-foot-long jet engine. The turbine would have come apart, spraying deadly metal in all directions. It would have been like a storm of ten thousand flying razor blades. No wonder parts of the turbine house looked as if they had been shredded.

And the shaft itself . . . ? A hundred sixty feet of rotating steel?

It would have gone *somewhere*. Maybe straight up in the air, like a giant spear.

It sure wasn't in the turbine house anymore.

He didn't want to think of the people who had been inside when it happened.

Behind the turbine house, a column of dark smoke rose into the sky. Between the obscuring mist and the smoke itself, it was hard to tell just what it was that burned.

He came to the southwest corner of the control structure. His path diverged from Wilbur's here: Larry would continue to head west to the number one auxiliary diesel behind the auxiliary structure, while Wilbur would detour south again around the remains of the turbine house to try to find the number three generator by the machine plant.

"Good luck," Larry said.

He didn't hold out a lot of hope for Wilbur's success. The machine plant was too close to the turbine house. Very likely it had been destroyed when the turbine came apart, and the auxiliary diesel structure with it. One or the other structure might even be the one that was producing the column of smoke.

But still, he had to make certain the safety backup systems were working. If only one of the three backup diesel generators went on, it was enough to secure a safe shutdown for the reactor. With that necessity in mind, the three generators had been placed far apart so that the same catastrophe could not overwhelm them all.

One of them, he thought, had to have survived. It didn't matter which one. So Wilbur had to try to get to the number three diesel, just on the chance that it was still intact.

Geysers shot out of the ground here, on the west side, but they weren't as numerous, or as forceful, as they had been on the other side of the building. Larry loosened his collar and tie, and then he and Wilbur each chose paths between the jets of water and began to run. Larry threw his arms over his head for protection in case one of the geysers decided to spit a rock at him. Pain shot through his right shoulder.

Water splashed up around his ankles as he ran. Where was

it all coming from? Larry wondered. Underground, yes, but from a hidden artesian system that had somehow escaped the geologists' reports, or . . . ?

A stone as big as his head splashed down a few feet away and Larry gave a jump, his heart thudding. He decided to think only about running. Pain jolted through his shoulder at every step.

Larry cleared the area where the geyser debris was raining down, and Mississippi's summer heat wrapped him like a suffocating blanket. He stumbled on something hidden under the water, recovered, and swiped at his glasses with his sleeve, trying to clear the droplets of spray. He panted for breath, not used to running, not used to any sort of real exercise in this heat. His heart bounced around his rib cage like a loose stone.

He blinked as he saw a bent form in front of him. A man in coveralls kneeling in the water, debris all over, his back bent, face close to the surface. It looked like he was praying.

It looked like he was dead.

Larry splashed closer. Slowed, heart rattling in his ribs. He stopped, panting for breath. Reached out a hand, touched the man on the back. "You okay?" he asked.

The man raised his head, and Larry's heart turned over in shock. There was a dividing line across the man's forehead, right at eyebrow level. Below the line the man's face was very pale, and his lips a bit blue, but he seemed otherwise normal. Above the line the flesh was bright red, and shiny. It was the most unnatural color Larry had ever seen, like an overripe red plum stretched tight and about to burst. Huge blisters had exploded over his skin, and some of them had broken and were weeping fluid.

Larry saw, as the man pulled his hands from the water, that the backs of the man's hands were bright red, too, and just as badly blistered.

"What happened?" Larry gasped.

The man blinked at him with pale blue eyes. "I was in the turbine house," he said. "Primary steam line went." The man's lobster-red hands fumbled at his collar in memory. "I used to work at a plant in Santa Barbara, so I knew it was a quake right off. Soon's I knew, I pulled my coverall over my face and ran for the door." The man's lower lip trembled. "Everyone else must've breathed the steam in, and died."

Larry stared at him in shock. A primary steam line rupture would have flooded the turbine house with thousand-degree steam straight from the reactor. If anyone had breathed it, his lungs would have gone into instant shock and he would have died within seconds.

When the turbine had, a few seconds later, torn itself into murderous razor-edged shards of metal, everyone around it was probably already dead.

"Dang thing blew up behind me," the man said. "I just kept running. Ran all this way." He looked down at the water in which he was kneeling, then slowly put his hands into the water again. "Hurts," he said. "The cool water helps." He bent forward, lowered his blistered forehead into the water.

"You've got to get help," Larry said. "You got to . . ." His mind flailed. "To get to the infirmary," he finished.

"Figure it's still standing?" the man said, his sad voice muffled by the water.

"I . . . don't know." The infirmary was in the administration building, southeast of here, behind the smoke pall of whatever it was that was burning. Larry hadn't seen it behind the smoke.

"I'll just stay here awhile, then," the man said. He sighed heavily, his body almost visibly deflating.

Larry splashed around him in agitation. "Listen," he said. "I'm coming back for you. I've just got to . . . I've got to run now."

"Take your time," the man said. "I ain't got nowhere to go."

Larry loped on, gasping in the humid air. His boots had filled to the ankles with water and they were like iron weights on the ends of his legs. The auxiliary building loomed up on his right, the building that held over thirty years' worth of Poinsett Landing's spent fuel in its stainless-steel-lined concrete pond. Larry looked at it anxiously as he jogged past. The buff-colored aluminum siding had peeled away here and there, revealing the ugly concrete beneath, but the walls seemed still to be standing. From the stumps of steel girders tilted skyward atop the flat roof, it looked as if part of the roof had caved in.

There were two separate pumping systems in the auxiliary building to keep cooling water circulating through the spent fuel. He wondered if either one of them was working.

First things first, he reminded himself. The reactor came before everything else.

Where was this *water* coming from? The geysers weren't throwing up enough water to cover the ground like this.

As he splashed around the corner of the Auxiliary Building he saw a group of a dozen workers standing behind the building. Panting, he approached them.

"Hey, Mr. Hallock." The speaker was Meg Tarlton, one of the foremen on the fuel handling system. Her red-blond braids peeked out from the brim of her hard hat.

"Hey," Larry said, and then he had to bend over, hands on knees, while he caught his breath.

"What *was* that?" Meg asked. "A bomb or something?"

"Earthquake," Larry gasped.

"Told you, Meg," someone said.

"How's the . . ." Larry gasped in air. "Fuel."

"It's a mess. Roof's caved in. Active cooling's down. Fuel pond's cracked in at least two places, but the leaking isn't too bad just yet. I don't think."

"You've got . . ." Larry straightened, tried not to whoop for breath. "You've got to get in there and make an inspection."

Meg's eyes hardened. "You're not getting us up on those catwalks again. Not till we know it's safe."

"But—"

"We had three people hurt bad. Jameel and some people just carried them to the infirmary."

"We're not going back in there, Mr. Hallock," someone said. "Just look at what happened to the tower!"

Larry's eyes followed the man's pointing finger, and his mouth dropped open in wonder. Little trailers of steam still rose above the cooling tower—what remained of it—but the elegant double hyperboloid curves were gone. It was as if the concrete skin of the upper tower had peeled away, like the rind of a fruit, in long diagonal sections, leaving behind only a skeleton of twisted rebar.

First things first! he reminded himself.

"Look," he said, "I've got to check the backup diesel. Meg, can you and a couple others help me with that?"

Meg nodded.

Larry pointed around the corner, toward where the lone survivor knelt in the flood. "There's a man back there, been badly burned. Can someone help him to the infirmary, or wherever it is that Jameel took those other people?"

Meg, who knew her people better than Larry did, made the assignments. The others following, Larry sloshed toward the backup diesel. Their route took them around a collapsed workshop and through a parking lot—water was up to the axles of the cars, and a geyser had coughed up a cone of white sand in the center of the parking lot. The cars were no longer parked in orderly rows: the moving earth had shuffled them like dominoes.

Well before Larry reached the diesel building he could see that there was going to be trouble. The walls and roof had fallen, and the only thing that kept them propped up was the steel mass of the diesel itself.

If the diesel were operating, Larry should hear it. It sounded like a locomotive.

The surface of the water trembled as an aftershock rolled beneath the land. The aluminum walls and roof of the diesel building rattled and creaked as the earth shivered. Larry stopped moving, arms held out for balance. Fear jangled through his nerves. He could hear the workers muttering behind him, and a splash as one of them fell.

The earth fell silent. Larry slogged forward.

He approached the diesel building, his pulse crashing in his ears. The steel door was crumpled on its foundation, clearly unusable, but there were wide gaps in the walls, and Larry stepped through one of these.

"Sir?" someone said behind him. "You maybe want a hard hat for that?"

Larry stepped into the broken building. His nerves gave a leap as the broken roof gave an ominous creak. The silent diesel loomed above him, tall as a house and 150 feet long if you counted the generator stuck on the end. Its mass propped up fallen roof beams.

Oily water shimmered around Larry's boots. There was a horrible chemical smell that didn't seem to belong in this scenario. He gave a sudden cough as something stung his throat. He tried to remember all the backup procedures he'd once memorized, the schematics of the diesel's systems. He hadn't dealt with any of this in years.

The roof gave another groan. Larry's eyes watered. "Mr. Hallock?" Meg called.

Larry backed out. "Batteries have spilled," he said.

The batteries were used to power the diesel's control systems once the big engine started. But the diesel hadn't started at all, which meant that the mechanical system running on compressed air had somehow failed. So why hadn't that worked?

He turned as he heard someone splashing up through the parking lot. It was Wilbur.

"Number three diesel's kaput," he said. "Fuel spilled, and it's on fire."

So that was the pillar of smoke behind the turbine house.

"Okay," Larry said.

"And the administration building's gone," Wilbur said. His staring eyes gazed out from the blood that streaked his face. "Just *gone*. Nothing but wreckage."

"Jesus," said Meg.

"It was the turbine shaft." There was awe in Wilbur's voice. "It must have tumbled through the air and . . . there's nothing left."

Larry put a hand on Wilbur's shoulder. Thought about the reactor core simmering in its boric acid solution, heat and pressure building. The possibility of leaks, jammed valves, heat building in the core.

The core turning to slag. Steam exploding out into the containment building. And who could tell, the way things were going, if the containment building was able to contain much of anything?

"Waaal," he said, "best get this ol' boy started, then."

He and Wilbur slipped into the diesel building again to check the compressed air cylinders. They were in a separate room, but were easy enough to find because the wall that separated the rooms had fallen to bits. In agreement with the massive redundancy that characterized the plant's design, there were three cylinders, each big as a house. The pressure gauges showed that two had discharged at some point in the quake. The third still held its charge, but the valve atop the cylinder was in the open position, showing that it had tripped and tried, but failed, to discharge. With eyes that stung from spilled battery acid, Larry peered through the darkened, ruined building and traced the couplings that connected the diesel to the third cylinder. The couplings ran overhead, in plain sight, and Larry traced them into the diesel room, past another valve . . . *there*.

When the roof had caved in, one of the roof beams had fallen across the valve. The weight had probably distorted the valve to the point where it wouldn't operate properly.

Everything in order, Larry thought. He had traced the compressed air system, and now he traced the roof beam. His eyes were streaming. Okay, he thought, the beam connects *there*, and . . .

A sudden shock threw them both against the air cylinder. Pain jolted along Larry's injured shoulder. He ducked and covered his head as, with a long metallic groan, more of the roof came down, metal panels falling like the blades of guillotines.

There was sudden silence as they waited for another shock. Larry's heart throbbed in his chest. The silence was broken by Wilbur's cough.

"Jesus," he said, "my lungs are burning."

"I got what we came for," Larry said. "Let's get out of here."

They sloshed out of the diesel building. Larry's stinging eyes blinked in the bright sunlight. "We need to move a roof beam," he said. "Can we get something from the machine shop?"

"I'd hate to dig through there," Meg said. "Can you show me what needs doing?"

Larry took a few breaths of clear air, then led Meg back into the crumpled building. He pointed out the beam, and Meg gave a laugh.

"My pickup's in the lot just outside," she said, "and I've got tow chains."

Meg splashed off to her truck. Larry stood for a while outside, breathed clean air into his aching lungs while he wondered whether it would be safe to wash his eyes in this water. There was more splashing as someone ran up, and Larry saw one of his control room crew.

"I've been to the secondary shutdown room," he said, "and it's flooded."

"Flooded?" Larry echoed, then looked at the water that was rising above his boots. Where was it coming from?

There was a roar and a splash as Meg drove up in her white Dodge Ram. Her crew helped as she shackled the beam to her truck, and then she shifted the Dodge into low gear and gave it the gas. Everyone stood back as the chains straightened and took the weight. The Dodge growled, its exhaust pipe almost under water. There was a long cry of metal as the beam began to move, as pieces of the roof spilled free with a cacophonous jangled sound. Larry held his breath. There was a clang as the roof beam pulled free of the structure, and Meg's Dodge leaped free, water surging around its thick tires, the roof beam dragging behind.

Then there was a compressed air hiss, so painfully loud that Larry held his palms over his ears, and a throaty, hesitant rumble from the diesel. Larry held his breath. The diesel coughed, spat, coughed again.

Then caught. The fallen roof rattled and shivered as the diesel began a businesslike throb. Fumes gushed up from a broken exhaust pipe.

Larry found himself in a cheering knot of workers. Meg spun the truck around, returned to the others with the beam dragging behind. A big grin was spread across her face. "*Yes!*" Wilbur yelled, splashing as he jumped up and down in the water. "*Yes!*"

Well, Larry thought. He had done it, by God.

But that only meant, when you got down to it, that he needed to get busy and do something else.

He looked down at the water, nearing the tops of his boots. He wished he knew where it was coming from.

ELEVEN

In descending the Mississippi, on the night of the 6th February, we tied our boat to a willow bar on the west bank of the river, opposite the head of the 9th Island, counting from the mouth of the Ohio we were lashed to another boat. About 3 o'clock, on the morning of the 7th, we were waked by the violent agitation of the boat, attended with a noise more tremendous and terrific than I can describe or any one can conceive, who was not present or near to such a scene. The constant discharge of heavy cannon might give some idea of the noise for loudness, but this was infinitely more terrible, on account of its appearing to be subterraneous.

As soon as we waked we discovered that the bar to which we were tied was sinking, we cut loose and moved our boats for the middle of the river. After getting out so far as to be out of danger from the trees which were falling in from the bank—the swells in the river was so great as to threaten the sinking of the boat every moment. We stopped the outholes with blankets to keep out the water—after remaining in this situation for some time, we perceived a light in the shore which we had left—(we having a lighted candle in a lanthorn on our boat,) were hailed and advised to land, which we attempted to do, but could not effect it, finding the banks and trees still falling in.

At day light we perceived the head of the tenth island. During all this time we had made only about four miles down the river—from which circumstance, and from that of an immense quantity of water rushing into the river from the woods—it is evident that the earth at this place, or below, had been raised so high as to stop the progress of the river, and caused it to overflow its banks—We took the right hand channel of the river of this island, and having reached

*within about half a mile of the lower end of the town, we were
affrightened with the appearance of a dreadful rapid of falls in
the river just below us; we were so far in the sock that it was
impossible now to land—all hopes of surviving was now lost
and certain destruction appeared to await us! We having passed
the rapids without injury, keeping our bow foremost, both boats
being still lashed together.*

*Account of Matthias M. Speed,
Jefferson County, March 2, 1812*

WHAM WHAM WHAM.

Omar lay in his front yard and watched his house shake to
pieces. The old double shotgun home was lightly built—no
need for heavy construction in a place where there was no
winter, no weather worse than a thunderstorm—and it was
not built to stand up to tremors on this scale.

All the work, he thought. *All the work in this heat. And now
it's falling apart.*

The brick chimney had tumbled down before he, Wilona,
and Micah Knox had realized what was happening, and had
run—staggered, really—out onto the lawn. Once there, it
proved difficult to keep on their feet, and so they lay down
in an open area, away both from the house and the magnolia
tree in front, where nothing would fall on them, nothing but
a blizzard of tumbling blossoms from the tree.

WHAM WHAM WHAM. The earth quaked and shuddered and moaned.

Wilona gave a cry as the old shiplap house was shaken off
its brick piers and came lurching to the ground. There were
crashes from the interior as furniture tumbled or slid. The carport caved onto the car with a metal whine. Omar reached out
and put an arm around Wilona's shoulders.

"Don't worry," he called. "We're insured." And wondered,
Are we? He didn't have the slightest idea what the policy had
to say about earthquakes.

Wilona just stared at the house, one hand to her throat as

if to secure Great-Aunt Clover's pearls, her one treasure. Her other hand clutched her white gloves, the only thing she'd snatched from the room on her way out.

Knox crouched on the quaking ground in a kind of three-point balance, like a football player waiting for a signal from the quarterback. His expression was a mixture of fear and excitement, like a kid on a roller coaster.

WHAM WHAM WHAM.

Shingles and chimney bricks tumbled off the roof. Paint flakes flew in little blizzards. Many of the clapboards shook right off the side of the building. Wilona's lace curtains fluttered through empty windows. Omar could feel his teeth rattling together with every tremor.

And then the shaking faded away. In the silence they were aware of a baby's shrieks, the frenzied barking of cur dogs, the blaring of a car horn. The quake was over.

But there was a rushing, and a coughing, and rubble burst from the yard of the neighbor across the street. It was like a mine going off, throwing debris arching into the air. Omar's heart gave a leap. He threw himself over Wilona as stones and chunks of wood rained down. A gush of water came up, blasting from the fissure as if from a fireman's hose. The neighbor's trailer, which had tipped to one side with its metal wall tortured and bent, gave a tormented booming rattle as the geyser tried to tear the sides from the building.

Mist began raining down. Omar stood up, tried to shield Wilona. "Let's move away from this," he said.

Knox stood, swayed. "What *was* that?" he asked.

"Earthquake, I guess."

"You got earthquakes, *too*?" Knox was staring. "Hurricanes and swamps and niggers just down from the trees and *earthquakes, too*?"

"Every hunnerd years, I guess," Omar said. He helped Wilona to stand, and she began to walk toward the house. He caught her arm. "Don't go back in the house, hon," he said. "It might not be safe."

"I want to call my Davey!" Wilona's glare was fierce. "I want to know my boy's all right!"

Omar blinked. Their son was attending LSU in Baton Rouge—could the earthquake have reached that far?

He drew her gently from the house. "Come to the car, hon," he said. "We can make phone calls from the police radio."

The mention of the radio reminded Omar that he was sheriff, that he was going to be needed here in this emergency, that people would be depending on him.

His mind swam. He had no idea what to do next. Numbly, while he tried to think, he began to steer Wilona toward the crumpled car port, away from the spouting water.

Knox danced in front of him. He seemed full of energy. His eyes glittered, and there was an intent grin on his face. "Hey, Omar," he said. "Let's get the carport off your car. You need to get to headquarters, establish a command post."

The words seemed to enter Omar's mind from a great distance. "Yeah," he said. "Guess I'd better do that."

"But what do *I* do?" Wilona asked.

Omar licked his lips. "Come along, I guess," he said. "The courthouse is probably the safest place around."

"Great!" Knox said. "You know—you should deputize me. You're gonna need a lot of special deputies in a crisis like this."

Omar wondered if this was something he could actually do.

"In fact," Knox went on, "disaster on this scale, you're gonna need a lot of paramilitaries." He gave a glittering smile, bounced up on his steel-capped boots. "You're gonna have trouble keeping order in this county—parish, I mean. You might just wanna call in the Klan. Everyone you can trust. Because sure as there is God in Heaven, nobody's gonna be looking after the white people of this parish but you."

Charlie Johns belly-crawled from his house as it rocked beneath him. He crossed the portico, tumbled down the stairs, and lay on the hot front walk gasping for breath. The earth heaved under him. Megan's car, in his driveway, was jumping up and down in place, as if it had suddenly been possessed by the spirit of a pogo stick. In fact, *all* the cars on the street were jumping up and down.

Charlie's head swam to the echo of thunder. There was a stench in the air. He closed his eyes and gasped for breath. He thought his head was going to explode.

The earth's motion ceased, but it was some minutes before Charlie could move. He opened his eyes—the sky was full of murk—and he tried to sit up. His head spun and he had to close his eyes again until the spinning stopped.

He wondered if a bomb had gone off. Or a tractor-trailer rig filled with liquid natural gas. The bad smell made him think it must have been gas.

Charlie opened his eyes. His house was before him, strangely shrunken. Part of it seemed to have collapsed. The big oak tree in the front lawn had split in half, raw white wood showing, but it still stood. The garage had fallen on his car. The ornamental brick on the front of the house had peeled off and lay in little dusty piles. All the windows were broken and the yard was littered with cedar shakes fallen from the roof.

He couldn't believe it. He had paid a lot for that house. It wasn't supposed to just *fall down*.

The sounds of shouts and screams came dimly to his ringing ears. He looked left and right, saw more ruin. All the houses on his quiet, expensive Germantown road were damaged. Windows gaped. Trees had fallen across hedges and rooftops. Chimneys sprawled across lawns. A three-story brick house, two doors down, had simply collapsed into a pile. Porches had fallen, and roofs leaned at strange angles. Stunned people lay stretched on lawns. Some people, somewhere, were calling for help.

Charlie stared dumbly at the carnage. It must have been a big bomb, he thought. Terrorists. No—probably the U.S. Air Force had dropped a bomb by accident. He would be able to sue for damages.

Megan's BMW 328i, he saw, sat in his driveway with its

hood and windscreen covered in cedar shakes from the fallen garage. She would be happy, he thought, the car hadn't suffered much more than a few nicks.

Megan.

She had been in the shower, he remembered. She was going to shower, and then they would make love on his big king-sized bed, and then they would open a bottle of champagne and wait for the caterers to deliver his canard à la Montmorency and Megan's croustades aux crevettes, and they would celebrate the fact that they were both very, very rich. While he waited for Megan to get out of the shower, Charlie sat in the front room to listen to the financial reports on CNN.

And then the bomb, or whatever it was, had gone off.

Charlie wondered where Megan was. Perhaps she was still in the shower.

He tried to get to his feet. His head whirled, and his stomach was tied in knots. Vomit stung the back of his throat. He took a few steps to the house and leaned on one of the portico's pillars, but the pillar swayed as he put his weight on it, and he saw now that the portico was no longer attached to the house, it had taken a few jumps onto the lawn, and there was a yawning two-foot gap, studded with nails, between the portico and the house proper.

"Megan?" he called. "Are you in there?"

He walked across the portico, feeling planks sag beneath his feet, and stepped across the gap between the house and the portico and into the front hall. Inside was a shambles: every shelf fallen, every glass object broken, the furniture moved around as if scrambled by a giant. The bottle of Moët had fallen from the bucket and rolled across the hall from the spilled ice.

"Megan?" he called.

He went to the back hall and looked down it. It was dark. Charlie flipped the light switch and the light did not come on.

There was a little closet off the back hall where the water heater and the furnace boiler were located. The door was open, and the water heater had fallen out and was sprawled in the hallway like a drunken sailor. Water spread across the thick carpet.

Charlie ventured down the hall and stopped before the water heater. He saw that the flexible metal gas line had been yanked taut when the water heater fell. He could smell a whiff of gas.

"Megan?" he called. "Are you there?"

He wondered if he should call a repairman, but then decided that the gas maybe couldn't wait. He leaned forward and turned the gas tap off at the wall.

Then he went back down the hallway, picked up the phone, and tried to call 911. The phone line was dead.

Charlie returned to the water heater and looked at it a while. He took a big stride and stepped over the fallen water heater, then continued down the hall to the master bedroom. The wet carpet squelched under his shoes.

"Megan?" he called. "Love?"

Everything leaned at a strange angle here, and it seemed to Charlie as if he were walking downhill. The house seemed partly to have fallen into the cellar. The doorframes were very crooked. The water from the broken water heater was all running downhill.

He paused at the door to the master bedroom. He was afraid to look inside.

Maybe, he thought, he should try calling 911 again.

"Megan?" he called.

He took a breath and looked around the corner into the master bedroom.

Acid flooded into his throat, and he turned away and fell to his knees and vomited.

Directly above the master bed and bath was the deck, with the hot tub. This was convenient, because the spa shared a lot of the plumbing with the master bath.

But the hot tub, which weighed over a ton when full, had gone through the deck, and everything was wet and Megan was dead and she was lying beneath the tub and there was no question that she was dead and the room was wrecked and the water was red and Megan was dead beneath the tub.

Tears stung Charlie's eyes. He got off his knees and went down the hall as fast as he could, stepping over the water heater and almost running until he got to the front room. He picked up the phone again, but the phone was still dead. Glass crunched under his feet as he ran for the front door, and then he crashed down because he stepped into the gap between the house and the portico, and he fell hard and felt a bolt of pain as nails tore at his shin. He jumped upright— nails tore at his trouser leg—and hobbled forward off the porch. He ran to the middle of the lawn and then stopped, because he didn't know where to go next.

The brick house that had fallen down entirely was on fire, big leaping flames jumping through holes in its curiously intact roof. Another building, across the street and two houses down, was also on fire, though the fire seemed to be confined only to one corner of the building. Smoke poured out the broken windows, but Charlie could see no flames.

People were in the streets running. Charlie recognized one neighbor, who looked at him and waved.

"Come on!" he said. "McPhee's on fire!"

Charlie stared after the neighbor as he ran. This was ridiculous, he thought. He was not the fire department. Someone should *call* the fire department.

He could feel the warm blood as it ran down his wounded leg.

He remembered that Megan had a cellphone in her car, so he walked to the BMW and opened the door and slid into the front seat. The car smelled securely of leather and Megan's perfume. He took the phone from its cradle between the two front seats and tried to call.

Nothing. Nothing but a distant hiss.

"Megan," he said, "are you there?"

Damn, she thought. Guessed wrong.

She should have read the earthquake report.

Major General Frazetta looked cautiously from beneath the dining room table. Took a breath. Took another. Waited to make sure that her words wouldn't turn into a shriek that she'd felt bottled up in her throat as the world shattered around her, as she felt their new house try to shake itself to bits, and then she shouted out, "Pat! You okay in there?"

From the room that Pat had designated as his workshop came the sound of something heavy shifting, of things tumbling to the floor. "Think so," came the mumbled answer.

Jessica crawled from beneath the table, noted as she rose to her feet that her hose had been ruined, and then made her way through the wrecked living room and hall to Pat's room. Pat was trying to get his lanky body from beneath one of his worktables that had fallen across him. Jessica helped to lever the table back upright—tools and bits of fragrant wood clattered on the floor—a fallen mandolin sang a plaintive chord—and then Pat got cautiously to his feet, brushed dirt off his shanks.

"Nothing broken, I think." He gave a ragged grin. "Thanks for the warning. Gave me time to duck."

Jessica had recognized the quake's initial strike—the primary, or P wave—the jolt that felt like a giant fist punching the house from underneath, that set the plates and saucers leaping on the kitchen shelves. She knew that the P wave was only the fastest of an earthquake's many weapons to travel through the earth, that the P wave would be followed by the shearing force of the slower secondary, or S waves, and then by the madcap dance of the Rayleigh and Love waves that could churn the earth like ocean breakers or spin objects in wild circles like the Tilt-a-Whirl at the fair.

And she knew, as soon as she felt the incredible force of that first jolt, the P wave that lifted her from the floor of the house and almost threw her through the kitchen window, that within seconds she would be experiencing all four kinds of movement at once. And so she dived beneath the solid dark wood shelter of the dining room table while shouting at Pat to take cover, that the big quake had come at last.

Only to have her words devoured by the express-train sound of the quake, by the shattering of glass and the crashing of shelves.

The mandolin sang again as Pat rescued it from the floor. "I've got to get to headquarters," Jessica said. "The road is likely to be a mess. It might take two of us to get through— can you drive me in the Cherokee?"

"Sure."

She looked at her watch, passed a hand over her forehead. It was just after five-thirty, and the quake had lasted more than ten minutes. *My God*, she thought, *the quake hit during rush hour*. Millions of people caught on the roads, on or beneath bridges and overpasses as they fell . . . And with all the rivers in spring flood, too.

"Go start the Jeep," she said. "Put the chainsaw in it. I'm going to change—put on my BDUs."

Damned, she thought, if she was going to confront a major national emergency in torn pantyhose.

The earthquake must have gone on at least ten minutes.

Eero Saarinen's Gateway Arch still stood above the Mississippi. If the old man had still been alive, Marcy Douglas would have kissed him.

One of the Frenchmen had suffered a heart attack. Everyone else had been so preoccupied during the quake that no one had noticed him until after the arch shivered to the quake's final tremor. The Frenchman was pale and glabrous and his lips were turning blue. Marcy's colleague Evan was giving him CPR. The victim's friends milled around loudly explaining the situation to each other in French.

Hot prairie wind blasted through broken windows, and only partially cleared away the smell of vomit. Several people had come down with motion sickness, including one little boy who had thrown up what looked like an entire bucket of popcorn. The arch did not normally move much—it would sway less than an inch even in the highest wind—but things were obviously different when bedrock was jumping around.

Marcy crawled to the station from which she controlled the tram, and used the telephone to call Richards, her superior, down on the ground level.

"We need to get paramedics up here," she said. "We've got a medical emergency."

"Good luck," Richards said. His speech was fast and breathy, as if he'd just run several miles. "There must be hundreds of casualties in town. The ambulance crews will have plenty of people to treat without climbing the Gateway Arch."

"What should we do?"

"Get your casualty down here. Our generators have kicked in—the trams'll work. Then get everyone else down to ground level as soon as you can."

"Can you send some people up to—"

"No. I'm not sending anyone *up* there!"

"But—"

"Besides, you can't believe how many people we've got hurt down here."

Marcy replaced the phone receiver, gripped the console, and carefully steered herself to her feet. A powerful wind blew through the shattered windows, flooding the observation deck with heat and dust. She walked with care—it felt as if she were stepping on pillows, expecting the floor to leap at any instant—to where the Frenchman was lying in the midst of a group.

"How's he doing?" she asked Evan.

Evan was in his late twenties, a white guy who had lived in Missouri all his life. "He's breathing all right," he said. "I think he'll be okay if we can get the parameds here."

"Richards wants us to get him down on the trams," Marcy said. "He doesn't think the parameds will get here for some time."

Evan pushed his glasses back on his nose. "That's gonna be tough," he said. "Can they send us somebody beefy to help carry—"

"Richards says no." She looked up in alarm. "Stay away from the windows, please!"

One of the children was bellying up to one of the shattered windows. He pointed out into the air. "Busch Stadium fell down!" he said.

Marcy pulled him back from the broken window, but she couldn't quite resist looking out herself. The view made her heart lurch.

Busch Stadium hadn't fallen down, exactly, but the roof had collapsed, and the rest was clearly damaged. City Hall looked as if a giant had gone over it with a hammer. Some of the older buildings—brick office buildings and hotels—had collapsed to rubble. There didn't seem to be a single intact window in the entire city.

Above the shattered cityscape, a few thin columns of smoke were beginning to corkscrew into the sky.

As the strong wind batted at her face Marcy thought about her apartment, the comfortable old brownstone she'd felt lucky to find and be able to afford. It was brick, and she wondered if all her belongings were now buried under piles of rubble.

She was lucky, she thought. She was lucky she was working the swing shift, lucky to be in the most solid structure in all Missouri.

"Marcy," Evan reminded. "We're in a hurry."

Marcy walked to Evan's station controlling the north tramway and thumbed on the microphone. She took on a breath.

"Ladies and gentlemen," she said, "we're sorry about the delay. We have a visitor who has fallen ill, so we ask you will be patient while he is loaded aboard a tram. After he has been sent to ground level, we will start regular boarding, and we'll get you all to the surface as quickly as possible."

Evan recruited one of the other Frenchmen to link arms beneath the sick man, forming support beneath his back and knees in a two-man carry. Marcy was relieved that she hadn't been requested to support half the man's weight on her skinny frame, but wondered if she should be insulted that she hadn't even been asked.

The casualty was carried gingerly down the stairs until an aftershock slammed the arch. The French rescuer lost his grip, and the invalid spilled to the metal stairs. His friends clustered around and began shouting at each other in French.

"I don't fucking believe this," Evan muttered. Marcy shoved her way through the crowd and tried to restore order. Evan and his partner lifted the victim again, shuffled him to the first tram, then laid him inside. Evan, the other Frenchman, and one of the women—the victim's wife, possibly—got into the tram car with him.

Marcy closed the tram doors and heard the rumble recede as the little train began its long trip to the ground.

"Excuse me?" The speaker was the young Japanese man. He was shy, and his voice was so low that Marcy could barely hear him above the blast of wind. "We are going down elevators?"

"Yes," Marcy said.

"Is not safe on elevators," the man said. "Is *earthquake*."

A number of the visitors had clustered around to listen to this exchange. "That's right," one man said. "We could get stranded."

"The Gateway Arch has its own emergency power supply," Marcy said. "I've been up here during two power failures in the city, and the emergency power cut in both times, and the people in the trams never even noticed."

"Is *earthquake*," the Japanese man insisted. "Must take stairs."

"There are over a thousand stairs," Marcy said. "We're twice the height of the Statue of Liberty. It's a *long way down*." The man seemed unconvinced, and Marcy wondered if she was at all urging the right thing. There were earthquakes in Japan all the time, and maybe the Japanese man knew what he was talking about.

She summoned as much authority as she could, squared her shoulders, looked at everyone from under the brim of her Smokey Bear hat. "It's much safer on the trams," she said, and hoped her voice was steady.

The phone buzzed. She picked it up, heard Evan's voice.

"We've got him down. I'm sending the tram back up."

"Good. I'm going to need your help to—"

"No way, Marcy. I'm gone."

Surprise took Marcy by the throat. "What—?" she managed.

"I've got a pregnant wife and two small kids in Florissant. That's my priority. I've got to be with them."

"Evan," Marcy said. "This is an emergency. We've got to get these people to the ground. You can't leave."

"The Park Service can sue me. See you later, maybe."

The telephone clicked off. Marcy felt her skin flush with anger, not simply at Evan's desertion but at the futility of his decision. Florissant was *miles* away, right through the inner city, and there was no way Evan could hope to get there in the horrid ruin St. Louis had become. All he had done by running off was to make himself useless, to his family and the tourists and everyone else.

Marcy called Richards's office, but no one answered. Neither did anyone else. Maybe they'd *all* run home.

The tram rattled back into the station. Marcy smelled smoke on the wind that was blasting through the observation platform. She opened the tram doors and thumbed on the microphone.

"We will start boarding the tram in a moment," she said. "Please form a line . . ."

Marcy was somewhat surprised to find that a line was actually formed—two-thirds of her visitors silently took up their places on the stairs.

She turned to look at the remainder. The Japanese couple, who seemed uncertain. A few others. And the elderly woman and her mother, both of whom looked very stubborn indeed.

Marcy approached the group. Licked her lips, tried to sound reasonable and persuasive. "The tram is safe, ladies and gentlemen. You've just seen it go down and come up. No one was hurt. No one was stranded."

The elderly woman's lips were compressed in a thin line. "I'm not getting into one of those cars again. I want to see the stairs."

"Ma'am," Marcy said. An aftershock rumbled up through the soles of her shoes. Just a little tremor, she thought, and decided to ignore it, but she saw her visitors turn pale, saw their eyes grow wide. "Ma'am," she began again, "there are a *lot* of those stairs. And I don't know how safe they are—there could be damage there."

"Elevator not safe," the Japanese man said. "Is earthquake."

The elderly woman's daughter looked angry. "I'm not sending my mother down in those elevators!" she said. Her voice was nearly a shout. "They weren't safe the first time!"

Marcy took a step back from this ferocity. She wished she were older and had more authority. She wished she were a football player and could just mash these people into the trams one by one.

"Please keep your voice down, ma'am," she said. "I don't want you starting a panic."

The woman lowered her voice to a hiss. "Then don't bother my mother!" she snapped.

Marcy backed away again. "I'll send this group down," she said. "That should show you it's safe."

"Not safe," the Japanese man repeated. "Earthquake."

Marcy went to her station and told the passengers to board the trams. None of them looked very happy. At the last second two of them froze, and one of them ran back to the observation platform with panic plain on his face. Marcy knew that she wasn't going to stop him.

"Please enter the tram, sir," she told the other. He was a burly older man, dressed in bright shorts and a kind of tam o' shanter. He carried a disposable Kodak camera, one of those that came in a yellow cardboard wrapper. His face was pale.

Marcy went down the stairs and touched the man on the arm. "Please go in, sir," she said. She saw that the nearest tram had two women already seated. "Those ladies need someone to look after them, okay?" she said.

"Hm?" he said, surprised. "Why yes, all right."

He allowed Marcy to lead him to the tram. She seated him between the two women and returned to her station. She closed the doors and set the little train rolling downward.

She picked up the phone and called to let someone know the tram was on its way, but there was no answer.

What were they all doing? she wondered.

Or maybe, she thought, they were all dead. The huge concourse and museum beneath the Gateway Arch were below ground level: what if the roof had fallen in? What if a pipe had burst, or the Mississippi found its way in, and the whole place was flooded? What if she was sending the visitors to certain death by drowning?

No. She had been on the phone with people since the quake. The concourse was above the level of the Mississippi even at flood stage. Nothing had happened down on the concourse except that people were very busy dealing with damage to the exhibits and to people.

Marcy turned to her remaining visitors. She counted nine, including the man who had panicked and run rather than board the tram.

She took a deep breath and began to argue. The trams were safe. She'd run them up and down twice and no one had been injured. The power supply to the Gateway Arch had multiple backups and had never failed.

Her heart sank as she spoke. She didn't convince a one of them.

No pencil can paint the distress of the many movers! Men, women and children, barefooted and naked! without money and without food.

Russelville, Kentucky, February 26, 1812

Nick and Viondi stood by the Oldsmobile. The car was in the crevasse, pitched over at an angle of maybe forty degrees, rear wheels still on the road with the tail in the air, the grille rammed into the side of the fracture. The front wheels hung in air. Something had cut Viondi, and blood ran down his face—the car had an air bag only on the driver's side. Nick and Viondi had got out of the car by climbing over the front seats into the back, and then leaving the car by the back doors, from which they could take the long, nervous step to firm ground.

It was hard to say how deep the crevasse was. The water table was high here, and water had filled the crack to within ten feet of the surface. The water was far from still—a storm of bubbles rose to the top, and foam was beginning to gather in stripes on the surface.

"Earthquake, I guess," Nick said, gazing down. His heart still throbbed in his chest.

"New Madrid fault," Viondi said. "Shit." He wiped blood from his face. "I gotta get back to St. Louis. Gotta get to my family."

"At least my family's well out of it."

Viondi gave him a quick glance, blood dripping down his face. "You sure about that?"

Nick hesitated. "The earthquake couldn't hit Toussaint that hard." He hesitated. "Could it?"

"We get out of here, then we'll know."

Nick looked at the car. "Wherever we go, it'll be on foot."

"Give me the keys." Viondi opened the trunk, took out Nick's suitcase, his own box of clothes, and the silver samovar, which he jammed down on top of his clothing.

"You're not going to take the samovar, are you?" Nick asked.

"Shit, man, it's solid silver. I'm not gonna leave it in an abandoned car in Buttfuck, Tennessee, that's for sure." His grim look grew more thoughtful. "Besides, if we can find drinkable water, we're going to need something to carry it in, and this is all we've got."

"Let me try to stop that bleeding before we go anywhere. I've got some Band-Aids and stuff in my bag."

There was nothing to clean the wound with, so Nick ended up using one of his T-shirts. He had some disinfectant cream, which Viondi patiently let him smear on the cut, and then he tried to close it with the adhesive strips. The cut was big, and blood kept pouring out while he was working, so Nick ended up using three different strips to try to hold the edges of the wound together. The adhesive strips, which he'd bought on sale, were what used to be called "flesh," meaning a light tan color intended to blend in with the skin of

Caucasians, and it contrasted strangely with Viondi's black skin.

The strips also had little green dinosaurs on them.

At least they stopped some of the bleeding.

"I guess we might as well go," Nick said. He put his satchel on his shoulder, picked up his soft-sided suitcase, then turned north.

"Hold on there," Viondi said. "We ain't going north. There's nothing there—we're miles from the highway or any big towns."

"There were some farms," Nick said. "And that restaurant."

There was anger in Viondi's look. "You want to bet that restaurant ain't floatin' down the Hatchie by now? And those farms—whoever lives there ain't gonna be in any better shape than we are." He pointed south, across the crevasse and the soybean fields. "Memphis is down that way. It's a big city. We can find a tow truck there, and people to help us."

Nick was confused. "How are we going to get over the crack? I can't jump that."

Viondi slammed the trunk with his big hands. "We got a bridge right here."

Nick was dubious, but Viondi put down his box, put one foot on the rear bumper, and climbed up onto the trunk. Nick held his breath, expecting at any second for the car to pitch nose-first into the crevasse, but all that happened was that the back of the car sank under Viondi's weight. Viondi crawled onto the roof, reversed himself, then slid his legs down the windscreen and onto the car's hood.

"There," he said. "Now pass me the box and the bags."

Nick put a foot on the rear bumper and passed Viondi their gear, and then Viondi belly-crawled backward down the length of the hood until he could stand on the other side of the crevasse. "Your turn," he said.

Nick felt his stomach clench. "Yeah," he said. "Okay."

He crawled slowly over the car, his heart giving a leap every time it shifted under his weight. But the bridge remained in place, and when he backed his feet to the broken pavement on the other side of the crevasse, he felt his breath ease.

Viondi handed him his suitcase. "Let's get moving," he said.

A shadow fell across the sun. Nick looked up, and was surprised to find how much of the sky was now covered with dark cloud.

"Maybe it's going to rain," he said.

And then he followed Viondi down the lonely, broken road.

The interior of the Gateway Arch was airless and musty and at least a hundred degrees. Sweat dripped from beneath Marcy's Smokey Bear hat, and her thighs ached. She'd been going down stairs forever.

"Careful," she told the people behind her. She pointed her flashlight. "The rail here is a little shaky."

There were 1076 steps altogether, one of those facts that Marcy had been obliged to memorize as part of her job. She hadn't bothered to count them as she descended, and she was glad. She didn't want to walk to the point of exhaustion and realize that there were still 600 steps to go.

The monumental skeleton of the arch loomed around her. Massive I-beams, giant stanchions, cross-braces of steel. The stair that wound its way down the arch rested in part on the framework itself, and wasn't going to move unless the arch itself gave way.

So far the stair had been safe enough. It was the little things that had been damaged. About two-thirds of the light-bulbs had shattered, leaving the stair a passage through gloom and shadow. The handrail had given way in places, and Marcy cautioned her visitors about putting their weight on it. Some of the smaller fixtures had fallen—bits of steel mesh, some cable, the lighter crossbraces. These could be worked around, with care.

"Take your time, now," she told her people. "We're not in any hurry."

She'd given one of her two flashlights to the Japanese man, and told him to keep to the rear of the column. Marcy kept the elderly lady right behind her, so that she could keep an eye on her, be certain not to overtax her, and make sure she wasn't about to drop dead of a coronary.

Marcy came to a landing, peered at the next flight of stairs, decided to call a halt.

"Everyone catch your breath," she said.

Simply catching one's breath was hard enough inside the stainless steel shaft. The heat was almost overwhelming.

Everyone clustered onto the landing, as supported by massive crossbraces it was clearly safer than the stairs themselves. "How much farther do we have to go?" a man asked.

"I don't know," Marcy said. "I've never done this before."

An aftershock slammed up through all the girders and beams and almost threw Marcy to her knees. She clapped hands over her ears as the metal around her began to shriek as if in pain. Something fell, somewhere, with a loud clang that echoed forever in the curving metal stairwell.

"I can't take it! I can't take it!" Marcy heard the words as though they came from far away. She looked up to see a man's distorted face, eyes so round that his irises stood out as tiny dots in a lake of white. "I want to take the elevator!"

It was the same man who had panicked just before entering the tram. He lurched on the landing, knocking into people bodily, and then he spun about, shoved aside the Japanese man at the tail of the column, and began to run up the metal stair in the direction of the observation deck.

"*No!*" Marcy shrieked, and lunged after him. She was not going to lose another one. Her shoe caught on a stair riser and she fell face-first on the metal treads, but her outstretched hand caught the panicked man's pants cuff. Marcy snarled as she clenched her fist around the fabric and pulled. The man was off-balance on the quaking stairway and fell. "*Get back here!*" Marcy yelled, and climbed up the man's body, putting all her weight on him as the man thrashed beneath her.

"I can't take it! I can't take it!" the man shouted.

Marcy straddled the panicked man and punched him in the face with her flashlight. "Shut up!" she shouted. He began to scream, a strange, scratchy wailing sound, as inhuman and metallic as the scream of the arch under tension. "Shut up, motherfucker!" Marcy hammered him with the flashlight again, then a third time.

The aftershock faded. The metal shrieking of the arch died away, and the man's screams faded at the same time. Marcy stared with fury into the panicked man's bloodstained face.

"I want to go to the elevator," he said.

"No way, asshole," Marcy said. "I'm not having *another* damn deserter." She grabbed him by his collar and hauled him to his feet, shoved him down the platform. "You walk ahead of me," she told him. "Now *march*."

Ten minutes later they shouldered open a bent metal door and stepped out into the concourse. Marcy gasped in cooler air, took off her hat, wiped sweat from her forehead. She heard moans of relief from her tourists.

The huge underground room was a mess. The glass ticket windows had gone, and the ticket counters leaned at strange angles. Displays had toppled, signs had come down, light fixtures had shattered. The floor was littered with tourist brochures, tickets, guidebooks, maps, and broken glass.

Marcy had never been so glad to see a wreck in her life.

She stepped aside and let her visitors file out of the stairwell. The elderly lady stopped for a moment, fumbled in her pocketbook. "I just wanted to say thank you," she said.

Marcy stared in surprise as the old lady held out a ten-dollar bill.

"No thanks, ma'am," she said. "We're not allowed to take tips."

Carrying her two flashlights, Marcy found her French party in the middle of the concourse, shouting at each other as usual. The heart attack victim lay on the floor, conscious but showing little interest in his friends. Other casualties lay nearby, maybe thirty of them. Some of them were very bloody, some unconscious. A number were covered in what looked like gray brick dust.

Marcy saw no one in khakis, no Park Service people at all. She glanced around her in shock. Could they all have run away? *All* of them? Had Evan started a panic?

She turned at the sound of shouts and saw two of her colleagues carrying an unconscious woman down the stairs and onto the concourse. Marcy's head lurched as she saw blood pouring from a wound in the woman's lower leg. Marcy ran and helped carry the woman to an empty space on the concourse floor.

"Where *is* everybody?" she demanded. "What's going on?"

"Parking structure collapsed," one of the park rangers said. He was gasping with the effort of carrying the injured woman. "There are dozens of people in there. We're trying to dig them out."

"We've got this one," the other ranger said. "Get out there and see if you can help someone else."

Marcy cast a last look at the bleeding woman and sprinted for the wide stair. The parking structure adjacent to the Gateway Arch was several stories tall and held hundreds of cars. If it had collapsed, there was no telling how many people were trapped in the rubble.

She ran out into the open and into a hot wind that blew burning cinders across her path. Heat flared on her exposed skin. Her feet slowed as she stared in horror at the wall of fire blazing on the other side of Memorial Drive.

Half the city seemed ablaze, everything from the tallest structures to the smallest heaps of rubble. She held up a hand to shield her face from the heat, and her palm turned hot. Clouds of black smoke curled up between her and the arch, obscuring its gleaming stainless steel skin. Hundreds of people swarmed across the highway toward her, crossing the park as they tried to get away from the fires. Others had collapsed on the grass, exhausted simply by the effort of getting here.

Marcy kept trotting toward the parking structure. Most of

the trees that lined the walkways had fallen, and she had to keep zigzagging around fallen trunks and limbs.

She glanced in the other direction, saw another cloud of dense smoke, growing from roots of flame, in East St. Louis. The *Casino Queen*, the huge riverboat that fed the East St. Louis economy with its gambling income, was lying on its side in the river. Its ornate smokestacks had fallen, and the ginger-bread on its balconies was broken. A few people were seen clinging to the part of the boat remaining above the water.

St. Louis's boats hadn't fared much better. The excursion boats *Tom Sawyer*, *Huck Finn*, and *Becky Thatcher* had been moored for the evening on the landing right under the Gateway Arch. Only *Becky Thatcher* seemed reasonably intact: *Tom Sawyer* had sunk at its moorings, and *Huck Finn* drifted downriver, trailing its mooring cables in the water. All had lost their stacks.

Marcy swerved around a fallen tree and came within sight of the parking structure.

It looked like a crater of the moon. A hideous pit filled with broken concrete and mangled steel.

Smoke burned Marcy's eyes. She slowed, gasping for breath.

"Evan!" she shouted. "Damn you!" And then, though her feet felt as if they weighed a hundred pounds apiece, she went down into the pit to rescue her visitors.

A neighbor girl knocked on the window of the BMW. Charlie looked at her in some surprise. The electric window wouldn't go down, because he didn't have the ignition key, so he opened the door.

The air smelled of smoke from the houses that were burning.

The girl was maybe fifteen and lived next door. Charlie saw her and her friends from his deck all the time. Charlie tried to remember her name.

"Are you all right, Mr. Johns?" the girl said.

"Yeah," Charlie said. "Everything's fine." He thought about Megan in the master bedroom, and his mind shied away from the thought.

"Fine," he repeated.

"My dad says we shouldn't go into our houses," the girl said. "In case there's another earthquake."

"Earthquake," Charlie repeated. It was an *earthquake*, he thought in surprise.

For some reason he hadn't even considered earthquake. He'd seen public service announcements on television every so often, usually late at night, but none of the locals seemed to take earthquakes seriously, and he didn't either.

Besides, everyone knew that earthquakes only happened in California and Japan.

"We're going to pitch a tent in the backyard and camp," the girl said. "We have a spare sleeping bag if you want one."

"No," Charlie said. "I'm fine. Thank you."

"We were wondering if we could get some water from your swimming pool."

Charlie blinked as he processed this strange request. He couldn't make any sense out of it. "Fine," he said finally.

"Thanks, Mr. Johns. See you later, okay?"

"Fine," Charlie said again.

He closed the door. Now the BMW smelled of burning.

He looked at the cellphone receiver he'd thrown down on the next seat, at the red lights winking. He picked it up again. He tried to call emergency numbers and nothing worked. He tried to call Dearborne, because Dearborne had been at the country club and perhaps hadn't realized they were all rich.

The phone didn't work. He threw it on the passenger seat in disgust.

Earthquake, he thought. His mum and dad would think it very strange when he told them.

McPhee's house was burning by now in a very lively manner. The neighbors had saved some of the furniture, which was all over the lawn and street, but could not save the house. There was a huge pall of rising smoke over downtown Memphis, as if a lot of things down there were burning.

Charlie realized he was hungry.

Too bad, he thought, that the caterers were going to be late.

TWELVE

This day I have heard from the Little Prairie, a settlement on the bank of the river Mississippi, about 30 miles below this place. There the scene has been dreadful indeed—the face of the country has been entirely changed. Large lakes have been raised, and become dry land; and many fields have been converted into pools of water. Capt. George Roddell, a worthy and respectable old gentleman, and who has been the father of that neighborhood, made good his retreat to this place, with about 100 souls. He informs me that no material injury was sustained from the first shocks—when the 10th shock occurred, he was standing in his own yard, situated on the bank of the Bayou of the Big Lake; the bank gave way, and sunk down about 30 yards from the water's edge, as far as he could see up and down the stream. It upset his mill, and one end of his dwelling house sunk down considerably; the surface on the opposite side of the Bayou, which before was swamp, became dry land, the side he was on became lower. His family at this time were running away from the house towards the woods; a large crack in the ground prevented their retreat into the open field. They had just assembled together when the eleventh shock came on, after which there was not perhaps a square acre of ground unbroken in the neighborhood, and in about fifteen minutes after the shock, the water rose round them waist deep. The old gentleman in leading his family, endeavoring to find higher land, would sometimes be precipitated headlong into one of those cracks in the earth, which were concealed from the eye by the muddy water through which they were wading. As they proceeded, the earth continued to burst open, and mud, water, sand and stone coal, were thrown up the distance of 30 yards—frequently trees of a large size were split open, fifteen or twenty feet up. After wading eight miles, he came to dry land.

*Extract from a letter to a gentleman in Lexington,
from his friend at New Madrid, dated 16th December, 1811*

Jason huddled between the lightning and the flood. He had lost track of the number of thunderclaps, the number of times lightning had blasted the top of the mound. Storm gusts blew dust, spray, mud, and rain, the alternations from one to the other coming with bewildering speed.

Jason clung to the steep side of the mound, away from the lightning. All he could hope was that one of the tall trees that loomed above him would not attract a bolt of lightning, topple, and kill him.

The water continued to rise. And on the northern horizon, Cabells Mound continued to burn.

There was wreckage, some of it still on fire, tangled with the row of trees to the north that marked the boundary of the cotton field. It was all that was left of the row of homes that Jason had lived in. The hope that Jason's mother might still be alive, somewhere in that wreckage, haunted his mind. *If only*, he thought, *I could get over there . . .*

But then what? If he were out there on those pieces of wreckage, what could he do for his mother, or even himself?

At least, he thought as windblown mud spattered his face, he wouldn't be *alone*.

When the lightning finally dwindled, the sky was so dark that it was not clear whether dusk had come or not. The mound was surrounded by a sluggish black river so wide Jason could not see its banks. He realized he was thirsty.

He wondered if he dared to drink the water.

He thought about the water jug in his mother's refrigerator, with the quartz crystal that was supposed to give the water magical powers. For some absurd reason tears came to his eyes at the thought of that jug, of the forlorn plastic container of magic water rolling along the bottom of the river. He pressed his head into the mud-spattered moss and let the tears flow down his face, let his breath fight past the hard lump in his throat.

From above the clouds, from above the darkness itself, he could hear the sound of a jet aircraft rumbling far overhead, like the echo of a vanished world.

Eventually he rose, wiped the tears from his face with a muddy hand, and carefully descended the mound's steep side. The water had stilled and seemed to be receding a little. He thought about bending over the surface of the water, anchored firmly to the mound with one hand on a tree limb, and easing his thirst.

No, he thought. There are dead people in that water.

He shuddered and drew back.

And then he saw, half-concealed by a fallen elm, the scrolled words. The letters were upside-down. Jason tilted his head, read *Retired and Gone Fishin'*.

Mr. Regan's bass boat.

Jason remembered the carport tearing away on the Regan's house, falling into the cellar along with the rest of the building. Apparently the boat had been liberated at the same time, though he didn't remember seeing it bob to the surface.

Weird hope fluttered through him, tentative as the wings of a new-born butterfly. With the boat, he could rescue his mother from the ruins of their home and take them both to someplace safe. Jason approached the boat, one foot sloshing ankle-deep on the steep slope. He climbed over the fallen elm, then was jerked back by a weight on his shoulder.

The telescope. He'd forgotten he was carrying it by its strap.

He disentangled the telescope from a tree limb, then hiked both feet over the bole of the tree. The boat floated upside-down before him, its aluminum hull scarred by collision with trees and debris. It was caught in a tangle of leaves and branches, and its bows were half-sunk beneath the waters.

Jason hung the telescope from a limb and splashed into the water. He tried to heave the boat over, but it was very heavy, his footing kept sliding away beneath him, and at one point he found himself swimming. He paddled back to the mound, but it was too slippery for him to climb, and eventually he hauled himself, hand over hand, up the length of a sapling.

He lay on the steep mound for a moment and panted for breath. The boat was too awkward and heavy to turn over by main strength. He was going to have to find another way.

He decided to try hauling it up onto the mound as far as it would go, then try to turn it over. He waded into the water, reached under the stern, and grabbed the stern counter with both hands. He heaved, throwing himself backward. Water poured off the boat, and it moved. Jason sat down, the stern of the boat in his lap. He dug his heels into the wet soil and scrambled backward up the bank, hauling the boat after him, gasping for breath after each heave. Sweat popped onto his forehead.

There was something springy in the feel of the boat, something that kept trying to pull the boat back into the water. With every heave, the boat's bows sank deeper into the water. Eventually Jason couldn't haul the boat any higher. It was caught, he realized.

He had to uncatch it, obviously enough. He scrambled out from underneath the stern, then waded out into the water, feeling his way around the port side of the boat. The steep mound fell out from under him very rapidly, and soon he was up to his chest. He gave a careful look at the bow of the boat, at the branches trailing in the water, to see if there was any dangerous current.

The water appeared to be barely moving at all. Jason slid into the water, kicking as he moved along the side of the boat. The bow ducked beneath the waters as he put weight on it. Underwater branches slashed at his kicking legs. He felt along the underside of the submerged bow, found nothing holding the nose of the boat under water. As he hung onto the submerged bow, the water was past his chin. He dog-paddled over, and began to feel along the starboard side.

Nothing.

Jason paddled back to the mound, climbed out of the water, and tried to catch his breath. Whatever was holding the nose of the boat down was clearly *underneath* the boat. He would have to dive beneath the boat to free it.

A cold tremor shook his nerves. He imagined being under the cold, dark water that had already killed so many. Groping in the blackness. He could so easily be caught and held underneath—by a branch, a cable, a piece of wreckage, anything.

He imagined drowning in the dark water, alone and lost, trapped under the river where he would never be found.

His gaze involuntarily turned northward, toward the line of trees where the wreckage of his house had been caught. The boat was his only way of reaching it, of finding whether his mother still lived.

The water seemed colder than it had before, and it made him gasp. Water lapped up to his lips, his chin. He felt his way along the overturned boat, took a gasping breath, and pulled himself under by his fingers.

He could see nothing in the murky water. He held onto the boat with his left hand and swept out with his right, trying to encounter the obstruction. Tree limbs lashed him—and for a moment he felt a pang of fear at the thought they might hold him under—but none of the limbs seemed to be attached to the boat in any way.

Jason surfaced, caught his breath, moved a little closer to the bow of the boat, and dived again. Again he held on with one hand and probed with the other. And this time he touched something different, something braided and slick.

Rope. Nylon rope.

He felt along its length, found a metal shackle hooked to an eye on the boat's bow. It was the rope that was used to winch the boat onto its trailer at the end of a day's fishing. Apparently the boat's trailer was somewhere underwater, carried along with the boat by the flood, and the two were still connected.

Jason was out of air. He pushed off from the boat toward the surface, kicking, but he ran into a tangle overhead, sharp and unforgiving branches. He batted at them as panic rose in his throat. Twigs stabbed at his face. His frantic kicks only seemed to lodge him more securely in the tangled, spiny nest.

Bubbles burst from Jason's lips. There was a throbbing ache in his throat. He snatched at the branches as his pulse beat in his ears. And then it occurred to him that he was going the wrong way, that he couldn't go *up*, that in order to get free he'd have to go down and then over.

He pushed at the overhead branches, trying to force himself down. His legs thrashed. He struck out with a breast stroke, trying to move laterally in the dark water. Invisible fingers clawed at his scalp. He thought of the hands of dead men and thrashed out frantically, more bubbles bursting from his nostrils and lips.

He came to the surface with thunderous splashes, gasping for air. He beat for the shore, dragged himself up the steep bank. Coughs racked his ribs. Nausea gripped his stomach.

When he had calmed, when his head finally swam clear of terror, he looked back at the water, saw the elm branch that had caught at him, and realized he'd probably been less than two feet under water. It had been so dark that he had felt he was much deeper.

He lay back on the bank, closed his eyes, tried to gather his strength. His teeth chattered from cold.

It was some time before he could bring himself to enter the water again, and when he did, it was on the opposite side of the boat from the tree limb. He ventured carefully, his fingers edging along the bows of the boat an inch at a time. He took a series of breaths, closed his eyes, and pulled himself under.

On the third swipe of his arm Jason found the rope. He followed it to the shackle, felt for the toggle that would release it. He found the toggle, tried to push it open with his thumb, rattled the shackle back and forth. It wouldn't come.

He was out of air. He pushed back from the boat and kicked to the surface, then treaded water while he caught his breath. Then he dove again.

He found the shackle more quickly this time, thumbed it open, tried to pull it from the metal eye at the boat's bow. The line had too much tension, he realized, for him to get the inch or so of slack needed to slip the shackle from the eye. So he reached to the bow, gripped the edge, and put his weight on it, made the bow bob in the water.

He reached out for the line again, and that's when he grabbed the dead man.

It felt wrong. Not the slick texture of the nylon line, but something soft and yielding and cold. He felt along it, trying to puzzle out what it was, and then he felt the cold fingers brushing light as gossamer against his wrist and he screamed.

He lunged to the surface in a boil of white foam. Water seared his throat. He clawed his way to the bank and lay retching. River water drooled from his mouth and nose.

Mr. Regan, he realized, had died with his beloved boat. Caught in the rope, apparently, and drowned.

Jason shivered on the bank and gasped for air. He sat up, spat out river water, and stared in at the boat in horror. He thought of old Mr. Regan lying under the water waiting for him, arms reaching out, eyes staring into the darkness, white hair floating. He thought of the distant flame-scorched rubbish on the horizon, and his mother clinging to it, clinging to life in the cold river water.

Without thought he flung himself into the river. He swam to the bow of the boat, put his weight on it, snatched for the mooring line, found it on the first grab. He felt slack on the line, and quickly he snapped off the shackle and let it fall.

The bow rose to the surface and brought Jason with it. He turned and swam straight to the mound, because he didn't want to see if Mr. Regan bobbed to the surface behind him.

He climbed onto the mound and caught his breath, and only then did he dare to look behind. No dead men floated in the water. Relief flooded his heart. He was going to rescue his mother, sail them back to California on the *Retired and Gone Fishin'*.

It was getting very dark. The sun must have set. Jason looked northward and saw that the fires of Cabells Mound had largely died down. He shuddered with a sudden chill and decided it was time to get his boat rightside-up.

He climbed to the stern, got a grip on the underside, and

heaved. There was a splash, a rain of water from the bow, and the boat moved. Jason ducked, got his feet and body beneath the boat, and straightened, giving a shout as the boat moved, rolling away from him.

With a great splash, *Retired and Gone Fishin'* landed on its keel. Jason's heart leaped.

He never could have turned the boat over on dry land. But the water had supported the boat's weight, and taken most of his burden from him.

The bass boat had clearly seen better days. It had platforms fore and aft, so that fishermen could stand and cast. There had been a padded swivel chair on each platform, but these had been torn away. Right amidships there was a small cockpit, with two forward-facing seats and a small jumpseat between them. The small windscreen in front of the driver's seat had been torn away, and the fore part was half-flooded with water.

Jason got into the boat, groped in the darkness for any equipment.

Nothing.

No engine, no paddles, no life vests, no fishing poles. No water, no food, no fuel. No way to bail out the water that filled the bottom of the boat. A steering wheel that wasn't hooked up to anything, a throttle that flopped uselessly back and forth like a screen door in the wind.

He wondered how he was going to get to the wreckage of his home. That cotton field might be fifty miles wide for all this boat was going to help him.

Pole along, he supposed. Or use a stick as a paddle. Or hang his feet off the back of the boat and kick.

Still, Jason could see no point in staying on the mound. It wasn't as if some rescue craft was going to parachute him an emergency outboard motor. If he stayed on the mound, who knew how long it would take for people to find him? The river would bring him to other people sooner or later.

He groped around on the flank of the mound for sticks suitable for paddles, and found several leafy branches that would do as well as anything else he was likely to find. He threw the branches into the boat, put his hands on the stern counter, and prepared to push off. Something solid banged him on the forehead.

He swiped at it and felt the hard plastic casing of his new telescope. He took the scope from where he'd hung it and, a bit self-consciously, hung it over his shoulder. Suddenly he felt like laughing. He looked down at the boat and imagined a crew of sailors waiting for his orders.

"We've got a *telescope*, men!" he said. "We're ready for sea *now*!"

And with a laugh, he pushed the boat off from the mound and jumped into the stern as it surged away.

The river was sluggish and still. *Retired and Gone Fishin'* turned slow circles as Jason fumbled his way over the boat. He found a locker that was reasonably dry, and put the telescope in it. The dying fires of Cabells Mound reflected red off the water.

He sat on the edge of the boat and tried paddling with one of the branches, but that only turned the boat in circles, and the effort was exhausting. The boat was too wide for him to paddle on both sides to keep it straight, not unless he kept jumping from one side to the other, and that seemed useless.

Jason tried hanging over the end of the boat and swishing the branch back and forth, hoping to propel himself along by lashing his tail like a sperm, but when he tried it nothing seemed to happen.

He looked at the bulk of the mound on his left, and it seemed farther away. He was slowly drifting south with the river, not north as he wished.

He threw the branch into the boat in disgust and heard it land in the water that splashed ankle-deep in the bottom. He was going to have to try kicking the boat northward.

He took off his sneakers and socks, then carefully lowered himself off the back of the boat. A shiver ran through him at the water's chill. He hung onto the metal plate to which the outboard was usually bolted, and he began to kick. Water splashed as his heels broke the surface.

He kicked steadily for a few minutes, but from behind the

boat he couldn't tell if he was on the right course, so he stopped kicking and pulled his head above the gunwale to take a bearing on the red glow of Cabells Mound. He seemed to be aimed more or less in the right direction, so he dropped into the water once more and began to kick.

That was the way it went for a long time. Kick for several minutes, take a bearing while he panted for breath, kick some more. The glow seemed to be getting a little nearer.

The air rasped in and out of Jason's lungs. His hands were numb on the metal plate. His head spun, and he felt the beginnings of a cramp threatening his left calf. He paused, hanging off the end of the boat, and tried to massage the cramp out of his calf with a half-paralyzed hand. He could feel his teeth chattering in the cold. There was an ache in his throat from his labored breathing.

A brief gust of wind flurried the surface of the water. The boat swung to the right, and Jason tried to kick to correct his course. He failed, and the boat swung farther.

He saw the Indian mound looming up close on his left. It shouldn't be there, he realized. It should be farther astern.

A flame of panic brightened in Jason's heart. He pulled himself above the boat's counter, tried to get a bearing. The fires of Cabells Mound seemed more distant. He looked frantically at the mound again, tried to get a bearing on it. The clouds above the mound were breaking up, with stars visible here and there, but the clouds were moving swiftly, and it was difficult to gauge motion relative to the water.

The boat swung to another gust. Jason's pulse throbbed in his ears as he turned his head to view the mound. He fixed his gaze at a star just visible above the tree-topped mound, tried to see how fast it was moving relative to the mound . . .

The star seemed to be flying in relation to the mound. Which meant that neither the star nor the mound were moving, it was *Jason* that was moving, Jason and his boat . . . The lazy current had picked up speed and intent, and was carrying him swiftly away from the wreckage of his home, away from any chance of rescuing his mother.

Jason gave a frantic yell and dropped back into the water,

kicking furiously to get the boat back on its proper course. Heaving the boat's slab side against the wind was difficult, and by the time he got the boat pointed in the right direction again he was already breathing hard, and he could feel the cramp building in his calf again.

He knew that he could not allow himself the luxury of weariness. He had to kick, and kick hard.

So he kicked, and from the first minute it was torture. His hands ached, his lungs were agony. Blackness filled his eyes. The cramp came in his leg and he clenched his teeth and ignored it, tried to keep kicking despite the muscles that turned hard as iron, that tried to tear his tendons from the bone. He didn't dare stop. The pain filled him and he *became* the pain, and the pain was in his heart and his mind and his body, and it filled the world and the night, and he kept kicking, because it would be worse pain to stop.

He shook water from his eyes and blinked at the bulk of the mound—he could *see* it sliding past, could see he was losing ground to the current. Mad determination brought a scream to his throat, a cry of hoarse defiance. Fresh energy seemed to glow in his limbs. The pain was not gone, but somehow it didn't matter now, he had managed to put himself somewhere else, to let the pain flow through him without touching him. He kept kicking, kept pushing the boat ahead of him, fighting the wind and the current, until he caught another glimpse of the mound again and saw that it was far away, far upriver, and he knew that all the effort had been in vain, that the current had him now and that the river was taking him away south, far from the fires of Cabells Mound, the floating wreckage that was his home, far from the muddy grave of his mother, who was, he knew, dead, a lifeless *thing* lying in the river mud, drowned or burned or broken, wreckage herself, flotsam, food for animals that swam or crawled in the muddy darkness . . .

So he threw one arm over the boat's stern and just hung there, legs dangling in the water, and let the pain claim him at last, the sobs tearing at his throat, as the boat turned slow pointless circles in the water that carried it to a destination that waited patiently somewhere to the south, concealed by the soft Mississippi darkness.

One gentleman, from whose learning I expected a more consistent account says that the convulsions are produced by this world and the moon coming in contact, and the frequent repetition of the shock is owing to their rebounding. The appearance of the moon yesterday evening has knocked his system as low as the quake has leveled my chimnies. Another person with a very serious face, told me, that when he was ousted from his bed, he was verily afraid, and thought the Day of Judgment had arrived, until he reflected that the Day of Judgment would not come in the night.

> *Extract from a letter to a gentleman in Lexington,*
> *from his friend at New Madrid, dated 16th December, 1811*

The Reverend Noble Frankland rose from his knees. His clothes were soaked with rain, and his knees with mud, but he had not felt that this was any moment to cease raining prayers and praise back to heaven.

Despite the downpour, the air still smelled agreeably of brimstone.

He reentered the radio station, walked across the littered floor to the control room. Though power had been restored, the station was mostly dark. Very few lightbulbs had survived the quake. The dials on the control panel—the ones that hadn't shattered, anyway—showed that he was still on the air. He fetched his old metal wheeled chair from across the room, dusted some broken glass off the green plastic seat, then sat before the microphone. His wet pants squished beneath him, and he gave a tug to one trouser leg. He put on his earphones, then spoke.

"Brothers and sisters," he intoned, "the Last Days have begun. These are the days of lightning and brimstone and shakings of the earth, the prophecies of the Bible coming true. We praise you, Lord Jesus, for letting us see this day."

As he spoke his hands automatically worked the potentiometers. During the lengthy time he'd spent praying on his knees he'd had time enough to plan what he was going to say once he returned to the mike.

"If anyone in the Rails Bluff area can hear me, the *first* thing I want you to do is thank the Lord's mercy for allowing you the opportunity to build His kingdom here on earth during the next seven years of Tribulation. And the *second* thing I want you to do is see to the safety of your family and your neighbors. And the *third* thing I want you to do, *if* your home is destroyed or damaged, or *if* you are afraid to be alone in this difficult time, or *if* you are in need of spiritual aid, I want you to come *here*—here, to the Rails Bluff Church of the End Times here on Highway 417. We will see that everyone is cared for and fed. We have enough supplies to support a large number of people, and we have the organization to make sure that everyone is cared for.

"If you don't have transportation, or if you're injured and can't move, try to call emergency services. If you can't get through, try to care for yourself as best as possible, and *we will find you.*

"If anyone from the Family Values campaign can hear me, I want you to look after those children and return them to their families if you can. If that's impossible, I want you to bring them here, to the Church of the End Times, where we will care for them till their parents can come for them.

"To any Christians in the Rails Bluff area—if you have no other duties, *come here now. We need you at the church!* We know how to organize you for survival here in the End Times—we have studied this problem for years!"

Frankland took a breath. "And now, let us all give thanks . . ."

He spoke a lengthy prayer, and then he found a sixty-second cart—a tape cartridge looped so as to repeat itself infinitely, usually intended for announcements or advertisements—and then Frankland broadcast his message again, recording it this time on the cart, making certain that it lasted a precise sixty seconds. Then he slapped the cart into the player and set it on infinite repeat. He listened to it once to make sure that it sounded all right, and then he took his earphones from his head.

It was only then that he heard the noise in the outside office. Someone had come into the station. He could see a large, shadowy form moving in the outer office.

Frankland's mouth went dry. In a movement that seemed to take forever, he reached into the drawer next to his chair and put his fingers securely around the custom grip of his P38 semiautomatic pistol. He eased the wheeled chair back from the control panel, but the wheels crunched over broken glass, and swift, angry reproach flashed through his mind at the sound.

The intruder halted at the sound, then moved down the corridor. Glass and wreckage crunched under his feet. Trying to breath in utter silence, Frankland thumbed back the hammer on the pistol and slowly raised the weapon. The intruder loomed closer. The pistol seemed heavy as sin.

"Reverend?" Hilkiah's voice. "You in there?"

Frankland let his breath sigh from his throat. His head swam with relief.

"Yes, Hilkiah. I'm here."

The big man groped uncertainly toward the doorway. "Are you hurt?"

"No." Frankland eased the hammer of the P38. "I'm just fine."

"Praise the Lord you're all right! I can't see a damn— whups, sorry, Brother Frankland—a dang thing in here."

Frankland put the pistol back in its drawer, rose from his chair, and shuffled through the rubble toward the door.

"Were you in town?" he asked. "What happened there?"

"Town's wrecked," he said. "The courthouse and the old Bijoux theater are the only buildings still standing, pretty much. A buncha houses caught on fire. Bet you we've got five, six hundred homeless people in this county, probably more."

The Bijoux was an old opera house from the nineteenth century, later converted to cinema, but abandoned now for years. It had a strong iron frame, and Frankland had once considered buying it for the site of his church.

"God bless it!" Frankland said as he barked his shin on a fallen shelf. "How about my wife? Our kids?" meaning the Family Values picketers in front of Bear State Videoramics.

"A few cuts and bruises, but they're okay. We were all knocked down when it started, but it was safer in the parking lot than inside the buildings, and we were away from the store fronts and the flying glass." He gave a chuckle deep in his throat, *hugh hugh.* "You shoulda seen them cars jump! Like they was trying to fly to the moon!"

"And the Piggly Wiggly? The video store?"

"Roof came down. We had to pull people out. Some busted legs and heads—I didn't stay to take count, I just helped round up the kids and then Sister Sheryl sent me here to make sure you were okay."

They emerged from darkness into the gloom of the outer office. "Where are the kids now?" Frankland asked. "Did you hear my message?"

"I don't got no working radio in the pickup, pastor. But Sister Sheryl was going to try to get them back to their families, then come here. And Dr. Calhoun had his bus there, and he was going to take care of the kids that live out of town."

If the bus doesn't break down somewhere in the middle of nowhere, Frankland thought. He sighed.

"We've got to get ready," he said. "I've told people to come here if they're in need. We'd better be set for them when they come."

He opened the metal door, let murky sunlight flood the room. "We need to clean the glass out of the church, so people can sleep there. Hang some plastic sheets on lines inside so the women can have privacy."

He looked across the road and saw Joe Johnson with a blade on his tractor, trying to shore up his leaking catfish ponds. Those catfish, he thought, they could feed a lot of people.

"Is it time to open the vault?" Hilkiah asked.

Frankland stepped into the parking lot and savored the sulfur in the air. Even though there were a number of vaults, all containing supplies laid under concrete until the End Times, Frankland knew which one Hilkiah was thinking of.

"Not yet," he said. "We don't want to scare people with all those guns before we have to."

Jessica rolled up to the headquarters of the Mississippi Valley Division in Pat's red civilian Jeep Cherokee, with her husband behind the wheel, half her senior military staff either in the back or hanging off the vehicle's sides, and Sergeant Zook, her driver, sitting on the vehicle's hood brandishing a Homelite chainsaw.

No one could say she didn't know how to make an entrance.

It had taken Jessica almost half an hour to get to her headquarters, normally a three-minute drive. The roads were badly torn, blocked with fallen trees, power poles, and landslides. The aftershocks that came every few minutes theatened them with further slides and falling trees. Only the Cherokee's four-wheel-drive made the journey at all possible. Along the way she'd picked up most of her staff, who lived on the same road above the WES, and found Zook, who after the quake had tried to fetch her in her car, but had got bogged down trying to negotiate a landslide.

The headquarters building was still standing, but Jessica suspected that this was going to be about the only good news. She bounded out of the Jeep before it quite pulled to a stop on Arkansas Road, and she headed for the group of soldiers she saw on the grass inside Brazos Circle. She was followed by a wedge of senior officers.

To the poor junior MP lieutenant on duty, it must have looked as if the whole Pentagon was descending on him. All the soldiers were in battle dress, BDUs, and most were wearing helmets, a sensible precaution in an environment where things might fall on their heads at any second.

The lieutenant had no good news. "We evacuated the building, General, because it's damaged and we figured it was dangerous to stay inside," he said. "Ground lines are down. Power's out. Most of our communications gear is wrecked, inaccessible, or without power. We got a Hammer Ace radio out of stores, but the batteries were dead, so we're recharging with the solar recharger . . ."

Jessica looked at the radio. It had a segmented antenna with a metal flower at the end, meant to communicate via satellite. Now useless, until they could recharge the batteries that were sitting in the solar array next to the radio on the lawn.

"How long is that going to take?"

"Quite a while, General."

Jessica looked at the red Cherokee. "Recharge it with the vehicle engine."

"Ma'am!" The lieutenant looked happy for an excuse to leave the cluster of senior officers.

"Just a minute, soldier," Jessica said. "How many personnel do we have on station?"

"You're looking at most of us, General. Most of our people went home at five o'clock, just before the quake."

They should know to report back, Jessica hoped.

No communication, no information. No information, no decisions. No decisions, no orders.

No orders meant waiting. Jessica was not very good at waiting.

"Have you tried cellphones?" she asked.

The lieutenant looked embarrassed. "Didn't think to," he said. "I don't happen to have one, and I guess nobody else here does, either."

"Right. Get that battery recharged." Jessica's cellphone was clipped to her belt. It was connected to the Iridium network: 66 satellites sent into canted polar orbits in the late nineties by a consortium headed by Motorola. The satellites were supposed to cover every inch of the globe, capable of patching into every active phone network in existence.

The disadvantage was that, if the local cells were down, the phones had to be used out of doors, because buildings would impede the signal to and from the satellite. Jessica considered that the advantage of instant communication with Moscow, say, or Antarctica, outweighed the disadvantage of having a conversation during the occasional rain-storm.

She unclipped the phone and turned to Sergeant Zook.

"Report to the motor pool," she said, "and sign me out a Humvee."

"Yes, ma'am."

"And I want a report on what you find there, particularly the earth-moving machines. I want to get the roads open around here so that our own personnel can report for duty."

She looked at the faces around her. "I hope some of you have experience in operating bulldozers and graders, gentlemen."

The colonels and majors looked at each other uneasily.

Zook trotted off, then stumbled as the sudden shearing force of an aftershock almost took him off his feet. As the earth began to growl, Jessica stood in place, feet braced apart, knees bent slightly. The ground felt liquid below her feet, like Jell-O. Vertigo shimmered in her inner ear.

There was a crash in the headquarters building as something very large fell. The aftershock faded, though the uneasy sensation in Jessica's inner ear continued.

"Come with me, gentlemen," Jessica said, and began walking for the headquarters building.

Jessica opened her cellphone, punched in her father's number in New York, and was delighted to hear a ringing signal. Her mother answered: Jessica told her that there had been a severe earthquake, that she and Pat were fine, but that she was very busy and couldn't talk.

"I know," her mother said. "It's been on TV."

"What do they say, Ma?"

"They don't seem to know much of anything."

"Do they know what cities have been hit?"

"We felt it here."

Jessica was horrified. "You felt it in *Queens*?"

"Your grandfather's Toby jug—the one he got in England during the war—it fell off the shelf and broke."

"In *Queens* ..." Jessica's mind whirled as she tried to understand the scope of it all.

"The TV says they can't raise anyone in St. Louis or Memphis. None of their, what d'you call 'em, affiliates. Chicago got shook up, and Kansas City. And this place that's named after the syrup, you know . . . "

Jessica looked at the phone in disbelief. "*Syrup*, Ma?"

"Kayro! That's it."

"Cairo."

"They said they got a radio message from someone in Kayro, wherever that is, and the town got knocked down and flooded."

Well, it would be. Cairo was at the junction of the Mississippi and Ohio and practically surrounded by water. Protected by flood walls, but an earthquake would breach those easily enough.

Jessica paused in front of the headquarters' glassed-in front. Most of the glass was broken or shattered. Jessica's mother began complaining about the incompetence of the Korean family that had just bought the grocery on the corner.

"I gotta go, Ma," she said. "I got work to do."

"Call when you can." Jessica's mother sounded resigned. "You know how we worry."

"Love you. Bye."

She closed the cellphone, clipped it again to her belt. Her staff were looking at her.

"The earthquake was big enough to break crockery in New York City," she said. "St. Louis and Memphis are out of communication, and that leads me to suspect that it was the New Madrid fault that slipped." Jessica looked up into their eyes, and wondered why every person she'd ever served with was so much taller than she. "This means, gentlemen," she said, "we're going to be coping with a three-hundred-year event. Maybe even a thousand-year event. Which means that we are involved in a calamity akin to that of a major war, with bloodshed, property destruction, and damage to communications all on a similar scale."

Colonel Davidovich, her second-in-command, blew out his cheeks in surprise at this notion. Jessica spoke on.

"We're going to have to assume significant damage to Corps installations throughout the MVD. As soon as we get into communication with the outside, I want to check the dams first—I want a complete list, however many hundred there are." Walls of water pouring down river valleys from broken dams was the vision that frightened Jessica most.

"We're in Vicksburg," she went on, "which is built on a bluff—reasonably solid ground, even if there's no bedrock. But most of the Mississippi Valley is built on goo. We're going to have to assume that the damage we've seen here is probably on a lesser scale than has been inflicted elsewhere."

Her staff looked at the building behind them, with its shattered windows and ominous-looking cracks, and for the first time looked intimidated.

"What I need now is an evaluation of the buildings here—HQ in particular. I want to know if it's safe to reoccupy the building. And even if the building is safe, we're still going to have to break some tents out of stores. So who's qualified to do an assessment?"

Davidovich and a couple others raised hands. She looked at Davidovich, said, "Right, you take charge of the survey party. Report to me when you've reached a conclusion about HQ."

Davidovich drew the others off for a quick briefing. Jessica looked at the wreckage of the porch.

"I'm going to go to my office," she said, "and get some maps and phone numbers."

She felt a presence hovering behind her and turned to see her husband. Pat wore an expectant look.

"Once the battery's charged," she said, "I guess you can head on home."

He looked dubious. "Not much for me there," he said. "And I'd as soon not have to make that drive alone." He rubbed his face. "Maybe I can make myself useful."

Jessica thought about it. "Right," she said. "In the absence of proper communications protocols, I hereby appoint you my message-runner."

"Jeb Stuart," Pat reminded, "had a banjo player on staff."

"He was in another army," Jessica said, "but I'll take that suggestion under advisement."

The Situation Room was still filling up. The Vice President's helicopter would be landing at any time. The National Security Advisor was in the building but had not yet arrived. The Secretary of the Interior was in Alaska, and the Secretary of Defense was on a tour of the Balkans. The Secretary of Labor was on his way from West Virginia. The head of the Forest Service and the chairman of the Joint Chiefs of Staff were stuck in traffic on the Alexandria Bridge, but hoped to be present within the hour.

But Boris Lipinsky, the Ukrainian-born head of the Federal Emergency Management Agency, had arrived at the same time as the President, and he and the President had a lot to talk about even without the others.

"We have less than three thousand employees in FEMA, sir," Lipinsky said. "We depend for the most part on volunteers, and on personnel supplied by other agencies."

"What can you do *now*?" the President said.

Lipinsky spoke slowly, with a pronounced Ukrainian accent. His blue eyes were vaguely focused on empty space, as if he were reading his words from an invisible Tele-PrompTer.

"Normally we act only in response to requests from the governors of individual states," he said. "But when I felt the shock earlier this evening, and received confirmation from the National Earthquake Information Center that a major quake had occurred, I alerted the staffs of the Catastrophic Disaster Response Group and the Emergency Information and Coordination Center.

"We have to assume," he continued, "that any emergency services in the affected areas will have been swallowed up by the catastrophe and be able to achieve very little of substance. The citizens can count on no help from the police, from National Guard, from hospital and ambulance services, or from electrical, transportation, or sewer workers unless they are sent in from outside the area."

Any emergency services swallowed up by the catastrophe . . . The President found the thought stupefying. He was a modern man, and the thought of existence without any of the most basic modern comforts—shelter, police and fire protection, electricity, running water, the telephone, *television*—it was almost beyond his conception.

Surely, he thought, it couldn't be that bad.

"Therefore, Mr. President," Lipinsky went on, "on my own authority, I began the process of alerting all response teams concerned with Urban Search and Rescue, Firefighting, Transportation, Health and Medical, Public Works, Hazardous Materials, and Mass Care. Such elements as Energy, Food, and Public Resource Support can wait until the full scope of the emergency is better determined. I also took it upon myself to alert the Public Health Service." Lipinsky raised his bushy eyebrows. "I hope this display of initiative meets with your approval, sir?"

"Yes," said the President, happy to finally have a chance to speak.

Lipinsky plodded on. "Most of our response teams will be ready to deploy into the affected areas within six hours. The deployment will be through MARS, so we will need to coordinate with DOD, U.S. Transportation Command as soon as possible. I hope that my staff will have recommendations for deployment within a few hours."

MARS was shorthand for military units under the authority of the Department of Defense. The President nodded and said, "Very good."

"We are contacting the regional phone companies. During a disaster of this scope, the phone lines are often jammed with calls from outside the area trying to discover if their friends and relatives are all right. This can prevent genuine emergency calls from going through. So we are asking the phone companies to close down long-distance service from outside the area. People in the disaster area will be able to call *out*, and they will be able to call each other and emergency services, but those from outside will not be able to call into the area unless they are calling on official business."

The President nodded again.

"My office has been trying to contact General Breedlove, our Defense Coordinating Officer, who is the military gentleman responsible for coordinating FEMA's teams with those of MARS. But he is on a fishing vacation in Arkansas, which is one of the affected areas, and may be out of communication for some time. Perhaps you, Mr. President, or some other person in a position of authority, will take it upon yourself to appoint a Supported Commander-in-Chief to manage the deployment of our civilian/military Joint Task Forces?"

There was a moment before the President realized that this was his cue to speak. Lipinsky's labored rhythms had a certain hypnotic effect, and the President had been lulled into a near-trance.

"I'll consider that when General Shortland arrives," the President said. "I want his advice on any military matters."

Lipinsky nodded. "Very good, sir. I must also ask you to appoint a Federal Coordinating Officer for each affected state. The FCOs will travel to each state and coordinate state, local, and federal disaster response."

"I presume you have recommendations?"

Lipinsky signaled to one of his aides, who came forward and opened a briefcase. "I have taken the liberty of making up a list of candidates that I consider suitable."

The President ground his teeth as he took a copy of the list and reached for his reading glasses.

Bureaucracy, he thought. You couldn't do anything without the bureaucracy. Everything had to be crammed into organization charts, boxes, lists, accounts, departments, labeled with acronyms, staffed by bureaucrats who used other acronyms as their titles.

A major disaster would take all those neat organizational charts and tear them into shreds. But he had to deal with them anyway.

What was the choice? Particularly now? The President could stand on his desk and scream, "Everyone help those people!", and people would probably try to do their best, but unless the efforts were organized and directed by all those people with the acronyms, little good would result.

And so the President resigned himself to his duty. He consulted with Lipinsky, appointed his FCOs, and once General Shortland appeared, the President appointed a Supported CINC to handle MARS deployments via the AMC and USTRANSCOM. Then SAAMs could be tasked to deliver US&R teams and other JTOs to affected areas. USACE personnel trained in Basic and Light US&R were placed on alert. Attempts were made to contact SCOs in their individual states. DOMS established a CAT in the Army Operations Center. USTRANSCOM SAAMs were tasked to deliver FCOs into the field.

And all along, information kept arriving as to the scope of the crisis. Memphis and St. Louis had been, apparently, flattened. Parts of Chicago were on fire. Little Rock was hard hit. Bridges, roadways, airports, and railroads were out. Even large military units seemed to have dropped off the map. *Millions* might well be homeless.

And almost all the military air missions had to be rescheduled. All airfields in the quake areas had been destroyed, and fixed-wing aircraft couldn't land. SAAMs—Special Airlift Assignment Missions, for those who lived outside the world of acronyms—had to be landed at the nearest intact airports, and the rescue teams, and their equipment, reassigned to helicopters.

Selected Reserve units were mobilized—engineers to rebuild runways and other vital transport, signal units, logistics commands, supply, transport, plus ground units to provide them with security. National Guard had already been called up by the governors of the quake-ravaged states.

At the insistence of the National Security Advisor, the entire U.S. military was put on alert. Terrorists or other enemies, he warned, might try to take advantage of the situation.

In the end, the President was thankful for the acronyms. They kept him from thinking about the *people*, the people trapped in rubble or cringing from the flames or watching the flood waters rise slowly above their children's knees . . .

"We have the word from the Earthquake Information Center, sir," Lipinsky said around midnight. "The quake tops out at eight point nine on the Richter scale."

The President blinked. "That's not so bad, is it?" he said. "I gave a speech in Monterey in '98, I think it was, and there was a five point five. Just a big bang and it was over. And eight point nine, that's, what, not even twice as large."

Lipinsky's bland blue eyes didn't so much as twitch. "The Richter Scale isn't numerical, sir," he said. "It's logarithmic. A three on the Richter scale isn't half again powerful as two, it's *ten times* as powerful. And a four isn't twice as powerful as two, it's a *hundred times* the size of a two. So the 8.9 in Missouri is therefore—" the blue eyes turned inward for just a half-second "—one thousand four hundred times the strength of the quake you experienced in Monterey."

Numerals swarmed through the President's mind. *One thousand four hundred times . . .*

Lipinsky went on. "In fact, Mr. President, the Information Center told me that the earth probably can't hold enough energy to deliver a quake larger than eight point nine." He looked solemn. "This is the worst the geosphere can do to us, Mr. President. There's only one earthquake in human history that compares with it, and that was in China four thousand years ago."

The worst natural disaster since the Bronze Age, the President thought. *And on my watch.*

"I need to get out there," he said. "I need to get into the field myself."

And, as his press secretary would no doubt remind him, he would need to be *seen* in the field.

The Secret Service would go nuts. The presidential bodyguard wouldn't want the President anywhere near a catastrophe on this scale. Assassins were the least of their worries, not when an aftershock could drop the Gateway Arch on him.

"Sir." One of his aides, holding a phone. "The chairman of the Federal Reserve would like a meeting with you tomorrow, as early as possible."

The President stared, a new realization rolling through his mind.

He had completely forgot that all this was going to have to be *paid for*.

Jason could feel the speed of the boat increase, hear the roaring ahead. He had been drowsing in the front seat, leaning forward on the boat's useless wheel, but the grinding of the boat over some debris had woken him, and once awake he sensed a change. The wind was blowing much more steadily, a cool fresh breeze with the scent of spray in it. The black river was moving fast, raising a chop that slapped water against the sides of the boat. In the fitful starlight Jason could see debris crowding the water, boxes and bottles and lumber, limbs and whole trees. In the dark Jason couldn't tell where the bank was, but he sensed it was close.

It was as if the river had spread itself out into a lake. And now someone had pulled a cork on the bottom of the lake, and it was all draining out at once.

The roaring sound increased. Water sloshed around his ankles as Jason stood on the pitching boat, holding on the wheel for support as he peered downriver.

A cold fist clamped on Jason's throat.

Ahead, even through the darkness, he could see the white water, the white-crested chop leaping higher than his head.

A gentleman who was near the Arkansas river, at the time of the first shock in Dec. last, states, that certain Indians had arrived near the mouth of the river, who had seen a large lake or sea, where many of their brothers had resided, and had perished in the general wreck; that to escape a similar fate, they had travelled three days up the river, but finding the dangers increase, as they progressed, frequently having to cut down large trees, to cross the chasms in the earth, they returned to the mouth of the river, and from them this information is derived.

*Extract from a letter to a gentleman in Lexington, from
his friend at New Madrid, dated 16th December, 1811*

In the hot Tennessee night, Nick could see the lights of
Memphis glowing on low cloud ahead, an angry red. At least
Nick *hoped* they were lights and not fire.

He hoped, but hope was fading. He'd already seen too
much.

As he and Viondi trudged toward Memphis, they began to
pass into areas with a larger population, but they passed
nothing but ruin. Every house was flattened. Sometimes the
homeowners stood numbly in front of their shattered
dwellings, or made vague attempts to fetch belongings from
the fallen structures. Some of them waved as Nick and
Viondi passed. Some were injured, but most of the injuries
seemed light.

The badly injured ones, Nick figured, never made it out of
their houses. Once Nick and Viondi heard someone calling
from a shattered storefront, some kind of clothing store. They
dug into the ruin, throwing bricks and ruined clothes behind
them into the street, and found an elderly Asian man with a
beam fallen across his legs.

There was no way to move that beam. All they could do
was promise that they'd contact the police or somebody to
help him.

At least the storefront wasn't on fire, Nick thought. Many
of the buildings were in flames.

Nick didn't want to think about people who might have
lain in those ruins waiting for the fire to reach them, calling
for help that never came. By the time Nick and Viondi passed
by, the buildings were already blazing. Anyone inside was
already long dead.

The road was often blocked by fallen trees or by crevasses,
and every vehicle on it had been abandoned. Furious rain-
storms pelted down on them, and they plodded on wearing
windbreakers dug out of their luggage. Lightning boomed
overhead even when it wasn't raining. When night came on,
there were no traffic lights, no street lights, no lights at all but

the stars and the flare of burning structures. Nick saw no police, no fire engines, no ambulances. Everyone out here was on his own.

And then, just ahead, Nick saw the lights of a police cruiser, its flashers illuminating the rubble that was once a brick Mobil station. The Mobil sign, dark, was still intact on its metal pole, and pulsed faintly, blue and red, in the flashing police lights. The Mobil station was a pile of rubble. Standing by the open door of the car was a state trooper talking into a microphone.

"Hey," Viondi said, and took a closer grip on his soggy cardboard box. He squinted ahead at the state trooper. "And the man's a brother, too. Looks like we finally got lucky. I'd sure as hell hate to walk up to a cracker cop on a night like this."

The dead boy kept staring at him with a face that looked like Victor's. And the old man—he didn't want to think about the old man.

Eukie James was trapped. He'd figured that out. He was trapped and he couldn't help Victor or Emily or Showanda or anybody.

"Damn it?" he said into the mike. "What was that about Latimer Street?"

The whole damn city was on fire. That was clear enough. All a man had to do was look at that glow on the clouds.

He thought about Victor and tears came burning to his eyes.

"Where was that?" Eukie demanded of the mike. "Where was that damn looting?"

And the dead boy kept staring at him with his son's eyes. Reminding him that there wasn't anything he could do.

It was usually quiet on these back roads. The worst thing he'd ever seen since he'd been patrolling here were some car accidents where nobody was badly hurt, even if a lot of metal got bent. His presence helped to keep the speed down, and people waved at him in a friendly way when he drove past.

And now this. Nuclear war or something, Eukie figured,

somebody finally pushed the button. Some asshole shot a rocket at Memphis, and the whole place had gone up in fire.

And there was nothing Eukie could do to help his family, who were probably right smack in the middle of that—what was it called?—*firestorm*.

He couldn't get to them. A whole forest of trees had fallen across the road both in front of him and behind, and he couldn't move the patrol car off this little piece of ground. He'd barely avoided a power pole that tried to fall right on the car—there was a big scar on the trunk where it had bounded off. He'd never before thought a public utility would try to kill him.

All that seemed to exist on his little strip of state road was the collapsed Mobil station with its little population of dead people. Eukie had heard the screams from the wreckage as soon as he pulled over to the side of the road after the nuclear strike, or whatever it was. He'd dug through the fallen brick Mobil station, gashing his hands on broken glass, till he'd found the kid, the little black boy with the staring eyes, no more than six years old. But even after he'd dragged the boy out of the rubble and wiped the brick dust from his face and tried to revive him with mouth-to-mouth—even after he'd pounded on the kid's chest and breathed for him and shouted at the kid to wake up—even after all that, the screams went on, and so Eukie finally worked out that there was someone else trapped in the building.

And then, digging farther into the wreckage, he found the old man, an old white-haired black man in overalls. Maybe he was the kid's grandpa. All the man could do was stare up with his yellow eyes and scream. He wouldn't talk, he wouldn't answer Eukie's questions, all he could do was take another breath and yell. So Eukie grabbed him under the arms and put his back into hauling him out of the wreckage. The old man gave one last full-blooded shriek and then fell limp.

And as soon as Eukie got him clear, he knew why.

The old man had left his legs in the wrecked station. Sliced off by falling glass or something. Eukie fell to the ground in shock when he saw the stumps spurting blood.

The man just rolled his head to the left and died. Eukie's hauling him out had completed the partial severing of his legs. Had sliced the arteries and killed him.

Eukie jumped up and felt himself all over to make sure he didn't have blood on him. If he found a wet spot, he tried to brush it off.

It was then that he noticed how much the dead boy looked like his own son Victor.

Fear tingled cold along his nerves. He ran back to the car, got on the radio. But nobody would listen to his ten-fifty-five, his call for an ambulance. All the other officers seemed to have plenty of ten-fifty-fives of their own. The air rang with ten-threes, commands to clear the air and let someone talk. But people kept jabbering away anyhow.

Maybe they weren't hearing each other properly, because Eukie's reception was very spotty. Sometimes that happened, the flat wet ground tended to soak up radio signals, but now there was a lot of static, too, as if there was some kind of serious electrical disturbance. There were a lot of ten-ones, people signaling they were having trouble receiving the radio calls.

Eukie sagged into the car and listened to all the calls. Darkness gathered around him. Every so often the ground would shake, as if another bomb was going off somewhere.

Ten-forty-three, *rescue call*. Ten-thirty-three, *fire*. Ten-eighty-three, *officer in trouble*. Ten-fifty-eight, *dead on arrival*. Ten-seventy, *chemical spill*. Ten-nine, *repeat*. Ten-three, *clear this channel*. Ten-seventy-two, *street blocked*. Ten-thirty-three-four, *hospital on fire*. Ten-fifty-three-one, *fire alarm*. Ten-nine, *repeat*. Ten-forty-six, *send a wrecker*. Ten-nine, *repeat transmission*. Ten-three, *clear this channel*. Ten-nine, *repeat*. And calls for which there were no ten-codes: *Power lines down. People trapped in building. Flooding on the riverfront.*

He looked at the dead boy, and he saw Victor's eyes.

Ten-eighty-one, *civil disturbance*.

Ten-sixty-nine, *sniper*.

Ten-eighty-three, *officer in trouble*.

Eukie grabbed the mike, thumbed the button. "Where?" he said.

"Looters." A breathless voice. "Latimer Street."

Damn. Eukie *lived* on Latimer street.

"You are authorized—"

"Ten-three! Stop transmitting, for Christ's sake!"

"—to shoot looters on sight. Repeat."

"Ten-one, dispatch. I am not receiving—"

"What?" Eukie demanded. "Where on Latimer Street?"

"Will you ten-three, damn it!"

"Shoot on sight. Repeat."

"Ten-one, dispatch. I am not—"

"God damn it!" Eukie took off his hat and threw it down the road. People were shooting on his *own damn street* and there was nothing he could do about it. He wanted to grab the shotgun out of the car and run south to Latimer Street to defend his family, but it was twenty miles away, and he knew he'd never make it through the kind of chaos he could hear on the radio. He stamped back and forth past the door of his car, tethered at the limit of the mike cord. He tried not to look at the dead boy with his son's face.

In disgust he threw down the mike and stalked down the broken road to find his hat.

"Where the hell—?" he asked the world. "What the hell am I supposed to do?"

He jammed his hat back on his head and gazed defiantly into the darkness. And then twigs and brush crackled as something moved ahead on the road. Adrenaline sang in Eukie's veins. "Who's that?" he demanded.

There was no answer, but the sounds got closer.

Eukie backed for a few steps, then turned and sprinted for his car. He was breathing hard by the time he dived head-first into the passenger compartment, grabbed the Remington shotgun, and racked in a round.

The ten-codes spat out of the radio. *Officer in trouble. Fire. Looters.*

Eukie turned on the driver's door spotlight and panned it across the darkness.

A white-faced cow gazed back at him.

A cow.

Eukie didn't know whether to laugh or cry. "Jesus," he said. "Jesus God Almighty."

The cow ambled past, oblivious to whatever had destroyed the city to the south. That cow, Eukie thought, was having herself an *adventure*. She had probably never been out of her pasture before.

"Jesus," he said again. He leaned the shotgun against the side of the vehicle. The radio continued to rattle out its ten-codes.

Ten-thirty-three-four, *hospital on fire*.

Ten-fifty-three-one, *fire alarm*.

Ten-nine, *repeat*.

Ten-forty-six, *send a wrecker*.

Looters.

You are authorized to shoot . . .

Victor's dead eyes gazed up at him from the broken pavement.

"What about Latimer Street?" he said into the mike. "What about that ten-eighty-three?"

"Ten-three! Ten-three!"

"Damn it," Eukie said, "what about Latimer Street?"

"Officer needs assistance . . ."

"Ten-three! Clear the air, whoever you are!"

"Listen, motherfucker," Eukie said. He could feel tears springing to his eyes. "What about *Latimer Street*? What's going down out there?" All he could see was Victor's dead face.

"Asshole!" the dispatcher yelled. "Ten-three when I tell you to ten-three!"

"What about my son?" Eukie demanded.

It was then that the looters came out of the darkness. "Say, brother," one of them said.

Fear and anger blazed through Eukie's veins. He spun and through his mask of tears saw the looter *looming right out of the darkness*, a *huge* man, big hands clasped around a cardboard box full of stuff he'd stolen, complete with a huge silver pot he'd probably killed somebody for. There was blood all on his face and clothes, probably from beating someone to death over that silver pot, and the looter had some kind of weird stripes on his forehead that strobed in the emergency lights of the car. The looter looked like the Frankenstein Monster.

And there was *another* looter right behind him, a tall man whose features were obscured by the darkness. And probably there were more looters behind, circling the car, trying to sneak up on Eukie while the first two distracted him.

All Eukie could think of was that Victor and Showanda and Emily were depending on him.

"Don't you move, nigger!" Eukie yelled, and reached for the shotgun.

The looter's eyes widened in surprise. And when Eukie fired, it was those eyes he used for an aiming point.

Nick's heart dropped into his shoes at the sound of the shotgun, and he stared at the scene in shock. The first round was birdshot, lightweight pellets, but it hit Viondi in the face. Viondi staggered back, dropping the cardboard box. The silver samovar clanged on the pavement. Viondi raised his hands to his eyes.

"Hey," Nick said, too surprised even to move, but the cop was shouting, *"God damn it, God damn it!"* and he jacked another round in the shotgun.

The second round was double-ought buckshot, twelve steel pellets each the size of a 9mm pistol round, and it struck Viondi full in the chest. He threw his arms wide and fell back into Nick. Nick dropped his suitcase and tried to catch Viondi, but Viondi's big body was all great ungainly weight, and Nick found himself falling with Viondi on top of him. He landed hard, feeling the impact slam up his spine, and while he was falling he heard the awful *click-clack* of another round being fed into the chamber.

"Hey," he said again, but the cop kept shouting.

"Stay away from my family, motherfucker!" And then another round went off, and Nick felt a breath of air on his face as the pellets whirred past his face.

Click-clack. Nick felt concrete bite his hands as he scrambled out from beneath Viondi's heavy body. The cop was standing right over him, and the barrel looked the size of a cannon. Nick stared for a long, cold eternity at his own death, an invisible fist closing off the air in his throat, and he saw the cop's brown finger twitch on the trigger.

Snap. That was all. No explosion. The shotgun had jammed.

"*Shit!*" the cop screamed, and he banged the butt of the shotgun on the ground.

Nick took off. He didn't know how he got to his feet, how he managed to start running, suddenly he just *was*, and he was running fast. And when the gun went off again, he just ran faster.

He could hear the cop's screams behind him as he fled into the night.

After a while, he realized he'd run off the road into a field, and that in the dark he couldn't find his way back.

And then, when he ran into the water, he couldn't find his way out of it.

Before nightfall Dr. Calhoun drove up to the Church of the End Times in his bus. "Heard your message on the radio," he told Frankland. "The Rails River bridge is out, and I can't get all my kids home. And they won't have homes anyway, because every home out here is wrecked, and so is my church, and so is my trailer."

"Your people are welcome," Frankland said.

The bus was full, adults as well as children. Calhoun had been trying to drop off the kids, but instead he'd ended up rescuing their families from wrecked homes.

"I've put Sheryl in charge down at the church," Frankland said. "She'll find room for your kids to sleep."

"Thank you, Brother Frankland."

Calhoun gave the news to his people on the bus. People began pouring out. Frankland recognized some of his own parishioners, adults and children both, and some of Reverend Garb's black kids, still in their white shirts and slacks. Frankland turned to Calhoun.

"Can you ask some of the men if they're willing to join some teams I want to send out to find the injured and bring them in? And also to scavenge for food and such? We should get back to the Piggly Wiggly just to get the food before it spoils."

Calhoun nodded his bald head. "That's good thinking, Reverend."

"I knew this would happen. I've been thinking about it for a long time." Frankland smiled. "In just seven years, Christ's kingdom will be established here on earth. And *we* can help, if we can get things organized fast enough."

"Well," Dr. Calhoun said, "as someone who just gave up being a pre-Tribulationist Rapture wimp, let me just say that I'm pleased to offer any assistance that you or the Lord may require."

Frankland smiled down at the shorter man. His heart glowed at the sound of this endorsement.

"Well," he said, "I'm sure I will be thankful for your assistance."

Larry Hallock gazed out at the flooded remains of the Poinsett Landing Nuclear Station, the broken double hyperboloids of the cooling tower that glowed softly in the night. The soft darkness and bright starlight gave the power station a majestic, almost ancient air, like the ruins of the Coliseum crouching beneath the Roman moon.

Water lapped at Larry's feet, and Larry wondered if it was still rising. It had kept rising after the earthquake, and finally Larry and everyone else realized that the levees had gone—some distance away, apparently, because the flood, however inexorable, came slowly. It was clear that the plant personnel would have to evacuate.

There was but one place to go. The buildings were unsafe, the roads blocked by fallen timber.

The only high ground was the old Indian mound that the archaeologists had insisted remain on the plant site.

It was there that the plant survivors fled. Those who could brought their vehicles, and the old mound now resembled more of a gypsy encampment than a gathering of highly trained engineers and technicians.

None of the paramedics in the infirmary had survived the destruction of the administration building. The senior administrators had either been absent during the catastrophe, or died in it.

Larry, if anyone, was in charge. He had done his best for the injured, sheltered them from the elements by putting them in a few pickup trucks that had camper shells. He had found some people with Red Cross or Boy Scout training to put in charge of his pathetic infirmary. He had counted heads, and had made a survey of the survivors' food (none) and water (ditto). He had seen to the digging of a pair of slit trenches to use as latrines.

And he had tried to make contact with the outside world. But nothing worked. Even cellphones were dead. He would have sworn that *somebody* among all these people would have had a citizens' band radio, but no one did.

There were a few radio stations that car and truck radios could pick up. Aside from one crazy preacher in Arkansas ranting—barely audible at this distance—about the end of the world, everyone on radio was discussing the earthquake, retelling over and over the few bits of news they seemed to think were certain. Memphis and St. Louis were hard hit, apparently—in flames, the radios said. Roads were out. Electricity was out. Communications were out. Floods, broken levees, fire. Even the Mexican station they picked up was discussing the quake in Spanish.

Larry and his cohorts were stuck on the mound till somebody came to get them. And surely, no matter how comprehensive the disaster seemed, it would be *somebody's* job— either at the power company or at the NRC or at one of the contractors—to remember that there was a nuclear power station at Poinsett Landing.

He had done all that he could do. He had ridden that mare in as many circles as she was going to go. There was nothing to do now but worry.

He was capable of worrying on the same level of thoroughness with which he did everything else. He had no reason to think that his wife Helen was anything other than alive and well. The quake had been bad, but their frame house in Vicksburg was sturdy, and Vicksburg was safe from flood on its bluff. There was no reason to think that Helen would not have escaped the quake: she would have known to stand in a doorway, or roll under a table.

The problem was that his imagination was too strong to find this logic in any way reassuring. Extrapolating from the way things had flown around the control room, he was fairly certain that his house would have been full of deadly missiles. He pictured Helen on the phone in the dining room, the sideboard flying at her, all deadly broken glass, crystal, and china. Or the heavy bookshelf in the living room toppling on her as she ran for the front door.

Or the water heater or the furnace—which so far as he knew were not secured to the floor, but just rested there— leaping into the hallway from their closet, spilling hot water and fire . . .

The worry gnawed at him. He needed something to do, so he made the rounds again, making sure his people were as comfortable as the night, the flood, and the insects would permit. The burned man that Larry had met was there, and in agonizing pain. Two worried coworkers were sitting on his arms to keep him from tearing the flesh from his scalp. All they had to give him was Tylenol. Larry couldn't think of any way to help the man.

Larry hadn't mentioned his own shoulder injury to anyone—it hadn't seemed important enough—but he found that his injured shoulder hurt less if he cradled the right arm in his left, so that's what he did. It didn't occur to him to ask someone to make him a sling.

He went to the edge of the mound and gazed out at the plant, giant concrete and steel islands in the flood. It was the darkest night he could remember. There were no lights anywhere, *none*. Normally the station was ablaze at night, floodlights illuminating the parking lots, air warning flashers on the cooling tower, the other buildings outlined by spotlights and illuminated offices. There were no lights on the river, no lights from nearby towns. The whole country had gone dark, and that meant the whole power grid was down. Not just Poinsett Landing, but *everywhere* for hundreds of miles around.

As a consolation, perhaps, there were the stars. Larry had never seen so many—just looking up took his breath away. He could see the broad swath of the Milky Way, the red glow of Arcturus, the bright yellow gleam of some planet or other, probably Jupiter. The stars of the Corona blazed with an intensity he had never seen, and Cygnus and Aquila wheeled about the pole.

It was to a sky such as this, he thought, which ancient Britons had in homage raised the monument of Stonehenge.

His shoulder ached. The thought of Helen kept rising to his mind.

He needed something more to do.

THIRTEEN

> *. . . the river was now doing what it liked to do, had waited patiently the ten years in order to do, as a mule will work for you ten years for the privilege of kicking you once.*
>
> *William Faulkner*, The Old Man

The Mississippi is lazy between Cairo and Memphis, and in no hurry to reach its destination. It moves in long, swooping, snakelike curves, heading generally south, but also turning east, west, and sometimes north. At the New Madrid bend it manages to move in all four directions, one after the other.

On occasion the river shortens its path. Sometimes the Mississippi, instead of taking a gentle curve around a bend or point, will decide to cut right through the point at its base, shortening its length and leaving, in its old course, one of the many picturesque oxbow lakes that ornament the Mississippi valley. On occasion the river has left a piece of Tennessee attached to Arkansas, or annexed a piece of Arkansas to the state of Mississippi.

Mark Twain, who noted that in his time the Mississippi shortened itself on average by a mile and a third per year, remarked that at this rate, in seven hundred years the Lower Mississippi would be only a mile and three-quarters long, and Cairo and New Orleans would share their streets.

Sometimes these shortcuts do not occur naturally, but are imposed on the river. Before the Civil War, some planters, resentful that their inland plantations were less valuable than those blessed with access to the river, brought their field hands out to the nearest point in the dead of night, armed with pick and shovel, to cut the river a new channel, giving themselves river access and stranding their neighbors on a newly formed oxbow lake. Sometimes these attempts succeeded. Sometimes they failed. Sometimes, whatever the outcome, the ambitious planter was shot dead by a neighbor firing in defense of his property values.

During the Civil War, General U.S. Grant tried to cut the river a new path across DeSoto Point in hopes that this would strand the rebel fortress of Vicksburg inland, making it useless to the Confederacy. He failed, but a few years later a flood rushed across his old works on DeSoto Point and carved the river a new path through Centennial Cutoff, ending Vicksburg's access to the river until the Corps of Engineers restored it a quarter-century later.

Later, in the twentieth century, the Corps eliminated the four Greenville Bends—Rowdy, Miller, Spanish Moss, and Bachelor—shortening the Mississippi's length by thirty miles and creating Lake Ferguson, named after the Army general who masterminded the project.

But these cutoffs were created artificially, attended by all the massive Corps engineering necessary to achieve a safe result and a deep, navigable channel.

When the river carves its own path, the result is less gentle. The path is cut across country, sometimes over a farmer's fields, sometimes through stands of heavy timber. The channel is narrow at first, full of shoal water, and the Mississippi rages through it, the weight of the entire river turning it to foam. There are rapids and falls, and the channel is littered with trees, rocks, snags, and stumps. The bank on either side is continually eroded and falls in half-acre chunks into the water. Large steamboats were sometimes sucked out of control into these new channels, flung through the new-made chutes, and either dashed to pieces on obstacles or spat out spinning into the old river.

South of Cabells Mound, the flooding Mississippi had cut through the bend called Uncle Chowder's, and the flood waters were about to drain through it as if someone had pulled a cork at the bottom of the river.

*   *   *

The boat dropped down a precipice and hit a mass of glistening black water stern-first. A fan of spray rose high and fell into the boat. The impact knocked the breath out of Jason as he clung to the wheel. He never realized that water could be so *hard*.

The sound of the rapid was overwhelming, loud as the earthquake. Spray filled the air. Jason could feel the boat's vibration up his spine, through his bones. A piece of wreckage—a whole *tree*, Jason realized—ground against the side of the boat, knocking it into a sideways lurch that brought another gush of spray into the boat. As the big tree surged past, tree limbs caught the bow and spun the boat around. Branches clawed at Jason's face.

Jason hung onto the wheel and wished that the boat had seat belts.

The torrent whirled around him as the boat spun helplessly in the channel. Something slammed into the boat, sent it airborne for a few seconds, then dropped it into a hole. Jason gave a yell as the steering wheel punched his sternum. He had barely caught his breath before the boat took another bounce—this time off the bole of a cottonwood that was somehow still standing upright in the middle of the white water.

He wondered how long the boat could take this kind of pounding before it was beaten into a shapeless hunk of metal.

Retired and Gone Fishin' careened down a chute of white water. The spray was so dense that Jason couldn't tell if he was underwater or not—the boat might have capsized for all he could tell. At the bottom of the chute the boat hit something hard, and the impact threw Jason back away from the wheel, against the seat behind. The boat was spinning like a yo-yo at the end of its string. Jason clawed blindly for the metal wheel as the world rumbled and shuddered around him. He pulled himself forward onto the wheel again, felt the boat lurch madly to port. His inner ear spun. He opened his eyes and saw that the boat was tipped on its right side, that the starboard gunwale was underwater, that another ounce of weight added to rightward side of the balance could capsize her . . . Terror clutched at Jason's heart. He flung himself to the left, threw his arms over the gunwale, tried to add as much weight as possible to the forces dropping the boat back onto an even keel.

The boat skated on its side for several long, terrifying seconds, then slowly began to tip to port. Jason gasped: he realized he'd been holding his breath. He slid back into the seat as the boat tipped, as its bottom slammed on water.

The terror ride continued: Jason clung on as the bass boat raced along between steep banks, smashed into rocks, trees, and less identifiable debris. Something huge and black loomed up—Jason realized it was a stranded river barge—and the boat slammed into it, grating along its rust-streaked side. Jason ducked as steel cable whipped over his head. And then there was one last, horrible grinding noise—the boat tipped on its port side, sending Jason clawing to starboard as a frantic counterweight—and then the boat was over the obstacle and was being pushed by the rushing river into wide, calm water.

Jason gasped for breath as the roaring faded behind him. His heart pounded in his chest.

He glanced around, saw nothing but starlight glinting off debris-filled water. There was six or eight inches of water in the boat, and no way to bail.

Though the rapids were falling behind, the boat was still moving fast. The river still had purpose, was still hurrying to get somewhere.

Jason was too tired to wonder what the river had on its mind. He nodded over the wheel and let exhaustion claim him.

Until a few hours later, when he woke to the sound of another rapid ahead.

The sound of the human voice, raised in praise of God, floated toward Frankland through the broken windows of the church. Sheryl had everyone there singing, children and adults both, to keep them occupied and out of trouble. What they lacked in harmony they made up in enthusiasm.

But Frankland had visitors. Sheriff Gorton was a lean, slit-eyed man of sixty who had been the town's mortician until his business had failed. There weren't enough people left in the county to keep the burying business profitable. He'd run for sheriff and got elected because his neighbors felt sorry for the way he'd lost his business after working hard all his life.

Gorton was also, Frankland knew, one of Dr. Calhoun's parishioners.

"I heard your message on the radio for people to come here if they was in trouble," Gorton said. "I wanted to see for myself what kind of facilities you had here."

Frankland explained that his church, house, and radio station had all been specially reinforced against earthquake, and that he had food supplies enough to last for weeks, maybe months. He had a big tent left over from his days as a traveling preacher, and a number of large surplus Army tents. All these would be set up if the church began to overflow. "This is the safest place you're going to find in Rails Bluff," he said.

Gorton nodded. "Can I send people here from town? We've got so many homeless . . ."

"I will provide for them," Frankland said. "Dr. Calhoun, Reverend Garb, and I have been conferring on how best to care for the people, and we are organizing everything now."

He hadn't actually talked to Garb yet, but he knew that Garb was perfectly reliable on the subject of the Tribulation and how to handle it.

Gorton looked anxious. "You don't have any doctors or nurses, do you? We don't have anyone who can take care of the injured except for old Maggie Swensen, who used to be a nurse before she retired. But she's in her seventies, and she's completely overwhelmed. We're putting the injured in the old Bijoux, but it's a real nightmare in there."

Frankland gave him a serious look. The county had lacked a doctor ever since old Sam Haraldsen had died—there wasn't enough money in Rails Bluff to attract a doctor. "No," Frankland said, "I regret to say that we have no one with any formal medical training. The boys and girls in the Christian

Gun Club learned first aid, though, and I will send some of them to you. Maggie can give them some work, and teach them how to do some things, and they can help take a load off her that way."

Gorton seemed relieved. "I thought I'd seen it all, you know," he said. "Korea, working around bodies. But this . . ." He leaned close to Frankland, lowered his voice. "Do you really think this is the end?"

Frankland nodded. "Earthquake, brimstone, fire from heaven," he said. "It's all in the Book."

Gorton was solemn. "That's what I thought, first thing. When the ground started to shake. Dr. Calhoun told us the signs."

"It's clear enough to those who can see," Frankland said. "And I'll tell you frankly—the odds of a person surviving the next seven years of Tribulation is not good. The Antichrist will rise, and the world will burn with fire. There is not any part of the planet that will not be consumed with war. The comet Wormwood alone will poison a third of the world's water. But what happens to their bodies doesn't matter, we need to prepare the souls of everyone here, so that they can survive the Judgment of God. That's the important thing now, whether they survive in the flesh or not."

Gorton tilted his hat back, wiped his forehead. "I've been worrying about that, pastor. You know, I think there are people down at the Bijoux who are dying. I would hate for them to die without the Word. And Pete Swenson's been killed, you know—buried in his church."

The Lutheran Church of the Good Shepherd, the graceful nineteenth-century brick building that had been greatly envied by those parsons in the vicinity who had not been blessed by such well-established congregations, had not been built with earthquake in mind. Frankland had taken one look at it, when he'd first moved to the district, and known it wouldn't survive the End Times.

He closed his eyes, said a little blessing for Pete Swenson. Frankland opened his eyes. "His entire flock will be needing consolation and guidance. I will go there directly. With you, if that's all right."

"That's good, Brother Frankland, that's good."

"I will round up some of the Gun Club members," Frankland said. "And they'll follow us down."

Hilkiah brought some of the Gun Club kids in his pickup truck to act as nurses, while Frankland rode with Gorton in his cruiser. On the way he told Gorton his plan to send out people to scavenge food and other supplies from fallen buildings, and bring injured people from outlying areas into the town. Gorton said that it all sounded fine to him.

"Only thing is, my people could be mistaken for looters," Frankland said. "We want you to be able to identify 'em, so that your deputies won't make any bad mistakes and people get hurt."

"I'll depitize 'em, if you like."

"That'll be good. That'll be good. But maybe I should just put white armbands on 'em, like I did with the Family Values Campaign."

"That'll work. I'll tell my deputies."

"We'll send them out tomorrow morning, then."

Frankland leaned back in the seat and smiled.

Things were going to work out.

The Old Man's voice sounded faintly in Jessica's headphones. "Have you been able to contact the St. Louis District or the Memphis District?"

"No, sir," Jessica said.

"How 'bout Rock Island?"

Jessica took a breath. "Not so far, sir."

"And your own headquarters has suffered considerable damage, especially in regard to its communications."

"Yes, sir."

There was a pause as Jessica's superior considered his next step. Jessica bit her lip. She had a suspicion that right in the middle of the worst natural disaster the United States had ever faced, she might find herself taken out of the loop.

Communications with other military and Corps of Engineer units had finally been restored through use of Jessica's lone satellite radio. But no word had come from the Corps of Engineers' St. Louis and Memphis district, those closest to the New Madrid fault system. It had been anticipated that these districts might fall victim to a major quake, unable to carry out their assigned tasks, and the Kansas City and Vicksburg districts were the selected backups. But Vicksburg itself had been hard hit, and no one had expected the Rock Island Division, north of St. Louis, to fall victim as well.

With all four of USACE's Mississippi Valley districts either victims or potential victims, the earthquake had seriously compromised the Corps of Engineers' ability to respond effectively in the crisis.

"General Frazetta," Jessica's superior said at last. "I am declaring St. Louis and Memphis to be victim districts."

"Yes, sir," Jessica said. "I concur."

"Should I declare Rock Island a victim as well?"

Well. It was nice of the Old Man to let Jessica express an opinion.

"With respect, sir," she said, "I think that may be premature."

"What's Rock Island's backup district?"

"Chicago, sir."

"Chicago's been hit, too," the Old Man mused.

Jessica was shocked. *Chicago?* No one had imagined that Chicago would suffer in a New Madrid shock. How big *was* this quake? She had told her officers that this might be a three-hundred-year event. A *thousand*-year event, more like. Or five thousand.

"Very well," the Old Man said. "I will reserve judgment on Rock Island, but I will tell Chicago they may have to assume Rock Island's responsibilities."

"Very good, sir."

"Now. Vicksburg."

Jessica's heart gave an anxious little throb. If the Old Man decided that Vicksburg was a victim district as well, then she might well find herself and her command handed over to their backup in Mobile.

The Mississippi Valley was *hers*, damn it. She wanted to keep it.

"Sir," she said, "we won't be able to do anything till dawn, anyway. I think we will be back on line by then. We are doing a good job of recovery here. I see no reason to declare Vicksburg a victim district at this time."

A voice yammered faintly on the radio channel, then faded. Whoever it was, he sounded panicked.

"You're certain of that, Jessica?" the Old Man said. "You know that you'll have to take on the Memphis District's responsibilities, too."

"Yes, sir," Jessica said. "It will take us some hours before we will be able to respond with efficiency, but once we've sorted ourselves out, I think we're admirably placed for running the Joint Division Team."

"Very well," the Old Man said. "If you're that positive."

"I am, sir," Jessica said, and hoped she wasn't deluding herself.

"What can I do for you," he said, "to make your job easier?"

Jessica had been waiting for this. "Communications, sir," she said. "And Prime Power."

Jessica's subordinates were almost entirely civilians, and her Prime Power—the actual military units under her command—consisted of only the 249th Engineer Battalion. If she was going to have to rebuild or reinforce most of the flood control structures between Rock Island and St. Louis, along with reconstructing roads, railroads, and airfields, getting power stations, communications, and waste treatment plants back online, the one battalion was clearly inadequate.

"General Shortland has put the entire U.S. military on alert," the Old Man said. "You can have your pick."

"Yes, sir!" Jessica said.

Well now. *That's* what she considered an adequate response.

By midnight Omar began to feel that he had things in hand. Wilona had called their son David and heard that he and the city of Baton Rouge had been shaken up, but that both David and the city had got through the quake all right. In Spottswood Parish, the courthouse and many of the larger buildings had come through the earthquake well enough, with just windows and fixtures broken, and sometimes doors jammed. But in the semitropical climate many of the buildings in the parish, including Omar's own, were lightly built, and many of them suffered. Homes and trailers fell off their pier foundations, and clapboards and roof shingles had been shaken off.

It could have been worse, Omar thought thankfully. And according to the radio, it *was* worse north of there, with whole cities flattened.

In Omar's jurisdiction, all that might be necessary was some carpentry, a few jacks to get the houses back on their foundations, and most of the parish would be back in business.

And tomorrow, Omar thought, he was going to get his own house fixed. The poor neighborhoods in Hardee were going to get repaired as well as the well-off areas in Shelburne City. And sooner, because the poor people were the ones living in the most heavily damaged buildings.

No one had been killed, so far as Omar knew, but there were broken legs and heads, and scores of minor injuries. Dr. Patel, whose office was soon overwhelmed, set up a clinic in the Presbyterian church. Other churches—those built sturdily enough to survive the quake, anyway—offered space for those unable to sleep in their homes.

Electricity and phones were still working in most parts of the parish. Between phones and the radio, Omar was able to get ahold of all his deputies. The local National Guard unit mobilized, and was able to help Omar's deputies in checking the parts of the parish that were out of communication, looking for damage and seeing if people needed medical attention.

The roads were in bad shape, with dropoffs and crevasses everywhere, but then the roads here were *normally* in sorry condition, and the parish road crews would work long shifts until they were all driveable again.

Wilona worked the night as an assistant, making sure there was coffee for the deputies and that messages got passed to the right people. And the Crusader Micah Knox had put himself to work, helping to direct traffic, volunteering to ride with the deputies and help bring people to the infirmary.

At least the kid had energy. Omar, who was soon yawning and keeping himself fueled with Wilona's coffee, had to admire that.

And then Knox came into Omar's office, a puzzled look in his green eyes. "I don't get it, Omar," he said. "Is your doctor here a nigger?"

"Dr. Patel?" Omar looked up at him. "He's from India."

Knox's mouth dropped open. "God-*damn*, Omar! I thought those wogs were only in the cities!" He shook his head. "They're everywhere!"

"Indians are Aryans, I think." Omar frowned. "Aren't they?"

Knox paced back and forth in front of Omar's desk. "What the hell is he doing here in Liberated America? Jesus—that man's *putting his hands on white women*!"

"Patel's all right," Omar said. "And if you can find a white doctor willing to move to Shelburne City, Louisiana, you just tell me, okay? We went without a doctor for two years till Judge Moseley got us Patel."

"I wanted to bust his damn hands after I saw him touch some of your women," Knox said. "I wouldn't want him to touch me, that's for sure."

"Well, he's not going to try to touch you, I guess. Patel's all right for setting busted legs, and that's what we've got mostly."

He and Wilona went to a white doctor in Vicksburg for their checkups, a habit they'd got into when the parish was without an MD. But Omar, as a deputy, had brought enough injuries into Patel's office to have seen that the man seemed to know what he was doing.

"So—" Knox stepped closer, lowered his voice. He kept jiggling in place, though, bouncing on his heels. "Shall we start calling? Get some paramilitaries here? Some of my boys, some of your Klan people?"

Omar thought of a couple dozen Knoxes running around his parish, and slowly shook his head. "I don't think we need 'em," he said. "We're in good shape. We've got the Guard out. We haven't had any reports of looting. Once we get the roads fixed, the power and phone lines repaired, we're back in business." He looked at Knox. "I reckon your people would be more useful farther north, where there's looting and such."

Knox thought about this for a moment, still bouncing on his heels. "Yeah," he said. "Looting." His strange eyes glittered. "I guess you're right, Omar." He dug in the pocket of his jeans. "I got a phone card ... I'll just make some calls from that pay phone out in the lobby, if it's working."

"Fine," Omar said. Knox bounced out of the room. Omar gazed after him thoughtfully.

Knox, planning who knew what with his buddies, made him uneasy, but whatever it was that Knox was planning, he looked to be doing it elsewhere.

A Micah Knox elsewhere was a Micah Knox that Omar didn't have to worry about. And Omar figured he had enough worries as it was.

FOURTEEN

There has been in all forty-one shocks, some of them have been very light; the first one took place at half past 2 on the morning of the 16th, the last one at eleven o'clock this morning, (20th) since I commenced writing this letter. The last one I think was not as severe as some of the former, but it lasted longer than any of the preceding; I think it continued nearly a minute and a half.

Exclusive of the shocks that were made sensible to us in the water, there have been, I am induced to believe, many others, as we frequently heard a rumbling noise at a distance when no shock to us was perceptible. I am the more inclined to believe these were shocks, from having heard the same kind of rumbling with the shocks that affected us. There is one circumstance that has occurred, which if I had not seen with my own eyes, I could hardly have believed; which is, the rising of the trees that lie in the bed of the river. I believe that every tree that has been deposited in the bed of the river since Noah's flood, now stands erect out of the water; some of these I saw myself during one of the hardest shocks rise up eight or ten feet out of water. The navigation has been rendered extremely difficult in many places in consequence of the snags being so extremely thick. From the long continuance and frequency of these shocks, it is extremely uncertain when they will cease; and if they have been as heavy at New Orleans as we have felt them, the consequences must be dreadful indeed; and I am fearful when I arrive at Natchez to hear that the whole city of Orleans is entirely demolished, and perhaps sunk.

Immediately after the first shock and those which took place after daylight, the whole atmosphere was impregnated with a sulphurous smell.

*Extract of a letter from a gentleman on his way
to New Orleans, dated 20th December, 1811*

The first big May quake—M1, as it was later known—began
at 5:19 Central Daylight Time as a sudden ten-meter bilater-
al dextral strike-slip motion along the whole length of the
twenty-five-mile Reelfoot rift, a subterranean fault structure
running beneath the Mississippi from Missouri to Tennessee.
The Reelfoot rift intersects several other faults or fault seg-
ments—the Bootheel lineament, the New Madrid north fault,
the New Madrid west seismicity trend, and others. The
Bootheel lineament in turn intersects the fifty-mile-long
Blytheville arch, an axial fault running more or less beneath
the Mississippi.

The original Reelfoot slip triggered further slippage and
upthrusting along all nearby faults, each fault contributing in
its turn to the intensity of the destruction—over 150 miles of
built-up tectonic energy cutting loose at nearly the same
instant. The shock waves from this massive disturbance traveled across mid-continental North America with admirable
efficiency.

Most earthquakes occur near the boundaries of the earth's
tectonic plates, the giant twenty-two-mile-thick pieces of the
earth's crust, which drift slowly and massively on the semi-
liquid mass of the planet's interior. The collisions of the
earth's plates throw up mountain ranges, cause deep frac-
tures in the earth's crust, and precipitate almost all the earthquakes in the world. California's famous San Andreas fault
runs along the boundary between the Pacific plate and the
North American plate, which are grinding against one another as they move in opposite directions.

The quakes generated at the edges of plate boundaries
tend to be limited in scope. The fractured nature of the earth
itself tends to disperse the tremblors, or channel them into a
small area. The great San Francisco earthquake of 1906 was a
stupendous 8.3 on the Richter scale, but most of the destruction was confined to a compact part of the Bay Area, and
deaths were limited to about 700. The San Fernando quakes

of 1994 were likewise restricted to a small area, and caused less than a hundred deaths.

But the Reelfoot rift and other mid-American fault structures are not situated on a plate boundary, like the San Andreas fault. They are square in the middle of a very solid continent, and when something hammers the bedrock of the Midwest, the North American plate rings like a giant bell.

There is nothing to stop the quake energy from traveling hundreds of miles from the epicenter. P and S waves leaped from the fracture zones at a speed of around two miles per second, and the terrifying Rayleigh and Love waves, though moving a little more slowly, propagated across the American continent and through the entire structure of the earth, met on the far side of the planet, then returned, circling the globe a half-dozen times before subsiding.

The particular structure of the Mississippi Valley contributed to the catastrophe. A hundred and ninety million years ago, the North American continent almost split in two along the line of the Mississippi Valley. Had this geological action continued, a rift valley would have formed, similar to the Great Rift Valley in Africa. But the continent seemed to have changed its mind. The rift never formed, but the geological action left behind weaknesses in the earth's crust, including the tangle of faults around New Madrid.

The Mississippi River, magnificent as it is, follows the course of what once was an even more magnificent bay, a branch of the ocean that reached as far north as Cape Girardeau, Missouri. Over hundreds of centuries, the Mississippi gradually filled this bay with sediment, creating the Mississippi Delta that stretches from Cape Girardeau to the Gulf of Mexico. The sediment—soil, mud, clay, gravel, vegetable matter, sand—is in some places thousands of feet thick.

When the Mississippi periodically flooded and covered a part of the Delta with a new layer of soil, the soil was intermingled with water and air. Over the course of many years, the water and air normally percolate to the surface and disperse. But if the Mississippi flooded again before this could take place, laying down another layer of a less permeable sediment—clay, for instance—then the water and air was trapped beneath the surface, and as more and more heavy layers of alluvial soil was deposited on top, this water and air was put under enormous pressure.

With layers of clay or other heavier sediment sitting atop a goo of soft soil mixed with air and water, the geology of the Mississippi Valley resembles nothing so much as a layer of bricks placed carefully on a foundation of Jell-O.

The bricks are perfectly stable, so long as nothing shakes the Jell-O.

But when the complex of fault structures beneath the Mississippi snapped, the carefully balanced structure was disrupted. Pressurized water and air blasted its way to the surface, resulting in the so-called "sand blows," thousands of geysers bursting through the surface to loft water, sand, coal, ancient chunks of wood, and rocks far into the air. More water found its way to the surface in less violent fashion, as M1's power liquified the alluvial soil.

It is common for sediment or fill to liquify during an earthquake. Otherwise solid structures, built on alluvium, suddenly find themselves supported by nothing more solid than soup. Sometimes they can tumble downhill like a winter tourist on an inner tube. Much of the property damage suffered during the Bay Area quake of 1989 occurred in the Marina District, a part of San Francisco built on fill.

All of the Mississippi Delta—*all of it*, from Cape Girardeau south—is alluvial soil. Structures everywhere suffered catastrophic failure. Levees, dikes, and flood walls were broken, or weakened. Riverbanks collapsed. Whole forests were laid low. Water geysering into the sky or welling up through the sediment poured off the saturated land to join rivers already filled with spring snow melt.

Even areas built on solid ground did not fare well. The Chickasaw Bluffs, standing above the Mississippi Valley in Tennessee and Kentucky, were subject to landslides that dropped trees, roads, and expensive houses into the valley below. Cape Girardeau suffered a failure of its flood wall, and the lower part of town was inundated. The old French town of Ste. Genevieve, south of Girardeau in Missouri, was likewise partially flooded, and lost several of its historical structures to the flood or to the quake.

The Mississippi town of Natchez, with its proud, pillared collection of antebellum mansions perched atop the loess bluff, windblown soil piled high in the last Ice Age, lost a small city park to landslide as well as a quintessential Southern mansion house, Rosalie, built in 1820. Natchez also lost its riverboat gambling venue when a landslide spilled right through the rough old port town of Lower Natchez and into the casino boat, sinking it at its moorings.

Buildings of unreinforced masonry are more susceptible to earthquake than any other type, and unfortunately the entire area struck by the quake rejoiced in tens of thousands of brick buildings, most of which were destroyed or damaged. Mobile homes were shaken to bits or pitched off their foundations. Frame buildings fared better than others, though some, in the worst-affected areas, were simply shaken to pieces.

Throughout the area, significant damage was suffered as a result of the failure of foundations. Most basement walls were not reinforced and simply caved in, the house falling atop them. Throughout the region, particularly in areas where the water table was high, houses had been set above the ground on small brick piers. The masonry piers either shattered in the tremblors, or the complex motions of the quake walked the houses off their foundations and dropped them onto the broken earth.

Approximately a million people were in their automobiles when the quake struck, most of them heading home from work. In many areas the road systems were destroyed in an instant. Bridges and elevated roadways fell or were mangled; roads were torn across by fissures; right-of-ways were flooded. The roadways were packed with desperate people stranded in their vehicles, far from their homes, away from supplies of food and water.

Rail transport suffered as well. Bridges fell, tracks were

torn or wrenched into pretzel shapes, depots were destroyed. The most economical and efficient method of getting food and other supplies to affected areas, by rail, was rendered temporarily unusable.

At airports, runways were destroyed, fuel depots ruined, control towers pitched to the ground, and hangars collapsed on aircraft. Radar installations were wrecked, or lost the ground lines by which they transmitted their data. Entire districts of the country disappeared from air controllers' screens. Aircraft, stranded aloft when their destinations were turned to rubble, began to call frantically for controllers to find them a place to land.

Following the shattering catastrophe of the quake came the swift catastrophe of fire. Propane tanks spewed their explosive contents through shattered couplings. Unsecured stoves and water heaters marched from their places, spilling scalding water and breaking their gas connections. Underground oil and gas pipelines were broken. Aboveground storage tanks ruptured. The unexpected lightning storm over Swampeast Missouri struck forests and buildings alike. And shattered buildings provided tinder that could ignite a conflagration.

Winds fanned the flames. Shattered communications and inundated emergency communication systems ensured that the fires would go unreported or unnoticed until they had taken hold. Broken water mains meant there was no water available to fight the fires.

Conflagration took hold everywhere in the stricken land, and on every scale. Isolated barns and houses burned, small stores and large, small towns and large towns, and the city centers of St. Louis, East St. Louis, and Memphis. Thousands of people, trapped in rubble or with their retreat cut off by flames, died in terror. Forests and prairie took fire as well, and with the authorities concentrating on quelling fires in cities and towns, there was nothing to stop the flames in the countryside but what Nature provided in the form of rain and flood.

The author Robert A. Heinlein once mocked what he

called the wooden fire escapes on Chicago's apartment buildings, unaware that he was looking not at fire escapes, but at wooden back porches equipped with stairs. But Heinlein may have had the last laugh when M1 shivered a part of the city to bits. Though Chicago, well away from the quake's epicenter, on the whole survived the quake fairly well, a fluke of geology carried the earthquake's full power to the northeast district of Rogers Park, and the heavy wooden porches, dry as tinder after years of weathering in the outdoors, turned to flaming deathtraps.

After the shattering catastrophe of the quake and the swift catastrophe of fire came the slow-motion catastrophe of flood. The Mississippi and its tributaries were full with snow melt, and spring rains had saturated the soil. Sand blows and soil liquefaction brought subterranean water to the surface. And when the levees and dams broke, river water had nowhere to go but to spill across country.

Flood is a disaster slow enough so that people can normally get out of its way, but in this case broken road and communications systems made it impossible to manage proper evacuations. Flood caught tens of thousands in their homes, and tens of thousands of others were caught in the open, trying to get away from their wrecked homes or their stranded automobiles.

Nor was the flooding confined to the Mississippi alone. The Father of Waters has 250 tributaries, including many that are mighty rivers in their own right: the Missouri, the Arkansas, the Ohio, the Red, the Des Moines, the Illinois. Each of these rivers has its own system of levees, locks, dams, and reservoirs, and each was filled with spring snow melt. The tragedy of the Mississippi, the flooding and destruction and death, was repeated many times throughout the country, from Iowa and Illinois south to Louisiana.

And sometimes flood was as sudden as fire. The Carlyle Dam in Illinois failed completely, causing a multimillion-gallon wall of water to roar down the Kaskaskia. Mark Twain Lake spilled through the shattered Clarence Cannon Dam, roared over the town of Louisiana, Missouri, into the

Mississippi, where it turned into a wave that obliterated Lock and Dam No. 24. The failure of Dam No. 24 in turn released the millions of gallons it had been holding, and the two united bodies of water spilled south toward St. Louis, already vulnerable due to the shattering of its floodwalls.

There were hundreds of little dams throughout the Midwest, many privately owned. Many were simple earthen embankments that held just enough water to support a herd of cattle, or to keep a creek from flooding a field, and others were larger. When the quake came, many of them failed. Though the breaking of these small dams did not cause catastrophic flooding, it nevertheless added to the burden of water carried by the already shattered system.

Perhaps the worst thing, amid all this loss and tragedy, was that for many hours following M1, none of the people in a position to aid the survivors, from the President through General Frazetta and on down the chain of command, were in a position to understand the full scope of the catastrophe, or to mitigate its destructive power in any way.

"We're fine, General. Shook up, but fine."

Jessica felt the tension in her neck ease as the words crackled out of her cellphone. The Kentucky Dam, holding back the combined waters of the Cumberland and Tennessee Rivers, was intact. If it had gone, pouring both Kentucky Lake and Lake Barkley into the Ohio, it would have created a colossal wall of water that would have turned the Ohio and Mississippi Valleys from Evansville to Memphis into one long, blank, lifeless smear of mud.

"I want the dam surveyed for damage," Jessica said. "And every other dam in the area."

"Yah. I'll get right on it."

"I need to make some other calls right now. But let me give you my number—call me *only if you've got bad news*, understand? If things are fine, I don't want to hear from you."

"You betcha. Guess you're kinda busy down there, yah?"

Jessica grinned. That *you betcha*, spoken in a classic Red River of the North accent, was far from a proper military response. But the Army Corps of Engineers, though operated by the military, was not entirely a military outfit. Most of the people who worked for Jessica in the Mississippi Valley Division—engineers, inspectors, architects, and lock masters, surveyors, boat captains, equipment operators, and managers—were civilians, and not subject to military discipline. Entire Corps districts saw a person in uniform only rarely.

A clash between military and civilian cultures was a constant possibility. Jessica preferred to think of this not as a disadvantage, but as a stimulating opportunity for cross-cultural discourse.

Jessica disconnected and batted moths away from her flashlight. She was squatting on the lawn in front of her headquarters building, looking at maps and lists of phone numbers spread out on the grass. Flashlights and the headlights of vehicles were the only illumination.

She called the Clarence Cannon dam again, and received no reply. "Fuckingskunksuckingsonofabitch," she muttered rapid-fire. Too many critical installations were out of communication.

"General Caldwell?" The voice came out of the darkness. Jessica looked up to see a man approaching. He wore civilian clothing and his eyes glittered strangely from behind thick glasses.

"I'm General Frazetta," she said as she rose to her feet. Caldwell had been the name of her predecessor, a tall, burly man who looked more like a sandhog than an engineer.

"I brought this, General. I knew you'd need it."

He held out something that glittered in the headlights. Jessica reached out a hand and something metal and heavy was placed in her palm. A heavy double-ended chrome-plated wrench.

"Took me a long time to find it," the man said. "But I knew you'd need it." He gave a serious nod, then faded back into the night. Jessica looked down at the wrench in her hand, then at the dark silhouette of the spectacled man as he vanished into the night.

The earthquake had shaken people up. She had met relatively few people since the quake, but a disturbing number of them weren't behaving rationally. It was as if the disaster was so far outside their experience that they had no way of reacting to it logically; the scale of the thing had unstrung their minds.

Something had to be done for these people, she thought. There were probably thousands of them.

But she had other things to do first.

She squatted down into the light of the headlights and began to press buttons on her cellular phone.

An aftershock woke Charlie some time after midnight. The BMW trembled on its suspension as the earth shivered for a good three minutes.

Earthquake, he thought. It was an *earthquake.*

How strange. Earthquakes were only in California and Japan.

He could still see downtown Memphis glowing red on the horizon, beneath a spreading gloom of smoke.

Charlie blinked and stroked the stubble on his chin. A sheen of sweat covered his forehead. He felt feverish.

More than the earth was moving, he knew.

Prices were moving.

He needed to get a *grip,* he thought. *Prices were moving.* There was money to be made. He needed to get to his desk and make some sales.

Stocks were going to *plummet,* he thought. Which meant there were going to be all sorts of cheap bargains to be picked up.

America, he further considered, was going to need to rebuild. Which meant that they would need dollars. Which meant that Charlie needed to buy dollars *right now,* because lots of investors were going to panic when they heard about the quake, and they would try to sell their dollars. So Charlie would buy, because the Federal Reserve was going to have to buy billions of dollars to finance the reconstruction, so the dollar would eventually go *up,* and he would profit. Which would result in depressed prices in places like London and

Tokyo, as American dollars came home, so he'd have to start shorting those markets.

And bonds. He needed to talk to his bond traders. Because the Fed would be loaning out its dollars at very low interest rates to finance reconstruction, and that would mean higher bond prices.

He considered other side effects. He would buy oil, lots of it. Refinery capacity would be reduced, and the price would be up. And foodstuffs, because a lot of agricultural land had just got trashed, so food prices would be rising.

He needed to move *right now*, because the whole situation could change by the time the markets closed tomorrow.

He picked up the cellphone again, tried to call Dearborne. Nothing. He called some of his traders. Nothing but a hiss.

Move! he thought, and pounded the car wheel in front of him with his fists.

Nothing moved in the still night. Nothing but the drifting cloud of smoke overhead.

As dawn approached, the news from the quake zone only grew worse. Huge fires raged out of control, both in cities and national forests. Communication and transportation were shattered. Millions in need, and no way to get aid to all of them.

"Mr. President," Lipinsky said finally, "I am afraid that the limits of our efforts are very rapidly being reached. There are large sections of the country—mostly rural—that will be on their own for some time. We cannot get help to them, not with our efforts concentrated in the cities."

The President licked his lips. "We can put more soldiers in the disaster area," he said. "Call up more reserves. Bring the National Guard in from other states . . ."

Lipinsky shook his head. "We can't put in more soldiers until there's a way to move them into the field, and to supply them once they get there. Right now we can only move our people into the badly damaged areas with helicopters, and we only have so many, and they have to divide their limited time between rescue, supply, and delivering our rescue teams to their objectives. Helicopters are also very delicate—they spend more time in maintenance than in the air." He gazed into the President's face. "Sir, I recommend that you address the American people. Tell them frankly that many of them cannot expect our assistance for some time to come. I think they will be safer for that knowledge."

The President clenched his teeth. "It is not my job," he said, "in the midst of the worst disaster in history, to tell the taxpayers of the most powerful nation in the world that their government *can't help them*!" He realized he was shouting, that the Situation Room had fallen silent.

He looked at the crowd of people for a moment, then realized how tired he was.

"Five-minute break," he said, turned, and left the room.

He went to one of the rest rooms, moistened a towel in cool water, and applied the towel to the back of his neck. His kidneys ached. He closed his eyes, then had to open them because he began to sway with weariness. He stared into the hollow-eyed scarecrow that stared back at him from the mirror.

"Let Lipinsky be wrong," he said.

He was the *President*, his mind protested. The President of the most powerful nation on earth.

So why was he feeling more helpless than any other time in his life?

The water rolled into St. Louis with the dawn. Farther upstream, just below where the waters of Mark Twain Lake had broken Lock and Dam No. 24, the flood had become a literal wall of water, foaming, eight feet high, that obliterated everything in its path like a bowling ball rolling down a pipe. But by the time the water reached St. Louis, it had moderated into a series of steep rollers, each one higher than the one before.

Most people were able to head for higher ground as the waters rose, but still thousands drowned. These were trapped in collapsed buildings and unable to flee: others were injured, caught in areas away from high ground, caught in the flood when they were caught behind uncrossable fissures, or caught in floating debris that carried them to their deaths.

Marcy Douglas watched the waves go by. She greeted the dawn from her post at the Jefferson National Expansion Memorial, standing below the soaring stainless steel Gateway Arch that marked the safe, high ground where neither floor nor fire had reached. Marcy had worked all night in the collapsed parking garage, pulling people free of the debris. She had seen men crushed in their cars, women trapped beneath falling concrete, children lying blue-lipped and cold, smothered beneath the arched bodies of the parents who died trying to protect them. She had helped to carry the bodies out as well as the survivors, but there was nowhere to lay them but on the grass of the Memorial park.

There were a few doctors and nurses among the crowd of refugees that had fled across Memorial Drive, and these did what they could for the injured. There was no medicine, no supplies, no beds, no blankets. But the doctors and nurses and Park personnel and a thousand ordinary people did what they could, and over the course of the night they performed miracles, and saved scores of people who otherwise would have died.

And so Marcy—with no sleep, no food, no rest—stood to greet the dawn, the red sunrise that gleamed on the Arch. She stood tall in her stained khaki uniform, her wide hat square on her head, and knew, through her weariness, that she had done everything possible for her tourists, for those caught in the parking garage, and for everyone else that had come within the boundary of the Memorial.

As Marcy watched the sun rise, she saw the long foaming waves rolling along the channel of the Mississippi. The brown water mounted higher and higher, nudging at the groaning wreckage of the *Casino Queen* and the *Tom Sawyer*. Marcy knew that the day would be long, and that her part was not over.

And a few miles south of where Marcy stood on the river, a man watched the waters rise and felt ice run up his spine.

His name was Stewart DeForest, and he was fire chief of the City of St. Louis. When he felt the first tremors slam into his home, even as the glass shattered and the furniture leaped, as shingles spilled from the roof and the house rocked on its foundation, he knew that his place was in south St. Louis, by the River Des Peres.

The Des Peres was a tributary of the Mississippi and formed the southern boundary of St. Louis proper. The Des Peres's flood protection was inadequate, and everyone knew it. If the Mississippi backed up into the Des Peres, the area near the river was threatened with inundation.

Mere flooding was not what frightened the fire chief. What terrified DeForest were the long white rows of liquid propane cylinders that crouched near the river. Each cylinder held 30,000 pressurized gallons of one of the most explosive substances on earth, and there were more than fifty of them, making for over a million and a half gallons altogether.

One leak, one spark, was all it would take to ignite the greatest conflagration that Missouri had ever seen. The catastrophe had barely been averted in the flood of 1993. DeForest was determined that it would be averted now.

Two characteristics of propane combined to make the situation dangerous. Propane was heavier than air, but lighter than water. When confined in its cylinders in a flooded area, propane would try to float to the surface. When released, it would lie atop the water in a dense cloud, caught between air and water.

If the area was flooded to a sufficient depth, the 30,000-gallon propane cylinders would rise, float loose from their moorings, then break their cables and bob with the current, ramming into buildings, trees, and other obstacles. Leaks were probably inevitable, and leaks would create a dense, flammable fog that would float downstream to the Mississippi in search of a source of ignition.

Against this danger, DeForest could do little. Over the course of the night he deployed his men on rafts and boats and temporary platforms. Fire hoses, nozzles set to maximum dispersion, played on the huge cylinders in hopes that this would diffuse any leaking propane. Propane was very slightly soluble in water: if DeForest could keep his artificial rain playing on the area, he might absorb some of the propane, and scatter the rest.

By dawn it was working well. The area had flooded to a little over three feet, then receded slightly. Breaks in the levees upstream and down were keeping the pressure off the Des Peres.

But then the water from Mark Twain Lake began rolling in—DeForest could *see* it, *see* brown waves rippling in from the Des Peres—and DeForest knew he was in a toe-to-toe battle with a holocaust.

The waters rose. DeForest told his men to stay at their stations and summoned other units. He called in police to make certain the area was evacuated.

The pumpers pulled flood water into their intakes, then spewed it out over the tank field. From his command post on a hill overlooking the tank field, DeForest could see the propane cylinders rising, straining at their moorings.

The water just kept on rising. DeForest deployed more hoses and called for more backup. He ordered a fire boat to wait at the outlet to the Des Peres, ready to catch any cylinders that floated that far.

He gave a start at the sound of a shot. One of the cylinders had broken a cable.

There was another shot, another. DeForest felt sweat gathering beneath his helmet. He blinked salt droplets from his eyes and began to pray.

God help *those people*, he thought earnestly. *God help us all.*

More shots, a metallic shriek. One of the cylinders broke free, began bobbing on the tide. It floated up against one of the other cylinders with a metallic clang.

"Can we corral it somehow?" One of DeForest's deputy chiefs, with panic in his eyes.

DeForest shook his head. "Do you know how much one of those things *weighs*? It will go where it wants. The only way we could move it around would be with motorboats, and I don't want hot motor exhaust around *any* of those cylinders."

More bangs, more cables parting. Weary hopelessness washed over DeForest. People down in the tank field were reporting the smell of propane. They asked permission to evacuate.

"Denied," DeForest said. "Put on your respirators, and keep that water pumping."

The huge unmoored cylinders were spreading like oil on the surface of a pond. Some of them caught in a line of trees on the edge of the property. Others floated off into residential areas. DeForest didn't have any way to chase them down. All he could do was hope that they would disperse so much that if one of them blew, it wouldn't set off any of the others.

But he knew too much about liquid propane to really believe in that hope.

He had a daughter in college in Wisconsin. A son lived in Colorado. Both were safe.

He began to mentally say good-bye to them. And to his wife, whom he had left in her housecoat on their front lawn, and whom he hadn't been able to contact since. He hoped she would be out of the blast radius.

Two of his men breathed in too much propane and collapsed. They were dragged to ambulances and replaced. The hoses continued to flood the area with gentle rain.

Even on his little hill, DeForest could smell an occasional gust of propane. It was everywhere.

The cylinders spread across the quiet inland sea. The waters were still rising. The city was very quiet.

And then he saw the flame rolling in from the direction of the Des Peres, a little blue wavy line that fluttered and shifted in the wind, but that raced like lightning toward the huge leaking cylinders.

DeForest turned to dive behind his car, and he thumbed the transmit button on his walkie-talkie and opened his mouth to tell his men to take cover.

It was a futile gesture.

The fireball, one and a half million gallons of liquid propane going up in an instant, was over a mile in diameter.

Five or so miles to the north, Marcy Douglas felt the earth tremble. She was working to clear fallen trees from a part of the Jefferson Memorial Park so that the area could be used as a helipad. Army helicopters had soared in just after dawn, and were questing for a place to land.

Marcy thought the tremor was just another aftershock, but then she saw the flash brighten the shining steel of the Gateway Arch, and turned south to watch in awestruck horror as the bright fireball rose over south St. Louis. Bright arching trails of flame shot out of the fireball, like Fourth of July rockets, as debris rose and fell.

The sound came a few seconds later, the colossal concussion that drowned out the roar of the helicopters circling overhead. The copters spun dangerously as the concussion caught them.

It is the Bomb, Marcy thought. *It is the End.*

The bubble of fire rose into the heavens, and its reflection turned the Mississippi to the color of blood.

Accounts from la Haut Missouri, announces a general peace among the Indians, it is said that the earthquakes has created this pacification.

Pittsburgh, April 18, 1812

"For then shall be great tribulation!" Frankland barked, "such as was not since the beginning of the world to this time, no, nor ever shall be!

"And except those days should be shortened, there should no flesh be saved: but for the elect's sake those days shall be shortened." He glanced down at his notes to make certain of the citation. "Matthew," he said, "chapter twenty-four."

Frankland looked from the pulpit at the crowded people in his church. People murmured and shuffled and grumbled, and a number of children were wailing. Frankland's amplified voice had no problem being heard over the cries of the children, however. He shouted over the cries for at least an hour.

He had begun his preaching at six o'clock in the morning, jolting the people awake with the sound and fervor of his call. He knew that the bellies of his audience were empty, that many had no rest. That was all to the good. It made them less likely to disregard his message. It was necessary to convince them, to terrify them, to make them want and need his guidance. Some of the grownups were weeping, he saw. Others stared up at him as if they'd been hit with sticks.

It didn't slow him down. He'd written the sermon *years* before. It had been waiting in one of the fireproof safes in the guest bedroom closet, in a manila envelope labeled *End Times First Sermon*. There had been many other sermons filed alongside it.

"For the elect's sake!" he repeated. "For the sake of those who remain true to Jesus' word, the Tribulation will be shortened! Otherwise *nothing would be left*! The catastrophes of yesterday would go on and on until *every last human being is destroyed*! But out of compassion for those who hold true to the Word, the Lord will have mercy on us, elect and sinners both. For God promises, later in the Book of Matthew." He looked down at his notes. "'Verily I say unto you, This generation shall not pass, till all these things be fulfilled.'

"And at the end of that time, Jesus will return in righteousness and reign for a thousand years. Amen."

Afterward he called for volunteers—strong, young able people—to go out into the county round to look for survivors, and to bring in food. He called for more volunteers from among the ladies to help with cooking. And he called for the older men to help with jobs of construction, raising tents and building latrines.

There were plenty of volunteers. He divided them into groups, and put them under reliable people from his own congregation. "Bring in radios," he told the leaders. "All the radios you can find. And if any of your people are carrying radios, tell them we're going to need them. We need all the radios so that we can listen to the news, and pass it on to the people."

And to keep them from hearing the word of the Devil,

which would probably be on every radio station but his own.
  Amen.

Nick shivered as dawn leaked over the eastern horizon. He
had spent the night in a cottonwood tree with black flood
waters rushing beneath him.

The levees must have broken, he thought. There were eight
or ten feet of water under him, and the water was moving
fast. Every so often the tree would shudder to the impact of
floating debris.

He thought about Viondi's body floating in the darkness,
past the broken Mobil station, heading south toward his
Aunt Loretta in Mississippi.

He thought about the Asian man trapped in his broken
storefront, pinned down by a beam, the waters rising past his
outstretched chin.

His left arm ached in the tricep region, and when he put
his right hand there it came away sticky. He'd been shot.
That crazy cop had shot him.

There didn't seem to be anything he could do about it. He
didn't even have his stupid pale Band-Aids with dinosaurs
on them.

Nick straddled a limb, leaned back against the bole of the
tree, and tried to sleep. The wound throbbed all night long,
and there were insistent biting insects, a truly amazing number of them, that kept him busy slapping them away.
Occasional aftershocks rocked the tree, causing him to clutch
at his bough and hope that the shock wouldn't loosen the
tree's roots and topple it into the water.

He must have finally fallen asleep, though, because when
he opened his eyes he found it was light, just past dawn.
Birdsong rang through the trees. Nick blinked gum from his
eyes and peered out at the drowned world.

He was in a grove, an old stand of cottonwood. His tree
bore so many leafy branches that it was difficult to see
through them. The area was brushy, and the tops of bushes
waved from the murky water below. Far off to his right—
southeast, to judge by the sun—there was a wide open area

covered with water. He couldn't tell if it was a flooded field, a lake, or a river.

There was a rustling out on the big limb that Nick was straddling. He looked out and gazed into a pair of brown eyes. He started and banged the back of his head on the bole of the tree.

Opossum, he recognized. With little pink-nosed babies clinging to its fur.

"Damn," Nick said, and rubbed the back of his head where he'd knocked it on the tree. The opossum gave a disappointed murmur and climbed higher into the tree, out of sight.

"Possum," Nick told it, "you don't want to get down now, anyway."

Loud bird calls barked from the next tree over. Nick hitched himself out on his limb to get a better view, peered between branches and saw a flock of guinea fowl, survivors from someone's farm. In another tree, he saw a pair of squirrels leaping from one branch to another, just above the sullen, bedraggled form of a hen turkey. He could hear the cawing of a whole flock of crows, but he couldn't see them.

All nature had gone aloft when the water began to rise.

No, he discovered, not *all* nature.

The corpse of a drowned deer, already stiff, floated half-submerged in the current.

Nick gave a shudder. At least the body wasn't that of a human being.

It occurred to him that there might be someone within hailing distance. Even someone else stranded in a cottonwood would be company. He cupped his hands to his mouth, turned his head in the direction he suspected was inland, then hesitated.

What does a person say under these circumstances? he wondered. "Help"? "Get me down!"? "I'm stuck in a tree"?

He settled on "Hello."

He called out his hello, waited for an answer, called again. Called in all directions.

Only the guinea fowl in the next tree answered.

He sagged on the bough, discouragement rising in him

like the rising flood. He was very thirsty, very hungry. His wounded arm ached. He tried to get a look at it in the morning light, but it was on a part of his arm that he couldn't see, no matter how much he tried.

He decided to check his pockets, make an inventory. Billfold with credit cards and ID. Money clip with a hundred and sixty in cash, more or less. Thirty-seven cents in loose change. House keys. These, and the Timex on his wrist, seemed to be the sum total of his resources.

He felt something in his shirt pocket, and fished it out. Opened the box. Saw the lily-shaped pendant on the necklace, saw dawn light winking off diamonds and rubies.

For Arlette. He looked at the golden lily in his palm. He would have to survive for Arlette.

Nick felt a stinging bite on the back of his right arm and slapped at it with the left. Felt another bite, made another slap. Then he felt a bite on his back, and after slapping it away looked behind him to see what was the matter.

His heart gave a leap. Down the bole of the tree behind him poured a red river of insects. There were so many that the tree seemed to shimmer with the reflection of their glittering eyes.

He spasmed forward along the tree limb, slapping furiously at his back and behind. There were red ants all over his body. He moved forward along the limb, feeling it dip under his weight, leaves trailing in the water. The mother opossum, from somewhere in the clump of leaves, gave a cry of warning.

Nick threw one leg over the limb, turned to face the tree, swung the other leg over. An implacable swarm of ants marched along the bark toward him. He beat at them with his palms, then slapped at his body where other ants were still biting.

He wondered where the ants were coming from and looked up: a huge glistening ball of ants pulsed on the bole of the tree, only a few feet above where he'd laid his head all night. The ants must have evacuated their nest when the river rose, carrying with them their eggs, pupae, and queen;

and now their nest was composed principally of their bodies, a ravenous scarlet sphere boiling with angry life, now wakened by the dawn and gone in quest of food.

There was a squawk above him, a flurry of beating wings, and a pair of grackles, cawing furiously, burst free of the foliage and thundered madly into the air. Apparently the ants had just invaded their perch.

For a moment he considered abandoning the tree in favor of another. But there was no guarantee that a new tree would be any more hospitable, or that he would be able to climb it as easily as he climbed this one.

Besides, something in him resisted dropping into the cold water below. He could all too easily get caught in brush or debris, and drown.

He reached behind him to one of the cottonwood's many small branches, and wrestled it back and forth until he succeeded in snapping it off. Then he used the leafy branch as a broom to sweep the tide of ants off the limb.

Another large bird squawked and flapped out of the tree. Nick didn't see what kind, he only heard it. The ants were hungry, or angry, or both.

There was more thrashing in the tree, and Nick saw a raccoon, big as a dog, bound out of one branch and to another, clawing madly to get a firm grip. Once safe on the new limb, the raccoon began a frenzy of frantic scratching.

"Be thankful, man," Nick said, sweeping with his branch. "It could be worse. They could be fire ants." The raccoon gave him a resentful look and kept scratching.

Nick looked up at the ant nest, the ball of glittering angry insects, and he considered attacking it directly. Maybe with his branch he could knock them into the river by the thousands.

On the other hand, maybe he'd just piss them off.

He decided it was worth a try. He edged along the limb until the knot of ants was within easy sweeping distance of his branch, and then he cocked the branch back and slapped it against the ball of ants.

He was surprised at how easily it worked—the seeming

solidity of the ball of ants had made him think they would be harder to dislodge. A large chunk of the ant nest was knocked off the tree and fell in the water. He was surprised that the knot did not disintegrate: the ants clung to each other, forming a nearly solid raft as the current swept them away.

When they hit another tree, Nick thought, they'd all climb it.

A catbird gave its mewling cry of alarm and fluttered to safety. Another bird burst from the higher branches, dropped low across the water before gaining altitude. Some kind of owl, he saw, a big one, with horns. Didn't like the ants, either.

He cocked his arm back, swept again. More ants spilled into the water.

He swept a third time. And then something flashed white and tan in the tree, and glittering fangs clamped on the leafy twigs. Cold primordial fear shot up Nick's spine.

Cottonmouth, he thought.

His father had taken him all over the world when Nick was growing up. Nick had grown up on Army bases in Europe, in Korea, and in Thailand. But he had spent much of his youth on bases in the American South. And, like every Southern child who shares his swimming hole with nature, he had learned terror of the cottonmouth moccasin.

Snake! some boy would cry, and there would be a flurry of arms and legs and white water, and the boys would stand panting on the shore while a cottonmouth, long and thick as a grown man's arm, prowled the water in search of something to kill.

Coral snakes and rattlers were shy, avoided humans when they could, and never bit unless threatened. A cottonmouth moccasin was afraid of nothing, would aggressively invade territory occupied by others, and would bite without hesitation. Their venom, unlike that of the copperhead, was deadly.

"A cottonmouth will bite you just to watch you die." That's what the old folks told their children. And when the children grew older, fear and hatred of all snakes was buried so deep that it might as well have been seared on their bones. A lot of the children with whom Nick had shared his boyhood swimming holes grew up to kill every snake they saw, whether they were poisonous or not.

That was what the fear of the cottonmouth could do.

Nick had never been as afraid of anything in his life as he'd been of the cottonmouths he'd seen when he was young. And that deep-buried fear had never gone away.

The distinctive white mouth tissue flashed again and again as the snake struck repeatedly at Nick's branch. The snake was a big one, too, four feet long.

Its thick body was covered with furious biting ants. It was in agony. And it was angry enough to kill.

Fear clawed at Nick's brain with fingers of fire. Nick kept thrashing at the snake with the branch. He couldn't think of anything else to do. His branch was too small and light to knock the snake off the tree, but at least the flailing leaves distracted it, kept it from biting at him. He found himself retreating along his limb, backing up until his butt came up against a nest of branches and he could back up no farther.

The cottonmouth advanced, half-falling down the tree as it writhed in pain. It gathered itself on Nick's limb, raised its head, hissed. Furious ants swarmed over it. Nick thrust the branch at it again, and it struck.

The raccoon gave a warning yelp and made a hasty jump for the water. It was as scared of the cottonmouth as Nick was.

For a half-second Nick considered following the raccoon's example. But the cottonmouth was an aquatic snake, it could swim better than Nick could. If it was angry enough to follow Nick into the water, then it could kill him easily, while he tried to thrash his way through the waterlogged brush below.

The cottonmouth writhed closer. Nick batted at the snake with the branch, but the leafy broom was too light to budge it from its perch. He could see his reflection in the snake's unblinking eyes, and felt his blood run cold. *Grab it behind the head*, he thought, that was the safe way to handle a snake, but he couldn't think of a way to grab its head without letting the cottonmouth strike at him first.

Nick reversed the branch, thinking perhaps that he could use the sharp broken-off butt end as a dagger. He held it like an icepick in his right hand, eight inches or so from the end, and gave a *huff* of breath as he stabbed at the snake. The sharp wood skiddered on bark, blunted itself. Leaves waved. The snake reared, hissed. Nick stabbed again, a cry of anger and fear breaking from his lips. The snake struck. There was an instant of terror as Nick realized that the snake was striking too fast for Nick to snatch back his hand.

And then the snake's jaw clamped down on the branch, an inch below Nick's little finger. He saw the two poison fangs digging into the smooth bark, saw beads of venom swell up. His heart gave a leap. *Now!* he thought.

He pulled the branch toward him, dragging the snake toward him by its fangs. The resistance was formidable: it was like pulling on a thick rubber band. But the cottonmouth was unwilling to let go of the branch, and Nick managed to stretch out the snake's neck until he could pounce with his left hand, grabbing the cottonmouth just behind the head, where it couldn't turn to bite him.

Nick dropped the branch, grabbed the snake halfway down its body with his right hand. The cottonmouth's glassy reptile eyes gazed into his, expressionless, as Nick tried to lift it so that he could fling it into the water below. But the tail was anchored around the tree limb, and muscles *pulsed* in Nick's hands, sinew flexing, testing his strength. The body was so thick that Nick couldn't quite close his right hand around it; he could feel the muscles working against his grip, trying to pry the fingers apart, and he clamped down, digging fingertips into the scaly skin, tugging at the snake as he tried to pull it from the limb.

Furious ants swarmed over the snake and Nick's hands, bit them both without mercy.

The snake dropped the branch and opened its mouth wide, the mouth tissues blossoming like a deadly white flower. It tried to turn its head to bite Nick in the wrist, but

Nick held it fast by the neck and wouldn't let it double back on itself. Drops of venom welled at the tips of the fangs. Its muscles pulsed, flexed, strained beneath Nick's fingers. And then its muscles surged, and its tail left the tree limb and tried to coil itself around Nick's right wrist.

Nick gave a yell of alarm as the snake's fat body writhed in his hands. He thumped his hand onto the tree limb, scraped the cottonmouth's tail off his wrist against the bark, then raised the snake in both hands over his head and flung it through the air.

"*Yaaaaaah!*" he roared, a scream of rage and triumph.

The cottonmouth curled in air, almost turning itself into a knot, and then hit the water.

There was a splash, a twist, and suddenly the aquatic snake was swimming, in its element. Its body surged effortlessly in the water, its head carried high, eyes focused . . .

Eyes focused on Nick.

Nick felt his triumph turn to disbelief and horror. *The snake was coming back to the tree. The cottonmouth was coming to kill him.*

"Stay out of my tree!" Nick shouted. Heat flushed his skin. "*My* tree!" He waved a fist. The snake kept coming.

Nick turned, snatched at the branches behind him. He grabbed one of the strongest and seized it, bending it back, fighting it. There was a crack as he tore it free. He stripped twigs and leaves from it, turned it into a club.

The cottonmouth pulsed its way to the tree, its head winding a path through the smaller branches so that the thick surging body could follow.

The first, leafy branch that Nick had dropped was still lying in his lap. He took that branch in his left hand and the new club in the right. He hit the club against the bole of the tree a few times, trying to get a feel for the weapon. He tasted bitter despair on his tongue: the club was far too light to smash the head of the snake.

The hopelessness brought defiance to his lips. "You want a piece of me?" he demanded of the snake. He snarled. "You come and get it!"

The cottonmouth's weaving head slid around the bole of the tree, its cold, inhuman eyes intent on Nick. The forked tongue flickered from the soft white mouth. Nick smashed at the snake with the club, hit it in the neck. The snake reared back, then dropped its head and surged forward.

Nick smashed with left and right, trying to confuse the snake with the leafy branch and then hammer it with the stick. The cottonmouth coiled protectively when it was struck, but then extended itself again and continued its motion along the tree limb. Nick hammered and hammered. The cottonmouth struck at the club and missed. Nick hammered at it, the hot blood bringing strength to his arm.

"You want a piece of me?" he shouted. "You want this tree?"

He smashed the club down on the snake's neck, pinning it to the tree limb. He snatched out with his left hand and grabbed the cottonmouth by the neck, just behind the head. The snake's tail whipped around, coiled around his wrist.

"You think I care if you grab me?" Nick demanded. The snake tightened on his arm. Nick held the snake's head with his left hand while he smashed at it with the club in his right. The cottonmouth's head darted left and right to the limits that Nick would permit, seeking escape from the blows. Then Nick lunged forward and smashed the snake's head into the bole of the tree with all of his strength. The snake's body spasmed on his arm. He smashed again and again.

"You want a piece of me, cottonmouth?" he demanded. "You come and take it!"

He smashed the snake's head against the tree until the snake hung in loose coils from his arm, until Nick's hand was scraped and bloody and the snake's forked tongue hung limply from its mouth. Then he wearily uncoiled the snake from his arm, held it over the water, and let it fall.

The Mississippi received it with barely a splash.

"*My* tree!" Nick shouted. "*My* damn tree!"

His cries echoed in the empty grove. Birds shrieked in answer.

He slapped ants from his hands, from his legs. Snapped off

another leafy branch, began to sweep the ants from his limb, from what remained of their nest.

The tree was *his*, and he was going to keep it.

He touched his shirt pocket, felt Arlette's necklace.

He would give it to her, see the sparkle in her eyes. He *knew* that now.

Hours passed. The day grew hot, and the ants grew torpid. Perhaps they'd found something to eat, or lost interest after the destruction of their nest. The insects that drove him crazy now were mosquitos, dancing around him in swarms.

Farther out on his limb, the mother opossum rustled its way through leafy branches and squawked at its babies. Every so often it would peer out to see if Nick had left. It always seemed disappointed when he hadn't.

The water level seemed to be dropping a little. The sodden tops of bushes were more visible. The water had ceased to run with its earlier swiftness, now lay still and dark, its surface reflecting the bright rays of the sun.

After sitting on his limb till his body felt like a giant cramp, Nick decided to climb a little higher and discover what might be seen. He clambered higher, heaving and sweating as he pushed his way through tightly woven branches.

This was really the sort of thing the snake would have done much easier.

The tree began to sway under Nick's weight. He was panting for breath, and he decided he had climbed enough. He planted his feet carefully and looked around.

Leaves still obscured much of the view. He pressed branches down, tried to clear the sight lines. North and south stretched trees as far as he could see. West he could see an opening, a flat space covered with water, but he couldn't tell whether it was the river, a field, or a clearing.

He turned east, and a chill shivered through his blood. There, across a flooded field, was the shattered Mobil station where Viondi had died. Its white, blue, and red sign still swung above the brown water.

The Mobil station was no more than a half-mile away. Nick

thought he'd wandered much farther in the dark. He must have been tracking in circles once he got among the trees.

There was no sign of the cop or his car. Or of Viondi. Or of any other human being.

He was king of the tree and all he surveyed. He gave a bitter laugh.

The sun was hot on his head.

Nick slapped at a biting ant and decided he might as well climb down. He found it harder to force his way down through the vegetation than it had been to climb up through it. He drove his way between branches, using his weight to force branches aside. He paused as he discovered the opossum below him, heading upward. They stared at each other for a moment, and then the opossum opened its mouth in a snarl, showing a surprising number of very sharp teeth, and then scurried off onto a side limb, its rat-tailed babies still clinging to its fur.

Nick felt like grinning for the first time that day.

He dropped back down to his old limb, then paused a moment to stretch, carefully testing his muscles. The wound on his left arm had stiffened, and the climb had set it bleeding again.

Standing in the tree, testing his muscles one by one, he almost missed the kid in the boat. He *would* have missed him, if he hadn't seen the white script, *Retired and Gone Fishin'*, through a gap in the leaves.

He knelt on his bough, looking at the boat in surprise. It had passed him in near silence, a big black aluminum boat with a shattered windscreen and no motor. In another few seconds, it would disappear into the flooded grove. A white kid stood in the stern, shoving the boat along with a long pole. His back was turned to Nick, and he clearly hadn't seen him.

"Hey," Nick said, and then, louder, "*Hey!*"

The kid jumped and spun around, and Nick felt a sudden knock at his heart.

The boy's face and hands were striped with black and red, as if they'd been horribly burned.

* * *

The man's voice, coming out of the empty cottonwood grove, nearly scared Jason out of his skin. He turned wildly, almost losing his grip on the pole, and stared out into the trees. He couldn't see anyone.

"Where are you?" he blurted.

"Over here." The voice was a bit more gentle. Jason shaded his eyes and looked in the direction of the sound, and he saw a disheveled black man crouched in a tree, a kind of horror in his staring eyes.

"Can you turn that boat around?" the man asked. "And get me out of this tree?"

Reluctance tugged at Jason's heart. "I guess," he said.

A stranger. An adult. A black man. Any of these would be reason to be wary.

He poled the boat around while he argued with himself. What were the odds that the guy was some kind of criminal or pervert? Here in the middle of a disaster, stuck up a tree in a flood?

It shouldn't matter, he argued, that the guy was black. It wasn't that he didn't like black people, he thought, he got along with the black kids at school just fine, even though they tended to keep to themselves. It was just that he didn't know who the hell this guy was.

Jason sighed. The stranger was a man needing help in the middle of a disaster. What more did Jason need to know?

As Jason poled the boat closer, the details of the stranger's appearance grew less encouraging. The man was splashed with mud and, maybe, blood; his clothes were dirty and torn, and his hair was sticking up in weird tufts. He was unshaven, his eyes were bloodshot, and his skin was covered with lumps.

Well, Jason thought, the guy's been chased up a *tree*, none of that is necessarily his fault.

But he found himself poling more warily, watching the treed man as the boat turned a circle and drifted slowly toward the cottonwood.

And the man, Jason saw, was watching him, with a peculiar intent pop-eyed stare that made Jason nervous. And then the man's expression eased, and he laughed.

"Boy," he said, "what you *got* on you?"

Jason looked down at his arms. "Mud," he said. "I was getting sunburned on the river, so I covered my skin with mud from a mudbank." The man laughed, and Jason felt self-conscious. "I saw it in a movie," Jason said.

"I saw your face covered with that stuff, I thought you'd been burned in a fire," the man said. "Scared the hell out of me. I was afraid I was going to have to get you to a hospital."

Jason smiled. "Sorry."

"We don't find any shade, I'll have to find a mud bank myself."

It was news to Jason that black people got sunburn—how could you tell?—but he supposed the man knew best.

The bows of the boat floated up beneath the treed man, and he carefully lowered himself onto the foredeck. The boat bobbed under his weight, and Jason took a step to keep his balance. Jason's passenger walked in a crouch across the foredeck, then dropped into the cockpit.

"Thanks," he said.

"'Sokay," Jason said.

The man brushed mud off the passenger seat, then sat. He moved his left arm with care, as if there was an injury. And it *looked* like blood.

"I'm Nick," the man said. "Nick Ruford."

"Jason Adams."

Nick Ruford nodded. "Glad you got me out of that tree. I was afraid I was going to starve up there." He licked his lips, looked down at the plastic bottles rolling in the bottom of the boat. "Is that drinking water?"

"It's from the river. It's all I've got to drink." He hesitated. "I drank some, and I didn't get sick."

"Guess I'll stay thirsty a little longer. Got any food?"

"No." Jason pushed with his pole, swung the boat around. The leaves of submerged bushes scratched against the boat's bottom.

"What's this stuff?" Indicating the broken boards that Jason had piled in the cockpit.

"Things I picked up out of the river," Jason said. "To paddle with." And then he added, "Do you know where we are?"

The stranger seemed surprised at the question. "In Tennessee. Not too far north of Memphis."

That far, Jason thought. That far in one night. It took over an hour to drive a car from Cabells Mound to Memphis.

"You look surprised," Nick Ruford said. "Where do you come from? Kentucky?"

"Missouri," Jason said. "Cabells Mound."

"Where's that?"

"I must have come sixty miles overnight."

The stranger looked dubious. "As the crow flies? The river doesn't move that fast. Not even if it's in flood."

Jason looked at him. "It moves that fast *now*. I went through two stretches of rapid, and moved real fast the rest of the time."

A new light dawned in Nick Ruford's eyes. "Rapids, huh," he said. "Bet you're glad you're out of it now."

"The rapids were scary, yeah." He remembered that second rapid, swirling close to a bank just as it began to cave in, a hundred feet of Mississippi mud falling into the river at once . . . the splash had been enough to knock the boat back into midstream, out of danger, but if he'd been there a second earlier or later, the boat would have capsized.

In the morning, when the speed of the river began to slow, he'd found some plastic soft drink bottles floating in the river, and he'd used them to bail. It was slow, waiting for each bottle to fill before emptying it overside, but he had nothing else to do.

Eventually Jason had come aground on the left bank of the river. He was beginning to get sunburned by then, and he'd covered his exposed skin with red mud. He'd found the pole—it was stuck in the crown of a broken levee, just standing there, he didn't know why—and he'd used it to pole the boat along until he came to a break in the levee big enough to pole the boat through. Which he'd done, hoping he'd find civilization on the other side, but he'd found nothing but wilderness.

Nothing but wilderness, till he found Nick Ruford up a tree.

The stranger licked his lips. "This your boat?" he asked.

Jason shook his head. He didn't offer any further explanation. He didn't want to think about Mr. Regan right now.

There were a lot of things he didn't want to think about.

He pushed, felt the pole dig into the Mississippi ooze, pushed the boat ahead. Let the pole fall back into his hands, not grabbing at it.

"How about your parents?" Nick asked.

"Well," Jason said, "my dad's in China." He felt defiance rising in him, looked down at his passenger. "My mother's dead," he said. He could feel his jaw muscles tighten. "She died last night."

The stranger held his gaze for a moment, then looked away. "Sorry," he said.

"Not your fault." Cold anger clenched at Jason's stomach, and he looked up at the sky as he poled the boat forward.

"You know this area?" Jason asked. "Anyplace we can go?"

The stranger shook his head. "I'm from St. Louis. I was just passing through."

"Well." Jason shrugged. "Guess we might as well keep on."

Jason kept the boat's bow pointed south. Insects whined.

The sun lifted toward its zenith, and moist heat smothered the world.

FIFTEEN

Between the first shock and daylight, we counted 27. As day broke we put off from the shore, at which instant we experienced another shock, nearly as violent as the first, by this the fright of the hands was so much increased, that they seemed deprived of strength and reason: I directed Morin to land on a sloping bank at the entrance of the Devil's Race Ground, intending to wait there until the men should be refreshed with a good breakfast. While it was preparing, we had three shocks, so strong as to make it difficult for us to stand on our feet; at length recovered from our panic we proceeded; after this we felt shocks during 6 days, but none to compare with those on the memorable morning of the 16th. I made many and minute observations on this earthquake, which if ever we meet, I will communicate to you, &c.

*Extract of a letter from John Bradbury,
dated Orleans, January 16th*

The sun woke Charlie, and as he opened his eyes he realized how thirsty he was. He opened the car door and stepped out. His wounded leg was stiff and it ached. The air still reeked of smoke, and the world was lit only dimly by the bloated red sun that sat cloaked on the dark horizon.

He needed to get to work, he thought. He needed to be at his desk the second the markets opened.

Charlie limped to the house, crossed the listing portico, and then hesitated as he looked through the open door into the interior. He thought of Megan lying inside. He didn't want to go in.

But he needed something to drink, something to eat.

He needed to use a toilet.

He would stay out of the back hall, he decided. He'd

just go to the kitchen and get some food, and then use the toilet off the living room, not the one in back.

As he stepped into the front hall, he felt reluctance dragging at his feet. He really didn't want to go inside.

The Moët bottle still sat in the front hall. The champagne bucket lay in a puddle of melted ice in the front room. Charlie's shoes crunched on broken glass as he went to the telephone, picked up the receiver.

Nothing. Still nothing.

He went to the kitchen. The quake had walked the refrigerator into the middle of the kitchen, and its door had been open all night. Some of the kitchen cabinets had fallen, and most of the glassware had jumped onto the floor or counters and shattered.

The cleaning lady was due tomorrow, he remembered. He'd have to leave her a big tip.

Charlie found one intact highball glass and went to the sink for a drink. He opened the tap and a third of a glass of water dribbled out. He looked curiously at the tap, then drank the water. He walked to the open refrigerator, and found that it contained two single-serving-size containers of Dannon yogurt, a couple cans of diet drink that Megan had put there, and some duck à l'orange left over from Friday night. The container of milk and a cardboard container of orange juice had tipped over in the quake and poured their contents out onto the floor.

In the door racks he found a small bottle of cocktail onions, anchovies, some low-fat salad dressing, and a couple of green olives floating alone in their jar.

He went to the pantry, which he had converted into a wine rack. Several of the bottles had been pitched from the racks and broken, but most of them were intact.

He shouldn't drink them, though, he thought. Not the reds. The quake would have shaken up the sediment.

He found a clean spoon and ate one of the containers of yogurt while standing in the kitchen and staring out the shattered window at his swimming pool. Now he knew why the neighbor girl wanted some of his water.

He'd have to remember to throw more chlorine into the pool, to keep it drinkable.

He used the toilet, flushed it, and picked his way back to the front hall. He needed to get in his car and get to work. He imagined the legend he would create by walking into the office unshaven, in his shirt sleeves and his torn, bloody slacks. It would show everyone how determined he was, how determined to make money.

But how was he going to get to Tennessee Securities? The garage had collapsed on his car, and he didn't have the keys to Megan's BMW, Megan had them . . .

His mind skittered from the memory of Megan like a cat jumping away from a spray of water.

He couldn't call a cab, because the phones weren't working. Maybe Charlie could get one of his neighbors to give him a lift.

He looked down by his feet and saw the bottle of Moët. He was still thirsty. He unwrapped the foil, removed the wire, eased the cork from the neck of the bottle.

He went outside and sat on the portico and drank the champagne from the bottle. I am still lord of the jungle, he thought. I guessed *right*. All I need to do is get to a terminal somewhere, and I can make *millions*.

He put the half-empty bottle down, and set out to find a car.

"Have you got a Web browser?" asked the man from NASA.

General Jessica Frazetta blinked in the dawn light. "A what?"

"Because the quickest thing we could do," the man said, "is just put the pictures up on our Web site as soon as we get them. You'll see them as fast as we do."

Jessica sighed. "What's the URL?" she asked.

In fact a Web browser was one of the things she possessed. One of her civilian employees had turned up, around midnight, with a laptop computer and an Iridium cellular modem. As soon as he arrived, his computer had been militarized for the duration of the emergency.

Right now Pat was using it, trying to glean useful news off the Net.

Jessica jotted the Web address in her notebook. "Thanks," she said. _____

"If you need any pictures in particular, let us know," the NASA man said.

"All I can tell you right now is that we need pictures of the Mississippi region between Hannibal and Natchez," Jessica said. "And major tributaries as well, particularly the Missouri, Ohio, and the Arkansas."

"I'll tell the boys," the man said. "Keep looking at our Web page, we'll put the pictures up there."

Jessica thanked him and closed her cellphone. She turned toward the military camp that was growing around the damaged buildings of the Mississippi Valley Division.

The air rattled to the sound of portable generators. A tent had been pitched everywhere a tree limb or a building wouldn't fall on it. Mess tent, communications, maps, hospital tent, clerical . . . A number of the tents were piled with furniture and equipment salvaged from the headquarters building, but which hadn't been sorted out yet. Communications and data retrieval systems were being kludged together out of gear pulled out of damaged buildings. Ground lines were still out, but at least radio communications had been restored. All that had been required was the return of her communications specialists, who straggled in over the course of the night. And the Old Man had assured her that she'd be getting a mobile communications unit from Fort Bragg as soon as it could be packed onto a helicopter and flown out.

Her command was sorting itself out, at least locally. What Jessica lacked was information on which to act elsewhere. Communications were wrecked in precisely those parts of the country she was trying to reach. The St. Louis and Memphis districts of the MVD were still out of communication, though Rock Island had finally reported in around three in the morning, and was loudly claiming that it was *not* a victim district. Jessica, whose insistence to her own superiors had been no less ardent, was willing to give them the benefit of the doubt.

Still, Rock Island was able to report the situation only in its immediate area. Jessica needed to find out what was happening elsewhere, where the levees had broken, where the floods were spreading.

She had thought of satellite maps first thing. But her first call to the National Reconnaissance Office, which handled military satellites, informed her that the NRO would not be of much use. So that each American satellite could cover the entire globe, each had been placed in six-hour polar orbits, fixed in inertial space while the earth turned under it. But the NRO, with its brief to provide data on enemies and rivals of the U.S., had never been *interested* in satellite maps of North America—if they wanted a map of North America, they'd contact Rand-McNally. So the satellites' orbits were timed to pass over North America at *night*, precisely when there was little point in taking pictures.

Jessica had been urged to contact the space agency NASA and the National Oceanic and Atmospheric Administration, which ran the weather satellites, and the privatized company LANDSAT, which sold satellite imagery round the world.

At least Jessica hadn't been urged to buy Russian photos. She'd probably have to do it with her personal credit card.

It took a lot of effort to get the right person at NOAA. "I've been trying to get ahold of *you*," Jessica was told finally. "But your people at the Pentagon gave me a number that isn't working."

"This is my cellphone." Jessica gave the man her number.

"I wanted to tell you," the man said, "that as soon as we get the images, we're going to be putting the latest pictures of the disaster areas up on our Web page. Do you want the URL?"

Jessica sighed. "Sure," she said. "Let me get a pencil."

"Mr. President," said the chairman of the Federal Reserve, "it is my sad duty to inform you that we cannot pay for the reconstruction of this nation's earthquake damage."

The President felt his weariness fall away in a surge of adrenaline. "I think you had better explain," he said through clenched teeth. He was very tired of people telling him what he *couldn't* do.

The chairman adjusted his spectacles. The President had chosen to meet him in the Oval Office, a more dignified venue than the noisy, chaotic Situation Room

"Sir," the chairman said, "if the reports are true—if *half* the reports are true—then I regret to say that there is not enough liquidity in the United States to support reconstruction. By which I mean to say—" he added with greater haste, as he saw presidential anger glowing—"by which I mean that *this* nation cannot pay for it. So London will pay for it, and Tokyo, and Singapore. And the rest of the world, probably."

"Yes?" the President said.

"American investments and commitments abroad will have to be withdrawn. Dollars will come home to finance reconstruction." The chairman gazed over the President's shoulder into the garden, and his nostrils twitched as if hoping to scent a rose. "There will be a lot of volatility in the currency and bond markets," he said. "Speculators are going to work this all out sooner rather than later. I may have to delay action to let the situation cool. But believe me, sir, that those dollars will come home."

"Thank you, Sam," the President said.

"I cautioned you last week," the chairman went on, "that though indicators were mixed, there might be a trend toward recession." He gave a heavy sigh. "I must inform you now that the recession is inevitable, that it will be worldwide, and that it will be deep and prolonged. Our investment dollars are a significant prop to the world economy, and we will have to knock that prop out just at the moment that economy has become vulnerable. The United States is the engine that drives the world economy, and now that engine is crippled."

Worldwide recession, the President thought. Factories closing, workers on the dole, emerging economies plunging back into darkness. And with economic desperation came political instability: riots, fanaticism, tyranny, terror, civil war, mothers bayoneted, and babies starving.

So, the President thought, the rest of the world, as well as the most needy parts of America, were on their own.

"We need a plan, Sam," the President said. "An economic plan that I can present to Congress when I call them back into emergency session. Because if we *don't* have a plan, they're just going to throw money at the situation, more or less randomly, and much of it will go to waste."

The chairman nodded. "I will work with your people. I believe that in the present emergency, the people will understand that the barriers between my office and the Executive Branch should be relaxed."

The President's phone buzzed, and he picked up the receiver and listened for a few moments. He said, "Thank you," and hung up. He looked across his desk at the chairman.

"The Israeli Defense Forces have just gone on full alert," he said. "They're calling up reserves."

The chairman looked thoughtful. "Are they attacking anyone?"

"We're not sure."

"Let's hope they're just being cautious, Mr. President. But my guess is that mobilization won't be the last. Other nations may well wonder if we have the ability—or the will—to stand by our security commitments."

The President gave the chairman a hard look. "*I* have the will."

The chairman gave a shrug. "Well. I will try to make certain that you also have the money."

"There's leaking around the base of the dam structure. Frankly, I do not like it."

Neither did Jessica Frazetta. Bagnall Dam held all of Lake Ozark at bay, and the thought of that huge lake spilling down its channel was enough to give her shivers.

"I don't see that we have any choice," Jessica said. She paced back and forth, cellphone held to her ear as she talked to the civilian engineer whose responsibility included the dam. "We've got to release as much water as possible, take the pressure off that dam."

"Yes, ma'am. But the Osage is already at a high stage, and that'll mean flooding. When it hits the Missouri, it'll probably flood all the way up to Jefferson City."

"At least Jefferson City will have warning," Jessica said. "Which is more than they'll have if the dam fails."

She had, at long last, heard about the failure of the Clarence Cannon Dam and the wall of water that had torn its way through the rich Illinois bottom land on its route to the Mississippi. Hundreds of people were missing. Nothing like that was going to happen again, not if she could prevent it.

"Very good, Miss Frazetta. I'll start dumping all the water I can."

Jessica rang off. Her ear ached from the many hours she'd spent with her cellphone pressed against it. It was very possible that she'd give herself a cauliflower ear before this was all over.

Her dutiful staff had prepared the morning SITREP, a copy of which she carried in her pocket. The Situation Report duly noted everything they knew or did not know, from which flood control structures had failed to how many of their own personnel were injured or missing. The list of "unknowns" was much larger than the list of items of which the staff were certain.

Jessica's stomach growled. She remembered she hadn't eaten since the previous day's lunch. And she hadn't slept since before that.

She went to the mess tent. The tent echoed to the chatter of a large number of women and children. Many of Jessica's returning subordinates had straggled onto base complete with their families and a fair selection of their possessions. Their houses and trailers had been wrecked, the district was in chaos, and Jessica could forgive them for figuring that if anyone in this situation was going to have food, shelter, and clothing, it would be the Army.

Jessica hadn't the heart to turn these refugees away. Besides, from a strictly utilitarian point of view, she could hardly expect her subordinates, almost all of whom were civilians, to give their all for the Army while they were worried sick about their families.

But she had made rules. *Everyone works* was the first. Adults were to assist Corps personnel in pitching tents, setting up gear, policing the area, and cooking. Older children helped as well, or watched the younger children. The only people excused were those too young to have a job, and those injured in the quake, who were sent to the hospital tent.

Jessica tried not to think about liability issues. Could she be sued if one of her civilians was injured by a falling branch? If one of the children tripped over a tent line and broke a leg?

She put out orders that non-Corps personnel were not to enter the damaged buildings on any of the various ongoing salvage operations. She figured that might limit her liability in at least one direction.

The mess tent's sides were rolled up to provide ventilation, and a few scavenged tables and chairs had been set up. Some young children in one corner were sitting in a circle and playing a game under the direction of an older child. The woman behind the improvised counter—a battered old folding table—looked at Jessica and smiled. "We've got oatmeal coming up, General," she said. "Would you like a cup of coffee while you wait?"

Jessica hesitated. She hadn't had coffee in eight years. Everyone said it made her too hyper.

Hell, she figured, the country *needed* hyper right now.

"I would absolutely love a cup of joe," Jessica said. "Black, with two sugars."

When Jessica was handed the white porcelain mug, she held it under her nose and breathed in the fragrance. Her mouth watered.

It tasted as wonderful as she remembered.

"It's impossible," said Mrs. Shawbutt, Charlie's neighbor. She was strangely dressed in a caftan, a wide-brimmed straw hat, and large dark glasses with pale blue lenses. "The roads are too torn up, the bridges are all out—there's no way you can drive downtown. And besides—" She looked significantly at the column of smoke rising on the horizon. "Downtown's on fire. The radio is saying people shouldn't try to leave their homes unless their lives are in danger."

"I've got to get to a phone," Charlie said. "Or a computer."

Mrs. Shawbutt shook her head. "Phones are out. Even cell-phones, I hear." She looked at him through her hornrims. "Have you been drinking, Mr. Johns?"

Charlie shrugged. "No water, love. I drank what I could find."

"You should be careful. You can get dehydrated if you drink alcohol."

"I'll get something later."

He gave his neighbor a wave and walked out into the street. No one was cooperating with his plan to get to work—he'd asked everyone he knew, and they'd all given the same answer. He looked at the Breitling on his wrist, saw that the New York Exchange would open in less than an hour.

"Might as well walk," Charlie muttered to himself. Surely he would find a cab somewhere. Or, if need be, a bus.

He remembered Mrs. Shawbutt in her big straw hat. "Be careful of the sun," he reminded himself.

He went back to his house to get a cap from the front hall closet. It featured the logo of the St. Louis Cardinals, and it was the cap he wore when he lost at golf to Dearborne.

Charlie put the cap on his head. He buttoned his collar and straightened and tightened his tie. He looked at himself in the hall mirror that, surprisingly, had neither fallen nor cracked. Brushed scuffmarks off his shoes. He was ready for work.

He stepped over the gap between the house and the front portico—have to call his insurance people when he got to his office—and then he looked down at the half-empty bottle of Moët. He hesitated for a moment, then picked up the bottle.

The heat of the day was already rising. Charlie could feel sweat gathering under his cap. He started down the street, the bottle swinging at the end of his arm. His stiff leg eased as he walked. He waved at the people he saw, who had slept in their cars or on their lawns.

He turned right at the corner, drank some champagne, and kept on walking. The huge pillar of smoke loomed right ahead of him.

This street was much the same as his own. All the houses had been damaged; all the chimneys had fallen; two houses had collapsed. One of the houses that still stood had been burnt out. The gutters were full of water—apparently a water main had broken.

Charlie looked ahead, saw something disturbing ahead, slowed. He approached the strange sight with a frown.

Right across his path was a crack in the earth, cutting left and right across the street, over curbs and through yards, and beneath one partially collapsed home. The crack was about three feet wide, and five or six feet down had filled with black, silent water. The ground had dropped three feet on Charlie's side, or risen on the other, because Charlie faced a little cliff of raw earth topped by broken asphalt.

Charlie took a drink of the champagne and looked at the chasm. He paced uncertainly back and forth.

It wasn't that wide, he thought. He could cross it in one jump.

Charlie's inner ear gave a lurch, and the ground trembled, just a little. Bubbles rose to the surface in the black water at the bottom of the chasm.

Charlie's heart thudded in his chest. Weakness shivered through his limbs. He took another drink of the champagne.

"I am Lord of the Jungle," he said. But in his mind all he could see was Megan's body lying in his bedroom.

Tears burned his eyes. The chasm had cut clean across his world.

He didn't remember when he turned around and began the walk home. But some time later he found himself standing on the walk outside his house, an empty Moët bottle in his hands.

He sat behind the wheel of Megan's car and picked up the

cellphone that was lying on the seat and began to punch in numbers.

No one answered.

Prime Power.

Helicopters circled overhead, judging the correct approach to the helipad that Jessica's people had chain-sawed and bulldozed across the road from the Post Exchange. Rotors flogged the air, beat at Jessica's ears. She grinned.

She was in *charge* of this. It was glorious.

Things were coming together. Once the choppers discharged their cargo, which would include state-of-the-art field communications equipment, she could really take charge of her division.

"Finally got a meteorology report, General." Her secretary, Nelda, had been working on this task, among others, ever since she'd finally walked on base at ten o'clock that morning in mud-streaked sweat pants and her most sensible shoes.

"Can you summarize?"

"A high-pressure system will start moving through early tomorrow morning. Forecast is cooler and gusty tomorrow, followed by several clear days."

Jessica nodded. "Good," she said. There would be a few good days for operations, at least, though she knew that there might be problems later on. A rotating high pressure front moving over the plains would, as it passed, pull a lot of hot, moist air from the Gulf of Mexico in its wake. When this air cooled it would dump a lot of rain on the western plains, which would increase the danger of flood.

But there would be at least a few days for the flooded areas to drain first. That was good news.

"Any luck getting ahold of CERI?" Jessica asked.

"Nope. None." Nelda had to shout over the throbbing of the helicopters.

One of the aspects of the Corps' earthquake plan involved coordination with the Center for Earthquake Research and

Information at the University of Memphis. CERI had not, however, been answering its phone.

Jessica suspected that the Center for Earthquake Research had been wiped out by earthquake. One of life's little ironies.

"The city engineer's office sent someone over to inquire about restoring Vicksburg's electrical supply."

Jessica shook her head. "We don't have enough generating capacity to do that."

"He meant helping to repair the *lines*. We mostly get our power from that nuclear plant south of here."

Jessica stared at her. "From *where*?" she said.

Nelda stared back, only now absorbing the horror that Jessica felt rolling through her heart.

"But," Nelda said, "surely it's somebody's job to look after the power plants." Her eyes widened. "Isn't it?" she said.

On the morning of Monday last the 16th inst. several shocks were felt—four have been ascertained by an accurate observer to have been felt in this city. The principal one, as near as can be collected, was about ten minutes past two o'clock, A.M. There was no noise heard in the atmosphere but in a few instances in certain situations—The shock was attended by a tremulous motion of the earth and buildings—felt by some for about one and a half minutes; by others about five; and my own impression is, that I am conscious of its lasting at least three, having been awakened from my sleep. Several clocks were stopped at two or about ten minutes after. Several articles were thrown off the shelves; crockery was sent rolling about the floor; articles suspended from the ceiling of the stores vibrated rapidly without any air to disturb them, for about nine inches; the plastering in the rooms of some houses was cracked and injured; the river was much convulsed, so much that it induced some of the boatmen at the landing, who supposed the bank was falling in, to cut adrift. The shocks in the morning were at about six or half after, one of them considerable. The vibration of suspended articles was, whenever room would admit them, east to west. Accounts from

Louisiana state, that the first shock was felt about ten min-
utes past 2, A.M. at Black river, thirty miles distant, and at
different places on the road to Rapids, where the trees were
violently agitated. It was also felt on the river at a consider-
able distance above and below Vidalia. The shock was also felt
as far up as the Big Black, and at the different intervening
towns; in the vicinity of Washington the trees were observed
to be much convulsed, nodding their heads together as if com-
ing to the ground.

Natchez Weekly Chronicle, *January 20, 1812*

The thing about helicopters was the way gravity kept moving around. G forces went up, down, sideways, and sometimes in circles. The shifts from one state to the next were
often very sudden.

Jessica *loved* helicopters. But then she liked roller-coaster
rides, too. She sat up front, in the copilot's seat, where she
could get a view of the world zooming past.

The pilot was happy to impress the general with a display
of his skills. He skimmed his Bell Kiowa over the WES,
banked, put the chopper's nose down, and headed south.
Adrenaline sang happily in Jessica's veins.

Pity she'd never had time to learn how to fly one of these
things.

"Just follow the river," Jessica said. She watched with
interest—this was the best view she'd had since the quake—
as the Kiowa Warrior sped over the flat, tree-filled country
below Vicksburg's bluff. At least a third of the trees seem to
have fallen. The roads were blocked with fallen timber and
cut by crevasses or sudden uplifts. Of the few structures
Jessica could see, most were heavily damaged, especially the
larger buildings.

She clenched her teeth at the sight of the broken levees, the
way the river continued to pour through the gaps. Those
were USACE levees, damn it, and Corps levees hadn't broken since the 1930s. And now when it happened, it was on
Jessica's watch.

She should have covered her ass. All it would have taken was a letter in her file, directed to her superiors, expressing concern about earthquake preparedness. "I was working on it from Day One," she could have said, "but my superiors didn't respond in time. And the record supports this."

Still, there was small comfort to be drawn. Jessica saw no sign of massive failure in the levees, no huge mile-long crevasses. The levees didn't look as if they'd broken all at once; they showed every sign of having been weakened, not destroyed, in the quake. And then river water, with the weight of the whole Mississippi behind it, pushed inexorably into the levees' weak points, strained the structures, crawled underneath to undermine the levees from below, put more pressure on them until at last they gave way. The flooding wouldn't have been catastrophically sudden, and Jessica hoped this meant people had a chance to get away from the rising water.

It also meant that once the floods subsided, repair would be that much easier.

The pilot's voice grated on Jessica's headphones. "There's your power plant, General." She looked up and saw the distinctive outline of a cooling tower rising above the trees, the graceful white double curves. But the grace was marred, she saw, part of it had peeled away like the rind of a fruit.

Her heart gave a lurch. She wasn't sure she was ready for this.

The Kiowa sped past the tower, and the pilot banked to give Jessica a view of the plant. Poinsett Landing was a wreck, most of its buildings broken, the river streaming through the wreckage. There was evidence of fire. The big black cube that held the reactor was intact, though—no shattered roof and pillar of murderous radioactive smoke á la Chernobyl, thank God—but the two big buildings leaning against the reactor, which she assumed were control structures, had clearly suffered degrees of damage.

The pilot's voice interrupted Jessica's thoughts. "This isn't a nuke plant, is it, General?"

"Yes. This is nuclear."

"Should we be wearing moon suits? Shall I get us some altitude?"

"I don't think that's necessary." She hoped.

"Yes, sir."

Jessica noticed, however, that the Kiowa began to crab slightly away from the reactor complex. A little caution in the pilot's hands. And then one of the hands pointed.

"Some survivors, General. On that little hill over there."

The Kiowa rotated in space while maintaining its bank, and Jessica saw a clump of people—waving, jumping up and down, probably screaming their heads off—on a flat grassy hill near the perimeter fence.

"Call your outfit," Jessica said. "Tell them we need a dustoff."

Larry Hallock let the others run waving and shouting as the Army helicopter roared overhead. He was too tired and hungry and sore to race around like a lunatic, so he just sat on the tailgate of Bill Henry's camper pickup, cradled his arm, and waited.

The burned man had died in the night, screaming. Some of the injured were nearly comatose. No one had been able to help.

He had expected rescue before now. Someone in the Department of Energy, someone in the power company. He had figured he'd see the first helicopters silhouetted against the red dawn.

Instead it had been hours. Things must be worse out there than he'd thought.

And while he waited, he'd seen that there was a current in the flood waters. Up till the morning they had been still, a calm brown lake that ringed the old Indian mound. But then the waters had begun to move. The debris that had been floating atop the water was carried away downstream, and as time passed the debris began moving by faster. Larry had watched to see if the level of the water was declining, if the current meant that the flood was draining away.

But the water level didn't fall, and the current grew in

power. Which meant that Poinsett Landing, the reactor vessel included, now sat on part of the bed of the Mississippi River.

There was a flurry of people running to their vehicles, and then cars and trucks began to clear an area on top of the mound. The roar of the chopper increased to painful levels, a jet whine combined with the flogging of the rotors, and Larry felt blasts of wind on his face. The copter—it seemed pretty small for something that could make such a big noise—settled with surprising grace onto the cleared space of the mound.

Larry dropped off the pickup gate and shuffled toward the helicopter, holding his injured arm. His neck and shoulder throbbed. Some of the other people had suggested he'd broken a collarbone, but it was impossible to tell without an X ray.

A door slid open on the side of the helicopter, and an officer jumped out. A woman, Larry saw with some surprise. A *short* woman. A short woman with a flier's helmet and Ray-Bans and camouflage fatigues and the stars of a general.

Larry blinked. When the government finally got around to moving, it moved with authority.

"Do you have any injured?" the woman general shouted. "And who is in charge?"

Lieutenant Grimsley was a National Guard second lieutenant with washed-out blue eyes and a dusting of acne on his cheeks. "Sheriff," he told Omar, "I'm supposed to tell you that we're pulling out."

"What?" Omar blinked at Grimsley sleepily.

Omar stood out in front of the courthouse, supervising the crews that were chainsawing away the fallen limbs of the lawn's blackjack oaks. The old trees had taken a beating, and a couple of them were going to have to be cut down.

The Mourning Confederate, looking somberly down from his pillar, had survived without a scratch or a crack. Omar liked to think of it as an omen.

"The President has called up our outfit," Grimsley said.

"We're heading north to help restore order in Arkansas." Grimsley seemed proud of this fact.

Omar tried to clear the weariness from his mind. He had caught a couple hours' sleep toward dawn, but he'd been wakened by an aftershock and the jolt of electricity the shock had put in his veins had kept him from getting back to sleep.

"But what about Spottswood Parish?" Omar asked. "We need you boys here."

"Sorry, Sheriff. But things here are pretty much under control, and I guess the President figured we'd be more useful up north."

Faggot President, Omar thought wearily. *This was just like that asshole.*

"When do you boys pull out?" he asked.

"Soon's we can load up the trucks with seventy-two hours' rations."

"Well." Omar offered his hand. "Good luck, son."

They shook hands. "Thanks, Sheriff."

A chainsaw stuttered as it caught an oakwood knot. Omar looked up, felt sweat trickle down the back of his neck.

He'd done his job, he figured. More than the President had. And voters would remember *that* come the next election.

Omar figured his career was right on track.

Omar was at the armory when the National Guard pulled out. All those guardsmen were voters—some were even his deputies—and he figured that it would be a good thing to pump a few hands as they loaded up.

The guardsmen were in battle dress and helmets, and they carried their rifles. All except one man, who Omar to his surprise recognized as Micah Knox.

"I'm heading north." Knox grinned. "Your Guard are giving me a ride."

"Great," Omar said.

Knox indicated the heavy duffel bag on his shoulder. "I went by your house and picked up my stuff," he said. "Don't worry about it."

"I won't."

"Your house is okay, by the way. Your buddy Ozie was there with his trucks and jacks. He said that you and Wilona can move back in tonight."

"Great." Omar looked at the duffel, at the way it weighed on the kid's shoulder, and knew that Knox had retrieved his firearms and ammunition.

Well. At least he was taking the guns out of town.

"Hey, Sheriff! Hold still for a picture!"

Omar turned to see Sorrell Ellen of the *Spottswood Chronicle* pointing a camera. He sensed Knox fade quickly from the frame. Omar stepped in the other direction just as the camera flashed.

Omar blinked as purple blooms filled his vision. "Dang," Sorrell said. "You moved."

"Why don't you get a picture of me saying good-bye to one of my deputies?" Omar said.

"That's good," Sorrell agreed.

He led Sorrell toward one of the trucks parked on the gravel drive in front of the armory. He saw Micah Knox fading away behind another truck, his heavy duffel bearing down one thin shoulder.

"Do you have any comments on the emergency?" Sorrell asked.

"Just that I'm very proud of the way my department has responded," Omar said. "We've kept order, helped save lives, maintained communications that were vital to the parish."

Sorrell jotted this down. "Several of your deputies are moving out with the Guard, aren't they?" he asked. "Aren't you going to be short-handed?"

Omar left that unanswered as he spotted one of his deputies, Frank Schwinn, in the act of loading gear onto the truck. He and Schwinn paused for the photo, and by that time Sorrell had forgotten about his last question.

Deputies, Omar thought. He was going to need to make some more, and he figured he knew just who to call.

Hell, he was their Kleagle.

SIXTEEN

Precisely at 2 o'clock on Monday morning, the 16th instant, we were all alarmed by the violent and convulsive agitation of the boats, accompanied by a noise similar to that which would have been produced by running over a sand bar—every man was immediately roused and rushed upon deck.
—We were first of opinion that the Indians, studious of some mischief, had loosed our cables, and thus situated we were foundering. Upon examination, however, we discovered we were yet safely and securely moored. The idea of an earthquake then suggested itself to my mind, and this idea was confirmed by a second shock, and two others in immediate succession. These continued for the space of eight minutes. So complete and general had been the convulsion, that a tremendous motion was communicated to the very leaves on the surface of the earth. A few yards from the spot where we lay, the body of a large oak was snapped in two, and the falling part precipitated to the margin of the river; the trees in the forest shook like rushes; the alarming clattering of their branches may be compared to the affect which would be produced by a severe wind passing through a large cane brake.

Exposed to a most unpleasant alternative, we were compelled to remain—here we were for the night, or subject ourselves to imminent hazard in navigating through the innumerable obstructions in the river; considering the danger of running two-fold, we concluded to remain. At the dawn of day I went on shore to examine the effects of the shocks; the earth about 20 feet from the water's edge was deeply cracked, but no visible injury of moment had been sustained; fearing, however, to remain longer where we were, it was thought much advisable to leave our landing as expeditiously as possible; this was immediately done—at a few rods distance *from the shore, we experienced a fifth shock, more severe than either of the preceding. I had expected this from the louring appearance of the weather, it was indeed most providential that we had started, for such was the strength of this last shock, that the bank to which we were (but a few moments since) attached, was rent and fell into the river, whilst the trees rushed from the forests, precipitating themselves into the water with a force sufficient to have dashed us into a thousand atoms.*

Chronicle of Mr. Pierce, December 25, 1811

Jason poled *Retired and Gone Fishin'* through the stillness of the trees. His passenger Nick had begun to drowse in one of the front seats. This was all right with Jason. He preferred to be alone with his thoughts. The cottonwoods gave way to pine, and the floods slowly ebbed, bringing the tops of bushes and saplings above the water. Other than Nick, he saw no human being.

Edge Living, Jason thought. He'd hung posters to Edge Living in his room, but he'd never known what Edge Living was: living like a refugee, bereft of food, water, and shelter; lost in a disaster that seemed to have overtaken the whole world.

That was the Edge, all right. And Jason didn't want it anymore.

Eventually the boat floated up to an unbroken green levee stretching left and right across its path. Dozens of cows, white with black splotches, grazed on the levee's grassy flanks, which they shared with large refugee flocks of birds. Jason looked in each direction and realized he'd floated into the channel of a small river. Turning right, he thought, would take him back to the Mississippi, and a left turn would take him inland. He poled the boat to the levee and felt the bow thud up its grassy bank.

Nick opened his eyes. "What's happening?" he said.

"Thought I'd go up the levee and look to see which way to go," Jason said.

"I'll do it," Nick said.

Jason was sick of the boat and wanted to go himself, but

Nick jumped out of the boat as if he wanted to make all the decisions, and so as Nick walked up the flank of the levee, Jason just sighed and leaned on his pole to keep the boat's bow pressed firmly on the grass.

"More water on the other side," Nick reported from the top. He looked inland, took a few more steps to get a better view. "Can't see much but trees," he said.

Jason scratched at the mud that coated his arm, sending flakes spiraling to the boat's deck. Insects hummed about his ears.

And then there was a bellow, and a yell, and Nick came pelting back down the bank. "Jesusjesusjesus!" he panted, and Jason looked in surprise to see an enraged cow topping the levee. The cow paused for a moment, its head swinging back and forth in search of a target, and then it spotted Nick again, lowered its horns, and began to charge down the bank. "Jesusjesusjesus!"

Nick shoved at the boat's bow, pushed it into the water, and threw himself headlong across the foredeck. The cow paused partway down the flank of the levee, its forefeet spread in challenge. The boat swung out onto the water.

Jason collapsed in laughter, the pole clattering under his arm. Nick glared at him from the bows.

"God damn it! This isn't funny!"

Laughter continued to erupt from Jason. The boat spun as it drifted across the flat, shimmering surface of the water.

Nick crawled across the foredeck and dropped into one of the seats. "It isn't funny," he insisted. "Bulls are dangerous."

"That's not a bull!" Jason laughed. He pointed. "It's a cow! It's got that bag thing between its legs!"

The boat spun lazily in the water and gave Nick a good look at the cow. "Okay," he said. "Okay. But cows have horns, too."

This struck Jason as the most hilarious thing he'd ever heard. Water sloshed in the bottom of the boat as he sat on a corner of the stern while the laughter bent him double. Nick glowered for a long moment, then ventured a reluctant smile. "Well," he said, "I've had no luck with wildlife today, that's for sure."

Jason clutched his aching sides. Dried mud flaked off him like a brown blizzard. He ran out of air and his laughter ran dry. A hiccup straightened him up in surprise, and then he began laughing again. Laughter and hiccups alternated as the boat spiraled down the river. Finally the laughter faded.

"Sorry," Jason said finally.

Nick looked resentfully at the cow. "I wish I could come back here and turn that cow into steaks."

Jason looked over his shoulder and remembered how hungry he was. He hiccuped. "Guess that's what the cow was worried about," he said.

Nick rubbed his eyes. "I think the cow was just crazy. That quake made everything crazy—people, animals, the river . . ." He shook his head. "Wish I'd kept that snake. Could've eaten it."

Jason looked at him. "Snake?"

"Never mind." Nick sat up straighter, peered over the boat's bows. "Are those cattails over there? Could you pole us closer?"

Cattails, Jason thought. Snakes. It occurred to him that his passenger could be as crazy as the cow.

He hiccuped.

He picked up the pole and trailed one end overboard, like a brake, till the boat's spinning motion ceased, and then he dug the pole into the creek bottom and propelled it toward the patch of cattails.

The tails' sodden heads were just above the water. Nick hung over the side of the boat and began pulling the cattails up from the bottom of the creek. He threw them flopping over the boat's little foredeck.

Jason watched Nick carefully in case he turned out to be crazy.

"Cattails are edible," Nick said. "We can fill our stomachs with these."

Jason looked at the slimy plants lying on the foredeck. "You first."

"Sure." Nick reached for another fistful of cattail, pulled it from the river bottom. "I've eaten cattail plenty of times.

When we visited my great-aunt in Mississippi, she'd fix us lots of wild greens. If we had some wild onion and poke-weed, we could have a salad." He looked red-eyed over his shoulder at Jason. "Poor folks' salad," he said, making his point. "Hold the boat steady, now."

Now it's my fault I'm not poor, Jason thought. *Listen asshole, I'm a lot poorer than you are. Bet you anything.*

Jason put his weight on the pole and swung the boat left and right until Nick had pulled up a whole armful of plant matter. Then he poled off while Nick resumed his seat, rinsed off a cattail, and started eating the shoot near the root. "You can eat the soft part, see," he said.

Jason nursed his hiccups and watched Nick warily. Nick tossed overboard the part of the cattail he wasn't going to eat, then reached for another.

"We going upstream or down?" Jason asked. "What do you think?"

He did not want to go back to the Mississippi. The river had destroyed his home, drowned his friend and probably his mother, had flung him down rapids and tried to kill him. He didn't want to see that river again.

"If we go inland," Nick said, "we don't know *where* we're going. We know what's *down* the Mississippi. There are bound to be people there who can help us. If we go inland, we could wander around forever and never find anyone in better shape than we are."

"The Mississippi's full of rapids," Jason said. "And we'd have to stick close to the bank because this pole won't reach too far."

Nick looked at the cattail in his fist. "I've got a daughter downstream, in Arkansas. I'd like to get to her."

Jason looked at him. "You're not planning on going all the way in this boat, are you?"

"Well," eating the cattail, "before we decide, maybe we should take stock of what we've got."

"I've got a telescope," Jason said. "*That'll* get us to Arkansas all right."

Nick gnawed on his cattail stalk as he began looking under

hatch covers. "What's this red thing?" he said, looking at the Astroscan.

"That's my telescope."

"Really? It's funny looking." He opened another hatch, pulled out a heavy metal box, and opened the lid. It was filled with fishing tackle.

"Well, there we go," Nick said.

Jason looked at the tackle box in surprise. He hadn't seen it there last night, not in the dark. "No fishing poles," he said.

"Don't need 'em. There's spare line—we can just hang it over the end of the boat and troll."

"Okay." Jason felt annoyance creeping round his thoughts. Why was Nick messing around with his boat? *He* should have found that stuff.

"So we catch a fish," Jason said, "how we gonna cook it?"

"Maybe we'll have sushi."

"Gaah." Jason made a face. He wished Nick would just sit down and let him pole. He had done fine before Nick came on board.

Nick grinned. "No, we shouldn't eat freshwater fish raw. Not unless it's a choice between that or starvation. We could get flukes that would eat our liver."

"Get *what*?"

"Flukes. Little worms."

"So we don't get to eat raw fish," Jason said. "It breaks my heart."

Nick opened more hatches. Water sloshed. "We can keep fish alive in these cages till we're ready to eat them."

Another hatch. "Batteries," Nick mused. "Why batteries?"

"To start the motor? Run lights at night?" Jason wasn't quite able to keep sarcasm out of his voice.

Nick bent over, tracing the cables from the batteries. He looked under the boat's front casting deck, then gave a grunt. He reached beneath the deck, grunted, pulled something from brackets.

What lay in Nick's hands looked like a little outboard, a tiny motor at one end, a propeller at the other. And an electric cord wrapped in a neat coil and tied.

Nick jumped up on the front deck, connected the motor to a bracket right on the bow. Plugged the cord into an ordinary electric socket sitting flush on the deck. Then turned a switch.

There was a kind of a muffled thud, and Jason felt the motion of the boat change. It straightened its course and picked up speed.

"We've got a little electric motor, see," Nick said. "It must be for trolling."

Jason let the pole hang from the end of his arm. "You mean we've had power all along?" he said.

"More or less. We shouldn't use it too much, though, we don't have any way of recharging the batteries."

Jason felt despair wrap around him like a black cloak. If he'd known the motor was there—if he'd just had the brains to search the boat until he'd found it—he could have got the boat moving last night and saved his mother. Or if he'd accepted any of old Mr. Regan's offers to take him fishing, he would have known the motor was there, and he could have used it right away.

And his mother would be alive and they would be on their way back to Los Angeles and he wouldn't be on this stupid boat with a stupid stranger.

"*Shit!*" he shouted. He raised his pole and threw it as far as he could. The water received it with a splash.

Nick looked at him in surprise. "Something wrong?"

Jason threw himself onto one of the cockpit seats. "Nothing," he said. He put his head in his hands.

He was an idiot, he thought. A total fuckdroid. If he'd just known the motor was *there* . . .

The boat made almost no noise as Nick edged it toward the floating pole. He shut off the electric motor as the pole bumped against the side, and then he reached for it, pulled it in, held the pole dripping in his hands.

"Maybe I'll pole for a while," he said. "That okay with you?"

"Sure." Jason edged away to give him room.

Nick looked at him. "Would you rather go inland, Jason?

Is that what you'd rather? Because I'll go where you want—it's your boat." He sounded as if he grudged that fact.

"I don't care," Jason said.

"I think it's safe enough on the big river now," Nick went on. "We can use the electric motor to get out of trouble."

"*I don't care,*" Jason insisted. The river, he decided, was his fate. It had destroyed his whole existence; if it wanted to take his life as well, along with that of the stupid stranger, then it was welcome to do so.

Jason moved forward, slouched in the shotgun seat. "I'm going to take a nap." He closed his eyes and tried to get comfortable.

He could sense Nick hesitating, on the verge of saying something more, but then came the splash as the pole dipped, and a surge as the boat began to move. Water chimed at the bow. Then there was a series of frantic splashes as Nick tried to adjust the boat's course, but the boat was traveling too fast for the pole to get a purchase on the bottom, so Nick had to wait for it to slow down before he could pole again.

Jason smiled to himself. The boat was heavy and awkward to move with a pole. It had taken him a long time to work out the proper procedure—give the boat a push, then let the pole hang over the stern and use it like a rudder to keep the boat on the right course until the boat began to run out of momentum.

Jason saw no reason why he should instruct Nick in this procedure. Let him discover it on his own.

More poling, more splashing. Shuddering and a grinding noise as the side scraped bark from a tree.

And what'll you do, Jason thought at Nick, *when the pole gets stuck in the mud?*

This had happened to Jason. Suddenly the pole stuck fast, but the boat kept moving out from under him, and as the adrenaline surged through his veins he had to make an instant decision whether to hang onto the pole, or stay in the boat. Fortunately he'd made the right decision and stayed with the boat instead of hanging above the flood atop the pole. And when he did that, when he let go of the pole, it had fallen and clattered into the boat on its own accord. And that's what had happened every time since.

Push, surge. Push, surge. Nick seemed to be getting the hang of it, and faster than Jason had.

Insects whined about Jason's ears. *Go bite the cows,* he told them mentally.

Then he heard an alarmed cry from Nick. The boat swayed. There was a clatter as the pole bounced off the stern, and then muttered curses as Nick picked up the pole. Obviously the pole had got stuck in the mud, and Nick had been forced into the same split-second decision that Jason had faced earlier.

Nick had chosen correctly. Jason didn't know whether he was sorry about that or not.

Strange kid, Nick thought. *Alone on the river with a bass boat, a telescope, and an attitude.*

Nick watched Jason's head slumped down on his chest. The boy was exhausted.

Mother dead and father in China. Nick didn't know whether to believe it or not. But he wasn't going to challenge the kid's story—if it was true, if Jason had just lost his mother in the quake, then Nick wasn't going to intrude on the kid's feelings.

His own feelings were screwed up enough, he figured, without his trying to cope with someone else's.

Push, withdraw, steer. Push, withdraw, steer. His wounded arm ached at each thrust of the pole, but the pain eased as the muscle worked at the simple, repetitive task. Nick tried to let the motion relax him, but sometimes he saw the trees tremble in an aftershock, or his memory flashed on Viondi dying, or he saw a thick creeper that reminded him of the water moccasin, and a wave of rage would shake his body like a terrier shaking a rat. He found himself standing on the boat's afterdeck with his hands clenched around the pole, his jaw muscles working, his eyes glancing left and right for an enemy . . . He told himself to relax.

And he *would* relax. He was too exhausted to stay tense every second. But then he would hear echoing in his mind the voice of the crazy cop, *Stay away from my family, motherfucker,* and next thing he knew he would be panting like a wounded animal desperate for shelter.

Relax, he told himself. *Relax. Just push the damn boat. That's all the situation calls for.*

He felt something wet run down his left arm. He must have reopened the wound. He kept moving and tried to ignore the sensation.

Gold shimmered on the water's surface like light on the rippling scales of a snake. He kept the levee on his left. At one point he came across an area where the levee had been washed away for a hundred yards or so. It looked, from the cross-section, as if it were made of little more than sand.

And suddenly the trees opened up, and there was the Mississippi, framed by hulking levee banks on either side. The sight took Nick's breath away, and in an instant he deeply regretted his notion of heading toward the big river instead of inland.

Too late now, he told himself. *Got to get to Arlette.* And he drove on, to the wide, debris-strewn river that opened up before him.

Jason awoke as the bass boat took the chop of the Mississippi. "Whassup?" he said as the bow grated against a torn, leafy bough.

"We're in the big river now," Nick said.

Jason blinked sleepily at the wide expanse of water. "Well," he said, "I *told* you it was a mess."

Nick had to agree. The Mississippi was enormous, a mile or more across, a swollen gray mass covered with debris but utterly without life. He couldn't remember ever looking at the Mississippi below Cairo without seeing traffic—usually there were towboats upstream and down—but now there wasn't a single boat on the river. The only trace of humanity was wreckage: barges that had come aground here and there, stacks of lumber that had once been parts of buildings, cushions and foam boxes and an entire grain silo—one of the modern all-metal types, with the flattish conical roof—that rolled along the river like a seal with its nose above water.

Navigation lights were half-submerged or toppled. Stone piers and groins, built out into the water to help control the current, had collected colossal amounts of debris and turned into menacing obstacles studded with broken branches and roots as sharp as knives. Buoys bobbed in the water, but Nick had no idea what they could be marking.

Most alarming was the amount of timber. Trees covered the surface of the river, like an entire forest taking a holiday swim. Tangles of timber piled up in drifts on the shore and on hidden reefs. Twisted roots threatened like black fangs. A lot of the timber seemed very old—it looked as if it had lain on the bottom of the river for centuries until the quake had thrown it to the surface.

The river might have looked like this two hundred years ago, Nick thought. Before anyone ever tried to tame it.

"Hey!" Jason was pointing ahead, downstream. "Look! Is that a towboat right there?"

Nick's heart leaped at the sight of a boat's superstructure standing against the treeline. *Food!* he thought. *Safety. A bed.* And communication—surely they had a way he could reach Arlette.

"All right!" Jason said. "We're out of this!" He stood, jumped on the foredeck, began waving his arms and shouting. Nick felt a grin break out on his face. *My God,* he thought, *maybe I can take a* shower. Suddenly a shower seemed the most desirable thing in the world.

And then, as he looked at the boat over Jason's shoulder, he felt his joy begin to fade. That boat didn't look *right*.

Jason's shouts faded. He lowered his arms.

The river brought them toward the towboat. It wasn't even a *boat* anymore, it was a wreck come aground on a shoal of debris. It looked as if the river had rolled the boat completely over at least once. The stacks were gone, and the roof of the pilothouse punched down on top of the superstructure as if a giant had sat on it. The boat was wrapped in steel cable and covered with river mud, and timber and debris were piled up on its upstream flank.

Defeat oozed through Nick's veins. Jason stood staring at the boat, and Nick could see all the vitality go out of his body, the shoulders slumping. "I thought we were rescued," he said.

"Soon," Nick said, his voice sounding hollow. "Soon."

From the river, Jason could see surprisingly little. Above the flooded treeline to the east stood the Chickasaw Bluffs, forested slopes with little habitation. Landslides marred the bluffs, raw earth and tumbled trees. To the west were trees standing in the flood: there was a levee back there somewhere, but it was out of sight.

Jason and Nick managed to keep the boat away from the obstacles without great effort. Nick hung fishing lines from the stern in hopes of catching supper. The sun began to fall away westward. In order to calm the pain of hunger, Jason tried some of Nick's cattails. They weren't bad, he decided.

And there, suddenly, it was. Memphis. It emerged quite suddenly from behind the tail of a long overgrown island, a sudden panorama that sent relief singing through Jason. Memphis, perched above the river on Chickasaw Bluff Number Four, its glittering stainless steel pyramid in the foreground.

A pang touched Jason's heart as he saw the huge thirty-two-story pyramid. It was the pyramid that his mother had believed would summon cosmic forces to keep them all safe from the destruction that would wreck California.

Whatever cosmic forces were summoned by the pyramid, they certainly hadn't helped Memphis much. Many of the buildings were mere rubble, and those still standing had all suffered significant damage. Even modern buildings that had withstood the earthquake were blackened with fire. Bright tongues of flame still licked from some of the shattered windows. Pillars of black smoke rose from deep in the city. Northward, a blue-green water tower leaned at a desperate angle. Near the waterfront, grain elevators lay shattered and covered with soot. It looked as if they'd exploded.

Jason's gaze lifted to the M-shaped span of the Hernando DeSoto Bridge, which looked like a giant McDonald's logo vaulting across the Mississippi from Memphis to Arkansas. Though the towers still stood, the approaches had partly collapsed, and pieces were missing from the main span. A part of the roadway dangled precariously from the span, tons of steel and asphalt that looked as if they were ready to drop into the water at the merest touch.

Stay the hell away from that, Jason thought.

"Let's get to the shore," he said. "Let's get off this boat."

"Check it out with the scope," Nick said, "and find us a place to land."

Landing, on examination with the Astroscan, was going to be hard to do. Between the boat and the broken bridge stretched a long line of wreckage scattered the east side of the river. And to Jason's horrified surprise, he recognized it as belonging to Mud Island—recently renamed Festival Island—the long island park that lay between the Mississippi and Memphis proper. The island where he and his mother had, a few weeks ago, spent a pleasant spring afternoon was now almost entirely covered by gray water.

Emergency sirens sounded over the air. A helicopter throbbed overhead.

The dam that controlled the Wolf River, which ran between Memphis and Mud Island, had broken, and the Mississippi had backed up into the Wolf River channel. The massive stone bulwarks that kept Mud Island secure from the high river were shattered, and Mud Island Park had been swept by river water from one end to the other. The monorail and bridges leading to the island were twisted wrecks; the World War II bomber *Memphis Belle* lay crushed under its shattered white dome; water drifted through the lower levels of the River Center. Debris had collected along every bit of wreckage, forming jagged driftwood islands. The river foamed along a hedge of wooden fangs.

"We can't land in that," Nick said as he inspected the shore with the Astroscan. "We'd get stuck in the wreckage."

Jason looked at the ominous, shattered span of the DeSoto and suppressed a shiver. "That means going under the bridge."

"We'd better pick the safest part of the channel, then."

Which, they determined with the scope, seemed about a third of the way across the river from the east bank. The overhead roadway looked intact at that point, with no dangling slabs or girders. The river was moving sluggishly, and between the electric motor and paddling with pieces of lumber they'd pulled from the river, they managed to position the boat on the approach.

The bridge came closer. Water roared around the piers. The air tasted sharply of smoke. Beyond the DeSoto Bridge, on a broad drive at the river's edge, flashed the lights of a dozen emergency vehicles.

Nick was concentrating on the bridge overhead, eyes narrowed as he scanned the roadway for anything that could fall on them. The hum of the little electric motor was obliterated by the roar of water against the bridge piers. The sound of water against the piers was very loud. Jason trailed his pole over the stern to keep the boat from swinging.

For a long moment Jason looked straight up at the webwork of girders that supported the roadway. His heart throbbed in his chest. "Not today, O Lord," he heard Nick murmur. And then they were past, out of the shadow of the Hernando DeSoto Bridge.

There were more bridges ahead, Jason saw. They should come ashore before they had to risk another bridge. He felt a fresh wind on his cheeks.

"We're moving faster," he said. "Do you feel it?"

A pair of loud bangs echoed from the girders above. Nick gave a start, looked forward. "Oh shit," he said, and stood to grab the telescope, pointing it toward the flashing lights on Riverside Drive.

Jason looked at the older man in surprise. Nick's hands shook as he aimed the Astroscan. There was a wild look in the eye he put to the telescope.

"What's wrong?" Jason said. He angled the pole to turn the boat toward the eastern shore.

"No!" Nick shouted. "Don't turn!" His knuckles were taut over the plastic housing of the telescope.

"What's *wrong?*" Jason straightened his course again.

Nick didn't answer. Jason heard him panting for breath as he stared through the scope. "Damn!" Nick stared at Jason, and Jason wanted to take a step backward, away from the violence he saw in Nick's reddened eyes.

"We're not landing here," Nick said. He vaulted onto the front deck, slammed the electric motor's tiller over to turn the boat toward midstream. Jason stared.

"We're not going to Memphis?" Jason stammered. "What—?"

"Look for yourself!"

"I—wait." He pulled in his pole and made his way forward, put his eye to the scope, saw only sky. He readjusted the Astroscan, saw the line of vehicles on the river's edge, police and an ambulance, uniformed men standing casually in clumps nearby. Whatever emergency had brought them there, the crisis seemed to be over.

Jason looked at Nick. "So?"

"You hear those shots?" Nick said.

Jason was thunderstruck. "Shots? Those were *shots?*"

Nick jumped into the cockpit, sat crouched down behind the broken windscreen as if to make himself less conspicuous. "Look down near the water," he said.

Jason put his eye to the scope again. The cops still stood and were just standing in groups. They certainly didn't look as if they were being shot at, or had just shot somebody. He panned the scope closer to the water, searched among the wreckage of the shore, and his heart jumped into his throat.

There were bodies there. Two men, their bodies dragged just clear of the water. Both men were black.

"You sure they're shot?" Jason asked.

"You heard the shots, right?"

"I heard—" He hesitated. "You sure those were shots?" Those men could have drowned, he wanted to say, they could be off a boat, maybe the police are just hauling them out of the water, but the words froze in his throat at the sight of Nick's look, at the intensity that made Jason shiver.

"I've heard a lot of shots lately," Nick said. "I should know what they sound like."

"I—" The words stopped up in Jason's mouth again. Nick was crazy, he thought. Nick was a *criminal*. Maybe he'd escaped from a prison or a chain gang or something.

The Mississippi tugged them with increasing force. The river was growing narrower, and the water had to run faster as a result. Jason looked in alarm at the bridge ahead—no, he saw, not just one bridge, but three of them very close together. None of them seemed to be in very good shape. Fallen spans were plain to see. He didn't want to get anywhere near them.

"Listen," Jason said finally. "They're police, okay? There are ambulances there—medics. They can get you fixed up." He pointed at the three broken bridges clustered just downstream. "*Just look at the bridges!*" he shouted.

Nick's mouth was set in a firm line. The cables on his neck stood out. "Do you *own* this boat?" he demanded. "I know I don't. That means that this boat is *loot*, and we are *looters*. In emergencies they *shoot* looters." He looked at the flashing lights on the shore, his face hard as stone. "I'm not going to get shot."

"But—" Jason's mind whirled. "What—we're not going to *attack* them. We're—"

Nick looked at him again, red-rimmed eyes searching Jason from head to foot. "Maybe you'd be okay," he said. "You're young, you're white. But it's open season on niggers out there, and I'm not going to float right up to them and get my ass shot."

Jason's blood turned hot. His heart churned in his chest. He gave a swift glance to the shore, bit his lip as he tried to decide whether he should swim for it. There was at least a third of a mile of water between him and the shore, and the water was full of debris—he'd have to dodge entire trees, with their roots and branches, and other wreckage as well. If he got tangled, there'd be no one to rescue him.

Nick's strong hand clamped on his wrist. "Don't think it," he said. "Don't jump."

Fear shot through Jason as he realized that Nick had read his thoughts. Jason tried to snatch his arm back, but Nick's adult grip was like a trap of spring steel that had closed around his wrist.

"Stop it," Nick said. His voice was deep and hard.

Terror burned hot in Jason. He tugged again, shouted "Let me go!"

"Sit down!"

"Let me go! I'm not your kid!"

Nick's steel grip forced Jason down, down into the seat next to Nick. Nick's eyes blazed. Jason saw the sweat that gleamed on Nick's forehead, the scratches and insect bites that marred his skin, the blood that flushed the eyewhites.

"You *sit*," Nick said. "You *sit right here*." His voice was fierce in its intensity.

"You're *kidnapping* me! You can't do this!"

"Just sit!" Nick leaned closer to Jason and hissed, "I'm not gonna die for you!"

The words froze Jason to his seat. A chill ran up his spine. His mother was dead, he knew, because of his ignorance, because he didn't know how to operate the boat and save her. So maybe he didn't know anything about this situation, maybe Nick knew better than he did what was safe and what wasn't.

He stopped struggling, turned away. Felt despair clutch at his throat. What did it matter if Nick was crazy? It was only what Jason deserved. "I don't care," he managed to say. "Do what you want."

Nick held onto his wrist for another few burning seconds, and then Jason felt the grip relax.

The wind whirled through Jason's hair as the river sped faster. He didn't care. Let Nick be in charge, if that's what he wanted.

Flotsam ground against the boat's hull. Nick pulled the electric motor out of the water to keep it from being wrecked in a collision. Knifelike roots threatened, then were swept away. The bridges' broken spans, piled on the bottom of the river, had attracted other debris. There were now islands beneath the spans, brandishing roots and branches and covered with foam, and the river had been compressed into thundering narrow streams, rapids almost.

And then a shadow passed overhead, and Jason's heart lurched. He looked up to see that they were already passing beneath the three bridges, and moving on a current of white foam. For a moment of paralyzing terror he looked up at a dangling set of railroad tracks, at a boxcar hanging from a stalled train as if about to launch itself down the tracks into Jason's lap. BURLINGTON NORTHERN, he read on the car, and then it was gone.

Jason sat up with a jerk. The boat bounced in the chop. Spray splashed Jason's face. Nick stood up behind the useless steering wheel, the pole in his hand.

Another shadow flashed overhead, and then the bridges were behind them. To Jason's surprise the speed and the chop only increased. The boat slewed sideways, and a lot of water came aboard. Nick poled frantically to get the boat pointed downstream again.

"Could use a little help here, Jason," he said.

Fuck you, Jason thought, but he stood anyway and looked for a piece of lumber to help steer. Then he looked ahead and felt his heart lurch to a stop.

Ahead was a vista of white water and fire-blackened iron.

The Harbor of Memphis was the second-largest inland port in America, after New Orleans. More than ten million tons of cargo moved through its facilities every year. The terrain on which it was built was largely artificial, created when the Memphis Harbor Project built a causeway and dike connecting the mainland to the 32,000-acre Presidents Island just south of the old nineteenth-century Harahan Railroad Bridge. The slack water below the causeway became Memphis's principal harbor, lined from one end to the other with the evidence of the city's booming trade: Memphis

Milling, Petroleum Fuel and Terminal Company, Archer-Daniels-Midland Grain Company and Riverport, Helm Fertilizer Company, Ashland Chemical, Marathon Oil, Memphis Marine, Chemtech Industries, Memphis Molasses, MAPCO Petroleum, Riceland Foods, Vulcan Chemicals. All the boats and barges that serviced all this commerce. And amid all this, under the Stars and Stripes, the U.S. Navy's Surface Warfare Center.

M1 swept through this collection of industry with an efficiency the Surface Warfare Center could only envy. The causeway was torn, the dike destroyed. The river poured through the wreckage, through the oil and gasoline pouring from torn tanks, through the chemical stew that spilled from terminal facilities and from capsized barges. Oceans of diesel fuel mixed with tons of spilled nitrate fertilizer, creating the explosive combination known to terrorist truck-bombers throughout the world.

Of *course* it caught fire. It was impossible that it would not. One spark, one little flame, one arc of electricity, one overheated exhaust pipe . . . no human agency could have prevented the catastrophe that followed.

And so the Harbor of Memphis burned long into the night, explosions flaring bright at the base of a towering 10,000-foot-high mushroom of black smoke. Grain silos flamed like broken rockets on shattered launch pads. Boats and barges were transformed into gutted hulks. Steel melted like wax in the heat. Aluminum burned like old newspaper. And through it all poured the Mississippi, spreading the flaming waters far downstream.

The fires were mostly out now, the fuel burned up. All that was left was wreckage, the blackened girders, broken concrete, shattered buildings, and razed boats caught on the black waterswept shore of the Island of the Dead.

Nick Ruford looked at the white water ahead of the boat, felt spray touch his face. His heart hammered against his ribs. "My God," he muttered, and clutched the steering pole more tightly.

"Get a paddle!" he shouted, but Jason was already in motion, grabbing one of the broken-off pieces of lumber he'd propped in the cockpit. Jason crawled onto the foredeck, ready to fend off any of the fire-blackened structures that were pitching closer with each heave of the river. The air reeked of chemicals and burning.

Nick stroked with the pole, tried to keep the boat in mid-channel, but a current seized the boat regardless of his efforts and whirled it toward Presidents Island. He and Jason frantically beat at the water, trying to drive the boat away from obstructions. There was a grinding cry of metal as the boat dragged itself across a submerged obstacle, and the boat lurched, pivoting on whatever had caught it. Nick staggered, felt himself hang over the edge for a perilous instant, one arm windmilling for balance . . . the boat lurched the other way, and Nick stumbled toward safety. The world spun giddily around him as the bass boat whirled in the current, and he sank to his knees on the afterdeck in a more stable position.

Jason was paddling furiously, trying to check the boat's spin. Nick tried to assist, dipping the steering pole into the water as a brake. When the boat stabilized, it was heading stern-first down the channel, and Nick had to turn around to see what was coming.

The prow of a barge loomed up in their path, a wall of fire-blackened iron.

Nick gave a shout and raised his pole to fend the barge off like a knight raising his lance at a joust. The impact almost threw him back into the cockpit. The stern of *Retired and Gone Fishin'* slammed into the barge with a clang of metal, and the boat swung broadside to the current, pinned against the iron wall of the barge. The blackened iron loomed over their heads. Whatever had burned the barge had burned hot, Nick saw; it had left melted steel droplets frozen on the hull like candle wax.

Spray filled the air. The boat was pinned against the barge, unable to move. White water surged close to the gunwale on the upstream side. Nick looked upstream, saw a tree whirling in the current, roots flashing in the air like steel blades. *If it's caught in the same current we are,* Nick thought, *it'll come right at us and squash us against the barge like bugs.*

"Jason! Do like this!" He pressed his hands to the barge's bow, then pushed out with his legs, tried to prop himself like a bridge between the bass boat and the barge. "We walk it out!" he said. "See?"

Jason imitated him, sprawling against the barge wall to drive the boat back with his feet. The steel was still hot to the touch, and its rough surface tore Nick's palms. He and Jason began walking the boat off the barge's prow, the bass boat moving in lurches as their palms marched like unsteady feet across the flat bow of the barge. Nick looked over his shoulder, saw the tree swooping closer.

"Move!" he shouted. The boat shifted under him and he almost fell, almost pitched head-first into the foaming gap between the bass boat and the barge. He caught himself at the last instant, his heart like a fist in his throat.

The boat thrust its nose out in the current, and with a heave of his arms Nick flung the barge away from him. The bass boat pitched in sudden motion, and Nick staggered and dropped to one knee for balance. The blackened side of the barge swept past. Behind him, Nick heard thunder as the tree crashed like a battering ram into the bows of the barge.

Nick had no time to feel relief. A line of pipes loomed in front of him, and he reached for the pole to fend them off. "Left!" he shouted. "Turn us left!"

The pipes swept past before he could make more than a few strokes with the pole. He had no idea whether the paddling helped or not. The air stank of diesel fuel. Ruptured metal tanks, flame-scorched, loomed above the port. Three towboats, burned to the water line, lay in the heaving water like corpses rolling in the tide. Another pipe swept past, its broken end gushing flame and a stain of black smoke.

The boat tried to swing broadside the current. Nick struck the water to keep the boat stern-foremost.

Then the boat began to whirl dizzily as it was caught in a

sudden eddy, and Nick could only drop to hands and knees and try to hang on. There was a crash as the boat struck floating debris, and then *Retired and Gone Fishin'* rebounded, spinning in the opposite direction—Nick's stomach lurched— then there was a brassy metallic shriek as the boat struck its starboard side against a pier stanchion. The starboard side heaved up, and Nick clutched the gunwale as the boat tried to dump him out. Foaming water poured over the port gunwale, filling the cockpit and driving the port side farther into the water.

Nick looked at Jason huddled in the water at the bottom of the cockpit, the boy's eyes wide as he gasped for air amid the foam. Jason's weight was driving the port side farther into the water. In another moment the boat would capsize.

"Up!" Nick shouted. "Get on the high side!" His feet scrabbled on the deck as he tried to heave himself up the starboard side, where his weight would help to stabilize the craft. Jason stared at him from amid the flying foam, and then he stood and climbed up the nearly vertical deck, his feet bracing against the cockpit seats as he threw his weight onto the high side of the boat.

Nick pulled himself up over the gunwale—Jason scrambled beside him—and then Nick threw a leg over the side of the bass boat as he tried to shift his weight still further. *Retired and Gone Fishin'* trembled for a long heartbeat on the brink of oblivion. And then the weight of its occupants told, and with a cry of metal the starboard side fell into the water and the boat spun free of the obstruction.

Nick had been ready for this, and threw himself back inboard as soon as he felt the boat shift under him. But Jason was unprepared—Nick heard a sudden cry—and he looked up to see Jason pitch almost head-first into the white water, and he reached out a hand and closed it around the boy's flailing wrist.

Jason snapped back to the boat with a wrench that Nick could only hope had not dislocated the boy's arm. Jason stared up at Nick in shock, his eyes dilated black with terror. Jason's free hand clamped on the gunwale. The boat spun around Jason's weight as if it were an anchor. Jason gave a heave, a wrench, and tried to haul himself inboard. Nick tried to get his free hand on the boy's collar and failed. Jason strained, a gasp of pain fighting its way past his teeth, and then his hand slipped from the slick metal gunwale and he fell back into the water.

Nick sprawled across the afterdeck gasping for air, still hanging onto Jason by the one wrist. *Do this right,* he told himself. *Do this right or die with the boy right now. It was you got him into this.*

Nick rose to his knees, grabbed Jason under one armpit, then the other. The world spun around him. "Kick!" he commanded, and heaved. Jason gave a cry and flailed the water with his feet. Pain shot through Nick's wounded arm as he tried to pull the boy aboard the boat by main strength.

Strength failed. Nick gasped in air as pain shrieked through his limbs, and then he let Jason fall back into the water.

He blinked foam from his eyes and tried to think. It wasn't the right *angle,* he thought, he was pulling with the wrong muscles. Feet were stronger than arms. He needed to use his feet.

He looked up and saw a blackened metal pier swirling closer. Sharp driftwood daggers brandished in air. With cold horror Nick realized that if he didn't get Jason back into *Retired and Gone Fishin'* he would be impaled on the driftwood spines by the weight of the bass boat.

Nick gave a yell and lurched as he got his right foot under him. Then the left. "*Now kick!*" he screamed, and as Jason thrashed with his feet Nick lunged backward with every muscle in his body, and pulled Jason from the foaming water to land on top of him.

Jason gasped for breath, his arms floundering. "Hang on," Nick told him, and then there was a wrenching crash as the boat piled into the pier, as wooden spears came lunging over the boat.

And then the boat bounded away from the pier, whirling into safer water. Nick rolled Jason off him and clutched for something to steer with.

The nightmare journey had only begun.

It took half an hour to clear the five-mile-long port channel. There was no time for Jason or Nick to absorb the colossal scope of the damage—there was scarcely time to react at all as the river tried to run them against piers or pipes, burned-out towboats, or whole rafts of barges tangled in steel cable. Nick fended off one obstacle after another, lunging with his stick, sobbing with weariness. All he could see of the port were glimpses caught in the moments between frantic activity: the silhouette of a broken grain tower against the horizon; a blackened crater, half-filled with water, that marked an explosion. In the back of his throat lodged the reek of burning, the reek of chemicals, the reek of hot metal. He hoped that none of it was the reek of burned flesh.

Nick lunged, pushed off, poled, paddled. Water foamed over the jagged steel that lined the waterway. When they passed the port and entered the Tennessee Chute that dumped them back into the main channel, they gave up trying to control their direction and just hung on for dear life. Waves poured over them as they clutched the gunwale of their spinning boat.

They never noticed, as the white water lessened and they found themselves on the calmer surface of the Mississippi, that they had just passed the broken, burned, flooded, and abandoned remains of the Memphis District headquarters of the U.S. Army Corps of Engineers, the organization entrusted with the control of water for this part of the Mississippi.

You had to say one thing for the man, Jessica thought: he was tough. Just a few moments after one of the paramedics had set his broken collarbone, given him some aspirin, equipped him with a sling made from a dish towel, and handed him a breakfast MRE, a Meal Ready to Eat, Larry Hallock was back at the helipad with some of his crew, ready to be flown back to Poinsett Landing to make a proper survey of the damage to the nuclear power station. He was flying in a big Sikorsky, with an amphibious hull that could float him anywhere he needed to go.

All he asked was that someone go to his house to make sure that his wife was okay. It turned out that one of his own people could do that on the way to his own family, so Jessica didn't even have to detail one of her own.

"Good luck," she said, there being little else she could offer.

A crewman took Larry's good arm and helped him into the chopper. Jessica stepped back and waved as the Sikorsky lifted from the grassy pad.

Her office, minus walls and her collection of diplomas, had been recreated in one corner of the headquarters tent. The scent of old canvas and fresh grass was invigorating. The tent's sides were rolled up for light and ventilation, and from Jessica's corner she had an excellent view of the bustling techs setting up her state-of-the-art satellite communications rig.

Working for an organization with the resources of the Defense Department was sometimes perfectly awesome.

"Jess?" It was Pat, with the portable computer in hand. "I've got a selection of those photos from NASA and NOAA."

"Set the 'puter down here."

Once Jessica saw the pictures, she knew why she hadn't heard from Memphis or St. Louis.

The rubble that was St. Louis was practically an island, the Missouri flooding toward it from the north and west, the Mississippi from the east. Much of Memphis was covered by a cloud of smoke, and what she could see through the cloud looked like rubble. She looked at the photos from the Harbor of Memphis, and she heard her breath hiss from between her teeth.

"God damn," she whispered to herself. "I was afraid of this."

Natural disasters do not just have a single result. There was a whole chain of consequences: earthquakes cause fires, fires cause deaths, broken levees cause floods, floods cause evacuations.

And industry, destroyed by earthquake, flood, or fire, had levels of consequence all its own.

Jessica feared she was going to have to call the President soon and advise him to do something she knew very well he would not want to do. She didn't want to have to do that: powerful people had been known in the past to execute the messengers who told them about problems they didn't want to know about.

What Jessica badly wanted was a choice. She had a feeling the situation wasn't going to give her one.

But she would give it all the opportunity she could. She would lay on a helicopter flight for tomorrow morning, and do the research with her own eyes and mind. And then, if necessary, she would call the President and give *him* his orders.

SEVENTEEN

The inhabitants of the Little Prairie and its neighborhood all deserted their homes, and retired back to the hills or swamps. The only brick chimney in the place was entirely demolished by the shocks. I have not yet heard that any lives were lost, or accident of consequence happened. I have been twice on shore since the first shock, and then but a very short time, as I thought it unsafe, for the ground is cracked and torn to pieces in such a way as made it truly alarming; indeed some of the islands in the river that contained from one to two hundred acres of land have been nearly all sunk, and not one yet that I have seen but is cracked from one end to the other, and has lost some part of it.

Extract of a letter from a gentleman,
dated 20th December, 1811

The second helicopter thundered into sight just as Larry Hallock was returning from his inspection of the Poinsett Landing station. Larry didn't pay it much attention. He was returning in a rubber raft to the big Sea Stallion helicopter that had brought him out here, which sat on the water and had to keep its rotor turning to maintain its position against the current. Even though Larry was just a passenger in the rubber boat, the chop raised on the water by the downblast from the Sikorsky's six huge titanium-edged composite rotor blades was enough to keep his head down, and his mind firmly on keeping his seat in the raft.

Besides, he assumed the second helicopter was another military outfit.

It was after two crewmen, careful to avoid his damaged left arm, helped him into the Sikorsky by its crew that one of them said, "We have a radio call for you, sir. From the other helicopter."

Larry made his way forward, and one of the crewmen handed him a headset. "Go ahead and talk, sir," he said—shouted, rather—as Larry put the earphones over his ears.

"Larry Hallock here," Larry said. With his right hand, the one he could use freely, he pressed the right foam pads over his ear so as to hear the reply over the thunder of the Sea Stallion's rotor.

"Larry? This is Emil Braun. Are we ever glad to finally get ahold of you!"

Larry only vaguely remembered Emil Braun, who worked for the power company that owned the Poinsett Landing station, but the relief that soared through him at the sound of the voice was still profound.

He wasn't alone anymore. He didn't have to carry the burden of what he knew by himself.

"We've been trying to get ahold of someone since the quake last night!" Emil Braun said. "But no phone answered. No radio. We couldn't get a vehicle anywhere near the plant. And it was hell finding a helicopter, believe me! Our own chopper was down for maintenance, and ten minutes after the quake, you damn betcha that every civilian chopper in the country had been chartered by *someone*!"

Larry eased himself onto a fold-down seat. He found Emil's troubles in chartering aircraft to be at the least remote, not to say quaint.

"We've got problems here, Emil," he said.

"I can see that. Can you follow me to corporate HQ in Jackson and give everyone a briefing?"

Larry paused while a crewman competently and efficiently strapped him into his seat for takeoff.

"I think the Navy will want their helicopter back, Emil," he said finally. "From here I have to fly to Vicksburg to brief the Corps of Engineers," he said finally. "Why don't you follow me, and I'll brief you both at the same time?"

"The Corps of Engineers?" Emil repeated. Larry understood Emil's uncertainty: the Corps of Engineers weren't exactly in the electric company's chain of command.

"We're going to need their help, Emil," Larry said as the

Sea Stallion's huge rotor increased its speed and began to move the big Sikorsky forward over the brown water. "We're going to need all the help we can get."

Bail, splash. Bail, splash. Sweat ran into Jason's eyes. *Retired and Gone Fishin'* had survived the Tennessee Chute and had floated into a far more gentle part of the river. There were signs of burning on both flanks of the river, and the treeline was full of wrecked boats and barges that had come spinning down the chute from the port of Memphis, but the current was easy, and the cottonwoods on the western side cast long shadows on the sunset-tinted water.

The air reeked of dead fish. There were hundreds of them within sight, pale bellies uppermost. Something had poisoned them.

Nick, having lost his appetite for fish, had pulled in the fishing lines he'd been trailing astern.

The cockpit had almost filled with river water, and now Jason's job, and Nick's, was to bail. Bail, splash. Bail, splash. Jason's arm ached as he lifted the plastic milk jug filled with water and tossed the Mississippi back over the side where it belonged.

At least it was going faster than the first time he'd had to bail out the boat, that morning. Jason then had held his motley assortment of containers under the water, waited for them to fill, after which he poured them out. Nick had shown him a better way, one so simple that Jason wondered why he hadn't thought of it. Nick tore off the tops of the plastic jugs and bottles, so that he and Jason could scoop them full in one motion, then throw the water over the side.

Simple, but one of those simple things that Jason hadn't known or thought of. If he'd just *known*, if someone had shown him the trick, he could have taken it from there.

If he'd known about the boat's little electric motor, his mother might—no, *would*—still be alive.

He didn't know enough to live through all this, he thought. He didn't know enough to help anyone. In fact, he thought, he knew just enough to get himself killed.

Maybe he should just throw himself in the river before he killed someone else.

"Hey, look." Nick pointed downriver, where lights gleamed against the darkening sky.

Jason straightened as he threw water overboard, and saw a towboat—intact, upright, apparently unharmed, sitting motionless on the river with its bow pointed downstream. His heart gave a faint throb at the sight. It was too weary and discouraged to express anything more.

Nick displayed a more active interest. He dropped his bailing jug and turned on the electric motor, then steered for the towboat, half a mile away.

As he neared the towboat, Jason gave up his bailing and sat wearily on the gunwale. Sweat trickled down the back of his neck. Stars glimmered faintly in the darkening sky. There were navigation lights glowing on the boat's mast, but Jason saw no other lights on board. It was only when he got very close to the boat that he realized it was aground on a bar in only a few inches of water, and its entire long tow of barges with it. It was as if the river had dropped out from beneath the boat and its barges and left them intact, still ranked in formation, on the mud.

Debris was stranded on the bar as well, though not as much as Jason might have expected. The main current of the river was elsewhere, and carried most of the wreckage with it.

Dead fish, though, were everywhere, lying in the shallows in schools. Jason figured he'd never want to eat fish again.

Retired and Gone Fishin' avoided the debris and came gently aground on the bar about twenty yards off the stern of the tow boat. Nick shut off the electric motor, stood, and waved his pole at the towboat.

"Hey! Ahoy!"

It was the first time, Jason thought, he'd ever actually heard anyone say "ahoy."

"Ahoy the towboat! Anyone aboard?"

The towboat answered only with silence. Nick shrugged, then bent to pull off his already-waterlogged shoes. "Let's pull the boat over the bar," he said, and jumped into the water.

Jason pulled off his sneaks and socks and dropped over the opposite side of the bass boat, then was surprised at the near-liquid mud that sucked him in nearly to his knees. Without the weight of its two passengers, *Retired and Gone Fishin'* floated free. Pulling one foot after another from the suck of the mud, Jason and Nick walked the boat up to the stern of the towboat, which Jason saw was named *Michele S.*

The towboat was slab-sided, with a tall, squared-off superstructure. The pilothouse stood four decks above a raftlike hull that barely seemed tall enough for someone inside to stand upright. It hardly seemed possible that such a top-heavy design could travel anywhere without falling over. There were ropes dangling over the side, and Nick used one to tie off the bass boat. While Jason pulled free of the mud and went straight up one of the ropes, Nick climbed first into the bass boat, then jumped from there to the rail of the towboat. Jason found himself smiling at the way Nick was breathing hard after just the little climb to the towboat's lowest deck.

They stood on the boat while mud and water dripped onto the steel deck. Nick caught his breath and *ahoy'd* again. The only sound was the water river rushing past the stern.

"Look," Jason said, and pointed. There were davits overhead, on the end of the superstructure, that had once held a—would it be *lifeboat*, intended for life-saving? A boat, anyway. And the boat was just as clearly gone.

"Wonder why they left," Nick panted. "You'd think they would be safer here."

There were doors leading into the superstructure from the main deck, and Nick opened one about halfway down the superstructure. He groped inside for a switch and found it. Light flickered on, revealed a narrow steel corridor.

"At least their batteries seem to have a good charge," Nick said. He ventured in, bare feet slapping on the deck. Jason followed, and felt a sudden glorious rush of relief, finding himself *safe*. Indoors in a place unlikely to fall down, a place that had electricity, that probably had beds, toilets, water . . . and, he realized, *food*.

His dormant hunger woke at this thought, a hunger that clawed and bit at his belly from within. Jason had never been so hungry in his life. "Can we find the *kitchen*?" he asked. "The galley? Whatever it's called?"

"That's just what I planned," Nick said.

They headed forward through the crew quarters. There were sleeping accommodations for six, but only four of the beds seem to have been used. Forward was a tiny toilet and a shower, then a room the width of the superstructure with a dining table. Jason's mouth watered.

The galley was right ahead, past some stairs. Jason went straight to the huge metal refrigerator door and opened it. Gallons of milk and juice sat on racks. He reached for one.

"Careful, there," Nick said. "The refrigeration might not be on."

It wasn't, but the milk was still cool. Jason tore off the cap and tipped his head back. He took one deep swallow after another from the jug. The cool sweet milk flowed down his throat. He had never tasted anything so glorious. Runnels of milk ran down his cheeks, splashed down his shirt. He didn't stop drinking until his lungs ran out of air, and then he just took a gasping breath and drank some more.

Eventually Jason had to gasp for air again. Then he had to cough, and cough again, and when he bent down to clear his throat, he found that his cheeks were hot, and there were tears in his eyes. And then he became aware of Nick watching him, and Jason slapped the cap on the milk jug and turned away. Tears blurred his vision, and he stumbled against a table. Sobs clawed at his throat like razors, and his limbs had turned to water. He stood there, leaning against the metal table, and let the grief come keening out.

Nick put his arms around Jason and thought, *Oh God, I don't need this. This isn't my boy.*

"Take it easy," he said. "Take it easy, okay? We're safe."

Jason turned to him, buried his face against Nick's shoulder. The sounds he made were like the whimpers of a dog caught in barbed wire, a pain so fundamental, so primal, that it caused the hairs to rise on the back of Nick's neck.

Damn, Nick thought, *damn. This is not my kid.*

"It's okay, Jase," Nick said. "It's not your fault. Just take it easy."

They stood that way for several minutes, Jason's cries raining down on Nick's heart, and then Jason turned away and sat slumped at the table, his face a swollen misery.

"You all right?" Nick asked. A stupid question, but Jason nodded anyway.

Give him some privacy now, Nick thought.

So Nick turned to the refrigerator and took out cold cuts, cheese, bread, and pickles. He made some sandwiches, put them on a plate, and put them in front of Jason. He took one of the sandwiches himself, and while he ate he made a thorough search through the refrigerator.

The cook of the *Michelle S.* was very organized. Meals had been arranged well ahead of time, though not cooked. There were at least four days' meals prepared, but the most inviting seemed to be the four thick sirloins waiting in a stack, along with vegetables and a sack of new potatoes.

Nick wondered if the boat's crew were all fat as Santa Claus.

The gas stove lit when Nick tried it. He cut up potatoes and onions and set them to fry in a skillet, and put a pot of water on the stove for boiling vegetables. He looked at Jason, still slumped in his chair, and the boy's pure misery made him want to offer comfort, but he didn't know what comfort he had in him. *Sorry your mother's dead, kid. Too bad about your dad being in China and all.* It didn't seem adequate.

Nick turned back to the stove. He stirred the potatoes, slathered butter over the steaks, and put them under the broiler. And then he went to explore the *Michelle S.*

He climbed, first, to the pilothouse. From behind the wheel he could see the river stretching ahead in the darkness, the square island of the barge tow sitting before the bows, black against the shimmering river. In the darkness

Nick couldn't see what kind of barges made up the tow.

He turned on the lights in the pilothouse and looked for a logbook or other indication of why *Michelle S.* had been abandoned. If there was a logbook, the crew had taken it with them when they left. He looked for a moment at the radio equipment and wondered about calling for help. But he didn't know how to use the radio, and it looked complicated, so he decided that maybe he would try it later, after he had time to find a manual or instructions of some sort.

Besides, he thought, anyone in a position to give help would probably be giving help to people needing it worse than he and Jason did.

He froze as a tremor rose up through the deck. Adrenaline clattered through his nerves. The broad shimmering river broke up into leaping silver waves.

And then the tremor faded, and the river stilled, but Nick's pulse continued to hammer in his ears. He dragged in a breath. The aftershock is *over*, he told himself.

He touched the necklace in his shirt pocket. *Arlette*, he thought, *I am coming to you*.

But still his knees felt watery when he went down the companionway to the galley. He stirred the potatoes, put frozen peas in the boiling water, turned over the steaks. Then he went down, to the engine space, where the towboat's powerful turbines bulked under the low ceiling, and the air smelled pleasantly of machine oil. Nick looked for the engine and electric system controls, and he found them. He started a generator to keep the batteries charged, the lights glowing, and to keep the refrigerator and the freezers working. He made sure that the water heater was on, and that there was water pressure for bathing and running the dishwasher.

He was much better at this sort of thing than at radios.

Then he returned to the galley and found Jason gobbling a sandwich. The boy looked at him through eyes swollen by sorrow and tried to grin.

"Smells good," he said.

"How do you like your steak?" said Nick.

* * *

Larry cupped his hand for the two orange ibuprofen tablets that the army corpsman was shaking into his palm. He slapped the tablets into his mouth, picked up a cup of water, and swallowed them.

Nervous eyes watched him from around the table set in Major General Jessica Frazetta's command tent. The table was covered with maps, many of them with pencil marks annotating breached dams, broken levees, shattered locks, flooded land, and the tracks of the rescue flights that were trying to pluck survivors from the chaos.

Larry put down his cup of water. "First, the good news," he said. "The reactor and containment structure is in good shape. Relatively speaking."

"The reactor can be restarted?" Emil Braun said hopefully. He was a bespectacled, pot-bellied man who did not look at all comfortable in the bright yellow jumpsuit he'd put on for his helicopter ride. He was looking for a happy ending, Larry could see, a way the company could restart Poinsett Landing and not lose the billions of dollars they'd invested in the plant, but Larry didn't have a happy ending to give him.

Larry licked his lips. "That reactor's not going to be restarted whether it's intact or not," he said. "As I will tell you in a minute."

"But—" Emil said.

"One thing at a time, please," Larry said, more sharply than he intended. Emil almost visibly bottled up his objection behind his plump cheeks.

Larry looked down at the sling that held his left arm. "My busted shoulder kept me from getting into the access penetration—" He looked at General Jessica. "That's a sort of an airlock built into the containment structure. It's the only one we could use, because the other access points were all under water."

Jessica nodded. "I understand. Go on, please."

Larry looked at Wilbur, who sat on his right. "Wilbur here went into the containment structure. We got all the readings we could by flashlight, with portable instruments.

Everything looks nominal. There may be damage to the reactor core, but if so there was no release into the environment."

Larry could see tension fading from the people around the table. No massive clouds of radiation drifting over the South, no Chernobyl on the Mississippi.

Larry felt a series of jolts, as if someone was repeatedly kicking his chair from behind. Before he could turn around to look for who was doing the kicking, he realized that an aftershock was going on.

His heart leaped. He looked up, saw nothing but tent canvas over his head. Nothing dangerous was about to fall on him, so he decided to stay right where he was.

Kick-kick-kick-kick-kick. Emil bolted from the table, ran into the field outside. No one else moved.

The aftershock faded. The general looked at Larry.

"You were saying, Mr. Hallock? No radiation released?"

"Not from the reactor, no," Larry said, and a wary look crossed Jessica's face.

"Go on, please," she said.

Larry looked up, saw Emil returning, an embarrassed smile on his face. Larry turned back to Jessica.

"I don't know what people here know about reactors," Larry said, "so I'll start with the basics, okay?" The general nodded. "Poinsett Landing is a boiling water reactor, which means that steam from the reactor is piped directly to the turbine, instead of going through a closed-loop thermal exchange system as in a high-pressure reactor. You follow?"

"Yes. Please continue."

"What that means is that steam from the reactor going straight into the turbine is then cooled by the turbine condensors, then recirculated to the reactor. So when the generator house was destroyed, there was a release of steam into the environment, and there was a certain amount of radiation in that steam. Not in the water, you understand, but in any impurities that may have been in the water. But since we use demineralized water in the reactor, there weren't very many impurities to begin with, and the radiation release wouldn't have been large. It may be of concern to anyone at the plant at the time of the release, but there is no real danger to anyone now."

"Very good," Jessica said, and Larry detected a well-concealed curiosity in her eyes. She knew that Larry had been at the plant when the steam was released, knew that the radiation was "of concern" to him. She knew that his health was compromised, and that he'd just brushed over the matter, and she wanted to know what it meant to him, how he was handling it.

Larry wanted to know these things himself. He hadn't had time to think about any of this as it related to himself, hadn't had time to *feel* much of anything. He'd been too busy.

One thing at a time. He'd deal with it when he had the opportunity.

Emil, who had returned to his seat, looked relieved at Larry's statement. Fewer liability problems for the company, Larry deduced.

"The real problems," Larry said, "are two, and the two interact in such a way as to make any solution a real mess. First, the stored fuel." He looked at Frazetta. "There's over thirty years' worth of spent nuclear fuel at Poinsett Landing. In fact we ran out of space for the spent fuel entirely at one point, but one of my colleagues came up with a new way of racking the fuel elements that increased capacity.

"Now, the spent fuel assemblies are stored vertically in racks under the water in the auxiliary building. The assemblies are in neutron-absorbing borated racks to assure that there is no chance of achieving critical mass and starting a nuclear reaction. And they're subjected to active cooling—water is circulated through the building to remove any waste heat."

"How hot *are* these fuel assemblies?" Jessica interrupted. "They're *spent* fuel, right?"

"When fuel assemblies first come out of the reactor, they're *very* hot, very hot indeed. It takes years for them to cool to the point where they can be safely handled. Now, the *good* news is that most of the fuel assemblies in the auxiliary building are very old, and if you need to, you can probably just have a couple strong men pick them up and carry them someplace else. But the *bad* news is that the plant underwent refueling over the last several weeks, and there are almost three hundred hot fuel assemblies sitting in the auxiliary building right now—with active cooling down, and the water level diminished due to leakage from the storage pond."

The look that Emil gave him was one of pure horror. "Are you *sure*?"

"I knew about the leaks last night," Larry said, "but I couldn't get on the catwalks to find out how fast the water was falling. Well, it fell pretty fast—this afternoon I could detect a *lot* of radiation coming out of that building just by flying over it in the helicopter."

Emil turned pale. Larry looked at the row of concerned faces that gazed at him from across the table.

"Here's what I believe happened," he said. "The auxiliary building lost active cooling, and lost enough water through its leaks to uncover the spent fuel. The hot fuel assemblies cooked—in fact they probably melted. There's no chain reaction—not enough fuel for that—but those hot fuel assemblies are cooking up gasses like iodine and xenon and various kinds of noble gasses. In the meantime some dissolved fuel, with radioactive cesium iodide content, has probably leaked into the Mississippi."

"So there's a *cloud* . . . " one of the Army officers said slowly ". . . of *radioactive material* . . . floating out over the countryside."

"A *smallish* cloud," Larry qualified. "This isn't Chernobyl. This isn't a meltdown, this is some nasty hot metal that's spilled and is putting out byproducts. This earthquake has probably killed a thousand times more people than will ever fall ill from this accident."

Emil put his head in his hands. "It isn't Chernobyl *now*," he said. "But by the time the press gets done with it, it *will* be."

"Better tell HQ to get their public relations people online," Larry said.

"Twenty years of liability suits," Emil said. "That's what we're talking about here."

General Jessica brought the conversation back to its proper theme. "What can be done, Mr. Hallock?" she asked.

"That brings me to the second problem, General," Larry said. "Which is that the Mississippi has shifted its course eastward, and that the power station is now smack in the middle of the river."

There was a long moment of silence.

"Are you sure?" Jessica asked finally. "It isn't just that the country is flooded?"

"I think that the level of the ground fell during the quake," Larry said, "and the river flowed right into it. Current's pretty brisk, too." He nodded at Jessica. "The river's your department, General Frazetta. You'd be in a better position to judge than me, but I reckon you'll find I'm right."

He looked at the others. "And the foundation of the reactor complex is not entirely secure. When the ground dropped, it didn't drop evenly; there's a perceptible list to the containment building and control structure. So—if you want the worst case—the action of the river might furthermore undermine the concrete pad the reactor's sitting on, and a reactor full of nuclear fuel goes skimming down the Mississippi like a hockey puck on ice."

Emil winced at this image. "I don't think," he said, "that's very likely to happen."

"Probably not," Larry agreed. Ache throbbed through his injured shoulder. He wanted this meeting over, and himself in bed. He took another sip of water.

"Here's what needs to be done," he said. "The reactor is fine as it is—we can just leave it undisturbed for ten years or so, give it time to cool off, then remove the fuel and turn the containment structure into a museum or a bird sanctuary or whatever you like. What needs to be done is to stabilize the foundation, and the way to do that is to build a big solid island around it. An island of stone or concrete or brick, twenty acres maybe, with a solid breakwater on the north end to keep the river from undermining it. I'll defer to the general—" nodding at Jessica "—as to the best way to accomplish this."

"That will take some thinking," she said.

"That leaves the problem of the spent fuel," Larry said. "What we need to do is fill that holding pond *now*, which will cool things off enough so that we can start other repairs. Demineralized water would be best." Poinsett Landing, he knew, had once possessed a facility for creating as much distilled water as they could ever need, but that had been destroyed along with the plant's other most useful facilities, like the beautiful, extensive machine shops that could have made any tool, appliance, or structure they would ever have needed during the course of the repair.

Larry looked at Jessica again. "If you can't ship about, oh, thirty tons of distilled water to Poinsett Landing to pump into that holding pond, I'd pump in river water. The impurities in the water will get hot, and some of that will leak out into the river, but that's better than what's happening now."

Jessica frowned as she considered the problem. "Could we use a fireboat? Just hose water in there?"

Larry nodded. "That's what I figured. Bring one up from Baton Rouge or New Orleans." He turned to the others. "That will buy us time. Time to survey the pond and discover the extent of the damage, to repair the leaks in the holding pond, clear the ruined roof and catwalks out of our way, and to work out a plan to remove the spent fuel. The actual removal will need to be done remotely, with machines or robots. There's a machine already in the building that would do the job, if it's undamaged and if we can get power to it."

Larry closed his eyes. Weariness sighed through his mind like wind across a distant prairie. He shook his head, then stood.

"Well, that's it," he said. "I'd be obliged, General, if you could give me a ride home."

Jessica looked startled. "Very well," she said after a moment's pause. "If that's what you want, Mr. Hallock. You seem to have got it all worked out."

Larry scratched his whiskered face. "It's just one thing

after another. It's not like I didn't have plenty of time to think, sitting on that Indian mound all night."

"Larry," Emil said, "I've got to take you to Jackson. You've got to brief people at the company."

Larry looked at him. "*You* do that. I've told you the situation and what we need. You provide it, and we'll be fine."

"But Larry—"

"I haven't slept in two days," Larry said. "I'm pushing fifty. I have a busted collarbone, and I'm in pain. I haven't seen or talked to my wife or my kids since the accident. I'm going home, I'm going to kiss my wife, and I'm going to collapse into bed and sleep till morning." He gave Emil a glare. "You got a problem with that, Emil?"

Emil made a last attempt. "What if we need to talk to you?"

"Is that a cellphone you've got there?"

Emil looked at the device peeking out of his jumpsuit pocket. "Um," he said, "yeah."

"Give it to me. Someone needs to say howdy, they can call me on your phone."

He stuffed the phone into his pocket and left the tent.

He'd done *his* job, he figured, and more. He'd come up with a plan. Let the others work out the details.

They gorged on steak, potatoes, peas. It was the best meal Nick ever had in his life. Then, because they were still hungry, Nick cooked another steak and they split it.

He looked at the boy opposite him. Jason had made some attempt to clean himself up—he'd washed in the sink and tried to scrub off the mud he'd used to paint his face and arms, though not very successfully. His hair hung in dirty strands down his forehead, there was grime caked into his knuckles and streaked on his arms, his clothes were stained with mud and river water. His eyes were red, and in spite of the mud he'd slathered over himself, he'd managed to get a good case of sunburn. Jason looked like a refugee from six months of war, and Nick supposed that he didn't look any better.

Nick looked at the boy, who was shoveling food into his mouth before he'd finished chewing the last forkful, and sipped thoughtfully at his own glass of milk. "Save room for ice cream," he said.

Jason looked up at him. "No problem," he said.

"I've got the water heater going," Nick said. "We should see what the crew has left us in the way of soap and shampoo, and shower while we can." He rubbed his chin. "I should shave. And there are probably toothbrushes around. And sunburn ointment. And some clothes that should fit us."

"Okay," Jason mumbled past a mouthful of steak.

"I don't want to tell you what to do or anything," Nick said, "but we should bathe and brush our teeth whenever we can. It keeps up morale. Keeps us from giving up."

Jason gave him a curious look. "Morale?" he said, as if he'd never heard the word before. "You're worried about our *morale*? Are you in the Army or something?"

"I was raised in the Army. But I was never in the service myself."

"Army brat?"

"My dad was a general," Nick said. "I learned some things about survival from him and, ah, from the military culture, you know. And I was in the Boy Scouts, too." He shook his head. "If I can remember all that stuff. It was years ago."

A wary look entered Jason's eyes. "So what do you do now?"

Nick saw the look—it was one he knew all too well—and felt surprise roll through his mind. The boy thought he was crazy, or a criminal.

Well. Nick had preferred to run a deadly rapid in an unpowered boat to asking help from the cops. There was a wound on his arm. And—his mind a little grimmer now—Nick was black, and the kid's only contact with black people was probably watching pimps and gangsters on TV. What else was Jason to think?

"I'm an engineer," Nick said. "Got laid off from McDonnell in St. Louis five months ago." He laughed. "I shouldn't have any trouble getting an engineering job now.

Not with so many things needing to be put back together."

Jason's wariness lessened somewhat, but Nick could see that the boy was still a bit on guard. But exhaustion was falling fast on Nick, and he didn't have the energy to deal with Jason's suspicions now. Nick stood. "I'm going to shower and shave," he said. "You think you could put the dirty dishes in the washer? If the crew comes back, I don't want them to find out we've made work for them."

"Sure." Jason, his stomach full, seemed content enough.

Nick went into the crew's little cabins and dug through some of the lockers in search of clothes that would fit him. Photos of the crew's families looked down at him from the walls. He looked at pictures of smiling families, of kids and spouses and parents, and wondered if those families would ever meet again, if there would always be one or more missing.

He found some clothes that fit fairly well, a disposable razor, some shaving cream, a comb, a towel. In a locker he found a first-aid kit with sterile bandages and disinfectant. In the shower he found shampoo and soap.

He stayed in the little shower a long time, enjoying the hot water, the clean scent of the soap, the pounding droplets that relaxed the muscles of his shoulders and neck. He cleaned the dried blood from the wound on his arm, winced at the sting. The wound itself seemed to be scabbed and, so far as he could tell, healing. At least it wasn't hot, or oozing pus. He slathered on the disinfectant and bandaged the wound.

Then he shaved and splashed on the Mennen's Skin Bracer he found on the sink.

The sharp, clean scent stung up a memory. His father had used Skin Bracer. At the remembrance, sadness briefly clouded his eyes.

In the mirror he looked better than the refugee he'd seen a few minutes ago, but he still looked as if he'd been worked over with a baseball bat. He didn't look much like a general's son, that was for sure.

He found Jason in the galley, eating a bowl of vanilla ice cream with Hershey's chocolate sauce. The dinner things were gone, and Nick presumed Jason had put them away.

The boy knew how to do a few things, anyway.

"Don't you ever stop eating?" Nick said.

Jason looked at him. "I didn't fill up on cattails, the way you did."

Damn, Nick thought. *Ask a question, get a zinger.* What was with this kid?

"I've been thinking," Nick said. "We can stay on this boat awhile, I guess, maybe till someone takes us off. The people who own this boat are going to come back before too long, I imagine. But in case something happens, we should have some emergency supplies ready to put in that bass boat. Canned food, fresh water."

Jason looked up from his bowl of ice cream. "If there's an emergency," he asked, "wouldn't we be safer here?"

"What if the water rises, and this boat goes floating onto some rocks, or into the trees? What if a snag punches a hole in the hull?"

Jason scraped the bowl with his spoon. "Okay," he said. "I guess you've got a point."

"I'll put it together. You might as well take a shower. See if you can find yourself some clothes."

Nick assembled his emergency food in plastic garbage bags. There were jugs of fresh water right on the shelf. He threw in a container of flour, another of sugar, another of salt. Matches and a skillet. Soap, scissors, sun block, a sewing kit he found in one of the rooms, a bag of disposable razors, and a mirror—*for signaling*, as the Boy Scout manual might say. He smiled at the memory.

He stowed everything aft on the deck, where *Retired and Gone Fishin'* was tied. Then, since he remembered seeing a long extension cord, he plugged it in, ran it over the side, and plugged in the bass boat's battery recharger.

If another catastrophe occurred, he thought, the boat's little electric motor could carry them away. At all of maybe three miles per hour. Maybe he should study the engine controls, find out if he could operate the towboat single-handed.

He could feel exhaustion floating through his mind like

fog. Stress, a wound, and a night spent in a tree had caught up with him. He would find one of the unused beds and turn in.

In the morning, he thought, he would figure out how to work the radio. Maybe he could make a radiophone call, or whatever they were called, directly to Arlette, surprise her as she was eating breakfast.

In the morning, he thought. *First thing.*

He found an unused bed, dropped his clothes to the deck, slid between fresh crisp sheets. Before he could turn off the light there was a gentle knock on the door.

"Yes?"

Jason stuck his head in. "Good night," he said.

"Good night, Jason."

"And thanks." Jason's words came slowly. "Thanks for pulling me out of the water. When I went in. You know."

"Sure, Jason. You're welcome."

Jason nodded, drew back his head, closed the door behind him.

Weird kid, Nick thought as he turned off the light. *Weird kid.*

Jason woke with a cry of terror bottled up in his throat. He gasped for air and stared wildly into the night. His heart throbbed in his chest like a diesel.

He listened to the stillness for a moment and tried to decide what it was that had awakened him. An aftershock? A cry for help?

Broken fragments of his dream rattled in his head. He couldn't feel anything but a sense of alarm.

Something must be wrong. He swung his legs out of bed, opened the cabin door, and padded down the hall to the crew's dining area. He opened a door and stepped out onto the narrow steel deck.

A cool spring night floated up around him. Frogs and crickets called to one another in the midst of the silence. The river glimmered like a thread of quicksilver in the moonlight. A distant navigation beacon blinked downriver, marking a channel that probably no longer existed. It was the only sign of humanity in the entire magnificent desolation of the Mississippi.

Nothing had happened, Jason realized. It had been a bad dream, that was all.

He made his way back to his cabin, imagining that it would take forever to fall back to sleep.

Somewhat to his own surprise, he found that slumber reclaimed him with ease.

Jason woke to feel gooseflesh on his arms. The weather had cooled during the night, and the sheet he'd used for a cover was not enough to keep him warm.

He blinked open gummy eyes and looked at his watch. 8:13. He smelled bacon. His stomach rumbled.

Time to get up.

Jason pulled on some of the clean clothes he'd found in one of the crewmen's lockers—they were too big, but he could roll up the legs of the jeans, and if the sleeves of the shirt hung down past his elbows, it would just help to protect him from the sun.

He strapped on a pair of sandals that he'd found—the other footwear was too large—then made his way forward. He found Nick sitting at the dinner table, looking through a stack of manuals. Dirty dishes were piled up in front of him.

"Smells good," Jason said.

Nick looked up from his manuals, his chin propped on one fist. Shaved, cleaned, in clean clothing, Nick looked a lot less like an escaped felon than he had the previous day. Maybe, Jason conceded, he really *was* an engineer.

"Bacon," Nick said. "Eggs. English muffin. Want some?"

"Sure."

"Want coffee and orange juice with that?"

"Juice, sure. I don't drink coffee."

Nick stood, stretched, yawned. "Young people don't need coffee in the morning," he said.

Jason frowned down at the manuals, tried to read them upside-down. "What are you reading?" he said.

"I'm going to try to work the radio. Maybe I can get a message to my family." He looked at Jason. "Your family, too, maybe."

"My dad's in China."

"I can't get China with that radio, I suppose, but I can get someone to try to pass a message to him. I know that the Red Cross does that sort of thing."

"I don't know where he is, exactly." Jason tried to remember his father's itinerary. Would he still be in Shanghai? Or was he in Guangzhong by now? He hadn't paid his father's schedule much attention since he found out he wasn't going himself.

Nick looked at him. "Any other family here in the States?"

Jason thought for a moment. Aunt Lucy lived in Cabells Mound, and he had watched Cabells Mound burn. Even if she survived, her home probably had not. Also she was elderly and wouldn't be able to look after him. There was another elderly aunt in upstate New York, but he hadn't seen her in years.

"My dad's the best bet," he said.

"Well," Nick shrugged, "I'll try. How would you like your eggs?"

"Scrambled."

Thoughts of his family left Jason downcast. When Nick went into the galley, Jason decided he didn't want to hang around waiting and being depressed, so he stepped out onto the deck and was surprised to discover that *Michelle S.* was now high and dry on an island. The river had dropped to a lower stage since the middle of the night, and the mud reef on which the towboat had grounded was now above the level of the water, a muddy plain that stretched several hundred feet in all directions. The island had caught a lot of debris, and its upstream flank was walled with driftwood, logs, and with what looked like a green-roofed metal storage shed, deposited on its side with a door hanging open.

The whole island was covered with dead fish. Flocks of crows and water birds were feasting on the corpses. Their croaks and calls were almost deafening.

The day was gray and cooler than yesterday, for which

Jason was grateful. A wind made singing sounds as it gusted over the superstructure.

Jason made his way forward to the blunt bow. The tow stretched out before him, fifteen long barges laid out three abreast, all lashed together with steel wire held taut by big ratchets. The nearest barges were domed with pale green metal, and a complex network of pipes ran fore and aft along their length. There was a short mast on the middle barge, with a red flag and a light on top.

Jason jumped up on the prow, balanced for a precarious moment, and then jumped across to the nearest barge. Metal rang under his feet as he landed. The wind gusted toward him, bringing a sharp chemical smell.

He sneezed.

There were a pair of huge blue rubber gloves lying on the barge near his feet. *Why blue?* he wondered. He wandered forward along the green roof of the barge. More blue gloves were scattered here and there. A gust of wind ruffled his hair. He sneezed again.

He jumped easily to the next barge in line. He wondered if it would be possible to skate on the barges, roll along the smooth metal tops and hop over the piping. Do it fancy, land fakie and jump the next pipe going backward. It would be easy enough to leap from one barge to the next.

Pity that the pipes were mostly horizontal. Otherwise he could ride them as he'd ridden the tower rail in Cabells Mound.

The next gust of wind brought a strong chemical sting to his nostrils. What was *in* these barges?

He looked up, saw the short mast planted on the barge in front of him. The mast's red flag, he saw, was metal, so it would always stay rigid whether there was wind or not. The flag had lettering on it. Jason jumped onto the barge—the chemical smell was stronger now—and approached the flag.

NO SMOKING

NO OPEN LIGHTS

NO VISITORS—EVER

A chill finger touched Jason's neck. Now he knew why

Michelle S. had been abandoned by its crew.

The gusting wind backed around to the southeast, and the chemical smell blew strong at him. Fumes raked the back of Jason's throat. He ran to the side of the barge and peered over the side, into the gap between this barge and the next.

A foul chemical lake lay beneath the barge.

One or more of the barges had broken open during the quake, or when the tow went aground, and had been leaking its cargo ever since. Until this morning the river had carried the stuff away, whatever it was, but now the river had dropped and the noxious mess was pooling on the surface of the tow's little mud island.

Jason whirled, looked again at the red flag through eyes that stung in the chemical reek.

NO SMOKING

NO OPEN LIGHTS

The barges' cargo *had* to be explosive. Otherwise the barge wouldn't be flying the red danger flag. Otherwise the crew wouldn't have abandoned ship.

NO VISITORS—EVER

Horror ran through Jason's veins as he thought of his breakfast bacon sizzling in a skillet over a blue propane flame.

He scrambled aft, the southeast gusts blowing the chemical smell past him. He cleared the gap between barges without breaking stride, then leaped from the barge onto the *Michelle S.* in one bound. He dodged around the superstructure and dived into the first door.

He heard the sizzling sound of bacon. Never had he found an ordinary, homely sound so terrifying.

Jason dashed into the galley, past a surprised Nick, and turned off the stove burners. The blue flames fluttered and vanished with a *whuff*. Nick stared at Jason's terrified expression.

"What is it? What's going on?"

"We're going to blow up!" Jason shouted.

"What—?"

Words exploded through Jason's gasps for breath. "Barges

leaking! Chemicals! That's why the crew ran away!"

Horrified comprehension snapped into Nick's eyes. "What chemicals?" he asked.

"*Who cares?*" Jason cried. "Just go outside and *smell*."

While Nick went out to investigate, Jason ran aft to where *Retired and Gone Fishin'* sat on the mud aft of the towboat. He untied the line securing the bass boat to the stern, and flung it over the side. He lowered himself over the rail, felt the mud squelch to his ankles as he landed. Nearby birds broke for the sky, a fleeing black cloud. Jason slogged to the bows of the bass boat and yanked away the extension cord that was recharging the boat's batteries. Acrid fumes drifted over him in waves.

Nick appeared on the deck above. "Catch," he said, and swung out a plastic garbage bag filled with emergency supplies.

Three more bags followed. Jason tossed each into the bass boat. Then Nick rolled over the towboat's side, tried to lower himself to the mud on the rope, and lost his grip. He tumbled helplessly into the soft ooze. Jason jerked his head away as mud sprayed over him.

"*Shit!*" Nick pulled himself free of the sucking mud and staggered to his feet.

Dragging the heavy aluminum boat over the mud flat was a nightmare. Getting traction in the soft mud was nearly impossible, and Nick and Jason often fell. Both were soon covered with ooze. Black birds swarmed around them and mocked them with their calls. Jason gasped for breath as sweat tracked mud over his face. His arms, legs, and back ached, and his brain reeled from chemical fumes.

Finally the bass boat slid into the brown water. Jason and Nick flung themselves aboard. The boat spun lazily as the current caught it. Jason crawled forward to the bow, dropped the trolling motor over the side, and started it, heading directly across the current to get as far away from the towboat as he could.

The wind blew fresh air over the boat, and Jason sucked it down gratefully.

Retired and Gone Fishin' made its way down the river, drifted around a bend. Jason and Nick lay gasping on the fore and afterdecks. *Michelle S.* disappeared behind a screen of trees.

"God damn, God damn," Nick repeated. "And we had clean clothes an' shit."

Jason sat up, turned down the speed of the trolling motor, and tried to wipe mud from his face.

Then a perfect sphere of fire rose from beyond the trees, and burst like a bubble over *Michelle S.* and its barges.

EIGHTEEN

At the Little Prairie, (a beautiful spot on the west side of the Mississippi river about 30 miles from New-Madrid), on the 16th of December last, about 2 o'clock, A.M., we felt a severe concussion of the earth, which we supposed to be occasioned by a distant earthquake, and did not apprehend much damage. Between that time and day we felt several other slighter shocks; about sunrise another very severe one came on, attended with a perpendicular bouncing that caused the earth to open in many places—some eight and ten feet wide, numbers of less width, and of considerable length—some parts have sunk much lower than others, where one of these large openings are, one side remains as high as before the shock and the other is sunk; some more, some less; but the deepest I saw was about twelve feet. The earth was, in the course of fifteen minutes after the shock in the morning, entirely inundated with water. The pressing of the earth, if the expression be allowable, caused the water to spout out of the pores of the earth, to the height of eight or ten feet! We supposed the whole country sinking, and knew not what to do for the best. The agitation of the earth was so great that it was with difficulty any could stand on their feet, some could not—The air was very strongly impregnated with a sulphurous smell. As if by instinct, we flew as soon as we could from the river, dreading most danger there—but after rambling about two or three hours, about two hundred gathered at Capt. Francis Lescuer's, where we encamped, until we heard that the upper country was not damaged, when I left the camp (after staying there twelve days) to look for some other place, and was three days getting about thirty miles, from being obliged to travel around those chasms.

Narrative of James Fletcher, 1811

* * *

The black pillar of smoke that marked the burning *Michelle S.* slowly fell astern. The river was slow and lazy: having spread itself wide beyond its banks, it seemed intent on staying awhile. The surface was less crowded with debris than it had been the previous day: much of the wreckage and timber had caught in the cottonwood and willow tangle that grew in the flood plain between the levees and the river. But there was still enough flotsam in the water to be dangerous, and Jason and Nick kept a watchful eye. When he had scavenged food and other useful supplies from the towboat, Nick had equipped the bass boat with a pair of proper boat hooks, which made it much easier to fend off wreckage.

Jason's breakfast consisted of some canned pineapple rings from Nick's emergency cache. He tilted his head back, drank off the sweet syrup, and tossed the empty can over the side. The river received it with a dull splash.

The river was his fate, Jason thought as he watched the can pace the bass boat on its way downstream. He kept being thrown up on the shore, but then the river would take him again. He was beginning to develop a superstition about it.

Nick, he saw, sat on the stern deck, his hands dangling over his knees. The older man looked once again like a refugee, borrowed clothes soaked or splashed with mud, face and hair spattered, the newly acquired sandals ruined.

Edge Living, Jason thought. This was *real* Edge Living—no resources, no help from outside, and every second on the brink of extinction. There were people, he thought, out in the Third World he supposed, who lived their whole lives this way. What he had *thought* was Edge Living, the kind he'd celebrated on his posters, was a sick joke compared to the real thing.

Jason managed a grin. "So how's our *morale* now, General?"

Nick looked up, gave a rueful laugh. "Don't imagine it can get much lower," he said. He looked at the emergency supplies, then began to stow the cans and jars in the boat's cooler compartments.

"So what's the plan?" Jason asked.

Nick shrugged. "Find a place that doesn't blow up?" he offered, then sighed. "I wish I'd contacted my family when I had the chance," he said. "They're gonna be worried. They knew I was driving down to Toussaint."

"You have a daughter, you said? In Arkansas someplace?"

"Yeah." Nick's hand went to his shirt pocket, then fell away. "She's having a birthday tomorrow—today, I mean." Discouragement lined his mud-streaked face. "Guess I won't be there."

"Is she at school, or what?"

Nick looked down at his work as he answered. "She's with her momma. We're divorced."

Sadness drifted through Jason at the word, at the timbre of failure he heard in Nick's voice. It suggested that the divorce hadn't been Nick's idea.

Jason nodded. "I know divorce, all right. And birthdays. That telescope we're using—that was a birthday present from my dad. But I think his new wife picked it out for him."

Nick nodded. "Divorce is hard on the kids. I always been thankful my parents had a good marriage." He reached into his pocket, took out a box covered in muddy velveteen. "Here's what I got for Arlette."

He opened the box. Jason leaned close and saw gold glowing bright, the glitter of diamonds and rubies. Some kind of flower thing. "That's pretty," he said.

Nick had probably picked out the necklace and earrings himself, too. Jason could tell by the pride in his face.

Nick closed the box and returned it carefully to his pocket. "I wanted to give it to her today," he said.

"Well." Jason glanced around at the river, the dense ranks of trees that lined the channel down which they traveled. "We're heading in the right direction."

Nick rubbed his face, brushed at the drying mud. "They're worried for me. I know they are."

Jason felt an urge to be supportive. "We'll get there," he said.

"I just wish I'd used the radio last night. But I was so tired . . ."

"We'll find another radio. Or a telephone. Or something."

Nick shook his head. "I wanted to call her at breakfast. I wanted to get her before she went to school."

It didn't seem like much: talk to his daughter before school. But it was very clear that Nick had counted on speaking to Arlette, and now that he hadn't, he was so downcast that he couldn't seem to get beyond his failure.

With something like a mental shock, Jason found himself wondering if his own father had been through similar agonies. His parents' divorce had always seemed something they had chosen to inflict on him, yet another example of the random cruelty that adults always imposed on their children. That his parents might have been in pain themselves was a new and surprising thought.

"Fend off, there," Nick said.

Jason snatched up a boat hook and pushed away a large chunk of frame building, a shed or chicken house, that threatened to run aboard the bass boat. His shoulders flamed with sunburn as he shoved the building away. Once the boat was out of danger, Jason put down the boat hook and sat again on the foredeck. He was surprised to see Nick watching him with sober eyes.

"Yes?" Jason said.

"You did a good thing back there," Nick said. "You may have saved our lives."

Jason looked at Nick in surprise. He felt a flush mounting in his skin. He wasn't used to adults finding reason to praise him.

"Thanks," he said.

"A lot of people might not have figured it out. You knew how to put two and two together." He looked down the river. "We'll be okay if we just keep our eyes open."

Jason nodded and felt awkward. He really didn't know what to do when a grownup told him he was smart. It wasn't as if it had ever happened before.

Nick brushed at his face again, knocking flakes of mud to the deck. He looked around at the smears of Mississippi ooze that covered the boat and its passengers. "Maybe we better try to clean up," he said. "Wash off some of this mud. Clean up the boat."

"Okay."

"And then put on some sunscreen. I found some in the towboat."

"We're going to need to fend off first."

That frame building had come back, floating again toward the bass boat as if intent on climbing into the cockpit. Jason stood and picked up the boat hook. Nick's praise made him feel stronger, more capable. Fired with purpose.

He leaned into the boat hook and drove the wreckage away.

Messrs. Cramer, Spear & Eichbaum Printers, Pittsburgh
Gentlemen:
Your being editors of the useful guide, The Ohio and Mississippi
Navigator, induces me, for the sake of the western country
traders to inform you as early as in my power the wonderful
changes for the worse in some parts of the Mississippi river,
occasioned by the dreadful earthquake which happened on the
morning of the 16th of December last, and which has continued
to shake almost every day since. As to its effects on the river I
found but little from the mouth of Ohio to New Madrid, from
which place to the Chickasaw Bluffs, or Fort Pickering, the face of
the river is wholly changed, particularly from Island No. 30,
to Island No. 40; this part of the river burst and shook up hun-
dreds of great trees from the bottom, and what is more singular
they are all turned roots upwards and standing upstream in the
best channel and swiftest water, and nothing but the greatest
exertions of the boatmen can save them from destruction in
passing those places. I should advise all those concerned to be
particular in approaching Island No. 32, where you must warp
through a great number, and when past them, bear well over
from the next right hand point for fear of being drawn into the
right schute of Flour Island, Island 33, which I should advise
against, as that pass is become very dangerous unless in very
high water. Two boats from Little Beaver are lately lost, and sev-

eral much injured in that pass this season. Boats should hug the left shore where there is but few sawyers, and good water and fine landing on the lower point of the island, from there the next dangerous place is the Devil's Race Ground, Island No. 36.

Here I would advise boats never to pass to the left of the island and by all means to keep close to the right hand point, and then close round the sandbar on the lower end of the schute is very dangerous and the gap so narrow that boats can scarcely pass without being dashed on some of the snags, and should you strike one you can scarcely extricate yourself before you receive some injury. From this scene you have barely time to breathe and refresh, before you arrive at the Devil's Elbow, alias the Devil's Hackle, Islands No. 38 and 39 by far the worst of all; in approaching this schute you must hug close around the left hand point until you come in sight of the sand bar whose head has the appearance of an old field full of trees, then pull for the island to keep clear of these, and pass through a small schute, leaving all the island sawyers to the right, and take care not to get too near them, for should you strike the current is so rapid it will be with great difficulty you will be able to save, your boat and cargo.

Letter of James Smith, April 10, 1812

The morning's SITREP had a lot fewer unknowns on it. Information was starting to flow into Mississippi Valley Division headquarters. Most of the information was bad, but even bad news was better than waiting in suspense for the next unanticipated horror.

In addition to gathering information, Jessica had largely assembled her Joint Division Team, which would coordinate civil works projects and disaster relief throughout her assigned area. She'd appointed the JDT's Chief of Staff, Subordinate Command Liaison, the Chief of Operations, the Staff Engineer, the Counsel, Contracting Officer, the Chief of Public Affairs—who would coordinate press briefings from a tent reserved for the purpose, provided of course that the press could ever find their way here through the disaster area.

As called for in the plan, Jessica had even appointed an official Economist. Rather more useful in the current situation was the Clerical Specialist, who was now assembling out of stores the inventory necessary for the JDT's operation. The necessary inventory included Facsimile Machine (auto feed, programmable, plain paper); Binder Clips, large; Binder Clips, small; Correction Fluid, white; Forms, Tasking; and Rubber Bands, assorted sizes.

Jessica was pleased to observe a Pot, Coffee on the list. Before this emergency was over she planned to make a significant dent in the inventory's Cups, foam, 8 oz.

Morning birdsong—the throb of helicopters—floated into her command tent, as it had been doing since before dawn. Jessica finished her second cup of breakfast coffee and threw the Cup, foam, into the trash. She rose from behind her desk and sought out her husband.

Pat was in the communications tent, helping the techs with their Computers (Database for mission tracking). "Hey, runner!" she said.

Pat was gazing into the innards of a three-year-old—and therefore rather antique—IBM, and trying to fit a modem card into the slot. He looked up. "Ma'am?" he said.

"Tell Colonel Davidovitch that I'll be TDY for a few hours, okay?"

"Now?" he said.

"Yes," Jessica said. "Orders generally mean *now* unless otherwise stated."

"Yes, ma'am." He returned the modem card to its bubble wrap. "You know," he said, "Jeb Stuart had someone on his staff just to play the banjo."

"If I need a banjo player, you'll be the first one I'll call."

An aftershock bounced the ground as Jessica made her way to the helipad, one vertical jounce after another. Jessica weaved slightly as she walked and tried not to twist an ankle.

She had seen to the recovery of MVD headquarters, which was now capable of surviving without her for a few hours. Her new Helicopter (Transportation, for use of) waited for her. She wanted to make a personal inspection of her division.

And if things were as bad as she expected, she'd have to call her commander-in-chief and tell him what he needed to do.

"Sugar bear," said Sheryl, "I think it's time to put up my Apocalypse."

Frankland paused, his hand poised with the razor to shave the dimple on his receding chin. He had tried to make certain that men remained shaved, and that everyone wash their face and hands before meals. Good for morale, he'd thought.

"Yes," he said, "yes. I'll help you in a minute."

After he finished shaving, he helped Sheryl carry her linen scrolls from her workroom to the church. Frankland got Hilkiah and some of the others to drive wooden stakes into the ground, and Sheryl unrolled her opus and stapled the scrolls to the tall wooden stakes so that they formed a long, fabric wall, with occasional gaps so as not to provide a continuous surface that the wind could more easily damage.

Frankland was awestruck. There was the Apocalypse in all its glory, blazing in the brightest color: John of Patmos cowered before the Son of Man. Seven golden candlesticks burned in the darkness; seven angels held seven vials; four beasts each with six wings clustered about the Throne; four Horsemen rode across a petrified world; a red dragon with seven heads and seven crowns; a woman unfurled the wings of an eagle; a scarlet woman on a scarlet beast; Babylon laid in ruins; the City of God descending to the earth in a glory of light. All in the most astounding detail, down to the leering tongue of the Beast and the malevolent glitter in its eyes.

It was magnificent. More beautiful, Frankland thought, than the Whatchamacallit Chapel in Rome.

People were wandering up to look at it. Pointing, and marveling. Sheryl's face glowed with pride.

"I'm so proud of you, sweetie pie!" Frankland said. "It's the most gorgeous thing I ever saw."

"It's what we should all expect," Sheryl said. "It's what everyone will need to know in order to survive the next seven years."

"You should take the rest of the day off, sweetie pie," Frankland said. "Just stay here with it and be like, you know, a tour guide. Explain to the people what they're looking at."

"I'll do that."

Frankland gave her a big kiss, right there in public.

The Apocalypse glowed around him, on its wide linen walls.

There it was on the water, like a giant wedding cake built against the left bank of the Mississippi. Tier upon tier of white lace, twin stacks topped by elaborate gold crowns, an enormous stern wheel with its blades painted vermilion.

Nick gave a nervous laugh as the giant boat grew nearer. "That's the weirdest thing I ever saw. Right in the middle of all this wilderness."

LUCKY MAGNOLIA CASINO, said the scarlet letters on the side, in some old-timey script.

Jason looked at Nick over his shoulder. "Hey," he said, "want to play some slots?"

"We must be in Mississippi," Nick said. "Everyone from Tennessee comes down here to spend their money." The last time he'd driven Highway 61 south of Memphis, it seemed as if there had been dozens of casinos, each with its own stoplight on the highway, as if every driver in Mississippi was forced to halt in honor of the money flowing toward the state from the north.

When Nick had been a kid, driving to Mississippi to visit his grandparents, there had been nothing on that road but wilderness, cotton fields, and desolation. Now the wilderness was overflowing with gold.

Nick gave it some thought. "Casinos have restaurants," he said. "We could get more supplies. And we could prepare the food properly in the kitchen."

"It would be nice not to sleep on the boat tonight," Jason added. "I did it once, and that was enough."

"Right," Nick said. "Let's give it a try."

Jason crawled over the foredeck and started the trolling motor. As they came closer, they saw the casino had suffered earthquake damage. Some of the white gingerbread had fallen, and it looked as if the inshore stack would have toppled if it hadn't been held in place by cables. Several windows were cracked or broken.

The casino loomed over them. It looked as huge as an aircraft carrier.

"Hook on," Nick called, and he and Jason each reached out with a boathook and snagged the rail. They brought the bass boat alongside and tied it to a fluted pillar that supported the deck above.

Jason gauged his movement, then jumped to the casino boat and legged over the rail. Nick followed more cautiously. He peered through a window into the darkened interior. "Here's a restaurant," he said. "There's got to be a kitchen next door."

The first door was locked, but the second opened to a corridor that led into the restaurant. A stack of menus lay spilled near the entrance. The restaurant featured green faux leather booths and brass torchieres, their gleam dimmed by the gray light outside. At one end of the room, the remains of a buffet supper sat beneath swarms of flies at a cold steam table. There were plates and glasses on the white linen tablecloths where meals had been interrupted by the catastrophe.

"Here's the kitchen," Nick said. He walked past a waitresses' station and pushed through a swinging door.

The kitchen was cold and dark, lit only by a single cracked window. A row of burgers, grease and cheese congealed, waited on a counter for a waiter to pick them up. The flies hadn't got through the swinging door to find them.

The freezers and refrigerators were huge, with brushed steel doors. Nick opened one of the refrigerators and eyed its contents.

"We better stay away from anything that could spoil," he said. "The power's been off too long."

Jason wandered over to the range, turned the control for a

burner. There was a hiss of gas, and the repeated clicking of an igniter, but nothing lit. "We can cook," he said, "but I think this needs to be lit with a match."

Nick opened a freezer, pulled out packages of meats that were still frozen. "We got chicken, beef, fish, sausage . . . how about pork chops?"

"They all sound great to me," Jason said. Ever since their interrupted breakfast, he'd eaten only from cans. He opened a tap in the sink, felt his heart lighten at the pouring water. "We've got water, anyway," he said.

The tap water reminded him of an errand of nature. He turned off the tap. "I'm going to see if I can find a toilet," he said.

"You like broccoli?" Nick said, hefting a package.

Jason shrugged. Vegetables were all one to him. "Whatever," he said. "I'll see you in a minute."

He left the restaurant and padded along a thick carpet in an inner corridor, then walked down a ramp into a huge semicircular food court. Burger King, he saw in the dim light, Pizza Loco, Ragin' Cajun, Baskin-Robbins. Plastic tables and chairs lay scattered where the earthquake had thrown them.

It's like a mall, he thought.

Somewhere near the food, he thought, there had to be a toilet. He found it, did his business, then discovered there was enough water pressure in the sink to manage some washing. He cleaned his face and neck and arms and looked at his hair in the mirror, glued into thick strands by mud and sweat. He wished there was a shower so that he could wash his hair.

Maybe, after dinner, he'd come back and try washing his hair with hand soap. It would make it stick out funny, but it was better than wearing mud for mousse.

Jason stepped out into the food court again and paused for a moment. Beyond were the gaming tables, slots and video poker machines standing in silent ranks.

He wondered if any of the gamblers had left their money behind when the earthquake hit.

The thought seemed worthy of exploration. He walked

into the huge central room, fingers idly exploring the coin trays of the machines as he passed. He didn't find any money.

The blackjack tables had spilled cards and spilled chairs, but not a single spilled coin or token. Dice lay on the craps tables, and drinks sat waiting for gamblers to return, but there was nothing on any of the tables resembling currency. Jason concluded that the casino employees had done a very thorough cleanup before they abandoned ship.

Jason hopped up to one of the big roulette wheels and gave it a spin. It moved with silent ease. Two ivory balls sat waiting in a slot by Jason's hand, and he picked one up and hefted it. He'd never seen roulette except in the movies, and he tried to remember how the croupier had thrown the ball into play. He tossed it with a flick of his wrist, but the ball bounced right down onto the spinning wheel, caromed across, bounded back, and jumped straight into one of the slots on the wheel. Not very professional.

They should use a plunger and spring, Jason thought, *like in pinball.*

There was a loud crash, the sound of breaking glass, and Jason gave a guilty start and looked up wildly. He wondered if Nick had broken something, and then he heard a loud whoop echo through the cavernous room, and he knew that he and Nick were not alone on the *Lucky Magnolia*.

High-pitched laughter followed the whoop, and then the laughter was joined by a deeper voice. There were at least two other people aboard.

Without knowing why, Jason ducked behind the roulette table. He decided it was because he hadn't quite liked the sound of those laughs.

He wondered what he should do. Tell Nick, perhaps. But tell him what? That there were people aboard who laughed funny?

There was another crash. Jason felt his heart give a lurch. Cackling laughter filled the air, and then Jason heard footsteps. He hunched down behind the table.

"I'm getting tired of popcorn and peanuts," a man said.

"We shoulda brought Janine to cook for us."

"We shoulda brought a woman for each of us," said another voice. "They'd give us all the food and lovin' we want, allowing as how we're both going to be so rich."

In the dim light Jason saw two men leave one of the darkened rooms off the main room. The sign above the door, he saw, said *Paddlewheel Saloon*. The two headed aft, boots crunching on broken glass.

Heart in his mouth, Jason ghosted after them, keeping low. He smelled cigar smoke. Tables and ranks of slot machines helped screen him from the interlopers. As he passed the Paddlewheel Saloon Jason saw that the bar's colorful art nouveau window had been smashed by some well-aimed beer bottles. These were the crashes he'd heard.

Talking in loud voices of matters clear only to them, the two men walked aft to the tellers' cages, then walked behind the screen. Jason paused and wondered whether to slip back to Nick, or try to find out first what the two intruders were doing.

He thought about what might happen if Nick came looking for him, and his mouth went dry. Then he heard a series of metal banging sounds, like a hammer ringing on an anvil.

He slipped toward the last teller's cage on the left, close by the wall. Trying not to breathe, he peered through the teller's window and saw the two men at work.

The younger of the two men wore a T-shirt and jeans. Lank hair straggled out from behind his battered baseball cap, which he wore with the bill pointed aft. The older man revealed a substantial belly between his T-shirt and the blue jeans that were belted low on his hips. His burly arms were covered in tattoos, and a short cigar was clamped between his teeth. Spectacles glittered beneath the bill of his baseball cap.

Each took a swig from a bottle of Jack Daniels as they rummaged through canvas bags filled with tools. The two were working on opening the casino safe, trying to chisel and pry open its door. They had gotten a chisel between the door and its frame, and were striving to widen the gap.

"Gaw-damn!" the older one said. "They built this sucker good, didn't they?"

"Fill the boat with fifty-dollar chips," said the younger one. "Good as cash any day."

Boat, Jason thought. They had come in a *boat*.

"Lend a hand here, Junior." Junior, it appeared, was the older one. The two leaned on a pry bar for a moment, grunting, boots scrabbling for traction on the tile. Muscles stood out on forearms, in necks. The door didn't move. The two relaxed.

"Gaw-damn," breathed Junior. He bent to root in his tool bag.

The younger man laughed. "How many casinos do you reckon we can find this side of Helena?" he asked. "Ten? Fifteen? All with cash, checks, and fifty-dollar chips?" He gave a little hop of sheer enthusiasm. "Jesus shit howdy!" he said. "We're going to have to buy a Chevy Suburban just to haul it all around."

"We aren't going to be able to afford a third-hand Yugo," Junior said, "if you don't help me bust this safe."

Boat, Jason thought again. They have a *boat*.

It had to be on the starboard side of the *Lucky Magnolia*. He and Nick had tied up to the port side and hadn't seen another boat there.

He crept to the starboard side, keeping crouched down below the ranks of poker machines, then slid along the side. The main entrance wasn't hard to find: it was huge, a twenty-foot-tall glass alcove set into the side of the riverboat, leading to a ramp and white plastic tunnel that clearly led to the shore. Two sets of glass doors blocked the entrance, but one door in each set had been smashed open. More confirmation, if any were needed, that this was the way to the intruders' boat.

The area in front of the alcove was wide open, and light coming in through the glass walls lit it well. Jason waited until he heard the ring of hammers on metal again, then ran for daylight, fast as his feet could carry him. His sandals grated on broken glass and then he was in the tunnel, sprinting down the ramp into fresh air and freedom.

The tunnel opened onto a wide pontoon pier against which the gambling boat was moored. The pier was held against the levee by steel cables, and connected with a foot ramp that led to the levee's crown. A row of flags snapped overhead in the cool breeze. Jason looked wildly for a boat, and had no trouble finding it at all.

It was moored bow and stern to the upstream side of the pier. It was longer than the bass boat, maybe twenty feet, with a windscreen and cockpit and a white canvas top. A big hundred-fifty-horsepower Evinrude outboard was fixed to the stern, which was filled with big translucent plastic fuel jugs, each aglow with amber fuel. The motor was tilted forward to keep the prop out of the debris-filled water.

Triumph sang in Jason's blood as he gazed at the boat. He untied the stern line, then took the bow line in hand and walked the boat to the edge of the pier, where the *Lucky Magnolia* lay against huge rubber fenders intended to preserve its paint. Jason jumped from the pier to the gambling boat, clung for a precarious moment to the outside of the rail, then hopped the rail onto the *Magnolia*'s deck, the motorboat's bow line still in hand.

He walked the boat forward, passing the line around the fluted white iron pillars that supported the deck above, then walked clean around the bow to the port side, where he moored the boat next to *Retired and Gone Fishin'*.

He felt a warm satisfaction as he contemplated his handiwork for a minute, then spent at least five seconds thinking of ways to steal the intruders' tools while he was at it. But then he decided he'd better tell Nick there were thieves on board, before Nick decided to call him in for dinner or to use the toilet.

Jason slipped back into the *Lucky Magnolia*, careful to close the door quietly behind him, then made his way through the restaurant to the kitchen. Nick was still cooking, oblivious to everything that had occurred to Jason since he left the kitchen. The smell of pork chops sizzling in the pan made Jason's mouth water, and for a lightheaded instant he considered eating his meal before telling Nick about the two men trying to break into the safe.

Nick looked up at him, grinned. "You like coffee gravy?" he said. "Give you energy for the rest of the day."

"Nick," Jason said, "there are people on the boat."

Nick seemed pleased. "They belong to the casino? Or did they drift up like us?"

"They're thieves," Jason said, and Nick's grin vanished in an instant. "They're drunk, and they're breaking into the safe," Jason went on. "They're going to steal the money here, then rob every casino on the river."

Nick's eyes never left Jason's face as he reached to turn the flame off underneath the pan. "We'd better get back to our boat," he said.

"Let's put the food on a plate and take it with us," Jason said.

Nick walked to him, grabbed him by his shoulders, and turned him around. "March on outta here," he said, "and don't make any noise."

Just for that, Jason thought, *I don't tell you about how I stole their boat.*

Nick was so wary, skulking through the restaurant with such theatrical care, that Jason wanted to laugh. When they got into the corridor outside, the sound of banging and hammering on the safe could be heard clearly. Nick raised a finger to his lips—Jason wanted to laugh again—and then they slipped outside to where they had left the bass boat.

Jason went ahead so that he could see Nick's face when Nick realized what Jason had done. Nick stepped out, intent only on the bass boat, and then slowed, puzzlement plain on his face as his eyes moved to the larger boat. He stopped, one hand on the line that tied the bass boat to the *Magnolia*, and then a conclusion seemed to pass across his face. He turned to Jason, his eyes suspicious.

"This is their boat?"

"Yeah!" Jason laughed. "I took it!"

Nick's eyes narrowed. "You took their boat? You stole it?"

Jason was surprised by the suspicion in Nick's tone.

Defiance bubbled up in him. "Yeah!" he said. "I *stole* it! They're here to take money, and I took their boat! What's wrong with that?"

Nick looked thoughtfully from Jason to the stolen boat and back, then stepped close to Jason, put a hand on his shoulder. "You're sure those men are thieves?" he asked. "You didn't just take their boat and then make up a story about their being robbers?"

Jason jerked away. "No way!" he said. "They're here to steal!"

Nick looked thoughtful, then cast a glance back over his shoulder at the door. "Oh, sure!" Jason scorned. "Go ask them! Junior and his redneck buddy'll be happy to see you!" He waved his arms. "You heard them hammering on the safe! You figure they'll just say howdy and offer you some of their Jack Daniels?"

Nick turned back to Jason, and his look softened. "I believe you," he said. "We'd better leave."

Jason's heart leaped. He jumped for the new speedboat, and dropped into the white vinyl seat behind the wheel. "Hey," he said, "we've got push-button starting! Let's blast outta here!"

"No!" Nick said sharply, and then lowered his voice. "They might have guns. We don't want to make any noise. Let's just drift away, then start the motor once we're clear."

Nick used one of the mooring lines to tie the bass boat's bow to their new boat, and then he untied them from the *Lucky Magnolia* and pushed the boats into the current.

Nick crawled beneath the canvas cover to the seat next to Jason's in the cockpit. Jason, heart beating, watched as they slowly slipped past the huge gambling boat. His eyes strained at the windows for a glimpse of Junior or his friend.

Nothing. The *Magnolia* fell astern. He laughed, then turned to Nick. "Start the engine?" he said.

"I guess it's time." Nick made his way to the stern and tilted the Evinrude's propeller into the water. Jason pressed the start button.

Nothing happened.

Jason tried again and again, and then realized that there was an ignition lock, like the lock on a car, on the console. Junior or his buddy doubtless had the key.

Jason's heart sank. He'd gone to the trouble and risk of stealing the boat, and now it might as well be a raft.

"No problem," Nick said, when Jason told him of the trouble. Nick hopped back to the bass boat, got some tools out of one of the storage lockers, then returned and ducked under the console. "Move your feet, okay?" he said—Jason did—and then Jason heard him work with the electronics for a moment.

"Give it a try now," Nick said.

Jason pressed the button, the starter whined, and the engine coughed. Jason gave a laugh. He let up on the button and the engine died. He tried again, and the engine again refused to start.

"Give it some choke," Nick said as he clawed his way out from beneath the console.

Jason looked for a button labeled *choke*, found it, and pushed it. Then he tried to start the engine again, and again the engine died.

"Let's see what you're doing," Nick said as he settled into the seat next to Jason. Jason showed him. Nick reached over and pulled the choke button. "Pull it *out*, not in," he said.

And the engine started.

Still need the grownups, Jason thought as he pushed the throttle forward. *Damn it.*

But his heart leaped as the engine roared, as the boat began to speed through the sluggish water. He turned to Nick and grinned. "Where did you say your daughter lives?" he said. "Bet we can get there in a couple days."

Nick was looking over his shoulder at the bass boat bumping along behind. "Once we get out of sight of the casino," he said, "we should cut back our speed, save fuel. Maybe tie up or drift at night so we don't run into anything."

"Fine," Jason said. "Whatever."

And then laughed, because the boat was his and now so was the river.

* * *

Larry Hallock stood in the pilothouse of the fireboat as it eased its way toward the Poinsett Landing plant. The boat moved slowly, feeling its way through the ruined facility so that it wouldn't go aground on some half-ruined obstacle.

He could see the fire crew standing ready by their water cannon. They were in full firefighting togs, helmets, capes, faces masked, breathing from respirators. They had to be suffering from the Mississippi heat.

Which Larry knew firsthand, because he was suited himself. Not, thank God, in a complete radiation suit, one that looked like what the astronauts wore on the moon, but in something that was bad enough. He was in anti-C clothing—the C stood for Contamination—which consisted of heavy overalls, boots, gloves, skullcap, and a gas masklike respirator to keep him from breathing in any airborne contamination. The boots and gloves had been duct-taped to the overalls to make certain that no contaminated particulates got into his clothing. If any of the portable radiation detectors on the boat showed that he'd been contaminated, he'd be able to throw away the suit and walk away free.

But he was hot, even in the shade of the pilothouse. The respirator was claustrophobic. Sweat kept dripping from his forehead onto the inside lenses of his spectacles, and he'd wished he'd remembered to put on a sweatband before he donned the gear.

Larry wasn't alone in his misery. Accompanying him on the boat were separate teams from the power company and from the Department of Energy, all in their own anti-C apparel. The fantail of the boat looked like an astronauts' convention.

Helicopters thundered overhead. A nuclear accident was just the sort of thing to *really concentrate* the government's attention as well as the attention of the media, which with its usual efficiency was in the process of blowing the incident into mass panic. Larry figured that more people were going to die of heart attacks and strokes while listening to the television coverage than would ever die of radiation exposure.

The depth sounder made ticking noises as the boat edged closer to the auxiliary building. The helmsman fired the stern thrusters briefly to nudge the back end of the boat around, then paused, the boat hovering alongside the long, buff-colored flank of the storage building, its engines providing just enough thrust to hover in the current. The depth sounder reported fourteen feet of swift-moving water under the keel.

"I believe, sir," the captain said, in soft, deferential Southern tones, "that we may commence."

Larry had spent the night in his own bed, in his quake-damaged home. His wife Helen had survived the quake without so much as a scratch, but the house had not been so lucky. Most of the shingles had fallen from the roof. The rear porch had become detached and moved about five feet into the yard. All the windows had broken, and all the shelves had fallen.

Helen had coped perfectly well with his absence, however. The fallen books and smashed crockery had been cleared up, and the shelves set up again, this time fixed firmly to wall studs with anchor bolts. Nothing was going to fall again unless it took the entire wall with it. Larry was thankful that he'd married a practical girl who knew how to use his tools.

That morning, on his way to his rendezvous with the fireboat, Larry had flown over the Poinsett Landing plant and surveyed the collapsed roof of the auxiliary building, looking for places to rain water into the holding pond. He'd taken a number of Polaroid photographs from the air, and he reached into an envelope for these and blinked at them past the smeared lenses of his spectacles.

He made his way out of the pilothouse, then told the captains of each of the water cannons where to direct their attack. Pumps began to throb. Valves were turned.

And brown Mississippi water began to flow from the nozzles of the water cannon.

It took most of the day before Larry's radiation detectors suggested that the great reservoir of the holding pond had at last been filled, and the spent fuel's furious heat temporarily quenched. At this point Larry thankfully got out of his

anti-C gear; the teams of inspectors left the boat to enter the
auxiliary building to analyze the damage and dump large
amounts of radiation-absorbing boric acid into the cooling
water. Larry himself was spared this duty, both because of
his injury and because all the access routes to the building
lay under water and would have to be entered by people
using scuba equipment.

Operation Island, as General Frazetta had dubbed it, was
getting under way.

NINETEEN

On Wednesday, in the afternoon, I visited every part of the island where we lay. It was extensive, and partially covered with willow. The earthquake had rent the ground in large and numerous gaps; vast quantities of burnt wood in every stage of alteration, from its primitive nature to stove coal, had been spread over the ground to very considerable distances; frightful and hideous caverns yawned on every side, and the earth's bowels appeared to have felt the tremendous force of the shocks which had thus riven the surface. I was gratified with seeing several places where those spouts which had so much attracted our wonder and admiration had arisen; they were generally on the beach; and have left large circular holes in the sand, formed much like a funnel. For a great distance around the orifice, vast quantities of coal have been scattered, many pieces weighing from 15 to 20 lbs. were discharged 160 measured paces—These holes were of various dimensions; one of them I observed most particularly, it was 16 feet in perpendicular depth, and 63 feet in circumferences at the mouth.

Narrative of Mr. Pierce, Dec. 25, 1811

Nick was eating his breakfast—Campbell's Chunky Beef, straight from the can—when they motored free of trees and wreckage, and there was the bridge dead ahead, the span between its three great towers glittering like a spider web in the morning sun. Mouth full of soup, he nudged Jason, but Jason had already seen it.

The boy turned to him with a grin. "All right!" he said. "We're rescued!"

Don't be too sure, Nick thought, though his heart grew lighter for all his caution.

Jason looked down at his can of food. "Creamed corn,"

he said. "Couldn't you find something in the pantry that doesn't suck?"

Nick looked in their bag of supplies. "Want some olives?" he said.

After escaping from the *Lucky Magnolia*, they had motored south till nightfall, then cut the engine so as not to run onto debris. Morning found them out of the main channel and somewhere in the flood plain, surrounded by tall trees, with a bluff hard by the west bank. Or perhaps this *was* the main channel now. It was impossible to tell.

They started the Evinrude and motored carefully southward through the trees, the engine turning at low revs to keep the boat away from obstacles. A brisk wind blew through the trees overhead, but at the water's surface the air was almost still. Jason steered while Nick prepared their unappetizing breakfast.

"Hey look!" Jason said, excited. "Look! It's a city!"

Through his own rising excitement, Nick paged through mental road maps. A town on the west bank, built up on a bluff, with a highway bridge crossing the Mississippi.

"Helena," he said. "That's Arkansas over there."

He could see towboats and rafts of barges moored along the waterfront. Maybe one of them would let him use their radio, he thought.

Jason put his bowl of half-eaten creamed corn on the gunwale. "Let's blow this popsicle stand," he said, and reached for the throttle.

As they neared Helena, Nick saw the place had suffered in the quake. Parts of the bluff had spilled downward into the lower town, and all of the buildings he could see over the town's big floodwall were damaged. Some of the older brick buildings had collapsed. From the marks of soot, it looked as if other buildings had burned.

"That way!" Nick said, pointing, as a lagoon opened up on the right. He saw piers, masts, small boats. Jason turned the wheel and the boat heeled as it roared for the marina entrance.

The moored pleasure boats, rising on the flood, had suffered little damage, though some, parked on dry land in trailers, had been knocked over, and sat now half-full of water. Jason cut the throttle as he entered the lagoon, and the speedboat slid over glassy water. Silence enveloped them. Nick could hear wire halyards rattling in the wind against aluminum sailboat masts, the cawing of the flocks of crows that massed overhead, the hiss of water under the keel. There were no sounds of traffic, no footsteps, no sounds of voices. Beyond its floodwall, Helena was strangely silent.

There were buildings close in sight, though. Nick could see what appeared to be a regular residential neighborhood between the bluff and the big half-collapsed warehouses near the marina.

Nothing moved there. Nothing moved anywhere. Nick wondered if the town had been evacuated.

"No point in mooring here," he said. "Flood's cut us off from town."

The bass boat bobbing behind on the end of its tether, *American Dream* idled past the Terminal & Warehouse Co., moved along Helena's floodwall until it found a gap, a gate torn open by the quake—the river must have *poured* through here, Nick thought, though now the waters were gentle enough—and then Jason steered the speedboat through the wall into the town beyond. Frame buildings rose on either side, many of them leaning, knocked off their foundations. The boat's muttering exhaust echoed strangely from houses and trees. Crows gazed down at them from peaked rooftops, from black windows that had lost their glass.

"Man, this is weird," Jason said. "Where is everybody?"

"Maybe they all went up the bluff to get away from flood."

"I didn't see anyone moving up there." Jason looked thoughtful. "Maybe we can scrounge supplies out of some of those houses. Shall we check it out?"

Nick thought about it, decided he had no real moral objection to this course of action. The food was doing no good where it was. "Find a house that won't fall down on us," he said.

Jason motored up to a two-story frame structure with a

broad portico. The building's gabled design suggested it had been built before World War II, perhaps well before that. Jason nudged the boat's bow right up to the porch. Nick pulled up his trouser legs above his knees, jumped into the flood, moored the boat by its bow to one of the white pillars. Goose flesh crept over his skin at the touch of the cold water.

Water washed back and forth through the screen door. The front door with its knocker stood open, and broken windows gaped. Nick opened the screen and ventured inside.

"Hello?" he said. "Anyone here?"

There was a rustling sound on the second floor, but no voice answered. Nick stood in a living room flooded to a depth of two feet or so, with a high-water mark on the flowered blue wallpaper twelve or so inches above the current level. Plastic articles, papers, and paperback books floated in the water. White lace curtains trailed in the current. A steep carpeted stair led to the floor above.

Jason sloshed into the room. "Guess we're not going to do much cooking here, huh?"

"Maybe we should have gone up to one of the towboats. They're bound to have a watch on board."

"We'll try that next. But if we bring the towboat some food, they're more likely to help us out."

Jason sloshed toward the kitchen, then gave a yelp as he banged his shins on a submerged coffee table. As if in answer to Jason's cry, Nick heard the rustling sound again on the floor above. He waded to the bottom of the stair. "Hello?" he called.

More rustling. Crows cawed.

"Maybe someone's hurt up there," Nick said. "Maybe they can't call for help."

"Might as well look," Jason called from the kitchen. "The pantry's empty. Maybe the food's upstairs."

Nick put his hand on the newel post, then took two cautious steps upward. All he needed was to get shot as an intruder by some half-senile old lady. "He was *black*," she'd say. "I knew he only wanted a white woman!"

"Anyone up there?" Nick called. "We've come to help."

And then he added, "Me and the boy!" to let whoever it was know that he was okay, harmless, he had a kid with him.

"Me and the geek engineer," he heard Jason mutter behind him. Nick concluded that Jason didn't like being called "boy" any more than Nick did.

Nick climbed the stairs and stood at the end of the upstairs hall with water streaming down his legs. He heard rustling and flapping sounds, but by now he thought he could identify them.

"I think they're just birds," he said, and looked through the first doorway.

There was a mad rushing of wings, a cawing of panicked birds smashing into walls as they tried to escape through the shattered window. Nick's blood turned cold. He took a shaky step rearward, turned away, took Jason by the shoulders.

"Don't look," he said, talking loud over the flutter of wings. "Go back to the boat."

Jason looked up at him resentfully, and his mouth opened for a wisecrack, but something in Nick's tone must have got through to him, because he turned in silence and began walking down the stair.

Nick's pulse fluttered in his throat. There was a tremor in his knees. Then, slowly, he turned and looked into the room again.

A young black couple, he saw, and their baby. They looked as if they'd survived the earthquake but died afterward, in some kind of fit. Their mouths were open and their hands were bloody claws. The man's fingernails had gouged tracks in the cheerful blue checks of the wallpaper. The woman had died with her baby in her arms. A bottle of formula lay where it had fallen in the middle of a throw rug.

The crows had got to their eyes. Despite the dark blood-flecked hollows in their faces, they seemed to have died with peaceful expressions on their faces. They had fought for life while the fit first came, but then died quietly, resignedly, when the time came.

Nick realized he'd been holding his breath, and he let it out. Softly he turned from the room, and closed the door behind him.

He found two more corpses. An older child, a boy, lying dead in his Air Jordans beneath a portrait of Jesus. He looked as if he had torn at his own throat in an attempt to breathe, though he, too, had relaxed at the end, had died with a strange soft air of tranquility. In another room was an older woman, probably the mother of one of the young couple, who had crawled under her bed to die.

The crows had gotten to them, whole flocks of them. Unless Nick wanted to find some lumber and plank over the broken windows, there was no way to keep them out.

He closed the door and walked in silence down the hall, then down the stair. Jason waited silently in the boat. Nick sloshed through the water to the portico, then unmoored the speedboat and pulled himself up on the foredeck.

Jason looked at him questioningly as the boat drifted away from the portico. "They were dead," Nick said. "The whole family." He licked his lips. "It looked as if they were poisoned or something."

Apprehension twitched around Jason's eyes. "Glad we didn't take their food," he said.

"It may not have been the food," Nick said, and looked at the flocks of crows that circled overhead and perched on all the roofpeaks.

Jason seemed surprised. "What, then?"

Nick rubbed his chin, feeling the unshaven bristle scratching his palm. "I don't know yet. I want to look in another house."

In the next house Nick explored, the scene was even worse. The entire family had died in one upstairs room, clawing at each other as if they had been taken by a homicidal fit. There were a lot of children, at least half a dozen, but Nick didn't want to count.

When he came back to the boat, Nick couldn't speak, he just waved Jason to go back the way they had come. Jason motored back toward the gap in the floodwall and passed slowly through the open gate.

"Shall we try one of the towboats?" Jason asked.

Nick nodded. But, as they motored along the riverfront,

Nick looked ahead to see the crows atop a shrunken mound of clothing on the afterdeck of the nearest boat, and he felt the hair on his neck stand on end.

"No," he said. "No. Get back in the river. As far across as we can go. And don't steer anywhere where you don't see birds flying."

Jason looked at him wildly. "Why? What *is* it?"

Nick licked his lips. "Gas. A cloud of gas killed all those people when the flood trapped them in their houses."

Nick saw Jason turn pale beneath his sunburn. "*What kind of gas?*" he demanded.

Nick searched his mind, shook his head. "There must be a dozen things that could do something like this. Chlorine gas. Arsine. Hydrogen cyanide. One damn barge is all it takes. We've got to hope it's dispersed, that we haven't been breathing it."

Jason's eyes widened. He raised a hand to his throat, and for a moment Nick saw an echo on Jason's face of the horror that must have come to Helena, the realization that they had been poisoned and were going to die.

As soon as they were clear of the land, Jason opened the throttle and the speedboat roared east across the river. There they followed a series of bird flights south, past the silent city on the bluff. Past the broken houses, the silent boats and barges. Past a double row of gasoline storage tanks that had burned and died, past the flooded casting field, past the shattered, abandoned Arkansas Power & Light plant.

Past the circling, calling flocks of carrion crows that feasted on the city's eyeless dead.

Helena died by phosgene gas. Two common chemicals, sulfuric acid and carbon tetrachloride, were mixed in the broken warehouse of a chemical company, and in sufficient quantities to generate a cloud large enough, by nightfall on the day of the quake, to cover the entire town below the bluff. The gas is colorless, and the characteristic scent of musty hay was not thought alarming by those who had already survived a major earthquake, and who were busy rescuing neighbors and taking shelter from a flood. Phosgene is fatal in small quantities, and often takes an hour or two to do its work: by the time its victims felt any symptoms, they had suffered enough exposure to assure their own fate.

Phosgene attacks the lungs, specifically the capillaries. The victims choked and gagged as their lungs filled with fluid, and then, as the characteristic euphoria of oxygen starvation took them, died in a strange, contented bliss.

A few survivors staggered or drove up the bluff to alert the town to what was happening. Helena, West Helena, and nearby communities were evacuated and cordoned off, but with communications so disrupted, and the roads so badly torn, the evacuation order in effect commanded the citizens to march into the wilderness and attempt to survive there for an indeterminate period. Thousands of people wandered lost in woods and fields for days, afraid to return home for fear of being poisoned.

Ironically, by the time the evacuation got under way, the danger had largely passed. Unlike mustard gas, Lewisite, or some nerve agents, phosgene does not persist in the environment. But Helena's surviving civil authorities were in shock from M1 and easily panicked; they had no way of identifying the gas or assessing the danger; they gave the orders and hoped for the best.

Days later, half-starved families were still staggering out of the countryside.

On the second morning after the quake, Charlie took a bucket of water from his swimming pool and used it to flush his toilet. Then he threw some chlorine in the pool to keep it drinkable—he didn't know how much to use, he had a company who normally took care of this job, he just guessed. Then he looked in his refrigerator.

All that remained was Friday night's *canard à l'orange* in its foam container, and a can of Megan's diet drink, and the anchovies. He took the diet drink from the shelf and opened it.

Vanilla. He *hated* vanilla.

He drank it anyway, and then ate the anchovies, which made a horrid contrast with the vanilla drink. Possibly, he thought, he should get some more food.

But the nearest supermarket was on the other side of the chasm in the street, and he couldn't cross the chasm. He just couldn't. His heart staggered at the thought of it.

And then he remembered the little grocery store. It was maybe a mile away in the other direction.

He didn't know why he hadn't thought of it before. There seemed to be something wrong with the way he was putting things together.

Had to get a grip, he thought. He was Lord of the Jungle.

Charlie made sure his wallet was in his pocket, and then he put on his St. Louis Cardinals cap and began his walk.

No chasms blocked Charlie's way, though broad cracks ran across the road here and there. The neighborhood had been tidied somewhat: some of the fallen trees had been cut up and hauled out of the road, some of the broken glass swept up. Charlie heard the constant sound of chainsaws.

There was almost no traffic. Charlie saw only a few trucks moving, carrying supplies apparently, and a flatbed truck with a bulldozer on it. He saw no official vehicles at all, no police, no fire trucks, no National Guard.

As he left his prosperous Germantown neighborhood, he saw clumps of ill-kempt people standing on street corners, people who watched him in silence. Children and babies were everywhere, the children unbathed, the babies crying.

The store shared a little strip mall with a furniture store and a place that sold office supplies. All the windows were gone: the office supply store was boarded up, but the furniture store was wide open. As Charlie walked past the furniture store he saw people inside, apparently living there, sleeping in the bedroom displays. Two unshaven, shirtless men in baseball caps carried a chest of drawers across the parking lot. It didn't appear to Charlie that they were employees.

The windows of the convenience store were gone, but a

rusty old Dodge van had been parked along the side of the store, blocking most of the broken windows. The broken glass had been swept into the gutter. Charlie saw figures moving in the darkened interior, and he heard a radio blaring, so he stepped in.

The inside was still a wreck. The quake had knocked practically everything off the shelves, and items hadn't been replaced, just swept into crude piles.

NEW POLISY, said a sign just inside the door. CASH ONLY. The sign was written in black felt marker on the back of another placard.

"If you came for milk," said the man behind the counter, "we ran out yesterday."

"No," Charlie said. "Not milk."

"Beer's gone, too," the man said.

The man was a white man in his fifties who wore a baseball cap and a dirty white T-shirt. He hadn't shaved since before the quake, and he carried a long pump shotgun propped on one hip. CIGARETTES, said another sign over his head, $10 PACK. MARLBOROS $12.

The man was a profiteer, clear enough. Charlie wasn't bothered. It wasn't anything more than what he, Charlie, planned to do. Besides, he could buy and sell the whole store.

Behind him was a battery-powered radio on which quake victims were being interviewed. "It was a true miracle that I lived through it," a man said. "A true miracle."

All the canned goods had been piled in one area of the store. LITTEL CANS $7, the sign said, BIG CANS $20. The cans were all sizes, and it was difficult to say which of the medium-sized ones were big, and which were little.

"You want some flour?" the man said. "I got a little left, but not much. And some cornmeal. Sugar's gone."

"Flour?" Charlie said. "No." He wouldn't know what to do with it, had never baked anything in his life.

"My baby's buried in there somewhere," a woman on the radio sobbed. "We're praying for a miracle."

A door opened in the back of the store and a young man

came in. He had long stringy hair to his shoulders and wore a baseball cap and a large revolver prominently strapped to his hip. He looked at Charlie. "C'n I help you?" he asked.

"Canned goods," Charlie said, "and something to drink."

"You want a bag?" the young man said.

Dinty Moore Beef Stew. Vienna sausages. Heinz baked beans. Spam. It was all dreadful, but Charlie filled his sack with it. When he could get real food again, he could give the extra canned stuff to the cleaning lady.

"It was a miracle that my father survived," said a man on the radio.

Charlie put two plastic bottles of mineral water in another sack, then walked to the counter and gave the man his Visa card. The man looked at it with contempt.

"Can't take this," he said, showing long yellow teeth. "Cash only." He pointed. "See the sign?"

"The card's good, mate," Charlie said. "It's platinum."

"Ain't no way to call to prove that. Phone's down."

Charlie sighed, pulled out his Amex card, his MasterCard, his Eurocard, a couple hundred thousand dollars' worth of credit all told. "They're all good," he said. "I can prove they belong to me."

"Cash," the man said, "only."

Charlie eyed him. "Right, then," he said. "Tell you what. Charge an extra hundred dollars to the total."

The man thought about it for at least a half-second. Then shook his head. "Cash," he said. "Radio says the economy's gone crazy. I don't know them banks are still around."

"Of *course* they're around!" Waving a card. "This is *Chase Manhattan Bank*!" Waving another. "This is *American Express*!"

"You got a problem here, pop?" the young man said. He stood behind Charlie and to one side, hand placed casually on the butt of his revolver.

"Cash," the older man said. "None of your funny foreign money, neither." There was a sadistic glint in his eye: he was enjoying this, humiliating one of the rich he'd served all his life. *I'm working class, too!* Charlie wanted to say. But he knew it was pointless: Americans didn't know one British accent from another, thought everyone was a lord.

"Charge me double, then," Charlie said.

The man took the plastic bag of canned goods in one hand, moved it out of Charlie's reach. "You got cash or not?"

"I thank God," said a woman on the radio, "for the miracle that saved us."

Charlie reached into his pocket, took out his money clip. It held a ten, two singles, some change. The older man reached into Charlie's bag and took out a can of Vienna sausage. "This and one of the bottles, eleven dollars."

Charlie gave him eleven dollars. The man added it to a thick roll he produced from his pocket. Charlie looked in anger at the single dollar remaining.

"Sell you a lottery ticket for that?" the older man asked, and laughed.

The laughter followed Charlie out of the store.

Charlie Johns paced back and forth before the chasm in the road. His heart thudded in his chest. "King of the Jungle," he whispered to himself.

He needed to get *out* of here. He had eaten all the Vienna sausages at once, and they'd served only to make him more hungry.

He had a *car*, he thought, Megan's BMW. He could just drive away, drive till he found some place that would take his credit cards or his checks. Someplace *sane*, where the phones worked.

But he didn't have the keys to Megan's car, he realized.

Megan had them. And Megan was dead and in the back of the house and lying under the tub dead in the part of the house where Megan was dead . . . His mind whirled. He felt the need to sit down, and he found the curb and sat.

The keys, he thought, were probably in her handbag. And her handbag was lying in the room somewhere. He might be able to find it without even *looking* at Megan.

Charlie rose from the curb, swayed, and walked back to his house. He felt he required fortification, so he went to the kitchen first, to the wine rack, and opened a bottle of Chateauneuf du Pape. He drank half of it from the neck— good things in wine, he thought, real nutrition there.

The wine's flush prickled along his skin. With his stomach almost empty, the alcohol hit him quickly.

Get to the bedroom fast, he thought. *Grab the handbag. Run.*

In his haste Charlie stumbled over the water heater that sprawled in the back hall and almost went to his knees. He wrenched himself upright and kept on going, his shoes squelching on the wet carpet. Floorboards sagged under his weight. *Don't look,* he thought. He lurched to the door and stepped into the master bedroom.

"Oh God," he said, and closed his eyes. He turned and lurched blindly for the door. He ran into the door frame and felt a cracking blow to his head. He staggered through the door and down the hall, and then he fell across the water heater and vomited up his Vienna sausages and red wine.

Because there were flies now, a black cloud of them, and maggots, so many maggots that they crowded on each other and leaped a foot in the air and fell with the sound of soft rain.

Charlie staggered to the kitchen and his bottle of Chateauneuf du Pape, and he rinsed his mouth with the wine and then gagged and went to his knees as his stomach convulsed.

He went out of the house to the BMW and lay down across the two front seats. He still had the wine bottle clutched in his hands.

He could still detect Megan's scent hovering in the car.

After a while, he took another drink of wine.

The Comet has been passing to the westward since it passed its perihelion—perhaps it has touched the mountain of California, that has given a small shake to this side of the globe—or the shake which the Natchezians have felt may be a mysterious visitation from the Author of all nature, on them for their sins— wickedness and the want of good faith have long prevailed in

*that territory. Sodom and Gomorrha would have been saved had
three righteous persons been found in it—we therefore hope that
Natchez has been saved on the same principle.*

The Louisiana Gazette and Daily Advertiser
(New Orleans), December 21, 1811

"Remember to bring in the food! All the food!" Brother
Frankland called after the little convoy he was sending down
into the Arkansas Delta. "Bring all the survivors, but bring as
much food as you can!"

The trucks and four-wheel-drive vehicles crunched gravel
as they rolled out of the church parking lot and onto the
highway. Frankland's people—conspicuous in their official-
looking white armbands—were doing a good job of bringing
in survivors from isolated farms, along with as many supplies as could be scrounged from wrecked buildings or dug
out of collapsed cellars. It turned out that Frankland would
need as much food as his scavengers could provide.

They'd managed to plunder the Piggly Wiggly, though, of
everything edible that had survived the quake. The sheriff's
department hadn't interfered, being told that the people in
the white armbands were relief workers, and Piggly Wiggly
management were somewhere else. Sheryl was salting down
as much of the meat as hadn't gone directly into the stewpot,
and storing the flour in plastic garbage barrels, along with
bay leaves to discourage the weevils from eating more than
their fair share.

Not that weevils weren't a good source of protein in themselves.

Protein was also available in the local catfish farms. Since
the catfish farmers couldn't get their fish to market,
Frankland reasoned, they might as well donate their harvest.
But he hadn't spoken to any of them other than his parish-
ioner Joe Johnson, who was willing to contribute his income
for his soul's sake.

The food issue aside, things were going well. By now, the
second day following the quake, the Church of the End

Times had turned into a regular encampment, encompassing half the ten acres that comprised Frankland's property. Tents marched in disciplined rows. Latrines had been dug and screened with canvas or plastic sheets that crackled in the brisk wind. Reverend Garb had brought in his own parishioners to help out, and now there were black hands working alongside the white in getting the camp ready.

It was laid out like an army camp. The Army of the Lord.

Hilkiah was out on the fields planting a series of poles in the ground—planting them deep in quick-setting concrete, so that they'd stay upright during any future tremors. Then he'd string them with loudspeakers, so that everyone, throughout the growing compound, could have the benefit of the Good News simultaneously being broadcast on the radio station. Frankland, Dr. Calhoun, and the Reverend Garb took turns broadcasting, varying their message between urging refugees to make their way to town, asking listeners to donate supplies, and lengthy sermons on the End Times.

Near the church, a portable drilling rig—one Frankland had bought fifth-hand years ago—was putting in a new well. The quake had sheared the pipes from Frankland's two old wells, but he'd been prepared for that, and his cisterns would be sufficient till they could get new wells dug.

Things were much better organized here than in town. Rails Bluff had long since run out of emergency supplies, personnel, food, and fresh water. All Sheriff Gorton could do when refugees straggled in was to advise them to continue up Highway 417 to the Reverend Frankland's place. He was sending them in shuttles on Dr. Calhoun's bus, along with as many of Rails Bluff's own inhabitants as he could persuade to go.

Communication was nonexistent: the telephone exchange had been destroyed, ground lines were down, radios in the sheriff's cars didn't carry far enough to reach anywhere else, cellular phone relays were all gone. It was probably a blessing, Frankland thought—he could do his work here without worrying about corruption and evil broadcast from the outside, but he still felt sorry for those worried about loved ones they could not reach.

"Brother Frankland?"

Frankland turned at the sound of Garb's voice. "Brother Garb?" he smiled.

"Heaven-o," said Garb.

"Beg pardon?"

Garb gave a shy smile. "Heaven-o. It's a way of saying 'hello,' except it leaves out the 'hell.' It always bothered me that there was hell in hello."

Frankland nodded in admiration. "Heaven-o! That's great!" he said. "Did you think of that?"

"No, I heard that there was this county in Texas that voted to replace hello with heaven-o, and I thought it was a pretty good idea."

"Maybe we should make it official here in the camp."

"I'd be very pleased if we could." Garb adjusted his gold-rimmed spectacles. "I've just been speaking to that last bus-load of refugees that came up from town," he said. "Half of them are from below the bluff, down in the Delta."

Frankland nodded. "They can hear our message in the Delta? That's good."

Garb shook his head. "No, they didn't hear you. They came here because it was the only place they could go. The levees broke, and everyone in the Delta was flooded out."

Frankland shook his head. All those rich farmers growing cotton and soya in the Arkansas Delta, living off the fat of the land while their neighbors, and their neglected brethren in Rails Bluff, stayed poor. Now the rich farmers were refugees, and Rails Bluff their only hope.

"God bless them," Frankland said. That Wal-Mart super-store, he thought, must be flooded out, too.

"The ones who got out were those who live close to the bluff," Garb went on, "or who owned boats that could get them through the flooding. There must be many more peo-ple down there who have been stranded." Garb looked up at Frankland. "I was thinking that we should organize rescue groups with boats, just as we've done with jeeps and trucks.

Go out there into the flooded country, bring people in."

Frankland put a hand on Garb's shoulder. "Brother Garb, that's a brilliant idea. Bless you."

Garb smiled. "Thank *you*. I can ask some of the refugees to serve as guides, because they know the country. And of course they already have boats."

"Put our own people in the boats as well, make sure the thing's done right."

"*Reliable* people."

"Exactly." Frankland nodded.

It was glorious to have so many people here on his wavelength.

"I will organize it, if you like," Garb said.

"Thank you, Brother Garb." He hesitated. "Don't forget the Wal-Mart. Tools, supplies, food."

"Guns and ammunition."

"Amen," said Frankland.

There was the sound of a horn blaring from the highway, and Frankland looked up to see a pickup truck rolling in from the east. The driver waved a hand from his window as he turned into the church parking lot. Frankland could see another man in the bed of the truck. He and Garb trotted up to the truck as it ground to a halt on the gravel.

The driver hopped out. Frankland recognized him as the sixteen-year-old son of one of his parishioners, a scavenger who had been sent out east with some others. "We've got a casualty," the boy said. "We pulled him out of a wrecked car at the bottom of the Rails River Bridge. He must have been on the bridge when it collapsed."

"He's been down there for two days?" Garb said, impressed.

"He was about to drown when we pulled him out. The river's rising." The boy walked around the pickup and let down the tailgate. "It was a heck of a job getting him up the riverbank," he said. "We need a stretcher or something to get him to the infirmary."

"We don't have any stretchers," Garb said, "but I'll get a canvas cot."

Garb hustled away. Frankland looked into the bed of the truck and felt a rush of cold surprise.

Father Guillaume Robitaille. Personal emissary from the Prince of Darkness to Rails Bluff.

The priest was pale where he wasn't sunburned, and crusted with his own blood. His nose was mashed over most of his face, his eyes were black, his front teeth had been knocked out. He looked at the world without comprehension, from rolling, half-slitted eyes. He shivered and trembled and made little whining noises.

Frankland gave silent thanks to the Lord, who had put the great Roman Enemy in his power.

"We'll take Father Robitaille to my house," he said. "I want to look after him personally." He looked down at the priest.

"Heaven-o, Father," he said. "Heaven-o."

"Sweet Lord, look at that," Sheryl said. Frankland nodded.

Father Robitaille trembled and whimpered in their bed. They had given him water, though he'd thrown most of it back up, and they'd tried to feed him, but he hadn't been hungry, or maybe just hadn't recognized his meal as food. He seemed pretty far gone.

He was safe enough in Frankland's house, though. Like his church and broadcast center, it was steel-framed and set firmly on its foundation. It featured steel walls, steel window frames, steel doors and door frames.

Frankland hadn't intended it that way, but when he was putting the building up, he realized it wouldn't make a bad jail.

Or a drunk tank.

"When I was growing up in Little Rock," Frankland said, "there was a little ol' Catholic church between where I lived and where I went to school. And my folks told me that when I walked to school, I should be sure to cross the street when I got to the Catholic church, and walk on the other side, so that the Devil wouldn't jump out of the church and get me. And most of the other kids in the neighborhood had been told the same thing, so practically everyone crossed the street to keep clear of the Catholics." He chuckled. "Some of the braver kids would sneak up to the church, knock on the door, and run. Dare the Devil to come out and chase them."

Sheryl nodded. "Your parents knew what they were talking about," he said.

"Yep." Frankland grinned. "When I was a child, I didn't understand that it was just a, a what-d'you-call-it, a *metaphor*. There wasn't a literal Devil in there, not the kind with horns and tail—well, I *guess* there wasn't, I never looked. But my folks were right that if you went to the Catholic church, the Devil would get you in his clutches." He laughed. "You know, I've never been in a Catholic church to this day. Not even just to look around."

"Me neither," said Sheryl.

"Ba ba," Robitaille muttered through his broken teeth.

Frankland looked down at him. "Look at the Devil now."

"Hah," Robitaille said. His eyes came open, seemed to focus on Frankland. "Hah. Help."

Frankland leaned closer. "Yes. We're here for you."

"Help."

"We're here to *save* you," Frankland said. Which wasn't the same thing as *help*, not exactly.

"Ta," Robitaille said. "Ta. Trink."

"He wants a drink," Sheryl said.

Frankland poured a glass of water from the pitcher and held it to Robitaille's lips. Robitaille raised a hand to the glass and gulped eagerly at the water, and then his whole body gave a violent shudder, and he turned away, retching. Water spilled from his lips.

"*Cochon!*" he shouted. "*Qui es-tu? Un espèce de fou?*"

"He doesn't want a drink, teddy bear," Sheryl said. "He wants a *drink*."

"*Donne-moi un verre! Un verre!*"

Frankland straightened. "Well. Water's what he gets." He looked down at Robitaille. "Water's what we've *got*! It's *all* we've got!"

Robitaille began to cry. Fat tears fell from his blackened eyes. "*Je vais mourir! Donne-moi un verre! Je vais mourir si je ne trouve pas un verre.*"

"What's that language?" Frankland asked. "Latin, like the pope talks?"

"I guess."

Frankland refilled the glass, put the glass on the table within the reach of Robitaille's arms.

"I'm gonna let him calm down," he said. "Then maybe the two of us can have a real chat."

He and Sheryl left the room, and nodded to the guard that Frankland had put on the door. One of the older men in their church, a tough farmer who wasn't about to let a drunk priest sway him from his duty.

"Look after him," Frankland said. "Give him anything he wants except alcohol—and I'm afraid that's *all* he's going to want."

"Where would I find alcohol, Brother Frankland?" The farmer grinned.

"Somebody might have snuck some alcohol in."

"Well, I'll keep on the lookout."

"I appreciate it, friend," Frankland said.

Frankland made his way down the hall, past the extra furniture and breakable items they'd taken from the bedroom before they put Robitaille in the bed.

And then Robitaille, behind the steel door, began to scream, hoarse wails that prickled the hair on Frankland's arms.

"Dang," the farmer said. "That don't even sound human."

Frankland thought about that for the next hour or so, and then he decided it was a question to which he'd better find out the answer.

Jessica's stomach gave a pleasant rollercoaster lurch as her helicopter circled the Gateway Arch. The ruins of St. Louis were spread out below her. The blackened devastation of yesterday morning's propane explosion, where the fire chief and a couple dozen of his men were martyred, was plain to see. There was a circular crater in the center of the area, filled with water from the River Des Peres. Smoke rose from persistent fires. The morning's brisk southwest wind was whipping up flames that had died down the day before.

Still, there were parts of St. Louis that were more or less intact, standing like hollow-eyed sentinels above the rubble that surrounded them. The earthquake had laid entire districts in ruin, but spared others. It was like a game of survival roulette: if you put your chips, your house and family, in the right area, you could come through with some broken windows and fallen shingles, while other people's chips were swept off the board. The only problem was that no one knew which neighborhoods would be spared until after the game began, and by then it was too late for most of the players.

The riverfront was a wreck. And the Chain of Rocks Canal in Illinois, through which river traffic bypassed the rapids that infested the river north of St. Louis, was now unusable. The canal's banks had caved in, and so had the sides of the newly built Lock No. 27.

The grounds of the National Expansion Memorial were covered either with tents or helicopters. MARS had moved in force: the Memorial held a battalion of paratroopers from Fort Bragg and a thousand rescue workers from all over the world, all in addition to the refugees who had poured out of the ruined city. Other city parks were also filling up with rescuers and refugees. Airlift Command was having a hard time just keeping them fed, particularly as there were few surviving runways big enough to carry heavy fixed-wing transports. Even the tough and reliable C130s were having a hard time finding places to land. Almost everything had to be flown in by helicopter, and choppers were fragile craft that required a lot of down time for maintenance.

Jessica sympathized with Airlift Command. They were trained to supply a mere *army*. This was an entire *population*.

During the Second World War, the United States had at its peak supported 15,000,000 soldiers, but that was after years of military buildup. Now there were millions of homeless refugees on American soil and the government was being asked to take care of them overnight, and with the heart ripped out of the country's infrastructure.

"Take me down over the river," Jessica said.

Her pilot gave a redneck grin. "You want to go under the bridges, or over?"

For a moment she was tempted, and then she decided she would feel truly ridiculous if, during the greatest adventure of her life, she was killed by a falling railway tie. "Better go over," she said.

Jessica's stomach sank into a single location as the Kiowa Warrior settled into a smooth dive. G's tautened her grin.

She was going to have to learn how to fly one of these, that was clear. This was just too much fun.

The river was fast and carried tons of debris. Once they got south of the bluffs at Cape Girardeau, Swampeast Missouri spread out before them like a shimmering inland lake. There were a pair of waterfalls at Island No. 8, though the Mississippi was busy reducing them. Jessica asked the pilot to make a detour to Sikeston, west of the river, to look at the power plant. The Sikeston Power Plant had been built directly on an earthquake fissure that was clearly visible from the top of its smokestack. At the time when the plant was built, no one realized this was an earthquake feature. But even after the fissure had been properly identified, land atop it had been acquired for a housing subdivision.

Neither the power plant, the smokestack, nor the subdivision had survived M1. Brown water washed through the wreckage.

The next power plant south had been built at New Madrid, not exactly the best choice under the circumstances. It and the town were a flooded ruin. So was Cabells Mound. The river had cut the New Madrid bend and the bend at Uncle Chowder.

Jessica took a professional interest in the area south of New Madrid designated the New Madrid Floodway. The levee east of the floodway had been built with plugs atop the levee that could be removed in the event of dangerously high water, allowing the floodway to fill with water until the water reached a backup levee built five or so miles behind the river. This was to enable deliberate inundation so as to take pressure off other critical areas of the river.

Removing the plugs hadn't been necessary, not with the earthquake tearing away chunks of the levee. To that extent the New Madrid Floodway functioned as intended.

Unfortunately this hadn't helped populated areas, not with every levee in the district broken, including the backup levee behind the floodway. Everyplace that *could* flood *had* flooded. But because the flood was *every* place, it wasn't as bad as it could get in any *one* place. Once the water had a chance to spread out, it achieved a kind of uniform depth over the whole region. It was a lake, but the lake was fairly shallow.

Jessica had hopes for the levees farther south. Before the Swampeast drained—and judging from the extent of the flooding, draining should take some time—it should be possible to reinforce and repair most of the levees south of the Arkansas River. She had hopes of keeping the major cities dry from Greenville south. This would entail pouring all these billions of gallons of water back into their proper channel south of the Arkansas. She thought this was possible.

"Refugees to starboard, General," the pilot said.

There were about a dozen of them, at least two families. They were trapped, with their automobiles, on top of a flooded two-lane rural roadway. They had probably been there for two days. They were standing on top of their flooded vehicles, jumping up and down and waving their arms. Probably screaming their heads off, too.

Jessica's Bell Kiowa light helicopter was far too small to carry the refugees away, even if they dangled from the skids.

"Circle them and let them know they've been seen," Jessica said. "I'll contact the jarheads and call for a dustoff."

The helicopter rescue units operating in this part of the Mississippi Valley had been deployed by the Navy and Marines into a naval air station north of Memphis. Big Sikorsky Sea Stallions, able to carry over three dozen refugees and capable of floating on their amphibious hulls, were picking up people in isolated locales and delivering them to refugee centers well away from the earthquake zones, where they could be fed and housed without straining the capabilities of Airlift Command.

While Jessica's pilot banked into a turn over the stranded people, Jessica contacted the Navy, who informed her that there was a Sea Stallion flying on a search pattern over the Swampeast just a few minutes away. Jessica kept the Kiowa circling to mark the refugees' position. When the big Marine Sikorsky arrowed in from the northwest, Jessica resumed her tour of the Mississippi, crossing the river to look at what remained of Memphis.

The Memphis Pyramid, she saw, was sitting in a lake. The old nineteenth-century Pinch District, surrounding the pyramid, was little but rubble, each building looking like a little crumbled brick pyramid paying homage to their huge silver neighbor. Mud Island was MIA. Beale Street, home of the blues, had been obliterated.

The random pattern of destruction that marked St. Louis, some parts destroyed and others standing, was not present here in Memphis. Here, the earthquake had spared nothing.

The Kiowa hovered at low altitude over the Harbor of Memphis while Jessica studied the wreckage, absorbing the company names on wrecked facilities, on ruptured storage tanks and half-submerged barges. Helm Fertilizer, she read. Ashland Chemical. Vulcan Chemicals. Chemtech Industries. Marathon Oil.

Even from the Kiowa, floating a hundred feet over the burned harbor, she could smell the chemical soup below.

She hovered for a sad moment over the wreckage of the Corps of Engineers' Memphis District headquarters. Eight of her own people, she knew now, had died there when the harbor turned to a holocaust.

Below Memphis was a burning towboat and barge tow that had just caught fire. A chemical slick oozed downriver from the burning barges.

Everywhere there were wrecked barges, burned grain elevators, suspicious stains on the water. There were dozens of oil and gas pipelines, Jessica knew, that ran across the bottom of the river. Who knew how many had ruptured?

At Helena, Jessica buzzed the wrecked chemical plant. South of Helena was the Union 76 Oil Company facility at Delta Revetment, the Port of Rosedale, the storage tanks of the Bunge Corporation and the waste discharge of the Potlatch Corporation at De Soto Landing in Arkansas, the port terminal and tank storage at Arkansas City. The Port of Greenville, snug in a slackwater horseshoe bend created by the Corps of Engineers, was choked with the spilled residue of its commerce: Farmkist Fertilizer, Cooper-Gilder Chemical, Warren Petroleum, and more than a dozen barge and shipping firms. It was a miracle that the port hadn't gone up in flames like the Harbor of Memphis. The town was evacuated until its port either blew up or was declared safe. Madison Parish, in Louisiana, featured a large complex of oil and chemical storage facilities.

And in Vicksburg, Jessica's headquarters, the port was choked with marine commerce, from Phoenix Rice Oil at the northern end to Mississippi Power and Light at the south, by way of the Ergon Refinery, Citgo Petroleum, and Neill Butane.

By the time the Kiowa spiraled to its landing in Vicksburg, Jessica knew what she had to do.

"Heaven-o," Frankland said, and Robitaille began to scream.

"He cries in pain when you speak the name of heaven," Dr. Calhoun said, and frowned at the man writhing on the bed.

The stench in the room was appalling. Sweat, urine, vomit. Frankland steeled himself against it.

"Donne-moi un verre! Au nom de Dieu, un verre!"

The three pastors looked down at the priest, each holding a well-worn Bible. "He just keeps talking that Latin," Frankland said. "I figure the Devil speaks Latin like the Pope."

"That's French," Calhoun said. "He's from Cajun country, remember."

Frankland looked at Calhoun dubiously, then decided the precise language didn't matter anyway. "Well," he said to Calhoun, "you're the college boy."

"Pour quo êtes-vous là? Qu'est-ce que vous faites? Des diables!"

"Did you hear that?" Garb said. "He said *devil*, I think."

Calhoun stepped closer to the bed, passing a hand nervously over his bald head, and then straightened and spoke in a loud, commanding voice. "Who are you?" he demanded. "What is your name? I demand this in the name of the Lord!"

"Don't touch me! Don't touch me!"

The English words sprayed between Robitaille's broken teeth. He shrank from his three visitors, backing across the stained sheets to the far wall.

"Why don't you want us to touch you?" Garb said. "Why do you try to hide from the name of the Lord?"

"Vous voulez que je meurs!"

Calhoun adjusted his gold-rimmed spectacles. "Why don't you try touching him with the Bible?"

Calhoun nodded. "Good idea, Brother Garb." He stepped forward and tried to press his Bible to Robitaille's head. Robitaille gave a cry and tried to bat the Bible away with his hands.

"C'est le singe! Le grand singe!"

Calhoun pulled Robitaille's hands away and firmly pressed the Bible to Robitaille's forehead. Robitaille shrieked, seized Calhoun's wrists. For a moment there was a frantic struggle.

"Get away! *C'est le singe!*"

Calhoun pulled back. Robitaille gasped for breath, eyes rolling wildly in his face as he tried to back himself into the headboard. Calhoun turned to the others, his face grave.

"Well," he said, "I guess that settles it." He looked at Frankland. "Brother Frankland, praise Jesus for letting you see this."

"Thank you, Dr. Calhoun," Frankland said in relief. He had needed his colleagues to assure him that his diagnosis was correct, that this was not merely a case of the DTs. They had all worked with alcoholics, they had all worked with people going through withdrawal. But this one was, clearly, different.

Now all could agree that Father Robitaille had been possessed by an evil spirit, presumably a demon flown up from Hell.

The Devil *could* get you if you went into a Catholic church, Frankland thought. In Robitaille's case, it wasn't a what-d'you-call-it *metaphor*, it was a genuine devil. It had led Robitaille into false worship, into alcoholism and probably other sinful behaviors. It cursed and gibbered in foreign tongues and shrank from the Bible and the name of the Lord.

Garb bit his lip. "The question is, how do we get rid of it?"

There was a moment of silence.

"Well," Frankland said, "our Lord cast seven devils out of Mary Magdalene, and a legion's worth of devils out of the two possessed men. And he gave this power to his disciples."

Calhoun passed a nervous hand over his bald head. "But how's it done, exactly?"

None of them had ever had direct experience with demons before. In preparation for this moment, each had looked into his Bible and discovered that there were no actual directions for casting out spirits.

"Well," Calhoun said, "in Mark, our Lord says, 'Come out of the man, thou unclean spirit.'"

Frankland considered this. "Shall we try it?"

They faced Robitaille and chanted the phrase in unison. They tried it several times. Robitaille only whimpered and muttered as he cast terrified looks around the room.

"There's got to be more to it than this," Frankland said.

"We don't dare let a demon spy on us," Garb said. "What we're doing here is too crucial."

Frankland looked at Robitaille again. He had curled up around a pillow, and was crying. "What can we use to help us?" Frankland asked.

"The Lord's name," Garb said.

"The Lord's Word," said Calhoun, brandishing his Bible.

"The Lord's . . ." Frankland stumbled. "Prayer?" he finished.

"All three," Calhoun said firmly.

They worked on Robitaille for an hour, with vigor and persistence and pure-hearted dedication, but it didn't seem to help.

It took some time to get a hold of the President. Jessica kept getting the brushoff from various aides and assistants. She didn't want to think about how many leaps in the chain of command she was making by placing this call.

"It is a decision that only the President can make," she kept repeating. "I must speak to him personally."

Jessica was told that the President was speaking to the press about the tragedy while taking a boat ride past the flooded Memphis Pyramid. Let it not be said, she thought, that he was ever at a loss for photo opportunities. Jessica wished she'd stayed in Memphis and dropped in on the President while he was making his tour.

"Listen," Jessica said, "the President *appointed* me to this job, in person, just a few weeks ago. The *last* thing the press wants to hear is that I resigned because the President would not speak to me on a matter of vital national interest."

She wagged her eyebrows at her husband, Pat, who sat across her desk with a highly impressed look on his face. He didn't very often have the opportunity to see her turn into Major General Frazetta, the Fire-Eating Army Engineer. She covered the mouthpiece of her phone.

"What's for lunch?" she asked.

"Mystery meat on a bun," Pat said. "Macaroni and cheese. Mixed veg. I haven't had these kinds of meals since high school."

"That's because you never experienced the joy of national service. A few years in the Army would have taught you to appreciate chicken á la king and chipped beef on toast."

"If today's army were sensible—like that of Jeb Stuart—I would have served."

Jessica grinned. "Could you get me some lunch?"

"You bet."

"Make mine with extra mystery meat, will you?"

Pat nodded and was off. Jessica returned to her phone and her war with the Executive Department.

In due time she heard the velvet tones of her boss. "Jessica," he said, "where are you?"

Ninety minutes, she noted. Damn. She had *clout.*

This was a good thing to know.

"I'm in Vicksburg, Mr. President," Jessica said. "At my headquarters."

"I'm told you needed to speak to me. What can I do for you?"

"A couple things, Mr. President. First, you'd make my job a little easier if you asked Congress to move along my appointment as President of the Mississippi Valley Commission."

"Okay," the President said. "I can do that."

An undertone of impatience had crept into the President's soothing tenor. Jessica had only asked about the MVC appointment by way of delaying her real request, which took a certain amount of nerve.

"But what I *really* need you to do, sir, is this," she said. She took a deep breath. "I need you to order the evacuation of the entire Mississippi Valley from St. Louis south to the Gulf of Mexico."

Pat returned with Jessica's second cup of coffee, and she sipped it gratefully. "I didn't hear all of that," he said, "but it sounded as if you wanted to evacuate every city on the Mississippi. New Orleans and everyplace."

Jessica nodded. "I do."

"But New Orleans isn't flooded. And there's no danger from quake down there—" Pat looked at her. "Is there?"

Jessica shook her head. "Don't think so, no."

"So the levees are safe? They'll hold?"

"Probably they'll hold. I'll do my damnedest to make sure they do. But that's not my problem—the problem is that all those cities, and every little town in between, get their water from the river. And the river isn't just a river, it's *the biggest sewer in North America*. With this many refugees, you're going to see every disease you can think of going into the river. Cholera, typhus, typhoid. Any industry you can name sits on the river bank. Petroleum, fertilizers, flammable chemicals, raw sewage. *Nuclear power*, even."

Pat looked at her. "You're going to have to evacuate those cities . . . because of *pollution*?"

She looked up at him. "I presume the big cities can chlorinate their water enough to keep out the diseases, but I doubt the small towns have even that capacity. And even the cities can't handle the other stuff. Heavy metals. Nitrate fertilizer. Chlorinated chemicals. Pesticides, petroleum products. Phosphates, ammoniated compounds. Plastics. Toluene, benzene, fuel oils. Polychlorinated biphenyls, from places that haven't phased them out. Corrosives. Hexavalent chromium—" she shook her head "—now *that's* a nightmare. And on top of all that, we've maybe got nuclear isotopes from that plant downriver."

"Jesus," Pat said.

"Enough to keep every Hazardous Materials team in the country busy for twenty years," Jessica said.

Pat's eyes were wide. "So what did the President say?"

Jessica's helmet felt very heavy. "He said he'd talk to his people and get back to me. But what can he do?" She shook her head. "I don't know how many millions of people live on the Lower Mississippi, but we don't have the capacity to ship fresh water to them every day, especially when there's an all-out emergency just up the river."

"How long is it going to be before people come back?"

Jessica leaned back in her chair, looked morosely at her crowded desk. "The river will clean itself. It does that. But it will take months." She looked at her husband sadly. "Months if we're lucky. And that means months with the entire middle of the country out of commission, living on handouts in refugee centers."

TWENTY

As we passed the point on the left hand below the island, the bank and trees were rapidly falling in. From the state of alarm I was in at this time, I cannot pretend to be correct as to the length or height of the falls; but my impression is, that they were about equal to the rapids of the Ohio. As we passed the lower point of the island, looking back, up the left channel, we thought the falls extended higher up the river on that side than on the other.

The water of the river, after it was fairly light, appeared to be almost black, with something like the dust of stone coal— We landed at New Madrid about breakfast time without having experienced any injury— The appearance of the town, and the situation of the inhabitants, were such as to afford but little relief to our minds. The former elevation of the bank on which the town stood was estimated by the inhabitants at about 25 feet above common water; when we reached it the elevation was only about 12 or 13 feet— There was scarcely a house left entire—some wholly prostrated, others unroofed and not a chimney standing—the people all having deserted their habitations, were in camps and tents back of the town, and their little watercrafts, such as skiffs, boats and canoes, handed out of the water to their camps, that they might be ready in case the country should sink.

Matthias M. Speed, March 2nd, 1812

The President gazed at the solemn faces that ringed the conference table in his hotel in Louisville. "What I need, people," he said, "is for somebody here to tell me that General Frazetta is crazy. Wacko. Out of her mind."

The others looked uneasily at the table, at their papers, at each other. "It can't be done, sir," offered the Senate's Minority Leader. "We can't evacuate the whole Mississippi

Valley. And in the middle of an emergency like this one? That's *insane*."

The President looked at Lipinsky. "Boris?" he said.

Lipinsky drew his bushy brows together. "I fear, Mr. President," he said, "that General Frazetta may have just presented us with our only sane course of action."

The President felt the others take a breath. "Well, people," he said. "Well."

"But we lack data, sir," Lipinsky said. "I will order my HAZMAT teams to test the water immediately and continually."

The President had flown to the Midwest shortly after word came that south St. Louis had blown up, and taken with him select members of his administration and the congressional leadership of both parties. If his nation's cities were going to explode, he was going to be on the scene. And so he had visited St. Louis and Memphis; the Vice President and First Lady had gone to Chicago and Springfield, respectively; and tomorrow, after the military made absolutely certain it was safe, he would visit the graveyard of Helena.

And of course he had made a point of being *seen*. Not for crudely political reasons—though those played a part—but because the news of his activities could bring people hope.

He was still cynical enough, however, to tell the First Lady and the Vice President that after he had to return to Washington, they were "to remain on PCD"—Permanent Compassion Duty, visiting every refugee center, hospital, and relief effort in the emergency zone; feeling the public's pain, preferably on television and in prime time.

"We will need time to prepare an evacuation on this scale, sir," said the supported CINC. "And most of our transport is already committed to bringing personnel and materiel to the devastated zones. The recommitment alone will take days."

"I need you to begin the logistical planning now," the President said, "before Boris's teams assess the danger." *Fortunately,* he thought, *the areas we need to evacuate are the areas south of the quake zone where the transportation infrastructure is still largely intact.*

"This is *crazy!*" the Minority Leader proclaimed. "That means shutting down industry and commerce throughout the middle third of the country."

"General Frazetta," the President said, "suggested that vital industry and ports like New Orleans could be kept open. We could ship in enough fresh water to do that."

"We can't, Mr. President!" the Minority Leader proclaimed. "The disruption will be—" Words failed him.

The President looked at him. "Are you prepared to go on television and tell the American people that it is their duty to our economy to poison themselves and their children by drinking contaminated water?" He leaned forward, looked at the man. "I'd like to see you do that, I really would."

The Minority Leader fell into glowering silence.

The President leaned back in his chair. "I'm not going to authorize any action right away," he said. "But I want plans made, just in case Boris's HAZMAT teams find out that we need to move a lot of people, and fast."

"Des bestioles! Des bestioles dans le bouffe!"

"Out," Dr. Calhoun cried, "unrighteous one, Spawn of the Pit! Leave this man in peace!"

"Il y a des bestioles partout!"

"I command you in Jesus' name!"

"Ayaaah! Des bestioles! Des centaines! Des bestioles dans le bouffe!"

"Out!" Frankland shouted, and brandished his Bible. Father Robitaille gasped for air, then let out a howl.

Despite the persistence of the exorcisms, and the unexpected flair shown by Dr. Calhoun for the work—Frankland had to admit that "Out, unrighteous one, Spawn of the Pit" was pretty darn good—Robitaille's demon seemed content to remain in residence.

The room stank of spilled food and vomit, soiled bedding and unwashed humanity. Robitaille hadn't kept any food down, and he'd just flung his latest meal to the floor without even trying to taste it. Just a sip of water brought on the dry heaves. And despite this lack of nourishment, he still demonstrated surprising power and mobility. Sometimes it required the weight and strength of all three exorcists to keep him on his bed.

"Des bestioles! Des bestioles!"

"Out! Out!"

"Des bestioles! Des bestioles!"

"Out!"

Frankland felt himself flagging. Robitaille was wearing all of them out. If this went on much longer, the smell alone would gas the three exorcists to death.

He summoned his resolution. It was the demon, he thought, or him.

Wearily, he wondered if "Desbestioles" was the demon's name.

"Out, Desbestioles, out!" he shouted. "In Jesus' name!"

But it didn't seem to help.

After Nick and Jason fled from the dead city of Helena, the bodies began to rise. Apparently the corpses had been there all along, rolling along the bottom of the river, but now they'd decayed to the point where they came to the surface. They were bloated, horrible dough-figures, facial features submerged in swollen flesh, splayed fingers fat as sausages. Nick told Jason not to look, and Jason did not give him any resistance. Nick kept his gaze away from the corpses himself.

He didn't want to look down at a body and recognize Viondi.

More than a dozen of these macabre figures appeared in just a few hours, and it was as if the boat somehow attracted them. The bodies kept closing with the boat as if trying to invite themselves on board. Finally Nick decided to keep the motor going all the time, at low speed so as to conserve fuel, so that he could maneuver clear.

"River won't let us go," he heard Jason mutter. Jason crouched on the foredeck, rubbing his forearms.

Nick closed his eyes and saw Arlette with the water crawling up to her chin. He snapped his eyes open.

There were other corpses in the river: a surprising number

of birds, wings stiffened in startled attitudes of half-flight. Whole flocks of them floated like feathery rafts, or spun in whirlpools. They weren't just water birds, but land birds like crows and hawks. Nick even saw a bald eagle.

"I'm glad we didn't catch any fish the other day," he said. "Yes?"

Nick indicated a nearby raft of floating birds. "Remember all those dead fish the other day? I bet these birds ate them."

Jason looked at the birds and swallowed hard. "Yes," he said. "Yes, I see what you mean."

Nick thought of Arlette, of Manon. All the things that could befall them.

No chemical plants in Toussaint, at least. Whatever happened to Helena wouldn't happen there. And surely there couldn't be severe quake damage that far into Arkansas. Surely the bodies weren't rising on the bayou that flowed past Arlette's home.

Surely, Nick told himself. Surely that was the case. But he didn't *know,* and in the absence of knowledge his mind filled with fantasies, fantasies of Arlette trapped in the cellar as it collapsed, or caught in a burning building, or swept away by flood.

He needed to *know.*

Jason stood in the cockpit, pointed frantically astern. *"Boat!"* he shouted. "It's a *boat!"*

Nick gave a surprised look over his shoulder. There was a towboat flanking through the bend behind them, exhaust pouring from its stubby stacks as it shoved its pack of barges downriver, moving fast on the heels of the drifting speedboat.

"Yes!" The boat rocked as Jason began a kind of lunging dance. *"Yes!"*

A grin rose to Nick's lips. He pushed the throttle forward, felt the big Evinrude respond. He cranked the wheel over and the boat heeled into a turn. Jason gave a whoop and jumped up on the gunwale, balancing with one hand on the struts for the canvas cockpit cover. He edged forward till he was on the foredeck, and then he jumped up and down, waving his arms.

The towboat came on. The water at the bow of the barges whitened as the tow increased its speed.

Better get out of the way, Nick thought. *Bet those barges can't slow down so good.*

He swung wide. Jason gave a disappointed shout. Nick swerved back to pass the towboat on its port side.

The towboat was a big one, increasing speed now that it was in a straighter section of the channel. White water surged under its counter. Nick counted eighteen barges in its tow. When Nick cut the towboat's wake, the boat rocked so much that Jason had to crouch on the foredeck to keep his balance.

Nick saw a dark silhouette in the pilothouse, but he couldn't see if the crewman had seen him or not.

"They're not stopping!" Jason yelled.

Nick spun the wheel and rolled into the towboat's wake. He pushed the throttle forward—the boat skittered on the water, the bass boat swinging like a pendulum on the end of its tow rope—and then he leaped the wake again, the boat's fiberglass hull banging down on the brown river. The river seemed a lot harder than it had been at lower speeds.

Nick roared up alongside the towboat. Jason stood again, shouted and waved his arms at the figure in the pilothouse. Nick wished he had an air horn to blow, or some other means of alerting the towboat's crew.

Nick swung closer. Jason waved.

The man in the pilothouse turned, stared out the side window. He'd clearly seen the boat.

The crewman opened the door, waved and shouted. He was a big man, with a big round belly in his green overalls. It looked as if he were waving the speedboat *away.*

"Stop!" Nick could barely hear Jason's words over the cry of the Evinrude and the roar of the towboat's engines. *"Stop! Help us!"*

The crewman waved the boat away again. Nick felt anger reach for his heart. Who was this man to deny them help?

The man went into the pilothouse again. The towboat's roaring engines increased in volume. The towboat was moving faster. Nick cranked his own throttle forward.

"God damn it!" Nick shouted. What was wrong with that man?

Jason waved and shouted. The man in the pilothouse resolutely ignored him. Nick wondered wildly what he could do. He and Jason were like a pair of mice trying to stop a charging elephant.

The man in the pilothouse ducked his head. He seemed to be talking into a handset. Jason howled abuse. "Fuckdroid! Cocksucker!"

A door opened in the superstructure, and another man appeared. He dropped down a ladder with practiced ease, then came to the gunwale. Nick maneuvered the speedboat closer. The crewman shouted and made gestures for the speedboat to clear off, but Nick couldn't hear what he was saying. He saw Jason's shoulders slump, though, and saw the boy turn aft.

Nick maneuvered away from the towboat, then cut the throttle and let the big boat's wake overtake him. The speedboat rose as the wake slapped the stern counter.

"What was that?" Nick demanded. His ears rang with the sound of the speeding engines.

Jason slumped into the cockpit. "Hazardous cargo," he said in a quiet voice. "It's too dangerous to take us aboard."

Disappointment whispered through Nick's blood. "Well," he said, "we know all about hazardous cargo, I guess."

"Don't want to blow up again."

"I guess not."

Nick watched the white water boiling under the swiftly receding stern of the towboat, and sadly turned the wheel.

"The river won't let us go," Jason said. "Every time we try to leave, it takes us back."

The day of the corpses was not yet over.

Two more towboats passed that day, one heading upstream, one down. Neither were pushing barges, and both were moving fast, water creaming at their bows. Nick didn't try to intercept them. They seemed too determined to get to where they wanted to go.

Which is why it seemed so surprising when, after more dull hours on the river, they found a towboat that didn't seem to be going anywhere at all.

The boat just sat there behind its tow of barges, facing upstream. Nick was too disheartened to find this sight encouraging. Even Jason seemed only moderately interested.

But as they got closer, signs looked more auspicious. The radar unit atop the pilothouse glittered silver as it spun. They could hear the subdued sound of the boat's powerful engines, see exhaust rising from the stacks. And when Jason stood and gave a hopeful wave, Nick almost jumped out of his skin as the boat responded with a blast on its horn.

Someone came out of the pilothouse and answered Jason's wave. Only then did Nick permit himself to feel hopeful.

They came right up to the boat before it was clear why the boat wasn't moving. The boat and its tow had gone gently aground, like the *Michelle S.*, and lay in only a few inches of water. The crew had carried lines astern of the boat, probably to help back her off.

None of the barges, Nick saw, seemed to contain chemicals.

The boat's skipper met them at the gunwale. He was a short, broad-shouldered white man—"more back than leg," as Nick's grandmother would have remarked—and Nick felt a little warning tingle at the sight of him, that *crackers with guns* vibe.

Below his bushy mustache, the captain's face split in a wide grin.

"Welcome to t' *Beluthahatchie*, podnah," he said in a barking Acadian voice. "Y'all been on the river long?"

Beluthahatchie was a small towboat, with a crew of four and a tow of twelve barges. The captain was the bandy-legged Jean-Joseph Malraux of Pointe Coupée Parish, Louisiana. Three hours after the earthquake, *Beluthahatchie*, moving cautiously upstream in the dark, had come aground in what was supposed to be a deep channel.

"We had the depth sounder goin' all the time," the captain said, "but the river shallowed too quick for us to stop. It takes a while to stop all these barges, you know." He barked out a laugh. "You wouldn't believe the dumb-ass things these people do. Run their little motorboats right up in front of us, and expect us to stop for 'em." The booming Cajun voice rang off the towboat's superstructure, *da dumb-ass t'ings dese people do. Run dere liddle modorboats . . .*

"The whole river's changed," Nick said. "There are rapids upstream, new channels . . ." Crewmen helped him over the side, and he stood on the solid deck, feeling a strange astonishment at this sudden change in his fortunes.

"Thanks," Jason said as he jumped to the deck.

"This your son?" the captain bellowed, tousling Jason's hair, and then he laughed at his own joke. "Come on and have some chow," he said. "I'd like to hear about river conditions northaways."

"Thank you, Captain," Nick said. Jason, flushing a little, finger-combed his hair back into shape.

"Oh hell, podnah," the captain said. "Call me Joe."

"I was wondering," Nick said, "if I could use your radio to call my daughter and let her know that everything's all right."

"Where is she?"

"Toussaint, Arkansas."

Captain Joe gnawed his mustache thoughtfully. "I don't know where that is, exactly, but if it's in Arkansas, there's a good chance the phones won't be working. Even Little Rock got hammered bad, I hear. I got a crewman with relatives all over Arkansas, and he can't reach any of 'em. But c'mon—" He gestured with one long arm and turned to climb a ladder. "We'll give it a try. If your girl's anywhere near a working phone, podnah, we'll find her."

As Nick followed Joe to the pilothouse, he felt as if his feet weren't quite touching the deck. He had the breathless sensation of viewing some strange, swift-unfolding miracle.

A few minutes later he was wishing Arlette a happy birthday.

* * *

It was easy. A communications firm caught the towboat's radio signal, shifted it over to the phone lines for two-way communication, and charged a small fee.

"Cost my company about six bucks," Captain Joe said. "I figure they can stand the freight."

"Daddy?" Arlette cried at Nick's voice, and then, to someone else. *"It's Daddy! He's on the phone!"*

A thousand-ton weight seemed to fall from Nick's shoulders. He could *feel* his heart melting, turning to warm ooze within his chest. The breath came more easily to his lungs. He felt two inches taller.

"Hello, baby," he said.

"Where are you? Are you okay?"

"I'm okay, baby. I've been on a boat on the river with . . ." He looked at Jason. "With someone I met," he finished, saving that explanation for later.

"On the *river*?"

"The Mississippi."

"But you were coming by *car* . . ."

"Nick!" Manon's voice, coming in loudly after the click of the extension picking up. "Nick, are you all right?"

"I'm fine. A little sunburned, that's all."

"Thank God!" Manon said.

"He's on the *river*," Arlette explained to her mother. "On a *boat*."

"I'm on a towboat right now," Nick said. "The captain let me use his radio. But we've been drifting on the river for a couple days."

"Are you with Viondi?" Manon asked.

There was a moment of silence. "No," Nick finally said. "Viondi didn't make it."

"Oh, Nick," Manon breathed.

"I'm sorry, Daddy," said Arlette.

Nick licked his lips. "The car wrecked in the quake," he said. "I got out by water. Somebody picked me up." He looked at Jason again. The boy was trying not to look at him, to give him privacy. "We've been on the river, and we just now got picked up by a towboat."

"So you're okay," Arlette said.

"Yes." The sounds of the voices were bringing visions to Nick's mind. The big clapboard house just outside of

Toussaint, with its oaks and broad porch. Arlette by the phone in the kitchen, dressed in a checked cotton blouse and blue jeans worn white at the knees. Manon upstairs in the bedroom, pacing back and forth at the full length of the phone cord the way she did, with the lace curtains fluttering in the window behind.

Fantasies. Nick couldn't know whether they were real or not. But they *felt* real, very real indeed.

"I'm sorry I missed your birthday yesterday," he said.

"It wasn't much of a party. Not with the way—well, not the way things are here."

"But you're okay? And Ed, and Gros-Papa, and . . ."

"We're all fine," Arlette said. "The house came through the quake okay. But we're on an island now. We don't have electricity, but they managed to repair the phone exchange, at least for the houses in town."

"We have food from the store," Manon said. "We have enough boats, we can get away if we want. But there doesn't seem to be anyplace to *go*—"

Arlette's excited voice broke in. "Maybe you can sail here in your towboat!"

"I'll do that, baby," Nick said, "if the captain will let me." And his eyes sought Captain Joe, who stood beaming in a corner of the pilothouse with his hands in his pockets.

"You tell your girl that I'll do what I can," he bellowed without knowing what had been asked of him. "Anybody who got a *Gros-Papa* is a fren' o' mine!"

Nick talked to Arlette for a long while as the captain beamed and grinned. The words just seemed to float out of him. He was having a hard time not floating away himself.

Eventually the words wound down, and he saw Captain Joe standing with a pensive expression on his face, and the man on watch staring neutrally out the window.

"I should go, baby," he said. "I think I've been using the captain's radio long enough. I'll call tomorrow if I can, okay?"

He brought the call to an end. Captain Joe turned to Jason. "You want to make a call, son?" he asked.

Jason gave a short little shake of the head. "No one to call," he said, and left the pilothouse.

Captain Joe gave Nick a look, brows raised. Nick only shrugged.

"Let's get us some chow, podnah," Joe said.

No word from the President. Jessica hadn't been expecting any as yet: the decision to evacuate was a big one, and she hadn't expected that it would be made overnight.

Morning birdsong—helicopters—floated through the open sides of her command tent. She looked at the weather photos that Pat had just pulled from the Internet and frowned. The big high-pressure system had stalled right over the Midwest, and that meant continued warm and sunny weather over the disaster area. That was good.

What was bad was what was happening behind the front. The clockwise rotation of the high-pressure zone was pulling up moisture from the Gulf of Mexico—you could *see* it, the swirl of cloud, there on the photos, a curve from the Gulf sweeping west, then east again over the Dakotas and Minnesota. Once the moisture was over the western plains or the Rocky Mountains, the air cooled and dropped the moisture as rain.

Some of those areas had been getting rain every day for a week. Lots of water raining down into Mississippi and its tributaries, joining the ice melt pouring down from the Rockies.

What this meant was that the floods weren't going away any time soon. The rivers would stay full, and that would delay repair work on the levees and bridges, prevent people from returning to their homes, and hamper the evacuation.

Well, Jessica thought. It was time to work out what she *could* do.

The river below Vicksburg was still under her control, even though she'd lost everything north of it. But she could use the controlled part of the river to affect the flood to the north.

When rivers flowed fast, it was for one of two reasons:

either there was an enormous weight of water behind them, pushing the water down its channel at greater speed; or the path of the river was *steeper*. When a riverbed was steeper, gravity pulled the water along it at increased velocity.

Jessica didn't want to increase the volume of water, which would only increase flooding. But she could make the river steeper. She could release water through the Old River Control system in Louisiana.

Old River Control was one of the Corps of Engineers' most colossal and long-term projects. It was designed to keep the wandering Mississippi firmly in its place.

Over its history, the big river shifted its path through most of the state of Louisiana, always seeking the steepest, short-est route to the sea. It settled into its present path around 900 A.D., around the time of a large earthquake on the New Madrid fault; and when human settlements were built in the years since, they tended to take the Mississippi's route as given.

By the mid-twentieth century, it had become clear that the Mississippi was ready to make a leap out of its bed and carve itself a new route to the sea. Most likely, it would bypass Baton Rouge and New Orleans and spill out into the Gulf in the vicinity of the modest town of Morgan City, well to the west of New Orleans. The salt ocean would pour upward into the river's old bed, turning the New Orleans waterfront into a narrow, twisting bay that would soon fill with silt. Whole sections of Louisiana would be turned into unpro-ductive salt marsh—all the fresh-water plants and animals dying in an unprecedented ecological catastrophe—and New Orleans, the nation's largest port, would be stranded in the midst of the dying land, its economic raison d'etre gone and its drinking water turned to salt.

The river's weak point was in middle Louisiana, where the Mississippi, the Red River, and the Atchafalaya came within a few miles of one another. Old River Control was a giant engineering pro-ject built to straddle the three rivers, sending water east or west as the situation demanded. The Morganza Floodway, with its 125 gates, could shift 600,000 cubic feet of Mississippi flood per second into the

Red/Atchafalaya system, thus preserving southern Louisiana from flood. Or, if the Mississippi was low, water could be shunted from the Red into the Father of Waters, which made certain that New Orleans remained a deep-water port. To take advantage of the water moving from one system to the other, the Murray hydroelectric plant had been prefabricated in New Orleans, at the Avondale Shipyards, and shipped north on barges to take its place in the Old River system, the largest structure ever to be floated on the Mississippi.

What Jessica needed to do was shift a lot of water from the Mississippi into the Atchafalaya Basin. This would lower the level of the river in Louisiana and make its path steeper, thereby draining the flooded lands more quickly.

She would dump as much water as she could while still retaining New Orleans and Baton Rouge as deep-water ports. If Morganza's 125 gates weren't enough—and she didn't believe they'd all been open together at any point in their history—she could open the Bonnet Carré Spillway above New Orleans, which could shift two million gallons per second from the Mississippi into Lake Pontchartrain.

That should do it, she thought with satisfaction.

Get this river moving.

They were fond of frying on the Beluthahatchie. Nick, sticking his head into the galley to ask for a glass of water, saw chicken, fish, potatoes, and okra all sizzling away. He took his glass of water and wandered off, stomach rumbling with hunger.

He found Jason straddling the gunwale near the stern, where their boats had been tied up. He was listlessly watching the water as it streamed astern in the growing darkness. Swallows in search of insects skimmed just millimeters above the surface.

"You okay?" Nick asked.

Jason nodded.

It was hard enough, Nick thought, being father to his own child. But it was clear enough, he reflected, that there was no one else here who was going to do the job. He put his glass down on the gunwale and looked at Jason.

"Your father may be in China," he said, softly as he could,

"but I know he's worried sick about you."

Jason turned away, gazed out at the far bank of the river, the last red light of the sun that touched the tops of the distant trees. "I don't know how to reach him."

"He may be on his way back," Nick said. "I would be, in his place."

"What could he do?" Jason asked. "I'm here on this boat. He'll be in China, or California, or someplace else. But he won't be *here*."

"Just relieve his mind, Jason. I know how I felt until I talked to Arlette just now, so I know how your father feels. He's got to be in agony. Call where he works, call the American Red Cross and give them your name. *They'll* get ahold of him—that's what they *do*."

Jason looked down at his hands. "If I call," he said, "I have to tell him that my mother's dead."

Nick felt a lump in his throat. Nick put an arm around the boy, hugged him for a moment. Jason accepted the touch, but otherwise did not respond. "I'll call first and tell him about your mom," Nick offered, "if you don't want to do it."

Jason shook his head. "That's my job, I guess," he said. He sighed. "I'll probably just get his answering machine, anyway."

Nick dropped his arm, looked into Jason's eyes. "When he plays that machine," he said, "And finds out you're alive, he'll be the happiest man in the world. Believe me."

There was a sudden glare of light as *Beluthahatchie*'s lights came on. Not just the navigation lights, but floodlights as well, the superstructure clearly illuminated. The captain was making certain that his stranded vessel was visible to any other traffic on the river.

Jason blinked in the strong light, started to say something, then fell silent. Swallows flitted over the water just beyond *Beluthahatchie*'s pool of light. Then Jason tried again.

"When you were talking to your daughter," he said, "you said somebody—I don't remember the name—the person didn't make it." He looked at Nick. "Was that your wife?"

Nick shook his head. "Viondi," he said. "My best friend.

He was . . ." His voice trailed away, and he tried again. "A cop shot him. Thought he was a looter, I guess, but all he was carrying was his own stuff from the car." He touched the bandaged wound on his arm. "Man tried to shoot me, too, but I ran."

"I'm sorry," Jason said.

"Me too."

"I was kind of mad at you," Jason said, "because you had a family, and I didn't. But I guess you've lost somebody, too."

"Yes."

"And that's why you didn't want to go near the police the other day."

Nick's nerves hummed to a memory of the terror that seized him then, had clamped down on his mind and made him steer the bass boat away from shore.

"That's right," he said. "I was scared they'd shoot me then and there."

Darkness swallowed the far bank. Jason's shadowed expression was hard to read. "We've been rescued," he said. "So tell me—*why do I feel so awful?*"

"Till now we were just trying to survive," Nick said. "Now we have time to feel." Strange, he thought, to think of emotion as a luxury.

"Almost makes me want to go back on the river," Jason said. "As long as I was on the river, I didn't have to think about things. The river was, like, our fate. It wouldn't let us go, but it kept us safe."

"We made it, Jason," Nick said. "There's no reason to feel bad about that."

Jason seemed unconvinced. "I guess," he said.

He gazed out onto the river. "I keep thinking I could have saved my mother," he said. "If I'd known about that trolling motor, maybe I could have taken the boat through the flood and pulled her out of the house. If only I'd known a little more about how things worked."

"That's not your fault, Jase. It wasn't even your boat. You can't be blamed for not knowing that motor was hidden under the deck."

"I suppose," he said reluctantly.

"We're not to blame for being alive. It's not our fault. And the people who didn't make it, it's not their fault, either. They'd be with us if they could."

Jason looked out at the dark river. "I know," he said.

Well, Nick thought, *either this has made an impression or it hasn't. No sense in beating a dead horse, no less a live one.*

"Hey," he said. "Cook's frying up a feast for us. I stay on this boat much longer, I'm going to gain fifteen pounds."

Jason gave him a wry look. "You're telling me it's time to eat, right?"

"Only if you're hungry. You want to stay out here and think for a while, that's fine."

Jason hesitated for a moment, then threw his leg over the gunwale and dropped to the deck. "Might as well have dinner," he said.

Nick had underestimated dinner on the *Beluthahatchie.* In addition to all the fried food, there was potato salad, red beans and rice, corn bread, and icebox pie for dessert. Nick couldn't understand why all the crew didn't look like blimps.

Nick and Jason told Captain Joe what they knew of the river north of their location. He was impressed that they'd survived the poison gas at Helena—he'd been worried that it was still there, clouds of the stuff hovering over the river like fog. The captain told them what he and his crew had heard on radio broadcasts. "Ain't no harbors on this river no more," he said. "All wrecked or closed. When I got the boss man on the radio, he told me to get this boat into the Ohio as soon as I can get her afloat. Nearest berth's in Cincinnati."

"There are rapids between here and Cairo," Jason said. "I went down them."

"Waterfalls, too," Joe said, to Jason's surprise. "But they ain't so bad as they were. Old Man River, he gon' wear down them rough spots. By the time we get afloat again, I figure them chutes are gonna be safe enough for *Beluthahatchie.* Maybe I'll have to moor the tow somewhere where I can pick it up later—boss man says I can do that—but we'll make Cincinnati okay, I guess." He looked at his watch and gave a shout of joy. "It's eight o'clock! Time for *Dr. Who.*"

They watched in surprise as Captain Joe jumped up from the table and headed aft. Nick looked at the other crew.

"Might as well join the captain," one of them said. "He likes company when he watches TV."

They followed Captain Joe into a little crew lounge aft of the dining room, where they found the captain digging through a cabinet filled with a large collection of videotapes. "You like *Dr. Who*?" he asked.

"Never seen it," Nick said.

"Well, podnah, you got yourself a treat in store. I watch *Dr. Who* every night at eight, unless I got business or a watch to stand."

Nick didn't make much sense of the video—it seemed to be a middle episode of a series—but he enjoyed Captain Joe's narration, a continuous discourse on the various actors who had played the Doctor over the years, the changes in the theme music, and footnotes on the various minor characters. He talked more than he watched the television, but Nick figured that Joe had seen the episode a hundred times anyway.

As the closing credits ran, Jason rose from his chair. "Thanks for the show," he said.

"I hope you liked it."

"I was wondering," Jason said, "can I ask you for a favor?"

"I reckon you can *ask.*" The captain grinned.

"I wonder if I could use your radio." Jason hesitated. "I thought about someone I could call."

"I can do that," Captain Joe said. "Just wait till the tape rewinds here, and I'll take you up."

Nick decided not to go with Jason, to give the boy some privacy. He waited in the lounge, staring at the empty eye of the television. Jason returned after ten minutes or so, just stood in the doorway while his eyes brooded over the little lounge.

"Everything go okay?" Nick asked.

"I got the answering machine," Jason said.

"You said that you might." Nick gestured at the TV set, the recorder. "You want to watch a tape or something?"

Jason shook his head. "I'm going to take a shower, if I can."

The boy left. Nick let his head loll back on his chair, raised a hand to touch Arlette's necklace in his breast pocket. One day soon he would give it to her. He knew that now.

It was just possible, he supposed, that now he would actually manage to relax.

"Charlie?" It was his neighbor, Bill Clemmons, the father of the girl who'd talked to him yesterday—or was it the day before? Or the day before that?

"Yeah, Bill?" Charlie, sweating in the driver's seat of the BMW, gave his neighbor a smile. "What can I do for you?"

"You doin' okay, Charlie?" His neighbor seemed concerned. Looked at the empty wine bottles in the car.

"I'm fine, Bill. Thanks for asking."

Bill had a smear of white on his nose, zinc oxide against the sun. "I didn't know if you'd heard," he said, "they've got a refugee center down at Cameron Brown Park. They're pitching tents and distributing food."

Charlie kept the smile plastered to his face. *Never let them see you down,* that was his motto.

"Thanks for telling me," he said. "Did the radio mention when they're going to get the phones fixed?"

Bill shook his head. "They're workin' on it. The phone companies are bringing in lots of workers from out of state. But transportation is so busted up that priority is being given to food and shelter."

"Well," Charlie said. "I guess there are plenty of homeless people."

"You think you might head on down there?"

Charlie shook his head. He could not see himself at a refugee camp, living in tents, holding out his begging bowl for rice as if he were a starving African farmer. This was not a place for the Lord of the Jungle.

All he needed was a place that would cash a *check*.

"I'm doing fine, Bill," Charlie said.

"You sure, Charlie?"

Charlie winked at him. "You bet."

"Well," Bill said, "I guess you know best."

"Pastor Frankland?" said Farley Stipes. "We have a little problem—I caught a boy trying to steal some food."

After the discouraging hour with Father Robitaille, a difficulty like this was just what Frankland needed. He felt his heart lighten. "What did you do?"

Farley was one of the Christian Gun Club kids, sixteen and red-haired and very proud of his white armband. "It was Elmore—Janey Wilcox's boy. He's not even ten years old, and he was trying to get a candy bar from that stack of stuff we brought back from the Piggly Wiggly, all that junk food we ain't sorted through yet. So I ain't done nothing other than told him to wait for you. Doris Meachum is watching him."

"Does Janey know?"

"Oh yeah. She's really sorry, pastor. She wants to talk to you."

"I'll speak to her right away," Frankland said. "Why don't you see if you can't find Sister Sheryl? And then we want to round up all the kids—all of 'em, I think, to hear our message."

This was the kind of pastoral problem that Frankland liked: simple, straightforward, with a moral to be absorbed by all.

So he talked to Janey Wilcox and explained the situation. Janey was anxious and eager to please and full of apology. When Sheryl arrived, Frankland briefed her, and then the two of them rounded up all the children they could find.

While the boy Elmore apprehensively stood by, Frankland wished the children a hearty heaven-o, and he explained to the children—and to the couple dozen of adults who had turned up to watch—that things were different now. Some of you children, Frankland said, thought that maybe it was all right to take a cookie or a candy bar when you wanted it. And maybe in normal times it *was* okay, but these weren't normal times. There was an emergency, and there were a lot of people who needed to be fed, and only a limited supply of food. They had gathered all the food they could find to assure that all of God's people were fed. So it wasn't just anybody's food anymore, this was God's food. And people shouldn't steal from God.

And Frankland turned to Elmore Wilcox, whose eyes were beginning to fill with tears. And Frankland told the boy that he was sorry, but he was going to have to punish him for stealing God's food. And that Elmore shouldn't think that this was because Frankland hated him, or that anyone hated him. Everyone here loved Elmore, God and Frankland included. But everyone here had to see that people shouldn't steal God's food.

Now, Frankland went on as Elmore trembled, he was not going to punish Elmore himself, because he was a strong man and didn't want to cause injury. So his wife Sheryl would give Elmore his punishment.

They bent Elmore over a chair and Sheryl gave him twenty whacks with a belt. And then Frankland and Sheryl hugged the wailing child and assured him of God's love, and gave him back to his mother. Frankland went in search of Hilkiah, because this would furnish a reason to put an armed guard on the food supply.

"Well," he said, "I think it's time to raise that slab."

"I'll get the winch, pastor."

Frankland glanced over the encampment that surrounded the church. It was still clearly a work in progress. "I think we need to reorganize," he said. "Put the married women with children in the church—that's the safest place. Have the food supply nearby. Separate areas for the men and the women without children."

Because otherwise, Frankland thought, the teenagers were going to pair up and start sneaking off for reasons of which the Family Values Campaign would not approve. Probably the adults, too. Best just to keep the sexes apart.

While Hilkiah brought up a triangle, a block, and Frankland's pickup with the winch, Frankland found Sheryl and talked over the camp's rearrangement. "Teddy bear,"

Sheryl said, "we can move the tents around all we like, but what we really need is *food*."

"Maybe I'll get the boys out to that Wal-Mart tomorrow."

"We've got enough food for maybe six weeks as it is. If we can get catfish from the growers, that'll stretch our time. But at twenty-five hundred calories per day for each adult, and five thousand if they're doing any kind of hard work, we're going to be stretching it to get through the end of June. And if your people keep bringing in more refugees, then the situation will get worse."

"I can't leave refugees out there to die, sweetie pie."

"I know that."

"I can talk to the farmers. If they can plow under some of their cotton and plant foodstuffs . . ."

"They won't be ready in time, teddy bear," Sheryl said. "The soy is *already* in the ground and it won't ripen till fall."

Frankland frowned, hitched up his pants. "It's not their bellies that are important," he said. "It's their souls."

"Well," Sheryl conceded, "that's true. But if mammas can't feed their babies, that's gonna make 'em crazy."

Frankland considered it. "Cut back on the number of calories. If people are just lying around camp, they won't need as much. Just give the full ration to the scavenging and rescue parties."

"That might work for a *while*, but—"

"A while might be all we need, with the Lord's help. The Tribulation will last seven years, but there's no guarantee that any of us will survive it. If we can just give them all a good *start*."

"Pastor? Sister Sheryl?" Hilkiah said. "I could use your help with this slab."

The winch whined. The slab rose from the sod by the steel ring that Frankland had planted in it when he laid it there. Sheryl and Frankland helped move the slab to the side of the concrete bunker.

And there, below, were the guns in their cases. Rising from the pit came the smell of the heavy grease that Frankland had used to coat the rifles. His heart lifted. He looked at Sheryl.

"We'll get the food, darlin'," he said. "The Lord will reward us, I'm sure, for planting his kingdom here in Arkansas." He smiled. "Like Brother Hilkiah says, 'Trust in God and the Second Amendment.'"

So there was Magnusson, the long-faced proprietor of Bear State Videoramics, with his wife and teenage son, standing in the gravel parking lot and asking for food and a place to stay.

God is good, Frankland thought. He frowned at the Reverend Garb, who frowned back.

"I don't know," Frankland said. "Are you planning on distributing any pornography while you're here?"

Magnusson's face reddened. "You know I ain't," he said. "The store's wrecked, just like everything else."

"The thing is," Frankland said, "as long as your pornographic videos *exist*, I figure they're a danger to the community."

"Listen," Magnusson said. "The store is *gone*. Our home is a pile of bricks and lumber. We don't got any food. They told us in town that if we came up here, you'd feed us."

Garb nodded. "We do what we can for the community. But you see, it's *our* food—"

"We aren't the government," Frankland said. "We don't *have* to feed anybody. We're just a service to the community."

"And our duty is to the community, not to individual people," smiled Garb.

"So if someone is a *threat* to our community," Frankland said, "it's our duty to protect the community from that person."

"God judgeth the righteous," Garb said, "and God is angry with the wicked every day."

Magnusson's face had turned as red as his hair. "It isn't even your food!" he said. "I watched your people take it from the Piggly Wiggly. That's stealing!"

"That's *initiative*," Frankland said. "I haven't heard any complaints from the store management."

"They're *dead*."

There was a moment of silence.

"Listen," Magnusson said. "You *won*. Understand? I don't have *anything* anymore. All I want is some food for my wife and my boy."

Frankland stroked his chin and smiled. "We'll do that. But there's something I want you to do for us. I want you to take your truck back to town, and gather up every single one of those porn videos, and bring them back here. And then we'll light a nice bonfire, and burn every video, and you can apologize to the community for bringing that filth into our midst."

"And then," Garb added, nodding, "because you are no longer a threat to us, we will accept you into our community, and give you food and shelter."

Magnusson had gone pale. His jaw worked. His blue eyes glowed. "This is the most outrageous thing I've ever heard. You can't make those kind of conditions. This is America, damn it!"

Frankland nodded. "That's true. This is a free country. You have a free choice—to stay, or go."

"Leaving means starvation for my family!"

"Staying," Frankland said, "means repentance."

"Look up," said Garb, "and lift up your heads; for your redemption draweth nigh."

Magnusson glared from Frankland to Garb and back again. Then he hesitated. He glanced at his wife and son. He licked his lips.

Frankland smiled. He knew he had won.

The world had become a better place.

TWENTY-ONE

A gentleman attempting to pass from Cape Girardeau to the pass of St. Francis, found the earth so much cracked and broke, that it was impossible to get along. The course must be about 50 miles back of the Little Prairie. Others have experienced the same difficulty in getting along, and at times had to go miles out of their way to shun those chasms.

Narrative of James Fletcher

"I peddled pornography." Magnusson's voice, amplified by the speakers, floated through the yellow curtains into Robitaille's room. "I didn't care about the consequences."

"Yes, Father Robitaille?" Frankland said. "You wanted to see me?"

Frankland gasped for breath in the foul air of Robitaille's room. When the message came that Robitaille had asked to see him, he'd left his morning service, right in the middle of Magnusson's ritual confession.

Robitaille looked appalling. Gray, moist-skinned, with dark blooms around his eyes. The straggling whiskers on his face were more white than gray. The priest's tongue, dark and leathery, flickered out in a lizardlike way to moisten his cracked lips.

He wants to talk, Frankland thought. Robitaille's salvation, he thought, was hanging by a thread.

"Where am I?" Robitaille croaked.

"In my home. This is my spare room." He looked at Robitaille curiously. "Do you remember the earthquake? The broken bridge?"

The priest gave a long sigh. Frankland peered at him cautiously, wondering if the Demon Desbestioles had finally vacated Robitaille's body, or whether he was in for another battle with the forces of darkness.

"I corrupted children!" Magnusson cried on the PA. "I broke God's laws." Robitaille's eyes moved uneasily at the sound of the amplified voice.

"May I have some water?" the priest asked.

"Of course, Father Robitaille. Can you keep the water down?"

"I think so."

The porn-peddler Magnusson moaned about his sins and begged his neighbors for forgiveness while Frankland left the room and came back with a glass of water. Robitaille raised a scabbed, scarred hand to take the glass, but the hand trembled so much that Frankland sat on the bed, raised Robitaille with an arm around his shoulders, and held the glass to his lips. Robitaille took several careful sips, then began to swallow eagerly. But he coughed, and spluttered, and in the end pushed the glass away.

Frankland looked down. The consciousness of a miracle glowed inside him. This was the real Robitaille, he thought, the demon had gone.

"There's more water when you want it," Frankland said. "I'm glad you've come back to us."

Robitaille dropped with a sigh to his soiled pillow.

"Forgive me, Lord Jesus!" Magnusson wailed. "Forgive me, everybody!"

Robitaille's eyes wandered to the window. "What is that? Who is talking?"

"Brother Magnusson," Frankland said. "Bear State Videoramics."

"What—" Robitaille licked his lips "—what is he talking about?"

Frankland smiled and slapped his thigh. "He's doing penance. You should know how that works, right? Being a priest?"

Robitaille furrowed his brows, but the act of comprehension seemed too much for him. "I don't understand."

"It's the end of the world!" Frankland said cheerfully. "The flock must be purified. I make the sinners confess their sin, in public, so the people can learn."

Robitaille still seemed puzzled. "Make them? How make them?"

Joy filled Frankland. Two thousand years, and neither the Pope nor his followers had worked out *this* one.

"See, we need everyone pulling *together* on this," he said. "Times are critical. Nobody made any preparations but us. We can't have disharmony, we have to speak with one voice. Anything that acts against scriptural reason has to be controlled.

"So what I do is make examples. I show what happens if people step from the straight and narrow. So people like Magnusson, now, they confess or they don't eat. And their families don't eat, either. And they confess *sincere*, because we can tell the difference.

"And the neat thing," Frankland said, his enthusiasm growing, "after the first few, people got the idea. People are volunteering to come up and confess before the congregation. They talk about their problems with alcohol, with adultery—you'd be surprised how they talk. I get a kick watchin' 'em, I really do.

"It's working!" Frankland said. "See, I wrote it all down years ago! I have it on a schedule. *Day 5—people come to a realization of sin.* And that's what happened!"

Robitaille closed his eyes again. He looked very old and very tired. His lips moved, but nothing came out.

"What was that, Father?" Frankland leaned closer.

Robitaille made an effort. "You . . . can't," he said. "Can't do that."

Frankland looked at the priest in surprise. "Can't do what?"

Frankland could see Robitaille's eyes moving under the pale, closed lids. The words came as a forced whisper from his cracked lips. "You are presuming to judge the Mystical Body of Christ. That is for God alone."

Frankland reared back in surprise. The Body of Christ, he knew, was a fancy theological term for the congregation of Christian believers. He looked down at Robitaille. "I don't get it," he said. "I figured you'd *like* this part. That's what you do, isn't it? You listen to confession. You make people do penance."

Robitaille's lips began moving again. Frankland leaned closer in order to hear. ". . . not . . . how it works," he said. "Not just confession. Must be . . . truly contrite. Perform satisfaction to God." He shook his head. "Not public. Not . . . *this*. The Mystical Body of Christ is judged by the Lord alone."

Anger flared in Frankland. All these fine distinctions were pointless, he thought, the world wasn't about to allow for fine distinctions anymore. Good or evil, take your choice, pay the penalty. That's how it worked.

"Well," Frankland said, "not to engage in *debate*, here, Father, but this is the dang end of the world, ain't it? I can't have bad influences in my people—I want *everyone* to go to Heaven, not just the few with the strength to fight the Antichrist on their own."

Robitaille shook his head. His words were barely audible. "Can't . . . judge . . ."

"Evil is like a virus!" Frankland roared. "I'm doing quarantine! I show the people what evil can do! Evil's not a *mystery*, damn it! I know it when I see it!" He rose to his feet, waved his hands. "It's *you* who are judging *me*! You got no right!"

Robitaille said nothing, just lay there beneath his dirty sheet. His mouth had fallen open.

"Hey, Robitaille!" Frankland said. He shook the priest by the shoulder. "Robitaille, you asleep?" He laughed. "You *dead* there, Father?"

Apparently the priest was not dead. His chest rose and fell with his shallow breaths. There was a little drool at the corner of his mouth. He had fallen asleep.

"Dang it!" Frankland pounded the wall with a fist. "You *answer* me!" he demanded. "Who are *you* to judge, you ol' drunk!"

Robitaille lay inert. Frankland punched the wall again, then stalked out of the room, past the guard he'd put on Robitaille's door, and who had told him that the priest was awake and asking for him.

The guard watched Frankland with wide eyes as he stalked down the hall. "Robitaille okay?" he asked.

Frankland didn't answer. He walked out of the house, headed toward where his people were gathered on the grass beside the church. He heard Calhoun's voice on the PA, making a few announcements about the day's work details.

Hilkiah met him on the way. The big man looked grim. "Brother Frankland, I just heard something."

Frankland didn't break stride, made Hilkiah walk after him. "Yeah?" he snarled. "If it's trouble, I don't want to hear it."

"You know old Sam Hanson? The farmer, from out Baxter Road?"

"Yeah? He's here, ain't he?"

"Well, sure. And he's with his friend Jack MacGregor."

"So?"

Hilkiah hesitated. "Well, according to Brother Murphy, y'know, their guide, he heard the two of 'em makin' out in their tent last night."

Frankland stopped dead in his tracks and swiveled on Hilkiah. "You're telling me *what*, Hilkiah?"

Hilkiah seemed embarrassed. "Well. You know. They's queer."

Frankland looked at Hilkiah in astonishment. Sam Hanson was just an old soybean farmer, past fifty, and his friend Jack wasn't much younger. Neither of them were the slightest bit—the slightest bit of whatever homosexuals were supposed to be, effeminate or lisping or whatever. Granted, the two had lived together for longer than Frankland had been in Rails Bluff, but there hadn't been the slightest hint that there was anything deviant going on, everyone just assumed they lived together because they shared so many hobbies.

They tied flies, Frankland remembered, they'd won a prize at the county fair.

"Is Brother Murphy sure?" Frankland said.

"Oh yeah. He said they were kinda noisy. And it wasn't just Murphy who heard it, neither."

"Lordamighty," Frankland said, stunned. "I can't have this

going on in my camp!" A new determination seized him.

I know evil when I see it. You don't need to be a Catholic priest to know when Satan was among the people.

Frankland took off at a brisk stride toward where Dr. Calhoun was finishing off the morning service. "Wait up there!" he shouted. He reached around his back, took out his Smith & Wesson, waved it over his head.

"We got one more item of business!" Frankland shouted. "Sam Hanson, Jack MacGregor, get up here!"

Judge me, will he? Frankland thought. *I'll show him judgment!*

They were going to have themselves some righteous *atonement*, by God. And they were going to have it *now*.

Later on, after Hanson and MacGregor had been exposed, after they had wept and crawled and begged God's forgiveness and the forgiveness of their neighbors, after they'd been separated and sent off to work with two different parties, Frankland heard from the guard he'd put over Robitaille that the priest had died in his sleep.

"Dang it!" Frankland wanted to hit something, but there was nothing nearby, so he kicked the ground instead.

Robitaille had slipped away, had escaped Frankland's jurisdiction. Before Frankland could argue him around to his way of thinking, before he could get Robitaille to denounce the Catholic church and join his own.

Before he could save Robitaille's soul.

"Dang it!" Frankland said again.

If only he'd had another few more days.

"I have some preliminary figures, sir," said Boris Lipinsky.

"By all means," said the President. Lipinsky turned up in the Oval Office, every morning at ten A.M., to bombard his president with numbers. The President had gotten used to it by now.

He was staring out the Oval Office windows at the White House grounds. A light rain was falling, spattering the glass with tiny drops. He turned and sat himself behind Rutherford B. Hayes's desk.

"Please sit down, Boris," he said. "And if you can, try to keep it brief. I have to attend Congressman Delarue's funeral." Delarue, a party stalwart, had died of a heart attack during an aftershock while on a visit to his home district in Arkansas. Being what the government termed a "Vietnam-era veteran"—without, however, actually having served in Vietnam—Delarue would be buried in the military cemetery at Arlington, after a service in the capital.

Lipinsky spoke without referring to the notes in his hand. The President, who usually needed his briefing books to remind him of the reasons behind his positions on the issues, could only envy Lipinsky this ability.

"We believe the quakes in the New Madrid region have killed between fifteen and twenty thousand people. Almost two hundred thousand have injuries serious enough to require hospitalization. There are approximately three million homeless people in the New Madrid seismic zone, of whom over fifty percent are now living out of doors for lack of a safe structure to house in, and a further five million in need of one form of assistance or other, either food aid, ice, medical aid short of hospitalization, or emergency financial aid in order to purchase food or other basic necessities." He blinked behind his thick spectacles. "These figures are very preliminary, sir."

"Ice?" the President said. "Why are we providing people with ice?" He had pictures of cocktail parties at the government's expense.

"To preserve food, Mr. President. The victim areas range from temperate to subtropical zones, and—"

"I understand now, thank you. Continue."

Rain tapped on the Oval Office windows as Lipinsky licked his lips and continued. "Much of the area is still without electric power, particularly rural areas. The lack of electricity means that other utilities, such as water, gas, and sewage treatment, may be difficult if not impossible to restore. Lack of safe water and proper sanitation will almost inevitably result in epidemics of disease ranging from dysentery to cholera and typhoid."

The President sat up in his chair. "Those diseases are in the United States?"

"I fear so, sir. Particularly on a major waterway such as the Mississippi."

"You are taking—"

"We are taking every possible precaution, yes. Ranging from urging people to boil their water to preshipping the necessary medical supplies to centralized points within the victim areas." He shook his head. "But there are entire districts—all rural—where we have been unable to do anything. We lack the assets to put into the victim areas, and even if we had the assets, the infrastructure no longer exists to put them in place." Lipinsky solemnly shook his head. "Hundreds of thousands of people—maybe over a million—are entirely dependent on their own resources in this crisis. It is an ongoing tragedy to which we cannot even bear witness."

Ongoing tragedy . . . For a moment the President was outraged. Lipinsky spoke about *tragedy* in the same pedantic manner he spoke of *assets* and *infrastructure*.

These people are not statistics, the President thought in fury. But then the fury passed, and he sighed. He was slowly growing used to his own impotence. He looked up at Lipinsky.

"The—the nuclear plant in Mississippi? This situation is being dealt with?"

"I am informed that General Frazetta will implement a—rather novel—plan at Poinsett Landing. An artificial island will be built around the reactor to stabilize it."

They can do that? the President wondered. Well, he concluded, why not? "I want that problem neutralized," he said. Meaning the political problem as much as any other. "The full resources of the government, you understand?"

"Indeed, sir." Lipinsky, the President knew, understood the political dimensions of a nuclear catastrophe as well as anyone.

"And . . ." The President hesitated. "General Frazetta's *other* problem? The water supply?"

Lipinsky paused, the moment of silence adding gravity to his words. "Our HAZMAT teams are still testing the water, Mr. President. Any information is exceedingly preliminary."

"And the preliminary reports indicate what, exactly?"

Another pause. Then Lipinsky just shook his head. "Preliminary reports are not at all encouraging, sir."

So, the President thought, *it would get worse. Three million homeless, and it will get worse.*

Worse.

Charlie woke with a start in the middle of the night to the sound of the telephone ringing in his ear. He clawed for the receiver on the passenger seat, clutched at it, raised it to his ear.

"Hello?" he said. "Hello?"

He heard nothing, not even a hiss. Charlie looked at the phone in growing surprise.

No one had called him. The cellphone had rung only in his dreams.

Charlie threw the receiver back on the seat. "Got to get a grip," he advised himself, and opened the door to let some of the wine fumes out of the car.

He had been drinking the wine pretty steadily. It was the only food he had left. That and some hard liquor in a cabinet.

"Got to get a plan," he muttered to himself.

He stepped from the car to let the cool evening clear his head. Pain stabbed at him from his injured leg. He wandered over to his oak tree, split right up the middle, and looked at the world from between its two halves.

He was a *trader*, damn it. He needed some way he could do his *job*.

There had to be ways he could take advantage of this situation. He dealt in commodities all the time, and what everyone lacked at the moment was commodities. There had to be a way he could take advantage of that.

If only he had a place to start. A place where he could start trading. A *market*.

When the idea came to him, it was so beautiful that he

could only gaze in wonder at the picture that unfolded in his mind.

Charlie Johns, he thought to himself, *you are a genius.*

Charlie was back at the convenience store. In the twenty-four hours since he'd left with laughter ringing in his ears, the pile of canned goods had been reduced by about two-thirds. The cans remaining weren't the most desirable: they were things like cranberries and pickle relish sauce.

The young man was behind the counter this time, his gun still at his waist. Behind the counter Charlie saw television sets, stereo systems, boom boxes, a few home computers. "You found some cash?" the young man said. "Or you got a TV set or something, we'll take that, too."

"What I've got, friend," Charlie said, "is a way to get rich. What we need to do is establish a market."

The young man looked at him. "This *is* a market. Don't you *comprendo* no English where you come from?"

"This is *one* kind of market," Charlie said. "But what's going to happen, mate, is that you're going to run out of food soon. And then how are you going to make money?"

The young man shrugged. "We'll get a delivery sooner or later."

"But when?" Charlie said. "And how much is it going to cost you? See, the weakness is that you don't know the answers to those questions, so your market isn't stable."

"Junior? What's going on here?" The older man emerged from the back room, buttoning his jeans. He looked at Charlie, then scowled. "Oh," he said. "The Limey."

Charlie turned to him. "I was explaining to your partner here—" he began.

"My son."

"Your son," Charlie said, "that the market for your goods is unstable, because you don't know when you're going to get a delivery, or how much it will cost."

The older man reached into a back pocket, took out a round tin of Red Man, and put snuff in one cheek. "Yeah?" he said.

"So what you do in order to regain stability," Charlie said, "is establish a market in contracts to purchase goods when they're delivered. Or contracts to *deliver* goods, if people have goods that they can sell to you."

The two men squinted at him. "And how do I do that exactly?"

Charlie wiped sweat from his forehead. Hunger growled in his belly. "See, mate, what happens is that somebody comes in and wants to buy some bread. But you don't *have* any bread, and you won't until you get a delivery, so what you sell the man instead is a *contract* to sell him bread on a certain date, at a certain price. And then—"

"Wait a minute," the old man said, "they give me *money* for this contract?"

"Right, mate. Yeah. The man gives you money, or—" glancing at the electronics behind the counter "—something else of value. And then, once he has the contract, he can keep it or sell it. And if the price of bread goes *down* by the time you're supposed to deliver, you'd lose money on the physical transaction, but you could *make* money by buying an obligation at the lower price to deliver the same goods . . ."

"This ol' drunk's crazy," the young man said.

"No!" Charlie said. "This really works! See, if the price of bread goes *up* . . ."

A young, very pregnant woman came into the store. She was badly sunburned on her forehead and shoulders. She pushed a shopping cart that held a portable television set. "How many cans can you give me for this?" she said.

"Just let me set up this market for you," Charlie said. "I know how to do it. We can all make money."

"We got a customer here," the older man said. He walked to the pregnant woman, picked up the television set, looked at it. "Five cans," he said.

Charlie looked at them in annoyance. "Look," he said, "I'm sorry to interrupt the workings of this primitive system of finance you've developed here, but I'm talking *big money* here. This is the *futures market* I'm talking about."

The older man looked at Charlie from under the rim of his baseball cap and put the TV set on the counter. "Pay me cash money for something," he said, "or get out of here. I got business to transact."

Charlie couldn't believe this stupidity. "Just listen to me!" he said. "Millions of dollars are made every day in just this way! *I've* made millions of dollars just like this! It's *easy*! All you have to do is listen!"

The older man slapped Charlie across the face, hard. His hand was large and rough. Charlie stared in shock at the man, at the incredible red violence in his glare. The man grabbed Charlie's collar and rushed him through the door, shouting *get out get out get out*. Charlie caught a heel on the threshold and went over backward. Asphalt bit his hands, and his teeth rattled. The older man stood over him, red-faced and shouting.

"You're right out of your mind! Get out of here before I blow your brains out!"

Charlie wiped tobacco juice off his face. "You don't understand," he said.

"I know a drunken derelict when I see one! Now clear out!"

Charlie got cautiously to his feet, keeping his distance from the man. "I'm not a derelict!" he said. "I'm a millionaire!"

"You're a derelict *now*, rich man! You're a bobtail flush that ain't got nothing to sell but bullshit!"

Charlie backed away. His cheek stung. Bewilderment whirled through his mind. What was *wrong* with the man, he wondered.

He had to stop three times on the way home and sit on the curb to rest. He was *rich*, he protested to himself. He had guessed *right* about the market. So why couldn't he buy anything?

Cable snaked through the block hung below the triangle. The electric winch whined, and the great concrete lid rose from the bunker.

Below Frankland saw packaged food. Flour, beans, rice, condensed milk, baby formula, canned fruit and vegetables, vitamins. Two years' supply for two people. Plus seed corn and fertilizer so that crops could be raised after the food ran out.

The Rails Bluff area had finally run out of food. What had been plundered from the Piggly Wiggly, the Wal-Mart, and the cupboards of the residents would be gone within a day or so.

Frankland decided to open the bunkers of the Apocalypse Club. These were supplies laid aside for the End Times by his followers, people who had answered his radio appeals and who had intended to join him here in Rails Bluff when the end of the world was clearly nigh.

But they hadn't arrived, not one of them, and hundreds of refugees had come instead. He had to feed the people who were *here*, no matter who the food actually belonged to.

The Apocalypse Club had thirty sealed caches behind Frankland's home. Some belonged to the Elders, who had three months' supplies in their bunkers, and others to the Lions of Judah, with six months' supplies. Some belonged to the Roots of David, who had a year's supplies, and others belonged to the Seventh Seals, who had purchased supplies for two years or more.

Actually there were only three Seventh Seals: Frankland, Sheryl, and Hilkiah. Response to Frankland's radio appeals had not been as great as Frankland had hoped. Hilkiah had bought his supplies on credit from Frankland and was slowly paying off the debt a few dollars at a time.

If necessary Frankland would open them all. But he would set a personal example and start with the Seventh Seals, with his and Sheryl's own personal supplies, and work from there down the list.

Things were moving along too well for material considerations to impede progress now. It was just as he had written it down in his Plan, years ago. *Day 7—all unite in love and praise of Jesus and the Holy Spirit*. Everyone was pulling together. Everyone was praising God. Sin had been vanquished, in the persons of people like Magnusson and Hanson and MacGregor, and everyone had rejoiced in their repentance.

The only thing that Frankland regretted was the death of Robitaille. If he'd had a chance to work with the priest a little more, he'd probably have been able to bring him around.

Frankland bent and helped Hilkiah move the heavy concrete lid to the side. "There," he said. "Let's get it moved to the kitchens."

"Brother Frankland?"

Frankland turned to find Sheriff Gorton approaching, along with a well-dressed, white-haired man in a coat and tie. Other than for Frankland and the other pastors, who wore ties for services, ties had been pretty rare since the End Times had begun.

The stranger looked somewhat familiar, though Frankland couldn't place him.

"Brother Frankland," the Sheriff said, "this is Gus Gustafson, from the County Council."

Frankland wiped the soil from his hands and shook Gustafson's hand. "Pleased to meet you, Brother Gustafson," he said.

Gustafson glanced around the camp with ice-blue eyes. "It's quite a place you have here, sir," he said. "Quite an accomplishment."

"Thank you. But all glory goes to Christ Jesus and the Holy Spirit."

"Ye-es." Gustafson's blue eyes darted from one place to the other. "When I tell the rest of the council members what you've done here, I'm sure they'll be impressed. I think the county owes a vote of thanks to you for helping so many of our people." He cleared his throat, and his voice turned brisk. "But what I've come to tell you, sir," he said, "is that the state is now able to take some of this burden off your shoulders. We've managed to open a road through the piney woods east from the county seat, and from there to Pine Bluff and points south."

"Well, good!" Frankland said. "Can you send us some supplies? Because," he confided, "the food situation is getting a little critical around here."

"I believe what the government has in mind," Gustafson said, "isn't to send food here, but to send the people where the food is. You've heard about the President's evacuation order, right? Well, a refugee camp is being set up in the Hot Springs National Park. The whole county is being evacuated to there."

Frankland stared at Gustafson in amazement. "But the evacuation's all about water, right? We don't get our water from the river! We have wells—good wells!"

Gustafson cleared his throat. "The water's only a part of the situation, as I understand it. This area is still subject to strong earthquakes that can cause casualties and damage the infrastructure. It took a road crew three days to bulldoze through the piney woods to get to Rails Bluff from the county seat! The Emergency Management people would have a lot of trouble shipping food into an area this remote, and so it makes more sense to pull people out of the area to a place where they can be fed more efficiently."

Frankland gave an astonished laugh. "That's the government for you!" he said. "They never think about the people at all!"

Gustafson cleared his throat again. "Well, that's as may be. But tomorrow morning they're sending a big convoy of National Guard vehicles to pull everyone out of here."

Frankland shook his head. Poor old Gustafson just didn't get it. "You don't understand," he said. "The people here are *happy*. They're praising God. They won't want to leave."

Sheriff Gorton dug into the dirt with the toe of his boot. For the first time Gustafson looked surprised. "You're sure about that, sir?" he said.

"Oh yes."

"Well," Gustafson nodded, "in that case, just to ease my mind, I'm sure you won't mind if we ask them."

Sweat poured down Charlie's nose as he punched number after number into the cellphone. Nothing happened at all. Maybe he'd worn out the batteries.

He threw the receiver down, rubbed his unshaven face. He was *not* a derelict, he thought. Not.

Exhaust from the line of National Guard trucks blew over the camp. Frankland watched in black despair as the long line of people, clutching their small bundles and their children, began to move out of the camp, past the black walls of Sheryl's Apocalypse, toward the waiting vehicles.

"This isn't necessary!" Frankland called. "You can stay here! We have everything you need!"

"In the Year 70 A.D. the Temple was thrown down!" Frankland's own voice mocked him from the loudspeakers.

Uniformed Guard personnel helped the women and children into the trucks. Officers stood by with clipboards.

"Thank you, Brother Frankland, for all you've done." This was Eunice Setzer, one of his own congregation, shuffling from the camp with her three children.

"You don't have to leave, Sister Eunice," Frankland said as he put a hand on her arm. "We'll take care of you here."

"Sorry, Brother Frankland," she said with downcast eyes, and with a twist of her body slipped free of his grasp.

"Look at Sister Sheryl's Apocalypse!" Frankland cried. "Lift your eyes and look at it! The Beast. The Woman of Babylon! That's what's waiting for you! That's what's waiting for everybody! We want to *prepare* you for that!"

They walked by in silence, past the angels with their vials and trumpets, past the Four Horsemen, past the City of God descending in glory. They walked as if none of it mattered, as if the End of the World was not at hand.

"Betrayal!—verse ten!" Frankland's voice boomed from the loudspeakers.

Betrayal. St. Matthew had it right. Frankland was betrayed, and so was God.

"I'll be staying, Brother Frankland," Sheriff Gorton assured him. "They're not evacuating law enforcement, that's for sure."

Frankland readied himself for a last appeal, and he raised his arms in exhortation, but the words didn't come. The

Spirit went right out of him, something that had never happened before. The promise that God had made him, made him amid the fury of the rain and the lightning and the shaking of the earth, had come to naught.

He slumped and turned away. And then, out of the shuffling crowd, someone took him by the arm.

"Brother Frankland."

Frankland looked up, saw the pornographer Magnusson gazing at him with a peculiar expression in his face. The man had probably come to gloat over Frankland's defeat. "Yes?" Frankland said.

Tears glimmered in Magnusson's eyes. "I'm staying, Brother Frankland!" he said. "I'm staying with you! I owe you my salvation."

To Frankland's utter surprise, Magnusson threw his arms around Frankland and began sobbing on his shoulder. Slowly, Frankland put his arms around Magnusson and began patting him on the back.

"Praise God, Brother Magnusson," he said. "Praise God."

Ten minutes later, the National Guard officers blew their whistles, and the convoy began to move off, the inhabitants of Rails Bluff staring out the back of the trucks from under the olive-green canvas.

When Frankland called for a head count, there were eighty-seven people left in the camp, including the three pastors and their families. There were probably less than a hundred others this side of the piney woods, mostly farmers who refused to leave their land, along with a few people in the Bijoux Theater too sick to be moved and under the care of a National Guard medic.

The awnings of the empty camp flapped disconsolately in the morning breeze. Frankland walked along the lines of tents, gazing in disgust at the garbage left behind by the six hundred people who had left earlier that morning, the plastic Star Wars cups and plastic sheeting and stained foam bedding.

Day 8—the people confirmed and strengthened in their faith.

He had planned for *years* for this. For the moment when the world began to come apart, when the people would be lost and need his guidance. He had *given* that guidance. He had shared his own food with refugees who had nothing to call their own. He had preached to them from the depths of his heart.

And now *this*. They had abandoned him, all but eighty-seven loyalists. Abandoned him for *Hot Springs National Park*! What a humiliation.

No more betrayals, he thought. He had been naive. He hadn't foreseen the seductions that the liberal humanist/satanist government would offer to his people. Now he knew.

No more government! That was the answer. You could not serve God and Caesar. There would be no room in the camp for anything but the Lord and praising the Lord and preparing the people for the end of the world.

No more desertions. No one would leave again. The soul was what mattered, and Frankland was going to save the souls of everyone here. That was his charge.

And anyone else—any more *government*—who tried to interfere, Frankland would deal with it.

Personally.

Birdsong floated on scented air from the Rose Garden. The President sat behind the desk that had been given from Queen Victoria to Rutherford B. Hayes, the one made from the timbers of HMS *Resolute*.

He wished he were on the *Resolute* right now, with eight inches of solid oak planking between him and the rest of the world.

"It's your call, Mr. President," said Boris Lipinsky.

Solemn faces, arrayed in a half-circle around the desk, gazed at the President. It was one of those moments where, whatever their ambitions, these people were clearly glad to be on their side of the desk, and not his.

Reports had come in, over two days, from the HAZMAT teams that had been sent to sample the water pollution levels of the Mississippi and other rivers in the disaster area. The reports had been terrifying.

General Frazetta had been right. The Mississippi, along

with several of its major tributaries, had become an efficient pipeline for the delivery of every conceivable toxic substance to the water systems of every town and city along the river. There probably weren't enough water filters in the world to clean the pollutants out of the drinking water.

"Mr. President?" the Minority Leader said. "May I say a word?"

The President fixed the man with a look. "*No,*" he said.

Another few moments ticked past on James Monroe's bronze-doré clock. Then the President sighed and put his hands flat on Rutherford B. Hayes's desk.

"It's out of my hands," he said. "I cannot permit millions of people to drink poisoned water. I realize that shifting our efforts from managing a disaster to managing an evacuation is going to strain our resources to the maximum, but I want the evacuation to commence."

He looked at General Shortland. "You've got till tomorrow morning to get your plans finalized, General," he said. "I'll make the announcement at nine A.M."

Charlie Johns looked into the one container remaining in his refrigerator, the week-old pieces of duck, and wondered if it was all right to eat. It *looked* all right. It smelled like it had been in the refrigerator a while, but didn't smell *bad*.

Maybe if he drank some brandy with it. Brandy was a disinfectant, wasn't it?

The house was full of flies, and Charlie didn't want to think about the reason for that, so he took the food into the shady backyard along with a bottle of Martell. He sat in the shade under his Russian olive tree and ate the duck along with swallows of brandy. He dug bits of rice off the ribs, sucked all the remaining meat off the bones, gnawed at the cartilage. Then he sucked the bones for a long while.

He stared at the pool while he ate. The neighbor kids had been coming over to take drinking water from it, and they'd kept it clean of leaves and sticks and windblown junk. He'd thrown chlorine into it every day and figured it was still safe to drink.

The cramps started an hour later. He barely made it to the toilet in time. He shuddered and sweated on the toilet for hours as he emptied everything that remained in his bowels.

When the spasms finally ended, he barely had the strength to crawl to the car and drape himself across the front seats.

Jessica gazed from the old Indian mound at the transformation of Poinsett Landing nuclear station. From the wreckage and desolation of just days ago, Poinsett Landing was on its way to becoming the busiest port on the Mississippi.

Operation Island was proceeding at a truly astounding rate. While power company and Energy Department teams concentrated on the problems presented by the leaking storage pond, the Army under the direction of Jessica's engineers had been engaged in the work of turning Poinsett Landing into a river port. Portable quays had been moved into place, cabled to building ruins, to the auxiliary building or the control facility, or when necessary to the river bottom. Barges filled with supplies and necessary equipment had been warped alongside.

The clutter of plant workers' vehicles that stood atop the Indian mound blocked any serious and sustained use of the mound by Jessica's engineers. The world would have forgiven her if she'd pushed these vehicles into the drink in order to turn the mound into a giant helipad, but Jessica realized she was going to depend on these plant workers, and didn't want to commence their relationship by shoving valuable workers' property into the Mississippi. Instead the vehicles were airlifted to Vicksburg by huge Super Stallion helicopters. On return flights, the big copters—which had been developed to carry the heavy equipment for entire Marine divisions—had carried enough supplies for a small camp atop the mound, and material to start building jetties and anchorages for the barges and boats that would bring emergency material to the landing.

For the moment, everyone in the area had been evacuated to the top of the Indian mound. Operation Island was about to enter a new phase.

"Good news, General," said Larry Hallock, who had just returned from the auxiliary building in a boat. "And bad news."

And how many times had she heard *that* in the last few days, Jessica wondered.

Well. By now, she figured, she was equal to just about anything. World ends the day after tomorrow? Fine, we'll come up with a plan for disassembling the planet and recycling the materials in order to create the galaxy's largest shopping mall. Just give us a few minutes.

"Good news and bad news, Mr. Hallock?" Jessica said.

She *liked* Larry Hallock. He was proving indefatigable at a time when indefatigability was at a premium. Within twenty-four hours of the big quake, he had put together the plan to entomb his reactor and salvage the spent fuel, a plan so solid in its fundamentals that no one had been able to improve on it in the time since. Larry worked twenty-hour days supervising the work at the plant, his detailed knowledge of the plant site was unsurpassed, and he was always able to modify his plans to account for the limited materials available. After a day or so on the job, he'd thrown away the sling that had supported his broken collarbone and spent his days scrambling over scaffolding, jumping between barges, and climbing ladders.

Larry was the kind of soldier that Jessica always wanted in her outfit.

"Go ahead," she said. "Good news first, if you please."

Larry nodded. "We've cleared away most of the wreckage in the auxiliary building," he said. "We've cut away the roof that was damaged, and reinforced the parts of the roof that are still standing. We've rebuilt the catwalks, and repaired the two leaks we know about. There's probably at least one more leak that we *don't* know about, because water levels are still declining, but I expect we'll find it before long."

"Very good, Mr. Hallock. And the bad news?"

Larry hesitated. "The crane that we hope to use to extract the spent fuel suffered some serious damage. So the repairs will delay things. We're probably going to have to cannibalize parts from other plants and fly them out here."

Jessica nodded. "I understand."

"And the reactor complex has increased its list. By another half a degree."

Jessica bit her lip. The endless series of aftershocks continued to shake the soupy ground beneath the reactor's massive concrete-and-steel foundation, eroding its support. While its current angle of list placed it in no danger of toppling, Jessica was still uneasy. What if another major earthquake occurred? The danger was by no means remote—in 1811–12, there had been no less than *three* major earthquakes on the New Madrid fault system, all Richter 8.0 or greater. If another big quake hit, Jessica worried that the foundation pad beneath the reactor might begin to break up. If it shattered, the Poinsett Landing reactor might well decide to start rolling down the Mississippi.

The best way to guard against this danger was to get on with Larry's plan to turn Poinsett Landing into an island. But Operation Island, despite the name, had run into a critical shortage.

In the normal course of events, when something on this scale was to be created, enormous works of engineering would be constructed to shift the river into another channel. While Poinsett Landing was dry, solid objects—such as quarried stone—would be moved from a nearby source of supply to the construction site and laid in place to form the island.

This was purely impossible. Even when the nation's infrastructure *hadn't* been shattered by an earthquake, the technology to shift a river as mighty as the Mississippi from its mucky bed would have taken years to get into place. Whatever work was to be done would have to be done with the river right where it was.

Not only that, but there was little to build an island *with*. There was no solid ground in the Mississippi Delta, and no source of solid material needed to implement the "island" part of Operation Island. No quarries, no hills to dismantle, no sources of stone at all. When the Corps of Engineers constructed its dikes and levees on the lower Mississippi in the 1920s and 1930s, the stone used had been imported by rail all the way from Tennessee.

This was more difficult in the present day, when many quarries throughout the country had been closed as uneconomical, and when rail transport to the area had been severely compromised by earthquake damage.

It was then that Jessica realized that a lot of the necessary materials were already at hand. It didn't have to be a *pretty* island, it just had to be reasonably solid—solid enough to keep the river from undermining the reactor. The earthquake had shattered tall buildings, highway bridges, and masonry structures of all descriptions. The broken bits were going to have to be swept up anyway. So why not put them on transports and ship them to Poinsett Landing?

Poinsett Island would be constructed of the debris caused by the earthquake that had made the island necessary in the first place. That, plus some other necessary material to string it all together.

There was a pleasant irony in that, an irony that Jessica intended to appreciate to the full.

A roar began to sound from over the treeline to the east. Jessica glanced at her watch.

"Right on time," Jessica said to Larry. "Watch this."

A CH-53 Super Jolly helicopter appeared over the treeline, moving with deliberate speed toward Poinsett Landing. Slung beneath it in a steel mesh cargo net was ten tons of island material. Half of it was pipe casing intended either for oil or water wells. Much of the rest was broken power and telephone poles, plus the wires that held them together.

"Operation Island," Jessica said blissfully. Her words were drowned by the deafening sound of rotor blades.

The Super Jolly plodded out over the river, the downblast from its rotors turning the waters white. It hovered for a moment upstream of the reactor, over buoys that had been set as aiming points, then the net was tripped and, with a grating roar, ten tons of material spilled into the Mississippi. Pipes and power poles flung themselves like spears into the riverbed. As the weight was released the copter bounded upward as if yanked into the sky by an elastic band. White water leaped as the debris struck the surface of the river. The roar sounded like Niagara. Tall, confused waves leaped from the site.

All that was left, as the helicopter roared away, were the tops of pipe and poles, and some of the tangle of wire that surrounded them. The inchoate structure lay about half a kilometer upstream from the power plant.

Jessica did not want to start at the nuclear plant and built upstream. In such a structure there was the possibility that the weight of the structure would actually *increase* the water pressure on the buildings. Rather, in building something this unprecedented, Jessica had chosen to emulate the technique of the North American beaver. The upstream part of a beaver dam was built first, and the rest filled in afterward.

Jessica would build a solid breakwater upstream from the plant, a huge tangle of pipes, timber, wire, and earthquake debris. As with a beaver dam, the pressure of the river would eventually wedge everything into a solid position. Once this was constructed, she would backfill toward the power plant, eventually engulfing its structures.

No sooner had the Super Jolly cleared the area, moving much faster without its cargo, than another copter appeared, this one a Super Stallion. Jessica had arranged a regular relay of big heavy-lift helicopters rolling in from the nearest rail-head in Jackson, where tons of earthquake debris were being moved by rail. Each Super Jolly could carry ten tons, but the big Super Stallions hauled sixteen tons each.

In a matter of days, a fair-sized island would have grown up around Poinsett Landing.

Jessica felt a broad smile spreading across her face. "Isn't it *great*?" she asked.

PART TWO

TWENTY-TWO

I shall advise all those descending the river not to take the right hand of Island No. 38, as it appears entirely choked up with drift and rafts of sawyers. When through these bad places the worst is over, only fuller of snags, but mind well the directions in the Navigator and there will be no danger. Run the Grand Cut-off No. 55, in all stages of the water, and hug close the right hand point, this pass is good. Take the left of St. Francis No. 59, left of No. 62, right of large sand bar and Island No. 63, and right of No. 76, in all the different stages of the water. All these channels are much the best and safest. Should this be the means of saving one boat load of provisions to an industrious citizen, how amply shall I feel rewarded for noting this, whilst with gratitude I acknowledge the obligation we as boatmen are under to you for your useful guide, that excellent work The Ohio and Mississippi Navigator, much to be valued for its accuracy and geographical account of this immense country.

I have the honor to be, gentlemen, your sincere friend and humble servant.

James Smith (February 18, 1812)

Bored out of his mind, Jason strolled on the hatches of *Beluthahatchie*'s barges. Then he heard a yell, and turned to see one of the crew waving from the pilothouse.

"Hey, Jase! Your dad's on the radio!"

Jason's heart gave a lurch. He sprinted aft, jumping from one barge to the other until he clambered aboard the towboat and ran to the pilothouse. He grabbed the handset, raised it to his lips. He gasped for breath, spoke. "Dad?"

Jason's heart hammered a half-dozen times before the answer came. "Jason?" His father's intent voice. "Are you there?"

"Yeah, Dad. It's me."

"You're still on the boat. The *Beulah*-something."

"Beluthahatchie."

"I've been trying to get through to you for days. All the marine radio operators are jammed up with thousands of messages . . ."

"Frank," Una's insistent voice, breaking in on another line. "Ask how he *is."*

"I'm fine," Jason said. "Got a little sunburned, that's all."

There was another little pause. Jason realized that Frank and Una were still far away, maybe still in China.

"I was so sorry to hear about Catherine," Una said.

Jason was silent. He couldn't think of anything to say.

"Are you still in China?" he said finally.

Another pause. "Yes. In Guangzhong. If you'll get a pen, I'll give you the number of our hotel."

Despair floated through Jason as he jotted down the number. The least his father could have done was flown to the States.

"Are they treating you okay on the boat?" Frank Adams asked.

"Oh sure. Everyone's been real nice. They're letting me and Nick use their radio whenever we like."

"Nick?" There was a flicker of intent interest in Frank's voice. "Who is this *Nick*, exactly?"

Jason wondered where to start. "He's a refugee, Dad. I found him on the river." He paused, then added, "He's about your age, I guess." Trying to demonstrate that Nick was a responsible citizen, not someone who was going to lead him into trouble.

He knew better than to report that Nick was black, had been shot by a cop, and had been found in a tree. This would not boost his father's confidence in his choice of traveling companion.

"And you traveled together," Frank said.

"Yes. For a couple days. He's been trying to get to his daughter in Arkansas."

"And you were in a boat? Was this Nick's boat?"

"Uh, no."

So Jason had to explain about his neighbor's bass boat, and how he'd used it to get off the Indian mound and gone down the river without meaning to. And met Nick the next morning.

"So you were on the boat for two days?"

"Well, not *that* boat. We got another boat later." The memory of stranding Junior and his friend on the *Lucky Magnolia* was too wonderful to resist, so Jason told his father what happened, how he and Nick had found themselves on the casino boat with the two thieves, and how they'd stolen their powerboat.

"And Nick let you do this?" Frank Adams said. Jason was surprised by his father's frigid tone.

"Well," Jason said, "he didn't *stop* me."

"I can't believe he put you in so much danger."

Jason licked his lips, tried to get his thoughts in order. "He really didn't have much to do with it, Dad."

"Well, he *should* have."

"This Nick doesn't sound like a very responsible person," said Una.

"He didn't *know*," Jason said, "that there were thieves on board."

"He just *let* you walk into this danger?" Frank demanded. "Of all the *stupid, thoughtless* . . ."

"Nick's really okay, Dad."

"He is *not* okay." Firmly. "I don't know what the man was thinking of."

"I—" Jason groped for words. "You've got it wrong, Dad."

Frank went on as if he hadn't heard. "Now where is this boat you're on? This *Beulah Hatchie*, or whatever."

"Well," Jason said. "We're somewhere south of Helena. But the boat's aground on a sandbar at the moment."

"It's *what*?"

"But it's okay," Jason said. "It's not sinking or anything. It's just that the river changed, and—"

Frank Adams snorted. "I don't know how a *river* can *change*," he said.

"If you were here," Jason said, "you'd know."

Frank sounded as if he were trying very hard to be patient. "So what you're telling me is that you're stranded. You're not going anywhere."

"I don't think the captain sounds very competent," Una contributed.

"He's fine, Una," Jason said. "The boat's going to Cincinnati when we can get it afloat. And that shouldn't take too long, the captain says, because the river's rising."

"I'll tell you what's going to happen, then," Frank said. "When you get to Cincinnati, there will be a ticket waiting for you. And then you'll fly to Syracuse, and your aunt Stacy will be waiting for you."

"Aunt Stacy?" Jason couldn't believe he was hearing this. His aunt Stacy, who was actually his great-aunt, lived in upstate New York. Though she was kind, he couldn't see spending the whole summer with her. She was elderly and didn't get out much, and where she lived there was nothing to do.

"Why can't I come to California?" he asked.

"Our apartment is really too small for a family, Jason."

Horrid visions of staying forever with Aunt Stacy flashed through Jason's mind. "Wait a minute!" he said. "I was coming in August."

"That was just for two weeks, Jason," Una said. "If you're coming to stay for good, we'll need more room."

Hatred blazed in Jason's heart. He had never hated anyone so much as he hated Una in that instant.

"Una and I will look for a house," Frank said. "We'll have it all ready for you when it's time to start school in the fall."

Jason was appalled. "I don't even get to see you?" he said.

"*I can't come,*" Frank said. His voice was almost a shout. "*They won't let me come and get you.*"

Jason blinked. "What?"

"The government isn't letting anyone fly into the quake zone!" Frank's voice was almost a shout. "They aren't letting phone calls in. You can fly *out*, you can call *out* if you need help, but I can't get *in* to you. *They won't let me come!*"

There was a moment of silence. Jason could hear atmospherics hissing from the radio speaker.

"Once you get to Syracuse, I'll come see you," Frank said. "They'll let me fly there. But in the meantime the only way I can talk to you is to get a radio operator to try to call your boat."

"Fly me to California," he said. "I don't want to go to New York."

"We've been into that. There's no room in our apartment. I've talked to Aunt Stacy, and it's all arranged. Now could you hand the receiver to the captain of the *Beulah*-whatever, so I could talk to him?"

"He's not in the pilothouse at the moment."

"Could you go get him, then?"

From the sound of it, Jason's father planned to give Captain Joe some orders.

Which he did. Captain Joe opened the conversation with a cheerful, "Hi, y'all," but soon fell silent as Jason's father began to speak. This went on for some time.

When the conversation was over, Joe put his arm around Jason's shoulders and walked with him down the companionway. "Your poppa's got a lot of opinions," he said.

"Yeah," Jason said. "I know."

"He wants me to keep you away from Nick. He seems to have something against that man." He gave Jason a look from under one bushy eyebrow. "Is your poppa prejudiced or something?"

"No," Jason said. "He's a lawyer."

Captain Joe nodded. "Okay," he said. "Now I understand."

Nick heard Arlette's voice over the sound of hammering. Some of the family, she had explained, were up on the roof, replacing the shingles that had spilled during the big quake.

"We're trying to get the house in shape," she said, "because we don't want it to fall apart if we have to leave."

Sudden anxiety clawed at Nick's heart. "You'll be leaving Toussaint?" he asked. "When?"

"That depends on the bayou. Looks like it's getting set to rise. And I've never seen it run so fast."

He had wasted too much time, Nick thought as he rubbed the nearly healed wound on his left arm. He should have taken the speedboat to Toussaint after the first night on the *Beluthahatchie*. But it had been comfortable on the boat, and *safe*, and he'd been able to talk to Arlette every day. And every time he thought about getting back on the river again, a bloated body would float by.

He and Jason had been on board five days. He'd talked to Arlette twice a day.

And he'd tried to get in touch with Viondi's family, but there was no answer at Viondi's number, or his plumbing business, or at the numbers of Viondi's sons that Nick'd been given by directory assistance. He wondered if the whole family had been wiped out.

Finally, after several days, he'd got an answering machine at Viondi's business. He hated to pass on the news by machine, but he had little choice: he identified himself and told the machine that Viondi was dead, and that he'd try to call later.

When he called the next day, he didn't even get the machine.

"The phone exchange is sandbagged," Arlette said. "And we've got pumps running. But if the bayou gets much higher, we could lose the phones. Half the people here are living in the second floors of their homes already. So Gros-Papa is getting everyone organized to leave by boat. He and Gilly and Aunt Penelope are going to stay and look after things."

Nick bit his lip. "How are you going to get out? The river's a mess."

"We're not going to follow the river. We're going to follow the *road*. In our boats, it shouldn't matter if the roads are torn up or the bridges are out."

"Honey. The roads might be blocked. A lot of trees and power lines have fallen down."

"We can float around obstructions, Gros-Papa says. But we'll have chainsaws just in case. And plenty of food." Her voice turned reassuring. "We'll be okay, Daddy. We know where we're going."

Should have gone there, Nick thought. *Should have been there for her. And for Manon.*

"Besides," she added, "we've *got* to leave. Did you hear the President's address? We're getting our water from the bayou—we can't keep on drinking it, not with the fertilizer plant upstream."

The President should *be doing something,* Nick thought. *Something besides making speeches.*

"I'm coming to you, baby," Nick decided. "You just hang in there for another couple days, and I'll be there."

"I want to wait for you, Daddy." She hesitated, then spoke. "But it's the bayou that has to wait."

With Captain Joe's assistance, Nick plotted his river journey in the chartroom just below *Beluthahatchie*'s pilothouse. Down the Mississippi, up the White River to Lopez Bayou, and up Lopez Bayou to Toussaint Bayou.

"But it's not goin' to look like this, podnah," Captain Joe said. "Everything on the map is nice an' neat, but you can look right out this window here and see how *neat* this river is." He looked down at the map and tapped the Arkansas Delta with a big knuckle. "This is *all* goin' to be under water. It will be hard to find the channel. Some of the navigation markers are goin' to be missing, others will have moved. The White River may have shifted its mouth—already done it once—and you maybe won't be able to tell one from the other. There ain't no towns on that stretch at all. Your marks are gonna be these three lights—Clay Wilson, Smith Point, and Henrico Bar. If the lights are there at all—they could all three have been wrecked."

He shook his head. "If you get to the light at Montgomery Point, you've gone too far. This Napoleon light here—" tapping again with his knuckle "—that's on a town that the river took over a hundred years ago. Napoleon, Arkansas. You used to be able to see parts of it at low water, but now maybe even the *light* ain't there." Captain Joe looked at Nick and tugged on his grizzled mustache. "This river just went through a big change, podnah. Maybe Napoleon's above water again. Maybe some other town's under. This map will prob'ly just get you lost. All's you can hope to do is stay in the river and out of the batture."

"The what?"

Joe gave a laugh. "Batture's an ol' Louisiana word, podnah. Means the floodplain, between the levee and the river."

Nick looked down at the map, felt his jaw clench. "Can you give me some paper?" he asked. "I'd like to make some notes."

"Hell, podnah, take the maps." With a grand gesture, he tore three maps out of the spiral-bound Army Corps of Engineers map set. He opened more long, flat drawers in his map chest, withdrew more maps. "I can give you maps of the White and the Arkansas, too," he said, "but they ain't up to date. We ain't gone up there in years."

Nick looked at the captain. "Thank you," he said.

Captain Joe grinned, clapped Nick on the shoulder. "You just say hey to your little girl from me," he said, "and to her Gros-Papa, too."

Jason watched Nick after he'd come back from talking to his daughter, and he saw Nick's face glow with love and delight. In the evenings, he'd call his father and try to tell him that things on the boat were okay: that Nick wasn't some deranged stranger who'd try to get everyone killed, that Captain Joe wasn't the captain of the *Titanic* about to massacre them all.

He'd leave the radio vibrating with anger, and then he'd see Nick musing over a cup of coffee, his face still radiating love.

Then Jason would hate everybody, and find a place on the boat where he could be alone.

"You want to learn how to use that scope of yours?" Captain Joe asked after one evening's episode of *Doctor Who*.

Captain Joe took the rewound tape out of the player, archived it carefully with the others.

"You know astronomy?" Jason asked.

The telescope had been stowed under Jason's bunk since he'd been on the towboat. Sometimes, when he saw it, the anger boiled up in him and he thought about throwing it over the side. But somehow the scope hadn't ever seemed worth the effort.

"What I learned," Captain Joe said, "was celestial navigation. Useless on the river, but I didn't know I was going to be spending my whole career being a truck driver on the Mississippi, I thought maybe I'd go to salt water one of these days. I never left the river, but once I got into the habit, I kept lookin' *up*, y'know what I mean?"

Captain Joe switched off *Beluthahatchie*'s floodlights and took Jason and Nick aft of the stacks, where the boat's remaining lights wouldn't blind them. There he set up Jason's telescope and pointed it upward at the brilliant swash of stars overhead. This was the best viewing, the captain declared, that he'd ever seen: the quake had wiped out light pollution for miles around, and the factories and automobiles that produced other forms of pollution were wrecked or unused.

"Here, podnah. Look at this."

Jason put his eye to the scope. It took a moment for his eye to adjust to the faint light that had crossed millions of miles of space to reach him, and then awe filled him as the great globular cluster M13 in Hercules grew brighter in the Astroscan: a huge ball of stars, so closely packed together that they looked as if they had merged, with fine trails of stars sailing in all directions from the core.

"A million stars or more, M13," Captain Joe said. "All concentrated in a ball."

A million stars, Jason's mind echoed. In Los Angeles, a valley flooded with the light of a million streetlamps, he could go years without ever seeing so much as a single star. And now he was a looking at a million of them, all packed into the little eyepiece of Astroscan. He had no idea the universe held such bounty.

"How far away is it?" he asked.

"Globular clusters are all on the perimeter of our galaxy. Say maybe twenty-five thousand light-years."

"So the light from those million stars took twenty-five thousand years to get here," Nick mused from over Jason's shoulder.

A million stars, Jason thought again. *All in my eye at once.*

Captain Joe showed them other globular clusters: M81, M82, M51. The Blackeye Galaxy, M64, beautifully defined spiral arms, all made of stars, spinning out from a blazing center, and curling across its center a long dark cloud, like a streak of chocolate swirled into whipped cream.

"Billions of stars there, podnah," Captain Joe said. "Maybe even a trillion. That's one with twelve zeroes after it."

"And people?" Jason asked.

"Mos' likely. Or maybe not people exactly, but intelligent life. Seems silly to think we're the only ones, not when there's so much potential for life in the universe, and so much room. A supernova will throw out everything you need for life—I'll show you a supernova in a few minutes, here."

Jason wondered what his mother would have said if she'd looked through the telescope at the Blackeye Galaxy. She probably knew people who *talked* to the Blackeye Galaxy, who conversed with the people there like neighbors chatting across the back fence.

And all the aliens, according to his mother, believed just what his mother believed. Races throughout the universe embraced peace, drumming, reincarnation, astrology, pyramid power, and Atlantis. It was only the folks on earth who remained mostly unconvinced.

Surely in all those billions of stars, Jason thought, there was *somebody* who would disagree with his mother.

Captain Joe shifted the telescope, peered busily through the eyepiece. Then he laughed, clapped his hands together with a bang. "There we are!" he said. "I was wondering if I could catch the detail with this little scope, but we in luck tonight! Take a look at this, podnah."

At first Jason saw only a small fuzzy blotch, but as his eye adjusted to the lens he saw that the blotch was hollow, a ghostly smoke-ring hovering in the darkness.

"That's the Ring Nebula!" Captain Joe proclaimed. "I told you I'd show you a supernova, and there it is!"

"I thought a supernova would be brighter," Jason said, his eye glued to the strange apparition.

"That's supernova remnants, that cloud, not the supernova itself. What supernovas do is manufacture all the heavier elements, see—iron, oxygen, carbon—and they blast 'em all into space in a huge explosion. Our sun is made up of old supernovas, and so is earth and the other planets. *We* are made of old supernovas. All living things. If it weren't for those big stars blowing up, no life would exist."

"They *blow up*?" Jason said.

"Yeah. Give Nick a look, then lemme show you another one."

Jason stepped back from the telescope. A chill threaded remorselessly through his soul. The problem with his mother's philosophy, he thought, wasn't that people, or even aliens, disagreed with her; it was that the whole *universe* disagreed. She had thought of the universe as being no more complex than her own backyard, and no less welcoming; but she was wrong. Stars blew up regardless of whether people built pyramids; earthquakes shook the earth whether or not they chanted and burnt incense; bodies rolled lifeless along the chill bottom of the Mississippi whether they practiced astrology or not. Existence was filled with wonder and terror and incomprehensible violence, from his mother's backyard to the Blackeye Galaxy. Human comprehension was limited, and human life terribly fragile.

The stars burned overhead, arching across the destroyed landscape. Jason stared up at them in fascination and horror.

Captain Joe showed Jason the Veil Nebula next, but Jason's pleasure in the sight, the gorgeous phosphorescent threads that floated in the darkness, was tempered by the knowledge that this was the remnant of another supernova, something else that had torn itself to shreds at the behest of Nature.

He could feel a pressure in his mind. His internal scale was growing, pressing against the inside of his skull. He felt as if his thoughts were racing outward at the speed of light, trying to catch up with the universe. *A trillion stars . . .*

It was a matter of scale, Jason felt. He did not know how to relate what he'd seen, the universe of stars and galaxies and immeasurable distances, to the rest of his life, to Nick and the *Beluthahatchie* and the torn landscape, the sagging bridges and the bodies floating down the river, a raft for crows.

All things were mortal, he thought. That was what everything had in common.

Everything was mortal, and even a star could die.

Jason didn't see why he needed to go to Aunt Stacy's. It was just another pointless scheme of his father's to stick him out of the way where his father wouldn't have to think about him.

He helped Nick stock the speedboat with supplies for the trip to Toussaint. Canned food, lots of fresh water. Ice and fresh food in the bass boat's cooler. Blankets, clothes, rain gear, a pair of proper oars for the bass boat, a pair of flashlights, tools, insect repellent. Much of it went into the lockers of the bass boat, which Nick planned to tow behind him— "like a tender," as Captain Joe said. Anticipation glittered in Nick's eyes as he planned the trip to his family. Jason tried to stay cheerful about it for Nick's sake, but all he could think about was that Nick would soon be with his family, and that Jason would never be with his family—his *whole* family— ever again.

Nick was going to leave in the morning. The only adult who had ever talked to him as if he was a human being, not a little marching moron to be given orders, or tried to pay for his neglect with presents that he didn't even pick himself.

Jason felt a sudden yearning to be on the river again, to hide somehow on the speedboat and not come out until they arrived at Toussaint, at the place where there was a family waiting. But it was pointless to think about stowing away on a twenty-foot boat. It wasn't as if he wouldn't be seen.

He went to bed that night with fantasies of escape spinning through his mind. He thought about flying up into the night sky, free in Captain Joe's world of stars, the universe to choose from.

Jason woke to a knock on the door of the cabin he shared with Nick. "Better get up, podnah." Captain Joe's voice. "The river's risin' fast. We're gonna float off this sandbar, and we've got to get you onto the water before we head upriver."

"It's still dark," Jason said.

"River makes up its mind to do something, we gotta do it," Joe called.

Jason and Nick dressed in the dark. *Beluthahatchie*'s big turbines vibrated up through the deck. Jason reached under his bunk and grabbed his telescope by its strap. Outside the towboat sat in a pool of white light, crewmen bustling, winches tightening the anchor lines that had been trailed aft. The speedboat and the bass boat had been moored to the side out of the way, ready to be boarded.

"Godspeed, then, podnah," Joe said, and stuck out his hand. Nick shook it.

"Thanks, Captain. Thanks for everything."

Jason held out his hand. The words *take me with you* were on the tip of his tongue. "Good luck," he said.

"Thanks." Nick took the hand, then put the other around Jason's shoulders, gave him a brief, fierce hug. "You take care, Jason." He released Jason, looked at the telescope. "You going to watch me with your 'scope?" he said.

"Sure."

"I don't know if you'll see much. I won't be carrying a light."

Nick turned to the boat, then hesitated. He turned to Captain Joe. "Can I call my girl?" he said. "Tell her I'm on my way?"

Joe glanced over the side at the rising river, then nodded. "Make it quick," he said, and then he and Nick hurried forward to the pilothouse and the radio.

There was a sudden loud clatter as a winch hauled on an

anchor line. Jason jumped. His heart hammered. Light glittered on the river's wavelets.

Below him the speed boat tugged on its line, eager to be off. *Retired and Gone Fishin'* bobbed behind on its towline.

The river was terror. The river was liberation. The river was Edge Living, and his fate.

Jason walked aft a few feet, then went over the side and dropped soundlessly into the bass boat. He crawled under the casting deck forward. The space was narrow, with only an inch or two to spare. It was damp and it smelled bad. Water chuckled against the boat's chine.

Dad is going to be really pissed, Jason thought, and closed his eyes.

Paxton looked down at the dead body in the bar ditch. "God damn it, Jedthus," he said.

"Didn't meant to kill him," Jedthus said. "There ain't more'n three inches of water down there."

"Nigger asked for it," said Jedthus's new partner, a Klan boy named Leckie who hailed from Washington Parish, and whom Omar had made a special deputy.

Jedthus gave Omar a defiant look. "He was talkin' smack, Omar, and that's the truth."

Omar walked around the car that Jedthus and Leckie had pulled over for reckless driving, looked with his flashlight at the license plate. New Orleans, he saw. The car was a late-1970s Mercury with a battered paint job and torn upholstery.

Leckie turned his flashlight on the body. "We was just sittin' on him and whalin' on him with our flashlights," he said. "Guess he must've drowned in the ditch without our knowing it."

Fury howled in Omar's veins. *"Turn off that light!"*

Leckie stared at him in surprise, then obeyed. There was a moment of silence filled only by the night songs of insects.

Omar stalked again around the car, looked up and down the two-lane road. The Bayou Bridge was visible, a shadow on the night's darkness, a quarter-mile away.

These boys were going to put him in goddam prison, he

thought. Killed some stranger passing through, then panicked and called him to ask what to do next. They'd made him an *accessory*! His whole career, his whole life, could end right here.

What a fucking joke. He took off his cap, ran his hands through his hair. At least it happened late at night, on a stretch of road where there was almost no traffic at this hour.

"We could say he resisted arrest," Jedthus said. "We could say he attacked us."

"So you *drowned him*?" Omar said. "In a *ditch*? In *self-defense*? Oh yeah, they'll believe that, all right."

Jedthus blinked, turned away. Omar closed his eyes and tried to think.

"Okay," he said. "This *never happened*. None of us ever saw this car. None of us ever saw this boy. Okay?"

"Sure, Omar," Jedthus said.

"Now what you two do," Omar said, "is put this boy in the trunk of his car. And you take the car down the bayou, where nobody can see, and you shove the car in. Okay?"

"Yes, sir," said Leckie, and looked back at the Bayou Bridge.

"And I mean *far down the bayou*," Omar said. "Not just down to the bridge. Take the car someplace where nobody ever goes fishing. Where no teenagers go to screw. *Where nobody's been in a hundred years.* I don't care if you have to cut a road to get there."

Jedthus looked nervously at Leckie. "Yeah, Omar. We'll do that."

"Because if you screw this up," said Omar, "you two are going to spend the rest of your lives in prison being raped by big-dick niggers. You understand me?"

Leckie's eyes were wide. "Yes, sir," he mumbled.

"Now get moving," Omar said. "And police the damn area afterward. I don't want anyone tomorrow to find a thing belonging to this boy." He began moving toward his car. "I'm heading home to finish watching the *Tonight Show*."

Omar heard splashing sounds as Jedthus and Leckie

waded into the ditch to pat down the dead man, find his keys, and open his trunk. He opened the door to his car, prepared to step in, and then saw headlights glaring on the other side of the Bayou Bridge.

"Careful!" he called. "Car coming!"

Leckie and Jedthus straightened and stood self-consciously by the ditch, like guilty children. Omar cursed, slammed his door, walked toward the other two. Checked the sight lines, made sure the body wasn't visible from the road. Headlights glared in his eyes.

The car rolled past. A Buick, Omar saw, a white family with children. Everyone but the driver asleep.

As soon as the driver was past, Leckie and Jedthus bent again to their work. Omar heard Jedthus curse under his breath.

"No fuckin' keys," Leckie said.

Another set of headlights were coming. Frustration boiled in Omar's veins. "Have you tried the *ignition*?" he demanded.

Jedthus cursed, splashed in the ditch. He wrenched open the door and triggered a buzzing alarm. Omar's nerves jumped at the sound. Jedthus yanked keys from the ignition and the alarm stopped.

"Wait for the car to go by," Omar warned.

The car was a big white Chevy Suburban packed with someone's possessions, with more tied on top. Part of a couch hung out the back end.

"What the hell is going on?" Jedthus said. "This is a *week night*. What are all these people doing out here?"

"Another car," Omar said. Jedthus banged his fist on the trunk of the dead man's Mercury.

The car was a little red Honda hatchback with a black woman driving, a kid in the passenger seat, and more belongings piled in the back.

And behind the Honda were two more cars.

The cars just kept coming, eighteen or twenty of them, all packed with people or possessions. Omar went to his car and sat in the driver's seat, drummed his fingers on the steering wheel, and tried to think.

One of the cars slowed to a stop, and Omar saw the driver rolling down the window. Omar winced, withdrew farther into the car.

"Excuse me, officer," the stranger said. He was a little white man, elderly, with a frosted mustache.

"Yes?" Omar said.

"Is there a motel anywhere ahead?"

"Not in this parish, sir," Omar said. The man rolled up his window and went on.

Finally there was a break in the traffic, and Omar helped the other two pick up the corpse and drop it into the trunk. Jedthus was breathing hard as he slammed the trunk lid down, and Leckie looked pale and frightened, as if he was about to run off into the night.

"What is going *on*?" Jedthus demanded.

"They're evacuating," Omar said. "You heard that everyone on the river's got to leave."

Jedthus looked bewildered. "Why are they coming *here*?" he demanded. "We don't have anything for refugees here. And they're driving farther into the earthquake zone."

"This highway's a hurricane evacuation route. These people have just been following the signs."

Jedthus stared. "Jee-zus," he said.

"More cars coming," Leckie said.

"Dang it," Jedthus said.

Omar put his hand on Jedthus's shoulder. "Listen," he said. "Stay cool. Just do what I said, and take this car *way down the bayou*. And no one will ever know."

Jedthus looked at Omar and nodded. Omar went back to his car and started the engine.

When he looked in the rearview mirror, he saw another line of cars coming.

Nick watched *Beluthahatchie* fall astern as he drifted down the river. He hadn't started the outboard except for a brief burst to show that he *could* start it if he needed to. He didn't want to speed downriver at night and risk running into an obstacle or losing his way, so he planned to drift easy till dawn, then make his way by whatever landmarks were still visible.

Beluthahatchie's turbines revved, the sound filling the still river. Winches clattered. It was tricky pulling the tow off the mud, Captain Joe had explained, because all fifteen barges were held together with just a single steel cable. If the cable parted, the entire tow would come apart, and the whipping steel cable could cut a man in half.

The river had risen four inches in just three hours, according to the captain, which should more than float the tow. Captain Joe hadn't expected it—reports from upriver had indicated a much slower rise—but the towboat's captain was going to take advantage of the flood while he could.

Nick looked ahead and felt anxiety claw lightly at his nerves. He hadn't been able to reach Toussaint with his radio call. The water was rising there, too, Arlette had said, and was threatening to flood the telephone exchange. Perhaps all communication with Toussaint was out.

Captain Joe had said that he'd keep calling. All Nick could do was hope that he hadn't delayed too long in getting on the river, that Arlette and her mother would still be in Toussaint when he arrived.

Nick jumped at the sound of the towboat's horn blasting over the river. It sounded three times, the echoes dying away in the trees, and then *Beluthahatchie* began to move, its turbines whining as it backed away from the hidden sandbar. Then it paused while the stern anchors were taken up, the boat's outline glowing in the darkness; its horn sounded again and it began to move forward.

Nick raised a hand and waved.

The towboat moved slowly and cautiously, but nevertheless, in a few short moments, it left Nick alone on the river.

"Omar?" Wilona asked sleepily. "Who is that?"

"I'll find out, darling," Omar said.

He reached for the pistol he kept on the nightstand as the knock on the front door persisted. It was four in the morning, and he had left Jedthus and Leckie with their corpse around midnight.

They'd probably screwed it up, he thought. He could hardly believe that they were stupid enough to come here asking for advice.

And if it wasn't Jedthus knocking, it was someone else who had even less business knocking on his door. Black militants. Jew assassins. Even that crazy Micah Knox, wanting vengeance for the way Omar had treated him. Omar was famous now, which meant that people he had never met would want to kill him, just like they'd killed John Lennon.

Omar held his pistol ready as he slipped to the front window and twitched aside the curtains, saw the familiar face under the porch light. His heart leaped. He put his pistol on a side table, unlocked the door, and threw his arms around his son.

"David! What are you doing here?"

His boy grinned at him, patted him on the back. "Baton Rouge is being evacuated. My summer job's gone, so I thought I might as well come home."

Omar stepped back, grinned. "Why didn't you call?"

"I tried. The phones were all jammed. So I just came." David was a younger version of his father—tall, with broad shoulders, curling black hair, and movie-star features that got him a lot of girlfriends.

"David!" Wilona called from the bedroom. She rushed to embrace her son. Omar helped David carry his bags into the back room.

"The traffic was bumper-to-bumper almost all the way here," David said. "It looked like the whole state was on the move."

"They started driving through earlier tonight," Omar said. "I don't know why they're heading this way."

"I don't think they know, either. They're city people, you know? They'll just keep driving till they see something familiar, like a Holiday Inn or a McDonald's."

"Can I get you something to eat?" Wilona asked.

David nodded. "Yes, ma'am. I haven't had anything since lunch."

"I've got some cold ham and potatoes. I could reheat it in the microwave."

"Cold is fine, Mama."

"Heating it's no problem. You want some Co-Cola?" Retying her bathrobe, Wilona headed for the kitchen.

David and Omar looked at each other for a moment. Then David grinned. "I saw you on TV, Dad. You looked good."

"Thanks."

"There was a lot of talk on campus about you. You'd be surprised how many friends you have there."

Omar nodded. "I'm glad to hear it." *Campus.* He had a son who was on *campus.* No Paxton had ever been to college before.

Father and son, they were on the move.

They walked back to the front room and sat down. David looked around. "The house seems to have come through okay," he said.

"Your mama put a lot of work into making it look that way," Omar said. "But you'll be eating off a plastic plate tonight. All the china fell out of the cabinet and smashed."

David made a face. "I hope the insurance covers it."

"No. The policy has an exemption for earthquakes and floods."

"Bastards," David said. "Jew bastards."

"Here's your Co-Cola." Wilona, returning with a plastic party cup in her hand.

"Thank you, Mama." Smiling. David turned back to Omar. "Is there any more work I can do around the house? Or should I see if I can find a paying job somewheres else?"

Omar considered. "The National Guard shipped too many of my deputies up north. I've been swearing in special deputies. And with all these refugees coming through, we'll need more just to handle the traffic."

David grinned. "Sounds great," he said. "Kind of like working for the family firm."

It would be good to have somebody intelligent working for him, Omar thought.

Not like Leckie and Jedthus, who were probably up to their hips in the bayou right now, finding a place to hide a corpse.

*　*　*

The current was sluggish, and *American Dream* turned slow circles around *Retired and Gone Fishin'* as it drifted. Nick let the boat do what it wanted, and only tried to keep it in the center of the channel, between the dimly sensed flood plain on either side. The night was dark, but the stars blazed overhead with an intensity Nick had never seen. He could see dozens of nebulae with the naked eye, little bright clouds between the stars, and he could never remember seeing so many before.

He wished he had Jason's telescope aboard.

He felt a breath of wind on his skin, and then he heard a distant rushing sound ahead. He turned his head downstream, cupped hands to his ears. The sound *might* be wind through trees.

It might be rapids.

It might be a waterfall.

The wind freshened, fell, freshened again from another direction. The rushing sound grew louder. Nick strained his eyes for sign of white water.

Captain Joe hadn't received any reports of rapids on this stretch. Boats had been going up and down the river and hadn't reported white water here. It didn't make any sense.

Stay alive for Arlette, Nick thought. He dropped into the cockpit seat and started the engine. He turned the bow upstream and motored slowly for ten minutes. Then cut the motor and drifted again, till he felt the winds and heard the rushing. Then he did it again. And again.

Till dawn.

When the east turned pale he was surprised by the size and sluggishness of the river. The trees in what Captain Joe would call the batture sat deeper in the water than he'd seen them before. Debris floated aimlessly on the still water, turning small circles or pushed around by little predawn wind gusts. It was as if the river had almost ceased to flow, had become a lake three or four miles wide.

Almost. The water was moving south very slowly, taking

the boat with it. Nick folded back the boat's canvas top, then stood to peer ahead, scratched his bristly chin in thought. Something, he thought, was causing the river to rise, had floated *Beluthahatchie* off its bar. What could cause the river to rise four inches in just a matter of hours? Four inches over this huge expanse was a *lot* of water. Nick wondered if the Arkansas had changed its course, struck the Mississippi just south of here and backed up the water.

The sun blazed above the trees to the east, brightened the dark river with its touch. Nick could hear that roaring sound again. What was going on?

The southern horizon seemed indistinct, misty. Banks of fog?

Fear shivered up Nick's spine. He wondered if the mist was rising off rapids.

"Hey, Nick. What's happening?"

Nick turned and saw Jason sitting in the bass boat's little cockpit. His hair was tousled, and there was a sleepy smile on the boy's face.

Fury flashed like fire along Nick's nerves. *"What are you doing here?"* he roared.

Jason's eyes widened in surprise at the strength of Nick's anger, but when he replied his tone was deliberately casual. "Didn't want to spend the summer with my aunt. I thought I'd go with you."

"God damn it!" Nick banged a fist on the gunwale. *"God damn it, you're not my kid!"*

"Hey, it's okay," Jason said. He lifted his hands in appeal. "I won't get in your way. I can be useful. You know that."

Nick glared at him. "Now I've got to take you back to Captain Joe," he said. He threw himself into the cockpit seat, pulled out the choke.

"Hey, wait! You'll never catch the *Beluthahatchie*. You've been going down the river all night."

Nick didn't even bother to look at Jason as he shouted his answer. "No, I haven't! I've been staying in the same place all damn night long! And if you had any damn brains, you'd know that!"

"No! Wait!"

Nick punched the starter, felt the big Evinrude catch. He gunned the engine to drown out Jason's protests, then put it in gear. He spun the wheel, turned the speedboat upstream, and pushed the throttle forward. He felt the little tug that meant the tow rope to the bass boat had gone taut, and imagined rather than saw Jason being flung back in his seat as the bass boat accelerated on the end of its line.

The boat's nose rose as it gained speed. Nick could still hear Jason's shouts over the roar of the engine. He dodged debris as he roared upriver at top speed, smiling as he pictured the bass boat playing crack-the-whip on the end of its line. Run it into a few trees, he thought, serve Jason right.

Then he sighed. Who, he wondered, was he trying to kid? There was no way he could catch the towboat with its head start.

He pulled back on the throttle, then switched off the ignition. There was a rush of water as the speedboat fell off its bow wave.

"I'm sorry!" Jason called in the sudden silence. "I didn't think you'd be mad!"

"You didn't think at all," Nick said. Anger beat a slow throb in his temples. He stood, turned to face Jason as the boat lost momentum. "What am I going to do with you?" he said.

"Take me with you? Come on, Nick—I won't be any trouble."

That bright grin, Nick thought, must have got a lot of goodies out of Jason's old man. Rage burst like a firework in Nick's brain.

"*I'm not your father!*" he shouted. And then added, half to himself, "And your daddy's gonna kill me."

"Tell him it's all my fault," Jason said. "He'll believe that. He's used to blaming me for things."

Nick glared at the boy. "I suppose he's got reasons!" he said. He collapsed into his seat, shook his head. "I don't know what I should do."

Jason crawled onto the bass boat's foredeck, then began

pulling on the tow rope, drawing himself closer to the speedboat. "It'll be okay, Nick, really."

"Bullshit."

Jason clambered aboard the American Dream, dropped into the seat next to Nick. "Listen. You can say you didn't have a choice."

Nick looked at him. Fury simmered in his veins. "First town we come to—first landing, first boat, first inhabited damn building—I'm putting you off. I don't care if you have to live on somebody's roof for the next two weeks."

Jason opened his mouth, closed it.

"And another thing," Nick said, and he heard the echo of his father in his voice, General Ruford chewing out some subordinate, and he was pleased by the sound, "you better mind me from this point, boy, because if you don't, I'm going to kick your lily ass all over this boat."

Jason stared, swallowed. "Yes, sir," he said.

Nick hit the starter, felt the Evinrude growl, like one of his father's tanks. "Now," he said, "there's something weird going on downstream, so I want you to keep an eye out, right?"

"Umm. Shall I get my telescope?"

"You've got it with you? Okay. Yes."

Jason set up the telescope on the foredeck, peered into it, fiddled with the focus knob. Nick motored cautiously downstream, standing behind the wheel so that he could see to avoid debris. Sweat prickled on his forehead as the rising sun began to burn down on the flooded country.

Over the murmuring engine he could hear the rushing sound, and the southern horizon seemed indistinct and misty. He called to Jason. "What do you see?"

Jason looked up from the eyepiece, shook his head. "I can't tell. It's all weird."

"Is it rapids?"

Jason shook his head again. "I don't know. It looks like there might be white water."

Nick clenched his teeth. This didn't make any sense.

He motored closer. Puffs of wind gusted from different

parts of the compass. Nick put the Evinrude in neutral and throttled down so that he could hear better. Jason's eye was glued to the eyepiece of the Astroscan.

"It's an island," Jason said. "I think. It looks like water's breaking around something. And I see lots of driftwood piled up."

If it was an island, Nick thought, he could go around it. "Okay," he said.

"It's a big island," Jason said. He panned the scope back and forth, muttered something as he inadvertently shoved the inverted image the wrong way, then regained his view. Finally he sat up, looked at Nick.

"I don't get it," he said. "It looks like the island is right across the whole river."

Nick gnawed his lip. "Let me see," he decided finally.

He made his way onto the foredeck, knelt next to Jason, put his eye to the scope. The upside-down image bobbed uneasily with the motion of the boat. He saw tree roots, white water, mist.

Carefully he nudged the scope left and right, panning across the horizon. He could hear the roar of white water. The island looked huge.

He straightened. Rushing water dinned at his ears. His brain whirled, and then his mouth went dry as comprehension dawned. "Oh shit," he said.

"What?" Jason asked. "What is it?"

"It's not an island," Nick said. "It's a dam." He rose, the boat swaying under him, and made his way back to the cockpit.

Jason looked after him. "A dam? How can it be a dam?"

"Dam's made of driftwood," Nick said. "All that debris going downriver—a lot of it got hung up here. Maybe there was an island, or some rocks, or just a mud bar. But once the driftwood and other rubbish started collecting, it just kept stacking up. That's why the river's rising so fast. It's been dammed."

Nick bit his lip as he thought about the water piled up behind the dam. Millions of tons, all pressing on the haphazard accretion of rubbish that was holding them back. He knew how much power water could exert, how it would push through every crevice, prod at every weak point. Even well-built levees and breakwaters failed under the constant pressure of water: the driftwood dam, he suspected, wouldn't last long, not with the weight of the flooded Mississippi behind it.

And when the end came for the dam, he thought, *my God*. All the water pouring out in a flood and carrying the debris with it. A huge wave heading downstream, churning with tons of battering wreckage.

He was going to have to wait for the dam to burst, he thought. And then wait a long time after that, so as not to get caught in the flood or the wreckage the flood would carry with it.

Impatience twitched along his nerves. He wanted to get south, get to Arlette. Maybe he could find a way around the dam, find a chute of water he could ride south, or some way through the trees where the water flowed more normally.

But no. Even if there was a chute, even if he could get down the chute without mishap, that would just put him in the way of that deadly wall of water when it finally broke free.

Stay alive, he told himself. Stay alive for Arlette.

He turned the boat around, pushed the throttle forward. They might as well head for the treeline to the east, where they could tie up in the shade and wait.

Jason looked at him questioningly.

"Might as well have breakfast," he said.

The debris dam cracked around noon. There were a series of concussions, like bombs exploding. Flocks of birds flapped skyward in surprise. Jason and Nick both straightened, looked toward the sound.

Another boom sounded over the still water. And then they both heard the roaring, building over the trees, as water began to flow.

Jason turned to Nick. "Do we go now?"

"Too dangerous. Wait for the water to go down."

It dropped fast. Six inches in the first hour, judging by the high-flood marks left on the boles of trees. Every so often another blast from the dam echoed through the trees, as well as prolonged grinding noises, as if pieces of driftwood were being torn away from the dam with incredible violence.

By two o'clock the water was falling so slowly that Nick couldn't track its progress, debris was moving on the river at what seemed to be a normal pace, and the roaring sound had faded, replaced by the calls of birds in the trees. Nick decided that he may as well investigate.

The water was moving fast in the center of the river, and as Nick approached he began to hear the roaring sound again. Parts of the southern horizon were misty, presumably where the driftwood dam was still intact, but other parts were clear. Nick steered for the widest of the gaps, the Evinrude throttled down so far it barely kept headway. The roaring sound grew, and apprehension tingled along Nick's nerves.

Go or no-go? He stood behind the wheel, peered anxiously ahead. Half-submerged debris ground against the boat's side and set his teeth on edge. Suddenly he realized, from the strong breeze in his face, that the current was carrying the boat along at high speed.

Go or no-go? The decision might well be taken out of his hands at any second.

The boat dropped into a kind of watery chuckhole, bounced up again. Nick swayed on his feet, felt spray on his face. The Evinrude whined in protest. Ahead the water looked choppy.

"Can you see . . . ?" he asked Jason.

Jason shrugged. "Looks clear."

"Right." He pushed the throttle forward. He didn't want to barrel through at high speed, but he wanted enough momentum to get himself out of any trouble he might run into.

The river jostled the boat, slapping at its chine. Nick

blinked spray from his eyes, then opened them wide as the river yawned before him and flashed its teeth of white.

The boat pitched down, and Nick dropped abruptly into his seat. The propeller shrieked as the stern flew up into the air. Nick could feel himself flying. Ahead he could see nothing but a wall of foaming water. By his side, he heard Jason give a surprised yelp.

The boat smashed into the water, and the impact threw Nick forward onto the wheel. The boat buried its foredeck in the Mississippi, then surged sluggishly upward as water poured aft. A wave climbed the windscreen and hit Nick full in the face. The propeller dropped into water, caught, and threw the boat forward as water sloshed toward the stern.

Something smashed against the stern of the boat, and without even looking Nick knew what it was. "Untie the bass boat!" he shouted. He didn't want it climbing in the cockpit with him.

Nick caught a glimpse of a tangled thorn-hedge of foaming tree roots ahead, and calmer water to the right: he spun the wheel, threw the throttle forward. The boat slewed, banged on hard water as if it were a brick wall, then surged past the slashing roots with room to spare. Something bright and metallic loomed ahead—it might have been a grain silo that had lost its roof, or a gasoline storage tank—and Nick cranked the wheel in the other direction.

"Bass boat's untied!" Jason yelled.

American Dream smashed into the metal obstruction broadside, and then the propeller dug in and the speedboat leaped ahead. The sound of rushing water was loud, but not as loud as the pulse that beat in Nick's ears. Through the gleaming diamonds of spray on the windscreen, Nick saw another obstruction ahead—he cranked the wheel, felt the boat respond. A tree-root tangle swept past, then another. Then Nick was weightless again as the boat launched itself over a waterfall before pancaking onto the water with a hollow boom.

The timber dam hadn't just broken open, it had scattered bits of itself downstream, obstacles like tiger teeth waiting to impale the unwary. The water didn't pour through in a stream, it leaped down in stages, like a rapid.

Nick slalomed through the obstacles, his confidence growing as the boat responded to his commands. And then he was clear, the Mississippi opening up before him, choked with floating wreckage but still perfectly navigable. He laughed, turned to Jason.

The boy looked at him, eyes wide. "My God, Nick!" he said.

Nick grinned at him. "Glad we waited till it was safe, huh?" he said. He pointed. "And look there!"

The bass boat bobbed in the current, scarred and glittering with spray but still defiantly afloat. Nick pulled the speedboat alongside, and Jason caught the bass boat's trailing towline with a boathook and then tied it astern of *American Dream*.

Nick looked out at the river through the spray-bedecked windscreen. He reached for the throttle and pushed it forward. The boat's bow rose high as the Evinrude bellowed. *Arlette*, he thought, *I'm on my way.*

Larry stood above the holding pond in the auxiliary building. His boots were planted on the fuel handling machine that was used to shift fuel assemblies within the holding pond—in essence a giant overhead crane that ran on tracks, like the one in the reactor containment building but less robust. The machine had suffered considerable damage when the roof had fallen on it during M1, and putting it into working order had been one of Larry's greatest priorities.

Replacement parts had been a problem. Machines of this sort were intended to last decades, longer than the nuclear facility itself, and for that reason spare parts were not readily available, and such as had been available were stored in buildings destroyed by the quake and then flooded. Larry missed Poinsett Landing's huge machine shops, which could probably have scratch-built a Saturn V moon rocket, let alone parts for a big crane. In the end the parts were scavenged from other nuclear facilities and installed by Larry, Jameel, and Meg Tarlton. Power was provided to the system by a generator warped alongside the auxiliary building in a barge. Now the three of them stood on the machine's control platform, looking at the kludged-together control panel—part of which consisted of switches set into a raw-looking piece of plywood—and were ready to give the system its first test.

Larry raised his walkie-talkie to his lips, then paused while a helicopter thundered overhead. He caught a glimpse, through the open roof of the auxiliary building, of an Army Super Jolly helicopter with a load of earthquake debris.

The island that Larry had recommended be built around Poinsett Landing was rapidly taking shape, a steel, stone, and concrete ship's prow pointing upstream into the river. After the helicopter crews had a chance to practice their aim, and demonstrated to everyone's satisfaction that they weren't about to drop a ten-ton load on plant workers, Larry and his people had been allowed back into the building.

Larry waited for the helicopter sound to recede, then pressed the handset trigger. "Power up!"

"Power up, Mr. Hallock," the answer fizzed out of the speakers.

Elsewhere in the building, huge circuit-breakers were thrown. Lights gleamed on the control panel. Larry felt himself tense, waiting for the short, the pop of a fuse, the fizz of a misinstalled control system. Dim pain throbbed in his broken collarbone, and he rubbed the broken bone absently. It almost never bothered him unless he was under physical tension.

Nothing. No disaster. Larry's breathing eased.

"Just take her forward and back," he said.

Jameel approached the control panel, flicked switches, pressed a lever. With a hum of electric motors, the crane began smoothly moving forward along its tracks. He braked, then moved the crane back the way it had come.

"Nice," Larry said. "Now traverse the turret."

Larry leaned over the rail to peer at what he could see of the turret on the bottom of the crane, which was intended to traverse left and right so as to be able to drop the grab into any of the fuel storage racks in the storage pond. Another set of electric motors hummed. He saw the turret rotate, the grab on the end of its distended snout tracking past his field of view.

"Works fine," he said. "Swing it t'other way."

He waited for the snout to traverse into his field of vision, then called to Jameel to halt.

"Drop the grab," he said. "I'll tell you when to stop."

The grab was like a metal claw on the end of the machine's double chain. It was spring-activated so as to snatch a fuel assembly from its rack on contact, and would not disengage as long as the weight of a fuel assembly was detected at the end of the chain.

Jameel took hold of a lever screwed to the plywood control board and gave it a nudge. The bright stainless steel double chain clanked as it rolled out of the turret, the heavy grab swaying only slightly as it dropped to the water below. The Mississippi water in the holding pond lacked the brilliant clarity of the demineralized water that normally filled this space—the mud had mostly settled to the bottom, but its dark presence reflected little light and made it difficult to see into the water. *We're going to have to put a lot of floodlights down there,* Larry thought. *Otherwise we won't be able to see a dang thing.*

The grab smoothly entered the water, the chain unrolling above it. "Stop!" Larry called.

He didn't want to grab a fuel assembly by accident. He didn't have anyplace to put it.

There was a tremor, a rattle of roof panels, and Larry realized an aftershock was hammering the building. Larry's heart kicked into a higher rhythm as he felt the crane sway on its tall platform, and he backed hastily away from the rail he'd been hanging over.

The remaining roof beams and panels creaked. Fortunately, Larry noticed, he and the crane were under open sky.

The aftershock stopped. Meg gave a nervous laugh. Larry waited a few moments to see if it would begin again, then gingerly approached the end of the platform and looked down at the grab on the end of its chain.

"Bring 'er back up," he said.

Jameel stopped the chain, then threw another lever. There was a brief electronic hum from the winch motors, and then a hiss and a pop as one of the control panel fuses blew. Jameel jumped back from the control panel as if stung, then gave a nervous chuckle at his overreaction.

"Cut power!" Larry bawled into his handset.

Lights on the control panel died. Meg was already down on one knee, reaching for her tool box. "Just a short, Mr. Hallock," she said. "I'll have that fixed in a jiff."

While Meg and Jameel worked on the board, Larry took off his glasses and rubbed his aching eyes. There seemed no end to the problems. Solving one just meant another reared its ugly head.

The fuel handling machine was normally computer controlled, but the computer that did the job was now under the surface of the Mississippi. Control would have to be by hand and by eye, and that was going to result in awkwardness and lengthy delays in extracting over 1000 tons of nuclear waste from the pond.

Lost also were the records of exactly which fuel assemblies had been racked in which place, both those on computer file and the paper hardcopy, which had been stored in a destroyed building. Larry had no records that told him which of the rods in the pond below were the old safe ones, and which the new hot ones. He was going to have to drop radiation detectors into the pond on the end of a line to find out, and that was going to produce results that were messy and had a high degree of inaccuracy.

One problem after another, he repeated to himself. *You've only got to solve one problem at a time.*

At one time, he thought, that had seemed like a *good* thing.

TWENTY-THREE

There was one boat coming down on the same morning I landed; when they came in sight of the falls, the crew were so frightened at the prospect, that they abandoned their boat and made for the island in their canoe—two were left on the island, and two made for the west bank in the canoe—about the time of their landing, they saw that the island was violently convulsed—one of the men on the island threw himself into the river to save himself by swimming—one of the men from the shore met him with the canoe and saved him. —This man gave such an account of the convulsion of the island, that neither of the three dared to venture back for the remaining man. The three men reached New Madrid by land.

The man remained on the Island from Friday morning until Sunday evening, when he was taken off by a canoe sent from a boat coming down. I was several days in company with this man—he stated that during his stay in the island, there were frequent eruptions, in which sand and stone, coal and water were thrown up. —The violent agitation of the ground was such at one time as induced him to hold to a tree to support himself; the earth gave way at the place, and he with the tree sunk down, and he got wounded in the fall.— The fissure was so deep as to put it out of his power to get out at that place—he made his way along the fissure until a sloping slide offered him an opportunity of crawling out. He states that frequent lights appeared—that in one instance, after one of the explosions near where he stood, he approached the hole from which the coal and land had been thrown up, which was now filled with water, and on putting his hand into it he found it was warm.

Matthias M. Speed, March 2, 1812

* * *

When the trees opened up again to show the big white frame house on its little green mound, Nick was taken completely by surprise. His heart turned cartwheels.

"We're there," he said, and his voice seemed unbelieving even to himself.

They had gone up the White River—flooded, filled with more debris even than the Mississippi—then spent a night on Lopez Bayou. He had tried to keep track, by dead reckoning, of how far they had come, but he knew that his estimates had to be wildly out of true. He was more surprised than anyone when a stretch of water opened up just where he expected Toussaint Bayou to be.

They hadn't seen a soul the entire trip to Toussaint. Some flooded cotton fields, some abandoned farmhouses fallen into the flood, but no sign of a living human being.

Jason, in the other seat, turned to look at the big house with interest. Nick spun the wheel, aimed for the house.

One of the big oaks that shaded the house had fallen, he saw, but someone had turned the timber into a neatly piled stack of lumber. The windows had lost their glass, and the two brick chimneys had fallen. There had been some hasty repairs to the roof with plastic sheeting and mismatched shingles. Some of the outbuildings had collapsed into the flood. But the house itself was intact, and the sight of it made Nick want to laugh out loud.

"I've been meaning to ask," Jason said. "What's a Gros-Papa? If I meet him, I should know what it means, right?"

"It's French," Nick said. "It means Big Daddy. It's a name they have down here for grandfather." And then he added, "Tennessee Williams had a Big Daddy in one of his plays. I don't remember which one."

Nick cut the motor and ran the boat up onto the green slope below the house, then ran forward, tossed the mushroom anchor onto the grass so the boat wouldn't float away again, then jumped to solid ground. He held the prow steady while Jason jumped ashore, then realized he was staring at the boy with a silly smile, just a dumb happy guy standing on green grass in the sun, like any idiot about to see his daughter for the first time in months, and then he shook his head and started for the house at a brisk walk.

They approached the back of the house across a grassy plateau, walking toward the kitchen door. The town of Toussaint, such as it was, was on the other side of the house, and Toussaint Bayou curved around to meet it. The only sign of the town visible from where Nick walked was the water tower.

A rooster crowed from one of the outbuildings. Chickens scurried away from their approach.

"This is an old Indian mound," Nick said. "They built this house up here over a hundred years ago to keep above the floods, but they didn't know the mound was artificial until some archaeologists came up here in the fifties."

"There was a mound where we lived in Missouri," Jason said, and then an expression of loss crossed his face, and he fell silent.

Nick put his arm around the boy and walked with him through the grass, through the old shade oaks, to the kitchen door. The back windows had lost their glass, but screens were in place to keep out insects. The kitchen door, he saw, was open and the screen slightly ajar. Someone was home. He wanted to sing.

"Hello?" He opened the screen door and rapped on the frame. When no one answered, he stepped inside the big kitchen with its tall old wooden cabinets and its large modern range, and suddenly a graveyard chill ran up his spine, and he felt the winds of desolation blow in the hollow of his skull.

There was horror here. Somehow he knew it—there was a smell in the house, or a peculiar, ominous brand of silence, or some kind of spectral, psychic echo of terror . . .

Whatever it was, he'd felt it once before. In Helena.

He put a hand on Jason's chest as the boy was about to step into the kitchen, and held him back. "Stay here," he said. The boy's eyes widened in sudden comprehension and alarm, and he stepped backward, out of the doorway. Silently, carefully, Nick closed the screen door.

He could hear the buzzing of flies in the next room. If anything had happened to Arlette, he felt, his heart would tear open like the ground had torn in the quake, and he would die on the spot.

His nerves tingled as he walked past the big butcher-block kitchen table to the arched doorway that led to the dining room. There, by the dining table, he found Penelope, Gros-Papa's younger half-sister, who had moved into the house to look after him after his wife died. She had been shot several times in the back. She had her apron on when she died.

Gros-Papa lay in the front parlor, all three hundred pounds of him, in the jacket and tie he wore even on informal occasions. His silver-rimmed glasses were perched firmly on his stern nose. Shot in the chest. The watch chain he wore across his big stomach was gone and, Nick presumed, the watch with it, the watch that played "Claire de Lune" when you opened it.

Nick went to the gun cabinet in Gros-Papa's study, but the guns had all been taken. The drawers of the desk and file cabinets had been opened, and their contents strewn on the floor.

Gros-Papa's second son Gilly—short for Guillaume—was on the stair, as if he'd tried to run upstairs and been shot as he fled. Near misses had punched holes in the wall above the stair and knocked down a small watercolor that someone had made of the house a hundred years ago.

Nick's head swam. He hadn't really dared to breathe since he'd entered the house. He forced himself to take in a breath, and then he searched the house for Arlette and her mother. He went to Arlette's room first, found the closets ransacked, the drawers emptied. The scent of his daughter still hung in the room. His own image, a photo of Nick, gazed up at him from its frame.

The other rooms had been looted as well. Jewelry was gone, and probably money. Nick found no living persons, no additional bodies. Arlette and Manon and the others of the household were gone.

They'd evacuated, then. Got away before this had happened. Relief sang through Nick's blood. But the relief died as a horrifying thought rose in his mind.

Where had the killers come from? Arlette and her family were moving down the bayou by boat, toward the White River and the Arkansas. They had probably left sometime yesterday. If the killers had been coming up the White, they would have encountered the David family, and the encounter might well have been violent. But Nick and Jason had seen no sign of any violent encounter, or any encounter at all.

Which meant that the killers were coming *down* the bayou, traveling on Arlette's heels, possibly only a few hours behind. They hadn't turned down the White, because otherwise they would have met Jason and Nick. So that meant they had gone upriver, right on Arlette's trail . . .

He felt his lips peeling back from his teeth in a snarl. No. He would find the killers before they could find Arlette, and do what was necessary.

Nick went down the stair, avoiding Gilly's body, and then crouched for a moment next to Gros-Papa. He steeled himself, then reached out and touched the old man's large dead hand. Cool to the touch. He took the hand in his fingers and tried to raise it, but there was still a faint stiffness in the corpse: the rigor not yet passed. The death had been fairly recent, maybe last night.

Nick straightened, felt his head swim, then walked carefully back to the kitchen. Light glared in from the screen door. He paused by the butcher-block table for a moment, tried to clear his head and decide what he needed to do, and then he looked down and saw the envelope that rested on the table. The word *Daddy* was written on the back in Arlette's hand.

Much of his burden of dread fell instantly away. He felt physically lighter, as if someone had removed a burden from his shoulders.

Arlette had left him a message, and if she'd done that she wouldn't have been herded away at gunpoint. He picked up the envelope and headed out the screen door.

Jason stood in the shade of one of the oaks, pale and nervous. His lips were blue as if he'd been standing up to his neck in cold water. "What happened?"

"Three people killed," Nick said. And then, in answer to the question he saw in the boy's horrified eyes, he added, "Not Arlette. Not Manon. They must have left before it happened."

"Is it gas again?" Jason asked. "Poison or something?"

Nick's fingers trembled as he opened the unsealed envelope. He shook his head. "They were shot. Robbers."

"Oh, Jesus," Jason said. "Jesus, Nick, I'm sorry."

Nick's fingers were trembling so hard he couldn't manage to get the paper out of the envelope. He paused, took a breath, pressed his hands together with the envelope between them. Then tried again, and succeeded. His daughter's round, exuberant script opened before him like a flower.

> *Daddy,*
>
> *I am sorry but we have to leave. The phone exchange was flooded and I couldn't call you to let you know, and the water plant is flooded too and the water is not safe to drink. We are going in boats to Pine Bluff and I am drawing you a map.*
>
> *I love you and I hope to see you soon. Don't worry about me, I will be safe.*
>
> > *Love,*
> > *your daughter.*

Below the words were a row of hearts and then the map, which looked as if it had been traced off a highway map. Nick crushed the paper to his face, inhaled the scent of paper and ink and, maybe, Arlette.

Don't worry about me, I will be safe. It was up to Nick to make certain that remained true.

"Come on," he told Jason, "we have to hurry." And he began walking off before Jason began asking questions.

Nick didn't want to leave the bodies unburied, to leave the house open. But his duty was to the living, and every moment might count.

There was decay in Toussaint's general store, and for a moment Nick felt faint, expecting more bodies. But then he realized that the smell was coming from dead minnows in the galvanized bait tanks that lined one side of the store. The bayou hadn't reached high enough to wash the minnows out.

Toussaint consisted of about a dozen buildings grouped around a crossroads, most of them owned by the David family. People's farms and private residences spread for miles up and down the roads, and they all gave "Toussaint" as their address, but what passed for the village itself was tiny.

It was tinier now than it had been. The brick office building had been wrecked, along with its post office, and so had the brick filling station. The David family, who between them owned all these properties, had taken a couple big hits.

The general store had come off its foundations in the quake and had collapsed to one side. The roof sagged. Clapboards and shingles were missing. The flood had risen to the middle of the doorframe. Nick tied the boat to one of the supports of the sagging porch, then dropped into the cool water. He felt ahead with his feet as he carefully made his way into the store's interior.

When he returned he was armed with weapons that had been stored high above the flood. He had a Winchester Model 94 lever-action 30-30, a pump shotgun, and a couple of revolvers, a pair of .38s, one large and one small. He hadn't handled firearms since he'd left high school, and they felt heavier than he'd remembered, solid and purposeful. The weight of them in his hands didn't make him nervous, but he found they didn't give him an increased sense of security, either.

In a rucksack he carried boxes of ammunition, holsters for

the pistols, a cleaning kit, and a sling for the rifle. Holding all this over his head, he waded back to the front porch and put it all on the speedboat's foredeck.

Jason looked down at the pile of weaponry with a stunned expression, as if he was trying to work out what horrible, apocalyptic movie scenario he'd just wandered into. "Jeez," he said.

Nick hoisted himself onto the boat. Water sluiced from his soaked clothing. "Can you take the boat down the bayou?" he asked. "Back the way we came? I've got to sort out these guns."

"Yeah. I guess."

Nick untied the boat and then carried his gear into the cockpit. He loaded the larger of the two pistols, put it in the holster, and clipped the holster to his belt in the back. He practiced drawing it a few times, but he saw Jason looking at him, and he quit.

It's not like he was going to turn himself into a gunfighter overnight.

He worked the action of the rifle, dry-fired it a few times, then loaded it and the shotgun, leaving the chamber empty in each instance so that the gun couldn't fire accidentally. He left the long guns on one of the bench seats that ran the length of the cockpit, then moved forward to sit in the bucket seat next to Jason.

"Have you ever used firearms?" he asked.

"No. My parents just didn't—don't—have them around. Muppet and I were going to go shooting over the levee when the water dropped but—" Jason swallowed. "We never got to it."

"In that case, I don't want you touching the guns."

"No problem."

"I *really* don't want you touching them."

"*Okay!*" Jason said, his voice loud over the roaring engine.

"I need to confirm this, Jason. Because your record at following orders isn't very good."

Jason glared at him, his cheeks reddening. *"I won't touch your guns, okay?"*

Nick took a long breath. Maybe his insistence on this would just make Jason mess with the guns out of sheer contrariness, but he thought he needed to make his point. "Maybe I can teach you how to use them when we get the time," he said, conciliating, "but until then I want you to take this very seriously."

Jason nodded again. Then he turned to Nick and said, "What are we doing, exactly?" he said. "Are you trying to get into a fight or something?"

Nick looked at Jason in surprise. He had been so absorbed in his own grim thoughts that he hadn't considered how this would look to the boy. Finding his in-laws murdered, loading the boat with guns, then heading down the bayou, all without a word of explanation.

Jason probably thought that Nick was involved in some kind of gang war and bent on vengeance.

"No," Nick said. "No, not at all. I'm trying to get to Arlette and her family, and protect them from the robbers who killed her relations. Those robbers might still be around, and I don't want Arlette to be without help."

A look of relief crossed Jason's face. "Okay," he said. "I understand."

"Good."

Jason looked ahead and steered the boat around a tangle of cypress trees that the quake had cut off just above water level.

"Faster," Nick said, and Jason looked surprised again. "We need to go faster."

They found the place where Toussaint Bayou opened out onto Lopez Bayou, then instead of turning left, to retrace their path, they turned right, following Arlette's map. Nick kept wanting Jason to go faster. Jason didn't mind: he liked standing in the cockpit as he boomed up the quiet bayou, scattering ducks and herons and sending the boat's big wake surging out among the trees.

Nick was nervous and had a hard time sitting still in the passenger seat, and eventually he took over the driving.

Jason went to the back of the boat and ate his lunch out of cans, and looked thoughtfully at the guns that sat on the bench seat opposite his own.

In the movies, he thought, there were a number of things that happened during every big disaster. And one of these involved some bad people with Really Great Hair, who, the very first thing broke into biker stores and stole all the cool leathers. And then they got some guns and some wheels and went on a general rampage until the good guy chilled them out in the last reel.

Something like those bad guys had happened to Nick's in-laws. The cinematic prophecy seemed to be coming true.

Jason looked at the guns and wondered if Nick was the hero who was destined to destroy the bad guys at the end.

No, he thought. He knew who he and Nick would play in the movies. *We're the bad guys' victims*, he thought. *The people the bad guys kill on their way to dying at the hands of the hero.* That's who they were. *Corpses.*

He turned away from the guns and looked ahead, at the still, silent bayou ahead. He didn't want to think about the guns anymore.

It proved fairly easy going up the bayou. The obstructions had been cleared away by chainsaws and axes, presumably by the David party, and for the most part this left a channel wide enough to take their craft upstream. On occasion Jason was called to shove some piece of wreckage out of the way, and Nick tapped the steering wheel impatiently until the obstacle was clear and he could gun the engine ahead.

By late afternoon they came to a two-lane road that dead-ended on the bayou. This, Nick said, was where the David party had turned south, and turned south himself.

The road was narrower than the bayou, and choked with debris. Some of the debris had been cleared by the Davids, but some had just been shoved aside and drifted back, and other debris had floated into place since the Davids had passed. The road, though flooded, was elevated several feet above the surrounding country, and Nick tilted the Evinrude forward to keep the propeller from striking the roadway.

It was hard going. Jason stood on the foredeck and tried to clear away the obstructions with his pole. Within minutes he was bathed in sweat. Nick detoured off the roadway and around the obstructions where possible, but often this just led them into dead ends, or areas where the trees were too thick to permit passage.

When Jason was exhausted, Nick took his place on the foredeck, and Jason steered.

The sun was far to the west when they came to a debris field, hundreds of tree trunks piled over and across each other into a huge lumber raft that stretched as far as they could see. It looked as if a thousand beavers had labored on the dam for a thousand years. There was no way through the mass, and no indication that anyone had ever tried.

Nick looked at the obstruction in despair. "Did they go around?" he asked. "Or did they turn back?"

Jason looked left and right in the fading light. "Let's see if we *can* go around."

They tried, but every attempt to leave the roadway was blocked, either by falling or standing timber. It didn't look as if anyone had tried to get through.

"Where did they go?" Nick moaned. Shiny cables stood out on his neck, and sweat made big blotches on his T-shirt. "Where did they go?"

"They had to have turned back from here," Jason said. "They probably went farther up Lopez Bayou, then tried to cut south on another road."

Nick bit his lip. "If they'd gone the other way, to the White, we'd have run into them," he said.

"Right."

"Turn the boat around, then." Anger entered his voice. "We've wasted the whole day."

"It's getting dark, Nick."

"*Just go!*"

The return journey began. Jason turned the boat around, banging into the trailing bass boat in the narrow passage, and crept forward toward the first obstacles. Nick stabbed furiously with his pole at the floating debris until it was completely dark and he couldn't see it anymore.

"Flashlight!" he called. "Give me a flashlight!"

Jason passed forward one of the two flashlights. They kept going down the roadway, while Nick juggled his pole and the flashlight. Jason could hear Nick cursing under his breath as the bow ground against debris. Finally Jason saw Nick's shoulders sag in the fading light of the flash.

"*God damn it!*" Nick jabbed at a floating tree trunk as if it were an enemy to be impaled on his spear. "This is useless!"

Jason said nothing. Nick's pole clattered on the foredeck.

"Eat," Nick said. "Sleep. We'll get an early start at first light."

Nick stalked aft, the flashlight reflecting the fury in his eyes. Jason pulled the bass boat up close and climbed aboard to get access to the stores.

When he had stowed away, Jason thought, he'd expected to spend the summer in some big farmhouse, with Nick's daughter and in-laws. Instead he'd been thrown back into the river again, and he was trapped on a small boat, in a dead-end waterway, with a heavily armed man who was in a bad mood. To put the icing on the cake, there were a bunch of murderers loose in the area.

It occurred to Jason that leaving the *Beluthahatchie* might not have been the smartest thing he'd ever done.

After their meal Nick didn't insist they continue their journey to the bayou, but he was too agitated to sleep. He paced up and down the short length of the cabin, pausing occasionally to pick up one of his guns or drum his hands on the steering wheel.

Eventually exhaustion claimed Jason, and he fell asleep despite Nick's restlessness.

He woke with a full bladder hours later. Nick was asleep on the bench seat opposite. Jason rose stiffly from his bed, stepped aft, leaned against the fiberglass hull, and relieved himself into the water. He looked up and saw past the overhanging branches of the trees the stars wheeling overhead.

He looked for M13—*a million stars*—and found the cluster easily enough, a bright smudge against the hard, brilliant light of the stars. Twenty-five thousand light-years away. No matter what happened here—no matter what catastrophes, horrors, anguish—whatever lived in M13 wouldn't know about it for twenty-five thousand years, not even if they were interested.

He finished and zipped his pants, but he still stood gazing skyward, looking into the silent beyond.

And then the night's darkness faded. Suddenly the entire country began to glow, as if hidden floodlights had suddenly switched on, bathing the still waters and the trunks of the trees in golden radiance. The suddenness and silence of this ghostly flourishing was breathtaking.

"Nick!" Jason called. "Look!"

"Wha?" came Nick's sleepy voice.

"Look!" Jason could see leaves outlined perfectly in the glow, the patterns on tree bark, the vines coiling up the trunks.

"Oh my God," Nick breathed in awe.

And then the quake struck, and the world again turned dark.

A roar filled the air like the earth moaning in pain. Spray spilled into the boat as the water turned white around them. The air filled with leaves and twigs. Debris ground against the hull, and Jason fell, heart hammering, into the bench seat next to him.

"Get into cover!" He heard Nick shout, but all he could do was cling to the side of the boat as it leaped up and down to the music of the quake. Tearing sounds filled the air as tree limbs began to crack and fall.

Nick's strong hand grabbed Jason by the arm and pulled, and suddenly Jason was able to move. He crawled forward, past the driver's seat, and wormed into the damp space below the foredeck. Nick crawled in after him. A falling limb dropped onto the bulwark where Jason had been lying, then ground against the hull as it slid into the water.

"It's a bad one!" Nick shouted in his ear. Jason knew that already.

Jason clamped his eyes shut. The boat vibrated, banging up and down on water that seemed hard as concrete. His inner ear spun as the boat slewed to the push of the water. He could feel his teeth chattering.

Something heavy mashed the boat's canvas top, and he gave a cry at the thought of being killed here, in the darkness. The cold waters pouring in as he struggled, trapped, in the close little space under the forepeak. He gulped down a sudden flood of stomach acid that had poured into his throat.

"It's okay!" Nick chanted. "It's okay, it's okay, it's okay!" But Jason knew it was pretty clearly *not* okay.

He heard the shriek of wood as a tree limb tore free, and then the limb thundered off the gunwale as it splashed into the water next to the boat. The boat tilted alarmingly to port. Jason gave a shout as Nick rolled onto him, squeezing the breath from his lungs.

"It's okay!" Nick said. "It's okay!" The boat righted itself, and Nick's weight fell away.

"It's okay!" Nick said.

Jason bit his knuckle to keep from screaming.

The earth roared on, and the boat danced to its anguished tune.

TWENTY-FOUR

During the day there was, with very little intermission, a continued series of shocks, attended with innumerable explosions like the rolling of thunder; the bed of the river was incessantly disturbed, and the water boiled severely in every part; I consider ourselves as having been in the greatest danger from the numerous instances of boiling directly under our boat; fortunately for us, however, they were not attended with eruptions. One of the spouts which we had seen rising under the boat would have inevitably sunk it, and probably have blown it into a thousand fragments; our ears were continually assailed with the crashing of timber, the banks were instantaneously crushed down, and fell with all their growth into the water. It was no less alarming than astonishing, to behold the oldest trees of the forest, whose firm roots had withstood a thousand storms, and weathered the sternest tempests, quivering and shaking with the violence of the shocks, whilst their heads were whipped together with a quick and rapid motion; many were torn from their native soil, and hurled with tremendous force into the river; one of these whose huge trunk (at least 3 feet in diameter) had been much shattered, was thrown better than an hundred yards from the bank, where it is planted into the bed of the river, there to stand, a terror to future navigators.

Narrative of Mr. Pierce, December 25, 1811

Captain Jean-Joseph Malraux hummed Bernard Herrman's theme music to the film *Jason and the Argonauts* as he steered *Beluthahatchie* down the channel of the Ohio River. The pilothouse was dark around him except for the glow of the instruments. The lights of Bay City were falling astern, and the mass of the Shawnee National

Forest loomed dark and silent off to port. Joe kept one eye cocked on the depth indicator as he steered, making certain not to run onto any more unexpected sandbanks looming out of the river's channel.

His company had given him permission to moor his tow of fifteen barges to the St. Francis revetment, where it could be picked up when the river was safer, and so he had only the fast and highly maneuverable *Beluthahatchie* to worry about. He was happy to be out of the Mississippi with its shifting channel, its hidden reefs, and its masses of saw-toothed debris. The Ohio was in bad shape as well, with the bridge at Cairo lacking a span and Locks and Dams No. 52 and 53 both broken. But the Corps of Engineers had been clearing the wreckage, the river was high enough so that the dams weren't necessary to keep the channel full, and all the wreckage was heading to where Joe had been, to the Mississippi. And now that he was above the intact Smithfield Lock and Dam, the Ohio was smooth sailing.

The worst part of the last two days, though, had been calling Frank Adams on the marine band to tell him that his kid had gone missing. Frank had reamed him up one side and down the other. He had used language that would make a longshoreman blush, as Joe, who had known plenty of longshoremen in his time, could testify.

And then, when Joe had refused Frank's demand to turn his boat around and head back to conduct a search for his missing son, Frank's language had grown even more violent, and Joe's temper had finally snapped, and he'd given Frank the company's phone number, and told him that the company had lawyers who were *paid* to take that kind of abuse.

Joe felt kind of bad about that. Frank had just been looking for someone to blame, which was understandable enough.

But it wasn't Joe's fault. He had looked after Nick and Jase as well as he could. It wasn't his fault that they had left *Beluthahatchie.* And damned if he was going to let some Los Angeles shyster tell him that it was.

Cincinnati, he thought hopefully, in the morning. And then a lot of downtime, while barge traffic languished and the Mississippi was made safe again. Time in which Captain Joe would probably not be employed.

At least it would give him a chance to get his video collection in order.

Bernard Herrman kettledrums boomed through his mind. He pictured the Argonauts' galley moving up the river, drums beating time to the oars, while invisible gods and goddesses bickered overhead.

The door to the pilothouse opened, and his bowman came in. "Coffee, skip. And some beignets."

"Thanks," Joe said. He had barely slept in the two days since *Beluthahatchie* had got off its sandbar in the Lower Mississippi. He was the only crewman aboard certified by the Coast Guard, and he wanted to be on hand at every moment of the treacherous passage.

The bowman, who shared his watch, dropped the coffee cup into its waiting holder, and put the plate of beignets within Joe's reach. Joe reached for one of the beignets, but they were fresh from the deep-fryer and burned his fingers. He dropped the beignet and licked confectioner's sugar from his fingers.

And then the water began to dance around him, thousands of little wave-crests criss-crossing the river's still surface in the light of *Belutha-hatchie*'s floodlights. He could feel a trembling run through the towboat, shiver through the wheel beneath his fingers. To port and starboard, whole forests waved madly in the darkness.

"Aftershock," he said to his bowman. He had seen this before.

But the aftershock didn't die. Instead the wave peaks grew taller, and Joe could see foam forming in streaks along the surface. The vibration increased. The plate of beignets threatened to slide onto the floor, and Joe's heart beat like the *Argonauts'* kettledrums. His hand hovered over the engine throttles, but he didn't know whether it would be safer to throttle up or down, so he decided not to make a change.

"Go get the other watch," he told the bowman. "I want as

many pair of eyes up here as possible." The aftershock could stir up all kinds of crap in the channel.

The bowman nodded and left the pilothouse in a hurry. Spray bounded over *Beluthahatchie*'s blunt bow. And then the pilothouse door slammed, and the bowman was back, his eyes wild.

"Big wave!" he shouted, one finger pointing aft. "Just behind us!"

Joe's hand slammed the throttles forward before he looked over his shoulder. The turbines roared to a higher pitch as Joe craned his neck aft, searching the leaping water for sign of the overtaking wave.

Joe's heart gave a lurch. There it was, a big black wall moving across the leaping, foam-flecked water. It had to be at least fifteen feet high, and it was about to climb right up *Beluthathatchie*'s ass.

Tsunami. The great sea-wave caused by an earthquake.

Joe had never heard of a tsunami on a *river* before.

"Sound the collision alert!" Joe yelled. He didn't want to take his hands off the controls, but the off-duty watch needed to be ready for what was going to hit them. The other watch, plus any other human being within hearing distance of the signal.

The bowman threw himself across the pilothouse and the alarm blared out. White water boiled under *Beluthahatchie*'s counter as the turbines redlined. Joe peered at the great wave rising astern, tried to judge its speed relative to the boat.

Still overtaking. Damn it.

The bridge telephone rang. The off-duty watch, trying to find out what was happening.

"Answer that!" Joe snapped. Calculations leaped through his mind. If the wave rolled over the towboat's stern, it could sweep *Beluthahatchie* from stern to stem, bury it beneath tons of water. The boat might survive that, he reckoned, or it might not. And if the wave caught the boat broadside, *Beluthahatchie* would almost certainly capsize.

There was one possible escape, Joe thought. And that was to keep forward of the crest, by using the wave's own power.

He gripped the wheel with one hand, the throttles with the other. The bowman, shouting into the bridge telephone, was looking aft with eyes wide as saucers. *"Hoo-aaah!"* Joe shouted in a voice intended to be heard on the other end of the telephone. *"Hang on! We goin' surfing, podnah!"*

Joe pulled the throttles back, saw the wave loom closer. He let it come till he felt the wave just begin to lift *Beluthahatchie*'s stern, then throttled forward again. Turbines shrieked. The boat rose, and Joe felt a flutter in his stomach, panic rising in his throat.

Joe throttled way back. The boat continued to lift. The foaming curl at the wave top loomed closer, then stopped, hanging over the stern. Exultation screamed through Joe's veins.

"Yeeow! Hang ten, baby!"

He adjusted the throttles so that he was neither climbing the face of the wave, nor dropping forward. The power of the wave itself was doing most of the work.

Joe's inner ear swam. There was a sense of movement swirling on the other side of the pilothouse windows, and Joe felt panic burn along his nerves. He threw the wheel over, shoved the throttles forward. The boat straightened.

Joe took a gasping breath. He had almost lost the boat. If he'd let the wave push him to one side or the other, he'd have swung broadside to the wave and been rolled under.

Debris boomed on the bottom of the hull. The boat swayed: Joe corrected. The bowman was standing in the pilothouse staring aft, his knuckles clenched around the telephone.

"Put that down and call the Coast Guard!" Joe said. "Tell them we got a tsunami on the Ohio heading for Golconda! *Move* it, there, podnah!"

The bowman lunged for the radio. Joe's head lashed back and forth, peering behind to make certain the tsunami wasn't about to fall on them, staring forward into the night to see if the wave was going to run them right onto an island.

"Careful baby baby careful just a little more a little more *juice gaw-damn* . . ." Words burbled from his lips in accompaniment to his thought. The blackness off the port bow was broken by light. Joe peered at it, trying to make certain the light wasn't a reflection on the pilothouse glass . . .

Golconda. *Already.* He didn't dare think about how fast they were going.

Whoah. He juiced the throttle, swung the boat to starboard. He'd almost lost it there.

And if that *was* Golconda, he thought, that meant he was coming up on a big island that sat smack in the middle of the river. And if he made it past the island, the river was going to make a sweeping ninety-degree curve to the right, and that meant the big wave was going to get *complicated* . . .

Adrenaline screamed through his veins. He goosed the throttle, shaved the wheel just a little. Joe wanted to steer down the face of the wave, moving laterally to port as the wave kept rolling down the channel. He needed to get well clear of that island before he impaled the boat on it . . .

"Whoah whoah whoah you *cochon* just a little baby there you go . . ."

He was inside the wave's curl, heading slantwise down the wave. Golconda was dead ahead. Now if he could just head the boat a little to port, get it moving straight again . . .

"There you go baby there you go *aiaaah* surfin' USA careful there *goose her yaaah* . . ."

The boat swayed, the wave crest looming on over her, and then *Beluthahatchie* leaped down the wave, picking up speed. Joe's laugh boomed in the pilothouse.

Golconda was past and the island flashed up to starboard. Joe heard the grinding, grating, booming noise as the tsunami pounded over the island, ripping it and its timber to shreds.

"*Roi de la riviere! C'est moi!*" Joe felt like pounding his chest in triumph.

The island caused the wave to lose cohesion, caused ripples and back-eddies to build under the crest. Joe twitched the wheel and throttles to keep *Beluthahatchie* on course. And then the island was astern, and the tsunami shuddered as it met its twin, the wave that had creamed along the Kentucky side of the island. Joe felt sweat popping on his forehead as the boat surged beneath him.

"Yah, baby, *roi de la riviere!* Surf's up!"

He tried to decide what to do about the upcoming bend. He didn't want to be where he was, near the north bank of the river, when the river turned to the right—he would get caught between the bank and the tsunami and pounded to bits against the timber in the floodplain. So what he needed to do was cross over the front of the wave again and get as close to the south bank as he could . . .

"Here we go here we go on t'udder side . . ."

He was traveling along the front of the wave again, the turbines carrying him to starboard, white water creaming behind. The wave's curl hung overhead, looming over them like a white-fanged monster about to drop on them from above.

"*Skip! What are you doing?*" the bowman demanded, staring at the curl in horror.

"Hang on podnah." Joe skated right across the front of the wave, speed building. Then he turned the wheel, got the wave behind him, felt the boat lift . . .

He could see the silver surface of the water curving to the right. *Damn* they were going fast.

Water boiled white to port as the tsunami slammed into the outer bank of the river bend. There was a rending, crashing, as if the wave was trying to tear the riverbed itself from the earth. But the part of the wave pushing *Beluthahatchie* seemed to be speeding up, going faster as it skiddered around the inside of the river bend. The boat swerved violently, and Joe steadied it just in time, a bellow of terror and exultation rising in his throat.

The roar to port continued. Joe worked the throttles. "Yah baby you go papa say you go . . ."

The wave kept going, rolling across the curving river to smash into the north bank in a fountain of white foam. Trees went down like ranks of soldiers before machine-gun fire. But *Beluthahatchie* was flung away, across the river's inner curve and into the calmer upper river, like a watermelon seed squeezed between the fingertips.

Joe throttled up, intending to get clear of the turbulent

water behind him and the reduced reflection of the tsunami as it bounced off the north bank. He looked into the terrified eyes of his bowman and gave a wild laugh.

"The Argonauts ain't got nothin' on me!" he shouted, and reached for the horn button so that *Beluthahatchie* could trumpet his joy, send the sound ringing from Kentucky to Indiana and back again, the triumphant cry of the old river man who has beaten the elements, and is bringing his boat safely home . . .

About 2 o'clock this morning we were awakened by a most tremendous noise, while the house danced about and seemed as if it would fall on our heads. I soon conjectured the cause of our troubles, and cried out it was an Earthquake, and for the family to leave the house; which we found very difficult to do, owing to its rolling and jostling about. The shock was soon over, and no injury was sustained, except the loss of the chimney, and the exposure of my family to the cold of the night. At the time of this shock, the heavens were very clear and serene, not a breath of air stirring; but in five minutes it became very dark, and a vapour which seemed to impregnate the atmosphere, had a disagreeable smell, and produced a difficulty of respiration. I knew not how to account for this at the time, but when I saw, in the morning, the situation of my neighbours' houses, all of them more or less injured, I attributed it to the dust and soot, &c which arose from the fall. The darkness continued till day-break; during this time we had EIGHT more shocks, none of them so violent as the first.

> *Extract from a letter to a gentleman in Lexington, from*
> *his friend at New Madrid, dated 16th December, 1811*

As soon as the first jolt wakened her from sleep, Jessica was moving. She wasn't sure whether she'd rolled off her cot as she intended, or whether the tremblors kicked the cot out from under her. No sooner had she landed than the ground rose and punched her in the ribs. She reached blindly for the helmet she'd placed on the ground by the cot, felt it under her fingers, and jammed it on her head.

And then pain rocketed through her skull as something lunged under her helmet rim and smacked her in the eye. Sparks shot through her vision. She lay back, stunned, the helmet partly fallen from her head. There was a strange corkscrew motion to the earth this time, something that she didn't remember from the last big quake, and nausea rose in her throat.

Arms came around her. She felt herself being drawn protectively against Pat's shoulder.

That hadn't happened in the last quake, either. She huddled against him like a soldier in a bombardment sheltering against a basement wall.

The earth roared like a wounded bull. Pain throbbed through Jessica's injured eye with every shudder. She heard cracking and snapping sounds, and then rough canvas covered them like a blanket. Their sleeping tent had come down around them.

Which was not unexpected. Though her home had come through the first big quake reasonably intact, she had slept under canvas every night since, and she'd advised everyone else to do the same until the danger of a major aftershock was long over. Being draped by canvas, and at the worst getting hit by a falling tent pole, was a far more preferable fate than having a wall fall on you.

Jessica could hear Pat's teeth rattling next to her ear. The earth rolled under her in waves, giving her a little toss at each peak.

This was *not*, she thought, a mere aftershock. This was another major quake, one that felt at least as strong as M1.

The earth's roaring faded. The temblors gradually decreased, although from the way her inner ear still reeled, Jessica suspected they hadn't diminished entirely. She pushed her helmet back onto her head, began to shift in Pat's arms, aiming toward the front flap of the tent.

"Sorry I hit you," Pat said.

"You hit me?" she said.

"With my elbow. I was reaching for you, and the quake just picked you up and threw you at me."

Jessica blinked her wounded eye. Sparks flashed in her vision. "I'm going to get a shiner at least."

"Sorry."

She kissed his unshaven chin. "That's okay. Worse things have happened in earthquakes. Let's get out of here."

She belly-crawled beneath the fallen canvas, found the flap, made her way out into the night. Cool drops of dew anointed her bare feet as she helped Pat emerge from beneath the canvas.

The camp was in an uproar, a babble of voices rising up on all sides, orders and curses mixed with shouts of bewilderment and cries for help. Almost all the tents had fallen, and fresh fissures had gouged themselves across the landscape. Jessica saw that the satellite transmitter/receivers were down, and she ran across the stretch of ground and rounded up soldiers to set things up again.

If any of them saw anything unusual at the sight of a major general helping to wrestle satellite dishes into place while dressed only in her helmet, olive-green boxers, and tank top, they did not venture to say so.

Once she had the receiver dishes up again, Jessica wouldn't have to spend the first three or four hours trying to find a way of communicating with the rest of the country. All key personnel, throughout the area affected by M1, had by now been equipped with modern satellite-based communications gear, ranging from Iridium cellphones to the state-of-the-art Army mobile communications center here in Vicksburg. They could be in contact in a matter of seconds.

Generators coughed into life. Lights flashed. Tents were raised, and communications techs manned their stations.

Jessica was back in touch with the world.

Dams first, she decided. If dams had broken, then alerts would have to go out fast. After that, she would contact district levee superintendents. Then transportation, check as many bridges as possible. And then . . .

Horror struck her. *The evacuation*, she thought.

There were tens of thousands of people on the road. Maybe not all in their automobiles when the earthquake hit—maybe they were in motels or campgrounds, sheltering in churches or other refugee centers, or just sleeping in their cars—but they were all in transit, between their homes and the areas that had been set up to receive them.

They were cut off, without any way to call for help.

The evacuation, she thought again. *My* evacuation.

She may have just sent thousands of people to their doom.

The first shock bucked Omar up off the mattress, then dropped him down again. The house shook as if an explosion had gone off just outside. Wilona screamed, and adrenaline rocketed through Omar's veins. For a moment he groped for the gun he kept on the nightstand, and then he heard the express-train roar of the onrushing quake and knew what was coming.

When the express train hit, it had a sideways snap to it that sent the bed crashing against the wall. There was a crash of shelves falling. Wilona screamed again. Omar was terrified that the chifforobe on the far side of the room would walk across the floor and fall on them. "Get under the bed!" he shouted, but the bed was traveling in wild corkscrew circles, and to get off was only to be run down. He felt Wilona clutching at him. Glass smashed. Omar heard the doors of the chifforobe slapping back and forth. In the darkness he saw a flash of white as one of the ceiling panels swung down like a trapdoor, and he rolled partly atop Wilona to protect her in case the ceiling came down. Her nails dug into his skin. The mirror on the wall exploded, sending shards over the room. The crazy corkscrew motion was making Omar sick to his stomach. Wilona wept and shrieked in his ear. Another ceiling panel fell, bounced off Omar's shoulders. There was a roaring crash as one of the magnolias shed a limb onto the roof.

He just held on, for long minutes, until the motion faded. And then he got unsteadily to his feet, and rushed across broken glass to David's room. He hadn't heard anything from his son at all, and that seemed ominous.

When he looked at the empty bed he remembered that

David, now a special deputy, was on duty tonight, on call at sheriff's headquarters.

Omar began to check the damage. When the old double shotgun home had been jacked back up onto its foundation after the first quake, it had been supported by new brick pilings and hardwood wedges, and this time the foundation held. But otherwise the damage was far worse: half the clapboards were shaken off the walls, almost all the shingles were gone from the roof, the ceiling and wall panels were torn away, and parts of the floor buckled or caved in.

And none of it insured, Omar knew.

He went back to his bedroom and began pulling on his uniform. He knew that Spottswood Parish was going to have a long night.

Charlie Johns lay asleep in Megan's BMW, a bottle of wine near his hand. The earth rumbled—the car leaped and shivered—but Charlie stirred for a moment, only a moment, and then slept on.

Earthquake, he thought vaguely. *Ridiculous. They only happen in California.*

The shock faded, and night sounds resumed.

Next to Charlie, on the passenger seat, the cellphone gave an almost-silent purr. Its batteries were too exhausted to ring loudly; the sound was only a whisper, the barest touch of sound to Charlie's ear.

Charlie slept on. The phone purred again, and again, and again. And then fell silent.

When Charlie woke, he thought he heard Megan's voice.

The President rolled toward the phone on the nightstand. "Get me the First Lady," he said, "the Vice President, and whoever's in charge at the CDRG."

And then he looked at the clock. Five minutes after two.

He felt a panicked throb in his chest. That was a *quake*, he thought. His experience in the National Cathedral, and the days he'd spent touring the disaster areas in the Midwest, had sensitized him to earth tremors. The first temblor that shivered up through his mattress had awakened him from sound sleep.

And he had felt it *here*, in the White House, which meant it was another big one.

He kicked off the covers, felt for his slippers with his toes. And then a woman's voice spoke in his ear.

"Mr. President? This is Beverly Maddox at the CDRG. May I help you?"

"Did you feel that quake? Do you have any information?"

There was a moment's pause. "I felt no quake, sir, but I'll check."

And then, before the President could say anything more, heard the click, and then syrupy music. She had put him on *hold*.

"Jesus Christ!" the President barked in amazement. Nobody *ever* put the President of the United States on hold.

There was another click, and then the voice again. "Nobody here felt a quake, sir. I take it you're not calling from D.C.?"

"Don't ever put me on hold again!"

Stunned silence filled the line.

"I will remain on this line," the President said. *"You will find out about the quake and report to your commander-in-chief as soon as you have the information."*

"Yes, sir. Uh . . . sorry." And then he heard her put down the phone and shout to someone else in the office.

There was a click as another call came through. The President changed over and immediately heard the voice of the Vice President, calling from Jackson, Mississippi, where he'd been based in his current round of Compassion Duty.

"Did you feel the quake?" he said. "That was a *big* one."

"You're all right?" said the President.

"Just shook up. The bed was jumping around, and the drawers jumped right out of the bureau. Secret Service came rushing in to see if I was all right, and they could barely keep their feet."

The President found himself wondering if they'd tried to wrestle the earthquake to the ground.

"I felt it here," the President said. "That's why I'm calling."

And for once, he thought, *I'm ahead of the curve. I know more than FEMA does.*

And then it occurred to him that this, more than anything else, was frightening.

The first large May quake, M1, had been followed over successive days by thousands of aftershocks, four of which were deemed strong enough to deserve numbers of their own, causing damage rated at 7 or better—out of a possible 12— on the Mercalli Scale. But the M6 shock, ten days following M1, was a major earthquake in its own right.

M6 began at 1:02 A.M., Central Daylight Time, as an eleven-meter right-lateral strike-slip motion on the Blytheville Arch, a fifty-mile-long fault structure running more or less under the Mississippi, and centered on Blytheville, Arkansas, just south of Swampeast Missouri. M1 had loaded the Blytheville Arch with tectonic energy which the Arch now discharged. On the Richter scale, the quake reached a force of 8.5, one-quarter the size of M1 at 8.9, but still the equivalent of the Alaskan quake of 1964, one of the greatest quakes of the twentieth century. As during M1, the solid structure of the North American continent transmitted the destructive force of the quake hundreds of miles. The Arch directed most of ·its energy toward the south and west, into Arkansas, Mississippi, Louisiana, and Kansas, which suffered greater property loss than they had during M1. These powerful shocks in turn released additional energy stored along the Oklahoma Fault, resulting in significant destruction as far west as Oklahoma City and Wichita Falls. But the directional nature of the temblors meant that northern Missouri, including St. Louis, Illinois, and Iowa, were spared a repeat of the leveling caused by M1, though destruction there was certainly bad enough.

Memphis, close to the river and the center of the Blytheville Arch, received another pounding.

The slippage of the Blytheville Arch transmitted to other subterranean fault lines via the Bootheel Lineament, which connects all other fault structures in the area. All the faults suffered further slippage, though a particularly severe shock was created along the Reelfoot South seismicity trend. This fault hammered western Kentucky and Tennessee—shaking unlucky Memphis from north as well as west—and created a pair of tsunamis, one that roared up the Ohio River, another that launched itself up the Mississippi, destroying the old river town of Cairo, which fortunately for its inhabitants had been evacuated due to flooding.

Other effects of M6 were similar to M1: ground liquefaction and geysering, widespread destruction to timber and other natural resources, and significant infrastructure damage. Buildings, levees, bridges, and other structures weakened by M1 and its aftershocks now collapsed. Damage in Mississippi, southern Arkansas, Kansas, and Louisiana exceeded that suffered in M1.

In some respects M6 was more merciful than its predecessor. Most of the population were asleep, not on the highways returning from work. The people had been suffering quakes for ten days and knew how to react; they knew to avoid weakened structures, and had evacuated low-lying areas subject to flood. A survivable satellite-based communications network was in place throughout the area. Emergency rescue and medical teams were deployed and already in the field. Loss of life was in the hundreds, not in the thousands. There were fewer catastrophic fires, and none that leveled whole areas of cities.

But in other respects, M6 was a social catastrophe. It struck in the middle of the largest evacuation in the history of North America. Tens of thousands of people were caught somewhere in the process of evacuation, and though most of these people were not injured, they were isolated, unable to leave the areas where the quake had stranded them.

They were dependent, for every basic necessity, on the kindness of strangers.

Frankland spent the quake praying. On his stomach, because the temblors would not let him stay on his knees.

There was a nasty whiplike snap to the movement of the earth this time, something calculated to take the world off its feet.

Frankland prayed that the Lord's will be done, that His kingdom would soon come. As the quake went on he prayed that his sins would be forgiven, that his wife's life would be spared. He could hear the metal-framed church shrieking and rattling, and he prayed that the church roof wouldn't fall in on the women and children.

He prayed that the Lord would be merciful on the hundreds of deserters who had left the camp, who had abandoned the faith of their fathers and accepted the false comfort of the godless government. He prayed that the Lord not drop these faithless, worthless, miserable people in crevasses, or strike them with his lightning, or break their bones, or cause buildings or trees to fall on them, or permit the ground at Hot Springs National Park to crack and release the magma that lay beneath the surface, so that the faithless deserters who had not remained true to Christ would not burn forever in God's righteous hellfire.

Finally, as the shaking went on and on, and every thought was driven from his head, he just repeated *Lord Lord Lord* to himself, until suddenly the earth had ceased its groans and the world rang with silence.

And then the silence was broken by the screaming of children. Hundreds of them, wailing out of the night.

He spent the next few hours ministering to the hysterical children, who had been shaken from their dreams by a repeat of the trauma that had cost so many their homes, their belongings, and their loved ones.

Afterward Sheriff Gorton came to report. *He* had not deserted his faith; Gorton stayed in the camp and had been driving every day to his job at the county seat. But now he seemed in shock, pale, his watery eyes wide. "The Bijoux's gone," he said.

The sick people who hadn't been able to evacuate were in there, along with the National Guard medic who had been detailed to look after them. And now they were dead.

"God's mercy upon them," said Frankland. "I guess we're on our own, now."

Which was not, he considered, a bad thing at all.

It was fifty minutes after the quake that the President—pacing up and down in the situation room while he waited for senior staff to arrive—finally heard from the First Lady's party.

He did not hear from the First Lady herself, but from one of her advance people in Jonesboro, Arkansas, where the First Lady had gone to present awards to members of a local radio station.

After the quakes, people had begun to swarm into the disaster area to help with the business of rebuilding. Contractors, lumber dealers, homebuilders, roofers, heating and cooling specialists, hauling and freight companies, dealers in foodstuffs and fuel, all planning on making a profit at helping the victims of the quake to rebuild.

They were all, in some sense, profiteers. They did not leave their homes in safe parts of the country and travel, over dangerous roads, to hazardous areas without the intention of being rewarded for their services. If they wanted to make a normal profit, they would have stayed at home.

Services out of the ordinary, they reckoned, deserved profits a little out of the ordinary. But the devastated areas had been so thoroughly destroyed, leaving such total damage, that repair and restoration very swiftly became a sellers' market. Price gouging had become common. The suffering population had become enraged at the newcomers' attempts to milk them for the few remaining pennies in their pockets.

There had been a move to freeze prices in the affected areas at pre-earthquake levels. But all that meant was that the people who had come to repair earthquake damage, deprived of the hope of extra profit that had caused them to leave home in the first place, would return home.

What the Jonesboro radio station had done was simply to start reporting prices in the area. All they did was quote numbers. Basic foodstuffs, lumber, roofing supplies, all the necessities for surviving the Year of the Earthquake. If a foodstore or a contractor was demanding unreasonable prices, that was reported, too, and people knew to avoid them. The radio station had restored a buyers' market. Price-gougers were left without customers.

The Jonesboro program had been such a success that other stations began to imitate them. Essential supplies and services were still available, but prices had fallen all across the earthquake zone. It was one of the great successes of the recovery effort.

And so the radio station was deemed worthy of a visit from the First Lady, who was still shuttling about the devastated area on Permanent Compassion Duty. She was scheduled to appear on the radio station the next morning. Her plane had been landing on the repaired runway at Jonesboro at the very moment when M6 struck, and a crevasse had opened directly in its path. The plane's nose wheel had dropped into the fracture, the plane rolled and burst into flame.

The First Lady and everyone aboard had been killed.

"Do you understand, sir? Mr. President?" The aide who had called the President was crying.

"Yes," the President said. "Yes, I heard you."

Softly, he put the phone in its cradle. And sat behind Rutherford B. Hayes's desk, hands on his knees, and listened to the slow, inexorable ticking of the casement clock on the wall. He waited in that posture for twenty minutes, until an aide appeared to remind him that the emergency working group was waiting in the Cabinet Room.

"I'll be along in a minute," the President said.

But he didn't move. He sat there, behind the big desk, and listened to the clock as it ticked away the seconds of his life.

Larry's helicopter circled around the brightly lit spectacle of Poinsett Island. *That* was good, he thought, at least they hadn't lost power.

The earthquake had sent his bed careening into the bedroom wall shortly after one in the morning. He and Helen had clutched at each other while the earth thundered at them. At the penultimate jolt, the house had given a huge lurch as it fell off its foundation. Furniture and kitchenware crashed.

None of the shelves fell over, even as their contents spilled to the floor. Helen's anchor bolts held.

As soon as the quake died, Larry groped for his clothes, his boots. He knew he had to head for Poinsett Landing.

Helen was going to be left with home cleanup again.

There weren't many people who stayed at Poinsett Landing overnight. All of them, under the direction of Meg Tarlton, were safely on the Indian mound when Larry landed and staggered out of the aircraft into an aftershock that kept trying to buckle his knees. He pursued his path grimly until he saw Meg walking toward him beneath the light of the floods, swaying as the ground jounced beneath her with every step.

"What's happening?" he demanded.

The two of them lurched like inexpert dancers to the rumbling music of the aftershock. "I can't get near the plant, sir," Meg said. "The piers and the barges are too dangerous. Some of the barges got loose, and a couple of the others were sunk."

"Dang it," Larry said.

"No radiation releases, though. First thing we checked."

The aftershock faded. Larry stood on the edge of the mound and shaded his eyes from the nearby floodlights. He looked out over the water and could plainly see the damage to the little port that the Corps of Engineers built around the nuclear facility.

The portable harbor was lightly built, made of material that could be hauled or towed into place, and the morning's earthquake had chewed it up considerably. Some of the barges had drifted off, still lashed to broken chunks of quay, then come aground on partly submerged ruins. Others had, seemingly, disappeared downriver. Bits of the quays were tilted up on edge. Others had disappeared.

One towboat, ablaze with light, was heading away from the plant with deliberate speed, turbines whining loud in the still night. Larry wondered if it was going after lost barges or simply fleeing the scene.

"Lucky it happened at night," Meg said. "Nobody's out there now."

Larry said nothing, just turned and began to walk back to the helicopter.

He was going to have to radio Jessica and tell her that her little harbor, of which she had seemed so proud, had just been shattered.

It took Omar and Wilona over three hours to get from their home to Shelburne City, a journey far more difficult than it had been following the first big quake. Chasms or sudden upthrusts were scored across the highway, and the parish road crews had to attend to them before Omar could move onward.

The traffic was another problem. The quake had struck with the evacuation in full swing, and the road was filled with cars from the southern part of the state. Hundreds of them, filled with families and possessions, pets and paintings and the family silver, all stuck on the road, unable to move on because the quake had gouged rents across their path. When one fissure was filled in, the cars would all surge along to the next chasm, then clump up in another disorderly mass. And when these people saw a police car moving along, they naturally tried to flag it down, or crowded around it, to ask Omar what to do, where they could stay, how far to the next town.

Nor were the refugees the only folk who needed help. This quake had caused significant damage to the area's lightly built homes. Omar suspected that half the parish was homeless, at least for the present.

It was fortunate that Omar had his radio, and he was able to deploy his department as well as conditions permitted, and also to contact other parish officials.

He also contacted his son David, who had come through the quake just fine, and was now involved in driving the injured to Dr. Patel's clinic.

When Omar got to Shelburne City, he was shocked at the damage. Ozie Welk's bar, south of town, was a pile of ruined lumber, with several pickup trucks parked out front, and Omar wondered if the roof had dropped on Ozie and his customers. Half the storefronts on Shelburne Street had collapsed. The Commissary's roof had fallen in. All the blackjack oaks in front of the courthouse were down. The Mourning Confederate had pitched head-first off its broken plinth. The courthouse itself displayed some jagged cracks in its load-bearing walls.

"Do you think it's safe?" Wilona asked as they entered.

Omar only shrugged. He had too much work to do to worry about whether the courthouse was going to fall on him.

Information came in. Electric power was restored, at least to the courthouse and a couple of blocks around. The injured were brought to Dr. Patel's clinic, but because the building was unsafe, they were put on areas of lawn or side streets where nothing was likely to fall on them. No one quite trusted the churches or the schools not to fall down, and indeed some of them already had.

It was toward dawn that the worst piece of news came in, passed on from the state police. "The staties say that the District Levee's gone, right at the Parish Floodway."

Omar reached for the radio that sat behind his desk. "This is Omar," he said. "Says which?"

"District Levee's gone. A two-hundred-foot crevasse, they said. The highway's cut."

On the south end of the Parish Floodway, the highway ran for almost seven miles along the top of the District Levee. With the levee broken, the evacuation route to Arkansas had been cut off, and much of the land behind the levee would have been flooded. This also cut them off from the northern third of the parish, with about a third of the parish's population of seven thousand. There was only one sheriff's car out there to help police all those people. Omar guessed that meant they had become Arkansas' problem.

And with refugees continuing to pour up the highway

from the south, that meant that Spottswood Parish had become a bottleneck on the evacuation route, a trap for everyone who entered.

A random bunch of Louisianans, Omar thought. Mostly from the cities. And bringing city problems with them—crime, disorder, and negritude.

Jesus, he thought. Inner-city niggers. They'd probably start selling crack to the kids on the playground.

Omar had to get those people turned around, get them out of his parish before they ate the place out like a swarm of locusts.

First he called the state police, told them of the situation, and asked them to get a roadblock put up south of the parish line, turn new refugees back before they entered the trap. Omar was told that the staties were fully occupied dealing with aftereffects of the quake, but would set up the roadblock as soon as they had the personnel to do it.

As soon as they get their asses into their white Crown Victorias, Omar thought. He did not have a great deal of confidence in the staties. For one thing, they couldn't even decide what they were *called.* They had *State Police* on the rear of their cars, *State Troopers* on the front fenders, and *Louisiana State Police* on the front doors.

How could you trust these people for anything? They didn't even know who they were.

So Omar directed Merle to set up a roadblock on the far side of the Bayou Bridge and to turn people back there. It took an hour and a half for one of the patrol cars to get that far south, and the officer reported that the Bayou Bridge had lost some of its superstructure in the quake, that it trembled when they crossed, and that they were worried about getting back safely.

"I'll get the bridge inspected when I can get someone from the parish down there," Omar told them. "Just keep people off it, for God's sake."

"That's going to be a tough job, Omar," Merle said. "Some of these people abandoned their cars miles back and are coming in on foot. The rest say there's nothing behind them but wreckage."

"There's nothing but wreckage *here*. You tell them to wait there, okay?"

"Ten-four. I'll do what I can."

Omar kept on working. In the pale twilit hour just before dawn, Omar felt the bang, then heard the onrushing-train sound of a quake, and as he stared for a horrified moment at the wall of his office, he remembered the cracks he'd seen in the thick courthouse walls, and then adrenaline slammed into his body and he dived under his desk.

The earth groaned for a long moment, shaking the courthouse like shrimp in a pan, then fell silent. Omar stayed motionless for a moment, waiting for the roof to come down as he listened to the light fixture overhead creak as it swayed back and forth, and then he crawled from cover. His limbs shivered. He reached for the radio receiver behind his desk, turned up the volume to listen to the reports.

The Bayou Bridge has fallen, Merle said, along its entire length, cutting Omar off from the southern quarter of the parish and the five hundred or so people who lived there.

The center part of Spottswood Parish was now an island, with hundreds of strangers trapped by the flood, and no way to get them off.

"Old River's gone?" Jessica said. She stared blankly into the red dawn rising east of Vicksburg as she held her Iridium cellphone to her ear. "What do you mean, *gone*?"

"Low Sill, Morganza, Auxiliary Control came through okay," her informant told her. "The Murray hydroelectric plant's rode it out, too, but it's offline because they lost too many transmission wires, and they're losing water pressure through the turbines. The river went *around* the systems built to control it."

"God damn," Jessica said. Fury burned along her nerves. She took off her helmet, flung it on the ground. The ballistic material bounced well on the springy Mississippi turf.

Old River Control. The Corps of Engineers' greatest project, its greatest fortress against the enemy that was the river.

But when the river attacked, it hadn't attacked the fortress, it had gone around. Bypassed the frontier fortresses and struck directly into the heartland.

Jessica kicked her helmet toward the communications tent. She told her informant to call her as soon as he had any hard information, then put away her cellphone.

"I want all chopper wing commanders here ASAP," she ordered. "We've got a lot of rescue missions to run." She looked at one of the radio operators. "Get me the jarheads and the swabbies," she said. "We're going to need their copters, too."

"Mr. Hallock reporting, General," said another operator. "From Poinsett Landing. He wanted to speak to you."

Jessica picked up the radio receiver and blinked. Stars shot through her left eye. Ever since Pat had elbowed her eye during the quake, she'd both been developing a magnificent black eye and seeing flashes.

It was probably all right, she thought. Stars were what you were *supposed* to see after being hit in the head. Right?

"Mr. Hallock?" she said. "This is General Frazetta."

Larry's New Mexico drawl hissed over the speakers. "I've inspected the auxiliary building," he said. "We lost some of the scaffolding in there. Otherwise things are stable for the moment, 'cept that we've sprung another leak. Or maybe that ol' leak we could never find got bigger, I can't tell. Anyway, we've got the pumps going, and we're keeping the water and boron levels high."

"Roger, Mr. Hallock. Good work."

"We'll look for the leak and patch it if we can. But your port is a real mess, ma'am, and my people are afraid to go out on those quays."

I don't blame them, Jessica thought.

"And," Larry went on, "we checked the containment building. It's listing at another two degrees."

Jessica took a slow, careful breath. *Two degrees* . . . A two-million-ton reactor leaning like the Tower of Pisa.

"Roger that, Mr. Hallock," she said, her mouth dry. Star shells flashed in her left eye.

The last two problems—the fragility of the temporary harbor and the dangerous position of the reactor—could be fixed by accelerating Operation Island. Keep the big Sikorsky helicopters dropping tons of rubble twenty-four hours per day. Build a *real* harbor, make the reactor complex part of something solid.

But that meant the helicopters would not be free for other tasks, such as searching for refugees. People could die if she kept the heavy-lift machines moving rubble from one place to another instead of helping the victims of the quake.

But that's what she *had* to do. A worst-case accident at Poinsett Landing could poison the Mississippi for the next five hundred years.

"Mr. Hallock," she said, "I'm going to accelerate Operation Island. I want you to move your personnel out of the area, except for those you need to fix the leak and to keep the auxiliary building stable."

There was a pause. "Roger that, General."

"I'll see you later, Mr. Hallock."

There was another pause. "Good luck, General Frazetta."

Jessica nodded. "And to you," she said.

He had to put them somewhere, all these refugees. There weren't many choices. And so Omar found himself visiting the Reverend Dr. Morris.

Dr. Morris preached at the African Methodist Episcopal Church of Spottswood Parish, and was a white-haired black man of unimpeachable rectitude and gravel-voiced eloquence. It was fortunate for Omar that few people had listened to Morris at the last election.

Morris knew that Omar was coming—one did not do these things unannounced—and waited for him on the front lawn of the ruined brick California bungalow that had once been his parsonage. Next door, his church, of frame construction, had largely survived, though it had lost its steeple, most of its shingles, and all of its windows.

Dr. Morris was surrounded by his family and several of what Omar assumed were his parishioners, forming a half-circle behind him, like a bodyguard. Morris, or his friends, wanted witnesses to the meeting of their parson and the Kleagle.

Like Omar was going to go berserk and start throwing fire-bombs. *These people*, Omar thought, *should know better.*

Gravel crunched as Omar turned into Morris' driveway. He stepped out of the car, adjusted his hat, tried to mask his unease. He was here in the role of a supplicant, and he didn't like it.

He walked toward Morris, and behind his sunglasses he scanned the silent, hostile black faces that surrounded the minister. "Dr. Morris," he said, "Miz Morris," and touched the brim of his hat to the reverend's lady.

"Sheriff." Morris nodded. His wife gave a nod that seemed civil enough, though her unblinking eyes didn't leave Omar's face for a second.

"We've got a lot of refugees in the parish," Omar said. He turned, scanned the cars lined behind them on the road. "You can see that yourself. We've got to put them somewhere until they can be evacuated. I thought that the land where you hold your camp meetings might be suitable—you have facilities there, yes? Toilets and water and such?"

Dr. Morris nodded. "Yes. And we have grills for outdoor cooking, and a kitchen to serve hot meals. Though I don't know whether the cookhouse survived last night."

"Can you open the property on short notice, Doctor? We've got to put these people somewhere before they start keeling over of sunstroke."

The preacher nodded. "I can do that, Sheriff," he said.

"Thank you, Dr. Morris. I'll tell my men to give you an hour or so before they start sending people over."

Dr. Morris nodded. "Very well, Sheriff. We'll have the place open, and we'll do what we can for the people."

Omar touched his hat to Mrs. Morris again, then returned to his car.

All summer long, the A.M.E. ran camp meetings at their site north of Shelburne City. Whole families of black people from all over the South-Central U.S. drove to the meetings, pitched their tents, and spent their money at the Commissary and the local BBQ and burger joints. It was one of the few mainstays of the local economy that hadn't gone to hell in the last twenty years. Even the Klan was happy for the addition to the revenues of the parish.

Camp sites, toilets, running water. Exactly what the situation called for.

Omar was less happy with the subject of his next visit. Mrs. LaGrande Davis Rildia Shelburne Ashenden, the last member of the family that had run the parish for the last nine or ten generations, and—he suspected—a far more dedicated and skilled political opponent even than Dr. Morris.

The river was all over the goddam place. Stars flashed in Jessica's left eye as she peered down at the flooded Atchafalaya country from her seat in the Kiowa. She was on a personal reconnaissance, and it was as bad as it could get. It was 1927 all over again.

And on her watch. She tried not to think about that.

Before M6, Jessica had every expectation of penning the runaway river in its proper banks somewhere north of Vicksburg. Except for a few places like Poinsett Landing where the river had found a new channel, the levees were mostly intact from Vicksburg south, and Jessica had made certain they were inspected to make certain they would hold, and any weaknesses shored up or repaired. Any water that got behind the levees could be siphoned off by the various winding bayous, like LaFourche or Boeuf, that paralleled the Mississippi, then drained off into the Mississippi or the Red.

But M6 had wrecked that. Jessica had to get the river back in its banks somewhere south of the Old River structures in central Louisiana, which meant that the whole focus of her effort had shifted a couple hundred miles south of where she'd intended.

Goddam goddam goddam. She'd had to give up everything north of Baton Rouge. Her jurisdiction—the part of the twenty-three-hundred-mile river that actually obeyed her commands—had shrunk to the two hundred and fifty miles north of its outlet. A little more than one tenth.

The rest was flood and swamp, refugees and ruin.

"Please sit down, Sheriff Paxton," said Mrs. Ashenden. "May I offer you some tea?"

"Yes, ma'am. Thank you." He hitched his gun out of the way and sat carefully on an antique rococo armchair.

Mrs. Ashenden sat opposite Omar on a matching loveseat. Its curved legs were in the shape of animal legs, each clawed foot holding a carved wooden ball. Mrs. Ashenden was in her sixties, with white hair, a soft, languorous voice, and piercing blue eyes that glittered like diamonds. Her age had not dimmed her mind, and Omar imagined that her control of Garden Club politics had not weakened at all.

"We have our own blend that's come down from the Rildia family—we have it mixed in San Francisco and shipped here. Would you like to try it, or would you prefer Earl Grey or, ah, something else?"

"Whatever you're having, Miz LaGrande," Omar said.

Mrs. Ashenden turned to her maid, an elderly black woman named Lorette, and said, "The Rildia blend, then. And some of the macaroons, please."

"Yes, ma'am," Lorette said.

While Mrs. Ashenden spoke to the maid, Omar glanced over Clarendon's front parlor. The big house, with its heavy post and beam construction, had survived the two big quakes very well—Miz LaGrande's ancestors—or the two hundred slaves they owned—had built for the ages, had hauled huge cypress-wood beams to the building site and dug them deep into massive foundations. Other than broken windows and a couple of fallen chimneys, Clarendon had done very well. Even the front portico, with its four mismatched pillars—why did he remember the term *distyle-in-antis*?—still stood to proudly greet Omar as he drove down the live-oak alley toward the house. The oak alley itself had not done nearly as well—at least half the trees were down.

The interior appeared to have come through the quake intact. The mantelpiece and tables seemed a bit bare—presumably they had been cleared of breakables, either by the quake or by the housekeeping staff. But the furniture looked unscarred, and the cut crystal of the overhead chandelier seemed to have survived without a scratch.

"I wanted to say," Mrs. Ashenden said, "how much we enjoyed your Wilona, when she called the other day."

Omar looked at his nemesis and smiled. "She told me how much she enjoyed the visit. It was very kind of you to invite her."

Mrs. Ashenden tilted her head, gave Omar a birdlike look. "I'm surprised we haven't seen *you* here, Sheriff Paxton." Her ice-blue eyes glittered.

"I've had no reason to take your time, Miz LaGrande," Omar said. No reason to crawl to Clarendon for favors when he could take what he wanted by other means, he meant. He let Mrs. Ashenden absorb this for a moment, then glanced deliberately around the parlor.

"You seem to have weathered the quakes very well," he said.

"Yes. Mr. Oliver Shelburne built well when he built this place." She smoothed her lap. "I won't be able to serve you off the Wedgwood, I'm afraid. We had too many pieces of the creamware broken in the first quake, and some of it is impossible to repair, so we put everything in storage until the danger is over. It is fortunate that the pre-1830 Waterford came through all right, though some of the more modern crystal was damaged."

All our McDonalds cups came through just fine, Omar was tempted to reply. *Even the Darth Vader.* But he just smiled and told Mrs. Ashenden that she'd been lucky.

"Yes. Particularly during last night's horror. I understand many in the parish have lost their homes."

"Yes. And that's what I wanted to talk to you about."

"Ah. Here's our tea."

Lorette arrived with tea on a tray and poured. Omar asked for sugar, no cream, and got a sugar cube dropped into his cup with silver tongs. He stirred the dissolving lump into his tea—he knew from Wilona that his silver teaspoon was to a pattern made exclusively by a firm in Vicksburg since the 1840s—and he glanced at his cup as he raised it to his lips. Even if this was the second-best china, it was still impressive enough: thin and delicate as the petals of a flower, gold-rimmed, with a design of a shepherd frolicking with a shepherdess. Omar could crush it to powder by closing one hand, and for a moment— only a moment—he was tempted to do so.

Mrs. Ashenden had seen him study the cup. "It's Sèvres," she said, "but it's soft-paste, not *porcelaine royale*, and our set is incomplete."

"It's very fine, ma'am," Omar said. Mrs. Ashenden was lucky she had inherited the porcelain, the silver, and Clarendon, too, because if she hadn't, she might well be wandering the parish bereft as any refugee. Her husband, the late Herbert Temple Ashenden of Fort Worth, had gone through their combined fortunes like a hailstorm through ripe wheat. He had lost most of their money in the oil business, and then dropped the rest in a scheme to turn the Shelburne cotton fields into an exclusive hunting resort here in Spottswood Parish, a place carefully groomed to support quail, deer, duck, trout, and who-knew-what. He'd built a lodge and preened the country, and imported or otherwise attracted the game, and then found that no one came.

Rich people, it seemed, had better places to spend their time than Spottswood Parish. The scheme leaked money like a sieve. Ashenden, along with his blond girlfriend, a former Miss Concordia Parish, died in a car crash in Mississippi. Most of the old Shelburne plantation had been sold to pay his debts, and now belonged to Swiss Jews who had demolished the lodge, chased off the wildlife, and put the land back into cotton.

Omar had heard that Mrs. Ashenden had a hard time coming up with the taxes on the property she had remaining, but had made an agreement with a cousin, one of the Davises, to leave Clarendon to her in return for having her taxes paid. Rogers Wilcox, who worked at the courthouse, claimed to have seen the legal documents when they were filed.

It was hearing this that had determined Omar to run for office. Mrs. Ashenden couldn't back her political favorites with money, only with words and sheer force of habit. It was time, Omar thought, that the old habits died.

Omar put his cup into his saucer. "What I wanted to talk to you about, Miz LaGrande," he said, "is the homeless people here in the parish, and the casualties."

Concern entered Mrs. Ashenden's voice. "Are there very many injured?"

"There are some who really need to go to a hospital," Omar said, "but we don't even have the clinic anymore. Dr. Patel's offices collapsed last night. I know this is an imposition, but we need a place to put the injured, and this is the safest building in the parish."

"Of course you may bring them here," Mrs. Ashenden said. "We have always done our bit in an emergency. We sheltered a great many people during the Flood of 1927." She gave a little smile. "It will be like the War Between the States, I fancy, when so many of our homes were turned into hospitals." A troubled look crossed her face. "But I don't have the staff here to care for people. Just Lorette, and Joseph, and the gardener."

"Dr. Patel and his nurse will be here," Omar said. "And we hope that the families will pitch in."

"Ye-es," Mrs. Ashenden said, a little vaguely, as if she were picturing to herself a horde of people swarming into her house to look after their relations.

"Besides the injured," Omar continued, "the parish seems to have acquired a lot of, ah, misplaced people. Evacuees who were on the road last night when the quake hit. I don't know how many, but there are hundreds. The Bayou Bridge is down, and the Parish Floodway's broken, so right now there's no way in or out."

"Mercy."

"We've got to put these people somewhere until we can get them shipped out, or until we can get the bridges rebuilt. Last time we used churches and the schools, but none of those buildings are safe anymore."

"Yes?" There was calculation behind those ice-blue eyes.

"I thought your lawns and gardens," Omar said, then added quickly. "You've got what—six–eight acres? Nice, flat, with grass. We can put people under tents or some other kind of shelter, and we can use your house as an infirmary and your kitchens as a cookhouse."

"Gracious." Mrs. Ashenden seemed surprised. "Don't you have anyplace else?"

"I've got Dr. Morris to open up the A.M.E. campground, but that's going to fill up pretty quick. And everyplace else in the parish is either wilderness, under water, or planted in cotton. You know what it's like around here. I can't put people in a cotton field, and I can't scatter them around, because I need to bring food and other supplies to a central point."

Mrs. Ashenden absorbed this. "But I don't have the *staff*. Not any longer. I don't have the means to take care of all these people."

"Well, Miz LaGrande," Omar said, "I suppose they didn't have the staff in the War Between the States, either, but they managed somehow."

He saw the glint of duty in her eyes, and knew he'd won. There was nothing more sacred to a Shelburne than the traditions of Southern Womanhood. In times of crisis, the lady of the manor opened her home to those in need, and that was that.

Omar helped himself to one of Mrs. Ashenden's macaroons on the way out. When he got into his cruiser, he turned to look at the massive front portico, the four giant pillars— *distyle-in-antis*—and he thought of Clarendon surrounded by a shantytown, refugees living under tents or blankets, screaming children breaking down the neat hedges and rolling in the flowerbeds, the boiling laundry and slit-trench latrines contributing their odor to the flower-scented Clarendon air . . . *wonderful*, he thought.

Just like the War Between the States.

When Omar got back to his office, he dispatched two officers to Miz LaGrande's to direct traffic, and another two to the

A.M.E. campground. Then he got on the radio and told his officers to start moving the refugees to the camps.

"Sheriff," came a reply, "how do we know which camp to send folks to?" Omar recognized Merle's voice.

"Well," Omar said, "if they look like an African Methodist Episcopal to you, send them there. And if they don't, send them to Clarendon."

There was a pause. "Ten-four, chief," came the answer. Omar could just picture Merle's grin.

Omar had actually considered sending all the blacks to Clarendon, just burying Mrs. Ashenden in niggers. But Clarendon was only half a mile from Shelburne City's town square, and he knew the merchants and landowners would complain if he packed the town with refugee blacks from the inner city. Best to keep them well out of town, in their own place.

Wilona put her head into the office. She looked exhausted, deep circles under her eyes, lines of worry at the corners of her mouth. Omar signed off the radio, then went to Wilona and put his arms around her.

"You okay?"

"Just tired. I'm worried about our house, with all these strangers around."

"The neighbors will keep a lookout." He kissed her. "I've been to Miz LaGrande's."

She brightened immediately. "Yes?" she said. "Did you talk with her?"

"I had tea," he said, "off the second-best china."

"Well," Wilona frowned, "the Wedgwood was probably in storage, to keep it safe."

Omar grinned. "That's what Miz LaGrande said."

She brightened again. "So what did you talk about?"

"We're going to set up a hospital at Clarendon, and put a refugee camp on the grounds."

Wilona's eyes widened. "It'll be just like the War!" she said.

"I think the crisis has passed," Omar said. "Why don't you go down to the squad room, lie down, and get some rest?"

"I should go to Clarendon," Wilona said. "I should offer to help Miz LaGrande with her work."

Omar looked at her sourly. It was as if Wilona was planning on nursing the wounded of the Confederacy. "You've got plenty enough to do," he said. "We've got a busted house, and if that isn't enough there's plenty to do here."

"But I could help at *Clarendon*!" Wilona said.

"It's not going to be a tea party," Omar said. "It's going to be a refugee camp with screaming babies and sick people and bugs. Probably there will be a fair number of criminals, too. No place for white gloves and pearls."

Wilona seemed unconvinced. "I think it could be lovely."

"Wilona," Omar said. "What is it you came in here to tell me?"

"Oh. Sorry. Tree Simpson needs you in the council chamber."

The room where the parish council met was a court room when the council wasn't meeting there. Tree—short for Trelawny—Simpson sat on the council. He ran one of the parish's two pharmacies, was a middle-sized man with a little grizzled mustache, and looked as if he hadn't slept in a week.

"We're not getting the Bayou Bridge replaced anytime soon," he said. "Every portable or collapsible bridge in the U.S. of A. has already been deployed into the disaster area."

"How about an evacuation?" Omar said.

Tree only shrugged. "I couldn't get ahold of anybody who had the authority to do a thing. I got someone who said he'd put me on a list for someone in logistics, so that at least we could get sent some food."

"Joy in the mornin'," said Omar.

"The rest of the council are getting food supplies together. Paying with personal checks. At least we'll be able to feed our guests later today. Oh." He looked up as he remembered something. "The governor's declared martial law in several parishes, including ours. If that makes your job any easier."

"Could be," Omar said.

There was a tap on the door, and one of Omar's special

deputies stuck his head in the door. "Sorry, Sheriff," he said. "But I thought I'd better tell you there's been a shooting."

It was clear enough what happened. The drifter had been digging through the fallen remains of Ozie Welks' storeroom. He'd run when Ozie had challenged him, trailed bottles of Miller Genuine Draft behind him as he fled, and then as he paused to hop over Ozie's straggling barbed-wire fence, Ozie blew the back of his head off with the shotgun he kept on the rack in his pickup truck.

The most natural thing in the world, shoot a stranger who was trying to steal your stuff. That's what you carried shot-guns *for*.

The stranger was a little man, white, with a wrinkled cot-ton shirt and a porkpie hat. He was maybe fifty, with a home-made tattoo on the back of one hand. Even in death, he still clutched a bottle of Jim Beam to his breast.

"That's a looter, all right," said David, one of the first on the scene. Wearing one of his father's spare uniforms, he looked more official than most of the special deputies, whose uniform consisted of a star and a gun worn over civilian clothes. David poked at the bottle of Beam with the toe of his boot. "Got the evidence right in his hand." David looked at Ozie with an admiring grin. "That's a good shot, Ozie."

"Some ol' drunk," said Ozie. "Couldn't live without the hooch for another minute." He had come back from helping a friend rescue some furniture from his collapsed mobile home, and he'd found the drifter looting his bar in broad daylight.

"Any ID on the body?" Omar said.

David shook his head. "We checked."

Omar looked at the looter. Sweat trickled down the sides of his nose. He let his gaze travel over the road, the cars pulled off the highway during the quake and then abandoned by people heading into town. "One of those cars is probably his," he said, "but there's no way to know which one."

"Shall we take the body to the coroner?" asked one of the deputies.

Who, come to think of it, was Tree Simpson. Tree had been appointed when the last coroner, a tire salesman, had been electrocuted in his bathtub.

"Bag it up," Omar said. "Show it to Tree. Then we'll shove it in the potter's field."

"Dang," David said. "That was a great shot."

Ozie looked grim. "I'm going to have to put up with a lot of shit on account of this, ain't I?"

Omar shook his head. "Not with a looter. Not at a time like this."

"Good." Ozie wiped sweat off his stubbly chin with the back of one arm. "Maybe nobody'll miss this boy at all."

Omar glanced up as a pair of cars drove by, each packed with families heading for Clarendon. The cars slowed, and Omar felt himself being scanned by the eyes of strangers. The Klan Kop, Komplete with Korpse.

He could feel their little tiny refugee brains drawing conclusions.

Strangers, Omar thought, refugees. Wandering around without supervision. Bound to get into trouble, and one of them had just got shot by a local. And unless Omar got things under better control, this body wouldn't be the last.

He walked to the car, unhooked the mike from the radio, and spoke to the guards he'd sent to his two refugee camps.

"Once people get into the camps," he said, "I don't want anyone to leave unless they can tell you the name of the local resident they'll be visiting. Unless they know somebody here, there's no place for them to go."

He held the microphone to his lips for a moment, saw the corpse lying by the vine-covered barbed wire. The Louisiana heat beat on his head.

"Tell them it's for their own protection," he added.

Bill Clemmons knew it was going to be bad when he saw the flies. He was carrying government food home from Cameron Brown Park in a wheelbarrow, and when he passed the BMW that his neighbor Charlie Johns had been living in, he saw clouds of black flies floating in and out of the open door. Thousands of them.

Bill hesitated while sweat tracked down his nose. He knew well enough what the clouds of flies meant. He was tempted to let it be someone else's problem.

But it *was* his problem. He couldn't have that next to his own house, his own family.

What went wrong? he wondered. What had gone wrong with Charlie Johns? He was too smart to die like this.

Bill started pushing the barrow again. He'd deliver the food, then he'd walk back to the park to inform the authorities about the corpse lying in the BMW.

By late afternoon Omar had a head count. Two hundred thirty refugees, mostly black, on the A.M.E. campsite. Four hundred and forty-three, mostly white, crammed into Clarendon's parklands, a stench unto the nostrils of Mrs. Ashenden. Thirty-one badly injured people had been moved into the house itself, where they could fulfill her Civil War fantasies—maybe, Omar thought, she'd feed them off the Wedgwood.

And then of course there was the dead man occupying a body bag at the coroner's office.

Omar didn't know how many natives of the parish were without homes, but it was well into the hundreds. Many had taken refuge with friends; others were camping or living in their cars.

Omar couldn't just round them up. After all, they were voters.

The strangers were all hungry. The parish had done what was possible to get food to them, but there wasn't that much food in the parish to begin with, less than a week's supply.

Fortunately Judge Moseley had been on the phone to the Emergency Management people, and they had promised for the next day a helicopter supply mission, food, tents, and medical equipment.

Omar had just been to the A.M.E. camp to tell them that help was coming tomorrow. His reception hadn't been very cordial. "There are some damned angry niggers here," Merle grinned as Omar got out of his car. The camp inmates, Merle implied, wanted assistance *now*, and they weren't taking any shit from Klan Kops.

Omar went into the camp and tried to talk to Reverend Dr. Morris, tell him that the government was shipping in stuff tomorrow, but that everyone would have to sleep in their cars tonight—but there wasn't just Morris, there was a whole *wall* of black folks, all of them talking. All the white people in the camp—and there were a few—were probably in hiding. Some of the blacks looked like *aliens*, with dreadlocks or strange headgear or crazy, incomprehensible speech. All of them seemed to know who he was. "You can't scare *us*, cone-head motherfucker," one big man chanted, the deep voice repeating the words over and over, sometimes varying his rhythm, mother*fucker* alternating with *mother*fucker. There were at least two people with video cameras, hoping to catch Omar in some brutality.

Adrenaline flared through Omar's veins as he tried to shout his message over the sound of the crowd. He felt his fingers tingle as he thought about his pistol, thought about the flap holding the pistol in the holster. He thought about firing the pistol into the air just to get everyone to shut up. He repressed the thought. These people could be armed, he thought. They could shoot back.

He delivered his message and left. Taunts rang in his ears as he stalked away. Merle stood by his car at the gate, his easy grin turned taut on his face. "Figured I might have to pull you out of there, boss," he said, and showed Omar the Ingram Mac–11 he was holding concealed behind his car door. The thing fired eighty zillion rounds per second, Omar knew, and not a one of them accurate.

"Jesus," Omar said. "You would have shot me along with all the others."

"The first burst would have gone over their heads," Merle said.

Omar was not comforted. He looked over his shoulder at the angry crowd, the video cameras that were still trained on him. "Put that gun back in the car," he said, "if you don't want it on the evening news."

"I'm gonna need more boys here for crowd control," Merle said.

Omar pushed his sunglasses back up his nose. Anger snarled through his nerves. "You'll get them," he said.

"Make sure they've got shotguns at least," Merle said. "These aren't *our* niggers we're dealing with."

Omar rolled his cruiser carefully over a barely-filled-in crevasse as he drove down Main, then turned onto Courthouse Road. Anger still shimmered in his nerves, though weariness was beginning to beat it down. The courthouse lawn, with its stubs and torn stumps of blackjack oak, looked strangely bare in the slanting western rays of the sun. A wrecker, with a crane on the back, had been backed onto the courthouse lawn. Probably yanking stumps or hauling wood away, he thought.

He would sleep in his office tonight. After sixteen hours of coping with one emergency after another, he didn't think he could face the wreckage that was his home.

The parking place that had been reserved for the sheriff and other parish employees had been filled by a truck full of building scrap from the collapsed Robbie's Barber Shop across Courthouse, so Omar turned the car around and parked next to the courthouse lawn. He got out of the car, crossed the broken concrete sidewalk, then stopped in surprise as he saw who was standing by the wrecker under the cracked plinth of the Mourning Confederate.

Micah Knox. The biggety bantam Crusader stood among a knot of strangers, a camouflage baseball cap cocked back on his burrcut head, the long sleeves of his flannel shirt rolled down to his wrists. And standing next to Knox, looming over him almost, was the tall figure of Omar's son, David.

David looked up and grinned as Omar approached. "Hey, Dad," he said.

"Hey," Omar said.

The wrecker had been backed up to the Mourning

Confederate, Omar saw. The bronze statue had pitched head-first off its plinth during the morning's earthquake and stuck in the soft ground like a spear. A cable had been wrapped around the statue, and the crane on the wrecker was about to lift the Confederate and set it upright.

"Micah said it wasn't right that the statue should just be left there," David said.

"Not in Liberated America," Knox said.

"I agreed with him," David said, "so I got ahold of Judd Criswell and got him to bring his wrecker."

"Micah?" Omar said. He looked from David to Knox and back. "You know each other?"

"Since this afternoon," David said. "Micah and his buddies came in on a boat this afternoon, down by the Bayou Bridge."

And David and his partner patrolled down there, Omar knew, looking out in case refugees managed to get across the bayou.

"We were pretty grungy," Knox said. "We'd been on the river almost a week." He grinned at David, fiddled with a gold watch chain looped between a front and back trouser pocket. "Dave here took us to your house so that we could get a shower."

"And they cleaned the place!" David said. "Set the furniture up, tidied up the broken glass. Nailed the ceiling panels and the box siding that come loose."

Knox grinned, bounced up on the tips of his toes. "Five people," he said. "Working for an hour, while Dave was off on his patrol. It's not as nice as Wilona would make it, but it's a lot neater than it was."

Omar looked at the strangers. "Who are your friends, Micah?" he said.

"Crusaders brave and true," Knox said. "We keep in touch through the Internet and arranged a rendezvous. They're all happy to be here in Liberated America."

He introduced them. They were all bigger than Knox. Some looked like serious streetfighters that Omar would hate to encounter in a barfight situation. They were all young and wore combat boots and bits of military uniform. Their ears stuck out from short-cropped heads. Two had bad acne, and all displayed lots of insect bites. None of them seemed particularly happy to be in Shelburne City, liberated zone or not.

"Where've you been?" Omar asked.

"Arkansas, mostly. We met up there, before everyone started evacuating. We just wandered around, then got a boat when we got caught by flood—" His restless hands touched his cap brim, his belt, his shoes. His voice turned louder. "Hey, you know Omar, this quake knocked ZOG for shit. No Feds anywhere. No FBI, no DEA, no judges, no marshals, no military. No Equal Opportunity Commission. Just the *people*, for a change. It's like the frontier all over again."

"Hey, Omar," Judd Criswell said from the cab of his wrecker. "Can we get moving, here? I got plenty work for this truck."

"You bet," David said.

The winch whined, and the bronze man slowly rose from the soil. The others pitched it over so it would land right-side up, and Criswell carefully lowered it again to the ground.

"There we go," David said admiringly. "Straight up-and-dicular."

The figure had survived remarkably well. The muzzle of the statue's rifle had broken off, but the bowed head, with its somber expression, and the body in its caped overcoat had come through unscathed. David stepped forward and wiped dark soil from the mustached face.

"Can't get it back on the pillar, I guess," he said. "But the least we could do was set the ol' boy on his feet again."

After Judd Criswell disconnected his cable and drove off in his truck, Knox drew himself to attention and gave the statue an elaborate salute. "Comrade, we salute you!" he said. "We have kept the faith! The struggle goes on!" The Confederate gazed at him with glacial sorrow.

Then Knox turned to Omar and gave another salute. "Micah Knox and detachment reporting for duty, Sheriff Paxton," he said. "Tell us what you want us to do."

"I mentioned you could make 'em special deputies," David said.

Omar hesitated. "I don't know rightly," he said. "You're not from around here."

"Neither are the Klan boys you brought in," David said. "I heard the radio calls from that African Methodist camp—sounds like you need more people."

Omar paused for a brief moment to admire the thought of Knox and his Crusaders National race warriors guarding the nigger camp—now *that* would be fun to watch—but he remembered the video cameras and reluctantly dismissed the idea.

"Okay," he said. "You boys can relieve some of my trained men, and they can look after the camp."

Knox's strange emerald pupils blazed from within their rim of white. "We *are* trained, sir," he said.

"Not for police work, son."

Knox accepted this judgment with reluctance. Omar took them into the courthouse, swore them in, and assigned them as partners to other deputies, then sent the deputies' old partners either to bed or the A.M.E. camp.

He was going to have to do something about that camp, he thought as he sat in his office and listened to radio calls crackling out. Too many guns out there. Too many strangers. Too much unruliness.

He thought about it, and an idea came to him. He smiled.

Knox and his Crusaders might be useful after all.

The morning after the quake, Nick and Jason continued their water journey. But the waterscape had changed completely: they floated through a forest of broken trees, stumps, and raw wood spears jabbing from the flood. The water was choked with wreckage, and it was very easy to wander from the roadway they had been following. After losing it and finding it several times, they lost it for good, and after that they tried to navigate by the position of the sun.

Eventually they stopped using the speedboat's engine, because it spent so much time idling that they reckoned they were wasting fuel. Because the speedboat was too wide to row, they moved to *Retired and Gone Fishin'*, which they could row with the oars that Captain Joe had provided them. They towed the speedboat behind on a line. They traded rowing with fending off wreckage and trying to clear a path for the boat.

It was hot, backbreaking work. Insects buzzed round them in swarms. They had no idea whether they were moving in a straight line or in circles.

The next morning was no better, but by noon they found themselves rowing through water that was perceptibly moving, trickling past the stumps and standing trees. They decided to follow the direction the water seemed to be flowing, even though it was in a different direction than the one in which they'd been going. The trees seemed to open up gradually, and they found themselves in what might have been a river, or a flooded road, or possibly even a section line cleared of trees, but at any rate seemed to be a straight path that was taking them somewhere. The sun seemed right overhead, and they couldn't tell whether they were moving east, west, or south.

They moved from the bass boat to the speedboat, though they didn't start the engine, just drifted with the current. They stretched their kinked and sore muscles, and shared a can of tuna, some pickles, and an orange.

Then the trees opened up to the right, and drifting into sight came an open field with an old Allis-Chalmers tractor standing in it, the water up to its motor. Visible in the near distance were the collapsed remnants of a farm and its outbuildings. And between the farm and their boat was another boat, a fifteen-foot open flat-bottomed aluminum fishing boat with three people in it.

Jason's heart leaped. "Look!" he said. Nick jumped up with a shout poised on his lips, and then he hesitated. A darker look came into his eyes.

"Get into the driver's seat," he said. "Take us close to them. But not *too* close."

Jason's mouth went dry as Nick reached for his rifle and

crouched down in the cockpit. Nick looked over his shoulder, saw Jason's expression. "I'm just being careful," he said.

Jason's heart hammered in his chest. He got into the driver's seat, pulled the choke, pressed the starter. The Evinrude started up with a roar.

The people in the other boat heard the engine start up, and they jumped upright and started waving. Jason coasted closer to them. All three were black, he saw, one older man and a pair of boys about Jason's age.

"That's close enough," Nick said.

Jason cut the engine and drifted. Jason watched Nick's hand clench and unclench on the barrel of his rifle. The three in the other boat waved their arms and shouted.

"Heaven-o!" they cried. "Heaven-o!"

TWENTY-FIVE

It was now light, and we had an opportunity of beholding, in full extent, all the horrors of our situation. During the first four shocks, tremendous and uninterrupted explosions, resembling a discharge of artillery, was heard from the opposite shore; at that time I imported them to the falling of the river banks. This fifth shock explained the real cause. Whenever the veins of the earthquake ran, there was a volcanic discharge of combustible matter to a great height, as incessant rumbling was heard below, and the bed of the river was excessively agitated, whilst the water assumed a turbid and boiling appearance—near our boat a spout of confined air, breaking its way through the waters, burst forth and with a loud report discharged mud, sticks, &c, from the river's bed, at least thirty feet above the surface. These spoutings were frequent, and in many places appeared to rise to the very Heavens. —Large trees, which had lain for ages at the bottom of the river, were shot up in thousands of instances, some with their roots uppermost and their tops planted; others were hurled into the air; many again were only loosened, and floated upon the surface. Never was a scene more replete with terrific threatenings of death; with the most lively sense of this awful crisis, we contemplated in mute astonishment a scene which completely beggars all description and of which the most glowing imagination is inadequate to form a picture. Here the earth, river, &c. torn with furious convulsions, opened in huge trenches, whose deep jaws were instantaneously closed; there through a thousand vents sulphureous streams gushed from its very bowels, leaving vast and almost unfathomable caverns. Every where nature itself seemed tottering on the verge of dissolution. Encompassed with the most alarming dangers, the manly presence of mind and hero-

ic fortitude of the men were all that saved them. It was a struggle for existence itself, and the mede to be purchased was our lives.

Narrative of Mr. Pierce, December 25, 1811

"Oh it's just lovely," Wilona said. "Miz LaGrande has moved beds in, and she's divided the big rooms into wards. She's so gracious to everybody, even the ones who are in pain and shouting for help." She shook her head. "Those poor people. Broken bones, most of them. Some bad burns. But Dr. Patel is wonderful! I don't think he's slept in days."

She looked down at her drink. "I'm getting used to Co-Cola warm, you know that?"

Warm because there was no ice. Electricity had still not been restored to Hardee, even though most of Shelburne City had power.

Some things never changed.

Wilona sat on the couch in the old double shotgun with her feet tucked under her. Omar sat with a warm beer in his easy chair, gazing with heavy-lidded eyes at the dead television set.

"We lost a little colored girl this morning," Wilona said. "No older than six. Her mama crashed the car into a power pole during the quake. I held the little girl's hand till she passed, and her mama held the other." A look of melancholy crossed her face. "Gone where the woodbine twineth," she sighed.

Omar said nothing.

"Mrs. Ashenden was so kind to the little girl's mama afterward. Sat her down in the kitchen and talked to her for half an hour."

"Did Miz LaGrande give her any macaroons?" he said. "Serve her off the good china?"

Wilona looked cross. "You are so tacky sometimes."

"*Everybody's* been working hard," Omar said. "The old lady shouldn't get any special credit. I've been dealing with criminals and drug addicts. I'd like to see Miz LaGrande do *that*."

"I think you're being too negative," said Wilona.

"Miz LaGrande's had her foot on my neck from the day I was born."

Omar turned his head at the sound of a car pulling up in front of their house. David let himself in through the screen door, took off his gun belt, and put it on the sofa as he kissed his mother.

"We were expecting you earlier," Wilona said.

"I was with Micah Knox and his buddies." David sat on the couch next to Wilona. "We had a few beers and chewed the fat for a while. He's an interesting guy."

"Be careful around him," Omar said.

David looked at Omar in surprise. "He agrees with *you*, Dad. That's why he's here."

"Just be careful. That's all I ask."

"But he's so polite," Wilona said. "So polite he's almost Southern. He and his friends helped fix up our house."

"David," Omar said, and looked at his son. "He's not one of *us*. Okay?"

David hesitated a moment, then nodded. "Okay, Dad," he said.

Omar turned to stare at the dead television again. "Maybe I'll just go to bed," he said.

The big military copters flew into Shelburne City in mid-morning. Judge Moseley had directed them to the fields adjacent to the big house at Clarendon—an easy landmark for the chopper pilots—and the parish had trucks available to receive the government's bounty. Surplus cheese, rice, butter, and flour were unloaded, along with powdered milk, dried oatmeal, baby formula, rolls of plastic sheeting, two crated generators, water purification gear, and some moth-eaten old military tents that smelled as if they'd lain in a government warehouse since the Korean War. Big plastic bladders of gasoline and diesel fuel were rolled off the helicopters, and a man from the Emergency Management Agency—he looked like the worst case of overwork Omar had ever seen, eyes red, beard scruffy, skin flaking from sunburn—handed out a case of

Iridium cellphones so that parish officials could stay in touch with each other and the world.

Then all the government people got back on their helicopters and roared away. They said they had work elsewhere, they would bring another shipment of food in a few days, and the parish should call if they needed help, but they left so quickly that Omar figured they didn't want to spend any more time in Spottswood Parish than necessary.

To hell with them, Omar decided.

He got some of the food on the trucks, along with most of his force of deputies and the specials, and rolled them onto the Hess-Meier cotton field opposite the A.M.E. camp. He had instructed the guards there not to permit anyone to cross the road until the food was ready to be distributed. Then he let the people cross, no more than twenty at a time, to get their names on a list and draw rations. He had the parents and children cross the road first. Once they crossed into the cotton field, no one was allowed to return to the camp.

Once they were all away from the camp, Omar gave the signal. And his deputies, including Knox and his Crusaders, swarmed into the camp to search for firearms and contraband.

When the refugees saw what was going on, there was an outcry, and they surged toward the road in a swarm—but there were deputies in their path, with shotguns, and Omar shouting on a bullhorn, telling the refugees that the search was for weapons and drugs, that nobody was going to be arrested or get into trouble, but that the camp had to be made safe.

He pulled it off, just barely. There were some young men who stood on the far edge of the bar ditch and glared, their bodies trembling with the urge to violence, faces and bodies frozen in fury while others swarmed behind them, shouting taunts and abuse.

Many of the refugees, he noticed, didn't seem concerned by the search at all. They were a lot more interested in the food.

Everything in the camp was searched, even the cars— Omar had brought a locksmith to get into locked vehicles and trunks. Almost fifty firearms were found, along with bags of reefer, rock cocaine, a little baggie of brown heroin, and a whole sack of paraphernalia, ranging from a marijuana bong in the form of Godzilla to a very well-used syringe.

With any luck, some video cameras would disappear as well. In his briefing, Omar had mentioned that this would not be an occurrence that he would view as a tragedy.

"Sheriff! Sheriff, what's this?" One of his special deputies bounded eagerly across the road, holding out a small screw-top bottle half-filled with white lumps. "Is it crack cocaine or what?"

Omar opened the screw top, held it below his nose, took a careful sniff. He screwed the top on and handed it back.

"Moth balls," he said.

The deputy was crestfallen. "I thought I'd found a big stash of something."

"Better luck next time."

Omar turned to the refugees and raised his bullhorn. "When the emergency is over," Omar told them, "you can apply to the sheriff's department for a return of your property. Please be ready to furnish a description."

Steel wool, he imagined on a form, *small blowtorch, crack pipe made from old Dr. Pepper bottle.*

Some of these boys, he figured, were natural sorry to the point where they'd probably apply to get their drugs back.

After the search had been made, and the guns and other gear toted out of the camp and put in the trunks of the deputies' cars, Omar and his deputies stepped back and let the refugees swarm back to the A.M.E. camp in one great mass.

The Reverend Dr. Morris, Omar saw, had left the group and was approaching. Without, Omar saw, his usual scowling escort.

"There are still some things we need, Sheriff," Morris said.

Omar nodded. "Can you give me a list?"

"Some people need medication. Insulin is the most urgent, but we've got manic-depressives, folks with hypertension, thyroid cases . . ."

"If you'll furnish a list to the parish authorities . . ." Omar began. He really wasn't in charge of medication, except for the illegal kind.

"I was hoping we could get Dr. Patel here to write some prescriptions."

"He's at Clarendon looking after the injured. I could talk to him, but maybe it's just better if you make up a list and visit him yourself."

"We also need shelter. We don't have many tents."

"We didn't get much in that line," Omar considered. The mangy tents that came off the helicopters had been delivered to the Clarendon camp. Omar suspected there was something in the way of a tent shortage in the U.S. right now.

"We can give you some plastic sheeting," he said.

"We'll take it. But I was thinking you might send us some cotton wagons. We could park them in the camp, put plastic sheeting or canvas on the top, and they could hold quite a few people."

"*Cotton wagons,*" Omar repeated.

There were scores of them in the parish, he knew. They were big open wagons with chicken-wire sides, used during the time of the cotton harvest to carry freshly picked cotton to the gins. Wisps of cotton blew across the roads at that season, caught in trees and fences, piled in the ditches like a strange summer frost. Cotton wagons choked the roads, slow-moving targets often as not drawn at five miles per hour by a tractor, sometimes even by a mule. The wagons were unlit and dangerous at night, the cause of many an accident as fast-moving cars piled into them from behind. The rest of the year the wagons sat in barns or fields, useless.

"I'll put out a call for cotton wagons, Reverend," Omar nodded.

Black folks wanted to live in cotton wagons, it was all one to him.

Omar returned to his car, saw the firearms piled in his open trunk. *Real* guns, he saw. Glocks, Colts, Remingtons. And all the ammunition you'd need to stage a small war.

Tomorrow, Omar thought as he looked at the guns piled

into the trunk of his cruiser, *we better do this to the white folks' camp.*

There was the sound of distant thunder to the north. The earth trembled to an aftershock.

Micah Knox strolled up, and with an elaborate gesture pulled a large gold pocket watch that was on the end of the chain he'd been wearing. He opened the watch cover, looked at the dial. Bells in the watch played "Claire de Lune."

"One hour and twenty minutes," he said. "Pretty efficient, Omar, with so many people who ain't been trained for police work." He snapped the watch shut and put it in his pocket. "I think we got some real potential, here. Don't you?"

"Your people will get more practice at Clarendon," Omar said. "That's where we're going next." He looked at his own watch. "We'll have a bite, then get there just in time for their noon meal."

He had less trouble searching the Clarendon camp, but he collected many more firearms. The Clarendon camp, he decided, was going to be more trouble: it was closer to town, and people kept wandering off the camp limits into Shelburne City.

He wondered if he could get the parish council's permission to fence it off somehow. The parish was a little short of food and hospitality, but there was plenty of fencing material.

Hunger burned in Nick as the boy Orville guided him to Rails Bluff. In Rails Bluff there were fourteen people who came off boats from Toussaint two days before, and according to the boy one of them sounded like Arlette.

Yearning filled Nick to the brim. He saw Arlette every time he closed his eyes.

Love, your daughter. And a row of hearts.

Orville was twelve years old, and he, his older brother, and his uncle the church deacon had been sent out the day before, after the second big quake, to look for refugees and guide them to Rails Bluff. Orville had joined Jason and Nick as guide, while the others continued their search. He hadn't looked twice at the firearms piled around the boat. Guns weren't anything to Orville one way or another, just a part of the background.

The way to Rails Bluff was difficult, but not as difficult as their earlier wanderings had been. Orville's father had blazed a trail through the wreckage, and though there was still a lot of tree trunks that had drifted back into the channel and needed to be shoved out of the way, it was easier with much of the work already done. And part of the journey was along the Arkansas River, which though flooded and nearly choked with debris was open to movement by small boats.

Jason was quiet, Nick noticed, but he did his job. Nick couldn't manage to concern himself with the boy's moods, though, not with his daughter's presence tingling through his mind.

There was a rumble, and the boat tilted to port as something large and solid thundered along its aluminum bottom. Nick cut the throttle and jumped to the stern to tip the outboard up, out of the water, so its prop wouldn't be sheared off.

"That's a sawyer," Orville said. "Log just under the water." He grinned. "Lucky we're not in a wooden boat! We'd have a hole punched in the bottom!"

The boat grated as it slid off the sawyer. Nick waited till the boat was clear, then cautiously dropped the outboard back into the water.

"I wonder if Tom Sawyer was named after one of those," Nick said.

"Who's Tom Sawyer?" Orville asked, without interest. Then he looked up. "There's the bluff. We just bear off to the right here, till you get to Rails River."

The bluff rose gradually above the flooded land. It had been covered by thick stands of pine, but most of the trees had fallen in the quake and lay tumbled on the slope, their torn roots revealing the bluff's red clay. It looked as if a bulldozer had run mad among the pine groves, leveling everything it could find.

They followed the bluff, and Nick found himself in a flooded river. The fallen girders of a venerable iron trestle bridge lay spread across the river's channel, with the wreckage of an old Lincoln washing around amid the rusting beams.

There was a kind of improvised landing below the broken bridge, a homemade pier supported by oil drums. A miscellaneous collection of boats were moored there, or run up on the bluff, and there were two guards on the boats. Nick didn't like the look of that, particularly the man who set Nick's cracker vibe tingling, the big white guy with the homemade tattoo of an angel on his biceps. But the other was black, which was reassuring, and the big man, who said his name was Hilkiah, said that one of their scavenging parties had been shot at two days ago, by some men who Hilkiah thought were probably trying to break into the safe at a rural grocery store.

Nobody had been hurt, the big man said, but the Reverend was being cautious. He wanted armed men posted on anything that anyone might want to steal.

Nick figured he knew who the Reverend was: he'd heard about the situation in Rails Bluff from Orville. A bunch of preachers, Orville said, were running Rails Bluff. Nick reckoned that he'd rather have his daughter in the care of preachers than some rural sheriff or town council.

"I'm looking for the people from Toussaint," Nick said. He couldn't keep it in any longer. "They were supposed to have been brought in a couple days ago."

The black guard nodded. "I drove 'em to the camp myself," he said. "There was a whole bunch of 'em, right? Three or four families?"

"How were they?" Nick said.

"They spent a couple days in boats, which was hard on the old folks, but they was okay." The man looked concerned, put a coffee-colored hand on Nick's shoulder. "Any of 'em family?"

"My daughter," Nick said. "And . . . her momma." Hesitating because he almost said "my wife."

"They probably just fine," said the guard. He looked at Hilkiah. "Should I take these folks to the camp?"

"Might as well," Hilkiah said. He looked down at Orville.

"You and your Uncle Tyrus find anybody out there?"

The boy shook his head. "No, sir. But we didn't get far—too many fallen logs in the way."

Hilkiah nodded, then looked back at Nick. "What do you have in the way of supplies? Food and water?"

"We're well supplied. We ran into a towboat that gave us provisions."

"And I see you've got three, four gallons of gas left. Well—if you'll help carry your stuff to the top of the bluff, we can get it in the truck and you on to your family."

The pickup was an ancient Chevy that looked as if it had been salvaged from some junkyard. It had a bumper sticker reading TRUST IN GOD AND THE SECOND AMENDMENT. The five of them managed to carry most of Nick's supplies from the boats, up the slippery red-clay path, to the back of the truck. Jason carried his telescope on his shoulder.

"What's that?" Orville asked.

"A telescope."

"That don't look like a telescope."

"Well," Jason said, "that's what it is."

"Can I look through it, then?"

"Maybe later."

Jason put the telescope in the back of the pickup, nestled it safely against the cooler filled with provisions. Nick looked at him.

"You okay, Jase?"

"Yeah. I'm just tired."

"You can rest up here if you want. We can carry the rest of the stuff up without you."

Jason shook his head. "I can do it."

"I see you've got a rifle and some other guns," Hilkiah said as they trudged down the path again. "We don't allow guns in the camp, but we'll take care of 'em for you." He nodded. "We take good care of people's guns," he said. "In times like these, when the Lord is testing us, people want to know their firearms are being looked after."

"They're not my guns, exactly—I picked them up for protection after I found some people murdered."

Hilkiah looked at him. "Wars and rumors of wars," he said.

Nick blinked. "Murder, anyway," he said, and thought of Gros-Papa lying on the floor with his watch chain torn from his vest.

Oh God, he thought, *I'm going to have to tell Manon.*

The earth thundered with an aftershock. The old truck bounced up and down on its springs.

Hilkiah remained behind. The black guard, whose name was Conroy, got behind the wheel of the truck. Nick took the passenger seat, and the two boys rode in back.

The road was torn across by fresh fissures, one every few hundred feet; these were rudely filled in with dirt, rocks, and timber, sometimes sawn-up power poles that had fallen and been chucked into the gap. Every building visible from the road was in a state of collapse. The young cotton grew untended in empty fields. The pine trees that lined the road in places had almost all fallen and been shoved aside.

The result was that the area's large population of hawks had very few places left in which to roost. There must have been a lot of vermin for them to eat, because every remaining power pole or tree had at least one hawk sitting in it, each carefully facing away from all the others.

Conroy turned to Nick. "Say, brother," he said, "you been anywhere near a radio or TV?"

"For a while I was." They had listened to the radio regularly when they were aboard *Beluthahatchie.*

"Is it true about what happened to the nuclear power plant over in Mississippi? That it's poisoned all the country south and east of here?"

"That's not what I heard," Nick said. "I heard there was some trouble, with a little radiation released. But that's all."

"Reverend says that the plant practically blew up. He says whole states are poisoned. And he says the rivers are poisoned, too."

"There is a problem with the water, yes," Nick said. "Pollution from chemicals and fertilizers, oil tanks, that sort of thing. That's why the Mississippi and parts of some other rivers are being evacuated."

"The comet Wormwood," Conroy said. "That's what poisons the waters. You can read that in the Book."

Nick didn't quite have an answer for that, so he fell silent.

The truck crawled over more crudely repaired asphalt. The Church of the End Times was a strangely ordered island in the sea of devastation. The small metal-walled church stood intact, as did the radio station, with its tall tower and the small metal house behind it. In and about the area were ordered rows of tents, awnings, and vehicles. If it weren't for the gaping rents that scarred the ground, the place would have looked as neat as a military encampment on inspection day.

Two middle-aged white men sat under a picnic table umbrella by the road. They rose to their feet as the Chevy approached, each lifting a rifle. Nick's nerves jangled a warning as he recognized modern assault weapons, AR-15s, the civilian version of the Army's combat rifle, the M-16.

Guns, Nick's nerves jangled, guns and crackers. The combination didn't look good.

Conroy halted the vehicle by the table, and one of the men peered in.

"Heaven-o there, Conroy," he said. "You got some new folks for us?"

"This is Nick," Conroy said. "The boy's Jason."

"Welcome to God's country," the man said, and held a callused hand through the window for Nick to shake.

"Thanks," said Nick. The jolt of adrenaline that he'd received at the sight of the assault rifles was still jangling through his veins.

A man's amplified voice shouted in the background. *"Is this the day!"* it shouted. *"Is this the day of the Lord?"*

The guard smiled with crooked teeth as he peered at Nick through the window. "Do you have any liquor, drugs, or guns?" he asked.

Conroy answered before Nick could make up his mind whether he wanted to answer the question or not. "A rifle, shotgun, two pistols," Conroy said. "I put them behind the seat."

The guard nodded. "Me and George have some tags here,"

he said to Nick. "We'll tag your weapons and put them in storage. You can get them out when you leave."

Nick thought for a long moment while the guard and his buddy George fooled around on their table for a ballpoint pen and their jelly jar of tags. He didn't want to give the guns up, not in a situation like this, not in some kind of religious camp guarded by men carrying Armalites.

But on the other hand, he thought, how else would he see Arlette? And why should he expect people in a refugee camp to allow guns inside?

The guards scrawled Nick's name on the tags and attached them to his guns with string. The ammunition went into a plastic bag and was likewise labeled.

Nick, who had spent the first twenty years of his life going past military checkpoints with his father the general, figured he could have shot the guards fifty times over while this was going on. His anxiety over the assault rifles eased.

"Are you ready for judgment?" the amplified voice asked.

By the time the two guards were finished, two more people had hustled up from the camp. One white man and one black. Nick left the truck to greet them.

"Heaven-o," the white man said. He was a big, burly man and would have been good-looking if he hadn't lacked a chin. He and Nick shook hands. "I'm Brother Frankland." His was the voice, Nick recognized, that was shouting from the speakers.

"Pleased to meet you," Nick said.

"This is Brother Garb from True Gospel Church."

Garb was soft-spoken and toffee-skinned, dressed neatly in a pressed white cotton shirt and gold-rimmed spectacles. Nick shook his hand. "I heard my family was here," he said to Garb. "I heard they came in the other day from Toussaint."

A bright smile spread over Garb's face. "Is Arlette your daughter?" he said.

Relief and joy seemed to float Nick right off the ground. "Yes!" he almost shouted. "Yes, she is."

"She's a smart girl, your Arlette," Garb said. "She said you might be coming."

"Where is she?"

"In the church, most likely, looking after the children. I'll take you."

Nick almost danced after the Reverend Garb, but then he remembered Jason, and he stopped. He turned to the boy, who had been standing in silence by the truck.

"You want to come, Jase?" he asked.

Jason seemed uncertain. "Sure. If you don't mind."

"I don't mind at all. I'd like you to meet my family."

Jason brightened, then hesitated again as he looked at the truck. "Don't worry," Frankland said. "We'll look after your belongings."

"What does the Book of Daniel tell us?" said the amplified voice. A generator roared. Garb led Nick across the gravel parking lot, past the radio station—"Arkansas' Voice of the Lord, 15,000 watts AM"—and toward the church. Nick saw that big crosses, twenty or more feet long and made from trees or fallen power poles, were scattered through the area, lying on the ground, with the crosspiece lashed or bolted into place.

The sight of the crosses, of the sort that men in white hoods burned on Southern summer nights, sent a shimmer of unease up Nick's spine. But there were plenty of black people around, he saw, and they and the whites seemed on friendly terms.

"What are the crosses for?" he asked.

"'The cross shall be your salvation,'" Garb quoted, then laughed. "The crosses are to save lives. You see these big chasms? If a chasm opens up underneath it, a big cross will bridge the gap, won't fall in. We're teaching everyone that when a quake hits, they're to jump onto one of the crosses and hang on till it's over."

"That's interesting," Nick said. He suspected that it probably would work, too, if the crevasse wasn't too large.

They passed a sheriff's department vehicle—nice to know that someone official was present—and then, in front of the church, set up like a kind of wall, Nick saw a pair of banners, all covered with brilliantly colored, astoundingly detailed scenes. Nick saw angels, demons, volcanoes, scenes of violence and fire.

"What's this?" he said.

"Sister Sheryl's Apocalypse," Garb said. "She's been working on it for years—careful, there." This last was said to Jason, who had come very close to one of the banners, his nose just inches away from the Antichrist branding the number 666 into the forehead of one of his followers.

"Come here, Jason," Nick said.

"That's *amazing*," Jason said. "You know, I bet you there are rock bands, heavy-metal types, who would pay a lot of money to put this on their album covers."

"Well, maybe." Garb smiled. "You should get Sister Sheryl—she's Brother Frankland's wife—to give you a tour of her art."

Nick was impatient to see Arlette, and he walked faster, giving the others no time to view the banners. Behind Sheryl's Apocalypse about a dozen children played in the area around the church. Nick craned his neck as he looked for Arlette. Garb led him into the church. The pews had been pulled back against the walls, and the space divided by blankets and towels hung on lines. Mattresses filled half the floor space. The place smelled of babies and disinfectant, and the crying of infants echoed off the metal walls.

Nick's heart gave a leap as he saw his daughter at the back of the church. She was bending over a table, folding laundry, dressed in a cotton shirt and cut-off blue jeans. She wore a kerchief over her hair and a frown of concentration on her face.

My God, she's grown, Nick thought. Arlette seemed a head taller than when he'd seen her last. And she'd thinned out—at Christmas she'd seemed a little chubby, the way adolescents sometimes get just before a growth spurt. But now she was almost up to his chin, and looked graceful as an athlete.

He sprang forward. Arlette looked up at that moment, and for a moment there was a little frown between her brows, as if she couldn't understand why this strange unshaven man with grimy clothes and matted hair was lurching toward her; and then her face lit up, eyes wide with surprise and delight . . . *"Daddy!"* she cried, and ran to meet him.

Her arms went around him and Nick's head reeled. Arlette had survived the terror of the quake, the hazards of the river, the killers that had followed from her home. She had come through all this, to *him*. His sense of relief was so overpowering that it almost staggered him. He felt weak as a child, and clung to Arlette as much for support as out of joy.

"Amen, brother," he heard Garb say. "Amen."

The timeless moment ended. Nick dropped his arms, then stepped back to gaze at his daughter. "You're looking fine, baby," he said.

Her chocolate-brown face broke into a smile. "Thank you, Daddy."

"I've got something for you. A present."

Nick reached into his breast pocket, pulled out the battered cardboard box that he'd brought from the jeweler's.

"Happy birthday," he said.

And there it was, what he'd waited for these weeks, what he'd dreamed about when he touched the box in his pocket—he saw it at last, the shining glow that kindled in her eyes as she gasped and raised the necklace to the light that came through the broken windows of the church.

"It's beautiful!" she said, and hugged him again.

"Turn around," Nick said, "and I'll put it on you."

She turned and swept hair and kerchief off the back of her neck. Nick worked the clasp with clumsy fingers, and she hooked on the earrings.

When she turned around to face him, her smile was brighter than the gems he'd given her.

"Very pretty, young lady," Garb said, and suddenly Nick was aware of the other people watching, Garb and Jason, other young girls and nursing mothers and a large number of children, all of whom had nothing better to do than watch Nick's reunion with his daughter. Nick turned to Jason, feeling suddenly awkward.

"Arlette," Nick said. "This is my friend Jason. He got me down out of a tree the morning after the earthquake."

"Hi," Arlette said. "Thanks for rescuing my daddy."

Jason mumbled something and shook Arlette's hand.

Arlette turned back to Nick. "Did you come from Toussaint? Did you see Gros-Papa and Penelope?"

Nick felt his exhilaration die like a moth shriveled by flame. "Yes," he said. "Yes, but I should talk to your momma."

"She's working in the kitchens," Arlette said. She turned to Garb. "Could you spare me for a little while?" she said.

"Ask Mrs. Perkins," Garb said.

Arlette bounced away, spoke to an elderly black lady— Mrs. Perkins took a moment to admire the necklace and earrings—and then returned.

"She says I can fold the diapers later," she said.

"Got you working already, huh?" Nick said.

Arlette looked serious. "Diapers are going to be a problem. You can only reuse the Pampers so many times, and there aren't a lot of old-fashioned diapers around. So some of the ladies are making them out of old clothes."

"Nick," Garb said, "I'll leave you with Arlette, all right? Come look for me after you've talked to your family, and we'll get you a place to sleep and a place to stash your stuff, okay?"

Jason was standing there looking like he didn't know what to do, so Nick put an arm around him as they followed Arlette from the church. Their route took them over a four-foot-wide chasm. Its banks had partly fallen in, which made it even more of a hazard, but the fissure had been spanned by a wooden bridge, stoutly built of fresh lumber and complete with handrails.

Nick had to conclude that the camp was very well organized.

"*Seven angels!*" shouted the voice over the loudspeaker. "*Seven angels with seven plagues!*"

Nick's stomach rumbled to the scent of baking bread. The kitchen area was shaded by bright picnic awnings, and featured a number of mismatched gas ranges that looked as if they'd been scavenged from wrecked buildings—mobile homes or RVs, possibly, since they were being run off containers of LP gas. There were also grills that could burn charcoal or gas, and a large black smoker so big that it might have once been the boiler of a steam locomotive. Nearby was the dining area, more awnings sheltering long folding tables and benches that looked as if they'd been taken from the nearby grade school.

"Momma?" Arlette called

In the shade beneath the awning, Nick could see Manon only in silhouette, and she was among other women, but he knew her at once—knew the way her chin lifted at the sound of Arlette's voice, knew the arch of her back, knew her familiar pose, one hand resting on her hip. Knew the contralto voice that cried from the shadows.

"Nick! My God!"

Manon rushed from beneath the awning and threw her arms around him. He held her to him and welcomed the moment of bliss before the memory of the house at Toussaint returned to darken his mind.

Manon drew back, held him at the length of her smooth mocha arms. "You don't look *too* bad," she judged.

Which was the sort of phrase that she, and her whole family, used instead of compliments.

"This is Jason," Nick said. "He pulled me out of a tree."

Manon turned to Jason and smiled, pink gum showing beneath her upper lip, the familiar little imperfection that sent a shiver up Nick's spine. "Welcome," she said in her regal way, as if the whole camp belonged to her.

"Ma'am," said Jason.

She looked from Jason to Nick. "Have you eaten? I can sneak you a little food, I think."

"We had some canned stuff," Jason said.

"If you've actually *eaten*," Manon said, "I guess I shouldn't give you something till mealtime. Food isn't—it's kind of scarce, to tell the truth."

"Unclean spirits like frogs!" called the loudspeakers. *"Frogs from the mouth of the dragon!"*

"Manon," Nick said, and then a lump came up in his throat, and he had to start again. "Manon, are there any more of your family around? Because I need to talk to them. I've come from Toussaint and . . . there are things you need to know."

The men, it turned out, were all away from the camp, assigned to gangs scavenging for supplies or looking for refugees. The women were present, either in the kitchens or working elsewhere, and Manon brought them together under the awnings, at one of the dining tables. Nick looked at the faces of the women that circled him, saw the queenly bearing of the three David women, and the less assured faces of the two others, born into less exalted circles, who had married David men.

"It's bad news," Nick said, and for a moment he hesitated. "The people at Toussaint," he said finally. "Gros-Papa, Penelope, Gilly—they've been killed."

He looked at them, saw the shock and pain move in waves across their faces. Saw tears tremble in Arlette's eyes. He took his daughter's hand.

He and Gros-Papa hadn't been friends—the old man had made it clear from the start that Nick wasn't good enough to marry his youngest daughter—but Gilly and Penelope had been kind to him when he and Manon traveled to Toussaint for the obligatory David family reunion every August. But the old man was such a *fixture*, a kind of immovable pillar of firmness and probity and old-fashioned righteousness. A world without Gros-Papa was a different world, even for Nick.

"What happened?" Manon asked. "Was it the big quake the other night?"

"No." He looked at her. "I'm sorry, baby," he said. "They were killed. Murderers, robbers—I don't know."

The women looked at him in horror. "*No!*" Manon's sister turned away with a sob.

"It looked like the—the killers were following you down the bayou," Nick went on. "I was trying to catch up—either to protect you or—or fight them off, somehow."

My God, Nick thought to his own immense astonishment, he had been chasing after murderers, in an open boat, armed with guns he'd swiped from the general store. Now that he'd actually spoken his intentions aloud, it sounded like the most insane thing in the world.

"That was good of you, Nick," Manon said. Then her eyes brimmed over with tears, and she reached for the stunned Arlette, drew her daughter's head to her shoulder.

And then the wailing and crying began, the spontaneous flood of grief and mourning that swept over the David women and their kin. Nick watched helplessly, unable to think of anything that would help, anything that would comfort them—anything except to hang onto Arlette's hand, to let his daughter know that she mattered to him.

At least they were together, he thought. At least they were a family again, even if they were a family in mourning.

Jason was surprised by the intensity of the grief, by the way that Nick's family—or ex-family, he supposed—gave way to tears and cries and utter misery. After a while he began to feel uncomfortable. He wanted to be sympathetic, but he didn't know these people, and it looked as if they weren't going to stop anytime soon. He quietly told Nick he would go check out their belongings, and slipped away.

Jason crossed the chasm on the wooden bridge. The Reverend Frankland's voice bellowed out of loudspeakers, but between the loudspeakers' distortion and Jason's ignorance of the subject matter, he couldn't make out what the reverend was talking about. Whatever it was, Jason wished Frankland would save it for Sunday.

He returned to the highway to find that Conroy and his truck were gone. The guns had been taken to wherever guns were taken here, and the food had been added to the food store. The rest of their belongings, such as they were, had been laid on the grass by the side of the road. The two armed men at the entrance, loafing under their picnic umbrella, were presumably standing guard over their possessions.

The earth shivered with an aftershock. Jason balanced warily, then began to breathe again.

"The Reverend's assigned you to the young men's camp," one of the men said. He rose from his lawn chair. "I'll take you there when you're ready."

Jason shrugged. "Might as well go now," he said. All he had to take with him was the Astroscan, a blanket, and some mess gear. He took the spare bottle of sunscreen and left behind other medical supplies like aspirin and bandages, figuring that Captain Joe had given them to Nick. He slung the Astroscan over one shoulder.

"Son?" the man asked. "I've been meaning to ask. What is that thing?"

"A telescope."

"It don't look like a telescope."

Jason sighed. "I know."

He followed the man over some planks thrown across a pair of fissures—not the elaborate plank bridges he'd used before, but then these fissures weren't as impressive, either—and to an area marked off with string. Inside were rows of tents and awnings, and one large awning, with a plastic ground cover beneath it, where bedrolls, blankets, mattresses, sheets of plastic, and pillows had been piled.

"That's where the boys put their stuff in the daytime," the guard said. "You can put your gear there, and it'll be all right. When people get back, you'll be given a place to sleep."

Jason looked at the site, at the trampled grass and orderly rows of tents. *Welcome to your future,* he thought.

"Thanks."

"Ain't any boys here right now," the man said, looking around. "They're out on a work party."

Jason frowned. "What kind of work party are we talking about, exactly?"

"The boys your age mostly work at salvage. Sorting through rubble, getting food and other useful stuff out of ruins. Some are working with livestock or at planting food crops." The guard rubbed his chin, looked down at Jason. "I don't suppose you know much about farming?"

"I'm a city boy," Jason said. "You want an Internet connection, or a computer upgraded, you talk to me."

"Uh-huh." The man looked blank, as if he'd never heard the word "computer" in his life. He hawked and spat onto the grassy ground. "Well," he said, "I'll do that. In the meantime, you just make yourself at home till the other boys come back."

"Right. Thanks again."

The guard made his way back to the gate. Jason walked under the big awning, plastic crinkling under his feet, and he found a place for his belongings in the shade. Then he went for a walk along the lines of empty tents. Frankland's voice boomed out from loudspeakers. Large wooden crosses were set out at intervals in case of earthquake.

There was nothing to do and no one to talk to. During a moment when the reverend paused in his address, Jason heard a girl's laugh on the breeze, and he remembered that even if there were no boys here, he could maybe talk to a girl or two. He walked toward the borders of the camp, then thought about his telescope. He didn't want to leave it behind in an unguarded place. So he picked it up by its sling, then headed toward the church.

There were a series of camps, he found, laid out along the highway, each with posts and string as boundaries, with wide grassy lanes between them. He passed through another camp, also deserted, that was much like his own, then entered the one with women and children, around the church. The other camps, Jason thought, were set out as if to protect this one.

He wondered if Arlette was back to folding laundry, and looked into the church by one of the side exits. There she was, at the end of the aisle, her eyes focused on her work. The smell of ammonia and the cries of children almost sent Jason back to the camp, but Arlette looked up at that moment and saw him. She gave him a smile, though it was clearly an effort, and Jason stepped into the church, and put his telescope under the table where she was folding laundry.

"I'm sorry about your grandfather," he said. "And the others."

"Thank you." Her eyes were puffy with weeping. "It was a surprise."

"My mother died," Jason said, "in the first quake."

Arlette pressed her lips together, smoothed a child's T-shirt on the table. "Daddy said you'd had a bad time."

"Shall I help you with the folding?"

"If you like."

He folded a pair of blue jeans, added it to the pile. Arlette picked another shirt from a plastic laundry basket, laid it out on the ironing board. Jason looked up at her, at the necklace and earrings she still wore, the strange contrast to her plaid shirt, blue jeans, and kerchief.

"Your dad's been great," he said. "I don't know if I'd have made it without him."

"He said the same about you."

"He did?" Jason felt a rush of pleasure. "Sometimes he seemed to get pretty impatient with me."

Arlette nodded, her lips set in a private smile. "Yes," she said. "He does that."

The voice on the loudspeaker rose to a chorus of "Amens," and then there was a click and the sound died away. Arlette gave a sigh of relief.

"Sermon's over?" Jason said.

Arlette leaned close to Jason, a conspiratorial glint in her eyes, and lowered her voice so that no one could overhear. "The mothers here convinced Brother Frankland that the loudspeakers had to be turned off for an hour in the mornings, and in the afternoons, so that the children could have their naps."

Jason leaned closer to join Arlette's conspiracy, lowered his own voice. "So," he said, "what's it really like here?"

Arlette hesitated. "Well," she said finally, "it's Brother Frankland's camp. Brother Frankland's food. So we play by his rules."

"And what are they, exactly?"

Arlette looked uncomfortable. "I've only been here for two days. I really shouldn't judge, but I think he and the others are doing their best."

Jason considered. "I suppose it beats being out in the wilderness in a boat," he said.

Arlette looked up at him, nodded. But her eyes, he saw, were troubled.

"Brought you some more clothes," a voice intruded. Two more girls entered, both white, both in their mid-teens. They carried a plastic laundry hamper between the two of them, and set it next to Arlette. They looked at Jason, then at Arlette.

"Throw him back, girl," one of them advised. "He's too small."

Jason flushed. The girls, laughing, bounced back to their work. Arlette tried to conceal her smile.

"Well," she said, turning to the pile of laundry, "looks like we've got our work cut out."

TWENTY-SIX

At half past 6 o'clock in the morning it cleared up, and believing the danger over I left home, to see what injury my neighbours had sustained. A few minutes after my departure there was another shock, extremely violent—I hurried home as fast as I could, but the agitation of the earth was so great that it was with much difficulty I kept my balance—the motion of the earth was about twelve inches to and fro. I cannot give you an accurate description of this moment; the earth seemed convulsed—the houses shook very much—chimneys falling in every direction. —The loud hoarse roaring which attended the earthquake, together with the cries, screams, and yells of the people, seems still ringing in my ears.

Extract from a letter to a gentleman in Lexington, from his friend at New Madrid, dated 16 December, 1811

The radio calls were confused. *Officer in trouble. Shots fired.* But it was David calling. Omar recognized his voice.

Omar spun the wheel of his cruiser and mashed the accelerator to the floor. Turned on the flashing lights as acceleration punched him back into his seat. There was a jar and a cry of metal as the car bottomed out on a partly-filled-in crevasse. Omar didn't slow down.

In front of the A.M.E. campground he found a half-dozen vehicles with flashing lights, all casting long evening shadows across the highway. A big car, an old 1972 Oldsmobile with one primer-gray fender, had crossed the highway and was nose-down in the bar ditch. There were bullets stars in the windows. The driver's door was open and a body lay by the door.

David stood nearby, his arms akimbo and his cap tipped forward over his eyes. There was a smile on his face. Omar saw him unharmed and felt his racing heart begin to ease.

A knot of deputies, some of them Omar's specials in civilian clothes, stood around him in a knot. One skinny black man was seated on the asphalt at the rear of the car, his hands cuffed behind his back.

Omar parked and almost vaulted from his car. He ran to his son.

"Are you all right?" Omar called.

David looked at him, his smile broadening. "I'm okay, Dad. Just shot a guy, is all." He gave a little laugh. "It's martial law, right? It's okay."

Omar looked at the dead driver, saw a young black man, maybe twenty, with splashes of bright Technicolor blood all over him. Then he glanced at the camp, saw the wall of men, the hostile black faces, the stony eyes.

The smell of food floated on the air. The camp had been served their supper just before this happened, and Omar saw plates being carried by some of the onlookers, but nobody seemed to be eating.

Reverend Morris stood among them, his face long, a brooding in his eyes. And for some reason the calm sorrow on Morris's face seemed more frightening than fury on the dozens of faces that surrounded him.

Omar looked at David again. David, standing easy, smiling among his friends, among the neighbors who'd known him since he was a boy.

"Okay," he said. "We take pictures of the scene. Then bag the deceased and send him to Tree Simpson." He took David's arm, drew him aside. "And you tell me what happened." *And then we work out what to tell everyone else,* he thought to himself.

An amateur cop, son of the King Kleagle of Louisiana, had just killed some black kid. Omar knew that there would be consequences to a story like that, whether David was justified or not, whether there was martial law or not.

In fact, he couldn't think of any *good* consequences at all. Which was why it was important why David's story had to cover all the bases, and why everyone else had to tell the same story as David.

Omar was relieved when David's story sounded okay. A couple bad boys had got stir-crazy in the camp, decided to go for a joy ride even though there was noplace to go. Were in their car before anyone knew they'd got into the parking lot. And then ignored shouted orders to stop, until David drew his firearm and shot the driver.

"Everyone here saw the same thing? They'll all back your story?"

David shrugged. "Sure. It's what happened."

Omar nodded. "Good," he said. "Now what I want you to do is give me your pistol, then go to my office at the courthouse. We'll do the paperwork."

David looked at him in surprise. "I don't get to keep my gun?"

"Not one that's been used in a shooting, no. And you're off-duty until Tree Simpson rules the shooting was justified."

Omar collected David's gun and sent him off to Shelburne City. He sent the handcuffed boy in another car. He told the deputies they'd each have to give a statement at the end of their shift. He sent one of the deputies back to Shelburne City for a camera, then told the deputies who had rushed to the emergency, and who weren't normally assigned to the camp, to go about their normal business.

"Boss." Merle's voice quiet in his ear. "I need to tell you something."

At Merle's hushed tones Omar felt his heart sink. His son, he thought, trembled on the edge of the abyss.

"What is it," he said, and the words almost failed to leave his throat.

Merle drew him aside. "David got a little carried away, there," he said quietly.

Omar licked his lips. "Tell me."

"The kid drove off, okay? David drew and fired, and the car went across the road and into the ditch."

"It's martial law," Omar managed. "That was justified."

Merle nodded. "Sure, Omar. But what David did next was

maybe a little, I don't know, *dire*. See, that Negro wasn't dead when he crashed the car. David pulled him from the car and shot him twice when he was lying on the road."

Omar's mouth went dry. He took off his hat, wiped sweat from his forehead.

Merle put a hand on Omar's shoulder. "I'll stand by your boy, okay? We'll look after David. He'll be all right."

"Any witnesses?" Omar said.

"Some of the other deputies. They'll be okay." Merle looked sour. "But some people in the camp, yeah. They saw it. And Morris, he saw it, too."

"Reverend Morris," Omar repeated.

"Yeah. Morris. He was in his car, about to leave the camp just when the whole thing happened, got a bird's-eye view." Merle nodded toward the camp. "There he stands, with the others. Watching us like a black buzzard settin' on a power line."

Omar closed his eyes, felt himself sway like a willow in the wind. Even with his eyes shut he could feel the touch of Morris' hooded gaze.

"I'll talk to him," Omar said, "and we'll see what he says."

He crossed the road and took a long stride across the bar ditch and walked through the grass where the people at the camp had parked their cars. As he came closer he could see the tension grow in the knot of people around Morris, see the shoulders hunching as if against a blow, the fury blaze brighter in the stony eyes.

There were white people in the camp, Omar knew. A few, anyway. Where were *they*?

Omar politely touched the brim of his hat. "Reverend Morris?" he said. "I understand you may have been a witness to the shooting?"

The preacher's eyes did not leave Omar's face. His words were enunciated with care, with great precision. "I saw the crime," he said. "Yes."

The crime. Not the accident or the pursuit or the shooting. *The crime.*

Omar felt his face prickle with heat. Kept his voice under control, kept his hands calm, thumbs hooked over his belt.

"Do you want to come to the courthouse and make a statement?"

"Possibly," Morris allowed. "Possibly I will make a statement. Possibly I will reserve my statement and give it to the federal authorities at a later time."

Omar's head swam. He licked his lips, managed to speak. "Why would you do that, Reverend?" he asked.

Morris hooded his eyes and pretended to consider. Black bastard was enjoying it, Omar thought. *He couldn't beat me in the election, but he's got me whipped now. Whipped like a cur dog in a hailstorm.*

"I saw your son shoot that boy," Morris said. "He put two bullets into him without reason. What would be the point of giving a statement to *you*?"

"You tell him!" a woman called from the back of the crowd. "You tell him!"

There was a chorus of assent. Omar stiffened. Behind his sunglasses he looked at the faces in the crowd, tried to memorize them. The faces he already knew he was going to need to remember.

The hostile masks swam before his gaze. His heart fluttered in his chest.

"If you want to make a statement," he told Morris, "you can make it any time."

Omar turned his back carefully and walked away through he grass and between the parked cars to the highway. He nad turned his back on more than the camp, he knew; he had turned his back on his life, his position. Every thing he'd achieved, every advancement to which he'd clawed a path. His future.

"Is there anybody else from Shelburne City in the camp right now?" Omar asked Merle.

"There were some church people in there, but they left before the shooting. Morris is the last."

"Nobody leaves the camp," Omar said. "Nobody but Morris."

He got in the car and got on the radio. He got ahold of Micah Knox, and told him that he and the rest of the

Crusaders were relieved from their regular duty and should meet him on the highway by the John Deere dealership north of the Corp limit.

Omar knew that his own life—that everything he'd built and stood for—was already lost. But if he had to move heaven and earth to do it, he was going to save his boy.

Trucks began rolling into the compound in late afternoon, bringing people back to the men's camps. Jason was introduced to the leader—"guide"—of his unit, a lanky red-haired man named Magnusson. Mr. Magnusson had a band on one arm that had probably once been white. Though he looked and for the most part smelled as if he'd been working in the hot sun for days, his chin was shaven blue and there was an alert look in his eyes. He called everyone by their surnames, as if first names were too much to bother with.

"We'll be heading in to dinner when we're called by the PA, okay?" he said. "We're the Samaritans."

"Samaritans," Jason said. "Right."

"Thing to remember is, you don't leave the camp unless you're working, or unless you're called. People are doing important work out there, and they don't need you bothering them."

Jason didn't like the sound of this. Everyone was supposed to stay behind a fence made of string?

"When can I see my friends?" he asked.

"Morning and evening services." Mr. Magnusson squinted as he looked down at Jason. "What denomination are you, by the way?"

Jason hesitated. He had a suspicion a truthful answer—his mother's belief in pyramid power and Atlantis, and his father's lack of any religion whatever—would not be received well.

"What kind do you have around here?" he asked.

"Well, Reverend Franklin, he's sort of his own denomination—or he's multidenominational, depending on how you look at it. He's Charismatic and Fundamentalist, anyway. We've also got Baptists and Pentecostals, okay? Lots of

Lutherans, but our pastor was killed in the first quake, so we've kind of split up among all the others. The Catholics—uhh, the same. Not that there were so many Catholics to begin with." He narrowed his eyes and looked at Jason. "You're not Catholic, are you?"

"I'm Presbyterian," Jason said.

"Well," Magnusson said, "we ain't got any of those. So I guess you'll just have to pick a congregation from the ones we got." A gleam entered his eye. "I'd recommend Brother Frankland's," he said. "He saved *me*."

Jason had hoped that Presbyterianism might leave him out of this issue altogether. "I'll pick the one that my friends join," he said.

Mr. Magnusson nodded. "Fine. Any questions?"

Jason pointed at the man's arm. "What's the white armband mean?"

"It means I'm in charge. Any more questions?"

"I guess not."

"Good," he said. "I want you to buddy up with someone who will show you the ropes and keep you out of trouble. And that someone will be Haynes over there." He pointed to a skinny, freckled boy in a baseball cap. He lowered his voice, bent to Jason's ear. "Now Sam Haynes lost his parents in the quake, okay? So what I want you to do is look after him, all right?" He put a hand on Jason's shoulder.

"Okay," said Jason, confused by this brisk, overefficient manner of intimacy.

Mr. Magnusson straightened, shouted out. "Haynes! Heaven-o! I want you to meet Jason here."

Sam Haynes was a few years older than Jason. Jason shook his hand. Haynes didn't seem to have much to say. "I want you to show Jason the ropes," Mr. Magnusson said. He picked up a roll of large-sized plastic garbage bags, tore a bag off the roll, then handed it to Jason. "This is your ground cover. You sleep on this."

Jason looked at the bag. "Right," he said.

"You two go have fun now."

Jason slung his telescope over his shoulder and prepared

to follow Haynes to whatever fun might be found in this place.

"Hey!" Mr. Magnusson called after him. "Adams!"

Jason turned around. "Yes?"

"What's that *thing* on your shoulder?"

Jason looked at the Astroscan and decided he was already fed up with this place. "It's a portable nuclear reactor," he said.

Mr. Magnusson hesitated. His eyes narrowed, as if he was trying to decide whether or not to size up Jason for a liar. Jason tried to assume an expression of earnest good intentions.

"A nuclear reactor, huh?" Magnusson said. "Like the one in Mississippi that blew up?"

"Well," Jason said, "not as big."

Mr. Magnusson hesitated again. He propped his wiry arms on his hips. "*That* one ain't going to blow up, right?"

Jason tried to exude authority. "Not if people don't mess with it," he said.

"Well." Mr. Magnusson chewed his lip. "You don't let anyone touch it, then."

"I won't." Jason decided he'd better ease away before his guide had time to think about this, so he gave Mr. Magnusson a little wave and headed into the camp.

Haynes wasn't much company. He didn't seem interested in whether Jason had a nuclear reactor, or indeed in anything else. He just pointed out a place under an awning, near his own, where Jason could stretch out his plastic bag to sleep on.

"Or you can pick any place that's empty. Plenty of empty places."

"Yeah," Jason said. "I noticed that." The camp seemed more than half-deserted, as if it had been laid out and equipped for a much larger group of people.

"When do we eat?" Jason asked.

"Soon, I hope." Haynes dropped onto the grass, then flopped onto his back. He pulled his baseball cap down over his eyes. "Let me know when we're called."

There were about a dozen Samaritans altogether. They and another group called the Galileans were called to dinner a couple hours later. The meal consisted of a modest piece of baked fish, some mixed vegetables out of cans, and a large scoop of white rice, all served on a compartmented plastic tray that, Jason suspected, had been plundered from a local school. Water to drink, though younger kids got a small glass of milk. During the meal a gospel choir practiced beneath a nearby awning, sometimes swinging into a gorgeous mass harmony before the conductor, dissatisfied with something, stopped them and made them start again.

Jason ate his meal in less than five minutes and asked the others if he was allowed more. He wasn't.

He had eaten better when he was a refugee.

Mealtime lasted fifteen minutes, after which the Samaritans took their trays to a galvanized trough, washed the trays, rinsed them in another trough, and stacked them for the next shift. After this, Mr. Magnusson marched them back to the young men's camp.

After that it was another long wait, till it was time for church.

It was a long empty road between the A.M.E. camp and Shelburne City. Reverend Morris' old Ford could be seen for half a mile, even in the fading light, and that was enough.

Micah Knox pulled in front of Morris in a pickup truck he'd borrowed from Jedthus. Another one of the Crusaders pulled out behind the Ford, then tapped its bumper from behind. And then, when everyone had stopped to examine the accident, Omar drove up in his cruiser, parked opposite the Ford, and stepped from the car.

Most unexpected was the lack of surprise in Morris' eyes. There was a strange silent confirmation in those eyes, as if Omar was only attesting to the truth of the reverend's opinion of him when he raised his pistol and fired it five times through the window.

After that, the pickup rammed the Ford broadside until it tipped over into the bar ditch and rolled onto its roof.

Gasoline was poured into the interior and set alight.

An accident. That's what would go on the report. Failing light, an old man in an old car, on an old earthquake-torn two-lane blacktop. He must have lost control.

Omar would let someone else find the wreck, report the accident, fill out the papers. He would be miles away.

"Beautiful!" Knox said. He stomped up and down the asphalt in his heavy boots, uneven teeth bared in a grin. "Just like in *Hunter*."

"There are more witnesses in the camp," Omar said.

"Beautiful!" said Knox.

Firelight danced in his shotgun eyes.

Omar arranged for charges to be dropped against the boy who had been in the car with the driver David had killed. He turned him over to Knox and one of his friends to be driven back to camp, and he was never seen again.

No one would miss him. He'd been released from jail, the camp wasn't expecting him back, and that was that.

He had gone where the woodbine twineth.

Omar used the shooting incident that day, plus the earlier shooting at Ozie Starks', as leverage with the parish council and got permission to fence off the two refugee camps. That night he arranged for chain link and barbed wire, fence post diggers, and extra personnel. Extra cars. Extra guns.

They would start the ball rolling first thing in the morning.

Nick spent the rest of the afternoon floating. A glorious sense of well-being had fallen on him, and he felt almost free of gravity, bounding over the torn surface of the Arkansas bluff like an Apollo astronaut skipping over the surface of the moon. He had come through fire and water to find Manon and Arlette, through snakes and a hail of buckshot, past madmen armed with guns and a city choking on poison gas. They were alive, and he was alive, and they were alive together.

He had seen Manon's smile and the glow in Arlette's eyes when she looked at her birthday present. He was happy, and he wanted to bask in his happiness.

But he couldn't. Manon and her family were in mourning, and Nick had to conceal his joy, had to pretend that sorrow flooded his heart instead of delight. His was a difficult happiness to conceal; he had to try to remember not to let a ridiculous grin break out on his face, or make too light-hearted a remark.

He helped Manon with her work, happy just to be around her. Supper had to be prepared, in an improvised kitchen, for something like a hundred and forty people under the instruction of an elderly white lady who had once been in charge of a school cafeteria. The old woman was very careful of her calorie counts: she ordered rice, vegetables, and fish to be weighed out very carefully.

"Twenty-two hundred calories per day for everyone except the people who have work assignments," Manon explained. "Five thousand for nursing mothers, or for folks searching the swamps, raising food, or toting bricks. Milk only for growing children, since we don't have many dairy cattle in the area."

"That's not a lot of calories," Nick said.

"It's enough to get by, they tell us. But we're all going to be fashionably thin when we get out of this."

Nick looked at her, and his hand twitched with the impulse to pat her butt. "I always thought your weight was fine just where it is."

A smile twitched at her lips. "That's one of the things I liked about you."

Nick hadn't told anyone that he and Manon were divorced, so he'd been given a place to sleep in the married men's camp. Married men were assigned to the same work units as their wives and their children, which allowed families to meet during meals. The group that Nick shared with Manon, rather oddly called the Thessalonians, ate last of all, after the lady Thessalonians fed everyone else.

Even the late, scanty meal did not dim Nick's joy. He was with his family. That was all that mattered.

After supper was over, just as the sun was touching the western horizon, the PA called everyone to a religious service. The church was too small to contain everyone, so they all sat to one side of the steel church building, on the grassy sward between the church and the young men's camp.

The chorus—massed voices combining the choirs of all the local churches—opened with a rousing version of "Lord Help Me to Pray." Arlette and some others bounced up to clap along, but most people seemed too tired.

After the song ended the Reverend Frankland bounced up on a box, beaming left and right. "Heaven-o!" he said, and his people chanted "Heaven-o!" right back at him. He thanked the massed choir, promised more music for later, and began by welcoming Nick and Jason to Rails Bluff, and asked them to stand so that people would know who they were. Nick rose, feeling awkward, and saw Jason standing about a hundred feet away. People shouted out, "Welcome!" and "Glad you could make it, brothers!" Nick waved, mouthed the words "Thank you," and sat again.

Then Frankland spoke of the deaths of Gros-Papa and the others, murdered in Toussaint just a short distance away, and asked for a moment of silence to pray for them.

"Who told him about your daddy?" Nick whispered to Manon after the silence ended. "I never mentioned it."

"Someone else in the family, I suppose." Manon said. "Or maybe your friend Jason. You'd be surprised how fast word spreads in this place."

"What's he saying *now*?" Nick wondered, because what Frankland seemed to be saying was that Gros-Papa's death had been predicted in the Bible, specifically in Matthew, Chapter Twenty-Four.

"Did he really say your papa was in the *Bible*?" Nick whispered.

"Hush," Manon said.

"Which means we must beware!" Frankland proclaimed. "The world outside Rails Bluff is becoming a more and more dangerous place. The other day some of our people were shot at, and now we receive news of a mass murder almost on our doorstep. We must venture out only with care, brothers and sisters. The earthquake predicted in Revelations Six has come to pass. And following the earthquake, as predicted in Revelations Chapter Eight, has come the poisoning of the waters—even the *President of the United States* admits that the waters have been poisoned—and has commanded the people to flee the lakes and rivers.

"*'Woe!'*" Frankland said, pitching his voice a little differently to make it clear he was quoting, "'woe, woe to the inhabitants of the earth.'" He looked at a list in his hand. "Let me give you the news of the Last Days."

He then gave the day's headlines—the evacuation thrown into chaos by earthquake, cities knocked flat, homeless people wandering the earth in search of food and shelter, the stock market dropping into a bottomless pit, investment and savings wiped out, radiation drifting over the South, armies poised in the Middle East, ready for war.

And to each piece of news Frankland related another piece of the Bible, discussing each of the day's events in connection with prophecy.

Nick listened in amazement. He turned to Manon to ask if this happened *every* night, but her sharp glance warned him not to speak. So he looked out over the crowd, to see if they were as astonished by this as he was. Some were listening with great attention, but most seemed only tired and bored.

Jason, sitting amid a group of strangers, had a scowl on his face.

Frankland finished with a lengthy prayer for the well-being of loved ones outside Rails Bluff. "We'll have lights out in twenty minutes," he said. "Everyone please be in their beds by then, except for those who are on guard duty."

The choir cut in then, moaning out a melancholy arrangement of "I Don't Know Why I Need to Cry Sometimes" as everyone stood to leave. "Is that *normal*?" Nick asked Manon, pitching his voice low so that strangers couldn't hear him over the sound of the massed choir.

Manon glanced around before answering. "Normal for this place," she said.

"The man's off his rocker."

Manon bit her lip, then took his hand between her two

hands. "Baby," she said, "whose food is your child eating?"

Nick looked at her, then gave a slow nod. He looked down at Arlette, standing between them, and put his arm around her.

They were safe, they were together, they were getting their calories. For this, Nick could put up with an eccentric interpretation of current events.

He saw Jason approach them through the dispersing crowd. The boy seemed more amused than anything.

"Boy," Jason said, "that was pretty trippy."

"Ssh," Manon said, and gave him a look. "Not so loud."

Nick put a hand on the boy's shoulder. "Look," he said, "we're eating the man's food. So we take his sermons seriously."

"If he wants me to be all that serious," Jason said, "he can give me bigger portions."

"*Hush,*" Manon said. Her look was severe, all that commanding David heritage gazing down her nose at the boy.

Jason hesitated for a moment, then said, agreeably enough, "Yes, ma'am," though his response seemed more a result of calculation—perhaps even politeness—than intimidation.

Out of the corner of his eye, Nick saw Arlette give Jason a shared look of—of what? Not encouragement, exactly, but complicity. The alliance of a pair of adolescents against the absurdities of the adult world.

Nick was more sympathetic to Arlette and Jason than they knew.

"Listen," he said. "We're guests here, okay. We just do as we're told till we figure out what's what."

Jason shrugged. "I won't make trouble," he said.

"Good," Nick said. "Make sure you don't."

There are crackers with guns here. Due caution is necessary. That was the message he tried to put into his voice.

Jason said goodnight and made his way to his camp. Manon and Nick walked with Arlette to the string boundaries of what Frankland called the young ladies' camp, and kissed her goodnight. Her arms went around Nick's neck.

"Goodnight, Daddy. I'm so glad you're here."

A bubble of happiness rose in Nick's heart. "Happy birthday, baby," he said. "Sweet dreams."

He kissed her cheek and sent her off into the soft May night. The voices of the choir hung magically in the air. Joy whirled through Nick's senses. He looked at Manon, saw on her face a thoughtful little smile.

"Yes?" he said.

She shook her head. "Nothing, baby."

"Are you all right?"

She took a long breath, let it out. Shook her head. "I guess so."

Nick put his arm around her waist, a motion that felt so easy, so natural, that he was almost surprised at himself. She accepted it, rested her head briefly against his shoulder, then gently detached herself.

"Married women's camp," she said. "It's right here."

"Can we talk?" he asked. "About what's going on here? Why is this camp so empty? Where did everyone go?"

"One of the ladies told me there were many more people here after the first quake. But the government evacuated most of them."

"Leaving only Frankland's hard core?"

"I suppose so." Manon looked uncertain. "But more people came in after the second big quake, including my family. So now it's about fifty-fifty."

"Can we talk about what we're going to do?"

Her eyes were serious. "Not yet," she said. "Wait till you've been here a day or two."

"Okay."

"Sleep well, Nick." She reached out, touched his hand for a moment, then withdrew, walking into the married women's camp.

Nick stood for a moment and savored the touch on his hand, the memory of Arlette's kiss. The choir's distant chant quivered in his soul.

And then he made his way to the plastic sheet that served as his bed.

* * *

The aftershock jolted Jason awake. He woke with his heart in his throat, eyes staring wide into the darkness. Then someone screamed, screamed right in his ear.

He sat up, felt the earth shudder under him. It wasn't a bad shock—he knew, he was from California, and besides he'd become an expert on aftershocks by now—but why was someone screaming?

The screamer was Haynes, the buddy Mr. Magnusson had assigned him. The boy was sitting up and uttering one terrified shriek after another, full-blown animal screams vented into the night. They rang in Jason's ears.

"Hey," Jason said. "Hey, it's all right. It's not bad."

Boys ran past, sprinting for the big wooden crosses that had been stretched at intervals on the ground. Jason wanted to tell them not to bother, that the aftershock was fairly mild. But Jason couldn't be heard because Haynes kept screaming, one wail after another, pausing only to fill his lungs. Jason could see tears on his face. He patted Haynes' back. "Hey. You're dreaming. It's *okay*."

Other boys were screaming, Jason now heard. Boys all through the camp, and through the little kids' camp next door. The shock had jerked them into the world of nightmare, into memories of the loss of their homes, their property, and sometimes their families. The eerie sounds bubbling up in the darkness around him made Jason's hair stand on end.

"It's *okay*!" Jason shouted, patting Haynes on the back.

Haynes stopped for breath, gulped in air. Then he turned away from Jason, dropped to the ground, and began to cry.

"It's okay, it's okay," Jason repeated. He couldn't tell if Haynes was awake or not. He might still be stuck in some nightmare.

Jason was awake now, that was for sure. The wails and sobs echoing through the dark scared him more than the aftershock.

Haynes seemed to calm down a bit, and Jason tried to get back to sleep. That didn't seem likely. Seemingly at random a boy would wake up shrieking, and someone else would answer from across the camp, and soon there would be a chorus of cries and sobbing and wailing. Jason began to feel a kind of pressure on his mind, the pressure of dread, slowly increasing. He didn't want to be like these other kids, wailing in the night, desperate for the touch of comfort, desperate to live in a world where the earth did not move.

Jason yearned for dawn.

The wails and cries didn't stop. Jason took his plastic sack and his blanket to another part of the camp, away from the awning and out under the stars, and there he stretched out on his back, his head pillowed on his hands.

The stars wheeled overhead, beautiful and implacable like all nature. He gazed up and tried to remember their names.

He must have closed his eyes, because next thing he knew it was dawn, and the PA system was booming out instructions for all groups to report to the church for services.

"I was a pornographer! I made a profit out of poisoning the minds of children!" Mr. Magnusson's voice boomed through the still morning air. The man walked back and forward, holding the microphone to his lips. The dawn glinted on his thin red hair. There was a strange, strained smile on his face, as if he knew he was supposed to be happy but couldn't recollect why.

"I did my best to destroy my community!" he said. "All I cared about was the money!"

There was a regular section of people who cheered and applauded. "Tell it!" they yelled, and "Praise God!" Among those cheering was Frankland.

Jason sat crosslegged on the beaten grass and watched in amazement. He had just dragged himself from the young men's compound, and hoped that breakfast wouldn't be too far away. Frankland had started off with some announcements. Jason, still trying to crank his eyes open, hadn't paid much attention to these, and the next thing he knew the repentant pornographer was strutting out before his cheering section.

Magnusson couldn't have been *in* the pornography, Jason

decided. He couldn't feature anyone paying money to see Magnusson naked.

"But then the earthquake happened, and my business was destroyed!" Magnusson said. "And soon I learned that God was sending me a message!"

The burden of the message, it appeared, was that the man had to stay clear of pornography. As this message was elaborated at length, Jason believed he could see tears on the former pornographer's face.

This guy is in charge of me, Jason thought. *He is my* guide.

Everyone applauded when the message ended. Some of the applause seemed more enthusiastic than others. Frankland stepped forward and thanked the pornographer for his contribution. Then he looked into the audience and called on someone named Jonathan.

Jonathan was a boy about Jason's age, one he'd seen around the young men's compound but not spoken to. The boy said that he used to worship Satan, and listen to Satanic music and do Satanic things like animal sacrifices, but now he knew that Jesus was Lord and not Satan, and he trusted Jesus to get him through the Last Days. Frankland hugged Jonathan when he was done, and almost everyone applauded.

After Jonathan came a volunteer, a weathered-looking woman named Cora, who said she used to run around and do drugs, and hang around with people who ran around and did drugs, and she *had the tattoos to prove it!*—there was laughter at this—but now she was *clean for Jesus*, and if there was a single man out there who believed in the Lord, monogamy, and the Harley-Davidson motorcycle, she would like to meet him. There was more laughter, but Frankland seemed a little embarrassed by this solicitation, and he announced that they were out of time, and sent everyone to breakfast.

Omar had the camp surrounded at dawn, deputies and special deputies and Knox's Crusaders. All were conspicuously armed, shotguns or rifles displayed. Merle carried his little submachine gun slung under his arm. Once everyone was in place around the silent camp, the fence-builders moved in and started putting up chain link in a long shimmering curtain around the camp, starting with the north and east perimeter, where the camp backed onto an area of hardwood forest.

"It's a good thing, the fence," Knox said with his feverish grin. "It's psychological. It divides *us* from *them*. The *mud* people from the *real* people." He nodded. "The fence is a *good* thing," he said, as if trying on the concept one more time. "A *good* thing."

Omar didn't answer. A dull ache throbbed in his head, and a sharper pain griped in his stomach. It felt like the worst hangover he'd had in his life, even though he hadn't been drinking.

It was the heat, he figured. He'd just got too used to air-conditioning.

When the fence builders started work there was a lot of movement in the camp, people rushing about in and out of the outlandish shelters they'd made of cotton wagons. People stared and pointed at the circle of deputies with their guns. There was a lot of noise, a few angry voices raised above the others. It was time for the inmates' morning meal, but the volunteers from the A.M.E. church, who usually prepared the meals, had been stopped outside town at a sheriff's department roadblock. Omar would just as soon have given the refugees their meal—if that would have kept them quiet—but he didn't want anyone in the camp telling the A.M.E. people about David and the shooting, because once any version that wasn't Omar's version got out, there would be all manner of hell to pay.

Omar planned to keep Hell strictly behind that chainlink fence.

"See, what you want to do," Knox said, "is alternate random rewards with random punishments. It's all about behaviorism." He looked up at Omar from under the brim of his cap. Sweat covered his face with a silver sheen. "You heard about behaviorism," he said, "right?"

"I have a feeling I'm about to," Omar said, and wished Knox would just shut the hell up.

Knox bounced up and down on the steel-capped toes of his boots. "Behaviorism's *science*, see," he said. "Real science. They worked it out with rats. See, Omar, people—and rats, I guess—they assume that when something happens, there has to be a *reason*. If something good happens, there has to be a reason for it. And the same with bad things. So if you reward people for no reason, other people will figure there has to be a reason for it, and they'll try to behave, so they can earn a reward. And if you punish people at *random*, for no reason at all, then the *other* people think there has to be a reason, so they'll be extra-careful not to do anything to piss you off.

"So what you do, see—" Knox grinned "—is give some little girl a box of candy. And then you beat the shit out of her big brother. And anyone who sees it will think that the little girl and her brother both *deserved* it, somehow. They'll start to blame the *brother* for what *you* did. They'll say it's *his fault*. They'll say, 'Why are you making trouble? Why can't you be more like your sister?'" Knox cocked his hat onto the back of his head and grinned at Omar again. "That's how you control a big group of people, like you got here. You use science and turn them against each other."

"Really," Omar said. His headache throbbed behind his eyes.

"I read about it in a book about the Holocaust," Knox said. "The Nazis used behaviorism on the Jews. They'd punish Jews at random—beat them, shoot them, whatever—and the *other* Jews would say, 'Oh, it's all the fault of those trouble-making Jews, the Jews who aren't like us! They're making trouble for everyone.' Did you ever see *Schindler's List*?"

"Nope," said Omar. "It's propaganda, anyway."

"It's got a great scene of behaviorism at work. There's this SS officer named Amon Goeth, and he's in charge of a prison camp. Every so often he gets up on his balcony with a rifle, and he shoots some Jew at random. Just guns him down!" Knox's grin turned admiring. "So then the *other* Jews start working faster and harder, because they figure that Goeth shot the first Jew for being lazy, and the shooting was the dead Jew's fault. It's a great movie! I practically had an orgasm in that scene."

"Uh-huh," Omar said, and gave Knox a suspicious look. Didn't he know that the movie was made by a Jew?

"Amon Goeth was a kind of tragic figure," Knox went on. "He was on top of the world. He could kill anybody he wanted, all the women wanted to fuck him, and everyone was paying him money for privileges. He was like a king! An Aryan king! But then he fell in love with this Jewish girl, and his whole life was destroyed." He looked solemn for a moment, but then brightened. "But he returned to the true faith in the end. He shouted 'Heil Hitler!' before the Mongols hanged him."

"Mongols?" Omar said, surprised.

"You know. Russians."

"Oh."

"A great movie, *Schindler's List*. Sort of an instruction manual for the Holocaust. Shows you everything you want to do, and all the mistakes you want to avoid."

Omar felt sweat trickle down his temples. The sun was burning a hole in the top of his head, right through his hat, and it was barely morning.

"Of course," he said, "everyone knows the Holocaust didn't really happen."

Knox looked at him in surprise. "You think that?"

"Don't you?"

"No! I mean, I know we have to *say* we don't believe it, because that's the way politics work and we don't want to frighten the bourgeoisie, but I think the Holocaust was real! I think it was the greatest thing in human history!"

Omar felt a shock running along his nerves, almost a physical shock. He'd never heard anyone say something like that before.

"I'd like to go to Auschwitz," Knox said, "and just roll around in the dirt. It's holy ground, man! I'd like to take some of the dirt back with me and put it on an altar and *wor-*

ship it. Auschwitz was *real science*, Omar. The Kraut-eaters had their act together there. Real science." He tapped Omar on the arm, stared up with his strange green eyes. "That's what you need here, Omar. Science."

"I guess." Revulsion for Knox shivered through him. Even if the Holocaust actually happened, even if it was a good thing, Knox was carrying it a mite far with all this worship of Auschwitz dirt.

The sun burned Omar's head and shoulders. The metal barrel of his Remington shotgun, resting against his shoulder, was beginning to scorch a hole in his flesh. He shifted the gun, rested the butt on his hip. He couldn't understand how Knox could stand it in his long-sleeved flannel shirt. The shirt was dark with sweat stains, and Knox had a strange chemical-bog odor, but he refused to wear anything more suitable to the climate.

"Snake!" Knox screamed, and jumped six feet. Adrenaline jolted through Omar and he leaped to the side himself, his eyes scanning the grass near Knox to find the poison monster.

"Snake! Snake! Snake!" Knox said, doing a frantic dance in his heavy boots. Omar spotted the snake whipsawing its way through the grass, and breathed easy.

"That's just a little ol' bullsnake," he said. "It won't hurt you."

"Oh God, I hate snakes!" Knox said, still dancing. "I'm getting out of here."

He marched away. Omar wanted to laugh.

Some Aryan superman, he thought. Scared of bridges, snakes, and who knew what else?

Omar strolled away on a walk along the camp perimeter. His deputies had kept the inmates away from their vehicles, which were parked on the grass parking lot and along the highway, and he walked along between the row of deputies and the cars. Crowds of people were moving in the camp, he saw, and there was a lot of murmuring and gesturing going on.

They hadn't found a leader yet, though. No one to tell the others what to do, no one to speak for them. Omar looked for the people he'd marked the day before, the ones who had witnessed David shooting the runaway and who would have to go where the woodbine twineth. He thought he saw some of them, but he couldn't be sure.

"Hey. Hey, Sheriff."

A man called to him from the verge of the invisible perimeter between the camp and the line of deputies. He was a middle-aged white man, bespectacled, nervous-looking. Somehow he'd been mistaken for an African Methodist Episcopal and put in here, or maybe he'd come with a black person or something.

"Get back there!" said the nearest deputy.

"I want to talk to the sheriff. Please."

"That's okay," Omar said. "I'll talk to him." He strolled up to the white man. "What can I do for you?"

"I was wondering," the man said, and then hesitated. He lowered his voice. "Can you put me someplace else? Someplace with—" He lowered his voice even more. "Someplace with more Caucasians?"

Omar grinned. And then his amusement faltered, because he realized that the man was a witness to what David had done. Or a potential witness, or at least someone who he couldn't sift out from the real witnesses.

He would *never* sort them out, he realized with a chill. He hadn't thought that out before, not in so many words.

Nausea shivered along Omar's nerves. He looked at the nervous white man and knew him for doomed. *You are doomed*, he thought at the man, but his thoughts lacked conviction.

"I'm afraid not, sir," he said. "There's no other place to put you."

"Please, Sheriff!" the man blurted. "I know who you are! I've seen you on television. Can't you—can't you help me?"

If the man had only asked yesterday, Omar thought, before dinner.

"Sorry," Omar said. "There's no better place than this." *Not for you*, he added mentally.

"They took my fountain pen!" the man said.

Omar looked at him. "Your what?"

"Someone stole my fountain pen! It was a Diplomat! German! It had a lifetime warranty!"

Omar couldn't entirely suppress his grin. "Would you like to file a report?" he asked. Filing a report would keep the man busy, anyway.

"I'll loan you my Bic," he added.

The white man gave Omar a disgusted look. "Never mind," he said, and stalked away.

You are doomed, Omar thought at his retreating back. It was easier thinking that, after he had made the man so ridiculous.

He looked right and left, saw the fence-installers working fast.

Fences are a good thing, he thought.

"Here." His guide, Martin, handed Nick a blue bandanna. "You'll be needing this."

Nick took the bandanna from his team leader's hand. "What for?" he said.

"Tie it around your mouth and nose. We're going to be digging out bodies."

Nick looked at the bandanna for a moment, then felt his stomach turn over as he remembered Helena. He put it in his shirt pocket till it was needed.

Martin had clerked in an auto parts store before the quake had made him "guide" to the Thessalonians—the Second Thessalonians, actually, since the team had been divided into two. Martin was around thirty and white and very blond, with pink skin flaking from sunburn and what looked like a permanent angry red stripe across his nose. He had a wife back in the camp, and four kids. There was a dirty armband on his left arm, a whistle on a chain around his neck, a walkie-talkie clipped to his belt, and in the small of his back a holstered semiautomatic pistol of a businesslike aluminum shade.

The pistol, he explained, was for snakes or mad dogs. He and Nick were riding in the back of a pickup truck to the town of Rails Bluff, where they would be scavenging items from the remains of the town.

And digging out bodies. Nick wasn't ready for that.

Whose food is your child eating? Manon's words rose in his mind. His job was to preserve his family. If he had to do it by watching former porn salesmen humiliated, or by digging dead people out of ruins, then that was what he would do. He would be a good soldier, do his duty, and keep his head down, because he owed it to Arlette.

Rails Bluff was a desert of fallen power lines, dusty piles of brick, cracked concrete, shattered glass, torn trees. The pick-up pulled up before a largish ruin in what had been the downtown section. A fallen marquee, tumbled letters and broken bulbs, showed that the place had been a theater. Piles of bricks, timber, roofing material, and tools showed that people had been working here.

"The people who weren't staying at the Reverend's camp were mostly in here when the second big quake hit," Martin explained. "The Reverend wants to give them a Christian burial. There might be medical supplies and food in there, too."

Martin dropped the tailgate and Nick lowered himself out of the truck. Glass crunched under his work boots. The First Thessalonians and some other crews rode in, and Martin and the other guides began to organize things. Nick tied the bandanna over his face, put on the gloves he'd been given, and began his work.

The morning's breakfast—a largish lump of oatmeal, served with a spoonful of raisins—sat like a stone in Nick's stomach, at least until some of the First Thessalonians uncovered the first body, and then the oatmeal began to turn cartwheels. The body—an elderly white lady, starting to bloat—was pulled from the ruin, wrapped in plastic, then covered with a sheet. Nick turned away from the scene and concentrated on tossing bricks into a wheelbarrow and keeping his breakfast down. Aftershocks rumbled continually through the earth.

Martin was cheerful and encouraging as he led his crew. During the course of the morning two more bodies were recovered, and precious little else beyond a few blankets and some battered kitchen gear. At noon a truck arrived from the camp, with peanut-butter-and-jelly sandwiches on homemade bread, two for each worker, and a wheel of white cheese off which the men carved chunks with their pocket knives.

"Hey," one of the Second Thessalonians said, peering into his sandwich. "At least we got jelly today." He looked at Nick. "Sometimes it's just peanut butter."

"I don't think we've met, officially," Nick said. "I'm Nick."

"Tex." Tex had deep black skin and broad shoulders, with grizzled hair under a tall-crowned straw cowboy hat. The two men sat on the tailgate of the pickup—facing away from where the three bodies lay on the broken street—and began to eat their sandwiches.

"I been hoping to ask," Tex said, "if you heard 'bout what was happening on the outside."

On the outside. It sounded like the language a man might use in prison.

"I listened to the news on radio until a few days ago," Nick said. *Be cautious,* an inner voice warned.

"We could listen to the news on the truck radio," Tex said, "but Martin won't let us." He chewed his sandwich thoughtfully. "Is it true about the nuclear plant that blew up over in Mississippi?"

"They had some problems," Nick said, "but it wasn't Chernobyl. A very small amount of radiation released, nothing of any great concern."

Tex wrinkled his eyes in thought. "You sure it didn't blow up, and the government covered it up?"

Nick looked at his sandwich. "Earthquake or no earthquake, we still have a free press. There must be a hundred reporters with radiation detectors camped out around that plant. If there were even modest amounts of radiation released, it would have been on the radio twelve hours a day."

Tex scratched his jaw. "We've all been sort of wondering, you know, where the reverend gets his news."

"There's been no big nuclear accident," Nick said. "That's for sure."

Tex nodded. "And the poisoned waters?"

"Well," Nick said, "the quake threw a lot of bad stuff in the water. Jason—my, uh, friend—Jason and I went through a lot of it on our boat, and some of it has to be pretty nasty. The government is evacuating places that get their drinking water from the river, but if you get your water from wells, you should be all right."

"So we safe here, from the poison."

"From the poison," Nick said, "yeah." He sipped from his cup of water and cleared the peanut butter sticking to the roof of his mouth.

"We can't listen to the radio?" he asked.

"The reverend collected them all when we came into camp. Cellphones, too, though none of those were working. He said that the noise would upset the children, and it was better if he just told us what was happening."

Nick looked at Tex cautiously. "What do you think about that?" he said.

Tex chewed thoughtfully. "What I got, see," he said, "is a farm that got destroyed three nights ago, and a momma who just lost her husband, and four kids who just lost their grand-daddy. And if the man who feeds my family don't want me to listen to the radio, then I guess I don't listen to it, and I don't think much about it, neither."

Nick nodded. "I understand," he said.

"Besides," Tex said, and shrugged his big shoulders, "where is there to go? The roads and bridges are gone. We got poisoned water and floods north and east. South and west we got the piney woods—pines was so close together you could barely get between 'em anyway, and now the quake knocked 'em all down, so it's nothin' but a big tangle that people can't get through. I can't get through it with my family, that's for sure."

Nick nodded. The quake had knocked the middle part of the country back two hundred years. With transportation and communications gone, each little community might as well be an island all to itself.

"Do you know," Nick asked, "if the reverend, or anyone else, is trying to communicate with the outside?"

Tex just shook his head.

"Hey." Martin walked around the truck. There was a grin on his face, but a wary determination in his eyes. "Y'all don't need to talk about this."

Be cautious, Nick's inner voice said. "Well," he answered, "I'm new here. I'm just trying to work out the rules."

"That's good." Martin nodded. "But if you need to know things, you should ask the guides. That's what we're here for, to guide you." He hitched up his belt, and Nick remembered the holstered pistol he wore behind his back.

"I wanted to know if we can call our families outside Rails Bluff," Nick said.

"No communications," Martin said. "There's no way."

"There's a *radio station,*" said a new voice. "If the Reverend Doctor Brother His Holiness Frankland could just be persuaded to use his radio station to call for help, we could have food and fuel and medicine brought in."

Nick looked at the new man. He was a red-faced, balding man with a large stomach and a loud voice.

"We got all that now, Brother Olson," Martin said. "People were worried about things like insulin, but it turned out that Reverend Frankland had a whole refrigerator of the stuff. Every time food supplies start to run short, he opens another bunker, and there's the food. The reverend's been preparing for this for *years.*"

"So why are we digging in the ruins for beat-up old cans, if we have so much?" Olson asked. "And why can't we just send a message, on Brother His Holiness Frankland's *radio station,* to let our families outside the area know that we're okay? I've got a sister in Mississippi that must be worried sick about me and my whole family."

Martin shook his head. "Take that up with Brother Frankland. But if I were you, I'd just give thanks to the Lord that you're with us, where it's safe." He looked at his watch, clapped his hands together. "You guys better finish. We need to start workin'."

Olson kicked a chunk of brick fifty feet, then stalked away. Nick washed the last of his sandwiches down with water and began clearing rubble. The truck that had brought their lunch left with three bodies in its bed.

A couple hours after lunch Martin blew his whistle. He'd got a call on his walkie-talkie: there was a situation near the camp.

Someone had died. There was an emergency. And now everyone had to catch fish.

Trouble began at mid-morning, when the fence-builders began to assemble the fence that would cut off the people in the camp from their vehicles. Several clumps of refugees surged forward, shouting and gesticulating. The deputies waved them back. And then people among the crowds began to throw things, first whatever they had handy, and then fist-sized whitewashed rocks that were used to line the camp-site's fire circles. The fence-builders retreated. The deputies looked nervous and clutched their weapons as they dodged the rocks being flung at them.

At the first sign of trouble Omar had made his way to Ozie Welks, who stood in the parking lot. Since the destruction of his bar he had been working full-time as a special deputy.

"I need you to shoot me a rioter," Omar said.

Ozie shifted his plug tobacco from his right cheek to his left. "You got it, Omar." He raised his .30-'06, sighted briefly over the iron sights, and squeezed the trigger.

Omar saw the bullet hit, strike right in the chest of a young black man with a stone in an upraised arm. There was a splash of dust and blood and the stone-thrower fell.

There were shouts. Screams and curses. A thrashing of tents and awnings as people fled. Though a few people unloaded a stone before they ran, Omar heard most of the rocks thud on the ground as the crowd rolled back.

And then there were *more* shots, *bang-bang-bang*, as a man in dreadlocks—a huge black man, tall and broad-shouldered and amazingly fat—came running from the crowd, firing a pistol as he ran. His cheeks and stomach and dreads bounced with each step. Deputies dived for cover as bullets sang in the air around them.

"Him, too," said Omar.

Ozie sighted, fired. The bullet hit the fat man in the hip and dropped him to the ground, but the man still thrust out his pistol, still fired until the slide locked back on an empty magazine; and then Ozie shot again and hit again in the center of the man's naked chest, and the man kicked twice and died.

"Semper fi," said Ozie.

None of the deputies had been hit, despite the man who had managed to fire off a full magazine. Shooting a handgun while running full-tilt toward an armed enemy was a terrifying sight, but not the most tactical thing the gunman could have done.

A shriek came from somewhere in the camp, the sound of a woman in terror. The sound raised the hackles on Omar's neck. "What the hell?" he muttered.

He moved forward, across the line of the uncompleted fence, gestured his deputies forward. "Get that gun!" he said, pointing to the dreadlocked man. The crowd shrank from the advancing, armed line, receding like an ocean wave to reveal a young woman sprawled across a three-year-old child. The child was wailing, too, her face so contorted by pain and fear that the tears almost leaped from her eyes. There was blood on the child and on the mother. One of Ozie's bullets had gone through the target and struck the little girl.

In the arm, Omar thought. The wound couldn't be that critical if the child had so much strength to scream.

"My baby!" the woman wailed. "My baby! Oh Jesus help my baby!"

Omar stopped dead as he stood over them. *Give her a box of candy,* he thought inanely.

Yes. Yes, that made sense.

"My baby! My baby! They shot my baby!"

He bent, encircled the mother's shoulders with his arms. "We'll get your girl to the doctor," he said. "Come along, now."

He rushed her out of the camp. Beckoned to Merle. "Take the girl to Dr. Patel," he said, then added, in a low voice, "Don't let the mother talk to anyone else."

"You got it, boss."

"Bring them back when the doctor's finished."

When Merle had raced off, siren crying and lights flashing, Omar called Jedthus.

"I want you to go to town," he said, "and bring me a bag of candy. Here's five bucks."

Jedthus looked thunderstruck. "Omar? A bag of *candy*?"

"Yeah."

"*Now?* With a riot going on?"

Omar looked at the silent camp, the people huddled in whatever kind of cover they could find on the flat ground. Huddled as far away from him as the fence would allow. "Do you *see* a riot going on, Jedthus?" he asked.

Jedthus sighed. "What *kind* of candy?"

"Milky Way. Snickers. Whatever's in the Commissary."

After Jedthus departed, Omar had the two bodies dragged out of the camp and covered with plastic sheeting. This was bad police procedure, to take the two bodies away from where they'd been shot before they could be photographed and seen by the coroner, but Omar figured the riot excused his actions.

Besides, he didn't give a damn about the two dead people and he figured no one else would, either. He let them lie in plain sight, where the refugees could see them, while he called the fence-builders back to work.

This time there wasn't a riot.

Omar watched the silent, resentful people in the camp, and he thought about what Knox had told him. Use science, he thought, turn them against one another. There were over two hundred people in that camp, and they had to be kept quiet and obedient and isolated.

Science, he thought. Science would save his son.

The sun hammered Omar's head. His stomach churned. He wished he had sent Jedthus for Alka-Seltzer as well as candy. He went into his police cruiser and turned on the air-conditioning, and the cool and silence helped him to think. By the time that Jedthus returned with Omar's bag of candy, he thought he had his plan worked out.

The heat and the lack of food combined to keep the camp quiet. People splayed out under awnings and in the camp's shaded picnic areas, trying to stay out of the heat. Aftershocks shivered the tops of the trees. By one o'clock in the afternoon the fence was finally finished, a shimmering twelve-foot barrier of chain link with only a single gate that led out into the parking lot and the highway. The fence-builders began stringing razor-wire along the top.

"Five hours, twenty-two minutes," Micah Knox said, looking at his big musical pocket watch. "Pretty neat, considering we had a riot and everything."

Omar got his bullhorn from his car and advanced to the gate.

"Now you saw what happened when there was trouble," he said. "Three people got shot, and one of them was a little girl. So I don't want any more trouble, any more rocks or guns, because the folks who will end up paying for it will be the families here.

"So here's what I want. I want you to choose a council to help run the camp. Responsible folks, family folks. Ten will do. And I and the parish will deal with the council, and the council will deal with the rest of you.

"The council will arrange for y'all's distribution of food. I am going to leave now to get you some food supplies, and when I come back, I hope you'll have chosen some people that I can turn this food over to."

He left them to think about that for a while. The two bodies were loaded into the back of a pickup truck to be carried to Tree Simpson, and Omar arranged for the fat man's pistol—a boxy-looking Glock 9mm, weapon-of-choice for gangsters and gangster wannabees—to be bagged for evidence and brought along with the bodies.

"I'll be along to see Tree in just a minute," Omar told his deputies, and sent the truck banging on its way.

He himself stopped by the Reverend Morris' wrecked California bungalow, where he found the church people waiting with the shipment of food they'd brought in for the camp's meals. When Omar pulled into the driveway, he saw them assemble in the area between the house and the church, surging around his car before he could get it parked. They were stiff with barely suppressed hate and anger.

Omar got out of his car and tipped his hat to Morris's widow. "I'm sorry about your husband, Miz Morris," he said. "He was a good man."

"Thank you." Mrs. Morris' tone was strained but not impolite. "But when may we bring the food into the camp?"

"Yeah!" one of her supporters said. "The food!"

"There are babies in the camp," Mrs. Morris continued, "and they need their milk."

"There's been trouble at the camp, Miz Morris." He frowned at her. "And I need to ask you—do you have any reason to believe that someone may have wished your husband harm?"

Mrs. Morris looked surprised. She raised a hand to her wrinkled throat. "What do you mean?" she asked.

"He was last seen in the company of a young man from the camp," Omar said. "And now Dr. Morris is dead and the man is missing." He waited for that to sink in, then added, "I will have Tree Simpson take a good look at your husband's body, and we'll see if there is any reason to suspect foul play."

He looked at Mrs. Morris, then lifted his eyes to the others, her family, and some of the church workers. "I didn't see the accident site myself," he said, "so I didn't have any reason to be suspicious, but after what happened at the camp this morning I began to wonder. There was a riot, you see—a real riot, and my deputies were shot at, and two people were killed. And a little girl was wounded. *A little girl!*" He raised his voice, tried to sound outraged. "Maybe you saw my deputy taking her and her mother to the doctor."

He saw barely perceptible nods from several of the group.

"There are bad folks at the camp, Miz Morris," Omar said. "Drug dealers, thieves, gangsters. I suspect one of them killed your husband. I don't think I can allow civilians like yourselves into that camp anymore. It would only put you in harm's way."

Mrs. Morris absorbed this slowly. Her lips trembled, either with emotion or words that she hadn't quite formed.

"I will have the parish take over delivery of the food," Omar said. "It's government food anyway. You people have been good enough to volunteer to prepare and distribute it, but I can't put you in danger any longer. Not once they start shooting at us."

He got on the radio and gave orders for his deputies to take possession of the food, then drove to the courthouse to meet with Tree Simpson.

"Give Ozie a chance," Tree said with a weary grin, "he'll put an end to the population explosion single-handed. What is it—three dead men so far?"

"I'm not here to talk about Ozie," Omar said. "I want to talk about Dr. Morris."

Tree looked surprised. "What about him? I was going to send the body to the funeral home."

"There may have been foul play there," Omar said. "Could you give the body another look?"

Tree looked dubious. "It was burned pretty bad," he said. "I don't know if I could find much on my own. Normally we'd send the body to Baton Rouge for a proper autopsy, but I don't know if we can do that in the circumstances."

"Just give it a look. There may be something there. An exit wound, a shank left in the body. Something."

"Exit wound?" Tree frowned dubiously. "The back of the head was gone, but that could have been because the brains boiled in the fire and the head exploded." He shrugged. "I'll see what I can find."

Omar left Tree's office with a quiet triumph singing in his blood. Things were working out.

He would blame Morris' killing on someone who was already dead, the runaway boy that Knox and his people had killed yesterday, sent where the woodbine twineth. And then what he'd tell Spottswood Parish was that the boy was still at large, still armed, still murderous. And that would end any kind of friendly relations between the local community—particularly the local black community—and the refugees in the camps.

What Omar intended to do next was to divide the people in the camp from one another.

On his way out of town he stopped by the Commissary and bought some Alka-Seltzer, and he dropped it in a bottle of water that he also purchased and drank it off. It didn't help. When he returned to the camp, he met with the council that the refugees had chosen to represent them. All black, mostly middle-aged people, more women than men.

They had no experience, he guessed, at organizing and feeding hundreds of people. It would all go wrong—not enough cooked, or too much, or it would be badly distributed. And when the inevitable screwups came, when people got angry, it would be against their own leaders.

While the food was being carried into the camp and delivered to the camp committee, the little girl who had been shot was delivered along with her mother to the camp. The bullet had hit the fleshy part of the upper arm, but it hadn't broken the bone, and the girl was fine now that Dr. Patel had given her some stitches, some painkiller, and a tetanus booster.

The little girl was sleepy with the painkiller and the aftereffects of her fright, and her mother carried the girl in her arms as Merle walked her into camp. Omar followed with the bag of Three Musketeers candy that Jedthus had brought him, and waited till the mother was in plain sight of the people gathered around waiting for their meal.

He tipped his hat politely to the mother, and addressed himself to the sleepy little girl. "This is for you," he said, and handed out the candy. "You be sure to share it with your friends, okay?"

The little girl took the candy and looked at it with an air of incomprehension.

"Thank you, Sheriff," the mother said.

Omar smiled and tipped his hat again. "All in a day's work, ma'am," he said.

"Pretty slick, Omar," Knox said admiringly as Omar left the camp. "You've been paying attention, huh?"

Omar ignored him and went to his car and turned the air-conditioning on high. He felt like hell.

TWENTY-SEVEN

On Sunday night the 15th inst. the earth shook here so as to shake the fowls off their roosts, and made the houses shake very much, again it shook at sunrise and at 11 o'clock next morning, and at the same time the next day, and about the same time the third day after.

Accounts are brought in from the nation that several hunting Indians who were lately on the Missouri have returned, and state that the earthquake was felt very sensibly there, that it shook down trees and many rocks of the mountains, and that everything bore the appearance of an immediate dissolution of the world! —We give this as we got it— it may be correct—but the probability is that it is not.

Clarion, *Friday, February 14, 1812*

The President stared at the coffin that softly gleamed in the subdued lighting of the East Room, nestled beneath a huge bouquet between the Eliphalet Andrews portrait of Martha Washington and Gilbert Stuart's portrait of her husband. For a moment, a weird, wild grief struck him, and the President wanted to fling himself onto the coffin and wail and tear his hair. Then, just as suddenly, he was again himself, the President of the United States, standing on the polished floor in the silent solemnity of the Executive Mansion. In the morning, the gates of the White House would be opened and the public would file through the East Room, thousands of people sharing in the ritual of mass mourning.

More than the First Lady would be mourned tomorrow. Many thousands had died across the middle of the nation. Some were buried beneath unexcavated rubble; some were buried anonymously in mass graves; and many would never be found.

Tomorrow's funeral of the First Lady, here in the White House and taking place under the universal eye of television, was only the most public of the funerals for earthquake victims. All those who lost loved ones, or who waited in gnawing uncertainty, would now have a chance to participate in the rite of public mourning. In the public mind, this funeral might come to stand for them all. That was why, over the strong objections of the President's security detail, the public funeral had to be held in the White House, the tragedy brought fully into the national home.

And—though even Stan Burdett was too tactful to say so— the President was enough of a politician to know that this was something of a public relations bonanza. In the past, the nation had presidents who, as in the cliché, claimed they shared the citizens' pain. Now the tens of thousands who had lost so much in the quakes knew that the President was one of them. He, too, had lost a loved one in the tragedy.

The President expected that his next set of approval ratings would be at an all-time high. He would have prodigious coattails. The Party would stand to gain in the next elections.

The President, however, had not yet made up his mind whether he really cared about this or not.

"Sir?" The Marine colonel who had been put in charge of the funeral arrangements stood by, the subdued lights gleaming on the buttons of his blue full-dress jacket. "Mr. President? Is everything suitable?"

The colonel, the President remembered, had been reviewing the arrangements for the funeral, talking all this while. The President hadn't heard a word.

Well. It probably didn't matter anyway.

The President cleared a particle of grief that seemed to have lodged in his throat. "Yes," he said. "Yes, it's fine."

The President walked across the gleaming parquet floor to the coffin and laid his hand upon its smooth surface. He made the gesture only because he knew it would have seemed odd if he hadn't. Whatever was actually in the coffin, the burnt offerings that had been raked from the remains of Air Force Two, bore no resemblance to the woman with whom he had shared his life. For some reason the President found this a comfort. He would have been far more disturbed had he thought of the First Lady—the woman who had shared his life, his career, his bed—lying cold, still, and recognizable, in her familiar blue suit with its familiar corsage, all locked in the mahogany-and-bronze box.

Also because it was expected, he bent his head for a moment, and clasped his hands in an attitude of prayer. In reality his mind was pleasantly numb. Whatever of the outside world intruded on his thoughts, it seemed to come through a layer of cotton wool. Since his wife's death he had been operating largely on automatic pilot, making decisions in a world that seemed strangely devoid of consequence or purpose.

Yet he managed to make decisions. Most of them did not require a lot of thought—most situations had obvious enough answers, and when they didn't, he was resigned to the fact that decisions taken in an emergency were necessarily taken on the fly, with incomplete information, and that consequences would have to be dealt with as they occurred.

I say come, he thought, *and they cometh; I say shove off, and they shoveth. And in the end, the world seems to spin on its axis whether they cometh or not.*

He looked up at the tactful sound of a throat being cleared. It was one of his aides, reminding him of the meeting of his foreign policy working group. He finished his prayer—his public, nonexistent prayer, his dumb-show for the peace of mind of the Marine colonel and any other onlookers who wanted the President, in his grief, to behave "normally," whatever that meant—and as he made his way out he stopped by the colonel to thank him for the care he had taken with his arrangements, and said he would see him tomorrow. Then he walked with his aide down the length of the Jefferson Pavilion to the West Office Wing and the Oval Office.

The foreign policy working group consisted of the Secretary of State, the National Security Advisor, and various representatives from the Pentagon and the Department of Commerce.

For once, the President thought, he was able to attend a meeting without Boris Lipinsky droning on at his elbow.

The President greeted the working group in the Oval Office, accepted their condolences on the loss of the First Lady, and seated himself behind Rutherford B. Hayes' desk. He turned to the Secretary of State. "What's on the agenda?" he said.

"Firstly, Mr. President," the Secretary said, "I'm relieved to report that Israel, Syria, the Palestinians, and Iraq have been persuaded to reduce their state of military alert."

"Good work. Thank you, Darrell."

The Secretary smiled in acknowledgment. "We've got alarming news from the Balkans, sir. We are receiving bulletins on the persecution by Macedonia of its Albanian minority."

"*Which* Macedonia?" the President asked. The Greeks held onto the view that *their* Macedonia was the real one, with the state that called itself Macedonia being made up entirely of imposters. The Greeks were more or less alone in this view, but still the distinction created a degree of uncertainty in the terminology.

"The Former Yugoslav Republic of Macedonia," the Secretary clarified. "Though the Greek Macedonians would probably be happy to persecute *their* Albanians as well, come to that."

"And what form does the Former Yugoslavs' persecution take?"

"Attacks on villages by paramilitaries. Minor ethnic cleansing." The Secretary sighed. "I regret to say that minor ethnic cleansing, unless checked, often turns into major ethnic cleansing."

And, he did not need to add, an ethnic cleansing that would further destabilize a region that was already one of the most explosive places on earth. If Macedonia became unstable, Greece might very well intervene against the small nation that dared to usurp the name that Greece considered its own. The Serbs, friendly with the Greeks, might seize the opportunity to restore their hegemony in Bosnia and

Kosovo. Turks might view any larger conflict as their chance to adjust their borders with Greece. The Serbs were loathed by the Bosnians, Croatians, Kosovars, and Albanians, and the Montenegrins didn't think much of them either. All of these might view with favor the chance to reduce the influence, territory, or army of Serbia.

The Balkans had already graced the planet with the First World War. A certain degree of concern, the consensus considered, was definitely in order.

The President, swathed in his strangely congenial mental habit of cotton wool, had difficulty summoning any degree of concern whatever. But he was aware that the President *ought* to be concerned about such things, and he made the appropriate responses.

"What can we do about it?" the President asked.

"There are already NATO soldiers in Macedonia," the National Security Advisor said. "Patrolling the borders of Kosovo and Albania at the request of the Macedonian government. But they are lightly armed, dispersed through the countryside, and vulnerable to retaliation should they attempt to intervene in any local matters."

The National Security Agency had been created as an activist organization by President Kennedy, frustrated by the cautious diplomacy of the career diplomats at State. Traditionally the NSA was interventionist, willing to charge into any crisis with any amount of force; while the woolly minded diplomats at Foggy Bottom preferred caution, more caution, and endless talk.

The two men in the Oval Office reversed this tradition. The Secretary of State was a bouncy activist, a kind of muscular missionary for American values who was willing to take troubles by the neck and shake them till their teeth rattled. The National Security Advisor, a military man, had always been far more cautious. The President had the impression that the general did not want to commit force anywhere in the world unless he had a million armed men, bases and supplies prepositioned, a resolution from the UN Security Council, and a forecast predicting six weeks of perfect weather.

The President often thought of his Security Advisor as his General in Charge of Saying No.

No, as far as the President could discern through the strange inconsequential mist that seemed to envelop him, seemed the proper response to this situation. "Let's dump this in the Europeans' lap," he said.

"Sir," said the Secretary of State. He bounced with impatience on his Federal period armchair. "The Europeans have shown themselves consistently unable to deal with ethnic conflicts on their own continent."

"Well," said the President, "let them *learn.*"

"Without us," Darrell persevered, "they have no leadership. They're a committee without a head—you can't run a crisis by committee. Not with a dozen or fifteen countries all having an equal vote with Luxembourg."

"If they need leadership, then lead them," the President said. "Give them orders, if you like. But don't commit American resources. They will understand the reasons."

The American people, with their economy in ruins and a large percentage of their population living in camps or wandering for an indefinite period as refugees, would not look kindly on an administration that committed its forces to the defense of the Albanian minority of the Former Yugoslav Republic of Macedonia. If the President tried, Congress would go berserk.

Albanians would die—die horribly, tortured and raped and bludgeoned—but the President knew that most congressmen would rather see fifty thousand Albanians publicly tortured to death on CNN than to have a single serviceman from their home district come home in a box. Probably most of them, like their constituents, could not even find Albania or Macedonia on a map.

It was the Albanians' loss that the planet's only remaining superpower was so pig-ignorant of the world, but there you were. Those who did not know history, the President thought, were doomed to watch it being made by other people. He smiled to himself in appreciation of this little private witticism.

The President became vaguely aware that the Secretary of State had shifted to another topic. "Russian paramilitaries, sir," the Secretary of State. "Infiltrating into Georgia in large numbers—infiltrating, hell," he added scornfully, "they're taking buses and planes. Mercenaries, former Spetznaz men, old Gamsakhurdians, Russian Mafia, South Ossetian and Abkhazian separatists . . ."

"Aiming at what?" the President said, interrupting because he saw no point in the list going on. It was one of the facts of post-Cold War geopolitics that he knew who these people were, that a revolt of Gamsakhurdians and South Ossetians was something for which he was intellectually prepared.

The Secretary shrugged. "Who knows? Maybe they're after control of the new oil pipelines, maybe they just want to keep the Georgians running scared. Maybe they want to annex Abkhazia. Who knows if the Russians even know what they're after? It's a way of keeping the pot stirring in the Near Abroad. If things turn chaotic enough, they may be able to find some advantage. Or loot, that being what a lot of Russian generals are after these days."

"And our options?"

"Our soldiers in Georgia are few and highly specialized," said the National Security Advisor. "They are certainly not prepared to intervene in any Georgian civil conflict."

The President blinked. He turned his gaze on the advisor. "We have military assets in the Georgian Republic?" he said.

"Certainly. Special ops people, trainers and advisors, and communications specialists listening in on communications in Russia, Ukraine, and other areas of interest."

The President supposed he shouldn't be surprised. He'd probably been told this at one time or another, and forgot.

"Well," he said, attempting something that was half a joke, "I suppose it would be unwise to start a conflict with Russia."

"We can't do anything for Georgia other than let the Russians know we're paying attention," the Secretary agreed. "The Russians would go ballistic if we interfered with their arrangements in the Near Abroad."

"Which does *not* include Latvia," the National Security Advisor added.

The President looked at him in surprise. "Joe?" he said. "Latvia?"

"I'm sorry, Mr. President," the Secretary said. "I must have been unclear. The paramilitaries are also moving into Latvia. We presume they will attempt to cause civil disturbances which the Russians can profitably exploit. A few years ago the Russian military ran war games in the region of the Baltics, in which they simulated taking over a small country. They called it 'Operation Return.'"

The President tried to focus on this problem. It seemed to require more than his current level of concentration could quite absorb.

"Latvia is only a little more than fifty percent ethnic Latvian," the National Security Advisor said. "The rest are mostly Russians or Belorussians. We presume that the Russian infiltrators will attempt to provoke conflict between the Latvians and the minorities, who will then ask for Russian protection . . ."

"Latvia and the other Baltics are within the West's sphere of influence," the Secretary said. "They're candidate NATO members, and the only reason they are not fully within our defense umbrella is that we have tried not to offend Russian sensibilities. The Baltics were part of the USSR, and the Russians would be very sensitive about these nations being made part of a Western military alliance."

"The Baltics are militarily indefensible," added the advisor. "Latvia's nothing but a plain with rolling hills—Russian tanks could be in the capital in a matter of hours. I have to question whether NATO should commit itself to defending that which cannot be defended."

"Enrolling the Baltics in NATO is the best way of protecting them," the Secretary countered. "Let the Russians know that if they roll their tanks over that Latvian plain, there will be *consequences*, that they'll have to take on all of Europe and the U.S. at the same time . . ."

The President's head whirled. The Secretary's vehemence

was making his head ache. He pressed his palms to his temples. "Gentlemen," he said. "It's a little late to debate the NATO issue now. The question is, what can we do in the current situation?"

"Sorry, Mr. President," the Secretary said. "But this is a clear challenge to the West and to your leadership. They want to discover whether we still possess the will to defend our commitments in light of the tragedy that has befallen us."

Will seemed to the President a perfectly absurd thing to want to possess. What did will matter in a world that could wipe you out without thinking? That could open a crevasse in your path and leave you a burnt cinder on the runway?

Will was meaningless. An absurdity. It flew in the face of Nature. And for a *nation* to possess will—*that* notion was even more ridiculous.

Still, the holder of the office of the President was presumed to possess something called will. The President supposed that he was obliged to pretend that something like will existed.

And then an idea occurred to him.

"Do you suppose the Russian President knows what his people are up to?" he asked. He himself, after all, hadn't known there were American soldiers in Georgia; perhaps the Russian President was similarly uninformed. Or indifferent.

The Secretary seemed interested in this idea. "It's very possible," he said. "The Executive over there has uncertain control over some of its departments, let alone things like paramilitaries. It wouldn't be the first time some ambitious minister or general blindsided his own leadership."

"Perhaps you should tell our ambassador to inform their President on the QT," the President said. "Point out what a PR disaster the whole thing could be if it went wrong, like in Chechnya." He turned to the Secretary. "It *was* Chechnya where they really screwed the pooch, right?"

"Yes, sir."

"Tell them that this isn't a public issue yet," the President free-associated. "But that it *can* be. Tell him, hey, his people have *already* screwed up their little operation, everyone's onto them, if he acts quickly, he can save face."

"But if the Russian President is the person behind it . . ."

"It won't make any difference," the National Security Advisor said quickly. "It's a way of saving his face whether he's a part of it or not. Just tell him the jig's up. There's no need to make a public issue of it."

"Not unless we *need* to," the Secretary said. Calculation gleamed in his eyes.

The President rose from behind the desk. "Let me know what the Russian President says," he said. "I'm interested."

I'm interested in knowing why he cares, he thought.

The others, startled, rose from their seats. "I have a big day tomorrow," the President said. "I'll leave the details to you gentlemen."

Maybe his idea was useful. Maybe it wasn't. He would probably never know.

The world could open at his feet and swallow him up, and it wouldn't make a difference to anything.

He left the room, made his way out through the West Office Wing into the White House proper, and went up carpeted steps to his own private apartments. He sat on his bed for a long while and tried to decide whether or not he really wanted to lie down.

He really couldn't tell. So, after thinking about it for a while, he did nothing.

Jason hadn't had a good day. Most of it was spent cleaning out a feed store. The roof had fallen in, but a team of grownups had cleaned up some of the wreckage, and propped up the roof so that it was safe to go inside. The Samaritans were employed in hauling out fifty-pound feed sacks, twenty-pound sacks of dog food—Jason hoped he wouldn't be eating it later—and sacks of useful seeds, which apparently people hoped to plant for food. Most of the Samaritans were older, bigger, and stronger than Jason, and the work was easier for them. Sweat dripped in his eyes and he panted for breath in the humid air. The roof creaked and groaned to aftershocks. By the time lunch break came, all he wanted to do was throw himself to the ground and try to sleep. Mr. Magnusson had to badger him into eating his peanut butter sandwiches.

During the lunch break, three of the other Samaritans asked him if he'd brought a nuclear reactor into camp with him. They pronounced it *nu-cu-lar*. He always told them yes.

After lunch Jason went back to hauling sacks, but shortly thereafter a call came on Magnusson's radio, and everyone was loaded into the truck to go somewhere else and harvest fish. Whatever a fish harvest consisted of, Jason thought, it had to be better than hauling feed sacks.

The fish emergency was across the road from Frankland's camp. When Jason stepped up the earth embankment onto the edge of the catfish pond, he looked at the pond in stunned surprise. There were *acres* of still water glinting silver in the sun, all divided into smaller ponds by earthen barriers. All of the water was *choked* with fish, tens of thousands of them.

And all the fish were dead, floating belly-up. They were so closely packed in places they formed shoals.

A number of adults, Jason saw, were gathered around a man who lay on the earthen bank by one of the ponds, next to a large, bright blue machine that looked like an oversized outboard motor. Jason was sufficiently exhausted that he didn't realize right away that the man was dead.

"Right," Magnusson said. "We've got to harvest all the fish, okay? So we can eat them, okay?" He grinned. "Big fish fry tonight!"

Jason's head reeled. The fish were *dead*. He were supposed to eat poisoned fish for dinner?

He raised a hand. "Mr. Magnusson?" he said. "What killed these fish?"

Magnusson looked at him, grinned. "It wasn't anything that'll kill us, okay?"

"What was it?" Jason asked.

"Oxygen starvation," Magnusson said. "They weren't poi-

soned, they strangled to death. So we can eat them, okay?"
He went on to explain that if the temperature and humidity
were right, algae could grow in the catfish ponds. The algae
used up all the oxygen, so the fish would die unless they
could get oxygen.

Joe Johnson, who owned the ponds, had died attempting
to save his fish. The blue object was, in effect, a large blue
outboard motor, electrically powered, with a propeller on the
end. It was called an aerator, and its propeller acted to thrash
air into the water so that the catfish wouldn't die. When
algae began to grow in his catfish ponds, Mr. Johnson had
tried to start his aerator, but had electrocuted himself by accident, and his catfish had died before anyone noticed.

Stupid way to get killed, Jason thought through his weariness. But then, he thought, what was the intelligent way to
die? Get blown up by your star?

Jason looked from the dead man to the acres of dead fish.
"We're not going to harvest them by hand, are we?"

Magnusson grinned. "Not exactly, no. We've got other
plans for *you*."

In a few minutes a truck arrived, with a crane on its bed. A
net was strung from the crane, and a team of men deployed
the net along the far side of the pond. Then the crane hauled
in the net, brimming with dead catfish, and dropped the fish
into the back of one of the pickup trucks that had brought the
work crews to the site.

"Right!" Magnusson called, and clapped his hands.
"Everyone get on the slime line!"

Jason realized with a certain listless revulsion that he was
not expected to rescue the dead fish from the ponds, he was
going to have to clean them afterward.

"Ten tons of fish!" Magnusson shouted. "And we're going
to save every pound, glory hallelujah!"

"Omar," Tree Simpson said. His voice crackled over the radio
in Omar's police cruiser. "Omar, I've got some information
for you. About Morris."

"Yes?"

"Well, you know, I thought I should maybe get the body X-rayed, to see if there were any bullets in it. But Dr. Patel's little X-ray machine is out of commission, so what I did—I'm kinda proud of this, actually—was to borrow Joe Roberts' metal detector. And when I passed it over the head, it started beeping. So I probed into the skull, and I came out with a deformed nine-millimeter round."

"I took a nine millimeter into custody today," Omar said. "From one of the rioters." The gun would test negative, of course, because the pistol that killed Morris was sitting on Omar's hip, but that didn't signify. All that meant was that there was more than one armed bad man in the camp: more information with which to terrify the good people of the parish.

"It may be a while before we can send it to the state police to test it."

"It'll wait," Omar said. "Thanks a bunch, Tree. This is real helpful."

Now he would tell Mrs. Morris that someone from the camp had killed her husband. He would put out a murder warrant for a man already dead, send out a bulletin, and then he would send deputies to everyone who lived around the camp, warning them of armed, murderous refugees. Don't talk to *anyone* from the camp, they would say, just call the police and we'll deal with them.

And then Omar would do what was necessary. He didn't want to think about it yet, because it would mean the end of everything he had worked for.

But he knew he would face it when the time came.

Jason was given a knife and instructions on the filleting of a catfish, a task more difficult than it sounded. The dorsal spine had to be avoided, and the tough skin, which had no scales, had to be peeled off rather than scraped. The easiest way to accomplish this was to nail the fish's head to a plank, then peel the skin off with a pair of pliers. Jason repeatedly demonstrated his incompetence at this task, so Magnusson reassigned him to another group that gutted the fish before the stronger, more experienced boys peeled them.

Others were getting the big smoker ready to smoke fish on an industrial scale, other fish were being salted, drying racks were being readied, and the kitchens were frying and baking fish as fast as they could be delivered.

Dinner was fried fish served with a ball of rice. For once Jason ate as much as he wanted. He suspected this generosity wouldn't survive the current emergency, and though the fish half-nauseated him, he made himself eat as much as he could. The work went on after dark, by floodlights strung up on the poles that held the PA speakers. Sister Sheryl's Apocalypse, the weird artwork with its iridescent, hallucinatory rendition of biblical scenes, glowed in the light of the floods and provided an eerie backdrop to the toiling workers. The Reverend Frankland's tones boomed from the speakers, either old recorded speeches about the upcoming Apocalypse or genial encouragement to everyone on the slime line.

An exhausted cheer rose from the camp as the last of the fish was cleaned about one in the morning. Jason's clothes were covered with blood and fish guts. He smelled like offal and his head swam with exhaustion. He'd cut his hands with the filleting knife, and no bandage would stick to him in the slime, so he just bled onto the fish until the wounds closed. He washed in a galvanized horse trough and threw himself onto the first piece of level ground that wasn't already occupied by a stunned figure.

If boys cried that night, Jason didn't hear them.

The Earthquake. —A letter has been received in this city, from a gentleman of the first respectability in Tennessee, which states that the Earthquake, so generally felt on the 16th of Dec. was so violent in the vicinity of his residence, that several chimneys were thrown down, and that eighteen or twenty acres of land on Piney river had suddenly sunk so low, that the tops of the trees were on a level with the surrounding earth. Four other shocks were experienced on the 17th, and one or more continued to occur every day to the 30th aft., the date of the letter.

Raleigh, (N.C.) Jan. 24

"It's been lovely," Wilona said. "Hard work, but lovely. I almost fainted when I helped Dr. Patel set that broken leg, but afterward Mrs. Ashenden said I was very brave." She smiled. "And all the patients are so understanding. So kind. Even the ones who are in pain. They know we're doing our best."

Omar listened to Wilona in silence while a headache beat through his temples. He had picked her up at the Clarendon camp and was driving her home for the night, after which he would drive back to his office and continue his planning session with Micah Knox.

"We've got about a dozen cases of diarrhea," Wilona said. "There's some kind of stomach bug going around. That's the most disgusting thing we've had to deal with." She gave a little laugh. "We had that with Davy when he was little, of course, but I'm out of practice. *Look out!*" she called.

Omar swerved to avoid the figure of old Cudgel, off tramping the road alone at night. Omar caught a glimpse of the hermit's yellow eyes in his lined, black, bearded face beneath his big hat. Cudgel carried a stick over his shoulder with some kind of dead animal dangling from it.

"Poor man," Wilona said.

"He's probably happier than most of us," Omar said.

Omar and Knox had been discussing the situation at the A.M.E. camp when Wilona got off shift. Knox had been full of ideas. Knox really knew his stuff, Omar thought. Omar would never have thought of half those notions in a million years.

As Wilona spoke of her day, Knox sat in the back of the police cruiser without speaking. Omar could hear the faint sound of Knox's fingertips tapping on his knees. Some part of Knox was always in motion, tapping to the furious speed of his mind. His distinctive scent—not just sweat from wearing flannel in hot weather, but maybe some weird kind of cologne, too—floated faintly to Omar in the front seat.

Knox was like a weapon, Omar thought. It was as if he was

purpose-built. Knox had nothing but his cause: no property, no family, no job, no hobbies, no one to love. He hardly seemed to sleep at night.

It was as if God had made Knox solely for Spottswood Parish.

Or maybe, Omar thought, it was the other way around.

"And the people who were there!" Wilona said. "Mrs. Hall. Jamie FitzWalter. And Judge Moseley's daughter, the middle one ... Amanda! Everybody from Mrs. Ashenden's bridge club." It was as if she'd attended a garden party at Clarendon, not spent a day tending the wounded. "There we were, all working together!" Wilona put her hand to her heart, looked at Omar. "Do you think I'll be invited to join the bridge club after this is over?" she asked. "Do you think that might happen?"

"You already belong to a club," Omar said.

"Oh, that!" Wilona said. "That's not the same thing."

Wilona wanted to play bridge, Omar thought, and drink tea off the Wedgwood and eat pastel-colored petit-fours with tiny ladylike bites. Instead her club played poker on Wednesday afternoons, drank beer, and met in Lillie Hutley's double-wide trailer on the highway north of Hardee.

"Won't none of Miz LaGrande's ladies ever vote for me," Omar said. "I'd keep visiting Lillie Hutley if I were you."

"I would not drop *any* of my friendships," Wilona said. "I *never* drop my friendships, though sometimes *they* drop *me*, like Amy Vidor did when her husband got his new job with Allstate and didn't have to depend on your pull with the parish. But I don't see anything wrong with making new friends."

"Well," Omar said, "if any of your new friends drop any information about who they're going to run against your husband in the next election, you let me know."

Wilona sighed. "Oh, darling," she said, "do we have to talk politics?"

Omar drove to their house in Hardee and drew the car up in front. David's car was in the driveway, parked carefully out of the reach of any falling branches from the magnolia.

Knox waited in the car while Omar went inside with Wilona.

David sat on Omar's easy chair, a can of Bud in his hand. There were some empties on the table next to him and an open case of Coors by his feet. He looked up.

"I helped Ozie shift his stock this afternoon. He gave me a reward."

"So I see," Omar said. Wilona ruffled David's hair and kissed his cheek.

"Nothing much else to do," David said, "since Ozie 'n me are both off duty for shooting people. For doing our jobs." David's tone was resentful, his face sullen. Omar felt a warning tingle run down his spine.

"Might as well just take it easy," he advised. "Or if you get bored, you could work with one of the groups that's cleaning up."

"Oh," waving a hand, "let the niggers do the sweeping." He grinned up at Omar, eyes lazy with drink. "Dang it, I was starting to get a taste for law enforcement. You want a beer?"

The thought of beer made Omar's stomach queasy. He'd spent the day living on Akla-Seltzer, but it wasn't doing him any good.

"I'll have a dope instead," Omar said. He got a Coke from the fridge—the electricity was back on, finally—and took another for Knox.

When he returned to the front room, Wilona was telling David all about her lovely day at Clarendon. Omar watched them for a moment, then let himself out and rejoined Knox in the car. He gave Knox his Coke and turned the car around to drive back to Shelburne City.

"That was interesting, listening to Mrs. Paxton," Knox said. "I guess everybody in this parish knows everybody else, huh?"

"Pretty much," Omar said.

"The thing that really surprised me is how blacks and whites mix down here."

Omar frowned. "What do you mean?"

"I thought this was the land of segregation!" Knox said. "But you people mix with blacks a lot more than we do up

North. Back home in Detroit, folks who hate the niggers don't have nothing to do with them. We don't live with 'em, don't talk to 'em, don't hire 'em, run 'em out of our neighborhoods if they poke their noses in. But you Southerners—you *say* you hate the Mud People, but you got 'em everywhere! You live right alongside them. You talk to 'em like they were *people*. You hire them instead of whites! *You let them in your house! You let them raise your children!*"

"*I* don't," Omar said.

"Well, that's because you have *vision*, Omar! You know how things can be made better for the white race. But the others—I bet that Miss LaGrande lets the Mud People right into her home."

"She's got servants."

"I wouldn't trust a black in my home! My God, and she's a *leader* in this town. What kind of example *is* that?"

Omar gave a little smile. "Miz LaGrande and I have never seen eye to eye."

Knox's busy fingers tapped a rhythm on the car seat. "That's cause you're a man of vision, Omar. You fight for the race."

I fight for my son, Omar thought.

"This is going to be *famous*, Omar," Knox went on. "This is going to really wake people up. Just like in *Hunter*. I wouldn't be surprised if this started the war to liberate America."

"No one's going to hear of it," Omar said. "Nobody's going to hear of it *ever*. I'm going to bury it all right here."

Knox considered this for a long moment, his only sound the tapping of his fingertips on the car seat. "I don't see it, Omar," he said finally. "There are a lot of people in this county—parish. I don't know how you're going to keep the lid on this thing."

"Let me worry about it," Omar said. "You just help me do the necessary."

Omar suspected that Knox had no real idea why Omar was doing what he was doing. Omar was defending his family, not his ideology. But Knox had no way to view actions other than through his beliefs, or through fantasies like *Hunter* or *The Turner Diaries*.

Knox wanted a revolution, a race war throughout the U.S. Omar figured that was desirable, just not very likely. The cause of the white race was lost. Omar just wanted to suppress a killing. If keeping David safe meant killing other people, that was okay. And if word got out, he'd take the rap himself rather than let David take the fall.

Omar wondered if Knox had a family, if he even knew what a family was.

And then he thought, who would miss Knox if he were to vanish? Who would miss *any* of the Crusaders?

Maybe Omar wouldn't have to take the fall. Knox, he thought, was made for this.

"Well, Omar," Knox said. "You know the territory. You're the Kleagle."

Omar only hoped that being Kleagle was going to be enough.

TWENTY-EIGHT

Tuesday 17th—I never before thought the passion of fear so strong as I find it here among the people. It is really diverting, or would be so, to a disinterested observer, to see the rueful faces of the different persons that present themselves at my tent—some so agitated that they cannot speak—others cannot hold their tongues—some cannot sit still, but must be in constant motion, while others cannot walk. Several men, I am informed, on the night of the first shock deserted their families, and have not been heard of since. Encampments are formed of those that remain in the open fields, of 50 and 100 persons in each.

Extract from a letter to a gentleman in Lexington, from his friend at New Madrid, dated 16th December, 1811

The day after the fish cleaning was devoted to cleaning up. Nick shoveled offal into trucks, to be carried off and used as fertilizer on the food crops that Frankland's people had planted, after which Nick was then carried off with the rest of the Thessalonians to the Rails River for a bath. He was given soap, but it was intended more to clean his clothing than himself. Feeling like a Stone Age villager, he cleaned and pounded his clothes with a stick, then laid them out on grass to dry in the sun. Then he and the others washed the truck, after which Nick returned to the river to wash off the sweat.

The smell of dead fish still clogged his nostrils. He felt as if he'd never get rid of it. After riding back to the camp, the Second Thessalonians were given the rest of the day off.

Nick went in search of his family. The cooks had been up most of the night and hadn't been excused their duties for the daytime, so he found Manon in one of the cook tents, wearily frying fish in a skillet. Stock pots full of fish bones bubbled on all sides.

"Well," she said, "at least we'll have plenty of catfish to eat." She looked up at Nick and lowered her voice. "I overheard some of them yesterday morning. Before the big fish kill, they were thinking of cutting way back on our calories. Except for nursing mothers, down to fifteen hundred a day. That's over the line into slow starvation."

"And now?"

"Now we're okay. But it's catfish for breakfast, lunch, and dinner."

I've got to get my family out of here, Nick thought. He didn't like what he was hearing about the place from people like Tex and Olson, and he especially didn't like what he was hearing from Martin, his so-called guide.

There were too many guns in this camp, and too little sense.

"The problem with massacres," Knox said next morning, "is that they always have survivors. *Always.* Even if you set up machine guns outside and start mowing people down, some people will escape. It doesn't stand to reason they should, but they always do. Somebody's going to get away. Look at history."

Something twisted inside Omar's gut. He put a hand to his stomach, grimaced. He needed more Akla-Seltzer, he thought.

"What you're telling me," he said, "is that it's hopeless."

"No, not at all. You can't kill large numbers of Mud People *all at once*, that's all I'm saying." Knox flashed his jittery grin. "You have to sneak up on 'em. Just clip 'em in small groups, and with as much cooperation from the victims as possible."

They stood on the highway within sight of the A.M.E. camp. Omar had set up a roadblock here, and another farther down the highway. Any traffic between the two would move only under escort from Omar's special deputies.

Not that there was much traffic on the road to worry about. With the highway washed out to the north, there was no reason for anyone to travel in this area unless they were one of the half-dozen or so families that lived between here and the Floodway; and their movement was restricted, because there was so very little fuel remaining in the district, and any additional gasoline had to come in by helicopter.

The roadblocks were Knox's idea. He remembered something the Germans had done during the Holocaust. There was a Jewish ghetto in some big city, Warsaw or Prague or someplace, and an important tram line ran through the ghetto. The Germans couldn't shut down the tram, because people needed it to get to their jobs, so they just painted the tram windows so people couldn't see out, and made sure that soldiers were on board the trams to keep people from looking.

What the people couldn't see couldn't bother them.

Omar's roadblocks operated on the same principle. People would pass the camp only when he wanted them to. He couldn't paint over the windows of their vehicles, but he could keep them moving down the highway, under escort, at a brisk enough clip to keep them from seeing much.

"You've got to control the information," Knox had said. "Whatever story gets out, it's got to be *your* story."

Omar's story was that the camp was full of dangerous, armed felons. Camp inmates had shot a little girl and killed a local preacher who was only trying to help them. The killer of the preacher was still at large somewhere in the parish. People who got away weren't *refugees*, they were *escapees*, or possibly even *murderers*. And for the good of the parish, these people had to be corralled by armed force.

That was Omar's story. And so far, no one had heard any other.

A sudden pain clamped down on Omar's midsection. He winced, put a hand to his stomach.

"You okay, Omar?" Knox asked.

"It's the heat," Omar said.

"Hey, it's only morning! That air-conditioning's made you soft."

"I guess."

Knox looked at the camp again. "The question is, who's going to be the most trouble," Knox said. "It'll be the young, healthy, unmarried men." He grinned wolvishly. "Like me," he said. "I've *always* been trouble. So what you do, see, is you separate the young men from the rest."

"How?"

"Put them out on a work detail. And then when they don't come back, you just tell everyone that they're staying on site."

"It's pretty boring in that camp," Omar said. "Bet we'd get plenty of volunteers."

"You make sure none of your volunteers have family in the camp, and they won't be missed."

"Tell them we're building *another* camp," Omar said. "For single men."

"That's good," Knox approved, "that's good!"

And send them, Omar thought, *where the woodbine twineth.*

He would use Knox and the other Crusaders for that. Afterward Knox and his people could disappear. Either wherever they came from, or—if Omar needed a scapegoat— they would be found dead, killed in a gunfight with the last of the camp inmates.

And David would be safe. Safe. Which was the only thing that really mattered.

"Hi," Jason said.

"Hey there," said Arlette. "*Ça va?*"

He'd just come back from the river, and his clothing, the stains of which he had been mostly unable to remove by pounding, were still damp from having been washed. The crotch of his jeans was particularly damp and uncomfortable, and the wet seams scraped painfully along his thighs.

At least he thought he smelled okay.

Arlette sat crosslegged on the grass on the shady side of the church, supervising a group of small children at play. She wore a blue kerchief over her hair. Her birthday-present ear-rings dangled from her ears, though she wasn't wearing the necklace—too valuable, he supposed, for a place like this, or too showy.

"Locusts!" shouted Frankland over the PA. "Locusts with the faces of men! Right there in Revelations Nine!"

Arlette's eyes widened. "What happened to your hands?"

Jason looked down at his wounds. "I never cleaned a fish before."

"That looks awful. Didn't your guide help you?"

"He didn't seem to care."

"*Cochon.* Let me get you some bandages." She rose smoothly, without using her hands, from her crosslegged position, took one of his wounded hands, led him into the back door of the church. There was a small storeroom there, free of the smells and sounds of the infants in the main body of the church. The room was filled with items taken from the church when it was converted to a refugee center: boxes of Sunday School texts, files, religious literature, a dusty box of sheet music atop an old upright piano. Arlette walked to a small table behind the side door, dropped Jason's hand, and found a plastic box marked with a red cross under a small table.

Jason watched as she browsed through the contents of the box. Frankland's amplified voice went on about locusts going about the earth slaughtering its inhabitants.

"At least you didn't ask me about my nuclear reactor," Jason said.

"*Mais non. Je reconnais des telescopes quand j'en vois un.*" She raised her hands to mime a telescope, peered at him through her curled fingers for a laughing moment, then dropped into the box again.

She began to apply dressings to his hand. "Why are you talking French?" he asked.

"I'm supposed to be in France right now, at school. I don't want to get out of practice." She watched as he tugged at the inseam of his jeans with his free hand. "You don't look too comfortable in those clothes."

"They're still damp from washing. Hey." A thought occurred to him. "Don't you have washing machines here? You were folding clothes yesterday—why did I have to wash my clothes in the river?"

"We don't have that many machines in working order— we have to pour the water into them with buckets—all we try to do is keep the towels and diapers clean. When eighty men get catfish all over themselves—" She grinned. "It's the river. Give me your other hand."

"Where do the girls wash?"

"The same place. When the men aren't there."

Arlette peeled tape off the roll, eyed it, and cut it precisely with a small pair of scissors. "I don't understand," said a loud grownup voice, "why I can't leave."

Arlette and Jason fell silent as the voice boomed through the side door. Jason caught Arlette's eye, saw her surprised look, then a confirmation of his own first instinct.

Listen. Be silent. If you don't call attention to yourselves, maybe they'll forget you're here.

Jason and Arlette knew these things. How to listen, how to hide, how not to be observed. Jason shuffled sideways, put the open door between himself and the outside. Arlette slipped farther into the storeroom to make room for him.

The voice that answered was Frankland's. "I never said you couldn't leave, Brother Olson. What I said was—"

"What you said was that me and my family couldn't have any food! And that's after we brought a trunk full of canned goods and a box of vegetables into this camp!"

Jason looked at Arlette. *We* brought food into the camp, he thought.

"That food is *gone*, Brother Olson," Frankland said. "It was gone within a couple days of your getting here. It is my job to feed the people in this camp, and with God's help I will do that. But it is *not* my responsibility to feed the people who leave."

"I have kin in Mississippi," the first voice said. "They can look after us. And if you can just give us a few pounds of that catfish—heaven sake, you got *tons* . . ."

"Mississippi!" Frankland said. "You've heard the news! The place is a poison desert!"

Olson's voice was stubborn. "All I need is take my boat down the river. Won't take more'n two, three days. All I ask is food and water for that time. My guns for protection. The boat's my own. That's less'n I came with, and you won't have to feed us forever. It's a bargain for you."

"Think of your children, Brother Olson!" Frankland said.

"You're going to expose them to—"

"Reverend," Olson said, "I'm a Lutheran, okay?"

"I understand, brother, but—"

"Lutherans don't *do* the end of the world," Olson said. "I think what happened is an earthquake, not the Apocalypse. My family will be a lot safer once they get out of the earthquake zone."

"I will not let you endanger your family! I won't!"

"What are you telling me?" Olson roared.

"I won't let you kill your children!" Frankland shouted. "I won't let them go!"

Olson was beyond words. A chill shivered up Jason's spine as he heard Olson give a low growl just like an animal, and then there was a chiming metallic thump as something heavy hit the steel wall of the church. Frankland was shouting something incoherent, but Jason couldn't make it out because Frankland's recorded voice had just reached a crescendo in its sermon on the giant locusts of Revelation. Then other people were shouting, and there were more thumps.

Jason felt Arlette's hand close around his. He looked into her wide eyes as turmoil raged outside. He could feel a drop of sweat trickling down the back of his neck.

"Cast him forth!" Frankland's voice was raised in rage. "Take him outside! Let him wander in the wilderness!"

"He'll take your children, too!" Olson shouted as people hustled him away. *"He'll take your children!"*

Jason and Arlette stood frozen in the storeroom. Arlette's grip was like steel bands wrapped around his hand.

Jason licked his lips. "I'm getting out of this place," he said.

Arlette's eyes were wide as they turned from the open door to Jason. "How?"

"I don't know yet. But there's no way I'm going to stay here. That's for sure."

Frankland's voice boomed over the loudspeakers. *"And thus do the locusts do the will of Abaddon, the Angel of the Bottomless Pit."*

The camp was abuzz after Olson's ejection. A hundred and fifty people had nothing else to talk about.

Nick heard details from Jason and Arlette. He also heard the camp-wide rumor that Olson had just been driven in a truck to the far side of Rails Bluff, then set free to wander without food, water, or weapons.

Olson's wife and children, in the married women's camp, were at the center of a weeping, wailing cluster of friends and kinfolk. Nick led Manon, Arlette, and Jason away from the sight, wandering out of the camp onto the borders of the field beyond. The cotton had been plowed under here, and food crops planted, but only a few tiny green shoots had risen from the thin soil. The loudspeakers' words were reduced to a distant rumble.

"I'm going to get out of here, Nick," Jason said. "I'm getting back on the river."

Nick frowned, scuffed at the soil with his shoe. "We need to work out a plan," he said.

Jason looked at him in surprise. "You sound as if you want to come along."

"Yes." Nick frowned. "I don't think this place is stable. I don't think it's healthy." He looked over his shoulder in the direction of Sheryl's artwork. "Have you seen those banners? The people here think all that stuff is going to happen, and happen real soon. And what I'm afraid of is that if it doesn't happen on its own, they're going to do their best to *make* it happen."

Arlette looked up at her father. "What about Aunt Sarah and Uncle Louis and—"

Nick looked at her. "I think it will just be Jason and me, baby," he said. "You and your mother are safe here for the present. What we need to get out is a *message*, not necessarily *people*. If Jason and I can get down the river—Vicksburg, Baton Rouge, a towboat with a working radio, *somewhere*— we can tell the authorities what's happening here, and they'll start shipping in food and medicine, and put someone other than a crazy preacher in charge."

"Nick." Manon's tone was grim. "You've seen all the guns around here. What if Reverend Frankland decides he doesn't *want* the government putting him out of business?"

Nick looked at her in surprise. He had been concentrating so hard on plans to get away that he hadn't considered what might happen once he got his message to the authorities. "Do you really think he would?"

"The government have been here *already*. They took hundreds of people out of this camp. But my guess is that Frankland didn't want them to go, and he's decided that no one else is going to leave. Not even the ones who aren't his hard core, like Olson and his family. Olson came in because his business was wrecked after the second big quake, not because he was a believer."

Nick nodded. "Yes," he said. "Yes, I see that."

Manon bit her lip. Anxious worry glimmered in her eyes. "And besides," she added, "I don't think the government has a very good record when it comes to dealing with religious fanatics."

The deadly litany rolled through Nick's mind: *Jonestown. Waco. Ruby Ridge.* He thought about Manon and Arlette caught in a crossfire between cops and Frankland's guards, and he gave a shudder.

Manon stood straight-spined in the field, her chin tilted high. A princess in exile. "I want you to get your daughter out of this place," she said. Or, most likely, commanded.

Nick pressed his lips together, felt determination well up in his soul. *We are going to put together one hell of a plan,* he thought.

"All right," Nick said. "From now on, what we do is keep our eyes open. We need to find out how everything is done here. Find out where the supplies are kept. The guns. Food stores. Work out schedules for the guards." He nodded. "We're going to put together the best escape plan in the history of the world."

Because the best plan, the most flawless plan ever, was the only thing that would keep Arlette safe.

Apparently Brother Frankland wasn't talking much after Olson clouted him in the jaw, because the morning service was run by Garb, one of the other preachers. The service ran on for almost two hours, not counting a space of time that was taken up with a long, rumbling, but nondestructive aftershock. Garb made a lot of announcements about how Brother Amos' baby was feeling a little croupy and could use some prayers; and how Sister Felicity's arthritis was much improved after the congregation had sent a little of Jesus' healing power her way. Jason drowsed through it but woke up to enjoy the music.

Garb's actual sermon, when he got around to it, had to do with "God's marching orders," and the penalties inflicted for "falling out on the march," especially during wartime.

At present, Jason gathered, it was wartime. Jason didn't remember enlisting.

After another hymn, ominously entitled "Marching with Jesus," Garb made an announcement that after today most of the salvage jobs in the area would be discontinued. After finishing today, all the salvagers were to bring their tools and equipment back to the camp along with any useful items they may have found.

Jason would have to tote feed sacks only one more day. That was a relief.

Then, out of the corner of his eye, he caught Nick's frown, and he realized that with the work details ended, they'd have no reason to be out of the camp. It was going to be a lot harder to escape if their movement was restricted.

Finally there was breakfast. "Religion," Jason said over his beans and fried fish. "I don't get it."

Nick, sitting opposite Jason at the long table, seemed surprised by the question. "Say what?" he said.

"What's the *point*?" Jason asked. "What's it *for*?"

Nick exchanged glances with Manon and Arlette. "I'm an engineer," he said. "I only have an engineer's answer."

"Tell me," Jason said. He was aware of Arlette's nearness, of the warmth of her sitting only a few inches from him on the bench.

"Religion is to help people behave better," Nick said. "The whole point is—" He searched for a phrase. "Moral instruction. Moses taught duty. Jesus taught goodness. The rest—

Heaven and Hell, the miracles, all that—is just to get people to pay attention. Some people won't listen to instruction unless you give them a show along with it."

Manon, sitting by his side, rolled her eyes and gave a kind of snort. "You men," she said.

Nick gave her a tolerant look. "I *said* it was an engineer's point of view."

"Religion's about *community*, you fool," Manon said. The *fool* was affectionate, Jason thought, or meant to be affectionate anyway, though at the sound of the word there was a flicker in Nick's eyes that suggested he didn't much like hearing it.

Manon leaned toward Jason. "It's about sharing," she said. "It's about a group of people being happy together, and grieving together, and praising God together, and experiencing all of life together. That's the point of all those announcements that Brother Garb made, so that everyone would know what was happening in the community." She nudged Nick. "It's not as if we get together every Sunday for a *lecture*. About our *morals*, for God's sake." She looked at Jason. "It's *fun*. We always had a big meal beforehand. Big meal afterward, with all the family for miles around. The preacher was our Uncle Joe till he retired, and he came for dinner with his wife."

"You go to church because it's family," Nick said. "I went because it was a *duty*. The same reason I was an Eagle Scout. It was something a general's son did." He shrugged. "Scouting was more fun."

"Your daddy turned every damn thing into a job," Manon said.

"Do you *believe* it?" Jason asked her. Suddenly he was desperate to know. "Do you believe in God? Adam and Eve? Noah? All that?"

Manon seemed a little surprised, so Jason went on. "My mom believed *anything*, see. She believed in reincarnation, in astrology, in Buddha, in Jesus, in the Tao. She believed in a woman in California named Pharaoh Nepher-Ankh-Hotep who had a spirit guide named Louise from Atlantis. Someone once told her that the UFO people had a huge city on the back side of the moon. I remember she once told my dad about this—this was before the divorce—and he went, well, the astronauts went around the moon, they would have seen it. And my mom went, see, they *did* see it, and they had pictures, but there was a cover-up. And my dad asked her why they covered it up, and she went, well, they *always* cover up the flying saucers, just like they did at Roswell, everybody knows that. And my dad asked why, and she said it was because the government was secretly working with the UFO people and letting them abduct people in return for scientific knowledge. And my dad went, the government would never be able to keep a secret like that, it's a *huge* secret, it's the most important thing *ever*, and the government can't even keep their five-thousand-dollar toilet seats secret, or the itching powder they tried to put in Fidel Castro's beard . . ."

Jason ran out of energy. Manon gave him a curious look.

"What did your momma say?" she asked.

Jason looked at her. "She said, 'That's why they killed Kennedy.'"

Manon looked surprised. "I don't understand," she said.

"I don't either. I don't think my mom really understood what she was trying to say. She was making it up as she went along, I think, once she heard about the moon base. The point is, she'd just *heard* about the flying saucers on the moon, and if she was going to believe in that, she had to believe in all the other stuff, too. That was the way she was." He looked down at his plate. "My parents got divorced right after that."

Manon reached over the table, took his hand. "I'm sorry, Jason," she said.

Jason shrugged. "Not your fault."

She looked at him. "You had a question, though. And I forgot what it was."

"It's about whether you believe it all. Or whether it's just, like, community."

Manon's voice was gentle. "Well," she began. "You know that the church is important to black people, right? Because for a long time we weren't allowed to meet anywhere else. They were afraid that if we got together we'd start a rebellion or ask for our freedom, or for the right to vote or something.

But they couldn't keep us out of church, because it was their religion, too. So the church was the only place where we were free to be ourselves."

"I didn't know that," Jason said. If that had ever been mentioned in class he hadn't been paying attention. He hated history. But they probably hadn't mentioned it. They never seemed to teach anything that mattered to people.

"What I meant to say," Manon went on, "is that the part of church that is community is very, very important. But there's community with the Deity as well."

"So you believe in God?"

"Oh yes."

"And Jesus?"

"Certainly."

"And Adam and Eve? Jonah and the whale? Noah?"

Manon hesitated, looked at Nick. "Well. I don't know."

"If an engineer can interrupt, here," Nick said, "I think stories like Noah and Adam have a different purpose from some of the other Bible stories. They were intended for *moral instruction.*" He looked at Manon pointedly. "Those stories were to teach us how to behave, and to make us think, but I don't know that they were intended to be taken literally."

"I don't think I believe in God," Jason said.

There was a moment of silence. He felt Arlette stir on the bench next to him.

"Why not?" she said.

"Because," Jason said in swift anger, "if God exists, he killed my mother. And your Gros-Papa. And lots of other people rolling along the bottom of that river."

Suddenly Jason couldn't stand to sit there any longer, looking into the others' shocked and concerned faces, so he rose and mumbled an apology and almost ran from the breakfast tent. He wandered out into the parking lot in front of the church, where the empty trucks waited to carry the Samaritans and the other teams to their final days' work. Waves of heat were already rising from their metal as they baked in the morning sun.

Jason stalked around the trucks as anger simmered through his veins. Then he opened the door of a cab and sat behind the steering wheel. Keys dangled from the ignition, and for a wild moment Jason considered starting the truck and roaring away, fleeing the camp and the people in it.

But no. There was no place to drive to. That was why the key was in the ignition—there was no point in locking a vehicle when there was no place for a thief to drive it.

He was stuck in Rails Bluff, until Nick figured out a way to escape.

Words boomed from the loudspeakers: "Let him which is on the housetop not come down to take anything out of his house."

Jason swung his legs out of the truck cab, slid onto the grass. His anger had passed, had turned to a dull throbbing ache in his throat.

He turned around the back end of the pickup truck, with its Tommy Lift tailgate down, and found Arlette standing there, a bit awkwardly, off-balance with one ankle crossed over the other. Jason stopped dead. He felt his ears flush with the memory of his rudeness.

"I thought I'd see if you were okay," Arlette said.

"I'm, uh, *tres bien*," Jason said. "I'm sorry if I was angry."

"I brought you the rest of your breakfast," Arlette said. She held up a bundle wrapped in a handkerchief. "I thought you'd need it if you're going to be working today."

"Thanks."

He approached her and took the bundle. Beans and fish all mashed together.

Well. It was a nice thought. And probably he would be hungry enough, sooner or later, to eat it.

"I'm sorry you're mad at God," Arlette said. She took a step forward, her hip resting against the tailgate of the truck. "I think I need God, myself. I want to think that there's something that connects me with the rest of the universe. Some spirit. Something."

Jason thought about galaxies whirling in the velvet dark. Threads like lace glowing in the sky. A cluster of a million stars that he could hold in his hand.

Arlette looked at him with almond-shaped eyes. "Haven't you ever felt something connect you with everything else?" she asked.

"Yes," Jason said. His pulse was a roar in his ears. "You," he said.

He took her in his arms and brushed her lips with his. Her slim waist burned against his palms. He kissed her again, and again, and then for a long time.

Arlette drew away.

"No," he said. "Don't stop."

Her lips tilted in a delicate smile. "There must be twenty people watching us. And if we go on any longer there are going to be a hundred."

"I want to be with you," he said.

"Later," she said. The smile turned mischievous. "Maybe."

She turned, looked at him over her shoulder. "Enjoy your breakfast," she said, and skipped away.

Jason stood for a moment, then looked toward the camp.

Twenty people, he thought. More like fifty.

Let them watch, he thought.

"Looks like your daughter's getting down with the white boy," Manon said.

Nick watched from under the kitchen awning as Arlette and Jason embraced by the pickup truck. Anxious-father vibes bounced around in his head, and he told them to be reasonable. They didn't listen.

"Well," he said heavily, "I'm not going to worry too much about it." And failed to convince even himself.

Manon turned to him, fire snapping from her eyes. "Not worry?" she said. "You know what kids are like at that age. Hormones going crazy, and there's nothing to do in this camp, nothing but . . . Damn it, Nick!" She blinked out at the sunlit field, where Arlette was drawing away from Jason.

"Arlette's too young for this," Manon said. "She's my baby." Her eyes were shiny.

"You were going to send her to France for the summer,"

Nick said. "Did you figure she'd only meet nuns over there?"

"She'd be chaperoned," Manon said.

"She's chaperoned *here*, honey," Nick said. He couldn't resist smiling. "She'll never be more chaperoned in her life."

"Nick," Manon said, "that boy is white."

Nick said nothing. Anxious-father voices sang an aria in his head. It's not about race, Nick told himself, it's really not. It's about a boy touching his daughter, that's what it's about.

"Oh hell, Nick," Manon went on. "This is Arkansas, that's what I'm saying."

"Yeah," Nick said. "I know." And if it was a black boy kissing a white girl, there would be fifty people here ready for a lynching, whatever Reverend Frankland might say about it. And even as things stood, there might be hell to pay, anyway.

Arlette turned from Jason and began to move away across the field. The tension in Nick's chest eased a trifle.

"Certain things you don't do here," Manon went on. "Not where a hundred people can see you. Not if you're young and—" She blinked tears. "Not even if you've been raised to think these things don't matter."

Nick stepped closer to her, put his hands on her shoulders from behind. Her muscles were taut as wire.

"I'll talk to Jason if you like," he said. He had the sensation that he was arguing with himself as much as with Manon. "And you can talk to Arlette. But Arlette's an intelligent girl. I think we can trust her." He began to massage Manon's shoulders, trying to break the tension he felt in the muscles.

"Besides, baby," he said, "here's what's going to happen. One way or another, we're going to get out of here. Then, for a while, we'll be in a boat, and Arlette can't be any more chaperoned than in a sixteen-foot boat with both her parents. And after we get back to civilization, Jason will go home to his daddy, and Arlette will be in Arkansas, and that will be that."

He felt Manon's sinew resist his fingers, and then Manon gave a long sigh, and he felt her relax, lean back against his strength. "Oh, why'd you have to bring that boy here?" she murmured. "He's going to be nothing but trouble."

"That's the truth," Nick said. He studied the nape of

Manon's neck, the loose tight curls that had escaped the kerchief in which she'd bound her hair. The sheen on her fine
mahogany skin, supple as the day they were married. He
leaned close to her ear.

"Jason's only thinking what's natchel," he said. "He's not
thinking anything I'm not thinking."

He felt Manon stiffen. "That's what I'm worried about,"
she said, and then, after a moment's resistance, she relaxed
again, her head lolling back against one of his hands. "Not
now, Nick," she murmured. "I can't deal with this now."

"Don't worry, baby," Nick smiled. "We're chaperoned."

There was a honk from the speakers, and then Frankland's
voice telling all work parties to assemble to the trucks.

"There," Nick said. "See what I mean?"

Jessica stood with Larry Hallock next to the Auxiliary
Building. Stood on dry land, her boots covered with dry
dust, not river mud. A hundred feet away an Army brass
band, gratefully reunited with their instruments after days of
debris removal, were exercising their callused fingers on
"Hail to the Chief."

Operation Island was a success. The twenty-four-hour airlift of earthquake debris had finally produced a plausible
island of twenty acres raised six feet above the river's current
flood stage. The last loads consisted not of debris, but of
gravel to provide a safe surface to walk on. Army bulldozers
were currently grading the surface flat. More material would
be added later, but right now it was more important to get
Larry's people into the business of getting spent reactor fuel
out of the Auxiliary Building and then out of the earthquake
zone.

A channel had been carved into the island just for this purpose. A little canal, wide and deep enough for a fully laden
barge, ran from the edge of Poinsett Island to the end of the
Auxiliary Building. There, a barge could be loaded with
flasks of spent fuel, then towed to safety downriver.

A barge was now being towed into place by a pair of bulldozers. Its rust-streaked hull rode high in the water, ballast-

ed only by the three huge steel flasks into which fuel units could be loaded.

Jessica felt good knowing that at least one thing had gone right. With Nature stomping on her every effort to control the river, with the evacuation she'd recommended shattered by a second major quake, *this*, at least, was something she could point to with pride.

Her very own island. Built of much more solid material than anything else in the river, Poinsett Island might well last hundreds of years.

"Looks good, General," Larry said. "Nice piece of work, here."

"Thank you," Jessica said.

"I like the shiner, too."

Jessica raised a self-conscious hand to her black eye. "My husband thinks it's kind of dashing," she said.

"Makes you look determined as heck."

They both glanced up at the sound of a helicopter. They had both grown so used to copters in Army green or Navy blue that civilian white seemed a little startling against the cloudless blue sky.

"Here comes the press," Jessica said without enthusiasm.

"Bet they like the black eye, too," Larry said.

Despite the media's voracious twenty-four-hour-per-day demand for information—or, in the absence of information, baseless rumor, innuendo, and sensation—Jessica had managed to keep the press at arm's length till now. She had appointed a press officer in Vicksburg to manage the information flow—the information went not just to the media, but to politicians demanding information about their districts—and Jessica had stopped by the briefings at least once per day to add a little personal, calming dimension to the day's news riot.

Much of her work with the press consisted of stamping out one terrifying, sensational rumor about Poinsett Landing after another. Stories about giant poisonous radioactive clouds floating over the South, or a river of pure liquid plutonium burning its way down the Mississippi, continued to persist in the face of any data to the contrary. *The biggest earthquake in human history isn't enough for you,* Jessica wanted to say, *you have to have Chernobyl, too?*

As if that weren't enough, she had to be very careful with place names. Foreign journalists had demonstrated an understandable difficulty in separating the Mississippi, a river, from the State of Mississippi, a political entity, and the Mississippi Delta, a geographical feature. As if that weren't confusing enough to information-saturated foreigners, it was also necessary to keep straight the State of Arkansas, the Arkansas River, and the Arkansas Delta, the Missouri River and the State of Missouri, and bear in mind that much of Kansas City was not in the State of Kansas but in Missouri.

Compared to that, Operation Island was simple. Operation Island was Jessica's showpiece. The press were going to *stand* on the island, prove to themselves that it existed, that the panic they'd been broadcasting was baseless and that the Corps of Engineers could work wonders.

Jessica didn't know about civilian morale, she supposed, but it would sure as hell do her *own* morale a lot of good.

The press landed, and were shown to their reserved area by their liaison people. Secret Service, conspicuous in neat summer-weight suits, had stationed themselves around the island. More Secret Service, equipped as snipers, stood atop the Auxiliary Building.

The sound of helicopter rotors chopped through the air. Big Marine copters appeared over the treeline to the east.

"Here comes your boss," Larry said.

Jessica looked down at her BDUs, brushed dust off the pants legs and the toes of her boots, then made sure her helmet was square on her head. The commander-in-chief was coming to give her work on Poinsett Island the official presidential seal of approval.

The Army brass band did some last-minute tuning, almost inaudible in the helicopter roar. Jessica made a smart turn and marched across the gravel to the place where the presidential helicopter was expected to land.

Offer condolences before you say anything else, she reminded herself. *The poor guy's lost his wife.*

Try not to talk every single minute, she told herself as the presidential party circled the island. *Let the man get a word in edgewise.*

He's a politician, she reminded herself. *He'll want to talk.*

The fact was, Larry thought, that a presidential visit lasts only a few minutes. But cleanup is a task that lives forever.

The afterglow of the presidential visit, the presidential handshake, and the presidential compliments had lasted all of maybe twenty minutes. After that, it was back to policing the power plant.

Larry stood on the fuel handling machine and watched Jameel as he rolled the big crane along its tracks. Floodlights gleamed in the murky river water of the fuel holding pond. The crane came to a stop.

"This is where you wanted us, Mr. Hallock."

"Test the turret," Larry said. "Let's make sure everything works."

Electric motors whined. Larry, hanging his head over the edge of the platform, saw the turret rotate beneath his feet. Nothing shorted out on the instrument panel.

"Waall." Larry grinned. "Let's find us a fish in this ol' pond."

He watched as Jameel expertly lowered the pincerlike grab on the end of its double chain. The first snatch came up empty, and Jameel made modest alterations to the turret position and tried again.

A light shifted from green to red on the plywood display.

Jameel's laugh boomed from beneath the brim of his Chicago Cubs cap. "Got ourselves a fish here, skip."

"Better reel her in, then."

Electric motors whined. Brown river silt, by now disturbingly radioactive, floated upward as the chain retracted. In the midst of the rising brown mushroom Larry could see the silver glint of a fuel assembly.

An older one, fortunately, one that had cooled considerably in the decades it had been sitting in the holding pond. Larry had dropped radiation detectors into the pond to locate areas of radioactive tranquility, and this was one of them.

With the fuel assembly still held safely below the surface of the borated water, the machine skimmed back on its tracks to the fill bay on the far end of the building. There, after three tries, Jameel managed to drop the fuel assembly into one of the slots on a thick-walled steel transport flask. The flask, when full, would then be passed out of the Auxiliary Building onto a barge, and then carried down the river, with other flasks, to the holding pond of the Waterford Three nuclear plant in St. Charles Parish, Louisiana. Waterford Three was a new reactor, had only gone online in 1985, and had reserve space in its holding pond.

Which would soon be full. But there were other nuclear facilities in the country, other holding ponds. All of Poinsett Landing's dangerous children would find a home in the end.

There was a little *click* as Jameel activated the solenoid that released the fuel assembly, then a whine of electric motors as he raised the grab on its chain.

"Get us another fish, sir?" he asked.

"You bet," Larry said. "I want another dozen before the day is over."

The President sat in his suite at the rear of Air Force One and watched the clouds through his window. The clouds were far below, very white, and danced an interesting pas-de-deux with their shadows on the green land below. The President was returning to Washington from having made his inspection of Poinsett Island, and he was doing what he preferred to do nowadays, which was to stare at unexceptional things in a perfectly tranquil, uninterested way.

The visit to Poinsett Island had been entirely symbolic, he understood that. He hadn't a thing to do with rescuing the power station, and his presence made no difference at all to the level of safety at the plant. His appearance was just a way of telling people not to panic. If the President wasn't scared of the big, bad nuclear plant, the public shouldn't be, either. His appearance assured the people that things were in hand. It associated the President with a specific *way* that things were getting better, and therefore led to increased confidence in the country and in the economy, and of course higher approval ratings.

It was his first trip out of Washington since the death of the First Lady. That had symbolic value, too. The trip told the nation that he was putting his personal sorrows behind and getting on with the business of the country.

His visit to Poinsett Island had been both meaningful and meaningless. It was nothing in itself; it was a waste of time and jet fuel and didn't contribute to the solution of the national crisis one iota, but on a symbolic level it stood for a great deal.

What the President hadn't quite worked out yet was what it all meant to *him*. He was beginning to suspect, however, that it didn't mean much of anything.

It was all clouds, floating past his window. Earthquakes, swallowing the world.

Clouds and earthquakes, he thought, were almost the same thing. Sort of. Weren't they?

There was a knock on his door. "Come in," he said.

Stan Burdett's bespectacled face peered around the door. "Urgent phone call, sir," he said. "The Secretary of State."

The President looked idly at the battery of communications apparatus with which his suite had come equipped. Stan entered the room, picked up a phone handset, pressed some buttons, and handed the handset to the President.

"Secure line, sir," he said.

"Oh, good," said the President.

"Mr. President?" The Secretary's voice buzzed in his ear. "I've got a situation here."

"Right, Darrell. What can I do for you?"

"The Chinese have just announced that in three days they will test-fire a number of their medium-range ballistic missiles over the island of Taiwan, to land in the Pacific."

"Oh," the President said. "Oh my."

"This is an overt military threat, Mr. President. This is a direct challenge to our resolve and to our overseas commitments. The Chinese are testing us."

"Best not flunk, eh?" the President said.

There was a buzz from another handset. Stan picked it up. "Stan Burdett," he said. Then he looked at the President and told him the call was from the National Security Advisor.

The President realized that the Secretary of State had been talking nonstop while his own attention had been directed toward the other phone, and said, "Hold on, there, Darrell, I have another call." He put the second phone to his other ear and said, "Joe, I've just heard. Darrell's on the other line."

"We cannot afford to lose Taiwan, sir," the National Security Advisor said. "It is too completely integrated with our own economy. They produce countless small electronic components that are incorporated into American brand-names. If Taiwan is lost, a lot of American manufacturing goes with it."

Well, the President thought, his hawkish Secretary of State and his dovish Security Advisor actually agreed with one another. This was a no-brainer. "Better not lose Taiwan, then," the President said into both phones.

"Those bastards!" the Secretary was shouting into his other ear. "They've been planning this for weeks! I've got it figured out! Remember just before the big quake, when the Chinese sold a lot of dollars and sent Wall Street into a tumble? They were making a point! They were trying to show that they could fuck with our economy, and that we had better think twice before we tried to interfere with their attempt to intimidate Taiwan!"

While this speech was going on, the President looked at Stan and said, "Stan, could you arrange a conference call? This is giving me a headache."

"We should mobilize the Seventh Fleet!" the Secretary said finally, when they were all on the same secure line. "Send our ships into the area of the Pacific where their missile will land, and dare them to try anything!"

The Advisor cleared his throat. "I don't think that would be wise, Mr. President. What if the Chinese actually fire? That would be a shooting war."

"They wouldn't dare!" shouted the Secretary.

"If we dare them to shoot, that puts ammunition into the hands of their people who would *want* to shoot. And our military options are extremely limited in that eventuality. For one thing, our nearest real base is Pearl Harbor. And for another, we won't be able to fly sufficient sorties off our carriers, not with the shortage of jet fuel that we're experiencing."

"Jet fuel?" the President said in surprise.

"Mr. President," the Advisor said, "we're been flying so many relief supplies into the disaster areas that there's a worldwide shortage of aviation fuel. The refineries are cranking it out as fast as they can, but our reserves are very low."

"What you are saying," the President said, "is that we have to keep the Chinese off Taiwan, but we can't fight a war over it because all our planes would fall out of the sky."

There was a moment of silence. "That wasn't *quite . . .*" the Advisor began.

"I think you have summed things up very well, Joe," the President said. "Now how can we accomplish what we need to do?"

It was very interesting, the President thought, doing his job without being *attached* to it. He had decided he would be President when he was nine years old, and he'd worked toward that goal with every conscious moment since, until he'd finally succeeded in his ambition. He used to care so very deeply about every aspect of being the President, of working out every angle of every situation. He had loved it all, the brainstorming, the defeats, and victories. He had given it his all. His *ego* had been involved.

But now his ego was gone. Just . . . *gone*. He was doing the same job, making the same decisions, but it just didn't have much to do with *him* anymore. This situation would be fascinating, at least if he were capable any longer of being fascinated.

In the end, he sent two carrier battle groups into the Western Pacific, though was careful to keep them out of the area where the Chinese missile was supposed to land. Both the Secretary and the Advisor seemed reasonably content with the situation.

"By the way," he asked the Secretary. "What are the Gamsakhurdians up to?"

"Sir?"

"You know. *Last* week's crisis. Georgia and Latvia."

"Oh. Sorry. I was going to brief you, but—"

"I know, Darrell. We're all very busy."

"The Russian President told our ambassador that he was shocked at what his people were up to."

"Do we believe he didn't know?"

"As long as it suits us to. Right now it suits us to the ground. At least some of the paramilitaries have been recalled. The rest seem without direction. We are assured that heads are rolling in the Kremlin."

"Latvia is safe," the President smiled.

"For the present, sir. Yes."

"The thought of a safe and free Latvia shall warm my cockles on frosty mornings. I'll talk to you later, Darrell."

He handed the phone to Stan Burdett, who put it on its cradle. The President turned, looked out the window at the clouds far below.

"China is attacking Taiwan on a symbolic level," he told Stan. "By firing missiles over it. We are defending Taiwan on a symbolic level by sending two carrier battle groups. The symbols will clash harmlessly somewhere in the Western Pacific, and no one will be hurt. It's all very dreamlike and in its way profound, isn't it?"

Stan looked at him, adjusted his thick spectacles. "May I join you, sir?" he said.

"By all means."

Stan sat across from the President, put a hand on his knee. "Are you all right, sir?"

The President looked at him. "My wife is dead, my oldest friend is dead, the country just had its guts ripped out, and the Chinese are shooting missiles in the direction of our ships. Other than that, all is well with myself and with the world. How are you, Stan?"

"You're not . . ." Stan licked his thin lips nervously. "You're not depressed?"

"Depressed? No. I am strangely placid. And you?"

"Because—you know—it would be understandable if you were depressed. If you were, say, feeling tired and run-down all the time, if all you wanted to do was sleep . . ."

"I don't sleep much," the President said. "You people won't let me. Why do crises always seem to happen at two in the morning?"

"I just meant *depressed*, you know," Stan said unhappily. "In the—you know—*clinical* sense."

"I'm not depressed in *any* sense," the President said. "I eat well and I sleep well, at least when I have the opportunity. I do my job. You just saw me deal with a major international crisis without pulling my hair out or going into a crying jag." He peered at Stan. "Are *you* depressed, Stan?"

"No, sir. I'm concerned."

"That's kind of you." The President patted the hand that Stan had left on his knee. "But you don't need to worry."

"Sir, I—"

"Do you know, Stan," the President went on, "I have inquired three times as to your well-being, and you have not answered at all?"

"Sir?"

The President leaned toward Stan. "How *are* you, Stan? That's what I was trying to get at. How *are* you?"

"Oh. I am—okay. I guess. Sir." Stan smiled nervously. "The thing is—Mr. President—you seem, I don't know—unengaged."

"Ah."

"As if you—as if you're just going through the motions, as if your real thoughts are elsewhere."

The President ventured a mild frown. "And why should that be a problem, Stan?"

The press secretary seemed startled. "Sir?"

"What's wrong with a president who's detached? Who—" The President made a stirring gesture with his hand. "Who goes through the motions. As long as they're the right motions, what difference does it make?" He looked out the window again, at the clouds below. "If I send two carrier battle groups to Taiwan, does it really matter to the carrier groups if my heart and soul are in it? Will it matter to the Chinese? Will the Chinese be able to look into my soul and determine whether or not the carriers matter to me? Or will the Chinese decide that what matters is the *carrier groups*?" The President patted Stan's hand. "I think they'll decide that it's the Seventh Fleet that matters. Not my level of engagement *with* the Seventh Fleet."

He turned, looked back at the window. "After all, when you're dealing with an earthquake, you don't inquire as to the earthquake's state of mind. You just *deal with the earthquake.* The Chinese will deal with the reality of the Seventh Fleet. I don't expect a problem."

Stan looked deeply unhappy. He took a deep breath. "Mr. President, I think that perhaps you should talk to somebody."

The President peered at him. "I'm talking to *you.* I talk to people all the time. Practically every minute."

"I mean a professional, sir. A psychologist. After all, you've been going through a lot. You—"

The President returned to his cloudscape. "I talk to enough people as it is, Stan. Now, what I need you to do is work out what you're going to tell the press about the Taiwanese crisis once we return to D.C. You heard what we're going to do, and I'm sure you know how to spin it. Unless you'd rather have Aaron Schwarz down at State give the briefing . . . ?"

"I'll do it, sir," Stan said quickly. He rose from his seat. He did not seem to have been comforted in the least by this conversation.

The President's eyes tracked the clouds. "Don't worry, Stan," he said. "I'm not asleep at the switch. I'm doing my job."

"Yes, sir." Stan made his way out, closing the door securely behind him.

The President looked down at the clouds, skating brightly

above the warm green earth. Clouds that were the same things as earthquakes. Sort of.

Weren't they?

Omar rented a backhoe from Judd Criswell to make certain the graves at Woodbine Corners were properly set up. As a man with a career in law enforcement, he very much appreciated the dangers of shallow graves. He chose a very remote part of the parish, in old Bart Cattrall's back sixty acres near the bayou. Bart used to plant the field in cotton, but two years ago he'd had a crippling stroke, and he'd let his land lie fallow two seasons now. He kept claiming he was going to plant it, but he never did.

By noon Omar figured he had things well in hand, but by one o'clock everything had gone to hell. The dozen or so cases of diarrhea that Wilona had mentioned in the Clarendon camp had turned into a hundred. And the day after that, three hundred.

All emergency personnel in the parish were mobilized to deal with the situation. Three hundred people on the neat Clarendon grounds, enhancing the charm of the gardens with uncontrollable diarrhea and intermittent vomiting. Omar would have laughed, except that he was hip-deep in the action along with everyone else, trying to keep the patients hydrated and alive with Dr. Patel's emergency solution of glucose and salt.

Thirteen people died. Six were elderly, and five were children. The remaining two, healthy adults, were just unlucky.

Miz LaGrande got sick as well. Omar hoped she'd croak, but the old lady hung on. Omar figured she was too worried about her guests stealing the silver to actually die.

Omar wasn't feeling so good himself. Some days he could barely drag himself out of bed. Sometimes his stomach pained him so much that it felt like a wolf eating his vitals. He tried Alka-Seltzer, Maalox, and aspirin. Nothing seemed to help.

There were certain advantages to the emergency. Omar pulled all his regular deputies into town to deal with the situation. He could only keep a skeleton crew of special deputies at the A.M.E. camp, because everyone else was trying to treat the outbreak of dysentery. It gave him a plausible excuse for not being around the A.M.E. camp, for not knowing officially what was going on there. He put the whole place in the charge of special deputies, all Klan or Crusaders. The only actual Spottswood Parish deputy he placed there was Jedthus, whom he instructed to rely on Micah Knox's advice.

Jedthus, Omar reckoned, was his most expendable deputy.

The outbreak at Clarendon was traced to the water supply. The Emergency people had sent water purifying equipment, but this had been taken to the municipal water supplies of Shelburne City and Hardee for the use of the taxpayers. Since the city main that led to Clarendon had been wrecked, Mrs. Ashenden had uncovered a pair of old wells on the property in order to keep her refugees in water. But neither she nor anyone else had been careful about keeping the camp's latrines at a safe distance from the wells, and now they were all paying the penalty.

It was just, Omar thought, like the War Between the States.

TWENTY-NINE

This morning, at about 9 o'clock, a friend of mine, Captain Franklin, Miss Webster, and myself, had just sat down to breakfast, when Captain F. observed, "What's that? An Earthquake!" at the same instant, we felt as if we were in the cabin of a vessel, during a heavy swell. This sensation continued for one or two minutes, possibly longer. For although I had the presence of mind to take out my watch, I felt too sick to accurately observe its duration. The feeling was by no means tremulous, but a steady vibration. A portrait, about four feet in length, suspended from the ceiling by a hook and staple, and about five eights of an inch from the side wall, vibrated at least from eighteen inches to 2 feet each side, and so very steady, as not to touch the wall. My next neighbour and his daughter felt the same sensation about the same time. The father supposed it was the gout in his head. The daughter got up and walked to a window, supposing the heat of the fire had caused what she considered a faintness. Two others that I have seen mentioned to have felt the same, but none of them had thought of an earthquake. The two last being mechanics, and up late, mentioned that they were much alarmed at about 11 o'clock last night, by a great rumbling, as they thought, in the earth, attended with several flashes of lightning, which so lighted the house, that they could have picked up the smallest pin—one mentioned, that the rumbling and the light was accompanied by a noise like that produced by throwing a hot iron into snow, only very loud and terrific, so much so, that he was fearful to go out to look what it was, for he never once thought of an earthquake. I have thrown together the above particulars, supposing an extract may meet with corroborating accounts, and afford some satisfaction to your readers.

P.S.—The lightning and rumbling noise came from the

*south—I have just heard of its being felt in several other hous-
es, but not any particulars more than related.*

Extract of a letter dated West River, January 23

"Heaven-o there, Jason."

Jason—sitting crosslegged on the ground, resting his mus-
cles after a day of hauling feed sacks, and waiting for the
Samaritans to be called for dinner—looked up at the Reverend
Frankland. "Uh, hi," he said.

"I want to talk to you for a minute, boy," Frankland said.

A shiver of fear ran up Jason's spine. He wondered if the
Reverend had heard about him talking to the gate guards
about where the weapons were stored. Or others about how
the guards were set, and who set them, and whether they
walked regular rounds or just wandered at random.

Maybe he was just going to get chewed out for kissing
Arlette. He had got the impression, from what some of the
other boys in the Samaritans had said, that they took race
pretty seriously here in Arkansas. Maybe as seriously as they
took religion.

A smile beamed down from Frankland's face, its effect
marred by the split lip and bruising that Olson had inflicted
on him. That and the lack of chin.

"There's a story, Jason," Frankland said, "that you brought
some kind of nuclear device into the camp."

A nervous laugh broke from Jason's throat. Looking into
Frankland's searching gaze, he concluded that this was no
time to stretch the truth.

"It's a telescope," he said. "But if I told the other kids it
was a telescope, they'd play with it and break it. So I made
up something to keep them away from it."

Little amused crinkles broke out around Frankland's eyes.
"That's a good one, son!" he said. One big hand patted Jason
on the shoulder.

"Uh, thanks," Jason said.

"But you shouldn't tell stories that scare people,"
Frankland said.

Jason looked up. Tried to make his face vulnerable. "It's the only thing I have to remember my father by," he said. "I didn't want to lose it."

Sympathy settled into Frankland's bruised face. He patted Jason on the shoulder again. "If your telescope is valuable, bring it to me when I'm free, and I'll lock it up for you in the big storeroom. You can get it back any time you like."

"I'll do that, sir," Jason said. "Thank you."

"And maybe some night you can bring out the scope and give a show for the boys and girls. It'll be good to keep their minds occupied with so much time on their hands."

"I don't know much about the stars yet, " Jason said. "But I'll tell them what I know."

"Great!" Frankland was already rolling away. "Heaven-o, Jason!"

"Uh," Jason said, "bye."

Jason thought for a moment. He didn't want to let his telescope go, but on the other hand it would be interesting to see what was in Frankland's storerooms, and how it could be got to.

And it wasn't as if he'd been stargazing much, anyway.

Jason told Nick about Frankland's offer later that evening, after supper, as they were walking by the perimeter fence with Manon and Arlette prior to Garb's evening service. It was about the only encouraging news Nick heard all day.

He'd spent the previous day sweating and sorting through the rubble at the Bijoux along with the rest of the Thessalonians, and talking to Tex and the other workers when their guide Martin wasn't listening. All he'd managed to find out was how tight Frankland had Rails Bluff sewn up.

The guns Nick had come with, and all those belonging to the others in the camp who weren't part of Frankland's clique, were all in a concrete-walled bunker, with a concrete slab over them. A tripod and tackle were required to lift the slab, so there was no reasonable hope of getting firearms from anywhere in the camp before they made their run for freedom.

Nick had spent today at the camp. Work details were over, and very few people were allowed out. Nick had talked to a number of people who had been here awhile—he said he was looking for a suitable job here in camp—and none of the news had been encouraging.

Food supplies were guarded. There was a guard on the improvised boat jetty at the Rails River. Nick had seen a Chevy Suburban with heavily armed men drive out in that direction just that morning.

The only cause for optimism was that the guard on the camp itself was lax. The guards' training was nonexistent, or dated from years ago in the military, and lack of calories and proper supervision made them lazy. There were no passwords, no proper checks, and the perimeter was chiefly defined by twine strung from wooden posts.

Nick imagined the guards were all good shots, though. They all had the ease of country people who had been raised around firearms and were comfortable with them. The question was whether they would fire at another human being who was only trying to get away, who wasn't trying to harm them.

He suspected that most of them wouldn't shoot. But Nick didn't want to risk his daughter's life on that supposition.

It would probably be relatively easy to slip out of the camp, he concluded—but then what? If they stole a vehicle they'd give themselves away the second they keyed the ignition. They didn't know the country. And if they were missed, people would probably go out looking, and the guards would be alerted. Manon might sneak some food from the kitchen, but it wouldn't be much. The boat slip was guarded by two men.

Nick wondered if he could fake a message from Frankland to the guards. *You are needed at the camp. Nick here will guard the boats.*

Would they believe that? Did they have some way of communicating with the camp to check? Probably they did, if the walkie-talkie that Martin wore was any indication.

Even if they didn't, he thought, he couldn't trust the

guards to be as stupid as he'd hoped. He'd have to be prepared to take them out.

Take them out. One of his father's expressions.

Daddy, what would you do? he wondered. *How would you get your family out of this?*

Get a weapon. Nick could almost hear his father's voice. Kill the sentries on the boat from cover, without warning, much safer than trying to fool them or bluff them. If you can't get a gun, get up close to them with a knife and attack without warning. Slash a throat. Cut an artery. Stab a kidney. Get their guns and a boat. Sabotage all the other boats, or steal all the fuel, then head for open water.

Nick's mouth went dry when he thought of it, and his knees went a little weak. They're just *people,* he thought. They aren't the enemy, they're just old boys with funny notions about the end of the world.

But it might come to that, he thought. *It just might.*

"Should I take the scope to Frankland?" Jason asked.

Nick nodded. "Might as well get a look at that storage place," he said, without any real hope it would make a difference. "Might as well. Maybe we can liberate something that will be of use." Maybe.

He looked at Manon and Arlette. Helplessness sighed through his blood. *How do I keep you safe?* he asked. *How?*

After two days of chaos, the dysentery at Clarendon had begun to get under control, and Dr. Patel had a few moments to collect his thoughts. He decided that he wanted to inspect the sanitary facilities at the A.M.E. camp. "We do not want this type of lamentable event to occur in both places," he told Omar.

The lamentable event was one that Omar had been hoping for all along. It had occurred to him that a nice epidemic could break out on the A.M.E. campgrounds and solve a lot of his problems, but it hadn't happened. The place had been intended for large camp meetings, and its sanitary facilities were properly laid out at safe distances from the water supply.

"Let's plan your visit for this afternoon," Omar said. "I've got to put on some extra guards so you don't get your throat cut the second you walk through the gates."

Patel gave him a thoughtful look. "Very well," he said. "Certainly."

The more Omar thought about it, the more he considered that perhaps Dr. Patel shouldn't be the only person to inspect the A.M.E. camp. Perhaps it was time to reinforce the notion that the camp was full of dangerous people who had to be confined behind barbed wire before they sacked Shelburne City like the Goths sacked Rome.

"Whatever story gets out," Knox had said, "it's got to be *your* story."

So he invited various members of the local establishment to join Dr. Patel on his inspection tour—a couple members of the parish council, Tree Simpson, one of Miz LaGrande's harpies who happened to run the local Red Cross, and Sorrel Ellen the reporter. Then he drove out to the corp limit and called Jedthus to a meeting.

"I want you to get on the bullhorn," he said, "and tell everyone in the camp that the Imperial Wizard of the K.K.K. is coming to pay them a visit tomorrow morning. Tell them we expect them to provide the Wizard with a real courteous Southern welcome, just like they were white people."

Jedthus looked puzzled. "Is this our *Grand* Wizard, you mean? Or is this someone from *another* Klan?"

You really are *expendable*, Omar thought wearily. And he explained, carefully, what he wanted Jedthus to do and why.

So that when the inspection party turned up next morning they were met by a full-scale riot, swarms of angry niggers howling and stamping and throwing garbage. And no one, not even Dr. Patel, even got near the gate. Miz LaGrande's bridge partner, the Red Cross lady, looked ready to have a stroke.

"Hell a mile, Omar!" Tree Simpson said, as he stared wide-eyed from the shoulder of the highway at the rioters howling for his blood. "What's going on here? What's wrong with these people?"

"They're a bad lot, I guess." Omar shrugged. "At least they ain't acting like they're sick. I figure we can let them look after their own dang bowels."

So the inspection party headed back to town and left the A.M.E. camp to Omar. Omar hoped that from this point they'd deal with the diarrhea at Clarendon and leave everything else to him.

Frankland had barely swung into his morning announcements when a loud voice called out from the audience.

"Reverend!" A voice. "Reverend Frankland!"

A young man in the crowd waved a hand. Studs Morgan, Frankland saw. The day before the quake, he'd bailed out on that assault charge.

A Catholic. One of Robitaille's flock, and before he'd got out of jail he had worked for Magnusson, at the video store. The rest of his family had evacuated to Hot Springs, but Studs had remained, looking after the family farm, because he and his family didn't get along. After the second big quake, the Morgan place had burned down, and Studs had come to the camp.

Frankland tried not to scowl. "Later, please, Studs," Frankland said. "It's not time for questions."

"What's being done about staying in touch with the outside?" Studs called. "I'm sure it would comfort a lot of people here to know that their families down in Hot Springs were safe."

And dang it, Frankland heard people in the crowd agreeing with him.

Tension sang along Frankland's jawline as he deliberately donned his brightest smile.

"Well," he said through the smile, "I'm afraid there isn't much of an *outside* to talk to, properly speaking. It's a real mess out there, Studs. You've heard the bulletins. We should all be thankful that—"

"You've got a *radio station*!" Studs shouted. "All you have to do is call for help!"

"There are other people worse off than we are," Frankland

said. "*Much* worse off. We have food, we have adequate shelter. Other people should be first in line . . ."

"We need a *doctor*!" Studs said. "What if we get sick? What if someone gets hurt?"

Frankland saw Hilkiah out of the corner of his eye. Hilkiah sort of *puffed*, like a cat confronting a growling dog. All his muscles swollen, his neck taut, the prison tattoos ready to pop off his flesh with the tension that swelled his arms.

"I'll take care of this, Reverend," Hilkiah growled.

No, Frankland thought. That would be a disaster. He'd have to win them over; he'd have to *convince* them. Force would make enemies of them all.

He was *right*. All he needed was the *rush*, the feeling of the Spirit flowing into his body. And then he could convince them, convince them as he always did . . .

Frankland held the microphone away from his face, turned to Hilkiah. "No," he said. "Not now. I've got to—"

And then Hilkiah's head exploded, a huge splash of red and white superimposed for a brilliant second on Frankland's retinal image of his aide. As the big body fell, as the crowd reacted in shock, Frankland heard the voice calling across the highway, from the deserted catfish farm.

"Send me my family!" the voice shouted. "*I want my children, Your Holiness, and I want them now!*"

The concussion slapped Nick's ears. He watched Hilkiah's body fall, and he thought *rifle*. As he turned and lunged to his feet in one strangely seamless motion, he knew in an instant what he had to do.

"Up!" hauling at Arlette's arm. "Up! Keep down and run this way!"

"*Send me my family!*" a voice called.

The crowd was reacting, stirring like leaves in a slow wind. There were screams and shocked looks. Nick had hauled Arlette to her feet by one hand under her arm. He reached with the other hand, slid under Manon's armpit.

"Up!" he said.

Oh God, he thought, *don't let the guards start shooting back.*

Those people wouldn't have any kind of fire discipline at all, he knew, they'd just start blazing away. The more bullets in the air, the more danger for everybody.

He had Arlette and Manon up and moving through the crowd. His hands were on their backs, pressing them down into a crouch to make a smaller target. Jason was scrambling to his feet, a wild look on his face.

There was a scramble at the head of the congregation, Frankland falling as if he'd tripped over something, the choir stampeding off their risers. Feedback shrieked over the speakers. And then one of the guards cut loose, a crackle of fire from one of the Armalites. It wasn't automatic fire, but it might as well have been, the rifle snapping away as fast as the guard could pull the trigger.

Another shot, a single deep boom sounding over the rattle of the Armalite, and the crowd screamed as Dr. Calhoun fell, clutching at his midsection.

"Run!" Nick shouted. He hauled at Manon as she tripped over someone's legs. "This way!"

There was more chattering fire from Armalites. "*Stop!*" Frankland's voice, an anguished shout over the loudspeakers. "*Stop that shooting!*"

"This way!" Nick panted. "Quick!" He tried to put his body between Arlette and the shooter, but he figured it was useless. A single bullet could tear through them both.

Another boom. There was a raw scream of agony, a sound that sent claws tearing along Nick's nerves, and one of the Armalites stopped firing.

A scoped rifle, Nick thought. A sniper just picking his targets with all the deliberation in the world, and he was probably well concealed by the earthen bank surrounding Johnson's catfish pond across the road. There was no way the guards were going to stop him, not the way they were using their weapons, firing fast and almost at random.

"*Stop the shooting!*" shouted Frankland.

The crowd was screaming, picking itself up, scattering in flight. To Nick they were just obstacles, slow-moving, stupid things blundering between him and his objective. He moved through them like an Olympic skier charging down the slalom slopes. Nick alone, of all these people, knew where he was going.

"This way! This way!"

Nick ran for the parking lot. Arlette, Manon, and Jason were with him. Manon's eyes were big as saucers, and she clutched at Arlette, trying to shield her. They leaped a four-foot crevasse rather than queue up for a plank bridge.

The firing, a part of his mind observed, had died away. But the noise level had vastly increased as over a hundred people screamed and shouted and ran like panicked animals for cover. But this was an old field, plowed flat over scores of years and still rutted from the last time it was sowed with cotton, and there was no cover really, nothing but the buildings and a few trees and the dangerous crevasses left by earthquakes. Not enough to shelter everyone.

There were also the vehicles parked by the road. But you couldn't run *away* to the parking lot, you had to angle toward the sniper to get there. Nick hadn't led his group straight to the parked vehicles, he first took them parallel to the highway until there were plenty of cars between him and the sniper, then led them into the shadow of the Reverend Doctor Calhoun's old bus, then on to a truck parked just beyond.

"You wait here," Nick said. He pressed Manon and Arlette down behind a big tire. The truck body itself would provide little protection against a high-powered rifle, but the engine block would, and the engine block was behind the front tire.

"*Send me my family!*" The sniper's high-pitched voice could barely be heard over the shrieks of the crowd.

"Just stop the shooting!" Frankland begged over wild feedback shrieks.

Nick opened the truck door, checked to see if there were keys in the ignition. There weren't. He passed a quick hand over the top of the dash, then over the top of the sun shade to see if the driver had stashed his keys there.

No luck. He needed to find another truck.

He herded the others to the next truck, checked there, found nothing. Moved everyone to the next.

Frankland and the sniper were shouting at each other, trying to negotiate.

Olson, he remembered. The sniper's name would be Olson. The loud, red-faced, blustering man. Now his bluster was backed by a large firearm, which elevated the bluster to a new level.

"We're going?" Manon gasped, realizing at last what Nick intended. "We're leaving the camp?"

"No better time," Nick said as he groped for keys.

"*That* one," Jason said, pointing to another truck. "I was in it yesterday." Nick led the others to the truck Jason indicated, opened the door and saw, gleaming in the ignition, the dangling keys. He turned back to Manon and the others.

"Listen," he said. "I'm going to start the truck and get it moving. I *don't want you in the truck just yet!* You move alongside the truck, okay? *Crouch right down!* Keep the engine block between you and the shooter. And when I give the word, you just pile in the cab next to me, and keep your heads down. Understand?"

Nick saw a series of nods. He looked in the wide eyes for comprehension and saw it.

Adrenaline flamed through his veins. Nick crawled into the cab of the truck and slid across the bench seat to the driver's side. He slammed down the clutch so hard that it hit the floorboards with a boom. His hands shook so much that it took him two tries to get a proper grip on the ignition key. He pumped the accelerator, twisted the key.

And the engine started. By God, it started.

Nick blinked sweat out of his eyes as he jammed the shift lever into first and let out the clutch. The truck shuddered and Nick remembered the parking brake—he slammed at it with his hand and the truck leaped forward. Nick juggled accelerator and clutch as he slowed the truck to match it to his family's pace on foot. He crouched down over the wheel, trying to make a smaller target, and he tried to keep other vehicles between himself and the catfish pond, keep more metal between himself and any bullets.

He ran out of parking lot and cover at the same time. He

put in the clutch and let the truck coast to a stop.

"Everyone in!" he said. "Fast now, fast! Heads down!"

Manon and Arlette came scrambling in, Manon on top in an attempt to shelter her daughter with her body. Jason came next, jamming himself in with difficulty next to the others, his task made more difficult by the hard red body of the Astroscan telescope he'd slung over his shoulder.

He had brought the scope with him that morning, Nick remembered, to have Frankland store it. And he'd kept ahold of it through everything.

"*Maggie!*" Olson's voice, crying over the battlefield. "*Maggie you get out here, you bring Liza and Dickie!*"

Nick let out the clutch before his three passengers had quite wedged themselves in, and Jason gave a yell and clutched at the dashboard as the truck leaped forward and threatened to spill him into the bar ditch. The truck swayed as it ran up the shoulder of the road, and Nick flung the wheel over and punched the accelerator to the floor.

His back tensed. Waiting for the bullet.

Nick shifted into second, then into third. Tools and planks in the truck bed boomed as the truck thundered over broken asphalt and a filled-in crevasse. The last of the camp, the unmarried men's compound, fell behind.

Gears clashed as Nick shifted into fourth. His lips skinned back from his teeth in a demon smile.

The sniper wasn't gunning for them. They were free.

Frankland tried to take a step and stumbled over Hilkiah's inert body. Another shot boomed. There was the weird whine of a bullet sheathing itself in flesh, but all he could see was trampling feet. He clutched the microphone in his fist. He knew that if he gave up the microphone, he gave up all hope of saving the situation.

"*Stop the shooting!*" Frankland cried. "*Stop!*"

Shots chattered out into the air, people firing wildly. The panicked crowd screamed as it scattered over the fields. Choir members sprawled over the ground as the risers on which they were standing were tipped by panicked singers.

Frankland scurried on hands and knees after the crowd, trying to get the solid bulk of his steel-framed church between himself and the sniper.

Some people ran past him, dragging Dr. Calhoun over the bloody grass. Calhoun had been shot, Frankland thought dimly. And a voice in him said, *Oh, iniquity!*

Another cry, barely audible over the panic, came from the man lying behind the banks of Brother Johnson's catfish ponds. *"Send me my family!"*

Olson, Frankland thought. It was Olson out there. Somehow he had not quite realized this till now.

"You'll get your family!" Frankland shouted into the mike. "Just stop the shooting!"

One of the Armalites ripped off a dozen rounds. "Stop that firing!" Frankland commanded, and the gunshots ceased.

He scurried around the corner of the church. There were thirty people lying there—Frankland saw Sheryl with a pistol in her hand, and Calhoun lying pale, and old Sheriff Gorton standing there with a mild, puzzled look on his face, as if he were trying to work out the daily crossword in the paper.

"Maggie!" Olson called. "Maggie, you come out here!"

Frankland looked out at the terrified crowd stampeding away from the site of the shooting, and he wondered if there was any way he could find Maggie Olson and her children anywhere in that panicked mass.

"Maggie!" Olson's voice again. *"Maggie you get out here, you bring Liza and Dickie!"*

Olson squeezed off two shots that rang on the steel sides of the church. Frankland looked over his head and saw two bullet holes.

The church wasn't cover at all. That high-powered rifle of Olson's could punch right through it.

"You'll get your family!" Frankland shouted. *"Just stop the shooting!"*

He had been the target, Frankland thought. If he hadn't turned his head when he did, to whisper into Hilkiah's ear, it would have been his own head that exploded under the force of the bullet. And if he hadn't tripped, he would probably have been gutshot instead of Calhoun.

The Lord had preserved him, he realized. And that meant that the Lord wasn't done with him yet, that the Lord still featured him in his plans.

Frankland and Olson shouted back and forth for long moments while the crowd dispersed over the camp and beyond. Eventually Maggie Olson and her two children were located and sent forward to her husband. Maggie wept as she dragged herself with slow steps across the asphalt highway toward her husband, and her youngest was hysterical, screaming against his mother's shoulder as she carried him toward the catfish pond where her husband had fortified himself.

"Now you just leave us alone!" Olson shouted after his family joined him. "You leave us alone, and we'll leave you alone! If you send anyone after us, I'll shoot him dead."

Frankland saw no point in replying. He looked at Calhoun lying gasping and pale. Hilkiah's corpse was barely visible around the corner of the church. The flies were already busy about his brains.

They hath taken my right arm, Frankland thought, *but I shall smite them sore with my left.*

He had better things to do than wonder if the phrase that just popped into his head was actually from the Bible or not.

There was a rushing sound in Frankland's ears, like a thousand angels in flight. He picked his way through the prone figures toward Dr. Calhoun, who lay surrounded by the crouched forms of Sheryl, the Reverend Garb, and several others. Calhoun was pale, and his skin was moist. Frankland crouched by him, saw Calhoun's midsection soaked in red. Someone's shirt was folded and pressed over the wound to stem the bleeding, but Frankland knew that bleeding was not the greatest danger facing a gutshot man.

Calhoun would die within a few days, and he would die of peritonitis because there wasn't a doctor in Rails Bluff capable of saving him.

Frankland took Calhoun's hand. "How you doing, Lucius?" he asked.

Calhoun licked his lips. "Praying," he said. Dust blew from his ginger mustache as he spoke.

"Well," Frankland said, and touched his colleague's shoulder, "we'll get the man that did this."

Calhoun nodded. "Olson," he said.

"Yes. Smite him. We'll smite him." The sound in Frankland's ears resolved itself into a band of angels singing a chorus of vengeance.

Calhoun nodded again. His bloody fingers tightened on Frankland's.

"I'll talk to you soon," Frankland said, "and we'll pray together, if you like. But right now I got a posse to put together."

Calhoun nodded. "Heaven-o," he said.

Frankland rose to his feet. His skull filled with the sound of angels crying for vengeance.

An unprovoked attack, Frankland thought. He just fired from ambush, without warning, and blew Brother Hilkiah's head right off. Frankland couldn't let Olson get away with that.

Olson and his family had to leave the safety of that catfish pond embankment sooner or later. And when they did, Frankland and his people would follow. Olson would find he wasn't the only person with a high-powered hunting rifle.

Frankland cocked his head up as he heard the sound of a rattling little motor echoing from across the road. A dirt bike, he thought, or an ATV. That was how Olson was making his getaway.

Olson didn't even have a proper vehicle. He'd found a gun in a ruin somewhere, and some little Japanese scooter, and that was as far as his luck would go.

Frankland felt his lips turning in up in a grim smile. Spoke the words that the angels sang into his mind.

"Vengeance is mine, saith the Lord," he said.

That was one quote he was sure of.

Nick put Arlette and Manon behind some bushes by the roadside near the broken bridge. "You wait till I call," Nick said. "Jason and I will talk to the guards."

And maybe kill them, Nick thought, *if they don't do what's needed. Kill them with my bare hands.*

He could do it, he realized. He could do exactly what was necessary. And he found that he was not surprised by this knowledge.

Jason dropped out of the cab to let Manon and Arlette out, then climbed back in. The telescope swung into his lap on its strap.

"Whatever happens," Nick said, "I need you to back my play."

Jason licked his lips. "What are you going to do?"

"I'm going to tell them they're needed at the camp." Which, he considered, had the virtue of being true.

He rolled the truck to the top of the bluff near the broken bridge, turned off the engine, set the parking brake. He could see the jetty down below him, boats bobbing in the water.

"Let's go."

He made his way down the red-clay path with Jason at his heels. It was still early morning and the Rails River gorge was deep in shadow.

"Hey there," a man said from the bushes that lined the Rails.

Hey there, Nick thought with sudden scorn. He could imagine what his father would have said if a sentry had ever hailed him with *Hey there*.

"Hey there," Nick answered. "Hey. We got some trouble at the camp."

Two men emerged from where they'd been sitting beneath the bushes. The speaker was a stranger, a grizzled white man maybe fifty years old, but the other was Conroy, the brother who had driven Nick and Jason to the camp on their first day.

"Hey there, Conroy," Nick said.

Conroy's unshaven face was uncertain under his baseball cap. "What's happening at the camp?"

"Reverend needs you back there," Nick said. "That Olson came back, with a gun."

Conroy and the guard exchanged glances. Hesitated.

"Better get moving," Nick said. "There's a bad situation there." He heard his father's voice in his head, tried to echo the commanding tones.

The guards' eyes snapped to Nick at the sound of command. Then Conroy looked down at the walkie-talkie clipped to his belt.

"Can't call from here," he said. "Have to go to the top of the bluff." The two guards looked at each other again. "I suppose we ought to check it out."

"The keys are in the truck," Nick said. "The boy and I will look after the boats for you. Hurry!"

Nick watched, heart throbbing, as Conroy and the other man labored to the top of the bluff. Conroy lifted the walkie-talkie to his ear, then Nick saw a shock run through his frame. He and the other guard hustled into the truck, started the engine, and drove off.

Nick turned to Jason. "Fetch Manon and Arlette. I'll get a boat ready."

There were a half-dozen or more boats, either tied to the plank jetty or drawn up on land, but only one boat actually possessed a motor. The rest of the outboards had apparently been taken to the camp and put into storage.

The one boat with a motor was *Retired and Gone Fishin'*, Jason's battered old bass boat. *American Dream*, the speedboat Jason had got at the casino, wasn't even there.

For a moment Nick considered shifting the outboard to another boat. *Retired and Gone Fishin'* was small for four people, and there was no canvas top as there had been on *American Dream*.

But then he thought of the delay. It would take time to shift a heavy motor from one boat to another, along with its fuel. The bass boat, whatever its other disadvantages, would be fast under power. He could probably stay ahead of any pursuit. And the bass boat had built-in storage compartments, and the silent electric motor that could be rigged to the bow.

And then it occurred to Nick to wonder where Olson would go once he got his wife and children free of the camp.

He would come *here*, Nick realized. Olson would have to get a boat and flee. It was the only way he would escape Frankland's revenge.

He was probably on his way. Conroy and the other guard wouldn't be able to stop him: Olson would riddle them before they even got out of the truck.

Nick's heart lurched in his chest. He turned to Jason, shouted, *"Hurry!"* and jumped into the bass boat.

The oars that the *Beluthahatchie* had provided were still there. There were plastic jugs of water in one of the boat's coolers, but the compartments were empty. The fifty-horse Johnson had two plastic jerricans full of fuel. Nick wondered if he could find more.

He ran from one boat to the next, checking each in turn. Nothing. Then he turned to the bank and was luckier—four more plastic jerricans sat in the shade under the bluff, ready to be placed aboard any boat that was running low. Next to the jerricans were a pair of box lunches intended for the guards' midday meal, a plastic jug of water, a roll of actual toilet paper, a blanket, and a bright orange plastic sun-shade held in place with rope and tent pegs.

Nick gave a breathless laugh at the sight. He carried the jerricans two at a time to the boat. By the time he finished his second run, Jason and the others had come down the bluff, and they brought the food and other supplies aboard, including the awning.

Nick got everyone on the bass boat, then cast off. The boat drifted gently down the Rails River as he readied the engine, primed the fuel, worked with the clutch and choke, then pressed the self-start.

As the outboard boomed into life, Nick looked at the joy and relief in the eyes of the others. His heart thrilled. It was the most glorious sight he'd seen in his life.

He moved forward into the cockpit and took the wheel. Spun the wheel to correct the boat's course, pushed the throttle forward.

They were on their way.

"Daddy!" Arlette's arms came around him from behind. "That was brilliant!"

"Man, Nick," Jason said. "The way you gave orders, you sounded just like a general."

Joy sang through Nick. He kissed one of the brown arms that embraced him.

"Next stop," he said, "civilization."

The bluff parted before them, opening like a curtain sweeping left and right over the stage, and they coasted into the Delta. The still, brown waters of the Arkansas floodplain were littered with wreckage, and Nick had to keep his speed down. He took comfort in the thought that pursuit couldn't go any faster. He put Jason on the front deck, with one of the oars, to pole off such of the flotsam as he couldn't avoid.

Retired and Gone Fishin' glided slowly and cautiously through perhaps three miles of maimed, flooded forest before catching a glimpse of the main channel of the Arkansas River through the trees.

It was then, just as Nick's heart was lifting, just as he was about to throw his head back and laugh his triumph to the sky, that he heard the sound of a big outboard booming into life just ahead.

Nick's pulse thundered louder than the engine. He stood in the cockpit to stare ahead, and despair fell upon his heart like rain as he saw a familiar shape easing out from between the trees. It was *American Dream*, with its hundred-fifty-horsepower motor that could run down the bass boat without even trying. And inside the boat's cockpit Nick saw at least three silhouettes.

One of Frankland's river patrols out looking for refugees, the same sort that had brought them to the camp in the first place.

Plans flailed through his mind. He didn't think, in this instance, the "Brother Frankland sent me to tell you to come back to the camp" ploy was likely to work.

"Oh, hell," Jason murmured. "It's Magnusson."

"The porno guy?" Nick said. He cut power as the other boat approached. Fleeing at top speed was a futile idea, and therefore reserved for the moment when everything else had failed. The other boat throttled back, then reversed briefly to check its momentum.

"Heaven-o there, Adams," Magnusson said. "What's going on?"

"There's shooting in the camp," Nick called out. "A war almost. Olson came back with friends and guns. Hilkiah was shot dead in front of the whole camp, and so was the Reverend Calhoun."

The others looked at each other in surprise. Whatever they'd been expecting to hear, this clearly wasn't it.

"So what are you-all doing?" Magnusson said.

Nick stood straight, squared his shoulders. You are *telling* them, he informed himself, you aren't asking their permission.

"We're getting to safety," Nick said. "We're not armed, and there's nothing we can do. If you've got weapons, you should go back to the camp and help restore order. But otherwise I advise you to stay away."

The other two men seemed uncertain, but Magnusson returned an answer quickly.

"I don't think you're thinking very clearly, sir," he said. "There's no safety on the river. It's dangerous, and that's why we're supposed to bring in anyone we find here."

"There isn't any warfare on the river," Nick said. "It's a lot safer than the camp." He nodded as calmly as he could at Magnusson, but he felt helplessness drain the strength from his knees, and he leaned slightly against the side of the cockpit in order to support himself.

A momentary aftershock shivered the tops of the trees. Twigs and leaves rained down on the water.

"Sir," Magnusson said, "I can't let you out on that river, okay? Not with your family. It's too dangerous."

"*People are dying at the camp,*" Nick insisted. "You don't believe me, you call them. You have a radio, don't you?"

"It don't work this far out," one of the other men said. "Trees and water just eat up the signal, I guess."

"I think you should come back with us, okay?"

Magnusson said. "We'll check out the situation, make certain that things are safe before we bring you into the camp."

So here it was. Nick drew himself up, tried to summon his father's authority.

"No," he said. "*No*. We're not going back."

"I can't permit you to leave, mister," Magnusson said.

Nick narrowed his eyes. Looked at the pistol holstered on Magnusson' hip. "What are your orders exactly?" he asked. "You supposed to shoot us or what? And what exactly gives you the authority to do that?"

And the question, Nick thought, was, Would they? Would they actually open fire?

The other two, Nick thought, probably wouldn't. They seemed intimidated by the situation. He couldn't see either of them raising a weapon against someone who wasn't trying to harm them. They would look for excuses not to.

Magnusson, though, was more problematic. Magnusson was the strong-willed one, the one with the white armband that marked him as a leader. The one who wailed in front of a hundred and fifty people about the evil pornography he had sold, and how Frankland had helped him see the light.

"You're coming back with us, okay?" Magnusson said.

"Calhoun is *dead*." Nick barked out the words like his father dressing down a recruit. "Hilkiah's *dead*. Other people died with them. And *Reverend Frankland's dream is dead!* There's nothing to go back to."

Fury blazed in Magnusson's eyes. *"That's not true!"* he snapped. One hand touched the butt of his pistol. *"You're coming back!"*

Nick's heart sank. He'd played it wrong. General Ruford had given too many orders. If Nick had stayed sweet and reasonable, he might have been able to talk his way out of this.

Now it was hopeless. General Ruford had failed, and it was up to Nick to make up for the general's failure. The only thing for Nick to do was to try to talk his way onto the other boat, then knock Magnusson down and get a gun, hold them all off at gunpoint or go down blazing . . .

Hopeless, but it was the only thing he could think to do.

Jason looked at Nick and *knew*. There was that resolution in Nick's face, that hard resolve that Jason had seen before on the river when he was trying to get to Arlette and Manon ahead of the people who had killed Gros-Papa. Nick was going to try something desperate, jump onto Magnusson and his gun maybe. Do whatever he could to save his family, and probably die.

Jason's head whirled. He needed to do something, he knew. Something . . .

"No way!" he yelled. He waved his arms and jumped from the foredeck down into the cockpit. The boat rocked under him. He had wanted just to distract Magnusson, to break the thread of tension he'd seen running from Magnusson to Nick. That, and maybe give Nick a chance to come up with a plan that wasn't based on getting himself killed

And then his eye lit on the red plastic case of the telescope, tucked behind the passenger seat. Wild inspiration seized him. He grabbed the Astroscan in both hands and held it over his head.

"This is a nuclear reactor!" he yelled. *"You hit this with a bullet, and we're all blown to bits!"*

There was a long, astonished silence broken only by the pounding of Jason's heart. Magnusson's eyes were wide and staring. Muscles worked on his unshaven jaw.

"Nick," Jason said, still glaring at Magnusson, "let's get this boat out of here."

Nick slowly lowered himself into the driver's seat and pushed the throttle forward. The Johnson rumbled and the bass boat began to move.

Looking over his shoulder, Nick saw Magnusson step forward, one foot on the gunwale. Then saw one of the others put a restraining hand on his arm.

The boat rolled from the broken forest into the bright sunlight. Jason faced aft, the telescope still held over his head. Nick felt a laugh rising like a bubble through his astonishment.

"Goodbye-o!" Jason howled over the stern as he waved the Astroscan over his head. "Goodbye-o!"

He turned to the others. *"Who's the genius?"* he demanded. *"Who's the genius? Who's got his own atomic bomb?"* He gave a whoop.

And then Jason looked down at Nick, at the man's trembling hands clenched on the wheel, and he felt the silent passage between them.

I was this close, he read in Nick's face.

I know, Jason answered silently. *I know how close we were.*

The hunt lasted most of the morning. Frankland and his people, traveling across country in pickup trucks and four-wheel-drive vehicles, in pursuit of Olson, who had his whole family piled onto one little beat-up ATV that wouldn't go twenty miles an hour.

Olson first of all tried to make for the piney woods to the northwest of town. Frankland knew that once Olson got his family into that dense wreckage, they might well die of starvation or frustration, but would be perfectly safe as far as pursuit was concerned. So Frankland first sent a column of hunters under Sheriff Gorton zooming down the highway to get to the woods first. They succeeded, and when Olson's ATV appeared, in a soy field south of the piney woods, he found Gorton's people waiting, behind the cover of their vehicles with their weapons pointing across their hoods.

Olson should have known, Frankland thought, that you can't fight the angels.

Olson slowed his vehicle, peered for a moment at the reception party ready for him, then turned the ATV around and buzzed away to the south. Gorton mounted his people and pursued cross country, careful to keep out of range of Olson's scoped rifle. Frankland was in touch with Gorton by radio, and had another posse under Garb waiting for Olson when he came. So Olson turned again, heading in about the only direction left, to the northeast. There wasn't much there for him, not unless he planned to descend the bluff and wade out into the flooded country below, but Frankland hadn't left him much choice.

Frankland himself waited there, between Olson and the bluff, with six trucks spread out and twelve guards under good cover. And when Olson saw that, and looked over his shoulder at the patient vehicles slowly following him, he turned again and went to ground, in a partially collapsed farm building belonging to a family called the Swansons.

Angels sang their triumph in Frankland's mind. The rebel Olson was in his power.

"Heaven-o!" Frankland called out, standing in the back of a truck and bellowing over the cab through cupped hands. He called for Olson to surrender, but there was no answer. So Frankland and Gorton sent in their posse. Frankland gave the advancing men cover, blasting away at the wrecked farmhouse with his Winchester from behind the cover of his truck. Angels cried their triumph at every shot.

The angels' song turned to a lament. Olson blew up one of the advancing trucks with a shot that hit the gas tank, almost roasting the three men inside. Olson killed one man sheltering behind another vehicle, and wounded two others. After that Frankland's people beat a retreat despite the reverend urging them on.

Then a siege began, with Frankland's people lying under cover at what they hoped was a safe distance and firing into the Swanson house in hopes of hitting their invisible enemy. Occasionally Olson would fire a round back to tell everyone to keep their distance.

Wait till night, thought Frankland. *At night I can get close enough to burn them out.*

This went on for hours, as the sun mounted hot into the sky and the land baked beneath them. Frankland's people hadn't even had breakfast, so he called the camp and arranged for food and water to be brought.

"Honey bear," Sheryl told him over the walkie-talkie, "I think you better get back here with some of those men of yours. Things here are going all to blazes."

"What do you mean?"

"You didn't leave enough guards to keep order *here*," Sheryl said. "People are wandering around outside the boundaries like they're not supposed to. A lot of folks ran off during the incident this morning and haven't come back. When you sent the dead and wounded back, that shot down the morale of the people who would have helped me. Some of the folks took some of our stored food and wandered away."

"Tell those people that the angels guard them," Frankland said.

"What was that, honey bear?" Sharply.

"If there is mutiny in the camp," Frankland said, "you have my authority to enforce discipline."

"How?" Sheryl demanded. "Nobody's paying attention to me."

"Shoot somebody," Frankland said. "Shoot *ten* somebodies. The angels will acquit you." And then he added, "When Satan rageth, surely he must be put down."

"I'm not shooting anybody till you come back," Sheryl said. "I want an army to back me up."

"Just send food and water," Frankland said.

"I'll bring it myself."

Sheryl brought supplies and somber warnings about what was happening in the camp. Before she left Frankland assured her that the angels were guarding them all.

All through the afternoon Frankland's people continued to fire randomly into the ruin. It was nearing twilight when Frankland finally heard a shout from the Swanson place.

"Stop shooting!" Olson's high-pitched screech. "You hit my girl!"

"Throw down your guns and come out!" Frankland said. "All of you!"

"Just take my girl!"

"No! All of you or none!"

"She's hurt bad! Someone come and take her!"

Frankland shouted "Open fire!" leveled his Winchester over the hood of his truck, and let fly. A regular volley rang out. Frankland heard screaming from Olson's wife, then shouts from Olson, then a shot from the farmhouse that cracked air right over Frankland's head. The screaming stopped.

The firing went on for a while. And then Frankland heard a strange throbbing in the air, and looked up to see a helicopter banking into a lazy turn over the bluff to the north. The helicopter was a small one, dark in color, but it had clearly seen something of interest below, because it finished its turn and began a shallow dive toward Frankland and the Swanson cabin.

"No," Frankland gasped. He could see it all too clearly. The Devil was coming to save his own. Flying through the air like the wicked angel he was.

"No!" he shouted, rising from his crouch behind his truck. "Shoot! Black helicopter! Government black helicopter! Shoot!"

"It's *green*, Brother Frankland," one of Frankland's men pointed out, but Frankland raised his Winchester, aimed at the oncoming helicopter, and pulled the trigger. He cranked another round into the rifle, fired, then fired again. Then he thumbed on his walkie-talkie.

"Black helicopter!" he shouted. "It's coming to rescue Olson! Shoot it down!"

More shots crackled out from the circle of trucks, along with a few cries of surprise or protest. Frankland fired twice more. The helicopter roared low over Frankland's head, close enough so that Frankland could see the government markings and helmeted pilot peering out of the slablike cockpit window. Frankland's rifle clicked on empty, and he frantically reached for fresh rounds in his vest and began to reload.

The helicopter passed over the area and began a steep climb. Shots dwindled away as the chopper passed out of range. "Brother Frankland!" someone called on the radio. "That was an Army helicopter! We can't—"

Frankland finished reloading and snatched the walkie-talkie from the hood of his truck. Angels chanted their anger in his ears. "Smite them!" he cried. "Let their tears be as ashes and let cinders be their end!"

"Brother Frankland!" Another voice. "You don't understand!"

"Heaven or Hell!" Frankland raged. Angels roared in his ears. "You go to Heaven or Hell! *Choose now!*"

Frankland dropped the walkie-talkie back onto the hood of the truck, then readied his rifle. The chopper reached the top of its climb, then spun in a lazy turn, the setting sun gleaming red off its rotor.

Frankland shouldered his rifle, wiped sweat from the pit of his eye. He put his eye to the scope and lined up the copter in the crosshairs.

The helicopter began another dive. Frankland could hear the whine of its jet engines above the throb of rotors, above the chant of the angels in his ears. He tracked the helicopter through his scope, saw sunlight etch shadows of the crewmen behind the smoked cockpit glass.

"I choose Heaven," he said, and pulled the trigger.

THIRTY

From what I had seen and heard I was deterred from pro-
ceeding further, and nearly gave away what property I had.
On my return by land up the right side of the river, I found
the surface of the earth for 10 or 12 miles cracked in num-
berless places, running in different directions—some of
which were bridged and some filled with logs to make them
passable—others were so wide that they were obliged to be
surrounded. In some of these cracks the earth sank on one
side from the level to the distance of five feet, and from one
to three feet there was water in most of them. Above this the
cracks were not so numerous nor so great—but the inhabi-
tants have generally left their dwellings and gone to the
higher grounds.

Matthias M. Speed (Jefferson County, March 2, 1812)

Jessica jumped as a bullet splashed off the windscreen of
the Kiowa. She could see armed men down below,
crouched behind vehicles. Some of them were shooting.
And some of *those* were shooting at *her.*

Bullets rattled off the helicopter's semimonocoque hull
as the Kiowa roared over the scene at a hundred knots.
"Hell of a lot of firepower, General," her pilot remarked.

Jessica winced as a round spanged off the cheek window below her feet. "Who *are* these people?" she muttered.

The Kiowa zoomed over the field and climbed up over
the Delta, out of range. Jessica's heart thrashed against
her rib cage.

A hot landing zone in Arkansas? This was deranged.

"Damage?" Jessica said, her eyes flickering over the
cockpit displays.

"I hear air through some holes in the fuselage," the pilot said. "Oil pressure's steady. No unusual vibration."

"Alert HQ to the situation," Jessica said. "Tell them to prep a dustoff in case we have to bail over the Delta."

"Yes, ma'am."

"I don't suppose that twenty-millimeter gun you've got has any ammunition in it."

"Sorry, General. We left the ammunition loads in Kentucky."

Oh well. That was just letting the adrenaline talk, anyway. Although the helicopter's cannon—if loaded—was perfectly capable of wiping out everything in sight on the field below, she could only imagine the penalties for any military officer who used such a weapon on civilian targets, whether they'd fired on her or not.

Jessica was already busy with the controls for the MMS, a kind of periscope unit inside the craft's rotor hub that carried video, infrared, and laser-sighting systems.

She turned on the video recorder, so there would be a record for later, and panned the area of the battle with the camera cranked up to maximum magnification. Saw the vehicles laid out around the half-fallen farmhouse, the rifles banging away. Presumably they wouldn't be firing at the farmhouse unless there was someone inside firing back.

Two of the vehicles, she saw, had racks of lights on top, maybe sheriff's department. Maybe there was a perfectly legitimate police action going on.

In which case, why had she been shot at?

While Jessica peered into the MMS display, the pilot gently tested his controls and control surfaces, shifting the Kiowa gently around the sky. "Are we going to have to dust off that farmhouse, General?" he asked.

"Negative. I'm not going to take us into a hot LZ without knowing what's going on, or who's shooting at us."

"HQ says they are warming up a Cayuse in case we need a dustoff. It's the only aircraft they've got available."

"Very good." Another light scout helicopter, damn it. If they had a Blackhawk or Sea Stallion available, a big ship with a reasonable chance of not being shot to pieces, she might have risked trying to rescue whoever was in the farmhouse.

"And ma'am—" The pilot shifted his chewing tobacco from one cheek to the other. "I don't mean to bring you down or anything, but our fuel situation will become critical in about five minutes and night is coming on fast."

"Let me know when we have to leave. Is there any way we can talk to those cops down there, or whatever they are?"

"We've got the secure UHF and SINCGARS only, General. Just military channels."

"Damn it." Eyes still on the display, she began searching for the map case she'd placed between the pilot's seat and her own. "Where the hell is this place?" she asked.

It was pure coincidence Jessica was there at all. She'd flown to Bald Knob to deliver instruction to a National Guard unit concerning the appropriate way to repair a levee, and on her return journey had flown over the Delta, as per her own standing orders to search for refugees whenever possible. The flashing lights of the police vehicle had attracted her attention, and the next thing she knew people were shooting at her.

She looked at the data from the AHRS display, which provided her position within a hundred yards or so, then down at the plastic-encased maps, gloved fingers tracking the coordinates. They were 4.3 kilometers northwest of Rails Bluff, Arkansas. Wherever *that* was.

She looked back at the MMS display and saw a half-dozen of the besiegers pile into a pickup truck and leave the scene. A grin tugged at the corners of her lips. "I'd say they have a morale problem down there," she said.

"Ma'am? The fuel . . ."

"Let me pan across this one last time," Jessica said, "and then we can get out of here."

She swept the video across the battlefield one more time, then took her hands off the controls. "Take us back by way of Rails Bluff," she said. "I want to see what's there."

Rails Bluff was a wreck, with no sign of life, though apparently efforts had been made to clear some of the rubble. Jessica took more video images for the record, though she suspected that twilight was degrading the image significantly. The surprise came a few miles outside of town, when a refugee camp floated into sight, a long line of tents and awnings stretched out along the broken highway.

"Is that one of *ours*?" Jessica wondered aloud. She couldn't remember anyone airlifting supplies to a place called Rails Bluff.

"Want me to get closer, General?"

"Negative. We've already been shot at once. Just let me get some pictures."

It was dark enough that the video unit wouldn't provide a suitable image, so Jessica used the FLIR, the Forward-Looking Infra-Red detector set into the MMS. She recorded the little burning lights that were stoves, generators, and human beings. And amid the camp, she saw a long tripod-shaped object standing into the night.

"Is that a radio mast?"

"Looks like it, General."

"Well." She panned the camp one more time, then folded the MMS back into the rotor hub. "Let's get back to HQ."

While the Kiowa was en route, Jessica spoke to headquarters and told them to check the FCC's web page to find out as much as they could about whatever radio station was licensed in Rails Bluff. And then to find out everything *else* available about Rails Bluff, including whether or not the state of Arkansas, the military, or anyone else had set up a refugee camp nearby.

Pat waited for her in the spill of the Kiowa's landing lights as the chopper came down onto the Vicksburg improvised helipad. He raised a hand to protect his eyes against dust kicked up by the rotor, and she saw a boom box in his hand.

On leaving the helicopter, Jessica suppressed the urge to jump onto Pat and wrap her arms and legs around his lanky body, and instead gave him a peck on the cheek.

He put an arm around her as his eyes surveyed the bullet splashes on her transportation. "You okay?" he said.

"All in a day's work," she said, a little too casually. "What have you got for me?"

He drew her away from the noise of the helicopter. "I've got something to play for you," he said. "We listen to this sometimes in the clerks' tent. It's not all disaster news, and it's kind of entertaining, in its own surrealistic way."

The Kiowa's turbines shut down, and Pat raised the antenna on the boom box and punched the power button. He held the speaker close to Jessica's ear. A crashing sound began to thunder from the speakers, a horribly distorted noise that suggested metal shelves being hit repeatedly with a baseball bat. A high-pitched male voice howled over the noise, distorted even more than the crashing sound in the background. Jessica wanted to cover her ears.

"Is this the day?" the voice cried. *"Is this the day? Is this the day of the Lord?"*

"Fifteen thousand watts AM," Pat said. "The Voice of Rails Bluff."

The Arkansas was slow and wide and choked with debris. Jason and Arlette worked on the bass boat's foredeck, each with one of Captain Joe's oars, fending off the trees, the chunks of lumber, the pieces of paneling or shingled gables that had once been a part of someone's home. It was slow and tiring work. Nick fretted aloud about the fuel they were using idling down the river this way. Jason was dreadfully aware of Arlette's presence, of the tantalizing warmth of the girl's bare legs as they moved next to his. It was as if his nerves were reaching out toward her, straining in her direction like new green shoots reaching for the light. He wondered if Arlette shared this awareness, or if this pleasant torture was for him alone.

He heard Nick and Manon in a whispered conversation in the cockpit, and then Jason heard Nick say, "Well, I hope you don't expect me to find a service station," and Jason felt a grin tug at his lips, a grin that he was careful to turn away from the cockpit. There were more whispers between Manon and Nick, and then Nick cleared his throat.

"Manon needs to pee," he said. "Jason, I'd be obliged if you'd keep your eyes to the front."

"And you, too, Nick Ruford," Manon added.

Jason strove to control his amusement. When he and Nick had been alone on the bass boat, this had not been much of an issue.

The boat took on a list to port, indicating that Manon was hanging her butt out the cockpit. Jason moved a little to starboard to help keep the boat balanced, crowding against Arlette. She gave him a glance over her shoulder—their eyes met for a moment, and she looked away. Their arms touched, and Jason felt the hair prickle on his arm at the touch of Arlette's skin.

There was a pause. Then a wail from Manon.

"I can't, Nick! Not here in the middle of the river!"

"Nobody's around to see you."

"I just can't!"

"There's no place else to have a pit stop out here," Nick said. "Not unless you want to hold it till we get to Vicksburg."

"Just take us over into the trees," Manon said. "Please, Nick, I can't pee out here."

Nick nudged the throttle forward and turned the wheel. The boat stabilized as Manon came inboard. Jason stepped back from Arlette, took a grip on his oar, fended off the garbage until they were in the shade of the trees.

Manon hung herself outboard again and managed to overcome her mortification at the procedure. After she was finished, Nick said, "Anyone else? Because I'm not taking this detour again."

"I'll go, Daddy," Arlette said.

"There's not much toilet paper," Manon remarked.

"Plenty of leaves and cattails," Nick said cheerfully. Manon made a noise of disgust.

Jason stood on the foredeck, eyes rigidly forward like a soldier, his oar grounded like a spear. *They sure sound married*, he thought.

It was slow going on the river. They passed a broken highway bridge, its span completely fallen, and shortly thereafter a shattered lock and dam, now abandoned. A towboat and a small fleet of barges were sunk in the lock, apparently having been caught there by the first big quake.

At nightfall they kept moving. Nick decided they were safer in the channel than anywhere else—if they moored beneath the trees, an aftershock could drop the trees right on them.

Eventually they grew tired and decided to drift. They had used two-thirds of their fuel and could no longer see any landmarks. Nick shared out the food he'd taken from the two guards—there wasn't much, and it didn't last long.

"This is the last," he said, "till we find civilization."

There was a roaring overhead, the sound of rotors flogging the sky. Navigation lights flashed against the blackness. A whole squadron of helicopters tearing away on some urgent errand.

If it were only daytime, they could have waved.

After the helicopters passed, Jason lay on the foredeck and looked up at the sky. He could spot M31 easily, and M13 and M3. Funny how easy it was when you knew how.

His eye searched for the Ring Nebula, but couldn't find it. He thought he could detect a smudge where Captain Joe had showed him the Veil Nebula.

A supernova. The Veil wasn't a veil but a shroud, draped over the corpse of its once-mighty star.

Jason gazed at the sky and felt on his mind the subtle pressure of its millions of stars. He wondered what his life meant in regard to that brilliant, diamond-hard, uncaring immensity. Compared to those stars, his life, his thoughts, his very existence was the merest nothing—no, a *fragment* of nothing, a spark that flared briefly and then was gone, unnoticed in the vast darkness.

His mother, Jason thought, had believed that she mattered, that the universe cared what became of her, that she and the universe were of equal importance. Frankland believed, as far as the universe was concerned, that he was a person of consequence, that he was chosen to carry out a monumentally important plan on behalf of the being who had created all this immensity.

If they had only looked up, if they had seen those millions of stars, perhaps they would have come to a different understanding. That life was not of consequence to anyone but the living, that there was no plan but what life made for itself.

Jason acutely felt his own fragility, his own lack of significance in the cosmos. But that consciousness, in some strange, paradoxical way, seemed a kind of liberation. Life mattered only to life. Life could choose its own meaning, give itself significance, attempt to preserve itself against the violence and destruction of the universe. Life could value *itself*.

Nothing else would, that was certain.

And life could treasure other life, as Jason treasured the lives of the others adrift on the little boat. They could guard each other's fragile spark, preserve themselves and each other.

Floating in that starry immensity, each was all the others had left.

After listening for a few minutes to Brother Frankland's Hour of Prophecy, and rerunning the Kiowa's recording one more time, Jessica decided that, whatever the dangers, she needed to send her rescue mission after all.

"We've got to dust off that farmhouse," she told her staff. "I don't know what the people in there did to get those others shooting at them, but I think we'd better do our best to part the combatants and sort out who did what later."

Most of her helicopters had returned from their days' errands, and after refueling she sent a half-dozen to Rails Bluff. Each craft was FLIR-enhanced so as to be able to navigate and maneuver at night without giving themselves away with spotlights or floods. Her own Kiowa was out of action until its ground crew could determine the extent of any damage, but since her pilot knew the country, she sent him as an observer on another craft.

The helicopters either weren't armed or had no ammunition loads, but Jessica was able to send a platoon of engineers armed with light weapons and grenade launchers, soldiers who could either fire from the helicopter doors or deploy on the ground. They were to avoid confrontation, and fire only if fired upon, but primarily they were to find out who was in that farmhouse and evacuate them if it was at all possible.

The other helicopters could support by making threatening, low-altitude passes over any opposition, by illuminating them with spotlights, or—if their lives were in danger—by returning fire.

After dispatching the mission, Jessica filled out the paperwork justifying the sortie—work that was inevitable and mindless, and therefore almost adequate for distracting her from the knowledge that she'd just sent her people into danger—and then she went to the communications tent to listen as the radio reports came in from Rails Bluff.

Her booted feet crunched the plastic sheeting underfoot as she paced. After a while she noticed that the crackling made the communications techs nervous, so she sat on a canvas chair in the semi-darkness and tried not to fidget. Disaster scenarios panned across her mind, her people flying into an ambush, fanatic bunkered Arkansas bushwackers letting them land, then mowing them down with entrenched weapons. Her rescue team pinned down in the farmhouse, the unarmed helicopters unable to properly support them.

The scenarios contrasted with the calm words of the chopper crews that floated toward her across the miles, illuminated in the commo tent by the soft glow of LEDs and liquid-crystal displays. The lights reminded her unpleasantly of the fireworks she'd been seeing behind her left eye, and she closed her eyelids so as not to stir her unease, but then the fireworks began to flash, like helicopters burning in the night.

"Want some coffee?" She heard Pat's voice.

Jessica thankfully opened her eyes. "Yes. Thanks."

He poured from a thermos into a plastic cup. She took the cup and held it below her chin, letting the aroma float up to her nostrils. Pat brought a chair, sat next to her, and silently took her free hand; their linked hands dangled between their seats.

She tensed and leaned forward as the copters turned off their running lights in the final approach to the target area. The leader hovered over the bluff, scanned the area with their infrared detectors.

"The farmhouse is afire," the observer reported. "I see no heat signatures in the area that resemble vehicles or human beings."

Jessica restrained herself from lunging forward to snatch up a microphone and start barking out orders. The sortie leader gave the orders that Jessica would have given anyway, to reconfirm the absence of human or vehicle IR signatures, then to advance cautiously in a dispersed formation so as to get a wider view of the area.

"I am on visual," another observer reported. "I see what appear to be two bodies in the yard of the farmhouse."

"I confirm." Another observer.

"An adult and what appears to be a child," the first observer said.

Jessica squeezed Pat's hand. *A child.* God in Heaven.

The sortie commander brought in a Huey to land in the yard while the others flew cover. Armed engineers piled out of the Huey on landing to secure the area, scout the outbuildings, and examine the corpses.

"A middle-aged man in civilian dress," the report came. "A little girl, maybe five years old. Both dead by gunshot."

At this point Jessica decided that it was time to give an order. She took the microphone and ordered the Huey to return with the casualties, keeping over the Delta and flying without running lights until they were well clear of Rails Bluff. The rest were to spread out and gather as much intelligence as they could without giving away their presence.

Jessica returned to her seat, took Pat's hand again, and gave thought to what she would do next. It was clear she must report this matter to her superiors. After that it was very probable that the matter would be taken out of her hands. Her authority involved civil engineering, not military operations. The area was full of military units that were getting really tired of looking after swarms of complaining refugees and their screaming children. Tired of repairing roads, cutting brush, and jacking up buildings that had fallen off their foundations. A lot of soldiers who just wanted to get back to soldiering. One of them would get the Rails Bluff assignment, she knew, whatever it turned out to be.

But she badly wanted to be a part of what happened next. She didn't want to turn the matter over to some hotshot who was going to get a lot of people killed.

Besides, she thought, *those motherfuckers shot at me.*

She turned to one of her radio operators. "Get me the commanding general, First Army," she said.

She was going to figure out a way to keep her hand in, whatever happened.

Jessica contemplated Matthew "Tex" Avery, the burly black man who, with his family, had been pulled by one of her helicopters out of a cotton field near Rails Bluff in the middle of the night. Tex had sprained his ankle falling into a crevasse as he ran with his family from the Reverend Frankland's camp, and now sat in a cot in a corner of the infirmary tent. His sprained, bandaged ankle was propped up in front of him on a folding chair, with a plastic sack of ice melting atop it. His abrasions had been cleaned and bandaged, and he'd been given a clean set of BDUs in a forest camouflage pattern. With his scraggly two days' beard, he looked less like a refugee than a guerilla fighter just extracted from the wilderness.

"Tex?" Jessica said. "This is Colonel Rivera. I'd like you to repeat to him everything you told me this morning."

Eddie and Rivera shook hands. Colonel Orlando Rivera was a stocky man who wore the sleeves of his tunic rolled up above biceps clearly sculpted by many dedicated hours at the curling machine. He commanded a Ranger unit that CG First Army had assigned to the liberation of Rails Bluff, and he had come in ahead of his command, which was still being pulled out of its rubble-searching duties in Greater Memphis and reunited with its combat equipment and transport.

The commanding general had said that Rivera was a reasonable type, a War College graduate, not a hothead, willing to work and play with others instead of stomping in and taking charge and committing heinous bloody massacre and otherwise acting like a macho stud. Jessica had been skeptical of this assessment, but so far Rivera seemed perfectly amiable.

And a Ranger, too, Jessica thought. And one with *biceps*. Would miracles never cease?

More important than the Ranger, perhaps, was the ruling she'd received from the Army's legal counsel. Her proposed action, the ruling stated, was legal. Martial law had been declared by the civil authorities in that part of Arkansas over two weeks ago, and never rescinded. The Army was allowed to get as martial as it felt necessary.

Jessica and Rivera sat crosslegged on the ground by Tex's cot while he went through his story. Rivera asked questions about the chain of command at the camp, the number of guards on duty at any one moment, how often the guards went on and off watch. Tex answered as best he could, but it was clear he had tried to keep as far away from the guards as possible and had little information on their movements.

Jessica and Rivera thanked Tex and returned to the tent Jessica had erected on the edge of the helicopter pad, where she had gathered everything available on Rails Bluff: all the maps, tapes of radio broadcasts, all the videos from the various aerial scouting missions, and all the interpretations of the data that had been provided by MARS sources.

Among the various data present was the fact that someone trained in photo interpretation had counted no less than ninety-six human-sized infrared signatures in Rails Bluff and vicinity. The Pentagon had people whose job it was to count things on reconnaissance photographs—numbers of tanks, antiaircraft missiles, and soldiers marching in formation— and Jessica had no reason to question the basic accuracy of the number.

That was a lot of people to get caught in a crossfire.

"The question is," Rivera said as he frowned down at the

information, "how many of them are armed? And of those armed, how many are willing to offer resistance?"

"Tex said that most of them had no weapons. That there was a hard core of supporters from the churches of the three preachers, but that everyone else was without arms, and that a lot of those were apathetic."

Rivera didn't seem reassured. "So how many is this hard core? Fifty? That still leaves a lot of bystanders." He looked grim. "Or hostages, however they want to play it."

Jessica looked at him. "We own the night," she said. One of the Army's unofficial mottoes, proudly proclaiming that they could move and fight as well in darkness as they could in the day.

Rivera looked at Jessica for a long moment, then nodded. "It's best that everyone wakes up tomorrow morning and finds out their camp's under new management."

"I think that's how it should be played."

He stroked his chin.

"Well," he said, "let's look at a map."

"There." Pointing. "The key to the position. This big tank, or whatever it is."

"Tex said it was a catfish pond," Jessica said. "Ten acres."

"That's where the sniper was, according to Tex. Just one man. We could put a battalion in there and they wouldn't see us unless we wanted them to." Rivera looked at the photograph. "Can we see any sentries on that embankment? If I were trying to hold that camp, I sure as hell would put people up there."

The latest photographs from Rails Bluff had just come in. Jessica had managed to get an Air Force RF-16, the reconnaissance version of the F-16 fighter, tasked to her command from a combat wing in Texas. The RF-16 had overflown Rails Bluff at high altitude, presumably without anyone on the ground taking notice, while snapping one detailed photo after another. The results had been flashed to Jessica's command tent, printed, and were on her desk within two hours of the sortie's landing.

Jessica took her magnifier, bent over the photo, looked down at the catfish pond through her left eye. There were strange little flashes in the corner of her eye, and she shifted the magnifier to the right.

"I don't see any sentries there," she said.

"That camp's spread out along the road, made up of smaller camps lined up in a long row. With the unmarried men at one end, the unmarried women at the other." Rivera grinned. "They're not so much interested in defense as keeping the single men and women as far apart as possible. We can flank the camps and cut one off from the next. Particularly if we can maneuver out of that catfish pond."

"Sorry to interrupt, General." One of Jessica's staff standing by the door and offering a folder. "The latest weather forecast."

"Thank you."

Jessica looked at the satellite photos, the attached isobar map, the analysis, and didn't know whether to feel relief or not. The strong high-pressure system that had been sitting on the south-central U.S. since just after M1 was finally moving. A big wall of low pressure was dropping out of the Rockies across the plains, bringing cooler, wetter weather.

It would be a relief to be out of the heat for a while. But as the whirling high-pressure area was shoved eastward, the moisture it had been sucking out of the Gulf of Mexico and dumping on the western plains would move with it. Torrential rains pouring across her entire area of operations weren't going to make her primary job any easier, not when half the country was flooded and the rest was bogged in the muck.

"This is going to help us," Rivera said. "In foul weather the camp sentries are going to be spending their time under cover, not looking for us."

"It may affect our ability to surveille the area."

"Can we get another photo mission scheduled before sunset? The long shadows would be valuable in showing us anything we've missed."

"The Air Force is cooperating." She gave a laugh. "They're

just like the Army—in the national emergency, the glamour units are tired of taking a backseat to the support elements." She glanced quickly at Rivera, suddenly aware that she'd just been tactless. *Keep your opinions to yourself,* she mentally snarled.

"No offense," she added.

Rivera grinned. "No problem," he said.

"They're coming," Frankland said. "The black helicopters are coming. They'll be back, and we have to be ready."

He had his most loyal people gathered around him on the highway in front of the church, and even there he had to talk loudly over the boom of the loudspeakers. He had cranked the volume up all over the camp so that the inmates couldn't ignore the Word. He knew he had only a short time to get his message across before the Pale Horseman rode into town with an unsheathed sword.

"It's been a whole day, practically," said Martin, the guide for the Second Thessalonians. "Are you sure they're really coming? Maybe the Army has other things to do."

"Don't you think Satan has an enemies list?" Frankland said. "Don't you think we're on it?"

He had felt the black helicopters hovering over him all night long. He'd felt the touch of their rotating wings on the back of his neck while he crept forward to the old Swanson place to light his gasoline bomb and throw it into the ruins. He felt it when Stone and his family fled the flames and ran into the bullets of his supporters. He felt it as he grabbed Stone's wife and surviving child and flung them into his truck, then lit out at full speed for the camp. He knew the enemy was there. He knew he had to get back to the camp and make ready. The terror of Satan's dark wings drove him on. That was why he'd left Stone and his daughter lying in the dust instead of bringing them back for burial. He knew he had so little time left.

"Satan never sleeps," said Magnusson. "I should know. I let some people get away yesterday because I let them bluff me. It was the Devil who put that bluff in the boy's mind, I know that for sure."

Frankland glanced over the highway. "What I want to do is make this place defensible. Sandbagged emplacements on the corners of the camps. Slit trenches for the people to shelter in." He pointed at the catfish farm. "And I want to emplace some of you *there*. I'm not going to let somebody with a gun catch us napping again."

Most of the guides and guards nodded and looked severe. A few seemed hesitant. Frankland looked at one of them, turned on his silky, persuasive voice.

"Do I *want* a battle?" he said. "No. But we haven't thought enough about our security, and yesterday we paid the penalty. I want everyone here *safe*. And they'll only be safe if we *make* them safe. Then we can be like the angels around the Throne, spending our days chanting 'Holy, holy, holy, Good God Almighty.' We'll be safe."

"'*Lord* God Almighty,'" someone corrected.

"Sorry," Frankland said, "I misspoke."

He wasn't sure whether he'd succeeded in motivating them or not. He made assignments, put people in charge of his new projects, then crossed the camp to his home.

Dr. Calhoun had been moved to the room where Father Robitaille had died. Calhoun was alive, his pulse strong, but he had been unconscious since morning and his abdomen was rigid and hard as iron around the bandaged entrance wound. He wouldn't live more than a day or two, and would probably never wake.

Sheryl and Reverend Garb watched in silence over the dying man. Garb looked somber. He had been very quiet since the incident the previous morning and spent much of his time in prayer. Sheryl wore her reading glasses and had her art on her lap, working nimbly with tweezers and tiny bits of postage stamp confetti. She had started a new project to keep hand and mind occupied—the Book of Daniel this time, Frankland noticed, the beast with seven horns.

"No change," Garb said in answer to Frankland's query. He held Calhoun's limp hand in his own.

"I'm trying to put the camp in a state of defense," Frankland said. "The forces of the Enemy will be coming for us soon."

Garb looked sadly down at the unconscious man. "I didn't think it would come to this."

Sheryl gave Garb a sharp glance over the rims of her spectacles. "You knew it was going to be bad," she said. "You knew that most of these people would die during the next seven years of Tribulation, no matter what we did."

"I suppose," Garb said.

"It only matters *how* they die," Frankland said. "If they have Jesus in their hearts, it doesn't matter what happens to them."

Sheryl dropped a yellow stamp-fleck onto one of the beast's horns. "Once the people leave us, teddy bear," she said, "they'll be back in the secular world." She shook her head. "Nothing there but temptation and sin, and most likely they'll die no matter what happens. Better they die here, when they're more likely to die in a state of grace." Her eyes flickered to the wounded man. "Like Dr. Calhoun," she said.

"Yes." Garb nodded sadly. "Yes, I suppose you're right."

"I'm going to prepare the camp for the end," Frankland said. "If we die, it's best we all die together."

"I'll be along in a minute, sweetie," Sheryl said. "I want to finish this horn first."

Frankland rounded up some of the Christian Gun Club and put his block and tackle over the last, untouched concrete bunker. He lifted up the slab and looked at what lay there. The others stood in sober respect.

And when he had opened the seventh seal, Frankland thought, *there was silence in heaven . . .*

M26A1, read the stencils on the box, *Fragmentation, 30.* Two cases at thirty per case. Hilkiah had acquired them two years ago, and Frankland had been careful not to ask how.

"Let's take the grenades out," Frankland said, "and then the .50 caliber Browning."

Mid-morning, the bass boat drifted at last into the Mississippi. The great river was sluggish, but at least it moved faster than the Arkansas. The amount of debris had increased, if anything, but on the wider, larger river it was possible to steer around it. Nick started the outboard but kept speed and fuel consumption low.

He kept a wary eye on Jason, who shared with Arlette the duties of standing on the foredeck and fending off debris. Jason had turned cooperative—he was obedient, cheerful, helpful, and had kept to himself his endless supply of smart remarks.

Nick found this ominous. That and the way Jason was relating to Arlette—the shared glances, the giggles, the way their arms or legs brushed together, as if by accident, as they worked on the foredeck.

Nick knew damn well what was going on. It was right there in front of him. But there was nothing he could object to, no inappropriate behavior, not so much as a kiss.

Just two young people falling in love. It made Nick grind his teeth. He ground his teeth so much that it made his neck ache.

There was no traffic on the river. None at all. The huge cypress and cottonwood trees coming down with the flood apparently provided too great a hazard to navigation.

At De Soto Landing, they gave a wide berth to a docking platform that thrust a hundred yards or so into the river. The facilities were big enough for tankers. Some of the big oil tanks on shore had burned. There was no sign of a living human being.

The boat floated downriver alongside the shimmering ribbon of oil that stretched out from the landing. The stench of the oil sank into the back of Nick's throat, a foul rasp he couldn't cough out even though he tried.

The river slowed to a crawl. The boat drifted, bumped aimlessly against debris, because Nick wanted to conserve fuel.

Hunger settled into Nick's stomach, became a part of him, a steady ache he carried always with him like a woman carries a child. He found himself thinking nostalgically of Brother Frankland's greasy fish and mixed vegetables. Food occupied his thoughts almost every minute. Not just for himself, but for his family. Rescue needed to come very soon.

A cooling breeze fluttered the surface of the water, brought light dancing on the river's skin of oil. The breeze was refreshing at first, the first real weather change in two weeks and a relief in the sweat-drenched, smothering tropical heat. But as the sky darkened and the breeze strengthened, flying into their faces from the south, Nick began to look for a way to shelter from the storm that was obviously building. Lightning flashed in the oncoming clouds, suggesting it would be unwise to remain in the main channel as the tallest electric conductor for half a mile in any direction. A gray chop rose on the river, tossing debris against the boat's chine.

It was clearly time to take a chance on the falling timber in the flood plain. The treeline on the east bank looked far too dense to safely enter, so when Nick started the Johnson, he maneuvered toward the western bank, crossing the track of the oil that had been draining from the broken tanks upstream. Oil-flavored spray spattered Nick's face as the bass boat shouldered into the chop. Thunder boomed from the sky like the bootsteps of God.

The bass boat reached the trees just as the rain cut loose, a drenching rainstorm that came down in floods all at once, without preamble. Within seconds it was too dark and wet to see more than a few feet. Wind howled through the broken tops of the trees, bringing a gentle drizzle of small branches and willow leaves. Nick and the others huddled in the little cockpit, stretching over themselves the orange plastic sun shade that they'd taken from Frankland's guards. Rain rattled on the plastic, little bright concussions like gunshots next to Nick's ears. Thoughts of cold drove thoughts of food from his mind. He was cold and hungry and wet, and as he shivered he could feel the others shivering, too.

The rain ceased around midnight, and with stiff limbs Nick and the others bailed out the boat. No stars were visible overhead. The downpour started again an hour later, as fierce as before, and continued intermittently past the gray, uncertain dawn.

When they finally shook the last drops off the orange plastic and looked around them, they found themselves in a flooded stand of cypress. The sun was invisible behind dark cloud, and they had no way of telling direction. Soon little wisps of mist began to rise from the water. The wisps thickened, then closed overhead like interlaced fingers.

The boat bobbed silently in the fog, lost and alone in the forest of silence.

The rain hammered down. Omar had set out pails and crockery for the leaks—his roof had not done well in the quakes.

Wilona was standing a night shift at Clarendon—probably sitting down to a session of tea and heartfelt gossip with Mrs. Ashenden as the rain drummed on the rooftop—so Omar was home alone, lying on the sofa with his shoes off and listening to Johnny Paycheck on the radio.

It was the endgame that he worried about. He'd isolated the A.M.E. camp. He'd made certain that no one but certain of his own people had access. Jedthus and Knox both told him that things were going well there, though they volunteered no details, and Omar asked for none.

But at the end, when the camp was empty, what then? He couldn't tell everyone that two hundred refugees had just flown away.

Timing, he thought. If the Bayou Bridge could be repaired soon, and he could know the date in advance, he could just claim that everyone had left of their own accord as soon as they could.

He heard booted feet stomping on the porch, kicking off the raindrops, and then David came in, banging the screen door and moving with the slow, overelaborate deliberation that gave Omar to understand that he was drunk.

David wore a plastic rain slicker over his deputy's star and one of Omar's spare uniforms. That morning, Tree Simpson had ruled that his shooting of the refugee was justified, and David had returned to duty as a special deputy.

Omar had made a point of assigning David to patrolling the highway between Shelburne City and the fallen Bayou Bridge, on the other end of the parish from the A.M.E. camp. He didn't want David near the place. When David asked him why, Omar said, "because if you turn up at the camp, we'll have a riot on our hands."

Which was not the real reason, but it was a reason that would have to serve for David.

"Hi, Dad," David said. He hung up the rain slicker and his baseball cap on the pegs by the front door.

"How was your evening?" Omar asked.

"Went out with the boys."

"Which boys?"

David went into the refrigerator without answering, got a beer, returned to the front room to sit in Omar's easy chair. Omar looked at him from his reclining position on the sofa. "Which boys?" Omar repeated.

"Knox and them."

"I thought—" Omar was about to repeat his instructions to stay away from Knox, but then he saw David's knuckles bruised and swollen, and he sat up.

"You been in a fight, son?" he asked.

David looked at his battered fists, then shrugged. "A little ramshagging, that's all."

Anger snarled in Omar's veins. "You just survived an *inquest*, sonny boy!" he barked. "Now you want to start getting into fistfights and maybe having people start thinking second thoughts about that killing you did? Who were you fighting *with*, anyhow?"

David gave a slow, drunken grin. "Nobody that'll complain. We was down to Woodbine Corners."

Omar stared at him in shock. David took a swig of his beer.

"We decided, hell, we'll save some bullets," he said. "We'll kill this batch with our bare hands. So we had a few drinks and got to business." He looked at his free hand, flexed the fingers meditatively. "It was a lot more work than we thought. It takes a long time, you know, to kill someone like that."

Omar's head swam. Revulsion squeezed his stomach, brought the tang of vomit to his tongue. He bit it down.

Then the anger hit, and he stood over David and slapped the beer from his hand. "*What are you doing?*" he demanded. "*Just what in hell do you think you're doing?*"

David stared up in amazement. Omar slapped him across the face. "Didn't I tell you to stay away from Knox?" he demanded. "Didn't I?"

The beer bottle gurgled as it emptied itself onto the floor. "What's the problem?" David demanded. "What's wrong?"

"Knox is *crazy*," Omar shouted. "Isn't that enough?" He clenched his fists and marched an angry circle around the room. Spilled beer soaked his socks.

"But Daddy," David said, "Knox believes the same as you. He believes the same as what you've always taught me."

Omar lunged across the room to stand over his son again, hand raised to strike. David flinched but didn't raise a hand to defend himself. Omar didn't bring the hand down; he left it in the air, in case he changed his mind.

"Knox is out of his head!" Omar shouted. "He's been wandering around the country stealing and killing! If you hang around him, you'll get killed or spend the rest of your life in jail! Did I raise you for that?" Omar demanded. "Did I, Davy?"

"He's a soldier!" David said. "He's fighting a war against ZOG. Just like you!"

"ZOG, shit! Ain't no ZOG and never was!"

Bewilderment shone on David's face. "I don't get it. If you ain't fighting for the white, why are you doing what you're doing?"

Blood flamed in Omar's heart. He panted for breath. He looked at the hand he'd raised, and let it fall.

"It's for you, son," he said. "You did a killing. Can't let no witnesses testify or they'll hang us both." He took a breath. *"I'm not doing this so you can get drunk and beat niggers to death! I'm doing it so you'll stay out of prison!"*

David licked his lips as he tried to comprehend this. "Knox says we're going to be famous. Knox says we're going to liberate all America starting with Spottswood Parish."

Omar straightened wearily from his crouch over David's chair, turned, slopped through the spilled beer back to the couch. He sat down heavily, staring at the wall opposite with the blue flowered wallpaper that he and Wilona had put up when David was still in grade school.

"Do you really think a dozen killers are going to turn this country around?" he said. "Do you really think that?"

"You've always stood up for the white man," David said. "That's all I'm doing."

"I've done what I can for myself in this place," Omar said. "Our family has been here for seven generations and we've never had anything to eat but shit from the people who run the parish. The Klan's the only answer for a man like me. But you—" He looked at his son. "You're in college. You've got what it takes to make it outside Spottswood Parish. You can leave this used-up old place. And that's what I want you to do."

David was still bewildered. "I ain't never heard you talk like this."

Omar felt cold beer seeping up his crew socks. "I want you to go away!" he shouted. "I want you to save yourself!"

"There's no way out of town, Dad." A reasonable tone had crept into David's voice. "The bridges are down. Besides, I don't *want* to leave. Not when we're all going to be famous!"

Omar stared at his son. "Famous?"

"With our pictures on TV and everything!" There was a drunken glow in David's eyes. "Then we'll disappear into the underground, like Knox does after he rescues some Jew money from a bank, and we'll wait to strike again. And then after the Liberation—"

"After the *what*?" Omar repeated.

"After we win. After the white man's in charge again."

Omar's heart beat sickly in his temples. His head whirled. He couldn't quite seem to catch his breath.

"My God," he said, half to himself. "My God in this world."

Micah Knox would pay for this, he thought. Would pay and pay.

David reached out, patted Omar in a comforting way on his knee. "Don't worry about me," he said. "Everything will be fine. You'll see. We'll come through, and maybe you'll even be President." He laughed. "Won't that be something! You and me in the White House."

Omar threw his head back and felt anguish twist in his heart like a knife. He wanted to howl his pain aloud.

"I wanted you to be better than me," he said.

David looked at him with drunken amiability. "Nobody's better than you, Dad," he said. "Nobody in this world."

Jessica's helicopter lurched as wind shear tried to fling it into the invisible Arkansas Delta below. Water coursed over the windscreen in streams, and blinking red and green navigation lights reflected off the slanted raindrops like a thousand distant stars. The command radio channel hissed in Jessica's ears, then crackled to the sudden flashes of lightning that lit the strange, featureless gloom in which the Kiowa traveled.

The rescue mission to Rails Bluff was underway. It was a little after two in the morning. Rivera's Rangers, with units of Jessica's engineers in support, were scheduled to be in position around the camp by five. The camp was due to be under new management, as Colonel Rivera had put it, by dawn.

Brightly colored star shells flashed in Jessica's left eye as the helicopter gave another lurch. She blinked, tried to will the flashing lights away. Gravity clutched at her stomach.

She enjoyed thrill rides, but this was absurd.

Lightning dazzled Jessica's eyes and thunder boomed through the cabin. "Jesus Christ," her pilot murmured, and then, "Sorry, ma'am."

I want my high-pressure system back, Jessica thought.

Suddenly the pounding rain ceased, and the remaining droplets were blown off the windscreen by prop blast. The Kiowa floated through cloud, a world of cotton-wool eerily remote from the rest of the universe. Enhancing the sense of unreality were the ghostly symbols on the heads-up display, navigation and other information projected onto the interior of the windscreen so that the pilot could read them without looking down at the instrument panel. Though the data from those displays, from the Inertial Navigation System and the Litton AHRS, tracking their location in the murk to within a hundred meters, kept the outside world a lot closer than it seemed.

"We have reached Point C," the pilot said. He touched the rudder bar with one foot while his hand made an adjustment to the collective. "Turning to course two-one-zero. Navigation lights—" A gloved hand reached for the instrument panel. "Off."

Jessica felt her mouth go dry as the night shadows closed in. The outside world was getting closer by the second.

The late-afternoon Air Force overflight had revealed that the Rails Bluff camp had made defensive preparations. Sandbagged emplacements had appeared on the camp's perimeter since morning, and some of the strong shadows inside the camp suggested that slit trenches had been dug here and there.

And worst of all, there were two sandbagged outposts planted on the embankment of the catfish farm across the road. One of them showed a tripod-mounted machine gun that could dominate the flat country for a thousand yards in all directions.

In the early evening Rivera, Jessica, and their officers made hurried revisions of their plan of operations. The machine gun had to be neutralized or taken out. Likewise the sand-bagged bunkers.

"Good thing we've got bad weather coming in," Rivera said. "Anyone in the camp's going to be under cover, and that MG is probably going to be wrapped in plastic."

We hope, Jessica thought.

The Kiowa gave another lurch, leaving Jessica's stomach about two hundred feet above her head. Jessica wondered if Rivera was still thankful for the rain.

We own the night. Jessica hoped it wasn't as empty a boast as *We control the river* turned out to be.

Rivera's voice crackled on the command channel. "Badger Team has landed and is taking position. All is copacetic."

"Roger that, Badger." Rivera's primary combat team had landed north of the catfish farm, out of earshot—it was hoped—of any sentries in the camp. That would mean a long slog through flooded fields to the camp, but that shouldn't be a consideration to people who Owned the Night.

Other reports came in as other teams landed. Jessica's Kiowa reached its landing point and began to descend. The cloud cleared, and below, in the infrared light of the chopper's FLIR, Jessica saw Rivera's helicopters spread over several acres of mud. Little glowing figures, Rangers, were setting up a perimeter.

Jessica's own engineers would be in support, and would not approach the Rails Bluff camp unless the Rangers called for them, or when the camp was secured. Likewise Jessica would leave Rivera to take care of tactical operations and only intervene with the capture of the camp if it was absolutely necessary. Which meant only if things went terribly, terribly wrong.

The Kiowa settled gentle as a dandelion seed onto the muddy field.

Jessica sighed. It was going to be a long night.

Rain drummed on Frankland's rain hood as he tramped to the door of the radio station. He wiped his boots on the mat and prepared to step inside, then hesitated with his hand on the doorknob as he heard a throbbing sound, distant but clear in the waterlogged night. For a moment his nerves hummed—black helicopters!—but then lightning cut loose somewhere to the west, freezing the world as if in a photo flash, and he shook his head and opened the door.

This weather was impossible. The black helicopters would come, he thought, but they could not come tonight.

Sheryl looked up from the reception desk. The desk light pooled on the long linen Apocalypse spread out before her. When the storm had blown up, after dark, Sheryl's magnum opus had suffered considerable damage from the wind before she and Frankland could rescue it and bring it indoors.

"The camp's going to be a real mess in the morning," Frankland said. "We'd better have a hot meal ready when people get up."

Sheryl nodded. "Already taken care of."

"How you doing, honey bun?"

Sheryl looked at him over the rims of her reading glasses. "Dreadful damage. Just dreadful."

"I'm sorry, sweetie. Is there anything I can help you with?"

"Just watch where you put your feet." A lot of the linen rolls had ended up on the floor for lack of anywhere else to put them. Frankland shuffled his boots from the fragile artwork.

"I'm going back to the studio."

"Mm."

He opened the inner door and walked down the corridor to the control room. Lights glowed, and dials clicked back and forth unattended as the station broadcast a tape that Frankland had made weeks ago, before the first great earthquake

Frankland felt an aftershock rumble up through his boots. That, he thought, must have been the throbbing sound he'd heard.

He took off his rain slicker, then unstrapped the AR-15 he carried across his chest to protect it from the weather. He propped the gun in a corner, took off his pistol belt—the grenades made it too uncomfortable to wear while sitting— and sat in front of the microphone.

He hadn't broadcast much new material since the first quake. He'd been too busy organizing the camp. But now that he knew the black helicopters were coming, Frankland felt he wanted to talk about what had happened, to explain his point of view and the necessity for everything he'd done.

Frankland wanted to leave a testament behind him. So that after the black helicopters came people would understand.

It was for souls, he wanted to say. The bodies didn't signify, it was winning souls for Christ that mattered.

And so he cued up a tape, positioned himself behind the microphone, and as the rain drummed on the roof and the building rocked to thunder, he began to speak.

When he broadcast the tape in the morning, the world would know.

The Rangers moved forward, hunched in their cloaks beneath squalls of wind and rain. While the pouring water streamed down the canopy of her helicopter, Jessica listened to her helicopter's command channel, the terse, breathless communications of the officers. Her hands clutched the sides of the seat as reports came in of the camp coming into sight, as night-vision and infrared gear was used to carefully scan the camp and spot any sentries who dared to stick their heads out.

There weren't many, it appeared. The camp was buttoned down against the storm.

"Coffee, General?" Jessica's pilot produced a thermos.

"No. Thanks." Much as she craved coffee at the moment, she was wound tightly enough as it was.

Jessica had read that Field Marshal Bernard Law Montgomery used to go to sleep the night before an attack, with strict orders not to be disturbed until the battle had already developed. She wondered how he managed it.

The smell of coffee filled the cockpit, activating Jessica's salivary glands. A mild aftershock rolled up the Kiowa's struts as commands hissed into Jessica's earphones. The Rangers were crawling forward toward the camp under cover of the intermittent squalls. They were moving toward the machine-gun nest at the catfish farm by crawling along the base of the earth embankment, so a lightning flash wouldn't silhouette them on the top.

"This is Badger Six," a voice crackled. "We have secured our objective on the northwest perimeter. The guards did not resist. Repeat, no resistance."

"Roger that, Badger Six." Rivera's voice.

Jessica's breath eased from her aching lungs. One corner of the unmarried women's camp was secure.

"Holy shit!" came Badger Six's voice again, very excited. Jessica jerked forward in her seat as if pulled by an invisible wire. "We got fragmentation grenades here! And a couple M-16s. Do you copy that?"

"Copy that, Badger Six." Rivera's voice was laconic.

"These people are loaded for bear, sir!"

"No chatter on this channel, Badger Six. We copy."

Another outpost fell in silence, then another. Then—Jessica

wanted to scream out her relief—the machine-gun nest on the catfish farm.

And then the rest. The camp's perimeter had been secured without a shot, without an alarm, without a single act of violence.

Relief sang in Jessica's veins.

Rivera began to position his teams to cut the camps off from one another, to secure the church, the radio station, and Frankland's house.

Jessica leaned back in her seat.

"I'd appreciate some of that coffee, soldier," she said.

They will say I have committed murder. The phrases rolled through Frankland's mind as he pushed back from the microphone. *Certainly I have killed, but I have killed justly. And God will judge me in the end, as he will judge all men. I have no terror of standing before the Throne of the Almighty.*

Frankland stood, stretched, felt his vertebrae crackle. His body was weary, but his mind still churned with ideas, with images. The spirit still sang in him, stirring his nerves, and he knew that it would be hours before he would sleep.

He rewound the tape to its beginning, then turned up the in-studio speaker on the tape that was already playing. He waited until the older recording came to a natural pause, then Frankland turned it off and cued the new tape.

"This is the Noble Frankland of the Church of the End Times." The voice came from the battered old speakers in the room. He turned down the volume, then strolled down the hallway to where Sheryl still sat behind the desk, working briskly with her tweezers.

"Any news?" he asked.

"No." She looked up from her work. "Rain's slackening off, I think," she said.

Frankland looked at his watch. It would be dawn shortly.

And then the door opened and a pair of armed men entered, rifles held across their chests, faces blackened and rain-streaked below the broad, dripping brims of their hats. "U.S. Army!" one of them said. "Nobody move!"

Frankland stared as his heart lurched into a higher gear. *Caught!* he thought. His rifle, his pistol, and his precious grenades were in the control room. He was helpless.

Another man entered the room, a pistol held lightly in his hand. "Colonel Rivera," he said. "U.S. Rangers. I understand you had some trouble here?"

Frankland could only gape. He couldn't understand how this could happen. He had *guards!* He had *outposts!* He hadn't heard a single shot.

Black helicopters! his mind screamed. Black helicopters of Satan! They had come in the night, and he and his poor people had been caught unprepared.

Now they would all live. Live, and sin, and go to Hell. When they could have died and gone to Glory.

"You—" The word hissed from Sheryl. She stared in outrage at the colonel's muddy boots planted on her artwork, right on the seven angels and the seven vials. "You—" She half-rose from her seat. "You're wrecking my Apocalypse!" she shrieked.

It was only then that Frankland's paralyzed mind recalled the double-barreled, sawed-off shotgun clipped under the desk, the shotgun that had been there all along, from well before the quake. He threw himself backward, down the hall.

The shotgun blasted out, twice. All three soldiers were caught in the broad swath of buckshot. Sheryl dropped the sawed-off, opened a desk drawer, took out a grenade, primed it, and pitched it straight out the open front door.

Frankland scuttled down the hall, on hands and knees, heading for his weapons. There was a flash and a bang outside the door. Grenade fragments whined off the station's steel walls. Frankland grabbed the Armalite, cranked a round into the chamber, then snatched up his gun belt with its grenades and pistol. He ran down the hall again toward the front room.

"Hang on, sweetie pie!" he said. "I'm coming!"

The Kiowa bored into the Arkansas dawn. Jessica could hear the grinding of her teeth amplified beneath her helmet.

Somehow, late in the game after all danger should have been passed, Rivera had somehow lost control and everything had gone to hell.

Rivera was dead, apparently, along with two other Rangers. Several others were wounded by grenade fragments. After everything had been secured—the outposts, the camps, the church, Frankland's home—there had been some last-minute screwup at the radio station. Shots fired. Grenades thrown. And the Ranger officer on the spot had ordered return fire.

Jessica had ordered support elements aloft as soon as she heard the news. Apache gunships and Hueys to provide close support, more Hueys carrying her engineers with heavier weapons and the body armor that the Rangers lacked.

It was over by the time Jessica's Kiowa first soared over the camp. Resistance had ended. The radio station was on fire, smoke billowing from under the metal eaves. Rangers were diving inside, braving the flames, to haul out the bodies of their comrades.

Fucking amateurs, Jessica thought. The people in the radio station had no idea of the firepower of a modern military unit, even a lightly equipped outfit like the Rangers. They'd thought it was going to be like the movies, like a Western gunfight, like Davy Crockett at the Alamo.

Instead, everyone in the radio station was probably dead within seconds after the Ranger commander had ordered his people to return fire. A kill zone. *Bang-bang-bang-bang-bang.* Just like that.

Ranger training was not for the faint-hearted. One of the exercises featured a fifteen-mile ruck march, with 100-pound field packs plus a rifle, that ended with three shots to the bulls-eye at a range of fifty meters. Compared to that, a little slog through the mud and a firefight against a few hayseeds didn't even signify.

The Kiowa circled the camp once, then dropped onto the highway in front of the church. Jessica dived out of the vehicle and ran for the church as fast as her short legs would carry her.

Then she stopped in her tracks. Put a hand in front of her right eye, then her left.

Half the vision in her left eye was gone, gone as if a black curtain had dropped across the world.

THIRTY-ONE

Our voyage was from various causes tedious and disagreeable, we being 28 days from St. Louis to this place, Mr. Comegys has fared worse, being two months. Our progress was considerably impeded by an alarming and awful earthquake, such as has not I believe, occurred, or at least has not been recorded in the history of this country. The first shock which we experienced was about 2 o'clock on the morning of the 16th Dec. at which time our position was in itself perilous, we being but a few hundred yards above a bad place in the river, called the Devils Race Ground: in our situation particularly, the scene was terrible beyond description, our boat appeared as if alternately lifted out of the water, and again suffered to fall. The banks above, below and around us were falling every moment into the river, all nature seemed running into chaos. The noise unconnected with particular objects, was the noise of the most violent tempest of wind mixed with a sound equal to the loudest thunder, but more hollow and vibrating. The crashing of falling trees and the loud screeching of wild fowl made up the horrid concert. Two men were sent on shore in order to examine the state of the bank to which we were moored, who reported that a few yards from its summit, it was separated from the shore by a chasm of more than 100 yards in length. Jos. Morin, the patron, insisted on our all leaving the boat which he thought could not be saved, and of landing immediately in order to save our lives: —this I successfully combatted until another shock took place, about 3 o'clock, when we all left the boat, went on shore and kindled a fire.

Extract from a letter by John Bradbury,
dated Orleans January 16th

"Sir! Sir! Mr. President!"

The President blinked awake, trying to adjust his eyes to the sudden glare of the overhead light. He had been dreaming so very nicely, too, a warm dream about—was it bread? Yes, bread. UFOs, it seems, were really loaves of bread, and the blinking lights were just the LEDs on the bread machines that made them . . . You could *eat* UFOs if you spread butter on them, that was the point.

"Sir? Are you awake?"

"Yes, Stan. What is it?"

There were a limited number of people who could wake the President. The names were on a list: the Secretary of State, the ambassador to the U.N., the Chairman of the Joint Chiefs, whoever was on duty at NORAD . . .

A relatively small list. The President very much regretted that he had ever put his Press Secretary on it.

"Calm down, Stan. And tell me what it is. And if it's the results of some kind of poll, I want you to march right out of here and—"

"It's not that, sir! It's General Frazetta! She's gone berserk!"

The President sat up in bed and frowned at Stan. "Berserk? My little Jessica, berserk? What's she done—" He smiled. "Gone and built another island?"

"She's conducting a renegade military operation in Arkansas! She's using Army Rangers and helicopters to attack some kind of church group!"

The President frowned. "Sounds serious."

"The Attorney General tried to reach you earlier, but he's not on the list to get you out of bed. He's mad enough to spit. He called me—I was in my office in the Executive Wing—and he practically chewed my ear off. Civil rights violations, abuse of power, separation of Church and State—my God, what a fiasco. I came right over."

The President considered Jessica Frazetta. Energetic, enthusiastic, overachieving. Sexy in a spunky, girl-next-door sort of way. And short. Really short.

He pictured her in a helicopter, spewing leaden death

upon the citizens of Arkansas. He pictured her grinning as she did so. The thought of it made him smile.

"Any casualties?" he said.

"Several dead, both Army and civilian. My God, sir, how do we spin this?"

The President lay back in his bed and pulled his covers up to his chin. "It's a no-brainer," he said.

"Sir?"

"We absolutely and categorically support General Frazetta's actions."

"*Sir!*" Stan was flabbergasted.

"Think about it, Stan. I appointed her to her present position. I was with her on her island, just a few days ago, shaking her hand and telling the world how wonderful she was. Implying that she'd saved the entire South from radiation poisoning. She's in an absolutely critical position—she's made herself damn near indispensable. I *have* to support her."

"But—this fiasco—"

The President closed his eyes. "It's not a fiasco *yet*. Right now it's a brave and courageous action taken in defense of civilian lives." The President smiled. "If it turns out to be a fiasco *later*, if she's really bungled it, then we'll say she misled us and cut her off at the knees."

There was a moment of silence. "Yes, sir," Stan said.

"Like I said, a no-brainer. Turn out the lights when you leave, Stan."

"Yes, sir."

The President heard Stan's feet crossing the room, and then the lights went out and the door swung softly shut.

The President sighed and tucked the covers up to his ears. He tried to remember the dream he was having.

Bread, he remembered. It was about bread.

A pair of Hueys throbbed away into the rising sun, carrying Rails Bluff's wounded. Including the Reverend Dr. Calhoun, who had been gut-shot two days ago, who had been in a coma for some time, but for whom—incredibly—no one in charge had ever thought to call a physician.

Crazy, Jessica thought. The man would rather die than let anyone know about his little operation here.

Fanatics. Jessica and her people were going to have to be very careful.

"Everyone gets patted down for weapons!" Jessica ordered. "When each is done, line them up on the road. Tell them rations and fresh water are coming!"

"O Lord!" cried a gangly red-headed man among the refugees. "O Lord, let me die with Brother Frankland! Let me pay for my sins!" The other refugees had cleared a space around him, looked at him with sidelong glances.

"O Lord! Take me now! I can't be saved without Brother Frankland!"

"Who the hell is that?" Jessica asked. "Another preacher?"

One of the grim-faced Ranger officers looked up. "He's been like that ever since the shooting. He keeps saying he was a pornographer and that he should die." He gave the man a grim look. "I think the others are good and sick of listening to him, but we can't shut him up."

Jessica rubbed her forehead over her injured eye. "Just make sure he doesn't try to kill himself," she said.

The camp was going to be a colossal administrative nightmare. Sorting Frankland's henchmen from the mere bystanders, and sorting the henchmen who had broken the law from those who hadn't, and in the meantime feeding the hungry and doctoring the sick—the legal issues alone, she suspected, were enough to keep several grand juries busy for years.

Officers hopped to carry out her instructions. Jessica rubbed her forehead over her damaged left eye while she reached into a pocket to pull out her Iridium cellphone.

She dialed Pat.

"Yes?" he answered at once. "Are you all right?"

"Yes. I came through it."

"We were listening to the radio. Frankland had just started this new rant, but it went on for only a couple minutes, and then we lost the signal. So I figured that the Rangers showed up right then. How'd it go?"

"It went about . . ." She looked around at the stunned refugees, the burning radio station, bodies of the Rangers lying under blankets. "About as well as we could rationally have hoped," she finished.

"That doesn't sound too good," Pat said.

"No," Jessica said. "No, I wouldn't call it good. It was the smallest and least destructive of a whole series of possible catastrophes, and that's all the good you can say about it."

"I'm glad you came through it okay."

Jessica turned, pulled her rain cape over her head, hunched away from the nearest soldiers. "Pat," she said, "I need you to make a phone call for me. I need you to call an ophthalmologist—probably one in Jackson—and make an emergency appointment. ASAP."

"Okay." Uncertainly.

"I need for you not to be overheard doing this." She bit her lip. "Pat—the appointment's for me."

Concern rasped Pat's voice. "Was there a fight? Did you get hit?"

"It's that shiner you gave me. I've been seeing flashes and . . ." She squeezed her eyes shut. "I've lost some vision in my left eye. I think it was the helicopter ride, it must have shaken something loose."

"My God, Jessie." Pat was thunderstruck. "My God, you've got to get here *now*."

"I can't. Things are a mess, and—look, you just make that appointment and let me know when I have to be there. And *don't tell anyone*. Because if the Army finds out, they're going to pull me off this job faster than you can spit."

There was a pause before Pat replied. "Are you sure that wouldn't be a good thing?"

Jessica clenched her teeth. "Everything's fucked up, okay?" she said. "Everything I've done has been destroyed or compromised or made a mess of. All I've been able to do is *watch*. I'm not leaving this job till I have a win, okay?"

"Yes," Pat said. "Yes. I understand."

"Make that call, okay? Take care of this for me."

"Right away."

"Good. Good. Because I need this."

"I love you, Jessie."

Jessica felt some of the tension ease from her taut-strung body. "I love you too, Pat."

She turned off the cellphone and pulled the rain cape off her head. The air smelled sweet, of rain and the grassy meadow.

Helicopters throbbed on the horizon, bringing in a company of military police, who would over the next day or two replace the Rangers and Jessica's engineers, leaving them free for other duties.

Jessica hoped to hell she wouldn't be blind by then.

Jason rubbed Arlette's arms, the friction of his palms warming the gooseflesh brought on by the clammy dawn. "Thanks," Arlette said in a small voice, and shivered. Jason wanted to put his arms around her, hold her close, keep her warm against him. But though he had huddled with her through the storm, flesh to flesh, in the tiny cockpit, so close that he could feel the chill cold of her thigh alongside his, smell the warmth of her breath beneath the improvised plastic rain canopy, still he did not quite dare to put his arms around her.

Not with Nick and Manon there, looking at him with weary, half-resentful eyes, as if they were on the verge of politely asking him to leave.

"Come here, baby," Nick said to Arlette. "Let me get you warm."

Arlette shifted across the little cockpit to sit on the edge of the cockpit next to her father. Nick began rubbing her bare arms, her back. Arlette sighed gratefully against his warmth. A pang of envy throbbed through Jason's heart.

Arlette sneezed. "Scat," her mother said.

"Thank you, Momma."

Arlette sneezed again.

"Scat," her parents said in unison.

Nick caught Jason's puzzled look. "'Scat' is Arkansas for 'Gesundheit,'" he said.

Jason nodded. "I kind of figured that out."

He rose stiffly to his feet from his perch on the edge of the cockpit, and gazed about at the fog-shrouded morning. Drops of water pattered down from the dark cypress trees, almost a rainstorm in themselves. The trees, standing on their thick stilt-legs and hung with vines and moss, were ungainly shadows barely visible through the mist. Some had fallen in the quake and lay like dead giants in the water, and elsewhere cypress roots, shorn off by tectonic force, stood in clumps like forlorn soldiers lost on a battlefield. Jason stepped up onto the wet front deck, looked down at the still, dark water, at his reflection fragmented by ripples. All the ripples were from the falling water, he realized. There wasn't so much as a breath of wind.

Hunger burned in his stomach. "What do we do?" he said.

"Get some *food,*" Manon said. "It's been two nights since we ate."

"We need to figure out where we are," Nick said. "The river's to the east of here, generally—maybe north or south is closer, but east will get us there—but in this fog we can't tell where east is."

"So we just *sit* here?" Manon said. "In the fog? And starve?"

"If you have a better idea," Nick said, "I would like to hear it."

"You should have planned better," Manon said. "You should have made sure that we had food with us when we got away from the camp."

"I wasn't the one who worked in the kitchens," Nick said. "You didn't put anything away?"

"*Can we not argue over this?*" Arlette demanded in a loud voice. "*Can somebody tell me why we're arguing?*"

The argument had the bitter taste of familiarity to Jason. *They sure sound like a family,* he thought. *Arguing about all the things they can't change.*

That was his family, too. What he remembered most about his family was the arguments. That and the long, terrible silences that followed the arguments, and the long absences when his father would vanish for weeks at a time, working eighteen hours a day in his office.

Nick's family seemed to be entering one of those familiar glacial silences. Jason rubbed the chill out of his upper arms.

"We could try to find some cattail," he said. His voice had a strange, hollow ring in the clammy mist. "Or some—what is it?—pokeweed?"

His voice vanished into the mist. The silence enveloped him. No one bothered to acknowledge his words.

He dropped to sit on his heels on the foredeck, hunkered against the tendrils of misery he felt floating around him, dank and clammy, like the mist.

Jason looked up for a moment as he noticed that one of the strange-looking cypress trees, standing tall on its knees in the flood, was moving along his line of vision. He looked up and found himself staring at the range of twelve feet or so into the beady eyes of a cormorant, one of a dozen who occupied the tree's lower branches—black, sinister silhouettes that sat in the trees as motionless, and as alien, as Easter Island statues, sentinels standing guard over unknown country.

Surprise brought an exclamation to Jason's lips. The cormorants didn't react, didn't even blink.

"Um," he said, to cover sudden embarrassment. "We're moving. There's a current here."

He heard the others shifting in the cockpit, testing the notion for themselves. None of them seemed to notice the ominous, long-necked figures in the trees that followed them with glittering eyes.

"The current is going downstream," Manon said. "All we have to do is go in the direction of the current, right?"

When Nick spoke, it was with slow reluctance. "Not necessarily," he said. "The storm just dumped a lot of rain upstream from here. When the flood hits us, it might spread out into the country as well as draining toward the Gulf. This current might be taking us further inland."

"That's not bad, is it?" Manon asked. "There are *people* inland."

"Maybe. It could be that we're just going further into the wilderness."

There was another moment of silence. "Nick," Manon said, "we have to get the child some food."

Jason turned away from the cormorants, saw Nick frowning in the cockpit. "I don't want to use fuel till we know where we're going."

"Anywhere is better than this."

"The fog will lift sooner or later," Jason offered, but the adults paid him no attention. It was as if they were locked in a kind of dance, and they couldn't leave the dance floor till the end of the music, and they couldn't change to a different dance because these were the only steps they knew.

Arlette, who knew the steps as well as the dancers, left her father's lap and joined Jason on the foredeck. They hunched in cold silence and watched the cormorants fade away into the mist. At the end of the argument, Nick started the outboard and began to motor along with the current. Jason and Arlette took their oars and stood on the foredeck to fend off floating debris.

At least the activity kept them warm. And Jason enjoyed just being in Arlette's company, working next to her on the foredeck.

The strange cypress-shadows floated past, as if in and out of a dream. Little aftershocks trembled in the still water, then faded. The motor's low rumble echoed from the invisible forest around them. Water streamed from the branches above. Jason was morally certain that they were heading in the wrong direction, that they were just getting deeper into the wilderness, but he was part of the adults' dance now, too, and there was no escaping it.

After an hour or so the cypress swamp came to an end. Instead of trees there was a tangle of bushes and low scrub, much of it covered with creeper and strung with floating debris. Nick cut the motor for a moment, and the boat drifted in the sudden silence. "What is this?" Nick asked. "Is it somebody's field?"

"If it's a field, it's overgrown," Manon said.

"The current's strong here," Arlette said, looking over the bow. "Stronger than in the cypress swamp."

The boat spun lazily in the current. Arlette reached out with an oar, pushed the boat away from a tangle of scrub. "It's a flood plain," Nick said. "We're in a flood plain."

"We're in the batture?" Manon asked, using the old Louisiana name for the country between the levee and the river. "That should mean we're near the Mississippi."

"I think we're going the wrong way," Nick said. "We're in a—what's the name?—floodway. The Corps of Engineers, or somebody, keeps this place clear of trees so that it can be flooded deliberately when the water gets too high. We're being carried off into an area that's been set aside intentionally as a place to store flood water."

"I think that makes sense," Jason said. *Not that anyone cares what I think,* he added to himself.

Manon's voice was uneasy. "Well," she said, "this really doesn't look like the Mississippi, what we can see of it. But what if we're in a river, and the current's taking us *to* the Mississippi?"

"That's possible," Nick said. "I'd rather not use any more fuel until we know for certain."

"Nick," Manon said, "I am so *hungry.* And Arlette hasn't had any food since the day before yesterday."

"I'm okay, Momma," Arlette said. "I'm getting used to it."

"We'll know soon where we're headed," Nick said. "If this is taking us to the Mississippi, we'll get there pretty quick. No mistaking the big river when we find it."

"I hate to do *nothing,*" Manon said. "Just sit here and do nothing."

Her voice trailed off into the mist. The current lapped against the bass boat's chine as it drew the boat into the pale unknown. Jason planted his oar on the deck and leaned his forehead against the smooth wooden haft. River water, trickling down the length of the oar, tracked its cooling path against his forehead. Suddenly Jason was very, very tired. He hadn't really slept during last night's rain, just drowsed against Arlette's shoulder while the rain rattled on the plastic sheet overhead; and the previous night's sleep on the metal foredeck had not been restful.

Jason lowered his oar to the casting deck, then sat on the deck. If nothing was going to happen, he might as well rest. He began to stretch out along the length of the deck.

"Wait, Jason," Arlette said. She put down her oar and sat beside him, her legs crossed. "Put your head on my lap," she said.

Jason felt suddenly awkward. He felt that he ought not to look at her parents, should not receive whatever signal their faces were sending. "Thank you," he said. He shifted himself on the foredeck and put his head in Arlette's lap, her crossed ankles below his neck. He looked up at her, saw an enigmatic Buddha smile on her inverted features.

"Comfortable?" she asked.

"Yes. Very."

He closed his eyes. He felt the warmth of her bearing him up, a yielding touch of softness in the cool mist.

The current rocked the boat lightly. For a moment Arlette's fingertips brushed his cheek, and he inclined his head slightly, like a cat, to strop his jawline along her fingers.

His thoughts whirled into the warmth of Arlette, into the touch of her fingers, and then his thoughts flew away and were lost to time.

When Jason opened his eyes he saw Arlette, the silent smile still on her face as she bent over him, drowsing. Her fingers lay curled against his cheek. In a pocket of her shorts he could feel the little jewelry box that held the necklace her father had given her. Above her was the whiteness of the mist. The current still chuckled against the bass boat's hull.

Without moving his head Jason looked left and right, and saw to his surprise that the mist had lifted slightly: it hovered about fifteen feet from the surface of the water, a perfect, featureless shroud of white that hung unbroken in the air, as if the world had simply dissolved into nothing a few feet over their heads.

Jason looked at Arlette against the backdrop of white and for the first time observed the little scar that disrupted the perfect arch of her right eyebrow, the length and richness of the lashes laid against her brown cheeks, the way her eyelids pulsed to the dream-movement of the eyes beneath.

Arlette must have sensed his scrutiny, because her eyes fluttered open. Jason watched the eyes as they sleepily focused on him, the mouth as the smile broadened.

"Hi," he said.

"Hi." Her chin tilted as she looked up. "We can see a little," she said. "Look."

He rose reluctantly from her lap, and Arlette straightened her cramped legs with a sigh. He saw that the boat was in a wide flooded channel, with a cypress swamp on one side and a line of cottonwoods on the other. The speed of the current had slowed, and the boat spun like an errant compass needle below the great sheet of mist above their heads.

Jason glanced at the other passengers. Nick was slouched in the cockpit, eyelids half-shut. Manon stood on the afterdeck, gazing in silence at the great, dark, silent mass of water. She gave a sigh, her shoulders slumping. "I think you're right, Nick," she said. "We're in the wrong place. This can't be a real river."

Nick opened his drowsing eyes, straightened in his seat. "We can head the other way. But I'd rather wait till we're absolutely sure before I use any more gas. I think we should just tie up to something till we can see the sun."

He rose slowly from his seat and rolled his shoulders to take the kinks out of them. He turned to Arlette. "Hand me that rope, honey."

Arlette reached for the neatly bundled mooring rope, turned to hand it to her father, and then said, "Is that some kind of house?"

They all followed her pointing finger. There was a structure of some kind in one of the cottonwoods, a boxy-looking object that clearly had not been put there by Nature.

"Looks like a kid's treehouse," Nick said.

"Kids build treehouses near their *real* houses," Manon said. A smile broke across her face. "I think we may be close to civilization here."

"If civilization hasn't been evacuated," Nick said. He started the engine and motored across the flood.

The object was in truth a treehouse, and a big one, a sort of split-level with two main rooms and a pitched roof of irregularly shaped, homemade wood shingles. The unpainted planks of the structure were green with age. Beneath, crosspieces of wood had been nailed to the bole of the tree as a primitive ladder.

"Look!" Arlette said. "Power poles!"

As the boat neared the treeline, the passengers were able to see farther into the mist a little beyond the trees. The line of cottonwoods was narrow, and behind it was an embankment, or perhaps a levee. On the embankment two power poles stood with their heads crowned by mist. The lines between them had fallen, and another pole, farther down the line, leaned at an oblique angle, strands of wire hanging limp like the arms of a man in despair.

Jason felt his heart stagger into a quicker tempo. These forlorn signs of a once-human presence—the weird old treehouse, the abandoned power poles—were enough to kindle his hope. Suddenly he couldn't leave *Retired and Gone Fishin'* quick enough. He wanted to leap to the shore and kick out, run down the embankment as fast as his legs would carry him. Or swarm up the tree to the strange old dwelling, stand on the roof, look for rescue as if from the crow's nest of a sailing ship.

"I'll check out the treehouse," Jason said.

"See if someone's home first," Nick said. He hailed the treehouse several times. No answer came. Nick maneuvered the boat to the cottonwood, touched it once, and Jason sprang for the homemade ladder.

"Watch out for snakes," Nick called. "In floods they climb high."

The thought of snakes didn't deter Jason. He practically ran up the tree, came to the platform where the treehouse rested. A weathered door of hammered-together planks, four feet high, was closed with a simple hook-and-eye. Jason hoisted himself onto the platform and unhooked the door. A strange smell, rotted vegetation and moldy fur, floated out of the old structure, and for the first time Jason hesitated. Then, slowly, he pushed the door open.

The hinges weren't metal, but oiled leather. Jason blinked as he gazed into the darkness of the interior. The small room seemed to be full of old junk. He crawled partway through the door and tried to make sense of what he saw.

There were homemade nets, a rusty tackle box opened to reveal old wooden fishing lures, some hand-carved duck decoys. Animal pelts and snakeskins were tacked up on the plank walls, along with pictures from a calendar, *Beautiful Black Women 1992*. Scattered on the floor were metal objects that Jason eventually decided were animal traps.

There was a narrow pathway through the clutter to the shack's other room, which had been built on a higher level. Jason crawled along the path to the upper room, where he found a stained old mattress with the cotton ticking sticking out of the seams, some plastic plates, cracked porcelain mugs, cooking tins for boiling water. They all looked as if they'd been scavenged from a rubbish heap. In one corner, on a little stand, were some small plastic statues of Catholic saints beneath a tacked-up card of the Virgin Mary. The Virgin was a strange contrast to the calendar girls, who occupied most of the rest of the wall.

The place smelled musty and unused. Jason guessed that no one had been in this place for months, if not years.

Jason backed out of the treehouse and stood on the narrow platform, craning to see through the trees. The mist was thicker here, but he could just make out, through a curtain of leaves, the embankment behind the stand of trees; and he could see that the top of the embankment was paved with a two-lane asphalt road.

He called out this news on the way down the ladder. Nick nudged the bass boat up to the cottonwood, and Jason jumped across.

"Anything in the treehouse?"

"Fishing gear. Animal traps. A few plates and pots." He looked at Arlette as he recalled the provocative smiles of *Beautiful Black Women 1992*, and looked away quickly.

Manon looked at Nick. "Should we take the pots? They'd come in handy if we find something to cook."

"They were pieces of junk," Jason said, "but they were better than what we've got."

Nick considered their course of action. "Let's check the road first. If we can't find anything there we can come back."

They motored along the line of cottonwoods, looking for a break in the vegetation, and found it soon enough: the embankment veered toward them, through the trees, but there it was washed out. The broken asphalt lay on the tumbledown slopes of the embankment as if trying to extend the roadway under water.

The other end of the washed-out road was lost in the mist. Nick drove the boat onto the grassy slope of the embankment. Jason slung the Astroscan over his shoulder, jumped off the boat, and helped Arlette and Manon disembark. Then he tied the boat to a sapling growing on the verge of the line of cottonwoods, Nick stepped off the boat, and they all climbed to the top of the road.

The blacktop stretched forward into the mist. It had not been in good condition before the earthquakes, and the quakes had buckled it in several places. On the far side of the embankment were still more flood waters, lying dark and featureless as far as the mist permitted them to see.

"That's somebody's field," Manon said. "There's no brush, like in the floodway. Somewhere around here there are people. All we have to do is find them."

They walked a few hundred feet along the road. Jason and Arlette fell back and let the adults walk in front of them. Jason felt his arm brush against Arlette's as they walked, and he reached out and took her hand. Her warm fingers curled around his. He looked at her, and they shared a smile.

The embankment continued to stretch before them, marked only by the downed power lines. A road sign came slowly out of the mist, and they paused before it.

SHELBURNE CITY 8 MI.

HARDEE 19 MI.

"Well," Nick said, "we may be getting somewhere after all."

THIRTY-TWO

The earthquake that was felt at Natchez on the 16th of December, has been severely felt above and below the mouth of the Ohio—we may expect detailed accounts of the damages soon. Travelers who have descended the river since, generally agree that a succession of shocks were felt for six days; that the river Mississippi was much agitated; that it frequently rose 3 and 4 feet, and fell again immediately; and that whole islands and parts of islands in the river sunk.

"An Observer," Tuesday, January 14, 1812

"You came from Rails Bluff?" the deputy said. "The place that's on the news?"

Jason saw his own surprise reflected on Nick's face. "On the news?" Nick repeated.

"The Army flew in there and took the place over. The radio hasn't been talking about much else."

Jason and the others looked at each other. If they had stayed in Brother Frankland's camp, they might be living safely and happily on government bounty.

"Was there any shooting?" Nick asked.

"Some, I guess. They needed the Army and all."

Well, Jason thought, *maybe it was smart to have left anyway.*

"Let's get these people to the camp," said the other deputy, the one without a uniform.

It was a strange, eerie world that Jason and his party had walked through, the mist floating overhead and graying the world in all directions, the floodway waters on one side and the flooded field on the other. When the police car rolled slowly out of the whiteness ahead it seemed to emerge from nothing at all, as if the mist itself had formed itself into the car, into the ghostlike occupants.

As soon as the car pulled to a stop in front of them and

the deputies swung out onto the road, Nick ran up to the deputies and told them he needed to get to a phone to speak with the authorities about the camp they'd just escaped from in Arkansas.

"Rails Bluff, right?" the uniformed deputy said.

This deputy, obese and wearing a khaki uniform, seemed relaxed and talkative, but his partner radiated hostility. The other man was young, in his early twenties, and wore a mixture of military uniform and civilian dress, with his deputy's star pinned to a hunter's camouflage vest. He wore wraparound shades and glared through them at the four refugees, arms folded on his chest.

"Let's get these people to the camp," the younger deputy said. "They can listen to the news there." He had a flat Northern voice that sounded a harsh contrast to the Southern speech Jason had been hearing for weeks.

The uniformed deputy hesitated. "Maybe we can take them to the camp in town," he said.

The younger man just scowled. "There's sickness in that camp. These people need to go to the *other* camp." He nodded at Nick and Manon. "They *belong* there. You know that."

"I guess." Jason could hear reluctance in the voice of the uniformed deputy.

Jason looked from one deputy to the other. He didn't know what he was sensing between the two, but he knew he didn't like the vibe.

"Take us to a hotel," Manon said. "I have a credit card. We can pay for hospitality."

"No hotels in this parish, ma'am," the uniformed deputy said. "Not in years. Sorry."

"Boardinghouse?"

"Full up since the quake."

"Perhaps we should talk to the district attorney," Nick said. "We can provide evidence about what was happening at Rails Bluff."

"Got to get you registered at the camp first," the younger deputy said. "I'll radio for a truck," he added, and ducked into the car.

The uniformed deputy looked at Jason for a moment. "We could take the boy to another camp," he ventured. "A camp for—for young folks."

Jason looked at Arlette. "Can my friend come with me?"

"I'm afraid not, son. It's for, uh, boys only."

Jason turned to the deputy. "I'm staying with my friends," he said.

The fat deputy gave him a strange look. Jason could feel a warning chill run up his spine. "I really think you'd like this other place better," the deputy said.

Jason decided that he would not go anywhere with this man. He took a step closer to Nick. "I'm sticking with my friends," he repeated.

The deputy just stared at him for a long moment, then said, "Fine. Your choice."

The other deputy left the car and spoke to his partner, without even looking at Jason or his party. "The camp's sending a truck."

There was a long moment of silence. The silent mist hovered about them, sealing off the rest of the world. Jason looked at Nick, at the others, and drew away from the sheriff's deputies. Nick and the others fell back a few paces as well.

"What's happening here?" Jason said in an urgent whisper.

Nick looked over his shoulder at the silent deputies standing by their car. The two men stared back, and Jason thought of the black-eyed cormorants sitting above the flood. "I don't know," Nick said. "Maybe they're sick of refugees here."

"That's not what it is." Manon stood stiffly, spine straight, chin tilted up, and touched Arlette's back. "Cracker cops," she said. "They don't like black people, that's all. Especially educated, well-spoken black people." She turned to Arlette. *"Souviens-toi qui tu es. Ces gents ne peuvent pas emporter ton amour-propre."*

Nick rubbed the healed wound on his left arm, the wound which—Jason suddenly remembered—had been inflicted by a deranged cop. "There's more to it than that," Nick said.

"There's something they're not telling us."

Jason shared Nick's suspicion. "This reminds me of Rails Bluff," he said. "Maybe we should just get in our boat and head back down the river."

"Not without food," Manon said.

Nick considered this. "Maybe we can just *buy* some food."

These speculations were still unresolved when another vehicle appeared from the mist, a small white Toyota pickup truck. Two more men got out, both with deputies' badges worn over civilian dress. Neither of them smiled, not even at the other deputies.

"We're here to take you to the camp," one of them said. "You-all got any more belongings than what you got with you?"

Manon walked toward them, head held high. "Not really," she said.

"Where's y'all's boat?"

"We were wondering if we could just buy food," Manon said. "Then we'd get back on our boat and head downriver to where we've got family."

There was a glimmer of interest in the deputy's eyes. "You got anything to buy food *with*?" he asked.

"A credit card," Manon said.

The deputy lost interest. "Nobody's taking credit cards. Cash or nothing."

"I've got cash," Nick said. A hundred and twenty-some dollars that had been sitting in his pocket since before the quake. "If you can take us to where the food is."

The deputy hesitated. "We can buy the food for you," he said.

Nick shook his head. "I don't think so," he said. There was some kind of racket here, police selling the refugees their rations, and he wasn't having any part of it.

The deputy gestured toward the truck. "Get in back. There's food in the camp."

"We're really not interested in going to this camp. Can you just take us to Shelburne City? We'll get along fine once we get to town. We're not *destitute*."

The deputies looked at each other. One of them shrugged. "Why not?" he said. "Get on in."

Jason felt a decided reluctance to get in the Toyota. The situation was too strange: the highway elevated above the flood, the mist that masked the world, the uncommunicative deputies, the attempt to separate him from Nick and his family, so reminiscent of Frankland putting him in the young men's camp . . . But his objections were unclear, even to himself, and so he found himself following the others, getting in the back of the truck.

Rainwater sloshed around in the bed of the Toyota. Jason perched uneasily, with the others, on the sides of the truck bed. Jason noticed a shotgun and a rifle in the rear-window rack in the truck cab.

The truck turned around and began moving slowly toward Shelburne City. As they moved farther into the country, the land on the right slowly rose and emerged from the flood, rows of immature cotton plants in red soil, the furrows silver with water. The highway left the levee top and continued into the country. Broad puddles shimmered on the blacktop. A few buildings appeared. Unlike Rails Bluff, where every building had been wrecked, the quakes here seemed to have left the buildings largely intact—windows and chimneys were gone, and shingles had been lost, but for the most part the homes seemed to have survived without major damage. Only some outbuildings, mostly ramshackle old barns, seemed to have collapsed altogether.

The truck slowed as it approached a roadblock, two vehicles drawn across the road with only a narrow space between them. A handful of deputies stood there, mostly in civilian dress or bits of military surplus, and they waved the Toyota through. The truck picked up speed as it drove down the highway, past a highway verge cluttered with abandoned vehicles, and then the Toyota swung suddenly across the highway toward the chainlink-and-razorwire fence that loomed behind the abandoned cars, and splashed and bounced across drowned ruts to the gate.

There was a somber refugee camp beyond the fence.

Huddled miserably beneath the low sky were scattered a strange collection of tents, awnings, and primitive wagons— *cotton* wagons, Jason recognized, cotton wagons with open sides of wire netting, and with canvas or plastic stretched on top to make dwellings.

Jason was shocked. The contrast with Frankland's orderly camp left him appalled.

The truck slouched to a halt in front of the gate, where another pair of deputies waited, both with shotguns couched in their arms. People—black people—watched listlessly from behind tent flaps, through the wire netting of the cotton wagons, from beneath blankets or sleeping bags tented over their heads and shoulders.

The deputies in the truck bounded out. "Everyone out!" one of them said. For the first time, Jason saw, he was smiling.

Nick and his family rose to their feet and stared aghast at the camp. "I'm not going in there," Nick said. "And neither is my family."

Without a word one of the deputies, standing behind Nick, reached into the truck cab and drew the shotgun out of the rear window rack. Jason cried a warning, but the deputy was fast: he slammed the butt of the shotgun into one of Nick's kidneys before Nick was aware of the threat. Nick gave a cry and fell to one knee. The deputy raised the shotgun again.

Fury flashed like steam through Jason's veins, and he screamed. Without thought he found himself flying through the air at the deputy that had hit Nick, arms outstretched to claw open the man's throat. Jason bowled the man over and their heads came together with a crack. The world spun in wild sick circles. Something hit him in the face, then a heavy boot stomped him in the stomach. He gasped and curled into a fetal ball, and then something dug into his throat and his wind was cut off. He clawed at his throat as the strangling-strap pulled him, half crawling and half falling, along the wet, rutted ground. Then he was flung onto the grass, and he heard the chain fence slam shut behind him.

Air sighed at last into his lungs, and he choked, began to cough. He pulled the ligature from around his throat and found that it was the Astroscan strap that he hadn't slipped off before launching himself at the deputy. For a while Jason was sick, puking up burning acid from his empty stomach onto the grass. He heard Arlette sobbing, Nick muttering. Tears blinded him. Then a cool palm touched the back of his neck.

"Take it easy, Jason," Manon said. There was a strange sadness in her voice. "We'll be okay. Just take it easy, *cher*."

After the pain came rage. Nick staggered to his feet, breath hissing through his teeth with the agony that throbbed through his kidneys. Blind anger almost sent him lunging after the deputies, who were backing away from the closed gate with their shotguns leveled. With his bare hands he would tear the gate to shreds, then the armed men.

Arlette must have seen the fury in his face, because she ran to him and flung her arms around him. *"No, Daddy!"* she cried. *"Don't!"*

And he didn't. He stood there, poised to launch himself at the deputies, and Arlette clung to him, her terrified, tear-stained face pressed to his chest. Then Nick shuddered as a wave of pain and nausea rolled through him, and he looked down at his daughter and raised a hand to caress the back of her head.

"It's okay, honey," he whispered. "It's okay."

The red rage faded from his mind as he stood holding Arlette and he became aware of Jason huddled on the ground nearby, Manon crouching over him, absently caressing his hair.

Somewhere a baby wailed. Nick glanced around, saw people approaching from all directions. Approaching cautiously, not yet convinced that shots wouldn't be fired.

Black, he saw, all black. And the deputies all white.

A dreadful certainty began to chill his anger, the certainty of nightmare. The river had cast him up on an unknown shore, where some madman's malevolent fantasy was being enacted.

A woman was walking up to him with a firm tread. She wore

boots and bib overalls and a yellow T-shirt. Her white hair was shorn close to her scalp, and her skin was a deep ebony.

"I'm Deena Johnson," she said. "Come with me, please. I'll take care of the young one, and perhaps I might find you some food."

Miss Deena Johnson performed some first aid on Nick's and Jason's abrasions, then found the newcomers some food: stale cheese and some kind of flat, greasy crackers that tasted as if they'd been buried in a pit for fifteen years; but it was the first food that Nick had eaten in almost two days, and he devoured everything that was put before him.

"Perhaps the young people might take a walk," said Miss Deena, "and Nick and Manon and I can talk grownup business."

She had an authoritative way of speaking, like the David women, that choked off debate before it began. Unlike the Davids, she had a way of not making it seem overbearing. Even Jason, who Nick suspected would bridle at being sent away because he wasn't old enough to talk with the adults, accepted Deena's ruling without protest, and left the dining tent along with Arlette.

Miss Deena reached into a pocket of her dress, pulled out a sheaf of rolled papers and a stubby pencil. She smoothed out the pages with her lined hands and put on a pair of reading glasses. Nick saw that the pages were filled with minuscule writing.

"Could I have your full names and addresses?" Miss Deena asked. "And your girl's name, and the boy, too?"

"Certainly," Manon said. She and Nick gave Deena the information, and Deena wrote it down in tiny print.

"There," she said as she rolled up the pages and put them once again in her pocket. "There will be a number of copies made and hidden. So that when we are dead, a record of our names may survive."

Jason walked fast through the tent city. The boot-scrapes on his face burned. There was a sharp ache in his throat when he tried to swallow. It hurt less if he swallowed while tilting his head to the left.

He was getting out of here. *Out and away.* He just had to figure out how.

There were two big structures on the campsite. One was a large tent with metal folding tables for meals, where they'd just had their little meal of cheese and crackers. Next to the dining tent was a huge brick barbecue pit and a small frame building—since the quakes much reinforced with a strange supporting structure of timber and metal pipes—which held a propane-fueled cooking range, sinks for doing dishes, and the wellhead.

The other structure was a huge tent intended for church meetings, but which now housed entire families. The rest of the campground was a litter of tents, plastic sheeting, and cotton wagons slowly sinking into the mire. The ground was so wet that it squelched beneath Jason's feet as he walked. Soaked clothing, bedding, and blankets had been strung up everywhere to dry, and now hung limp in the windless air.

There were outhouses, a tool shed, and some pecan trees. Hungry people had scrounged all the old pecans. There was a softball field, with bleachers and a screen behind home plate, but that was outside the wire fence.

There were lots of people in the camp, entire families with children. It was strangely quiet. Even the children seemed subdued, walking or playing quietly in groups, and only occasionally would a lone child's laughter ring out among the tents. The summer warmth had risen quickly from the damp ground and smothered the camp in sultry heat. The mist had risen farther from the ground, but still hung unbroken overhead, a bright white shroud that cloaked the world.

The strange silence that pervaded the camp kept Jason and Arlette from speaking as they made their way toward the back fence. Arlette kept her hand in her pocket, touching the box that held the necklace that Nick had given her. The camp had once backed onto a hardwood forest, but the chainlink wall now glittered between the camp and the trees, and the trees had been bulldozed back in order to clear a lane between the woods and the camp. A pair of deputies, neither in uniform, paced along the back fence of the camp. One of them had a shotgun in the crook of his arm, and the other—he drank Diet Dr. Pepper from a can—had a little black machine gun hanging on a strap from his shoulder. Jason walked slowly toward the fence, glanced left and right as he tried to find the weak spot in the camp's defenses.

Jason figured he wasn't going to stay here long.

"You don't go to fence," someone said. Jason turned, saw an elderly black woman crouched in the shadow of a homemade shelter made out of plastic sheeting. "Only camp committee's allowed to go to fence. You go to fence, they shoot you."

The woman had no teeth and spoke with a kind of pedantic emphasis, as if she were talking to an unruly house pet. Her eyes were hidden behind thick glasses.

Jason's nerves gave a shiver at this strange apparition. "Thanks," he said.

"You don't go near to fence," the woman said.

"Thank you, ma'am," Arlette said.

Jason smiled at the woman and crabbed off to the side. Walked along the inside at the fence, peering out. He felt the stares of the silent people in the camp, and they made him nervous. The trees that had been bulldozed down, he saw, had just been shoved to the back of the lane, piled up against the standing trees. Good cover there, he thought.

"Slow down," said Arlette. "There's no place to go."

Jason stopped, took a breath. "You're right," he said. Then, "I'm looking for a way out."

Arlette stepped up to him, touched the scrapes on his face where the deputy's boot had connected. "You okay?" she asked.

"Yeah. I'm fine." He swallowed, grimaced, touched his throat where the strap had cut across it. "My throat hurts, though."

"Thank you for trying to help my dad," Arlette said. "That was brave."

"I got pissed off," Jason said. "That man didn't even know who Nick *was*."

There was a pause. Jason saw sadness drift across Arlette's brown eyes. "He thought he knew everything that mattered, I guess," she said.

Jason looked at her and felt a restless urge to flee the moment, this unwanted intrusion of the difference that was at the heart of this perverse scene they'd just entered. What she meant was that the deputy had attacked Nick because he was black, and black was all the deputy saw, all he thought he needed to know. All the deputy thought he needed to know about *any* of the people in the camp, apparently.

And he, Jason, was white. And in a camp full of black people who were probably very unhappy with white folks right now. He didn't want to be mistaken for the deputy or one of his friends. He was surrounded by people who were, in the only way that now mattered, different from himself. He didn't want to be a member of a minority; he wasn't used to it, and he didn't want to think about it.

He didn't want it to matter that Arlette and her family were black. He didn't want it to matter that he was not. All he wanted to do was get *away* before it was necessary to deal with any of this.

"I'm getting out," Jason said. "I don't think it's going to be hard." He licked his lips. "You come with me, if you want. We'll get on the boat and get out of here. Get to Vicksburg and tell people what's going on." He reached out, took Arlette's hand. "Let's get out," he said. "Let's get out of here. These people are bad."

Arlette looked serious. "I don't want you to get hurt. There's the fence, and those men have guns."

"Chainlink fences are easy. Back in LA, I used to scale fences all the time so I could go skating. They're easy to climb, and if that doesn't work you can go under."

Arlette looked uncertain. "Let's find out what's going on first. Maybe we should talk to some people."

Jason glanced at the camp inmates, the eyes that watched him, that maybe judged him, that maybe put him in the same frame as they put the deputies.

"Okay," he said reluctantly. "Okay." *If we have to,* he thought.

* * *

Nick and Manon listened in silence to Deena Johnson's unadorned history of the camp. Partway through the story, Manon's hand moved across the table to take Nick's in her own. Nick squeezed her hand. At some point Manon had to take her hand back, because he was clenching and unclenching his fists, and he'd hurt her without meaning to.

Other people came into the tent while Deena was telling her story, either watching silently or adding details to the narrative.

"You can decide best how to tell the children," Miss Deena said. "But you *should* tell them, because if they do not hear it from you, they will hear it from others in the camp."

"Tell my daughter that a bunch of clay-eaters are going to try to kill us," Manon said. Anger burned in her words.

Deena looked at her. There was a terrible cold objectivity in her eyes. "Yes," she said. "Yes, or she will not know how to behave when the moment comes. Because we have decid- ed—we have voted—that we will no longer cooperate in any way with these people. No one will leave to work on this other camp of theirs, or to live in it, until someone is taken to the camp and returns declaring that it exists."

Manon's eyes grew shiny. Her chin trembled. "I will not—" she began to declare, and then turned away, blinking back tears. Nick took her hand again. He could feel his jaw muscles hard as armor.

"What is being done?" Nick asked Miss Deena. "What are you doing to stop them?"

The older woman shook her head. "It took us too many days to realize what was happening. And then it took us too long to get organized—the camp was like a committee of two hundred people, each with their own ideas. Some of us resisted on their own and were killed. And we have so few resources, so few weapons, so few people who have had mil- itary training." She looked at Nick. "I don't suppose you have a military background?"

A chill laugh broke from Nick. "I was raised in the military," he said, "and my daddy was a general." He looked at her. "But what I do for a living, Miss Deena—when I'm working—is design weapons."

PART THREE

J1

THIRTY-THREE

Nothing appeared to have issued from the cracks but where there was sand and stone coal, they seem to have been thrown up from holes; in most of those, which varied in size, there was water standing. In the town of New Madrid there were four, but neither of them had vented stone or sand—the size of them, in diameter, varied from 12 to 50 feet, and in depth from, 5 to 10 feet from the surface to the water. In travelling out from New Madrid those were very frequent, and were to be seen in different places, as high as Fort Massac, in the Ohio.

Matthias M. Speed (Jefferson County, March 2, 1812)

So Nick, in his capacity as military brat and weapons designer, was put on the Escape Committee, seven men who met more or less permanently beneath one of the pecan trees, at least until one or more of them got mad at the others and stomped out. There were no qualifications for being on the committee, only the fact they'd volunteered. They were an argumentative bunch—two were elderly, and had to have things repeated to them—and they were all full of ideas and scorned the ideas of others, and were all too aware that they'd probably only have one chance to organize a big escape. All of this—most of all the knowledge of their own responsibility—had created a paralysis that had resulted in very little being decided.

They were able to inform him chiefly of what would not work. He heard of the two boys who had tried to drive away, only to have one shot by the Klan Sheriff's son while the other disappeared. He'd heard of the man who had charged the cops shooting his pistol and been shot dead. He heard about the Klan Sheriff Paxton bringing the Imperial Wizard by to show off his camp. He heard about the twenty-eight men—all single, all without family in the camp—who had been taken away, allegedly to build another camp, and who had never been seen again. He heard of the junkie who had run out of narcotics, who had gone into a screaming fit, been carried away by deputies, and who had not returned. He heard of the diabetics who were running short of insulin, people who needed other medication, and of the mothers whose babies needed milk, and how terrified they all were that their supplies could be cut off. He heard of the man who wriggled under the wire one night and escaped into the country, and whose body was exhibited by the deputies the next day. "He was shot by a neighbor," a deputy told the camp. "We didn't have nothin' to do with it. The folks 'round here hate you; I'd stay in the camp if I was you."

Nick was told about the spotlights that were turned on along the camp perimeter at night to illuminate the lanes on all sides of the wire. He was told about the random bullets fired into the camp at night. He was told that the water table was about four feet below the surface of the water, which meant no exit via tunnel, a là *The Great Escape.*

All the Escape Committee had managed to do was prepare a signal. Occasionally they heard the thrum of helicopter engines, presumably some relief agency or other delivering supplies to Shelburne City. No helicopter had actually been *seen*, but next time one was heard, the committee planned to ignite a bonfire of tires taken from the cotton wagons, and hope the column of dense, thick smoke would attract attention.

It certainly seemed worth a try, Nick thought, even though one of the Escape Committee, a thin, intense man of late middle age who called himself Tareek Hall, insisted that this was only one of many death camps, that white America had chosen this moment to exterminate *all* blacks, that this was all a well-planned worldwide conspiracy. Tareek seemed very happy when he spoke his theory aloud. It obviously gave him great satisfaction to know that millions of people wanted to kill him.

Even paranoids have real enemies, Nick told himself.

Nick was told that the camp's assets in any future conflict consisted of three handguns that had so far escaped the deputies' attention, an assortment of knives, clubs, hammers, and other improvised hand weapons, plus the services of about twenty veterans of the armed services, aged from their mid-twenties to their sixties, none of whom had ever seen combat. A number of the refugees were country people who had been hunting all their lives and knew how to shoot a rifle, but few of these had even been in the military, and none had fired a shot in anger.

And there were about four remaining gangsters who, as they had arrived with their families, had not been shipped out like the other gangsters. They could be counted on for aggression if nothing else, though one was reluctant to surrender his pistol for the common good.

The Escape Committee had at least made a survey of the guards: which ones would talk, which could be bribed, which would respond only with anger, with blows, or by racking a round into his shotgun.

Two guards patrolled the back of the camp at all times. One on each side. Two in front. All were armed with shotguns, machine pistols, or assault rifles. Any of these weapons could perpetrate a massacre.

Three or four deputies manned the roadblocks on the highway to either side of the camp. Those four openly displayed scoped hunting rifles that could pick off anyone at long range. The roadblock guards were, in their way, more dangerous than the men patrolling the perimeter, because they could kill from a distance and because there was no way to reach them. Two of these men moved to the camp at night and mainly patrolled around the back, where an attempt to escape to the woods was more likely.

The seven argumentative men of the Escape Committee, after vetoing a lengthy series of complicated proposals, had finally thrown up their hands and decided to attempt a mass escape. They'd try to cut the wire, or with the sheer weight of the inmates bash down a part of the fence, and then everyone would pour out of the camp and run into the woods.

It didn't sound promising to Nick, and he said so. Nobody knew the country. They'd be running blind into the woods with killers firing at their backs. By the time any escapees got through the woods, the deputies could have a whole line of men waiting on the other side of the woods and catch them between two fires. No one knew how large the woods was, or how possible it was for people to evade capture once they were in the trees. Nobody knew of an escape route once they were away from the immediate area. There was no transportation out of the parish even if they did evade the deputies.

"I don't like it," Nick said.

"What else can we do?"

"I don't know," Nick said. He rubbed the old wound on his arm. "I don't know."

You need a rear guard, he thought. That's what his father would tell him. Bunch of civilians in flight, you've got to have soldiers who stay behind fighting to make sure they get away.

But you can't have a rear guard armed with three pistols and some clubs. That wasn't a rear guard—that didn't even achieve the dignity of *suicide*. It was pure absurdity. Even if the rear guard were brave, even if they made up their minds to sacrifice their lives, they'd last only a few minutes, and then the horrible pursuit would begin, the massacre would stretch over miles, armed men pursuing helpless people over the countryside.

We'll need to get their *weapons*, Nick thought. *Then we can put up a fight.*

"They're punks," Nick said, more to himself than to anyone else. "Punks," he repeated. "Punks back down when you show fight."

"Maybe some of them will. But some of those redneck bastards learned to shoot at their granddaddy's knee. The same place they learned to hate niggers."

"Let me think," Nick said. He wished his father were here. "How do they get food in?" he asked.

"They come every two-three days. They bring less food all the time, and never enough, so they can sell us food for money sometimes. But they bring more guards along with the food, and they come armed. March a few of us out of the camp to take the food, then march them back in. The guards hardly ever come in the camp themselves."

That seemed the best chance for getting weapons, Nick thought. Swarm through the gate and bowl those crackers over. They would take casualties, but that was going to happen no matter what.

"When did they last bring food?" Nick asked.

"Yesterday."

So he probably had a while, Nick thought, to let that plan mature. But not long. Not longer than overnight.

"Have we got a map?" he asked.

Where could you hide? Nick wondered. Where—assuming you had soldiers—could you hide them?

Back in the woods, certainly. Once you got back beyond the bulldozed area, the trees were relatively open, you could even maneuver your men back there.

The parking lot. Eighty or a hundred cars parked helter-skelter by the side of the road. You could hide people in the cars—if you could first get them out of the camp—then have them jump out from ambush.

And the cars provided mobility, too. If he could get people into the cars, they could drive to the roadblocks and fight the riflemen at close range.

Nearby buildings. There was an old tumbledown church—literally tumbled down in the quakes—less than half a mile south of the camp. If he could hide soldiers there, he could enfilade the southernmost of the two roadblocks.

The bar ditch by the side of the road. It didn't provide much cover, but it was better than nothing.

And the camp itself. When all was said and done, there was a surprising amount of cover in the camp. Tents, blankets, and opaque plastic sheeting could hide people from sight even if they wouldn't stop a bullet. And slit trenches could be dug secretly, inside the tents, to provide cover. The slit trenches would fill with water, with the water table as high as it was, but getting wet was better than getting killed.

It might be a good idea to dig slit trenches under *all* the tents. Hide the children there, till it was time to run for the woods.

His head pounded where the deputy had kicked him. The pain in his kidney made him walk bent over, like an arthritic old man. The barely healed wound on his left arm throbbed. He could feel the tension lying like iron in his shoulders and neck as he walked about the camp making notes on paper.

At the end of his tour, he looked at his notes and saw they looked like the scrawls of a madman.

Got to do better, he thought. *Got to do better, for Arlette and Manon.*

The grownups didn't want to talk much. Arlette approached several, with Jason tagging along, and each greeted Arlette, and some asked about her family and where she came from, but they evaded answering Arlette's questions about the camp.

"There's a big secret here," she told Jason. "I've never known black people to clam up like this. This isn't natural. This is not right."

They kept walking through the camp. Little insects raced along Jason's nerves with swift sticky feet. His heart gave a leap at the sight of some white people—there were actually white people in this camp, two men and a woman—and he almost ran up to them to say hello.

But he didn't. *Now I'm doing it,* he thought. *Now I'm rating people by their skin color.*

His mind whirled. *How do I get out of this trap?* he wondered.

A golden beam of sunlight suddenly illuminated the camp. Jason looked up, saw that the pall of cloud that had covered the world was beginning to break up. A modest wind stirred the humid air.

He saw that Arlette was walking away from him, heading toward three boys who looked a few years older than she and Jason. They were all taller and bigger, dressed like almost everyone else in an assortment of ill-fitting, ill-judged clothing. Their hair was uncombed and stuck out in tufts, and thin, youthful beards shadowed their cheeks. Reluctance dragged at Jason's heels as he followed Arlette toward the three.

"Hey," she said. "I'm Arlette."

"Sékou," one of the young men said. "This is Raymond." He did not bother to introduce the third.

"We just got here," Arlette said.

Raymond flicked Jason a glance from beneath heavy-lidded eyes. "Who's your friend?" he asked.

Jason figured he could speak for himself. He told them his name. The other boys ignored him. "How you get here, baby?" Raymond said to Arlette. "You come on a boat, or they open a road?"

"We were all on a boat."

"Come through that storm, huh? That must've been hard." He put an arm around Arlette. "You get all wet, baby? I dry you off."

Jason's hackles rose at Raymond touching Arlette. He didn't much like Arlette's acceptance of the touch either. "What we wanted to know," Jason said, "was what's going on here."

Sékou sniffed. "What's it look like, man? One-eighty-six."

Arlette stiffened. The third boy, the one whose name hadn't been mentioned, looked amused. He shifted his toothpick from one corner of his mouth to the other. "Boy's never been stomped by a cop before," he said.

This didn't seem much in the way of credentials to Jason. "I've been arrested, if you think that's important," he said, exaggerating somewhat. "I've come a thousand miles down the river in my boat. And this is the second camp some nutcase has stuck us in. We got out of the first one, and we'll get out of this."

"Shi-it," Sékou said, drawling the word out.

Jason decided he was not about to impress these guys no matter what, so he decided he might as well keep silent. Arlette flashed Raymond a smile—jealousy burned through Jason like a blowtorch—and then she shrugged out from under his arm. "Nice meeting you," she said. "I got to Audi."

"See you later," Raymond said. Jason followed her another thirty feet, and then she stopped under one of the old pecan trees and turned to him. He was surprised at the drawn look on her face.

"What's the matter?" he took her hands. "One of those guys say something?"

"One-eighty-six," Arlette said. "Sékou said that."

"And . . . ?" Jason said.

An inscrutable look passed over her face. "Don't listen to hip-hop much, do you? One-eighty-six—that's a police call. It means murder."

That's where Manon found them, clutching each other's hands beneath the pecan tree, and she took them aside and— her voice halting, tears welling slowly from her eyes—she told them what Miss Deena had told her.

What else we got to make weapons with? Nick thought. He could feel pain throbbing through the veins in his temples, a new viselike grip with each beat of his heart. There had to be more than sticks and stones. More than three guns. There had to be something.

Miss Deena was surprised when he burst into the cookhouse while she and some others were preparing the noon meal. "Gotta be something here," he said. "Ammonia, something."

"What do you want, Nick?" Deena demanded. "We are busy here."

"What do you use for a cleaner? Ammonia? Anything?"

Deena pointed with one bony finger. "Back there, boy. In the chest."

The chest was a heavy thing, tin nailed over a wood frame, probably used as a cooler for milk or drinks or bread in the days before light plastic coolers were invented. Standing next to it was a fifty-gallon metal drum with the red-and-yellow Civil Defense symbol on it. Inside were wrapped stacks of crackers, like the ones Nick had eaten for breakfast.

My God, he thought, *those crackers have probably been sitting in some basement since the Cuban Missile Crisis.* Someone had found them and shipped them to the camp to feed refugees. No wonder they'd tasted rancid.

Nick rummaged through the bottles in the cooler, read yellowed old labels on bottles that had sat here for, probably, decades.

Methanol. Oh, thank God. Somebody had been traditional in their choice of solvents.

"What else you got?" he demanded. "You got any fuel? Gasoline, oil?"

"They's a tractor," an old lady said. "Out in the tool shed."

Nick grabbed the methanol and ran out the door. The tool shed was thirty feet away. The lock had been broken during the previous night's rainstorm, so that the place could be used for shelter. The tractor—actually a lawn tractor with a 42-inch mower blade—had been shoved out onto the grass. There were some blankets and clothing inside on the soggy, oil-soaked wooden floor, but no one was in the shed at the moment.

Nick ran inside, saw the pair of five-gallon red plastic jerricans standing against the wall. His heart leaped. One was filled with gasoline, and the other was half-full. On a wooden shelf at head-height were three dusty cans of motor oil.

Pain beat a wild tattoo in Nick's skull. Madly he sifted through the contents of the shed.

Insecticide and a sprayer for fire ants. Gas-powered weed trimmer. Miscellaneous garden tools—from the selection remaining, Nick figured that the ones that could be used for weapons had already been taken. Bases for the softball field and fielders' gloves—the bats and helmets were gone. Cleaning rags. A piece of canvas so oil-soaked and rotten that no one had yet been desperate enough to use it for shelter.

Wildflower seed. A twenty-pound sack of Scott's lawn fertilizer, half-used.

Nick pounced on the bag of fertilizer like a parched man lunging for a fountain. *Ammonium nitrate.* He wanted to hold the dusty old bag to his chest and dance a waltz.

He stood, looked around the musty-smelling shack. It was a simple equation. Petroleum products plus ammonium nitrate equaled boom.

Boom, he thought.

Boom.

Carrying his bag of fertilizer and his plastic jug of methanol, Nick went to the Escape Committee, still in permanent session beneath the pecan tree, and told them he could make explosive.

"But explosive isn't any good without a way to detonate it. We need blasting caps, or something like them. I can make them, if we've got the right ingredients." He waved his bottle of methanol.

"Bombs?" one of the older men said. "Want to blow down the fence?"

"I had something else in mind," Nick said. He wiped sweat from his face. Pain beat through his head. "Antipersonnel weapons. Claymore mines, command detonated." He looked over his shoulder at the gate. "We kill them. Kill a *lot* of them, all at once. And then we take their weapons and we fight."

The seven men of the Escape Committee looked at him, silent for once.

Boom.

Nick made list after list. There was so much to do. Get the battery from the little tractor, so that he could boil the contents down to make sulfuric acid. Get Miss Deena to put out a call for aspirin, which could be used to make picric acid as a booster explosive for detonators. Chip bits of lead off the well pipe and the pipes in the cook shed, to make lead monoxide, which was a preliminary step necessary to make lead picrate as a primary explosive in detonators.

But the first thing on the list was to collect buckets of

human manure from the piles behind the outhouses. Because that could be turned into saltpeter, which was necessary for just about everything.

"You want your sand buggers?" one of the old men on the committee asked him.

"Hm?" Nick said.

"You want your sand buggers, you best get in line."

Nick looked up and saw that a line was forming at the dining tent, and he decided that though he had no idea what a sand bugger might be, he knew he was probably hungry enough to eat one. He rose from his crosslegged position under the pecan tree, and walked to the end of the line, still carrying his notes.

Manure, he thought, quite a bit of it. He hoped there was enough methanol to do all the work he needed it to do.

He looked up, saw Manon walking toward him. Her long hands rested on the shoulders of Jason and Arlette. From the solemn look on their faces, Nick could tell that Manon had told them what had been happening here in Spottswood Parish.

"Nick," Manon said as she approached. "Tell Jason that he'd be a fool to try to escape tonight."

Nick hesitated before answering. The objections he'd given to the Escape Committee in regard to their planned mass escape might not all apply to a single individual.

But the single individual could still get himself killed.

"I wouldn't leave without Arlette," Jason said. "But I think it could be done."

Arlette's name set alarms jangling along Nick's nerves. There was no way that Nick would let his daughter go over the wall before he could make it absolutely safe. "I'm working on something else," he said.

"What else?" Jason asked.

Nick looked uncertainly at the people standing with him in line. "I'll tell you later," he said.

It occurred to him that not all the people in the camp might be safe. He didn't know how much contact they all had with the guards, or—as far as that went—which of them might just be too talkative, too inclined to boast to his captors.

They stood in awkward silence in the food line till they received a sand bugger apiece—a patty of vegetable matter, fried like a hamburger and consisting mostly of potato with bits of onion and greens mixed in. With this was served a spoonful of baked beans and one of the strange, greasy crackers they'd had when they'd first arrived at the camp.

It all tasted awful. Nick ate every bite, then licked the plate. Then he took the others aside and told them what he was going to do.

Jason wanted to help, so Nick collected some plastic buckets and a shovel and went behind the nearest outhouse. Piled high was a decade's worth of manure covered with bright green grass and blazing red pods of hearts-a-bustin'-with-love. *Nothing like a shit pile,* he thought, *to make a fine flower garden.*

"Dig," Nick said. "Slowly."

Jason gave him a thoughtful look, as if wondering if Nick had chosen this moment for some strange joke, and then apparently decided otherwise and began to dig. Jason turned a few spadefuls while Nick peered into the pile, and was rewarded with the sight of a line of dirty yellow crystals running through the soil.

Yes, oh yes, he thought. Potassium nitrate. Saltpeter.
Boom.

Jason filled three buckets with crystal-laced dirt, then he and Nick carried them to the cookhouse, where Nick filled another bucket with wood ash from one of the campfire circles. He took a fifth bucket and punched holes in the bottom, put the bucket in a big saucepan, put a towel in the bottom of the bucket, and poured in a layer of wood ash. Then he put another cloth on top of the wood ash, filled the rest of the bucket with night soil. He told Jason to go into the cookhouse and asked them to boil some water, and when the water began to boil he poured it into the bucket a little at a time while Jason watched.

"What in heaven's name are you doing?" Miss Deena asked from the shadow of the cookhouse.

"Making saltpeter."

"You going to add that to our food? Think we're getting too sexy around here?"

"I'm going to do a magic trick." He looked up at her from his position hunkered by the bucket. "I'm going to make guards disappear."

Deena gave him a cold look. "Uh-huh," she said.

"You'll see," Nick said.

"I got that aspirin you wanted."

"I'd like to take a couple. For my head. I won't need the rest till later."

She gave him some aspirin. Nick swallowed them and poured hot water into the bucket. He repeated the procedure until he was out of earth.

When he was done, he poured the hot liquid from the saucepan to a clean saucepan, throwing away the dark sludge left behind. He went into the cookhouse and put the saucepan on a burner. Miss Deena and the other cookhouse crew watched him with suspicion.

"What now?"

"Crystals will start forming in the water after a while. We want to scoop those out with something clean. A paper napkin, or filters from a coffeemaker."

"Uh-huh."

"I'm going to need another burner. You might want to clear out for this next bit."

He found a glass baking dish. He put on some rubber gloves and pulled the caps off the battery he'd taken from the little tractor. He poured battery acid into the dish and turned on the burner beneath it. Sulfuric acid fumes began to fill the cookhouse. Nick sent Jason outside. Nick's eyes watered, and he tied a bandanna over his mouth and nose and stood outside the cookhouse till he saw white fumes rising from the baking dish. Then he dashed inside, turned off the burner, and took the baking dish outside and put it on the grass.

"That acid's *concentrated*," he told Miss Deena.

"Uh-huh," she said.

He looked at Jason. "Wait for it to cool, then pour it into a clean bottle. Make sure you've got rubber gloves on, and that your eyes and nose are protected. Put the bottle in the chest in the cookhouse, and don't let anyone touch it."

"When can I use my cookhouse again?" Miss Deena demanded.

"Use it now, if you like."

"Uh-huh."

Whatever Nick did next depended on having sulfuric acid and potassium nitrate, so he washed his implements, then left Jason watching the boiling saltpeter water while he went to report to the Escape Committee.

Leaves rustled overhead. Awnings in the camp crackled as the air snapped at them. The wind that had sprung up since the morning was growing brisk, providing the only relief from the day's sledgehammer heat.

"Things are coming along," Nick told the committee.

"Joseph here hacksawed some lead for you."

"Thank you, Joseph." He took a handkerchief from Joseph that held bits of lead pipe.

"That enough?"

"I think so. We don't need much." Nick put the handkerchief in his pocket, and the movement sent blinding, unexpected pain knifing through his kidney. He gasped, took his hand out of his pocket, and waited for the pain to ebb.

"You best hope you're not pissing blood tomorrow," Joseph said.

"Anything else you need?" said another man

Nick blinked away the tears that had sprung to his eyes. "Okay," he gasped, "okay." He blinked again. "I'm going to need an electrician or someone who can string wire without blowing us all up."

"We'll ask around." But Nick saw his audience craning to look past him, and felt a stir in the camp. He looked over his shoulder toward the gate and saw a line of vehicles moving along the road toward the camp: a sturdy old five-ton truck, a sheriff's department car, and a civilian pickup truck.

"Some kind of trouble," one of the old men said. "They's not bringing food."

Sudden anxiety for Manon and Arlette sang through Nick's heart. He looked over the camp, saw a young woman in a kerchief silhouetted briefly between two of the miserable cotton wagons, and trotted uneasily in that direction.

The little convoy pulled up before the camp. The larger of the two trucks backed up to the gate. A big, burly man in a deputy's khaki uniform got out of the police cruiser and raised a bullhorn to his lips.

"Our new camp is ready," he said. "The one your men were building. And we'd like to move the first families over there this afternoon." He consulted a clipboard. "Jerry Landis and family. Connie Conroy and daughters . . ."

Nick's mouth went dry at the thought that his own name might be called, but then he recalled that he had never been asked for his name, he was on none of their lists. He reached the area where he thought he'd seen Arlette and saw a completely strange girl wearing a kerchief. He stopped dead and peered around.

The camp inmates, instinctively drawn by the announcements, but fearful of the deputies' firearms, had formed a kind of half-circle at a respectful distance from the gate. Nick thought they would be better advised to be digging themselves into slit trenches. Somewhere a woman shrieked when her name was called; Nick could hear her sobbing and calling on Jesus to help her. Nick stayed well behind the mass of people, trotted along in hopes of catching a glimpse of Manon or Arlette.

Miss Deena was walking from the crowd toward the gate. She was absolutely erect, her white-haired head held high.

Admiration for Deena warred with anxiety in Nick's soul.

Nick finally saw Arlette and Manon together, with Jason, who was standing on top of a concrete picnic table peering over the heads of the crowd. Nick accelerated, caught up with them, put his hands on Arlette's shoulders. "Let's get out of sight," he said. "Miss Deena's going to tell them we're not going along with them anymore. This could be nasty."

Manon cast him an anxious look. "All right," she said. "Jason. Get down from there."

Jason clambered down with a show of reluctance. His face was swelling where the deputy had kicked him. Nick shepherded them toward the back of the camp. "Let's get under one of the cotton wagons," he said. He wished he could hide them all in a trench. Pain knifed his kidney as he crouched down, and he gasped in pain.

Crouching in cover, Nick didn't see the deputies' reaction to Miss Deena's announcement. He didn't see the argument, or the little red-haired runt of a man who led a group of deputies sprinting for the gate. But Nick saw and heard the crowd's reaction, saw them fall back with a kind of collective cry, then saw them run as shots began to crack out.

Nick's heart hammered. He clutched at Manon and Arlette, held them to his breast while Jason crawled restlessly left and right, trying to get a view of what was happening. "Get your head down!" Nick told him.

Then the crowd parted, and he saw deputies with shotguns at port arms running right for him. "This way!" he yelled. "Run!" He pulled Manon and Arlette away from the deputies, from beneath the far side of the cotton wagon, then urged them to run between a pair of tents. Shots cracked out. He heard a man scream. He remembered the flash as the shotgun went off in Viondi's face, the way the warm, bloody body had fallen into his arms. He remembered fleeing into the night, running from the light, to wherever the light would not find him.

"This way!" he cried. His heart pounded in his throat. People screamed and ran in all directions. Shots began coming from the guards posted around the camp. There was nowhere to run, but Nick knew they had to run anyway. A man with a gun loomed up in his vision, fifteen yards away. "This way!" he shouted, and ran past the cookshed into a tangle of tents and awnings. A rope caught his ankle and he crashed down into the rainsoaked earth.

Hunted. He was being hunted, and so was his family. He rose to his feet and began to run. Shots rang out behind him. People shrieked, and a whole mass of them surged across his path. He ran with them. He had lost Manon and Arlette. Desperately he called their names. He realized that the people were being driven, like cattle.

A fence loomed up in front of him, and Nick realized that he'd swung round in an arc and ended up at the front of the camp again, to the left of the gate. People flung themselves against the fence, then fell back at the sound of shots. Sobbing for breath, Nick looked for cover, found a fallen tent, and wormed his way into it.

Panic hammered in his throat. He had never felt so helpless in his life, not even when the first quake had torn the earth apart in front of the wheels of Viondi's car.

He looked out at the world through a piece of mosquito netting that served the tent as a window. He saw the group of eighteen or twenty people, terrified and bruised and bleeding, that the deputies herded together and threw onto the five-ton truck. The deputies made no effort to search for the people they were actually after, just took whoever they could find. Nick saw Miss Deena still standing by the front gate, standing like a soldier with her back straight and her shoulders back, her gaze unflinching and defiant as the weeping people were herded past her. Too proud to run, too contemptuous of the enemy.

Nick saw the little redhaired runt, the leader, stop by the gate for a moment, saw strange green eyes turn to Miss Deena. Saw the thoughtful consideration in those eyes.

Saw him raise his pistol and shoot Miss Deena in the face.

A scream of horror and rage rose to Nick's throat. It echoed the screams of dozens of others.

Then, as the gate swung shut behind him, the redhaired man took out a pocket watch and looked at it. "Six minutes!" he said. "Good work!"

Little chimes sounded through the air. Nick recognized the tune as "Claire de Lune" and felt his blood turn to ice, his thoughts to murder.

That little man, he saw, that baby-faced killer with the shotgun eyes, was carrying Gros-Papa's watch.

* * *

Nick crawled out of his hiding-place. Frustration and baffled anger throbbed in his chest. He felt soiled, utterly disgusted with himself. He had allowed himself to be driven like an animal. Terror had ruled his mind. He hadn't acted the part of a man. He hadn't behaved like a father who cared for his child. He'd crawled into hiding like a worm into its hole.

Gunsmoke tainted the air. Nick wandered through the stunned, sobbing refugees till he found Manon bent under a tree and weeping. He knelt by her, put his arm around her.

"I've never," Manon gasped through tears, "never imagined."

"Where is Arlette?" Nick asked. "Where is Jason?"

"I am somebody," Manon said. "I am a *person*."

Nick stood, bit his lip as he looked for Arlette. He hadn't seen anyone familiar among those being herded onto the truck, but anxiety sang through him until he saw Arlette and Jason emerging from behind an awning. He called out to them, hugged them both against him.

He wouldn't run again, he thought. Next time, he swore, it would be the guards who felt fear.

Crystals of salt were forming in the simmering water that Nick had drained from the night soil. Nick set Jason to scooping them out with a coffee filter. Nick began assembling material for his next bit of chemistry.

Miss Deena didn't die, not right away. She was laid under an awning near the cookhouse, along with an unconscious wounded man who had been shot in the stomach. There were some other wounds, all minor, and a few dead. Miss Deena's moans and incoherent cries floated through the door and she tossed restlessly on a bloody mattress. The woman who had walked with such pride, spoken with such forthrightness, would not be allowed to die with the dignity she carried in life. Instead she would die slowly, half-conscious and moaning in pain.

Nick could see a little shudder run up Jason's spine at every moan.

"I can do that job, Jase," he said. "Why don't you go find Arlette?"

Jason gave him grateful look and made himself scarce. Nick tied a towel around his head so he wouldn't drip sweat into his chemicals. He continued to pick out crystals of salt until he'd boiled most of the liquid away. Then he added methanol to the solution and filtered it through a paper coffee filter. The white crystals of pure saltpeter, collected on the towel, he laid out to dry.

While the saltpeter was drying, Nick got out the bottle of aspirin that Miss Deena had given him. He ground a fistful of aspirin tablets into a cup and mixed them with water to make a paste, then added methanol and filtered the mixture through a paper towel. He evaporated the remaining liquid out of the mixture, then added the white powder to the sulfuric acid he'd made earlier, then added saltpeter till the mixture turned red.

He refined the mixture further, cooling and straining and reheating, until he had picric acid.

While the refining process was underway, he began to make lead monoxide from saltpeter and the chips of lead pipe that Joseph of the Escape Committee had sawn for him. This required more methanol, more distilling and filtering operations. By this point his operations monopolized the burners in the cookhouse.

When he had picric acid, he used part of it to mix with the lead monoxide to form lead picrate.

"*Boom,*" he said softly to himself.

There it was. The lead picrate formed the primary explosive, the picric acid the booster explosive. Pack them together and they made a detonator. And that would set off the fertilizer explosive he would make next.

He had his weapons. What he needed now was a plan for using them that would leave his family alive.

He stepped out of the cookhouse to take a breath of air, and he saw a woman drawing a blanket over the terrible gunshot face of Miss Deena. Her agonies were finally over. The wounded man, the one shot in the belly, had died also, apparently without ever regaining consciousness.

Nick stared at the two bodies while pain throbbed through his skull. He had the sensation that he lived now in death's realm, that his father's passing had somehow opened a door into the world of night. The bodies were piling up. And the only escape, perhaps, was for Nick to start piling up bodies himself.

He turned his eyes from Miss Deena and walked away, out of sight of the corpses, and simply stood for a while, looking at nothing, taking deep breaths of the sultry air. He'd been looking at Manon for a while before his mind really registered her presence—when it did, he felt it as a small shock. There she was, her unforgettable profile, the proud Nefertiti arch of the neck. She was facing away from him, gazing at the hardwood forest behind the camp.

Nick approached her. She turned as he neared her, looked at him with an expressionless face.

"You okay?" he asked.

"What a question," she said. "No, I am not okay."

Nick felt sweat trickling down the back of his neck. "I'm not okay, either," he said.

She hesitated, then touched his arm. "What's going to happen?" he asked. "Are we going to be all right?"

"Some of us will get away," Nick said. "How many, I can't say. But some will. That's the best we can hope for."

Nick saw that Manon's eyes were shiny, that tears were rolling down her face. She looked away from him suddenly. He stepped closer and touched her face, wiped a tear away with the back of his fingers. "I'm sorry, baby," he said. "I wasn't thinking."

"That's all right," Manon said with a kind of sigh. "That was the General talking."

"I'm sorry," Nick said again.

She turned to him. "You don't think it's my fault, do you?" she said. "Because I wanted to go the wrong way up the floodway?"

Nick looked at her in surprise. "It's not your fault," he said. "It's *their* fault."

"Those bastards," Manon said. Her lip trembled. "Those

clay-eaters. They don't know us. How dare they judge us on one thing? I am a *person*."

Nick remembered her repeating that sentence, *I am a person*, after the deputies chased them through the camp. Clinging to her selfhood in the face of those who would deny it.

Manon's family had worked for generations to build their pride, to educate themselves, to maintain their high standards of achievement, to lead their community. And that didn't matter to the people on the other side of the fence, because they saw color only.

"I know," Nick said. Because color wasn't all Nick was, either. He was a father, an engineer, a man who loved. He was a father, at least, before he was a black man. He didn't have any issues with people who reversed the order of those values—that's who *they* were, and that was all right—but he always resented those who insisted that there existed values that were solely black, that black people who didn't adopt these values, and no other, somehow weren't black enough; that by choosing one life over another they were somehow betraying their ancestors; that he, by his choice of school, his choice of friends, his choice of a job, was betraying the brothers he'd left behind.

His mind spun. He wondered if the deputies—those people out there he was going to do his best to kill—ever accused each other of not being white enough. Probably they did.

"How *dare* they?" Manon said. "I have never felt so degraded."

"Because somebody overlooked this damn place," Nick said. Overlooked it for a century, probably. All it took for death to take a grip on a community was a handful of crazy people and a lot of other people who *weren't paying attention*.

Both in Rwanda and in Bosnia, the radio had told people to pick up weapons and kill their neighbors. And they *did*. All that was needed to unleash the savagery was for someone to tell people it was okay.

Wars were all ethnic now. That had been a problem at

McDonnell, maybe even the reason Nick had been laid off. You don't need a jet airplane to kill your neighbor; all you need is a shotgun and a machete and a voice on the radio to tell you what to do.

Whatever chaotic combination of circumstances had led to this situation in Spottswood Parish, it hadn't been planned this way from the beginning. Never mind what Tareek Hall might claim about a nationwide conspiracy, this camp and this situation had the feel of improvisation. This simply wasn't organized well enough to be a deeply held conspiracy. The coneheads and crackers that had gained control of this area were making it up as they went along, and that gave Nick a kind of hope. They might not have any kind of backup plan. If Nick could throw a monkey wrench into their scheme, their whole operation might fly to pieces. The Escape Committee had said there were a couple dozen guards at most, and some of them, like the Klan sheriff, hadn't been seen since before the troubles really began. The ones who were present were standing double shifts, and were probably weary by now. The total wasn't very many, not to keep a place like this going.

"The rest of the country has forgotten this place exists," Nick said. "We need to remind them somehow. There's got to be *some* way of getting news to the rest of the country. Radios, satellite phones, something."

Manon shivered and turned away, hugging herself with her arms. "There's nothing I can *do*." She said. "I went to college. I'm not a fool. But I'm useless. I don't have any skills that apply in this situation. All I can do is *watch*."

Nick came up behind Manon and put his hands on her shoulder, began to work the iron-taut muscles. "Look after yourself, that's your job," he said. "Look after the children."

"I can't even do that!" Manon said. "Not in a war! I don't know how!"

Nick felt her muscles leap under his hands. "Then save yourself for after the war," he said. "Save yourself for me."

Her muscles leaped again, and she cast him a glance over her shoulder. "Oh, Nick," she said. "Let's not."

Nick sighed. "Okay, baby."

"There are reasons we're divorced."

He let his hands fall from her shoulders. "You know," he said, "I'm not too clear on what those reasons were. Other than the legal ones, 'irreconcilable differences' or whatever."

She sighed. "We discussed it at the time."

"*You* discussed it. I don't think *I* discussed it much."

She half-turned toward him, gave him a resentful look. "You were a sweet man when I married you, Nick. But you changed."

"*I—*" he began in anger, then said, "*I* changed?"

"When your father began to die. You got frantic. You kept *turning into* him—turning into a general, into a man who gave orders and wanted everything exactly his way and no other."

"I didn't do that," Nick said.

"Yes, you did. Sometimes you were yourself—kind, loving—and then you'd snap. And you'd turn cold and start barking out orders."

Nick stared at her. "Why are you blaming my father? There was nothing wrong with my father."

"There was nothing wrong with your father, Nick, except that *he wasn't the one I married*. I married you, not the General." She put a hand on his shoulder. "Then I realized, okay, the General was a part of you. I tried to accept it, I really did. But I couldn't."

He looked at her and wondered why he couldn't think of anything to do with his hands. "My father was *dying*. Why couldn't I mourn him?"

"Mourning I could deal with. Being in the military, I could not. I didn't marry the Army, I didn't marry McDonnell, I married Nick Ruford."

"I never said things would be like Toussaint."

She lifted her chin. "Toussaint wasn't easy. You think being a David is *easy*?"

"You were in *charge* in Toussaint. Your family owned everything. Folks are a little more insecure out in the world. People outside Toussaint don't understand that you're supposed to be some kind of French royalty. People on the outside lose their jobs."

Manon's lips compressed in anger. "What's wrong with being in a secure place? I wanted Arlette to be secure. Growing up with her own people in Toussaint, having all the advantages I had."

"I wanted her to be in the real world."

"The real world can be so unkind to a young girl! It doesn't even know she's human. *This* is the real world!" She jabbed her finger emphatically at the soil, at the camp with its armed guards.

"And the bayou put Toussaint under water," Nick said. "You can't live in your magic kingdom anymore."

They fell silent for a moment, each communing with the sullen, solitary resentment that each cherished in their heart. Then Manon shook her head.

"Look, Nick," she said. "You need to be the General now, okay? That's what will save us. I understand that." She put a hand on his chest. "So you go and be a general. And when you don't need to be Army anymore, we'll talk about . . ." She hesitated. "Our future."

Nick looked at her without speaking. He was too weary and heartsick to find the words, perhaps too weary and heartsick even to return to his war.

He felt like he'd been fighting the war for years. Forever.

"I love you, Nick," Manon said. "I know you love me. But I don't know what's possible besides that."

He took her hand in his own, squeezed it, turned away. Knowing what was possible seemed the key thing. Nick didn't even know if life itself was possible, if anything was possible more than living a few hours.

"'Scuse me?" a young man approached, carrying a heavy metal toolbox. He had light skin, a scraggly beard, and a Spanish accent. "Are you Nick? The Escape Committee sent me—my name's Armando Gurulé. They said you needed some wiring done, and I'm an apprentice electrician."

* * *

"Well, Omar, some of it worked, and some didn't," Knox said. He gave a jittery little smile. "I know you had hopes for that camp committee bungling the food distribution, but they seem to have done a decent job—no complaints, no sign of dissension. Maybe some of the white folks in there taught them how to do it. And the niggers inside are getting more and more surly—I had hoped to keep 'em divided a little better, but it's not happening. Are you okay, Omar?"

Omar sighed. His skull was splitting. After his conversation with David last night, he'd got a bottle of bourbon out from under the sink and started hitting it pretty hard. And he hadn't been feeling so good to start with.

Knox's peculiar, semi-industrial body odor was making Omar's stomach turn flip-flops. Knox smelled worse than usual today.

"Maybe I've got a touch of that camp fever they've got at Clarendon," Omar said.

"Anyway," Knox said, "things didn't go so good this afternoon, with our third shipment to Woodbine Corners. We ran out of single men, that was the trouble. We had to start taking away families. There was resistance—we had to go in shooting—but we got our quota." He shook his head. "I think it's time to make a maximum effort. We need to liquidate that camp. Everyone there. Just get the whole thing over with."

It was early evening. Swallows flitted through the growing darkness. After the previous night's toad-strangler of a rain, the air seemed unusually soupy. Beyond a nearby fence were the massive machines of the John Deere dealership, all strange half-lit looming angles. Omar and Knox met here, in secret, every evening.

"People are going to—" Omar rubbed his aching head. "They're going to wonder where the camp's gone."

"Those Mud People are more dangerous if they stay," Knox said. "If a whole bunch of 'em bust out of there, we'd get most of them for sure. But what if there were survivors?" He shook his head. "No survivors. That's the plan. Then we deal with the cars—sink them or bury them or whatever—and we're home free."

Omar looked down at the little bouncing crop-haired man and he felt his insides clench in hatred. "No survivors," he agreed, and narrowed his eyes as he looked at Knox from behind his shades.

And this means you, he thought.

I remained at New Madrid from the 7th till the 12th, during which time I think shocks of earthquakes were experienced every 15 or 20 minutes—those shocks were all attended with a rumbling noise, resembling distant thunder from the southwest, varying in report according to the force of the shock. When I left the place, the surface of the earth was very little, if any, above the tops of the boats in the river.

Matthias M. Speed (Jefferson County, March 2, 1812)

The camp was strange at night, almost eerie. No one dared to show a light, no one dared to speak in a normal tone of voice. Sometimes Jason heard a child's cry, or hushed voices, or the slithery sound of someone moving in a sleeping bag. Sometimes the sounds reminded him of the noises that Deena Robinson had made when she was dying, and he shivered. Aftershocks rumbled on the northern horizon, though most were barely felt in camp. The chain link gleamed silver in the light of the spotlights that were trained on the lanes cleared along the sides of the fence. It was difficult to see anything beyond those lanes of light. All detail seemed to vanish into an exterior darkness, and the camp seemed to exist in its own world, a dark island afloat on a midnight sea.

Jason sat with Arlette in the warmth and anonymity of the night. He leaned against one of the camp's concrete picnic tables, and Arlette sat with her back to him, reclining against his chest with his arms around her while they whispered to one another. Jason was glad he didn't have to do more than whisper, because his bruised throat ached whenever he spoke.

"I'm almost sorry that I got talked out of going over the

fence," Jason said. "Our boat might still be where we left it, and I could be on the river by dawn. I could do all right living on water and some of those biscuits till I got to Vicksburg or someplace with a telephone."

Memories of being hunted through the camp made him shiver. He had almost run for the fence even then, terror making him want to disregard the deputies' guns.

"The roads are patrolled," Arlette said. "And our boat might not be there."

"I can avoid people in a *car*," Jason said. "And if the boat isn't there, I'd try to find someone friendly."

"The people here *aren't* friendly. That's what everyone says. People here shoot anyone they think's from the camp."

Jason hesitated and wondered how to frame his answer. The local crackers might well shoot a black man who they thought was some kind of dangerous escapee, but Jason suspected that they wouldn't kill an unarmed white boy. But Jason wasn't certain how to phrase that suspicion, not to Arlette. He didn't know how to talk about race. He didn't know the words that were permissible.

"They wouldn't shoot a kid," he said finally. "Not if it was just me."

"I trust my daddy," Arlette said. "He'll get us out of here."

"If it were anyone but Nick," Jason said, "I'd be out of here by now."

He remembered the fevered way that Nick labored in the cookhouse, the way his jaw muscles clenched as he worked with his primitive materials. It was as if nothing existed but the deadly task at hand. He hadn't even been disturbed by the moans of Miss Deena, sounds that had Jason nearly crawling up the walls. It was that fierce, exclusive concentration on the work that gave Jason a degree of strange comfort. He knew that Nick would not rest until he had accomplished everything that was possible.

"At least you and I are together," Jason said. He tucked his chin into the warm notch between her clavicle and jaw, and heard her give a little giggle at the sensation. She reached up a hand, touched his cheek, stroking the down along his jawline.

"Soft," she remarked. "You don't really have to shave yet, do you?"

"No, I don't."

"That's cute, that hair you got there."

"Thanks, I guess." His mind whirled at her touch. He kissed her cheek. She turned and her moist lips touched his. He kissed her avidly, dreadfully aware that they might have no time at all, that this could end any second. He wanted to melt into her, bury himself in her muscle and nerve. He yearned to obliterate himself in her.

He touched her hair through the kerchief, began to pull it down her hair in back so that he could caress her. Gently her fingers carried his hand away, rearranged the kerchief on her head. Jason felt a baffled amusement at this strange modesty. "I want to touch your hair," he said.

"No, you don't," she said. "I haven't looked after my hair in over a week."

"That's all right."

"No, it isn't. It's a mess. Every day's a bad hair day for me."

He let his hand fall from her hair, clasped it around her waist instead. "Okay," he said. "But I can still kiss you, right?"

"Sure."

"Could you lean on my other shoulder? My throat hurts if I turn that direction."

Arlette shifted her position. "It's okay if I kiss you from here?"

"Yes. And you can touch my cute little sideburns all you like."

Arlette giggled. "Okay."

She touched his cheek, then brought her lips to his. They kissed again in the clinging darkness. Then Arlette gave a cry of alarm and Jason's heart leaped; he turned to see a strange figure silhouetted against the stars, standing above them.

The man was burly, dressed in a long coat and a broad-brimmed hat. Jason saw a long beard silvered by starlight, hair tumbled over the shoulders, strange yellow eyes that gleamed in his black face. The man brought with him an earthy smell that Jason tasted on the night air.

"I come from outside, me," he said, in an accent so thick that Jason could barely make out the words. "I need talk the man in charge, eh?"

Nick sat in the cookhouse, making bombs. He had the overhead light on, but he kept the doors shut so he wouldn't attract attention. It was hot and stifling in the cookhouse, and his head swam with the scent of fuel. He worked slowly and deliberately, not daring to make a mistake.

Nick took one-pound coffee cans from the camp's meager stores, then packed them two-thirds full with an explosive made from fertilizer and motor oil. He put all his weight into compressing the explosive, because he wasn't sure if the picric acid he was using as a booster explosive would be "fast" enough, when exploded, to detonate the fertilizer, and the more fertilizer hit by the shock wave of the detonator, the better. He pushed his finger into the compressed explosive, and then in the hole he made he placed a homemade blasting cap. Each cap was made from one of the spent pistol cartridges that the deputies had scattered in the camp on their raid that afternoon, a fact that Nick considered poetic justice. Nick had punched the used primer out of the bottom of each cartridge with a nail and inserted an electric fuse put together by Armando Gurulé, the electrician's apprentice who had been stranded in Shelburne City on his way to look for a job in California. Once the fuse was in place, Nick then packed in charges of lead picrate and picric acid, the primary and booster explosive.

Nick put in some scrap paper to hold the explosive in place, then began packing in pieces of metal. Nuts, screws, bolts, nails, bits of pipe, old hacksaw blades, coins, more of the spent cartridges—everything the Escape Committee could scrounge, including their own wrist watches. Anything that might make a hole in a deputy if it was shot at him with sufficient force.

When he was done, he'd created homemade claymore

mines, a more primitive version of the notoriously effective antipersonnel weapon that U.S. forces had used in Vietnam. Each mine, when planted in the ground with its open mouth pointed toward an enemy, would spray out its scrap metal in the direction of the foe like a huge shotgun, shredding flesh with hundreds of small projectiles.

Nick had no certainty that any one mine would work—there were too many variables in these homebuilds, too much improvisation in the formulae, too many things that could have gone wrong in the assembly—but Nick hoped that enough mines would actually work to blanket the area occupied by the deputies when they next came into the camp.

There was a soft knock on one of the cookhouse doors. "Nick?" Manon's voice. "You in there?"

"Yes."

"Can I come in?"

"I'll come out. Just a minute."

He finished packing explosive into a coffee can, then rose and switched off the light. Blinking dazzled eyes, he groped for the door knob. He opened it carefully, then slid out of the cookhouse and closed the door behind him.

Fresh air. He took in a few deep, grateful breaths. He couldn't see Manon in the starlight, but he felt his flesh prickle as he sensed her nearness.

"Nick, I'm worried about the children," Manon said. "I haven't seen Arlette since nightfall."

"Where can she go?" Nick said.

"That's what I'm afraid of," she whispered. "What if that boy's talked her into going over the fence?"

Nick breathed in the fresh air and considered this. "We haven't heard shots, right?" he said. "So if they've gone, they've got clean away. We should be grateful they won't be here for what will happen tomorrow."

"Damn it, Nick!" Manon flared. "I want you to help me look! This is your *family*—this isn't an army, this isn't some soldier you've sent away on a mission; this is *our baby* we're talking about."

Nick looked at her. "If they've escaped, it's a good thing. Jason knows enough about survival and the river to get away if he can find a boat. If he can get to the authorities, he may be able to save our lives."

Nick's eyes were adjusting slowly to the darkness. He saw Manon outlined before him, her tall, proud figure standing by the corner of the cookhouse. "And what if they haven't tried their escape yet? What if they *didn't* try to escape?" Manon demanded. "What if they're together somewhere? Off in the night doing what they shouldn't?"

Nick took in a breath of night air. "Good," he decided.

"Good? Good? Is that what I heard you say?"

Nick licked his lips. "I wouldn't want either of them to die without knowing love."

There was a moment of silence, and then Manon moaned. "Oh, my God." He could hear the keen-edged grief suddenly enter her voice. "Oh, my God, that you would say they will die."

Nick's head swam. "I'll do my best to see that they don't," he said. He was tired, far too tired, to offer any degree of false reassurance.

"You're blaming me. I know you are."

Nick looked at Manon in surprise. "Why would I do that?" he asked.

"I know it's true."

"Daddy! Daddy!" Arlette's urgent whisper cut through the night. "We found someone! Someone from the outside!"

Nick looked up in surprise as Arlette and Jason came out of the darkness followed by a strange figure, a bizarre bearded apparition, as if a scarecrow dressed in second-hand clothes had come suddenly to life. To his astonishment, Nick saw that the scarecrow was carrying a gun over one shoulder.

"Bonsoir," the man said. "I am Cudgel, me. I come see how you get along."

Nick took Cudgel to the Escape Committee, and they set out to round up as many of the absent members as possible, along with any from the Camp Committee who could be found. Rumor spread swiftly, and a small crowd gathered, murmuring in the darkness as speculation spread among them. Cudgel seemed taken aback by all the sensation. Nick urgently whispered for everyone who didn't have business here to get away, that such a crowd would only attract attention and, maybe, bullets. Reluctantly, the crowd melted into the darkness. Jason and Arlette remained, and Nick saw a defiant look in Jason's eye. Nick decided he might as well let them stay. They'd found the man, after all, or he'd found them.

Manon stayed as well. Nick suspected that he would have a hard time prying her away from Arlette tonight, even if he were willing to try.

Cudgel sat down amid the remaining people, slid the rifle off his shoulder into his lap. He wore a battered wide-brimmed hat decorated with feathers, and his long hair was so tangled that it hung down his back like a wiry horsehair mat. His beard, spread over his chest, looked like Spanish moss, and his eyes glimmered yellow in the night. He smelled as if he'd been wrapped in newspaper and buried for twenty years.

"How'd you get here?" someone on the committee asked. "How'd you get past the guards?"

"I move quiet, me," Cudgel said. For all his outlandish appearance, his voice was soft, and he seemed a little intimidated by the presence of all these curious people. "You go hunting, you, you want nice goose *pour le dîner*, you sho-nuff creep that goose. You no let that bull-goose see you, that goose, so you creep him goose."

There was a moment of bewildered silence. It took Nick a moment to work out that "creeping the goose" was something done while hunting, slipping past the sentinel geese to get within shooting distance of the flock.

"I've been in your house!" Jason said suddenly. "Down in the floodway, that treehouse!"

Cudgel looked at him. "I live there sometime, *mais oui*. In spring I go for crawfish, me, in fall for shooting." He smiled, yellow teeth flashing in the starlight. "Plenty birds there, come autumn."

"Can you take some others out?" Nick asked. "Can you take some of the children to safety? Or some messengers who can try to find help?"

Cudgel thought about this for a long moment. "I consider that could be hard, me," he said. "You got a man can creep the goose for true?"

That looked like to set off an argument about who in the camp was qualified, and who not, and since Nick doubted that anyone in the camp had ever crept a goose or was likely to try, he wanted to cut the discussion before it got started.

"Why did you come here, Mr. Cudgel?" he asked.

Cudgel frowned. "I see them kill, them trash," Cudgel said. "Down Cattrall's old cotton field, *la bas*, by where I go fish sometime in *bateau*, that sixty acres down by the bayou. They line them up, them black boys, and—" He raised a hand, mimed a finger squeezing a trigger. Made a sound, *psssh*, like a shot being fired.

There was a horrified cry from Manon. Stifled groans from the others.

"*C'est vrai*," Cudgel said. "So I think, why for them do that, them. Saw the Paxton boy, son of the High Sheriff, that Paxton boy, so I knew them be Kluxers. So I come the camp here, me, see what I find." He smiled again. "Creep the goose, me. Talk you fellas."

"We need help," said a woman on the Camp Committee. "Can you help us? You've seen what they do. Can you tell someone?"

Cudgel looked thoughtful. "I pretty grand fella, me, down Plaquemines Parish. Everybody know Cudgel there. But here—" He shook his head. "Nobody know Cudgel. I don't got but ten cents, me. Ain't nobody listen Cudgel up here."

The woman persisted. "Can you take someone out to speak to the locals? Or phone for help?"

"No phone here, no," Cudgel said. "Not since the earthshake. But someone come out, some fella, come out the camp, I take him where you say, me."

"The A.M.E. people used to come here, bring food and look after us. Brother Morris and his family, other people from the community. Then they stopped coming. And the—the hateful things—began to happen. Can you get word to Brother Morris?"

"Morris, he dead, that Morris."

There was another collective sound from Cudgel's audience, another half-gasp, half-groan.

"They say he been shot, Morris," Cudgel said. "Say a man from the camp did the shooting, them. But I take a man wherever you say, me. I take him Morris wife, you want."

"Yes. To Mrs. Morris. Yes, that would be good."

Nick listened to this discussion with only partial attention. His mind was factoring Cudgel's presence into his plans, this strange, stealthy swamp man who lived by his wits and by hunting, who carried a rifle over one shoulder and knew the country like the back of his hand.

"Mr. Cudgel," he said, "I think we may have to fight, whether you get a chance to talk to Mrs. Morris or not. If we don't fight to defend ourselves, we may have more people taken from the camp and killed before any help can come. You have a gun, you hunt and trap—can you help us fight?"

There was a sudden silence in the small group. Cudgel considered Nick's words, then nodded. "I do what you want, me. But if you can fight, what for you here? You got guns, you men, why never you shoot a mess o' Kluxer 'long time back?"

"We only have a few handguns," Nick said. "Everything else was taken. But I'm making other weapons—claymore mines, if you know what those are."

"*Hé quoi!*" Cudgel said in surprise, and a moment later a sudden broad smile lit his face. He held up a hand, thumb crooked over his fist, and he pressed the thumb down. "*Took,*" he said, a little falsetto birdlike sound.

Nick realized, to his astonishment, that Cudgel was miming his thumb pressing the button of a detonator.

"I know them claymores, me," Cudgel said. "I serve in Army, fight them V.C. I fight in Delta, me, I fight in Vinh Long, in Can Tho." He raised his fist again, crooked his thumb. "*Took.* No more V.C. I creep them Congs, them V.C., just like I creep the goose. I get my name in Delta, me."

I get my name in Delta. Realization flooded Nick's mind as he looked into Cudgel's beaming face.

"Your name isn't *Cudgel*," he said suddenly. "It's *Cudjo*, isn't it?"

The man nodded. "Cudjo, *c'est moi*. I get the name in Vietnam, me."

"That's an African name," Nick said. "A warrior name."

Pride straightened Cudjo's shoulders, glimmered in his yellow eyes. "*C'est vrai*," he said. "I a warrior, me. Get in trouble down Plaquemines Parish, come here to live. Never touch them liquors and drugs no more, for true."

Astonished hope beat in Nick's heart. "You can help us fight, can't you?" he said.

"*Si*, with them claymores." He took the rifle gun from his lap and held it out to Nick. "You take my gun, you. Kill them Kluxers. I help."

Nick took the gun, looked at it in surprise. "I'm not very good with a rifle," he said. "But I'll make sure it goes to someone who can use it."

"Take these shells, you." Cudjo dug in the pockets of his old coat, dropped cartridges into Nick's hand. Little ones, he realized, .22s.

"I don't want to leave you without a rifle," Nick said. "I'm sure you can use this better than anyone."

"That my squirrel gun, there," Cudjo said. "Only a two-two. When I come back tomorrow, me, I bring my deer gun, yes? Thirty-ought-six."

Nick was almost blinded by sudden possibility. Even Cudjo's little .22 would make a difference to the camp. Fired from cover it could make the deputies keep their heads down, if nothing else. And when Cudjo returned with his deer rifle, his .30-'06, he could do a lot of damage from the cover of the woods, and with reasonable safety to himself.

Eagerness seized Nick. "Let me tell you what I'm planning," he said. He unrolled his entire plan for Cudjo, while the woodsman listened, nodded, and asked questions. Then Cudjo analyzed Nick's plan, took it apart, and reassembled it in an altered, more perfected form.

"Yes," Nick said. "Yes, I see."

"Kill them Kluxers, take them Kluxers out, before you push the people on, yes? You no run them into guns, you."

"Yes. I understand."

"Direction you want run, that depend. No use planning too much, plans go to hell when shooting starts."

No plan survives contact with the enemy, Nick thought. His father had said that. "I understand," he said.

"Can you take the women and kids to where it will be safe?" Nick asked.

"I try, me."

"But what about getting someone out?" someone else asked. "What about Mrs. Morris?"

"You give me someone, you, I take him," said Cudjo.

"It's important that Cudjo be there with his rifle," Nick said.

"If we can get word out, there won't be a need for guns."

Nick considered an argument in favor of keeping Cudjo near the camp instead of running errands. Cudjo was an *asset*; he was the most hopeful thing that had occurred in the camp's entire miserable history. Sneaking someone away with him, someone who might not be so good at creeping the goose as Cudjo, seemed an unnecessary risk to Nick's asset. And sending Cudjo off on an errand to Mrs. Morris's house, when he might be needed in the camp, seemed dangerous.

But on the other hand, the idea of contacting the outside was seductive. It meant no one inside the camp had to take any risks, or fight other battles. All they had to wait was for Mrs. Morris to call in the U.S. Cavalry. Nick could see how the others were attracted by the idea, how much they wanted to escape this situation without having to fight a war.

"Listen," Nick said. "We don't want to risk Cudjo. We don't want to risk him in the company of someone who's less expert at—" his tongue stumbled "—at creeping the goose."

Whispers flurried at him in urgent debate. The only person who held Nick's point of view was Tareek Hall, the conspiracy theorist, who said that there wasn't any point in sending for help, that the authorities were all part of the conspiracy anyway. But Tareek and Nick were clearly outnumbered.

"Send Cudjo out *first*," Nick finally said. "Your messenger can go next. That way if he's—" He was about to say *killed*, then changed it. "If he's caught," he said, "then Cudjo won't be caught with him."

There was more whispered debate, but Cudjo ended the debate himself. "I reckon Nick right, me. I be better alone, for true."

The committee members chose one of their number as their messenger, a thirtyish woman named Nora. She was small and nimble, had taught gymnastics, and it was hoped that speed and agility would aid her escape. The fact that she was a woman might make her less threatening to the locals she would approach for help. She listened eagerly when Cudjo gave her instructions—vague hints, really—for avoiding the guards' attention. Nick approached the chain link with Cudjo, then hesitated. "I shouldn't come to the fence," he said. "I might be seen."

"Can't see nothing, them guards," Cudjo said. "That light along the fence, it make dark behind. Can you see the woods from here, Nick? They should point their lights into the camp, those Kluxers, they want to see in here."

Nick gazed past the fence in surprise. Cudjo was right. The spotlights, trained parallel to the fence, created a comparative darkness on either side. The pathway along the fence was brightly lit, but the camp itself was shrouded, and so were the woods on the other side of the lane.

"You kiss you lady for me, yes?" Cudjo said. His yellow teeth flashed for a moment, and then he stepped from Nick's presence and was gone.

Nick stood in silent surprise, his heart hammering. For a long moment his eyes searched the darkness, and then he saw Cudjo crouched just inside the fence, his big hat slowly scanning left and right as he observed the guards. Then there was swift movement as he lay flat and rolled under the fence into the tall, untrimmed grass that grew beneath the wire.

For an instant, Cudjo was standing in the light outside the wire, frozen as if motionless. Then the man was gone.

Nick realized he was holding his breath, and he let the breath go hissing into the night. *Creeping the goose.* It had seemed uncanny, magical.

"My turn," Nora muttered. Her eyes were wide, and there was a tremor in her voice

"You don't have to go," Nick said. Nora was brave, he thought, she was lithe and fast. But she wasn't magical. She wasn't Cudjo.

Nora gave him a look. "Yes, I do."

Nick saw her do as Cudjo had done, crouch low by the wire while she looked left and right at the deputies. Then she was down, rolling under the wire. And up, arms and legs pumping as she ran for the woods.

There was a sudden boom, the blast of a shotgun stunning the night, and Nora fell onto the earth, a sudden, limp tangle of awkward limbs. Nick's stunned retinas retained an after-image of bright blood staining the air.

He heard groans, cries from the people around him.

There was another shot, just to make certain Nora was dead.

Then more shots, this time into the wire. Shot whined off the chain link, strange Doppler noises. Nick was on the ground then, crawling into cover, so he never saw the deputy walk up to Nora, pull his pistol, and shoot her in the head.

Nick lay in the night, pulse throbbing in his skull. His nerves leaped with every sound.

Finally he rose and made his silent way to the cookhouse, to finish building his bombs.

THIRTY-FOUR

As we were all wrapt in sleep, each tells his story in his own way. I will also relate my simple tale.

At the period above mentioned, I was roused from sleep by the clamor of windows, doors and furniture in tremulous motion, with a distant rumbling noise, resembling a number of carriages passing over pavement—in a few seconds the motion and subterraneous thunder increased more and more: believing the noise to proceed from the N. or N.W. and expecting the earth to be relieved by a volcanic eruption, I went out of doors & looked for the dreadful phenomenon. The agitation had now reached its utmost violence. I entered the house to snatch my family from its expected ruins, but before I could put my design in execution the shock had ceased, having lasted about one and three fourth minutes. The sky was obscured by a thick hazy fog, without a breath of air. Fahrenheit thermometer might have stood at this time at about 35 or 40 (degrees).

Louisiana Gazette *(St. Louis)*
Saturday, December 21, 1811

Flash. Flash. Flash. The laser pulsed on Jessica's retina.

"There." The doctor's voice. "Can you see anything now?"

Jessica covered her right eye. The doctor's face floated toward her out of the darkness. "Yes," she said. She didn't know whether to be hopeful or not. "But it's like tunnel vision."

"I've just started." Jessica lay back in the padded headrest and felt the doctor lean over her. "I saw you on television the other day," the doctor said. "With the President."

"Yes." Flash.

"What's he really like?" Flash flash.

"I don't know him well. I've only met him a couple times." She smiled. "But he *did* appoint me to my job, so I think it's obvious that he's a great statesman."

Flash. Flash flash flash.

"I voted for him," the doctor said. "But it was just a stab in the dark, you know. You can't really tell with those people."

The first time Jessica had met the President, all she had felt was the man's charisma. When he looked at you, your insides went all warm and tingly. You wanted to roll on your back and have him rub your tummy. Even for someone as professionally accustomed to alpha males as Jessica, the effect had been surprising.

All big politicians were like that, though. Jessica had met a few. They all carried that enormous top-dog energy. The lucky ones could project it on television.

This last time, though, the meeting on Poinsett Island, the President's affect had been different. It wasn't so much as that the glow wasn't there, but that it had gone somewhere that Jessica couldn't reach. Though there was nothing Jessica could put her finger on, she had the sense that, at least part of the time, the commander-in-chief wasn't home.

Hey, she told herself. *Give the guy a break. He's just lost his wife.*

Flash. Flash flash.

She had lost the last of the vision in her left eye on the return helicopter trip to Vicksburg. The doctor, though, had been encouraging when he spoke to Pat on the telephone. Jessica had probably detached a retina. It sounded frightening—and Jessica was *very* frightened—but the doctor assured Pat that the retina could most likely be tacked back on with a laser.

To Jessica's surprise, she didn't have to check into a hospital. Unless there was some complication, the procedure could be done in the doctor's office.

And that meant she wouldn't have to be absent from her command for more than few hours. By the time the paperwork for the procedure caught up with the Army—and that would take a long while, given the current emergency—she would have been back at her work for weeks, if not months. Which meant that it would be far too late to question her presence at her job.

Flash flash flash. "The vitreal humor," the doctor said conversationally, "that's the jelly in the center of your eye. Well, it was probably pulling away from the retina—it happens to most of us as we get older. But in your case the vitreal humor pulled the retina away with it. Probably the earthquake tore everything loose."

"Not the earthquake. It was a bumpy helicopter ride."

The doctor was amused. "We don't get many of those," he said.

Flash flash flash.

"How's that?"

Jessica blinked cautiously at the world. Reality seemed more or less intact.

"I can see," she said in surprise.

"You may have lost some detail," the doctor said. "Time will tell."

"I—*thank* you, doctor. Thank you."

"Lie back and let me take another tour of your eye," the doctor said. "I want to check and make certain I haven't missed something."

"Certainly." Jessica leaned back on the padded headrest.

"And another thing," the doctor said. "No more helicopter rides."

Jessica felt herself smile. She had *got* here on a helicopter, a smoother ride than driving the torn road between Vicksburg and Jackson.

"I'll see what I can do," she said.

"Okay," said Armando Gurulé, the electrician's apprentice. "I've made this double safe. To set off the claymores, you've got to throw *both* these switches, right?"

"Right," Nick said. He bit his lip, looked at the wires. "What if they cut power to the camp?"

Armando gave a laugh. "They can't. Look at the power line. They run their own floodlights off the same power source."

Nick nodded. "Good."

"So you throw the switches. And then all the claymores go at once. Boom."

"*Boom*," Nick agreed.

Nick blinked gum from his eyes. The sun was just beginning to rise behind the trees east of the camp. In the last hour of darkness he had buried his mines—he'd ended up with eleven—leaving nothing but the detonator wires sticking out of the ground. Armando had crawled after Nick and connected the wires to his homemade control board, then covered the gear with grass or bits of matting or plastic sheeting.

"I hope this works," Armando said. "I'm from the Dominican Republic, man. I don't understand this crazy scene *at all*. I keep thinking I'm here by accident."

"We're *all* here by accident," Nick said.

"I guess so."

Weariness dragged at Nick's thoughts. He hadn't slept at all during the night, and only fitfully on the boat the night before. The thought that he might have forgotten something important beat at his brain like a weak, insistent pulse.

"I'm going to talk to the committee," he said. "Then I'm going to try to get some rest. Make sure you wake me if the bad guys come."

"You bet."

Nick dragged himself to the pecan tree, told the combined Escape and Camp Committees that he'd finished his job. "I'm getting a little worried about security," he said. "What I've been doing isn't exactly secret. Probably most of the camp knows about it by now." He rubbed his weary eyes. "What if someone decides he can sell the information to the coneheads?"

"That doesn't make any sense," someone on the Camp Committee said. "They aren't going to let anyone out of here."

"People don't always think straight," Nick said. "All you need is one parent panicked for the safety of a baby, or an alcoholic who will do anything for a drink . . ."

"Or a white man who got put in here by mistake," said Tareek Hall. "Or who was planted in here as a spy by the conspiracy. Or some nigger traitor seduced by the conspiracy, like Martin Luther King or Malcolm X."

The others were too tired to argue, but they took Nick's point. "The deputies already said nobody but the Camp Committee can come near the fence," someone said. "All we have to do is enforce that from *our* side."

Tareek began to say something about microphones planted by the conspiracy, and laser beams in orbital satellites that could make people behave crazy, but there didn't seem to be anything anyone could do about that. "You people have to organize the fighters," Nick said. "I can't do that—I don't know the people. You have to find someone to enforce the rules. And you've got to do it yesterday."

"We got motivation," one man said. He pointed to the fence, where Nora's body still lay. "We know what happens if anything goes wrong."

Nick could barely breathe in the hot and humid air. His mind swam. "I'm going to try to rest," he said, and left them to their arguments.

He'd done what he could. Maybe later he'd think of something else to do, but right now he was too weary to think of anything but sleep.

He went into the storage shed where he'd found the fertilizer and motor oil and lay on the soft, oil-soaked planks. Sleep took him in an instant.

Nick was vaguely aware of Arlette waking him with some breakfast on a plastic plate, but he was less interested in food than in sleep. When he next woke the sun was high, and his body was soaked with sweat where it lay against the floorboards.

They didn't come, he thought vaguely. The deputies had not come. No one had discussed this possibility.

He sat up, and pain hammered through his stiffened body. He saw the plastic plate where Arlette had left it. It held two of the strange greasy crackers and a small mound of an opalescent gelatinous matter. He pushed the stuff around with one of the crackers and concluded that the mysterious substance was made from powdered eggs, but lacked the usual yellow food coloring that turned them into a reasonable facsimile of fresh, scrambled eggs.

Nick scooped some onto a cracker and took a bite. The taste wasn't bad, but wasn't good, either. He ate it all.

He wandered out of the cookhouse and saw people lining up for lunch. He blinked in the sun.

The deputies hadn't come. He had been so certain that the deputies would arrive that morning, would enter the camp and drive the refugees like cattle to the slaughterhouse.

It looked as if they would be given a breathing space. He should check all the work he'd done that night, make sure there wasn't something he'd overlooked in the darkness.

The plan could be refined. Everybody could be made to better understand their roles, to understand the necessity of what Nick needed them to do.

He set about the task.

Jason gazed at the woman's body lying beyond the fence. *One-eighty-six,* he thought. *Murder.* Stars eddied in his head. He could feel his breakfast surge in his stomach, and he swallowed hard.

He crouched on his heels on the grassy earth and looked at the body. He had seen so many bodies, he thought, bodies drifting down the river, blasted by bullets in Frankland's camp, bodies whimpering life away like Miss Deena, now this woman one-eighty-six'd by the guardians of this prison. The world was probably paved with bodies.

And not just the world, he corrected, but the universe. Sometimes stars blew up.

His throat ached, the pain greater than yesterday. Awareness of the precarious fragility of existence filled his mind. The woman had thrown her own existence away, deliberately tempted death by walking into the lane of death outside the camp. People said her name was Nora. Nobody seemed to know her last name.

Half her name, forgotten already.

Jason had not seen the killing. When Nick, Cudjo, and the others began to argue their various plans back and forth, Manon had firmly drawn Arlette and Jason away from the circle and brought them to a place where they could sleep under one of the cotton wagons. Manon also made a point of sleeping between Arlette and Jason, keeping them apart during the night. Her determination made Jason smile quietly in the darkness as he drifted to sleep.

The shots had torn Jason from sleep. Manon, beside him, woke with a cry, and Jason, in sudden fear, had put his hand over Manon's mouth and whispered "Be quiet!" in an urgent voice. He could see the starlight glimmering on her eyes as she submitted.

Don't let them hear you, don't let them see you, don't become a target. A child, powerless by nature, knows these rules by instinct.

Nora had disobeyed the rules and died.

What did you die for? Jason thought at the corpse. Life was a flash in the darkness, brief enough without throwing it away. Life was the only thing life had.

A modest aftershock trembled in the earth for a moment, then passed. Jason looked away from the corpse as he caught movement in the tail of his eye, Arlette walking toward him. *That's what you die for,* he thought with sudden certainty.

You die for what you love.

Jason rose and kissed Arlette hello. He put his arms around her. "How was Nick?" he asked, then winced at the pain in his throat.

"Asleep. I left his breakfast with him." She looked at the body beyond the fence, then turned her head abruptly. "Let's go someplace else," she said in a small voice.

There's no place else we can go, he almost said. But he said "All right" instead, and took Arlette's hand as they walked away from Nora, toward the front of the camp. There was an undercurrent of excitement, people meeting in small groups. Jason saw some half-concealed weapons, clubs and knives.

Nobody had included Jason in any of these schemes as yet. He and Arlette and Manon had a rendezvous, a place under one of the cotton wagons where they were supposed to meet in the event of an emergency. Other than that, Jason was at liberty, he supposed, to make his own plans, if he could work something out.

He could still try to escape tonight. Cudjo showed it could be done.

But Nora showed how it couldn't. He had to think about that.

He and Arlette paused in the shade of one of the camp's pecan trees. He kissed her again, looked into her somber brown eyes.

I would die for you, he wanted to say. Instead he tilted his head a little to the left, to ease the pain in his throat, and said, "How are you doing?"

"I'm okay." She shrugged. "Shots, bodies." Anger hardened her face. "I'm beginning to understand why you're mad at God."

"I'm not anymore," Jason said.

She looked at him.

"The universe is too big to be angry at it," he said. "It's like being mad at this tree for being a pecan instead of a magnolia. It's a waste of our time."

She glanced over one shoulder in the direction of the gate. Her eyes hardened. "Is it a waste to hate a murderer for being a murderer?" she said.

"Murderers are different," Jason said. "They're more our size."

Arlette gave a little sniff, tossed her head. "They're smaller," she said. "Much smaller."

"Yes," Jason said. He glanced over the camp, the people in their small, hurried groups. "I was surprised that you or your mom didn't talk to Cudjo in French."

A smile touched her lips. "I think his French was probably as funky as his English. I've learned *French* French, not

Cajun, and probably Cudjo speaks a pretty strange version of Cajun, at that."

"Captain Joe could have talked to him, I guess."

"From what I heard of him over the radio, he probably could."

He took her hands. "I'm glad we had a chance to be together last night, before Cudjo turned up."

"And before my momma came and separated us." She smiled.

"I don't think she's looking at us now," Jason said.

"No. I don't think so."

They kissed. Arlette leaned back against the tree. Jason pressed himself to her. Her presence whirled in his senses.

"God damn, girl," said a voice. Jason turned, saw the three boys Arlette had spoken to the day before.

"What are you doing with this boy?" Sékou said to Arlette. "You think his color's catching? You think those peckerwoods won't hurt you, you kiss him hard enough?"

Fury flashed through Jason. He faced the other boys, fists clenched by his side. Then he saw that Sékou carried a heavy stick, just hanging casually against his leg, and that the boy called Raymond had a hammer stuck through his belt, and he took a step back.

"Why don't you mind your own business," Arlette said.

"It's your business to be with black people," Sékou said. "You're disrespecting the race."

"Sisters gotta support the brothers," Raymond said.

Arlette looked at them. "Even when they're being as charming as you?" she asked.

"We're gonna fight for you," Sékou said, "so why are you hangin' with the little kid? Jason—" His tone turned mocking. "*Jason!* What kind of trifling Yuppie-ass name is that?"

Jason considered kicking the nearest one in the crotch and then running for it. He thought that probably some adult would call the situation to order before he got his head beaten in.

Anger flashed from Arlette's eyes. "Why don't you just leave us alone?" she said.

"Scandalous-ass bitch upset, now," said Raymond.

"Jason saved my life," Arlette said. "He saved my whole family from a boat full of crazy men. You want some respect, you go do something useful instead of fronting on this crap."

Raymond looked at Jason from under half-closed eyelids. "You better watch it with the white boy," he said. "They set up a nigga every time."

His pulse throbbed in Jason's ears. He felt his toes curl in his Nikes. Getting the range on Raymond's crotch.

"Jason's black enough to *be here*!" Arlette said. "He's black enough for *them*!" She flung a pointing finger toward the deputies. Arlette's eyes flared. "He's black enough to *die with you*!"

The others fell silent. Arlette glared at them for a moment, then took Jason's arm and steered him away.

"'Scandalous-ass bitch,'" she fumed. "You heard what they called me?"

Jason's mouth was dry. Adrenaline sang in his veins. He'd been a half-second from violence, and it would probably have been violence inflicted mostly on him.

"Thanks for sticking up for me," he croaked through his injured throat.

"You stuck up for *me* when it counted," she said.

Jason strove for words to express his surging feelings, the thoughts that whirled in his head. Found himself baffled. "This race thing," he said finally. "It's really fucked."

The diarrhea at Clarendon was responding to treatment. Dr. Patel went home for his first sleep in days, and Omar returned to his office. Omar had ordered David to stay away from Woodbine Corners—had sent him out patrolling with Merle, in fact, on the other end of the parish, down by the Bayou Bridge.

Merle and David were the two key people he absolutely wanted away from the A.M.E. camp. He wasn't going to go anywhere near the camp himself, especially not today. Deniability was an absolute necessity.

Containment. That's what Omar was after. Build a nice fence around everything.

Omar's head throbbed. A sharp icepick pain flamed beneath his sternum. Sometimes it seemed he could barely breathe.

It was ten in the morning. Knox and Jedthus and their people should be about their work by now. Work he did not, officially, know about.

That's why he was surprised when Jedthus walked into his office. Omar looked up in surprise. "What's going on?" he said.

Jedthus carefully closed the door before speaking. "We've been ready to go," he said. "You know, do the necessary at the camp. But Knox didn't turn up. He was supposed to join us at eight o'clock."

"Says which?" Omar was thunderstruck. "He's gone?"

"He's not gone, he's *asleep*."

"What?"

"I went to where he's been staying—Sunny Spence's old storefront, you know—and there he was. I tried to wake him up, but he just rolled over and went back to sleep."

"Is he sick?"

"He's—" Jedthus hesitated. "You'd best see for yourself, Omar."

Sunny Spence's Dress Shoppe and Gifts, on Beauregard Street, had been closed for five years. No other business had wanted to rent the building, so the place had remained boarded up till the parish, under emergency decrees, had opened the place to house refugees. It had survived the quakes remarkably well for a building that hadn't been maintained in ages. Omar had given it to the Crusaders as a crash pad.

Knox was asleep, lying atop a down sleeping bag behind the counter. Clothing and sleeping bags belonging to the other Crusaders lay around the store. A pistol, a shotgun, and a deputy's badge sat atop the counter, within arm's reach of where Knox lay. Knox wore only his undershorts and was curled up on his side in a fetal position.

"Hey Micah," Omar bent down—the movement sent pain ringing through his head—and shook Knox's shoulder. "Micah, it's time to get up." His nose wrinkled at Knox's acidic body odor. "Man," he said, "this boy needs a bath."

Omar shook Knox again. Knox gave a kind of sigh, and then his eyelids cracked open. "Oh, hi Omar," he said, then rolled on his back, smiled a little, and went back to sleep.

"Son of a bitch," Omar said. He straightened, and looked in stunned amazement at the needle tracks that ran up and down Knox's arms.

"God *damn*," he said.

"Yeah," Jedthus said. "We got us a junkie, Omar. You figure he's OD'd?"

No wonder he always wore long sleeves, Omar thought. And the way he smelled—that was the drugs coming out in his sweat.

Fury sang through Omar's nerves. "What's he using?" he demanded. It had to be an upper, from the way Knox was always jumping around. "Damn it," Omar said, "I *searched* this boy!"

Omar tore through Knox's belongings—upended the toiletry bag, flipped through the pages of *Hunter*, tore the laptop computer from its foam packing—before he thought to open the big, heavy 500-count bottle of aspirin that had fallen out among the toiletries, and shake out the Crusader's drugs.

There was a set of needles and a syringe—the works were real doctor's issue, not the sort found on the street and made from an eyedropper—along with a fire-blackened spoon and a baggie of brown substance, presumably heroin. There was another bag of pills: black mollies, methedrine. A third baggie with a minute amount of white powder remaining. Omar opened the baggie, tasted the substance. Crystal meth.

Speedballs, Omar thought. The classic speedball was a mixture of heroin and cocaine, but working-class stiffs used heroin and methedrine instead. You could go for days on the stuff until you hit the wall and crashed. The meth was acidic and ravaged the veins, and that would have produced Knox's impressive rows of needle tracks in fairly short order. Though it was possible he shot only the heroin, and snorted or swallowed the speed.

"Damn it," Omar said. "Why didn't I see this?" Knox's fidgeting, his slapping out rhythms on his knees or his chair, the way he kept talking, the words spilling out, the theories and the diatribes and the history and the fantasy, all run together, all confused . . .

Knox was deep in drug psychosis, wandering around the country, jabbering about revolution and race war while he robbed banks and spent the money on scag and crank. Omar wondered if the other Crusaders were junkies as well, if this was some kind of heavily armed, mobile drug posse.

Jesus. David had been around these people. David had fallen for their line, had wanted to join them in their underground, follow this drug-addled psychopath as he lurched from one crime to the next.

"What do we do, Omar?" Jedthus demanded. "We can't wake him up. We can't arrest him." He paced around the little store. "Do I go back to the camp? Do I do the—the operation without him?"

Omar stepped away from Knox. He wanted a breath of fresh air, wanted to get Knox's stink out of his nostrils.

If Knox wasn't present to run the operation at the camp, Omar thought, then Jedthus was in charge. Omar, however, wasn't inclined to trust Jedthus's judgment. The boy was on the right side, but bone stupid. Yet if Jedthus wasn't in charge, then Omar was in charge. And if Omar was in charge, then deniability went out the window.

Besides, he wanted Knox in control of eliminating that camp. Even if Knox was a psycho, he'd get the job done.

Knox was a weapon, Omar reminded himself. Made just for Spottswood Parish. And when his job was over—when the weapon had been fired—there would no longer be any reason for him to exist.

Omar took a breath. "Wait for Knox to wake up. Bring him some coffee and some food."

"But Omar," Jedthus said. "He's OD'd!"

"He's crashed," Omar said. "Speed freaks do that. They run for days, but they can't live without sleep forever." He looked around the Shoppe, at the sleeping bags, blankets, pallets, and belongings of the other Crusaders scattered around the dusty floor.

"Do you think they're *all* users?" Omar asked.

Jedthus thought about it. "They're not all as speedy as Micah, but sometimes they're hyped. Yeah. We're all on twelve-hour shifts; I wondered how they held up so well."

Omar walked to Jedthus, put a hand on his shoulder, and lowered his voice. "These people are not reliable," he said. "Knox is a psycho. I wouldn't trust any of them behind a dime."

Jedthus nodded. "Yeah. I understand, Omar."

"These kids are going to crack sooner or later," Omar said. "And that will be bad for us. Real bad. So just be ready—we'll have to do something about it."

There was a moment of silence while Jedthus processed this. Then he licked his lips. "You mean—"

"I mean that action will be taken. But not now. We've got to deal with the camp first. Okay?"

"Yeah." Jedthus tipped his hat back, passed a hand over his forehead. "Yeah, I understand."

Omar moved back to the table and began to stuff Knox's paraphernalia back in the aspirin bottle. "For right now," he said. "Just get Knox on his feet. Give him enough privacy to pop his pills or whatever. Then get out to the camp and do the job."

Jedthus's eyes turned hard. "I understand," he said.

"I'm going back to the courthouse and cover y'all's asses with the authorities, just like I planned."

"I'll give you a ride."

"No. I'll walk. You stay here with Knox."

Omar stepped out of the shop and a lance of sunlight drove straight through his brain. He swayed on his feet.

This is going to be over soon, he told himself. *Over.*

And then he'd feel better.

* * *

"Head for that gate," Nick said. "Fast as you can. Stop only to pick up guns and ammunition. Once you're out, get in among the cars. Some of you are going to have to run for those roadblocks."

The young men looked up at him, nodded gravely.

"Don't stop," Nick said again. "We're counting on you."

I am telling them how to commit suicide, Nick thought. He wondered if they knew that.

He had a military force of sorts, composed of almost all the able men in the camp, along with some of the women, all recruited overnight by the various camp committees. Nick was a kind of general, at least insofar as they all were supposed to be following his plan. They were divided into three groups. The Warriors—younger men and women, mostly—would hold off the bad guys while the others made their escape. The Home Guard—older but able-bodied—were supposed to look after the women, children, and old people, and escort them to a place of safety while the Warriors held off any pursuit.

The third group were the ones Nick had called the Samurai, though he privately thought of them as the Kamikaze. They were the ones who were trusted with the camp's meager store of firearms, because they professed themselves good with guns.

Their job was to kill guards. They said they were ready to do this. The odds said they would probably die trying.

It was small comfort that they had all volunteered.

"Don't forget," Nick said. "Keep moving. Don't get bogged down. We're counting on you."

His father would know just how to do this, Nick thought. His father had been trained in how to send people to their deaths. How to act. How to think about it all.

Just thinking about what was going to happen to his little army made Nick tremble at the knees.

He'd talked to all of them, he thought. The afternoon sun was burning down on him and making his head throb. He needed something to drink. The deputies still hadn't come.

His father would quote Sun Tzu, he thought. Chinese military strategy was one of his passions. Cold analysis, life and death, marches and battles, but written all in poetry.

To win one hundred victories in one hundred battles is not the zenith of achievement. His father loved that passage. *To subdue the enemy without fighting is the zenith of achievement.*

We've already lost the chance not *to fight,* Nick thought. *And one victory in one battle is all I ask.*

Okay, Sun? he thought. *Okay, Dad?*

Nick gave his doomed soldiers the floppy-wristed homeboy handshake—*My God,* he thought at the touch of palm on palm, *we are surely going to die*—and then he hobbled to the cookhouse. Pain throbbed through his kidney at every step. Drank his glass of water, then poured another glass over his head in hopes it would cool him off.

He shook his head, and droplets of water showered the ground around him. The air hung torrid and oppressive, so sultry that Nick felt as if he were moving under water. One of the workers in the cookhouse gave him a cracker and a scoop of rice, leftovers from the noon meal that he'd missed, and he ate them.

"Excuse me?"

Nick turned to the speaker, a youngish white man with short-cropped hair bleached white by the sun. Nick blinked at the strange figure. One day in the camp, he thought, and now the very fact of a Caucasian seemed odd. The man held out his hand.

"Jack Taylor," he said. Nick shook the hand.

"Nick Ruford."

Taylor's green eyes looked sidelong at the others in the camp. "Listen," he said. "I know something's up. And I want to be a part of it. You know what I'm saying?"

Nick looked at him warily. "Why ask me?"

"Because it's centered around you." Taylor licked his lips. "Look," he said. "Nobody will talk to me. And I understand why, okay. Nobody trusts me. But listen—" A dogged look entered his eyes. "My *wife* is black. My stepkid is black. My children are half-black. They're all in here with me. And you'd have to be crazy to think I wouldn't fight for them. I *want* to fight for them. I want to be a part of what's happening. Can you fix it?"

Nick thought for a moment. Taylor was sincere, he saw, and angry. But this fight, when it happened, was going to be a mob scene, a giant gang rumble. With the exception of a deputy or two, nobody was wearing uniforms on either side. In a mess like that, that blond head might be all anyone would see. Taylor could have both sides trying to kill him.

Nick looked for him. "How many kids do you have?"

"Two. And my step-daughter. They're all here."

Nick took a breath. "Jack," he said, "the best thing you can do in this situation is stick with your family. Try and keep them safe." *And let them keep you safe,* he added mentally.

"Damn it!" Taylor said. "Why don't you trust me?"

"I trust you fine," Nick said. "But when these people get out past that fence they are going to turn into a mob, and it's the mob I don't trust."

"I want to fight!"

Nick put a hand on Taylor's shoulder. Taylor shrugged it off. Nick sighed.

"Look, I can't give you orders. If you want to do something, listen for orders for the Home Guard. Somebody says Home Guard do this, you do it. But wait till the mob calms down first, or you'll get lynched."

Taylor turned and stalked away without a further word. Nick looked after him, sighed.

Lost one, he thought, *and the fight hasn't even started. What else* haven't *I done right?*

Nick found Manon sitting on the ground in the shade of one of the cotton wagons. He squatted by her and asked her how she was.

"All right. This is where the children and I agreed to meet when—" She hesitated. "When whatever is going to happen happens."

"That's good. Keep together."

She looked at him. There was a distant, mournful look in her eyes, the eyes of a woman much older than her years. He realized with surprise that she resembled her aunt Penelope, her father's half-sister, who had been twenty years older.

"I keep thinking about Frankland," Manon said. "About Rails Bluff. It was crazy there, but—" She bit her lip. "Frankland was different from these people. He was kind of goofy. He meant well. He wanted to build Heaven there, in his camp." She shook her head. "These people here, they set out to build Hell. And they built it. And nobody's even *noticed*."

Nick took her hand. "We'll make people notice," he said.

"I keep thinking about my family," Manon said. "We left them in Rails Bluff. And we thought we were the lucky ones."

"Baby," Nick said, "one of those deputies—the little one who shot Miss Deena, the skinhead—he's got your Gros-Papa's watch."

She looked at him in shock. "What?" she stammered. "What are you saying?"

"Some of these people, they must have been traveling around in all this chaos. Robbing people, and—" He shook his head. "They must have been in Toussaint before they came here."

Manon's chin began to tremble. She clutched at his hand. "Oh, Nick," she said. "Oh, Nick, you've got to stop them."

"Yes," he patted her hand. "Yes, I'll stop them. I'll stop them for you."

"We got this by express," said Nelda. She had a strange, expectant smile on her face. "I think you'll like it," she said.

Jessica put her cup of coffee on its desk, took the air envelope from her secretary, hefted the envelope. It was surprisingly heavy and obviously had a lot of paper in it. Jessica sighed—she'd just had her eye repaired that morning and wanted to avoid too much reading—and then she slid out the contents.

A magazine slipped through her fingers and dropped into her lap. Her own face scowled back at her from under the brim of her helmet. "Oh, my God," Jessica said.

It was a special edition of *Newsweek* dealing with the quakes and their aftermath. A particularly determined-looking photo of Jessica was on the cover, glaring at the camera through her black eye. The photo seemed to have been taken at the ceremony and press conference at Poinsett Island.

GENERAL J.C. FRAZETTA, it said on the magazine cover, AMERICA'S RIVER WARRIOR.

"Oh, my God," Jessica repeated.

"That nice Mr. Sutter wrote it." Nelda beamed.

Jessica stared at the picture of herself in shock. *I need to lose ten pounds* fast, she thought.

"Which one was Sutter?" she asked.

"He was here for several days, remember? He talked to all of us about you."

"Was he the one with the hair?"

"The hair. The face. The body. You know."

Apparently Jessica *didn't* know. She was surprised at herself. She'd been so busy she hadn't even had the chance to ogle a good-looking guy.

She'd probably seen only the press pass, and then did her best to politely ignore him.

She opened the magazine and scanned at random. "Frazetta's lucid briefings," it said, "did much to clarify the situation in the Delta during the days following the first May quake."

So *that's* what they did, Jessica thought in surprise. She'd had the impression she'd been talking to a roomful of deranged, bloodthirsty, invincibly ignorant maniacs who insisted on interpreting her every word in the most sensational, dangerous, provocative way possible. An opinion that seemed borne out by the next part of the article that fell beneath Jessica's eye.

"Sources report that Frazetta, inspired by her vision of turning Poinsett Landing into an island, ran over all opposition at one of her daily council briefings and successfully commandeered the resources to carry out her project."

Untrue! she thought. No one had objected to the project at all, at least not to her. And the project had been Larry Hallock's idea, not hers.

She briefly meditated a letter to *Newsweek* on this matter. *While gratified by your otherwise flattering portrait, I beg to state . . .*

"Such steamroller tactics," the article continued, "were unlikely to work with the President, whose defenses were put to the test when Frazetta personally phoned him to insist on the controversial evacuation of the Lower Mississippi . . ."

"Hey, babe," said Pat as he came into Jessica's tent. "I heard you got a present."

"It has a nice picture of you," Jessica said, presenting her husband his picture, which showed him with the banjo he'd brought to the camp.

His eyes narrowed critically. "Do I really look that old? I look like a *geezer.*"

"In my eyes you're forever young," Jessica said, and glanced down again at the article to read the summary of her "most controversial" decision: the intervention at Rails Bluff. There was a sidebar concerning the reactions of unnamed but highly miffed Justice Department officials, who claimed that the situation in Rails Bluff clearly called for Justice Department expertise, that the use of the military in a situation of this sort was a dangerous precedent.

Oh yeah, Jessica thought. Like the Justice Department could even *get* their people to Rails Bluff. *We'd have to carry them in our helicopters,* she thought, *and hold their hands all the way to the camp. And even then they'd bungle it.*

Still, she would have to bear the Justice Department in mind. Her superiors had warned her that the Civil Rights division was looking into her handling of the matter, in case she'd violated peoples' rights while freeing them from gun-toting lunatics, but she'd been too busy to worry much about it. Maybe she should talk to someone high up in the Judge-Advocate General's office and make sure her ass was sufficiently covered.

"Hey," Pat said, "no fair skipping around. Let's start at the beginning."

They read the article from beginning to end. Jessica decided she was pleased with it on the whole.

"Though it makes me seem like such a pushy broad," she said.

"You *are* a pushy broad," Pat said chivalrously.

"Yeah, thanks." Jessica reached for her cup of coffee.

"You'd better call your mom," Pat said, "and tell her to go to the news dealer and reserve her twenty copies."

"Twenty?" Jessica mused. "No—for Ma, more like fifty."

It was then that Nelda came through the tent flap again. Once again she had a pleased, *I've-got-a-secret* look. "General?" she said. "There's a call for you on the radio. Secured line. From the President."

As she rushed to the communications tent, Jessica found herself brushing at her clothes as if for an inspection. She picked up the handset, said, "Sir? Mr. President?"

There was a moment of silence as words passed back and forth between satellite relays. "Jessica?" he said. "How do you do?"

"I'm fine, sir. And you?"

"I am fit as a fiddle and strong as a bull. I dominate the world as a colossus. I rival the sun as a source of radiance, and I am a nexus of power acknowledged by all the world."

Jessica blinked, uncertain quite how to respond. "I'm pleased to hear it, sir," she said finally.

"The only cloud on the horizon, Jessica," the President said. "The only fly in the ointment, the only blot on my escutcheon, in fact the only taint on my total omnipotence, is the fact that someone has usurped my rightful place on the cover of *Newsweek*."

Jessica's heart gave a lurch. "In *fact*—" The President's voice rose in volume. "In *fact*, I shall have to devote much of my attention to *making that person's life a complete and utter hell on earth*."

"Um," said Jessica, paralyzed. "Well."

The President barked a laugh. "Congratulations, Jessica.

Well done. I really had you going there for a moment, didn't I?"

Jessica felt sweat trickle down her nose. "Yes," she said. "Yes, you did."

"My staff insisted that I take a few days off and relax at Camp David. That's where I'm calling from. It's so dull here that I have no choice but to amuse myself by making prank phone calls to my subordinates."

"I hope it's not *that* dull, sir."

"Well, no, not entirely, not with Chinese missile tests and the menace of the Gamsakhurdians. I just wanted to congratulate you on your celebrity. And besides, I got the cover of *US News and World Report.* Unfortunately those swine at *Time* decided to devote their cover to some little pasty-faced urchin being rescued from the roof of his momma's car by one of your helicopters."

"Better luck next time, sir," Jessica said.

The President laughed. "Yes!" he said. His voice was manic. "Better luck next time! Exactly!"

Jessica's head swam. This was decidedly strange. The President seemed to be calling her from well beyond the ozone layer.

"I wanted to give you a little friendly advice in view of your current celebrity," the President said. "You're going to start hearing from people now—people in *my* line of work, you understand."

"Yes, sir."

"They're going to want to talk to you about running for office. Maybe even for *my* job."

Jessica answered quickly. "Mr. President, I have never even for a moment considered—"

"Don't get your knickers in a twist, Jessica," the President said. "I don't give a hang if you run or don't. What I wanted to say is this—they won't be approaching you because they admire your brilliant political thinking. They'll be approaching you not because you're the best candidate, but because you're a *viable* candidate. Because of that *Newsweek* cover and because you've got a very prominent job where you can score a lot of points with the public. And it won't be about *you*—it will be about *them*, you understand? It's their job to find people like you and groom them for office. It's their job to approach people and awaken ambitions that people never knew they had, and the more ambition they can find in you, the more they can generate business for themselves. That's how these people work."

Jessica's head swam. "I understand, Mr. President."

"Now if you've always wanted to run for office, that's fine. I can even introduce you to some people—people who work for *my* party, you understand. But if you have never thought of a career in public service, then I urge you to think long and hard before you give any kind of answer at all to these people."

"The only career in public service I've ever wanted," Jessica said, in all truth, "was in the military."

The President cackled. "That's a good one, Jessica!" he said. "That's exactly what you tell those bastards! That's my little politician!"

Jessica blinked. "Thank you, sir," she said.

The President cleared his throat. "Now, if you don't mind one last piece of advice . . ."

"By all means, sir."

"If you value your career, Jessica, try not to shoot up any more churches. Because then even I won't be able to save your ass, okay?"

Jessica hesitated, trying to read the tone of the President's voice in order to determine whether he was joking again or not. She decided she might as well reply with the truth, pedantic though it might be.

"Well, Mr. President," she said, "it wasn't actually a church. It was a radio station."

The President paused for a moment, then barked out another laugh. "Oh, it was the *media*!" he said. "In that case, I'm sure they got everything they deserved!"

The conversation ended shortly thereafter. Jessica put down the handset and walked past expectant-looking techs to her tent.

Gamsakhurdians, she thought. The President had men-

tioned the menace of the Gamsakhurdians. She made a note
to herself to find out who the Gamsakhurdians were, and
what they were up to.

Once her present job was over, the President might need
an officer who was on top of the Gamsakhurdian situation.

She passed Nelda at her desk, then entered her tent and sat
behind her desk.

Pat looked at her. "What'd the man say, Jess?"

Jessica pitched her voice so that Nelda could hear. *Give her
a thrill*, she thought.

"He said it was okay by him if I run for President," she
said.

The President returned the handset to an aide, then looked at
Stan Burdett. "There we go," he said.

"Do you think she'll bite?" Stan asked.

"I think it's more than possible. Give her a couple days to
let it all sink in, then have Bill Marcus give her a call."

"Bill's the best in the business. If he can't talk her into running, I don't know who can."

The President leaned back into the deep leather armchair
and put his feet up on the coffee table. One thing you could
say for the semirustic decor of the presidential retreat of
Camp David, nobody cared if you got scuff marks on the furniture.

The President scratched his chin. A faint sadness penetrat-
ed his detachment. "Jessica's a nice lady," he said. "I should
feel like a complete shit for doing this to her."

But the Party needed a winner, and here was Jessica
Frazetta piling up endless good-will points throughout the
heart of the country. It was hard not to endear yourself to
people by feeding starving families and plucking their children from floods. In the next election, three senatorial seats
and a half-dozen governors' positions would be up for grabs,
all from the Mississippi Valley. Jessica had made herself a
viable candidate for any one of them.

"The only question," the President said, "is whether she
decides she's a member of the Party or not."

"She's always registered as an independent," Stan said. "A lot of those military types do."

"Well," the President said, "if she has the good sense to decide to come to the aid of the Party, I can help her out before she declares, pin a nice big medal on her—the Soldier's Medal, maybe? And if she decides she's a member of the opposition," he sighed, "then we conclude she blew religious freedom to tiny pieces when she went into Rails Bluff, and the attorney general takes her down while our hands stay clean."

He swung his legs down from the coffee table and rose to his feet. He looked at Stan. "It's a no-brainer," he said. "You want to go for a walk?"

Pine scent filled the air as the President strolled along the open paths. Wind floated through the trees with the sound of a mother hushing her child. It was pleasantly cool here in Catoctin Mountain Park, and a pleasant change from Washington, where summer heat and humidity was already smothering the city.

It was a beautiful, tranquil moment. But then *all* the President's moments were tranquil these days. All moments were more or less like the next. It was an illustration of the Steady State theory of the President's psyche.

The President let his eyes drift over the tree-lined crest of the Blue Ridge Mountains. Hawks circled overhead, thermals lifting their outspread wings. "The Chinese fired three missiles," he said. "They all landed more or less where they were intended to land. The U.S. Navy gallantly protected Taiwan by being nowhere in the vicinity. The Chinese government has announced that this round of tests is over, and it looks as if their military forces across the Straits have stood down."

"The Seventh Fleet saves the day," Stan said.

"But for how much longer?" the President asked. "We're in no state to fight a war. The quakes have wrecked all that. Even if we have the capacity, the people won't stand for it— we can't fight any kind of conflict while millions of our own citizens are condemned to living in tents. We're going to have to pull in our heads for ten years or more." He looked at Stan. "You're the expert on spin. How long can you spin that?"

Stan adjusted his spectacles. "Sooner or later, you think someone will call our bluff?"

The President watched clouds drifting beyond the Blue Ridge. He'd had an insight about clouds some days ago, he seemed to remember, but he could not bring it to mind.

"Some people have nothing left to lose," the President said. "Others have everything to gain. There's a worldwide recession in progress, and that will make some people desperate. And there are so many flash-points now. Conflicts are almost all ethnic or religious these days, and those are the kinds of wars that are most difficult to stop once they get started. Once you start to kill your neighbors, you can't *stop*, now, can you? Stopping just gives them the opportunity to kill *you*. And it's worse when *God* starts telling you to kill. You can't stop if it's God doing the talking. The Ayatollah business is really prospering. Like that fellow in Arkansas that Jessica had to put down. How do you stop someone who *wants* the world to end? There's no way to negotiate. There's no common ground."

"Sometimes, Mr. President," Stan said, "you *can't* negotiate. You just do what you've promised to do."

The President looked at him. "Are you suggesting that a politician should keep his promises? How unlike you. I'm almost shocked."

Stan frowned. "Only when your back's to the wall, sir. And then when someone calls your bluff, I think that person, or his followers, should be swiftly and efficiently reduced to smoking debris. If you pick your target properly—if it's someone you *can* reduce to smoking debris—it will make an impression on other like-minded individuals."

A smile drifted across the President's face. "I was just thinking how much I would welcome not having to be the head of the world's only superpower. And now you want me to start blowing things up."

Stan gave a tight little smile. "It should be a very controlled explosion, sir."

"Ah. Battling on the symbolic plane, but with live ammunition. Always a delicate business."

The President walked for a while in silence. Bluebirds flickered through the trees like bits of the sky fallen and blown about like snow.

"We shall have to try to strengthen our international institutions. NATO, the UN, the various regional alliances. I'll have to send Darrell abroad to talk to them all. Tell them we can *lead*, but that they will have to follow with more willingness and more force than we've seen heretofore." He shrugged. "Maybe it will work. I don't have a lot of hope, since nations tend to be run either by cowards or psychopaths, and we've mostly got the cowards. But it seems the best we can do, and if anyone can wring commitments out of them, it will be Darrell the Happy Warrior."

"He can be persuasive, Mr. President."

"He has the advantage of actually believing what he is saying." He stopped, frowned at the sight of hawks rising on the afternoon thermals. "And our *national* institutions could use some strengthening, as well. When I flew over the Mississippi Delta the other day, I saw nothing but islands. Everything that holds a people together was severed—communications, commerce, community. Boris Lipinsky tells me that large parts of the country will go for six to nine months without basic services—not even electricity. Not even telephones. And hundreds of thousands of people, maybe millions, will be living in refugee camps for much longer than that. You can't expect them to be civil forever, not under that sort of pressure.

"How many will fall through the cracks?" the President wondered. "How many thousands can just *disappear* without anyone noticing they're gone? That Arkansas pastor and his private refugee camp—that man had a *radio station* broadcasting across the whole Delta, and nobody noticed he was there. I wonder how many others are setting up in their eerie little tribal habitats without anyone seeing them? It was sort of like the Balkans, in a way. Except," he conceded, "that the Balkans are mountains and this was a river, but it was the same, almost. Everyone cut off from everyone else. In the Balkans, they've been hating and fighting each other for thousands of years, as far back as history goes. And in the Mississippi Delta—well, who knows? They're all on islands."

He looked at Stan. "How are you going to spin your messages to them, Stan, when there's no way to find your audience?"

Stan Burdett looked pensive. "There was a way once. People lived out there before there was electricity or radio, and they were still a part of the republic."

"They had a ruling class. All those planters. The people did what the planters told them." He smiled. "Like Judge Chivington's family. They could deliver fifty thousand votes; they ran that part of Texas like they were little kings. But nobody can deliver those votes anymore, not consistently. It's still corrupt there, but it's nothing like it was." He shrugged. "But now, who knows? Who knows what's out there?"

The President gave a big smile, then laughed. "If you spin a message but there's no one to hear it, is there a message? That's what we should be considering."

Stan seemed glum. "If you say so, sir."

"I had a dream about bread yesterday. Did I mention my dream about bread?"

"No."

"UFOs are made of bread. It's a true fact."

Stan just looked at him. The President clapped Stan on the shoulder. "Oh, never mind," he said. "Let's just walk along and enjoy the country."

Islands, the President thought, the Balkans. He was finding equivalencies everywhere.

The previous day's breeze had died away entirely, leaving a sultry, expectant stillness in its wake. Nick slept the latter part of the afternoon away beneath the pecan tree used by the Escape Committee. Aftershocks shivered the leaves over his head. The camp was quiet in the moist afternoon heat, everyone trying to stay cool, and the deputies didn't come. Nick's thoughts drifted like the distant clouds, remote from the world.

The longer before the deputies came, he thought as he lay beneath the tree, the more time the deputies had to make plans. Nick didn't like to think about that.

His father, he thought, would have a quote from Sun Tzu that was appropriate to the occasion. *If you have a clue, let the enemy think you are clueless. Let the enemy believe you are wise on the occasions when you don't know shit from Shinola.*

Or something like that.

The westward-drifting sun shone hot on his eyelids. He shifted beneath the tree, put the shadow of a branch over his face. The leaves rustled pleasantly overhead.

What is of the greatest importance in war is to strike at the enemy strategy. Sun Tzu's words, in the accents of General Jon Ruford, floated into his mind. So, he thought, what was the enemy strategy?

Obviously, to keep the refugees in the camp, and to keep the world from finding out what they were doing.

Escaping from the camp would strike at the first object of the strategy. But what would strike at the second?

Making phone calls to the media and the authorities, he supposed. But both were far away, and the locals phones supposedly didn't work, and even if the state police or the Army heard of the horrors in Spottswood Parish they might not be able to respond quickly.

There were a couple dozen deputies involved with what was happening in the camp, and some of them, like the sheriff, hadn't been seen in days. This suggested that the other inhabitants of Spottswood Parish—and there had to be thousands—either knew nothing of what was happening here, or were taking good care not to know. The Klan sheriff, or someone, was managing events so that it was difficult to find out what was happening here.

Nick wished he could grind the whole sordid scene right into the faces of the world.

Then he sat up suddenly. The sun shining through tree

limbs blinded him for an instant, and in the flash of unexpected light he knew how to proceed.

"We go to Shelburne City," he said aloud. Two members of the Escape Committee looked at him.

"I take the Warriors to Shelburne City," Nick said. "Just like Sun Tzu."

Nick remembered the details only vaguely. Back in ancient China, Kingdom A had been on the verge of defeating Kingdom B. Sun Tzu, who commanded the army of Kingdom C, was ordered to go to the aid of the beleaguered Kingdom B. But instead of reinforcing Kingdom B, he took his whole army and marched straight for the capital of Kingdom A, which forced the enemy to retreat from Kingdom B to defend their own country. Sun Tzu caught the army on the march and destroyed it, winning the war.

Nick had planned for the Warriors to stay in the area of the camp as a rear guard while the rest of the refugees evacuated to a more defensible area. But that was surrendering initiative to the enemy. It would allow them all the time they needed to gather their forces and respond.

What Nick needed to do was to force the issue by attacking Kingdom A. He needed to take the Warriors right into Shelburne City and seize a big, defensible building in as public a place as possible. The people in the parish couldn't ignore *that*. They would have to start asking questions. The enemy would have to respond to that first, they couldn't go haring off into the countryside looking for escaped refugees. They would have to meet Nick on their own ground.

Stumbling over words in his haste, Nick told his plan to the Escape Committee. Reaction seemed divided.

"Running into town like that, you could get surrounded by a thousand crackers," said one. "It could be like John Wayne at the Alamo."

"The Alamo was a *success*," Nick said. "The Alamo delayed things long enough for the rest of the Texans to get their act together and win the war."

In the end, Nick got his way. The others had no better plan to offer.

The shadows had grown long. People began to line up for dinner. "Best go get our sand buggers," one of the men said, and the Escape Committee rose to their feet and began to trudge toward the cookhouse.

The silence of the early evening was broken by the sound of truck engines, revving as they rolled along the broken roads from the direction of town.

There was sudden stillness in camp as everyone paused, frozen in the midst of their motion, to listen. Nick's pulse was suddenly loud in his ears. "They're coming!" someone said, and suddenly everyone was moving.

"Calm, people!" It seemed to Nick as if the reluctant words had stuck to the inside of his throat, and he had to peel them off with an act of will and throw them into the air. "No running! No shouting!"

Guards surrounded the camp. What they saw had to be refugees milling around, not fighters taking their posts.

Nick made himself walk carefully to the cookhouse, where Armando Gurulé had set up the master control for the claymores. He felt strangely lightheaded, as if he might topple over at any minute. At one point he realized he'd forgotten to breathe, and when he let the breath out and took in another the air was sweeter than anything he'd tasted in his life.

He found Armando standing by the control board in the shade of the cookhouse. People were running madly through the camp, parents scooping up their children and trying to find cover. Nick hoped that to the guards this looked like a normal reaction to an approach by the deputies.

Nick stood in silence. *Just let them get close,* he thought.

Two five-ton trucks pulled off the road in front of the camp, and began backing toward the gate. Over intervening heads, tents, and awnings, Nick saw some other vehicles and some Caucasian heads bobbing around. Nick didn't see the crop-haired runt who had Gros-Papa's watch, but that didn't mean he wasn't there. He glanced left and right and behind and saw, glimpsed through trees and tents and awnings, deputies taking up station on the perimeter.

To Nick's right, wrapped in plastic and blankets, were the

bodies of Miss Deena and the other gunshot victim. Nick felt a chill brush his spine as he saw them. Just behind him an old woman was flipping sand bugger patties on the big outdoor grill. She frowned at her work in a business-like way and wielded her big spatula as if there weren't a pair of bodies within thirty feet of her, and as if all hell wasn't about to break loose any second.

"Maybe it's a food delivery," Armando said.

"Maybe," Nick said. He didn't think so.

One of the trucks backed right up to the entrance. A big, thick-knuckled uniformed deputy—the man who had made the announcements yesterday—got on the back of a truck and raised a bullhorn to his lips.

"The other camp has been completed," he said. "And we're moving you-all there, so that the A.M.E. can have their property back and get this mess cleaned up. I hope there is not a repetition of what happened yesterday. So what I want y'all to do is get your needcessities, make a nice line on your side of the gate, then just set there and wait for your name to be called."

There was silence in the camp. No one showed any sign of gathering their belongings or getting into line. Then, from somewhere out on the right, Nick heard someone begin to boo, as if he was protesting a decision by the umpire at a baseball game. The voice was deep and resonant and rumbled through the air like thunder. More people began to take up the call. The sound rose from the camp as if the earth was mocking the sky. Catcalls and jeers filled the air. Some people began banging on pans or other metal objects. The clattering noise echoed from the trees, causing startled birds to take to the air. Somewhere, someone started blowing on a whistle.

Nick saw the deputy using the bullhorn again, but beneath the defiant tumult heard nothing of what the man said. He saw the man look down at someone else, lower the bullhorn, give a shrug.

They'll move now, Nick thought. He craned for a view, saw little over the intervening obstacles. He looked behind him, saw the old woman still minding her vegetable patties. "'Scuse me, ma'am," he said, and stepped up onto the brick wall of the grill, balanced between air and the gridiron.

An irregular line of deputies was moving toward the front gate carrying weapons. Last time, Nick thought, they came in shooting into the air, tried to stampede everyone.

He licked his lips, looked down at Armando. "Better get ready," he said.

Armando looked down at his control board, flipped one of the two switches that would trigger the mines.

The deputies were standing by the gate waiting for the big man, who had dropped off the gate of the truck, put down his bullhorn, and picked up a shotgun. Nick couldn't tell if the gate had been unlocked yet or not. The leader approached the gate with a lazy stride, then made a gesture with one arm and moved his shotgun to port arms.

Any second now, Nick thought. Waves of heat rose from the grill, almost smothered him. He could feel sweat popping out on his forehead. The catcalls from the refugees rose to a crescendo.

The gate swung inward behind a line of hustling deputies. The big leader pulled trigger on his shotgun once, firing into the air. That boom triggered more noise from the camp, catcalls mixed with a rising defiant screech. The hair on the back of Nick's neck rose at the sound, at the primal challenge that must have first sounded in Africa a million years ago, when one prehuman clan first challenged another for mastery of the savanna.

The deputies came into the camp at a run, weapons carried high. The crowd fell back, yelling and whistling. The attackers moved fast, faster than Nick had expected. Another second or two they would run right over the mines.

"Jesus!" Nick said in a burst of terror. "Fire!"

Armando threw the second switch. The mines went off with a deep concussion that staggered the earth like an aftershock—Nick swayed on his perch—and then the air was filled with weird whirring, yowling sounds, airy demons unleashed, as the mines flung their strange munitions, the screws and stones and bits of jagged metal, the nails and cable and used razor blades. Nick heard a sound like a tortured animal as something flew past his head.

There was an instant of silence. Nick couldn't see anything—there was dust and debris in the air—and then there was a shot, another deep shotgun boom.

"*Go!*" Nick shouted. "*Go! Now! Go, go!*"

A sudden howl rose from the camp, a song of triumph and blood and vengeance, and Nick saw a wave of people charging forward into the murky air. Nick's nerves answered with a mad song of berserk joy.

There were more shots, and Nick heard a crack close to his ear like someone snapping his fingers. With a sudden jolt of fear he realized that a bullet had just flown by his head, and that standing on the grille made him a perfect target. He swayed for a moment in sudden vertigo, then jumped to the ground to see Armando carefully turning both the switches on his control.

"If there was a misfire," he said, "we don't want them going off *now*."

"Gotta get up there," Nick said, as much to himself as Armando. There were a lot of shots now, including the sustained, stunning clamor of at least one of the deputies' machine pistols. Nick looked around for a weapon—he hadn't thought to provide himself with one—and saw the old lady carefully crouched down behind the brick walls of the barbecue grille, clutching her spatula as if it were a spear. It was probably the safest place to be in the whole camp.

Nick didn't want to wrestle the old lady for her spatula, so he gave up his search for a weapon and ran forward into the melee. The dust in the air had dispersed, and Nick saw a dozen bodies lying in the dirt. Most were deputies, but some were not. The bodies of the deputies were surrounded by clumps of refugees stripping them of their weapons. A pair of deputies retreated through the gate, a wave of club-waving refugees close behind. One of the deputies was wounded and had his arm around the shoulders of the second, who was supporting him in his withdrawal while firing back into the advancing crowd with a pistol. One of the pursuers sprawled to earth, and then with a series of triumphant cries the two deputies were engulfed by the wave of attackers. Nick saw knives and cudgels rising and falling, heard bone-chilling screams from one of the fallen.

He kept going. *Don't stop except to pick up a weapon.* That's what he'd told everyone. The heavy air labored through his lungs. *"Keep moving!"* he gasped. *"Keep moving!"*

The air was full of gunfire, but Nick couldn't see who was shooting, or at whom. He burst free of the gate—a yell of defiance rose to his lips—and then he was in the parking lot. Some of the cars had suffered cracked windshields from the claymores' munitions. Shotguns boomed. Nick crouched low between two cars.

Gather in the parking lot where there's cover. Take your car keys. Start your cars and get ready to move out on a signal.

That's what he'd told his army. But he didn't have any car keys, he didn't have a car; he'd have to wait for others. He leaned his back against one of the cars, tried to catch his breath, mopped sweat off his forehead with his sleeve.

"Warriors!" he shouted. "Warriors! This way!"

He wondered what was happening in the camp. Bullets snapping overhead convinced Nick that it wouldn't be wise to stick his head up and find out.

Whoever was firing the machine pistol had stopped. That was good, at least.

Nick heard a car door slam, then the grind of a starter and the roar of the engine. Bent in a crouch, he began moving in the direction of the sound.

And then he turned around the front end of a Chevy pick-up and came face-to-face with the enemy: the big deputy who had been giving the orders.

The deputy was in cover between the pickup and a Pontiac wagon. He crouched in front of the Chevy, leaning against its bumper. His hat had been knocked off, and his forehead badly gouged by one of the claymores' weird munitions. Blood ran down his face, spattered his khaki uniform. He still carried his shotgun in both hands. His left hand was bloody where the middle finger had been shot or blown or blasted off.

At the sight of the man, Nick's blood seemed to flash into steam. The deputy looked at Nick in surprise as Nick came running around the truck's fender. Maybe he'd been deafened by the mines and hadn't heard him coming. Nick could smell the man's sweat. He screamed and lunged at the man.

The deputy lifted the shotgun in both hands to fend Nick off, and Nick grabbed the shotgun and drove into the man, knocking the startled deputy on his back. They sprawled onto the soil of the parking lot, Nick on top. He scrambled to a crouch above his enemy, his hands still gripping the gun. The barrel was slick with the deputy's blood. The deputy writhed under Nick, trying to throw him off, bucking like a horse. Nick bore down with all his weight onto the shotgun, trying to press the gun against the deputy's throat and strangle him.

They both gasped for breath in the hot afternoon air. Nick drove the shotgun down, toes digging into the soil, slipping on the slick grass. His sweat dripped onto the deputy's face. The deputy blinked blood from his eyes, saw the barrel coming near his throat. His eyes widened as he saw the danger, and then Nick saw determination enter the deputy's face; the deputy gave a long, growling exhalation as he gathered his power and began to press Nick back like a weightlifter bench-pressing a set of barbells. To Nick's astonishment the deputy lifted him upward, pressing him into the air no matter how much weight Nick put on the shotgun.

Terror sang through Nick. If the deputy could throw him off, then he could finish Nick through superior strength.

The deputy's body gave a heave under Nick as he positioned himself for greater effort. From the way the deputy shifted, Nick realized he had one leg between the two legs of the deputy, and with a roar he shifted his own weight, pivoting off the shotgun as if it were a high bar in gymnastics, and dropped his knee with full force into the deputy's groin.

The deputy's eyes popped, and his breath went out of him in a great whoosh. Instead of bearing down further on the shotgun, Nick pulled at it, trying to snatch it out of the deputy's grip. *"Mine!"* he shouted.

The barrel of the shotgun came free from the deputy's maimed left hand. Nick tried a final wrench to yank it entirely free, but the barrel hit the chromed front end of the Chevy, cramping Nick's movement, and the deputy hung on with his big right hand. Nick yanked the gun back and forth, banging the weapon into the Chevy and the Pontiac wagon on the other side, until he realized that the deputy was reaching his left hand across his front, toward the pistol that was holstered at his belt.

"No!" Nick yelled. He hammered at the deputy's wounded hand with his right fist. The deputy gave a gasp of pain and surprise and snatched his hand back. Nick gave a wrench to the shotgun, managed to break it free of the deputy's grip.

"Mine!" he shouted, and smashed the butt of the shotgun into the deputy's face. The deputy gave a convulsive heave under Nick and almost threw him off. The man's hands clawed blindly upward, trying to grab the shotgun again or defend himself. Nick slipped the gun butt into the deputy's guard and smashed him again in the face. Blood spattered from the gouge on the man's forehead. *"Mine!"* Nick cried. *"My gun!"* He smashed another time. The deputy arched his back and Nick drove the gun butt again into his face.

"Mine! Mine!" The shotgun rose and fell. *"Mine! Mine, you bastard!"*

Nick stopped striking only when he ran out of breath. Both Nick and the deputy were spattered with blood.

A cry of savage joy rose in Nick's heart. He lurched to his feet, brandished the bloody shotgun over his head. *"Warriors!"* he screamed to the heavens. *"Warriorrrrrrrrs!"*

The shout was taken up by the other fighters now streaming through the parking lot. Some waved guns, others clubs. The shooting seemed far less intense than it had been, though a shot that snapped over Nick's head drove him again into a crouch.

He looked down at the deputy lying at his feet and felt his

raging triumph die and turn to cold, creeping horror. Dazedly, Nick read the plastic name tag on the deputy's uniform. *Jedthus C. Carter.* His head swam. He closed his eyes. He had done this, had beaten this man to death with his own weapon.

"Move! Keep moving!" People shouted to each other as they ran through the parking lot.

Nausea eddied through Nick's vitals. He put the shotgun down. He heard the thud of feet nearby. "Don't stop!" a woman's voice shouted close by.

Don't stop, Nick repeated to himself. *Don't stop except to pick up a weapon.* His own rules.

He reached blindly for the deputy's gun belt. The blood on the leather sent a surge of acid into his throat. His fingers felt thick as sausages as he tried to work the buckle.

"Go! Go!" someone shouted. "Get in the car!"

Go, Nick thought numbly. He finally got the belt open and pulled on it, rolled the deputy partly over and dragged the free end out from under. He rose to a crouch and stepped clear of the deputy and finally, now that he could look someplace other than the body, dared to open his eyes.

The gun belt dangled heavy from his hand. He saw the deputy's automatic pistol, a leather case for ammunition, another for hand cuffs, and a portable radio. Keys dangled from a spring-wound key ring.

"Warriors to the cars!" a woman shouted. "Home Guard give them cover!"

Those were Nick's own rules the woman was shouting. Nick listened dully as he blinked at the radio on his gun belt. Cars rumbled into life. Then Nick strapped the gun belt over his hips and picked up the shotgun and stepped from between the two vehicles, careful to keep his head down and lots of Detroit iron between himself and any likely enemy.

The deputy had a car, he thought. And these keys would fit it. It would be a good car, a fast car. And there would probably be ammunition and other supplies in it.

There was a shot from the southernmost of the two roadblocks, and a horrid scream from somewhere in the parking lot. Another voice began loudly to call on Jesus, a voice with a desperate keening edge that raised Nick's hackles. Nick bit down on the bile that rose in his throat at the sound, stuck his head up for only a brief instant.

There was only one police car in the area, parked next to one of the two trucks that had been backed up to the gate. During his escape Nick had run right past it without taking notice.

Nick ducked low, ran to the vehicle, and flung himself into the driver's seat. He kept his head below window level, picked what looked like a car key on the deputy's key ring, stuck it in the ignition, and turned it.

The engine roared into life like a beast emerging from hibernation. Air-conditioning began to blast cold air. The radio turned on as well.

"Miles," a voice said, "what's the situation now?"

"We got people runnin' all over the camp," another voice said. "I hear 'em startin' up some cars. We're keepin' their heads down, but I don't think we got any men left up there."

"Jedthus?"

"I don't know, Omar. I ain't seem him since the ruckus started."

"How about Knox an' them?"

"I think they're all gone, Omar."

There was a moment of silence. There was a bang from outside the car, then a sort of crunch from the radio, the sound of someone making a fast movement while holding the microphone.

"They're starting to shoot at us, Omar," the man said. "I think we may have to pull out."

"Fuck that," a third voice said, some distance from the mike. "I got bullets left."

"I'll leave it to you guys," said Omar. "I'm putting a posse together here, but if you think you need to hightail it out of there, you do that."

Run for it, you crackers, Nick thought. *Run for it, and we'll come for you.*

"Warriors to the cars!" people were shouting.

Nick opened the car door, stuck his head out, and shouted,

"Ready to move! If you're ready, honk your horn!"

He hit the horn, twice. Other horns began to take up the chorus.

The passenger door opened suddenly. Nick looked up in surprise, heart pounding. A man of thirty or so slid into the passenger seat—Nick knew he was among the Warriors, but didn't know his name. The man carried a big club and a large revolver, and there was a wild look in his eye.

"I'm ready, man," he said. "Ready to bust caps on some coneheads."

"Right," Nick said.

There was a chorus of horns outside, which Nick hoped were Warriors signaling they were ready, and not people blowing horns out of sheer exuberance.

"Let's go!" Nick bellowed out the door, and he put the car in reverse and began rolling it across the grass parking lot to the road. "Left and right!" he shouted. "Let's go!"

He shut the door and looked over his shoulder out the back window. Voices chattered on the radio, and Nick gathered that Omar, whoever he was, was having trouble assembling his scattered forces. *Don't worry, man,* Nick thought, *we'll be coming to you.*

Cars bumped onto the road and accelerated. They were heading for the two roadblocks north and south of the camp. The deputies at the roadblocks were armed with high-powered rifles that could kill at a distance, and Nick had reasoned that it was hopeless to shoot it out from the camp with that kind of firepower, not with the sorts of weapons that were likely to be liberated from the guards. Nick planned a vehicle assault, cars filled with Warriors charging the roadblocks to engage the deputies at close range, where the hunting rifles could be outgunned by pistols, shotguns, and if necessary clubs and knives.

Crossing the intervening distance, against those powerful rifles, was desperate. But Nick had already committed the Warriors to death, whether the Warriors themselves realized it or not. Enough of them would get through to kill the deputies, and that was all that mattered.

"Goddamn," Miles said over the radio. "They're pullin' out. They're heading for us."

"Clear out if you have to," Omar said.

The sheriff's car bounced as it backed onto the road. Nick swung the wheel, turned the car north, in the direction he hoped to help the camp inmates escape. He wanted that route to be open above all. There were already several cars ahead of him. Nick accelerated.

A lengthy series of shots rang out. Nick couldn't tell who was shooting: the guards or the escapees. Brake lights flashed ahead as the line of cars checked their speed. Nick growled his frustration and tapped the brakes.

One car rammed the roadblock. Cars swerved to the verge of the road, came to a stop. People burst from them, carrying weapons. Then the energy seemed to go out of them—they straightened out of their fighting crouches, let their weapons hang by their sides.

Nick pulled to a stop, ran from the car, and found out why the others had lost interest.

The deputies were already dead. One had been shot through the heart. The other had been hit in the midsection, crawled into the bar ditch, and bled to death.

Cudjo, Nick thought. Sitting in the woods with his deer rifle, picking off every deputy he could see.

There were crashes of metal-on-metal, a furious roll of gunfire from the other roadblock. Nick straightened, nerves leaping. He'd gone the wrong way.

"Get their guns," he said. "Get the ammunition. Bring their car."

By the time Nick got to the other roadblock, the fight was over. The driver of the first car to charge the roadblock had been killed by the rifles and his car spun off the road, but the second rammed the deputies' car, giving them the choice of jumping into the open or being hit by their own vehicle. The third car in line had hit one of the exposed deputies, throwing him fifty feet. He was hit so hard that he was literally knocked out of his boots. His partner had been run down in the field by a mob and shot to death. He carried a loaded rifle and a loaded pistol, but had been so terrified that he'd forgot to fire either one of them.

Nick got out of his car amid the crowd of fighters. They were jumping up and down, waving their liberated weapons over their heads, howling their victory.

Nick wandered among them, stunned.

He'd won. He'd won.

"Miles," the radio said. "Miles. What is your situation?"

Nick looked at the car. He got in the car, picked up the microphone, pressed the button on it with his thumb. Tried to still the tremor in his hand.

"Miles is dead, cracker," he said. "So are the others. What do you have to say to that, cracker?"

There was a moment of stunned silence. "Who *is* that?" said a voice. A voice that wasn't Omar's.

Nick felt his lips draw back in a savage snarl. "Jon C. Ruford, brigadier general, U.S. Army," he said. It was the least he could do in tribute to his father. It was all he could do to avoid mentioning Sun Tzu.

"You think I don't know about *camps*?" Nick said. "You think I don't know how to turn people in camps into *soldiers*?"

There was a moment of stunned silence. Nick forced a graveyard laugh.

"We got your friends' guns, cracker," Nick said. "We got more guns than *you* do now. You come visit the camp, cracker, and we'll make you real welcome."

He put the mike back on its hook. *Let them think we'll stay here at the camp*, he thought. *Let them think we're waiting for them.*

Please.

Fifteen minutes after seven o'clock, we had another shock. This one was the most severe one we have yet had—the darkness returned, and the noise was remarkably loud. The first motions of the earth were similar to the preceding shocks, but before they ceased we rebounded up and down, and it was with difficulty

*we kept our seats. At this instant I expected a dreadful catas-
trophe—the uproar among the people strengthened the colour-
ing of the picture—the screams and yells were heard at a great
distance.*

*Extract from a letter to a gentleman in Lexington, from
his friend at New Madrid, dated 16th December, 1811*

Jason spent the fight huddled beneath a cotton wagon with
Arlette, Manon, and a half-dozen other refugees. His nerves
leaped with every shot, every cry, every moan or scream.

He was glad to leave this business to the grownups.

At the start, right after the earth shuddered to the detona-
tion of the claymore mines, gunfire broke out all around the
camp as Nick's Samurai, with three handguns and one .22
rifle, opened fire on the six guards distributed around the
back and sides of the camp. One guard was killed, another
wounded, and a third fled unhurt. Two Samurai were killed
when guards returned fire. Bullets sprayed the camp, whining eerily as they tumbled after striking parts of the chainlink
fence.

Cudjo, by shooting two guards from cover with his deer
rifle, turned the tide. Fighters eagerly slipped under the
chainlink to seize the dead guards' weapons. The remaining
guards were killed as they ran for their lives across the
adjoining fields.

Jason hugged Arlette during the battle, both of them on the
ground, his cheek against the nape of her neck. It wasn't
romantic, it wasn't tender; it was two terrified people doing
their best to disappear into each other and into the ground.
He could feel Arlette gasp at each cracking shot, shiver as
buzzing bullets tumbled past. As the cars rolled out of the
parking lot and the fighting moved farther away, he could
feel her begin to breathe easier.

"It'll be all right," he whispered. For what it was worth.

She squeezed his hand, nodded. Pretending that he had
reassured her, while tears rolled down her cheeks.

They stayed hidden until they heard cars returning, until

the shooting was long ended and people started calling for everyone to come out of hiding. Jason rose into the long-shadowed day, and his heart gave a sudden leap of joy. He had lived through it. He would see another day.

"Take your belongings and go to the parking lot! Take some food with you if you can!"

Jason took his telescope, his only remaining property, from beneath the cotton wagon and joined the others as they marched toward the exit. There were bodies lying on the ground near the gate, all displaying that limp, careless, boneless sprawl that let Jason know these were real bodies and not actors in some movie. Manon took Arlette and Jason firmly by the shoulders and marched them quickly through the area, though Jason couldn't help but look at the bodies to discover if any of them were Nick. One of the bodies, he saw, was that of Sékou, one of the boys who had given Arlette grief for kissing Jason.

Jason tore his eyes from the corpse and looked straight ahead. He didn't want to think about Sékou, about how the boy had died fighting while Jason had huddled beneath the wagon.

When they came out of the camp, they found Nick in the parking area. He was wearing a gun belt, leaning on a shotgun, and giving orders. He looked like a highly successful field marshal in some dreadful, highly personal African bush war. Jason gave a cry of elation. Arlette raced up to him and flung her arms around him.

"Baby!" he said, and lifted Arlette off her feet as he hugged her. Then he carried Arlette to Manon and threw an arm around his ex as well.

"Nick!" she said, eyes wide with horror. "You're covered with blood!"

"It's, uh, not mine," Nick said. A shadow passed over the joy that glowed in his eyes. He turned to Arlette. "Careful, honey, you might get some on you."

"I don't care," Arlette said.

He lowered her to the ground. Nick saw Jason, and a smile crossed his face. "Hey, Jase," he said.

"Hey."

"You hang onto that telescope, okay, Jase? That scope is your luck."

Jason looked at the Astroscan in its battered red plastic case. "Yeah," he said. "Maybe so."

There was a lot of rushing around, car engines starting. Someone started one of the big five-ton trucks. Nick looked sharply to one side, and then his smile widened.

"Cudjo!" he said.

Jason turned to see Cudjo tromping toward them on his sturdy boots, his hunting rifle over one shoulder. Cudjo looked more strange in the light of day than he had at night, with his homemade canvas pants held up by suspenders, his moth-eaten, wide-brimmed hat, and a checked shirt that seemed made up of the remnants of other checked shirts all stitched together.

Cudjo held up a fist, crooked a thumb. *"Took,"* he chirped. And laughed.

"You come visit the camp, cracker, and we'll make you real welcome."

For a long, long heartbeat, Omar stared at the radio set in his office. All his people at the camp were dead, he thought. The Klan, the Crusaders, all of them. He could hear refugees howling and yelling over the radio until the signal abruptly cut off.

"Omar! Omar!" Eddie Bridges called. He was one of the deputies at Clarendon, trying to keep order amid all the sick people. Not a Klansman, not involved with the A.M.E. camp at all. "What the hell was that about?" Eddie demanded. "Did he say he was an *Army general*?"

Omar didn't have an answer for him.

He was almost thankful when the earthquake began to shake the world.

Nick walked to Cudjo, embraced him as fervently as he'd embraced Arlette. Moments of soaring relief floated through his mind, alternating with unreasoning jagged bolts of adrenaline lightning. "You saved it, man," he said. "You saved the damn plan. You saved fifty lives."

Cudjo seemed a bit taken aback. "You did the hard work, you fellas," he said. "You make the claymore, you fight the Kluxers *vis-à-vis*. I make the shoot from ambush, me." He shrugged. "That not hard, no. Not for hunter."

Nick stepped back, looked at Cudjo. "I need you to guide most of these people someplace safe."

"*Mais oui*, I do that, yes. Take you-all down bayou, me, take you across on *batteau*. Small *batteau*, my *batteau*, take all night cross that bayou, but you-all on south bank by morning. Lord High Sheriff can't follow you there, no, you be safe."

"Good. Good." Nick nodded. He glanced over his shoulder. "Is there a place in town I can take some of the fighters? Some place defensible. I figure the best chance of covering your withdrawal is to go right into Shelburne City and seize the most public building I can find."

Cudjo was surprised by this idea, but as he considered it an approving light began to glow in his eyes. "That sho-nuff gon' put the weasel in that chicken house, for true," he said admiringly. "But the Lord High Sheriff, that Paxton, he got his sheriff's men in the courthouse."

"Any place other than the courthouse?"

"There's Clarendon. Big ol' plantation house, that Clarendon, and that Miz LaGrande who live there, that Miz LaGrande, she hate Sheriff Paxton. Big refugee camp at Clarendon, that big house, all the white people go there."

Nick shook his head. "I don't think we're going to get any of these people to walk back into a refugee camp. Do we have anywhere else?"

Cudjo thought for a moment. "Carnegie Library. Big ol' place, that library. She got big lawns, that library, nice fields of fire, yes."

"How do we get there?"

"You go down highway, that highway, you turn left Jefferson Davis Street."

Nick gave a weary smile. "I'm not likely to forget the name of *that* street," he said.

"How 'bout the wounded?" A stout middle-aged woman came up to Nick. "We got some people shot up and no doctor. Some can't walk. These people gonna die if they don't see a doctor."

Nick bit his lip. "I don't suppose there's a hospital?" he asked Cudjo.

"No hospital in this parish, *mais non*. But they put sick people in Clarendon, that big house, there."

"And you say the lady who owns Clarendon hates the sheriff?"

"*Mais oui*. But your people there, they no be safe. Lord High Sheriff find them."

Nick turned to the woman. "I'm afraid we'll have to take the wounded with us. That's bad for them, but they won't be safe if they're not with us."

"Some of them are bad hurt."

"Yes, I know, but—" He stopped as he saw a bright, incongruous blond head crossing his line of vision. The white man he'd talked to that morning, walking across the grass with his black wife and three kids.

Wild inspiration struck Nick. "Hey!" he called. "Hey!" For the life of him he couldn't remember the man's name.

Jack Taylor stopped, turned, gave Nick an inquiring look. "Yes! You!"

Taylor told his family to wait, walked toward Nick. Nick looked at him.

"Your family get through okay?"

"Yeah." Taylor seemed surprised by being singled out this way.

"You have a car? You still want a job?"

Taylor gave a little incredulous laugh. "*Now?*" he said.

"I want you to go to Clarendon and talk to the woman who owns it—" He looked at Cudjo.

"Miz LaGrande," Cudjo said. "LaGrande Shelburne Ashenden, she."

"Mrs. LaGrande Ashenden," Nick repeated to Taylor. "I want you to follow us to Shelburne City in your car—not *with* us, see, but later. And then I want you to go to this plantation house called Clarendon and talk to Mrs. Ashenden."

"What do I say?" Taylor asked, wide-eyed.

"Tell her what's happened here. She's part of the local power structure, and she hates the sheriff. She'll be able to get word out." Another thought occurred to him. "No," he said. "Wait till after midnight. Make sure all our people can get clear."

Taylor considered this. "Okay," he said. "But I have to know someone will be looking after my family."

"We'll do that," Nick said. "We'll—"

Bang! The ground picked Nick up and dropped him again. "Incoming!" Cudjo yelled, and threw himself flat.

Nick dropped to the ground himself, hugged the long moist grass, but not because he thought the sheriff had somehow trained a howitzer on them.

It was the primary wave of another big earthquake. Nick knew quakes well enough by now to know that, at least.

He heard the secondary waves coming, a roaring sound like a great wind passing through a forest, and then the earth began to dance.

He had been dreaming more and more of New Mexico. The busier he got, the more demands his job made on him, the more his mind seemed to need that anchor, that sense of home. He woke in the morning to the scent of mountain flowers, to a memory of high meadows shimmering gold in the sun. And then rose to a day of heat, sweat, and Mississippi mud.

It was time to go home, Larry thought. As soon as he got things set up here, as soon as Poinsett Landing would relax its grip on him.

"I'll be with you in an hour or so," Larry said into his satellite phone. "Just as soon as we get this ol' barge tied up."

"I'll have something hot waiting," Helen said. "We just got electricity restored today, so I can actually cook."

The second barge of spent nuclear fuel was ready to start its journey to Waterford Three. This one contained several of the hot, partly melted fuel assemblies from the reactor's last unloading, and thus its mooring merited Larry's particular attention.

Larry watched as the barge eased its way out of the short canal from the auxiliary building to the west side of Poinsett Island. A pair of crewmen stood on the barge, minding the steel mooring and tow cables, while an Army backhoe drew the barge slowly to the Mississippi.

The barge would have to moor alongside the flank of the island overnight. There was supposed to be a towboat here to take the barge downstream, but some last-minute hitch with insurance had resulted in a delay. Larry didn't understand the problem: the *last* load had traveled to Waterford without special insurance, but now, somehow, things were different.

Larry explained this to Helen over his cellphone while he watched the barge slide into the Mississippi and swing with the current.

"A typical screwup," he concluded.

"Isn't it good," Helen said, "to deal with a *typical* screwup for a change? Instead of something new and completely unprecedented?"

Larry grinned and tipped his hard hat back on his head. "Waaal," he said, "I guess you're right." He watched the current swing the barge to its mooring place.

"Looks like we're going to be finished here in just a few minutes," Larry said. "I'll call for my helicopter."

Helen gave a chuckle. "Just listen to yourself," she said. "'*I'll call for my helicopter.*' You sound like Donald Trump."

"I'm still the same cowpuncher you married," Larry said. "And I'll prove it if we can ever get back to New Mexico."

"The company owes you a *long* vacation," Helen said.

"It surely does. And I'm planning to collect it as soon as I make sure this operation is working."

"See you in an hour."

"Bye, sweetie."

Larry clicked off his cellphone and stood watching the barge. The backhoe cast off the tow cable, and the cable was made fast to a tall steel stanchion that had been sunk and cemented into the close-packed rubble of Poinsett Island. The backhoe spun nimbly on its wheels, gravel flying, as it began its journey to shift an empty barge into the auxiliary building canal in order to take on another load of spent fuel.

Larry thought of horses. Low Die, sitting low on its hocks as it prepared to cut to the left. The backhoe, nimble as it was, simply was not an adequate substitute.

One of the men on the barge tossed a mooring line to one of the men on shore so that the barge would be moored more securely, bow and stern. Larry looked at the cellphone and began to punch in the number that would summon the helicopter pilot to carry him home to Vicksburg.

There was a crash as Poinsett Island jumped into the air. Larry felt his mouth drop open in surprise. Not *again*.

He heard the chuffing sound of the quake coming toward him and figured he wasn't going to be standing much longer, so he lowered himself to his knees on the gravel surface. When he looked north he could see Poinsett Island heave up in a long traveling wave that flung plumes of dust from its crest like foam.

The wave rolled under him, and he felt himself picked up, then dropped face-first to the ground in a spill of gravel and dust. Pain shot through his broken collarbone. Grinding and booming sounds slapped against his ears. Then another wave lifted him bodily—the feeling of that awesome force pressing him upward was at once breathtaking and terrifying—and then again he spilled downward in a slide of gravel. His hard hat tumbled off his head.

The air was full of dust. Larry glanced left and right through the sudden gray-brown haze and saw the barge vibrating in a sea of white water, the backhoe sliding backward as it fell off the crest of an earth-wave. He could see the operator's arms flailing inside the machine's roll cage. And then the backhoe toppled backward, its front scoop flying into the air. Larry watched in surprise. The machine was stable, and he didn't understand why it would somersault like that.

He found the answer when another wave lifted him, and with the advantage of height he saw that the sides of the canal leading to the auxiliary building had collapsed, and that the backhoe along with its operator had been tumbled into the water. *Got to help that poor man*, Larry thought, *before he's buried alive*, and he tried to rise to hands and knees and scramble across the gravel toward the canal. But the island kept jumping out from under him, and then he felt the ground under him start to slide, and water splash his face.

Poinsett Island was coming apart. It was rubble, and it was sitting on nothing but soft river mud, and the quake was shifting the rubble around. He needed to head toward the middle of the island before he slid into the Mississippi. He couldn't help the backhoe operator unless he first helped himself.

He tried belly-crawling away from the water, but he had no traction—the ground under him was shifting, sliding toward the river—sharp-edged stone and concrete cut his knees and hands. He gulped in air as the river boiled up around him, as the water took him and his view turned white.

Larry lunged upward, felt his head break the surface. Breath burst from his lungs and he gasped in foam-flecked air. The air filled with grinding sounds as the rubble island slid away into the river.

He blinked through water-splashed spectacles, his booted feet kicking as he trod water. He sensed a shadow behind him and turned his head just in time to see the laden barge swinging toward him, its black, rust-streaked sides looming tall as a house. It must have come unmoored.

Oh hell, he thought.

Larry raised his hands and pressed them against the side of the barge, as if he could hold it off him by strength alone. He knew it was futile, but it was all he could do.

The barge carried him back to the island, and crushed him against the merciless stone with all the weight of the steel hull and the big container flasks and the nuclear fuel.

Larry felt his rib cage cave in. Pain roared like a lion in his skull. He thought of plains and mountain flowers and the way Low Die shifted under him, all the powerful muscle and tendon under his control.

Stupid, he thought, *a stupid way to die.*

The barge rebounded from the island, releasing Larry to slide below the surface. As water poured into Larry's unresisting lungs, the barge spun on down the foam-flecked river, trailing on the end of its cable the mooring stanchion that had torn free of Poinsett Island.

THIRTY-FIVE

Messrs. Miner & Butler,

A very singular phenomenon took place near Angelica, in the country of Allegany, on Monday morning the 16th of December, which I will state, as related to me by one of the eye witnesses. Early in the morning, about sunrise as sitting at breakfast, he had a strange feeling, and supposed at first that he was fainting, but as his sight did not fail, he then concluded that he was going into a fit, and removed his chair back from the table. —He then had a sensation as though the house was swinging and observed clothes hanging on lines in the room were swinging, as also a large kettle hanging over the fire. He observed that his wife and family appeared to be greatly alarmed, and still supposing that it was in consequence of his apparently falling into a fit, but on enquiry found that all felt the same sensation. This continued as he supposed for at least 15 minutes. There was no noise or trembling, nor any wind, but only an appearance of swinging or rocking, as he supposed, equal to the house rocking two feet one way and the other. —One of his neighbors felt the same, and on the opposite side of the river, at the farmhouse and dwelling house of Phillip Church, the same motions and sensations were felt. Mrs. Church was in bed, and when she first felt the motion, and a strange sensation as if suffocating, she jumped out of bed, supposing the house was on fire. The motion was so considerable as to set all the bells in the several rooms a ringing, and an inside door was observed to swing open and shut.

The same motions were felt up the river, about eight miles above, at a house near a small brook; the people ran out of

*the house, and observed the water to have the same motion.
Accounts state, that the same motions have been felt at sundry
other places 30 miles distant.*

*I could relate many other similar motions felt and perceived at
the same time, but leave it for the present. How to account for it
I know not. If you think it worthy of notice, you may make it
public, and if the same or similar motions have been felt at other
places, doubtless it will be communicated. I should like to hear
it accounted for on rational principles.*

> *Christopher Hurlbut, Arkport, (N.Y.) Jan. 6*

"God damn, not again!"

Jessica sat with Pat beneath the kitchen table and listened to the house bang around them. They had moved back into their house only hours before—Jessica, her head echoing with the President's bizarre call, concluded that the emergency had ebbed to the point where she didn't need to be physically present at headquarters every minute of the day—and the quake struck just as they were eating their first home-cooked meal since before the emergency. Jessica had prepared tagliarini verdi ghiottona, lovely green pasta noodles with a sauce of onions, tomatoes, carrots, chicken livers, veal, and ham—the recipe called for prosciutto, which was not precisely available, but one of the civilians she'd helped in the early days of M1 had given her a smoked Cajun ham, which proved an effective substitute.

When the P wave hit and the house gave a sudden leap, Jessica and Pat slid neatly beneath the table before the S waves had a chance to reach them. Each kept a firm grip on priorities, and therefore retained both plate and fork.

"Right in the middle of fucking dinner!" Jessica muttered as the moaning quake enveloped them. Platters bounced loudly over her head. Something went smash in the bedroom. She was beginning to miss her helmet.

"At least there aren't any operations going on right now," Pat commented. His voice was as conversational as the circumstances permitted, shouting over the banging furniture and moaning earth.

"I hope I don't lose an eye," Jessica said. Rayleigh waves rattled her teeth as she spoke.

"I was hoping to keep your mind off that."

"That was good of you."

A wineglass walked off the edge of the table. Jessica snatched for it in midair, but the earth took a lurch at that instant and robust red wine splattered over the dining room floor. The solid Baccarat crystal, the sort of glassware out of which a major general was expected to serve her guests, didn't so much as chip.

She closed her right eye and peered out with her damaged left, tried to determine if she was losing any vision. But the earth was heaving and leaping too much for her to keep her eye focused on anything long enough.

The earth thrashed a few last times and then the vibrations died down. In the precarious silence, Jessica took a defiant bite of her dinner, handed the plate to Pat, and cautiously ventured into the front room to find her cellphone in the corner, having leaped from where she'd placed it on the coffee table.

It was already ringing.

She was in communication with her headquarters immediately, and with Washington in a few minutes. Her staff were well practiced by now; they smoothly gathered information and fed it to her as it arrived. Jessica had time to scarf her dinner before Sergeant Zook arrived with her car. Pat stayed behind to get the house in order. On her way to headquarters in the Humvee, she hit the speed dialer number for Larry Hallock, but didn't get an answer.

She tried three more times over the next hour, then tried some other numbers. She was unable to raise anyone at Poinsett Island. Then she got absorbed in her work, in the information flooding in and the deployments that needed to be made, and didn't try calling again.

It was while looking at a hastily made printout of Prime Power deployments that she absently raised her hand to her right eye and looked at the list with her left.

A chill whispered up her spine as she realized that her left eye had gone blurry. She looked at the list for the length of three long, slow heartbeats, then reached for her cellphone and hit Pat's speed dial number.

"Do you know the gentleman I saw this morning?" she said. "The gentleman in Jackson?"

"Yes."

"I need to see him again," Jessica said. "I need you to make the appointment."

"Are you—"

"It's not like it was last time," Jessica said. "The situation has improved, but I still need to see the gentleman."

"Jessica," Pat said, "you are not keeping this job at the expense of your sight."

"I hear you," said Jessica, and rang off.

Her phone chirped again the instant she returned it to her pocket. Her caller was Helen Hallock, Larry's wife, wondering if her husband had checked in. "When I last talked to him, he was about to call for his helicopter."

Jessica checked and discovered that the helicopter hadn't been called. She called her own chopper and took off into the waning light.

It was after the sun had already set that Jessica landed on Poinsett Island and made contact with the handful of people waiting there. They'd been cut off because their radio antenna had pitched into the river. It was then that Jessica discovered that part of Poinsett Island had slid into the river, that Larry Hallock was missing, and that a barge filled with murderously hot nuclear waste was drifting, untended, down the Mississippi.

The Mississippi Delta is filled with magnetic anomalies. Known as "plutons," these objects are believed to be extrusions of magnetic ore created by volcanic activity during the distant geological past. These structures are enormously dense, and they straggle along the middle Mississippi like pebbles being washed along a ditch. Their immense weight creates stress on the surrounding subsoil—and since the

Delta's geology consists of little more than layers of muck, there is very little save inertia to prevent a pluton from doing exactly what it wants to do.

Plutons have been associated with earthquake activity, particularly in places where no fault lines have ever been detected. A large pluton discovered off Cape Ann, Massachusetts, has been blamed for the earthquakes that struck Boston in 1727 and 1755, quakes that inspired a famous sermon by the revivalist Reverend Thomas Prince, "The Works of God and Tokens of His Just Displeasure," in which Prince demonstrated that the quakes were caused by the Lord's opposition to the sinful behavior of Boston's back-sliding Puritans. Another pluton beneath Charleston, South Carolina, has been held responsible for the giant earthquake that shook the southeastern United States in 1886.

The first June earthquake, J1, began at 5:54 P.M., Central Daylight Time, when a pluton, sitting atop gooey Delta sub-soil beneath Jonesboro, Arkansas—subsoil destabilized by the series of quakes—dropped six meters through slumping ground. The shocks caused by the passage of the pluton set off a familiar chain reaction as stored tectonic force was discharged throughout the various New Madrid fault structures.

J1 registered at 8.3 on the Richter scale, one-sixth the strength of M1 and a third the power of M6, but still equivalent to the great San Francisco earthquake of 1906. Its destruction was mitigated only by the fact that so much of the affected area had already been destroyed. Anything that was likely to fall down had *already* fallen down, and much of the population had been evacuated. Those remaining in the area were wise to the ways of earthquakes. Deaths were later reckoned to be in the 100-plus range.

Jonesboro, already hard hit by M1 and M6, was shattered. Memphis—by this point a near-desert of broken stone, torn roadways, refugee camps, and collapsed homes—received another pounding. More land slid, more fountains geysered skyward, more damaged buildings collapsed. Precarious infrastructure repairs, to power and sewer lines, to bridges and railroad tracks, were wiped out. Efforts by the Coast

Guard and the Corps of Engineers to mark a safe navigation channel in the Mississippi and other major rivers were brought to nothing as the topography of the river changed once again.

But relief workers were already in place. Supplies and funds had already been allocated. In spite of the quake's great size, remarkably little disruption took place, if only because everything had been disrupted long since.

Most of the survivors considered themselves lucky.

The earth shuddered, trembled, hummed. Children screamed. The long evening shadows were darkened by dust and debris.

One Mississippi, two Mississippi . . . Nick, without a watch, counted the seconds slowly to himself.

This was bound to disrupt the whole parish, Nick thought. Which would make things easier for him. The more emergencies the sheriff had to deal with at once, the better.

The world ceased its moaning after three minutes. Nick could hear the S-waves receding toward the south, the freight train moving away. Nick looked up, saw others cautiously lifting their heads. Children screamed as their parents tried to comfort them. Nick carefully raised himself to his feet.

"Everyone into a car!" he said. "Let's get ready to move out!"

He made sure that Cudjo was in the lead car. He kissed Arlette and Manon. He hugged Jason and rubbed the red casing of the telescope for luck, then made sure they were all three on a truck rolling south.

When the last of the Home Guard, the women, and the children were gone into the growing darkness, Nick waved the shotgun over his head and shouted for the Warriors to get on the road.

Bringing the war to the sheriff, Nick thought. To the capital of the enemy's kingdom.

Micah Knox lay half-submerged in the ditch. His heart pounded louder than the shots that still rang out over the fields. His men were being killed. Run down and killed by niggers. It was like every nightmare he'd ever had. He should help his friends, he knew.

But he didn't help. He didn't even move.

It was the snake that saved his life. As he and the others approached the gate, Knox saw a snake whipping through the grass just ahead of his boots, and his heart lurched and his steps faltered, and the others swept on through the gate while he pointed at the snake and stammered at them to be careful. He'd been ten paces behind when the bombs went off, and suddenly the air was filled with shrieking, screaming bits of sharp metal. He felt it tug at his clothing and flesh.

And then he saw the niggers coming, a howling black wave with weapons held high, and Knox let his shotgun fall and took to his heels. He ran back through the gate, through the parking lot, and across the road. He flung himself into the half-flooded bar ditch on the far side of the highway and wormed his way along it, sloshing through the warm water without daring to lift his head above the level of the ditch.

He stayed there. He stayed in the ditch, his nose barely above water, while cars raced past his hiding place and shots rang out. The shots died away. Cars ran back and forth. People shouted and cheered.

Knox didn't move. There were cuts on his hands, tears in his clothing. From the mines. He ignored them.

The earthquake came and Knox didn't move. He didn't move until the earthquake was over, until dozens of cars drove past, until he heard other cars drive off in the other direction, toward Shelburne City. And even then he didn't move. He stayed in the ditch, alone with his heartbeat and his terror and his breath. He didn't move until he heard birdsong in the trees, until he heard wind fluttering the grass on the shoulder of the highway. Until he heard nothing made by the hand of man.

He raised his head carefully, put his eyes at the level of the road, and looked for three seconds. Then he ducked down, crawled twenty feet along the ditch, then looked again.

The fields on either side of the road were empty. The camp

sat abandoned. The setting sun reflected in shimmering rose color on the fence. A few cars sat forlorn in the parking lot, or stretched along the road.

Vultures circled overhead, uncertain whether or not to land.

Knox rose cautiously, then ran in a crouch to the nearest car. Then to the next. The only cars that remained near the camp were those that wouldn't start, or those whose owners were dead.

And the car that Knox had come in. The Escort belonged to David Paxton, and Knox had been driving it for several days. The back window had been caved in by gunshots or by the mines' terrifying ammunition. No one had driven it away, because Knox had the keys.

Knox ran to the car, opened the door, scrabbled in the back for his duffel. He opened the duffel and brought out his overnight kit with his drugs. He opened the big aspirin bottle and shook out the contents. His hands trembled. He moistened a finger, and dabbed out the last of the crystal meth from the baggie. He rubbed the crystal on his gums, then shook out a pair of black mollies and dry-swallowed them.

It was only then that he noticed flies settling onto a corpse fifteen feet away. Jedthus, he saw, mutilated horribly.

He stared for a while, too shocked to feel fear, and then he straightened, took his bottle of aspirin in hand, and walked into the camp.

They were there, his friends, his action group. He had recruited them in Detroit, or they had recruited him, and they had traveled around the country doing the noble work of the white man. They had been killed horribly, beaten and torn, and lay like broken sacks of meal in the grass of the camp.

They hadn't died alone. There were nigger corpses lying in the grass as well, and Knox walked to the nearest and kicked the body in the head. He kicked it again, and then he got down on his knees and punched the dead face, and in a spasm of rage he picked up the arm of the corpse and bit it. He licked the arm and bit it again and licked it and bit it. Speed began to crackle through his synapses. He thought he knew what he wanted to do.

It was growing dark. Swallows darted over the camp. He looked for weapons but didn't find any. All he had was his .38 Special revolver hanging from his belt.

Well, that would have to do.

Speed sang through his blood. His body shivered and jittered. He was getting too hyper, so Knox went back to the car and cooked up some heroin and shot it into his arm. That mellowed him out fine. He could kill now, he thought. He needed to be hyper to want to do it, but he needed to be mellow so that he could do it well. Now he was hyper and mellow at the same time. He had reached the precise point of balance where he could accomplish anything he set out to do.

He put his things in David Paxton's car and got in and started the engine. David's father would take care of the nigs who went to Shelburne City. Sheriff Paxton was a man of vision and could handle things there just fine. Knox, therefore, should go looking for the others.

Most of the mud people had taken their cars north, away from Shelburne City and into the country. Knox would find them. Maybe take some trophies. That was clearly what the situation required.

Knox headed north. He kept his lights off so that the mud people wouldn't see him coming. He drove along the highway until it climbed the District Levee and dead-ended in the washout. He cursed and banged his fist on the wheel of the car.

Speed sang a song of death in his ears. He turned around and headed back the way he came.

They had to be around here somewhere. He would check every road, every lane, until he found them.

And then he would do what he had come to do.

After the quake had rumbled to its finale, Omar got on the radio and ordered all his deputies to report to his headquarters.

All seven of them. That's all that was left, if all the special deputies at the A.M.E. camp were gone. Seven, not counting himself and David.

What could he do with seven men? There were almost two hundred in the camp, and they now had the guns of his special deputies. Their . . . general . . . was right. Omar was outgunned now.

But he couldn't call in help, could he? The state police, the Federals, the Army . . . they wouldn't be on his side.

So, he thought. *Time to end it. Time to run.*

That's what he told David, when David came into the courthouse in response to his radio call. Omar took David into his office and told him it was time to run for cover.

"No!" David said. "I'm not leaving! They killed my friends! This is my fight, too! This is a fight for every white man in America!"

Omar shook his head. "Most of the white men in America aren't on our side," he said. "It's too late." He looked at his son. "We need to save the next generation, okay? Save the—" An aftershock rumbled for a few brief seconds. Omar cast a nervous look at the crack that ran up the exterior wall of his office. "Save the seed corn," Omar said. "We need you to carry on."

"Dad—sir—I—" David shook his head. "I don't want to run away. This whole thing is my fault, and I don't want to desert you when the chips are down."

"You're not deserting me," Omar said. "You're obeying orders. I am your Kleagle, and I'm sending you out of here with a message."

Omar turned to his desk and took out a piece of paper. He wrote the name and address of the Grand Cyclops of Monroe. He handed the piece of paper to David. "I want you to go to this address. Tell Otis there's been some trouble, and you need to hide out for a while. Don't go into details— either it'll be on the news or it won't, and if it's not, you don't want to start any rumors. I'll make contact if it's safe—and if it's not, he can pass you on to some other people who can look after you." He forced a grin. "You might even see me there in a day or two."

He walked past David and opened his office door. "Merle," he said.

When Merle entered, Omar closed the door. "Merle, I need you to get my boy across the bayou. Put him on the road heading south."

Merle nodded. "I'll take him across in my own boat."

Omar turned to David, found himself without words, and instead put his arms around his boy. "You keep safe," he said. Hopeless love and hopeless despair flooded his heart.

And then he heard shooting. A whole rattling volley heard clear as day through his screened-in windows. Thirty, forty rounds, all different calibers.

"What the hell is *that*?" David demanded. Omar was too astonished to offer an answer.

A few minutes later citizens began to swarm into the court-house, shouting out that they'd just seen a whole posse of niggers shooting guns into the air as they broke into the Carnegie Library.

"Hey," Jason said. "Hey, that's our *boat*."

He pointed out the side window of the little silver Hyundai. He saw the battered hull of *Retired and Gone Fishin'* sitting on a trailer outside a chainlink fence that surrounded a tumbledown clapboard business. The outboard was tipped up over the boat's stern. The homemade sign by the road proclaimed Uncle Sky's A–1 Metal Building Products and Agricultural Machinery Repair—No Drugs!

The place was padlocked and closed. No lights shone in the building or in the fenced yard.

"Stop!" Jason said. "That's our boat! We can put it in the water and get out of here!"

"I can't haul a boat and trailer," the driver said. "Not in this car. I don't have a trailer hitch."

Jason, Manon, and Arlette were crammed in the backseat of the small Korean car, stuck in the middle of the long cara-van of refugees following Cudjo away from the A.M.E. camp. They'd left the highway and were heading west along an ill-repaired blacktop road.

"We'll use one of the trucks behind us," Jason said. "One of them will have a trailer hitch."

"I'm not stopping," the driver said. "It's not safe to stop." He was elderly and peered anxiously over the steering wheel at the car in front of them. His wife clutched his arm in terror, with a grip so strong he could barely steer. She hadn't said a word since she'd entered the vehicle.

"Hush," Manon said to Jason. "Cudjo said he had a boat."

"That boat won't have a motor, I bet," Jason said. "If we get the bass boat, we can run to Vicksburg and go for help."

But no one was inclined to pay him any attention, so Jason tried to relax, squashed against the inside of the car, as the caravan moved west down a sagging, rutted two-lane blacktop, slowing to a crawl every so often to negotiate parts of the road ripped across by quakes. The country was mostly uninhabited cotton fields with rows of pine trees planted between them. The sun eased over the horizon, and the western sky turned to cobalt. The caravan moved south, then west again, on narrow gravel roads. Sometimes the cars splashed through areas flooded to the floorboards. Eventually the line of vehicles pulled to a straggling halt in an area filled with young pines. Jason could see car headlights glinting off flood waters to the right.

After getting out of the Hyundai, Manon and Arlette thanked the elderly couple for the ride. Jason couldn't stop thinking about *Retired and Gone Fishin'* sitting in Uncle Sky's yard. He saw Cudjo walk past with some men carrying rifles, and Jason trotted alongside, his telescope bouncing on his hip. A wind stirred the tops of the pine trees.

"Sir?" he said. "Mr. Cudjo?"

The hermit turned to him, yellow eyes gleaming in the growing night. "Boy, I want you stay with you mama."

"Could we use another boat right now? As we drove here, I saw the boat we came in sitting on a trailer. We could go back and get it."

"Put this truck 'cross this road, you," Cudjo said to the driver of a pickup. "You—" Patting the shoulder of one of his riflemen. "You, *la bas*, down in them trees, you. Stay quiet, you. Lord High Sheriff come, you flank him, yes? The rest of you, you stay here, behind truck, yes? You no shoot, you, you don't know who come. Could be Nick and them who come, yes?"

Then Cudjo turned to Jason. "You tell me 'bout this boat, you."

"It's a bass boat," Jason said. "We came down on it from Missouri. There's a fifty-horse Johnson on it, and we had fuel left. If we put it in the water, we could travel to Vicksburg, send for help."

Cudjo frowned at him. A gust of wind tugged at his long beard. "Where you see this boat, you."

"Uncle Sky's Metal Building Whatever," Jason said. "The boat was right in the yard. It wasn't even behind the fence, it was like somebody just dropped it there. The place was closed, nobody around. We could hitch the trailer to a truck and drive it off, no problem."

Cudjo's eyes narrowed in thought. "Skyler King, he a Kluxer, that man. But he an old man, that Sky, he live in Hardee with his daughter, that Rachel. Ain't nobody at his business now, no."

"That Sky place isn't five minutes from here," Jason said. "We can make a quick trip."

"Jason—" Arlette came up the line of vehicles, took Jason's hand. "Mama says—"

Jason squeezed her hand. "We'll go get the boat," he told Cudjo, "if we can have someone to drive us out there."

Jason and Arlette held hands on the bench seat as they were driven to Uncle Sky's. Their van was alone on the old road— it was a plush vehicle, carpeted and with soft seats, a Chevy that still smelled new. The driver in front of them was a young light-skinned man named Samuel who scanned the road nervously as he pushed the vehicle to high speed in between slowing down for partially repaired tears and crevasses. Every so often Samuel would drop a hand to finger the pistol at his hip.

"Here it is," Jason called. Jason leaned into Arlette's shoulder as Samuel swung the van abruptly into Uncle Sky's gravel drive. The headlights tracked across a yard over which was scattered building materials, agricultural equipment, then the battered bass boat on its trailer, parked on the grass to one side of the gate.

Samuel backed the van to the trailer. Jason left his telescope on the seat, and he and Arlette went out the van's sliding side door. Jason felt the night wind ruffle his hair. They went to the trailer, and Jason looked down to see that a padlock had secured the ball on the trailer, making it impossible to hitch the trailer and tow it away.

"Damn," Samuel said. "Wait here." He opened the hatch at the back of the van and began searching through his large toolbox for something to cut the padlock.

Jason hoisted himself onto the bass boat's foredeck. Rainwater sloshed in the boat's bottom. Jason hopped over the cockpit to the aft deck, then bent to inspect the outboard motor. From what he could see in the dark, the outboard was as he left it, but when he felt with his hand in the well near the motor he couldn't locate any of the jerricans of fuel they'd brought with them from Rails Bluff.

Jason straightened. "There's no gas," he said. "They probably took the cans inside. I'll go look."

The fence was two feet away, chain link twined with Virginia creeper. Jason launched himself at the fence, clung with fingers, dug his toes into the gaps between the chain link. He scrambled to the top, put both feet on the pipe that ran along the top of the fence, adjusted his footing, and raised himself to a precarious standing position, arms flung out for balance. The gusty wind tried to pluck him off. He grinned. "Wish I had my skates," he said. "I could travel on this."

"Be careful," Arlette said. Jason knelt, reached a hand down to Arlette. "Want to come up?" he asked.

"You better hope there's not a big dog in there," Arlette said.

"Woof woof," Jason said. He dropped his butt onto the pipe, then twisted around and lowered himself to the soft ground inside Uncle Sky's compound.

Samuel found a hacksaw and began working on the lock that secured the trailer.

Jason walked through the cluttered yard to the unpainted clapboard building. He stepped onto the porch that ran the length of the front. Planks sagged under his feet. He looked into the window, peering through a frame of his two hands pressed against the glass. He saw the glint of a glass counter, dark objects that were probably lawnmowers or lawn tractors. He walked to the front door and tried to turn the knob—

—Then jumped three feet as an alarm bell began to ring out. His heart hammered. The door had been wired. Jason gave a helpless look back toward the gate, saw Samuel and Arlette staring at him, Samuel with the tail lights of his van outlining his exasperated expression.

"Sorry!" Jason shouted over the clatter.

Then he walked to the end of the porch and peered around the side of the building. Another boat loomed there in the shadow of the building, a big eighteen-foot powerboat with a canvas top. Jason wondered about stealing it. It would certainly furnish more deluxe transport than *Retired and Gone Fishin'*.

The ringing bell was on this side of the building, right over Jason's head. The clamor rang in his skull. He clenched his teeth and walked around the boat, put a foot on the fender of the trailer in preparation to boost himself into the cockpit, and he saw that the tire on the trailer was flat. So much for driving off with it.

Jason boosted himself into the cockpit. A hulking outboard was tilted up over the stern. Jason groped in the recesses of the stern and found a pair of plastic jerricans—not, judging by the weight, the ones he had brought on the bass boat, but larger and holding more gasoline. "Bingo!" he shouted over the clamor of the bell, but he doubted that anyone could hear him.

One container was connected by rubber hoses to the engine, and the other was free. Jason took the free container and heaved it onto the gunwale, then lowered it to balance it precariously on the trailer fender. He jumped off the boat and managed to catch the jerrican just as it started to topple over. He took it in both hands and waddled across the yard with his knees banging into the container at every step.

He was happy to be distancing himself from the clatter of the alarm.

While Jason had been exploring, Samuel had finished cutting the padlock free, and he and Arlette had hooked the trailer to the van. "Here's some gas," Jason said as he brought the gas to the gate. He tried to squeeze it between the gate and the upright to which it was chained, but failed.

"It's too heavy to boost over the fence," he said. "Can you cut a hole in it?"

"I've got some wire cutters," Samuel said.

"There's another gas can where I found this one. I'll go get it." Jason trotted back to the powerboat. While the alarm bell blared through his nerves, he disconnected the gas can from the outboard by feel, lowered it out of the boat, and began to carry it across the equipment-filled yard.

Samuel had cut a modest hole in the wire of the gate, and he was bent over, dragging the jerrican through the gap. He was brightly lit by the headlights of his van. Arlette stood by, watching him. The clamor of the alarm filled the night.

And then a small car—its headlights were off—lunged out of the darkness by the road. Samuel sensed the car's approach at the last second and turned to face it just as the car drove him into the chain link. Samuel's arms were thrown out wide as the gate bulged inward beneath the thrusting force of the car, but the chain held and Samuel's legs were pinned against the mesh by the car grill. He pitched forward from the waist and sprawled across the car's hood. Arlette watched in stunned surprise, her mouth open in a cry that went unheard beneath the clanging alarm.

Then the driver's door flung open, and a crop-haired man lunged for Arlette and seized her arm. She tried to wrench free, but he brought his other hand up, with a small pistol. He shoved the barrel into Arlette's throat, and she froze, her mouth still wide in a frozen scream.

Jason stared at the scene, the heavy plastic container still hanging from his arms. The ringing alarm filled his skull. He couldn't seem to move. Astonishment and terror froze him to the spot.

The driver was one of the deputies, Jason saw. He remembered seeing the little man during the deputies' attack yesterday.

The little deputy was shouting at Arlette. Jason couldn't hear the words over the urgent alarm. But when the deputy swiped Arlette across the face with his little pistol, hot rage surged through Jason's veins. He dropped the heavy container on the ground and ran for the gate.

The deputy backed Arlette to the side of the van, was pressing her against the driver's door. Jason crouched behind an old Allison-Chalmers tractor parked near the fence. He saw headlights reflect off the little black gun in the man's hand, felt helplessness jangle through his mind like the clap of the bell. He looked for a weapon, saw nothing in the darkness.

Jason saw a violent movement, the deputy punching Arlette with the pistol, and he heard Arlette scream over the clamor of the alarm. Jason's nerves wailed. He clenched his fists. All he had to do, he thought, was get the man to let go of her for just a second.

He climbed the tractor, crossed over the seat and stood on the big rear tire next to the fence. The wind flurried at him, whipped his hair. The deputy was twenty feet away along the fence. He had Arlette pinned to the van with his left hand around her throat; the right hand brandished the pistol in her face. He was turned away from Jason. "Where are they, bitch?" The demand was barely audible above the clattering alarm. "Where are they all hiding?" Arlette cringed away from the pistol. There was blood on her face.

Jason took a giant stride into space, landed on the top rail of the fence. For a moment he balanced wildly, pigeon-toed on the rail, arms spinning like windmill blades, and then he managed to shift one foot and gained a firm purchase. Weird triumph sang through his soul.

Clicked in!

He took one step along the pipe, then another. Then a third. The deputy kept howling questions, prodding Arlette with the barrel of the gun.

Land fakie, Jason thought as he took another step. *Land fakie and mule-kick the son of a bitch.*

The deputy must have seen Jason out of the corner of his eye, because he turned and looked up just as Jason took his last, swift step. Jason pivoted on the rail, saw little pebble irises in the wide, astonished eyes as he hurled himself into space. Jason saw the little gun swing toward him as, spinning in the air, he lashed backward and downward with both feet. *"Run!"* he screamed at the top of his lungs.

Run. Everybody run.

It felt like a giant hand slapping him out of the sky. Suddenly he was on the ground, amid moist grass, teeth rattling from the impact. He'd brought the deputy down, too, because the man was lying there with a half-dazed expression on his face. Arlette stood over them both, staring. *"Run!"* Jason screamed again. He saw the hand and the gun outflung on the grass and launched himself at the weapon, putting his weight on the deputy's arm. He sank his teeth into the man's wrist. The flesh had a strange, metallic taste.

The deputy gave a shout and punched Jason in the body with a fist. Agonizing pain crackled along Jason's nerves. He tried to hang on, but he felt himself growing weaker, weaker with each clang of the alarm, with each impact as the man's fist hammered into his side. When the arm and the gun slipped out of his grasp at last, it felt like trying to hold flowing water in his two hands.

Concussions slapped at Jason's ears. He felt himself wince with each shot, felt tears squeezed from his eyes. He couldn't seem to breathe. Couldn't breathe at all.

Jason blinked tears away. To his surprise he was looking at the deputy again.

The deputy was lying on the ground. And he was dead, small blank irises staring at the sky from his white, startled eyes.

* * *

"Well, excuse me, then, General," the towboat captain barked. "I was told to pick up a barge filled with nuclear waste that had got loose during the quake. Well that's what I come for, so when I was directed to a barge filled with nuclear waste I picked it up. And now this guy says it was the *wrong* barge of nuclear waste, and acts like it's my fault."

The towboat captain was a red-faced man in a baseball cap. His chin bristled with gray unshaven whiskers. He glared at Emil Braun, the power company executive. Braun glared back through his thick spectacles.

"This is the *empty* barge," Braun said. "Those containers haven't been filled with waste yet."

"Why is that *my* fault?" the captain demanded.

"Wait a minute," Jessica said. "The radwaste is *still missing*?"

Emil Braun had been sent by the company to take charge at Poinsett Island in the absence of Larry Hallock. The towboat and its captain had been near Poinsett Island before the quake, on their way to retrieve the barge of nuclear waste that had just been unloaded from the Auxiliary Building. On the night of the quake, when the few people remaining on the island had finally realized that the barge was missing, Jessica responded by sending out helicopter patrols to scour the river downstream from the power station. A drifting barge had been located toward morning, and remained in the choppers' spotlights until the towboat could take it in charge.

Now Emil Braun, having checked the numbers, was assuring everyone that the wrong barge had been rescued.

"The captain picked up the wrong barge," he told Jessica.

"I picked up the barge y'all *told* me to," the captain said.

Jessica reached for her cellphone. "Can you give me the numbers of the barge we're looking for?"

Braun looked at a clipboard filled with computer printout. "You bet," he said.

Jessica gave the orders for a complete helicopter sweep of

the river between Poinsett Island and Baton Rouge. Then she told the towboat captain to get his boat on the river and be prepared to undertake another rescue.

"I picked up the boat y'all told me to," the captain said. "I don't got to pick up another till my company gets another contract."

"You picked up the wrong barge!" Braun insisted. "The contract wasn't filled!"

"*Enough!*" Jessica said in her major general voice.

There was silence. Jessica looked at Braun. "Okay," she said. "What happens if this radwaste gets into the river?"

Braun licked his lips. "Well, that depends on whether the fuel assemblies get broken or not. The rods are full of little uranium pellets, and those could spill out. And *if* the pellets were from the really hot fuel assemblies that just got removed from the reactor, then there would be a steady source of contamination in the river until the pellets eroded completely. But," he added judiciously, "that's not *likely*. I don't think. Quite frankly, I do not believe any studies have been done in regard to this eventuality."

Jessica nodded. "So what could happen is somewhere on a scale between nothing at all to radioactive contamination of the lower Mississippi that could go on for years."

Braun nodded. "Um. I guess."

Jessica turned to the towboat captain. "This river is under martial law," she said. "You can contact your company and tell them to generate a new contract if you have to, but contract or not, you're going after that barge."

The captain began to speak.

"Don't make me put a guard on your boat!" Jessica snapped. "And don't think you can just sail away, because I'm going to be flying right above you, in my own helicopter, until that barge is found and brought under control."

The captain hesitated, then spoke. "Yes, ma'am," he said.

THIRTY-SIX

Previous to my leaving the country I heard that many parts of the Mississippi river had caved in; in some places several acres at the same instant. But the most extraordinary effect that I saw was a small lake below the river St. Francis. The bottom of which is blown up higher than any of the adjoining country, and instead of water it is filled with a beautiful white sand. The same effect is produced in many other lakes, or I am informed by those who saw them; and it is supposed they are generally filled up. A little river called Pemisece, that empties into the St. Francis, and runs parallel with the Mississippi, at the distance of about twelve miles from it, is filled also with sand. I only saw it near its bend, and found it to be so, and was informed by respectable gentlemen who had seen it lower down, that it was positively filled with sand. On the sand that was thrown out of the lakes and river lie numerous quantities of fish of all kinds common to the country.

Narrative of James Fletcher

Jason sat in the cockpit of the bass boat. Midnight-black water hissed along the boat's chine. Jason had turned his body to port because he'd been wounded in the back and he couldn't sit properly in the seat, not without agonizing pain. He rested his chin on his left shoulder and upper arm. He tried to breathe, but it wasn't easy—he had to take shallow, rapid breaths, because deep breathing had become impossible. He just couldn't seem to expand his diaphragm far enough to take a full breath.

Cypress floated across his line of vision, alien shadows reaching for the sky with moss-wreathed fingers. Stars floated overhead, shone in the still waters of the bayou.

He had been shot, it seems, when he'd jumped onto the deputy. The bullet had gone into his lower back on the right side and come out near the top of his right shoulder. The entrance wound was smallish and the exit wound a great tear across his shoulder. From the murmured, half-overheard conversations of the grownups, the chief question concerned what the bullet had hit on the way. Probably it had struck a few ribs. The chief question was whether or not it had punctured a lung. Jason's inability to breathe properly seemed an ominous symptom, though the fact he wasn't spitting blood seemed cause for optimism.

He could feel Arlette's hand stroking his head. She was kneeling behind him on the afterdeck. Barring a few cuts and bruises she was all right, had come through it all unharmed.

Her voice came into his ear. "Ça va?"

"Ça va," he said. "Okay."

The deputy was dead. Still lying on the grass, probably, starlight reflecting in his startled eyes. Samuel had shot him. Samuel hadn't been killed when the car hit him, he hadn't even been badly hurt. He'd had the wind knocked out of him, that was all. The chain link had absorbed the force of the hurtling car.

When Samuel had got his wits and breath back, he'd seen Jason fighting with the deputy on the ground. He'd reached for the pistol he wore and got it free of the holster and taken aim and shot the deputy as soon as the little man had wrestled his own gun away from Jason and stood. It gave Samuel a clear shot.

Samuel had got his breath back, but Jason hadn't. He was in pain and the muscles of his back had swollen hard as iron and he could barely breathe.

And maybe he'd been shot in the lung. Was Jason dying? It was a question that seemed of great interest to the grownups. Jason himself was past thinking about it, though.

The grownups had put the boat in the water. Manon was piloting, and Arlette was aboard, and a man named Bubba who said he'd worked on towboats as a bowman and knew the Mississippi.

They were going to Vicksburg. They were going to Vicksburg to put Jason into a hospital and get help for the refugees in Spottswood Parish.

Moss-shrouded cypress floated past, tall in the water. Stars glittered at their feet.

Jason leaned on the side of the cockpit and tried to breathe.

The library smelled of dust and decaying book paper. It was a better fortress than Nick had expected—there were iron grills over the windows, which would certainly keep out unwanted visitors as well as the larger munitions, like tear gas grenades. The front door was solid cypress wood and so invulnerable that the Warriors had been unable to break it down: they'd had to pry off one of the iron grills, go in through a window, and open the door from the inside. The walls were thick concrete, covered with plaster that had partially peeled away in the quakes.

"Keep a lookout," Nick said. "Two to each window. Nobody show a light."

He took his own station behind the reassuring oaken solidity of the reference librarian's desk. In front of him, on the desk, he propped the radio handset he'd taken from the deputy Jedthus. Carefully, wary of the pains in his stiffening body, he lowered himself into the librarian's padded swivel chair.

He picked up the phone. Nothing. Just as Cudjo had said, the phones were out.

He sat in the chair and glanced around. There had been surprisingly little quake damage to the building. The shelves were metal and bolted to the floor and still standing. A great many books had spilled to the floor, and papers from the librarians' desks. All the windows were shattered—probably in earlier quakes—but the iron grills would work better than glass to keep out whatever needed keeping out.

There were three different channels on the police radio, which Nick could reach with pushbuttons. He shifted from one to the other, but the sheriff's deputies kept all their calls on Channel One. There were calls about earthquake damage and injuries, all of which the sheriff relayed to other emergency services, most of which seemed amateurish and improvised. There was chatter about putting up roadblocks around the library, about evacuating people who lived in the neighboring buildings. Nothing whatsoever about sending deputies after the refugees that had fled from the camp.

Nick heard nothing about sending in a negotiator, nothing about trying to find out what Nick and the Warriors actually wanted. Nick wasn't particularly surprised.

Darkness slowly fell. The library grew full of shadows. Flickering on the wall behind Nick was firelight reflected from the burning police vehicle that Nick had driven onto the front lawn of the library, then set on fire.

Nick didn't know whether it was a signal, or bravado, or something else. It had just seemed the thing to do.

The other cars were parked closer, nestled right against the library, in case the Warriors decided they needed a fast exit.

"Anyone have a watch?" Nick asked. "What time is it?"

It was after ten thirty. Cudjo, he hoped, had got the refugees well into cover by now. Nick rose from his chair and winced at the pain that shot through his kidney. He hobbled to the front window, but stayed well under cover as he shouted, "We'll talk! Send somebody to talk to us!"

"What you doing?" said Tareek Hall from somewhere from the depths of the library. "We want to kill those crackers, not talk."

"Send someone to talk!" Nick shouted out the window. "We want to talk!"

"The fuck we do," said Tareek.

At least he wasn't shouting out the window.

Nick turned to Tareek and limped toward him. "I'm going to try to get other people here," he said. "Someone from the Army, the Justice Department. Major network media."

"Shit, they're all part of the conspiracy anyway," Tareek said.

"If the Army's part of the conspiracy," Nick said, "we'll be dead in an hour or two no matter what we do. We can't match their firepower for a second. But you don't know the

Army, and I do. I grew up in the Army. And I do not believe they are a part of this."

"Shit," said Tareek in disgust. "You still don't get it, do you?"

Jedthus's radio began to chatter. Nick limped back to the librarian's desk to listen. Nick's offer to talk had been heard and was being reported to Omar, the sheriff. Omar just acknowledged with a "ten-four" and otherwise made no comment.

That was all right, Nick figured. He could wait.

Omar looked across the lawn at the Carnegie library from the relative safety of Georgie Larousse's living room. The smell of the lasagne that the Larousse family had eaten for dinner made his stomach turn over. His head throbbed. He had no idea what to do.

He couldn't seem to *think*. That was the trouble. All the careful fences he'd built were breaking down, and he didn't know how to rebuild them.

All Omar had managed to do so far was choke off any attempt to talk to the people inside. But he didn't know how much longer he could do that. The parish council could decide to overrule him at any time, and he suspected that the only reason they hadn't was that they were distracted by earthquake repair work.

And he had called in as many local Klansmen that he could get ahold of, people like Ozie Welks, who hadn't been directly involved with the business at the A.M.E. camp because they'd been looking after their businesses and families in the wake of the disaster. They were armed, reasonably committed, and dangerous so long as they stayed sober, but Omar knew perfectly well that he couldn't launch them at the library without getting them all massacred.

I had no idea about the deaths at the A.M.E. camp, he said to himself. Rehearsing his defense. *That must have been Jedthus Carter and those skinhead friends of his. I had no idea who those people were, but Jedthus said they were private security guards and I was so short-handed that I had to employ them.*

"How about we gas 'em?" Merle suggested. "Shoot some tear gas in there, then gun 'em when they come out?"

"Grills on the windows," Omar said.

"Oh."

Merle seemed surprised. Probably he hadn't been inside the library since he was in grade school.

An aftershock rattled the shelves in the Larousse kitchen.

Did anyone see me at the A.M.E. camp after the second day following the quake? Omar thought to himself. *None of your witnesses can put me there. I was dealing with the epidemic at Clarendon that whole time and didn't have any time to spare to deal with the situation anywhere else.*

He considered this defense to himself. It was possible he could get away with it, he thought, if he had the right jury.

Maybe, he thought, maybe it was just time to run for it. Keep things going here as long as he could to guarantee David time to escape, and then follow him over the bayou and away.

"Is there a back door or something?" Merle said. "Is there a basement and a way into it? If we could get someone in there, he could gas the place out before they knew anything about it."

Omar thought about that one. "Let's see if we can get the keys from the librarian," he said.

Nick listened to the plot developing over the police radio. He didn't know whether the sheriff had completely forgotten that his radio security was compromised, or just figured that the car radio Nick used had burned up with Jedthus's car. In any case it seemed not to have occurred to him that Nick might have taken Jedthus's handset.

A party was going to creep up to the rear of the building, let themselves into the back door, and start flinging tear gas grenades up the back stair into the library. Then another group would charge the building and shoot down the Warriors as they came staggering out.

It was easy enough to counter the scheme. But as Nick placed his soldiers in the windows and told them to keep alert, he felt sadness drift across for the poor fools who were going to try to storm his stronghold.

They'd even waited for moonrise, so that they could be spotted all that much more easily.

His people saw three figures slipping across the back lawn, aiming at the rear door, and held their fire until they couldn't miss. A volley of shots boomed out, echoing in the wide space of the library. Nick felt his ears ring. One of the party fled, and the other two lay stretched out on the lawn.

The larger storming party never left their assembly area behind one of the residential homes across from the front of the library. Instead they swarmed into whatever cover they could find and started shooting, a truly impressive amount of fire that crackled through the night, but all completely useless, most of it going into the air or thwacking solidly into the library's concrete walls. *Poor fire control*, Nick thought. The Warriors fired back, increasing the racket. It required some effort for Nick to get his own people to stop shooting. Eventually the deputies' fire dwindled away.

No one inside the library had been hurt. The sharp smell of gunpowder stung the air.

Nick asked someone for the time. It was a little after two in the morning.

"We want to talk!" he shouted out a window. "Send someone to talk to us!"

Warm night air drifted through the Larousse house. Return fire from the library had knocked out most of the front windows, letting out the air-conditioning. Omar's headache beat at his temples.

Merle had been killed trying to sneak into the library. Omar felt as if he'd just had his right leg shot out from under him. He didn't know what to do. Those people in the library, under their . . . their general . . . were just too heavily armed.

"What I want to do, Omar," said Sorrel Ellen of the *Spottswood Chronicle*, "is volunteer to talk to those people."

"No, Sorrel," said Omar. "No way."

Sorrel gave his high-pitched laugh. The grating sound sank into Omar's head like a sharp knife.

"I'm a trained interviewer," Sorrel insisted. "I can find out what they're up to."

"I know what they're up to," Omar said. "They're a bunch of killers. They killed my deputies, and if—" He gave up. "Sorrel, I'm too busy to talk to the press right now," he said. "I need you to leave the building."

"But this is your headquarters! Your nerve center! I want to be present at your decisions!"

Omar firmly took Sorrel's arm and led him to Georgie Larousse's kitchen door. "Keep your head down as you go," he said. "Those people are killers."

And there, as he saw to his deep surprise, he saw Miz LaGrande crossing the lawn and heading in his direction.

"Mrs. Ashenden!" he said.

Even in the predawn darkness Miz LaGrande looked frail, not quite recovered from the dysentery. But she was dressed finely in a linen summer dress, with her hair done and a straw sun hat pinned in place, even though there was no sun. She carried a little clutch bag, and she was crossing the Larousse back lawn with precise steps of her sandaled feet.

Omar's special deputies, the heavily armed locals he'd summoned to his aid, stepped back to permit the old woman to pass.

"What are you doing here at this hour?" Omar asked. "You've been ill—you should be in bed."

Mrs. Ashenden walked to the back door, looked up at Omar. "May we speak, Sheriff Paxton?" he said.

"I'm very busy, Mrs. Ashenden. We have a bad situation here."

Her lips pursed. "So I gather. That is the situation we need to discuss."

Omar's head whirled. He drew back from the door. "I hope we can make this brief," he said.

Mrs. Ashenden entered, and Sorrel Ellen, damn him, turned around and followed her. "This is not a safe place for either of you to be," Omar said. "We've got a bunch of cold-blooded killers in the library, and—"

Mrs. Ashenden carried with her the scent of talc and rose water. "I have had a visit, Sheriff," she said crisply. "From a refugee who had been at the A.M.E. camp."

Omar stood in astonished silence. *Think!* he told himself.

"The gentlemen described some of the activities inflicted on the people in the camp," Mrs. Ashenden said. "The shootings, the riots. The—the activities that provoked this violent response."

Sorrel blinked for a surprised moment at Mrs. Ashenden, then reached for his notebook.

"I don't know anything about that," Omar said. His voice seemed to be coming from another place, from far away. "I haven't been to that camp in days. You know that. You know I've been at Clarendon."

She looked up at him, eyes glittering in the moonlight. "That's possible," she said. "But in any case I fear that the situation has gone beyond our ability to cope with it. We shall need to open negotiations with those people in the library, and also summon aid from the emergency authorities, perhaps the national government. They can send in soldiers, FBI men, trained negotiators."

Keep the fence up, Omar thought. *Keep it up till dawn, at least. Then get over the Bayou on Merle's boat and get out of here.*

"They are murderers, ma'am," Omar said. "They killed my deputies. They killed Merle out on the lawn not two hours ago. I am not negotiating with them."

Mrs. Ashenden gave a precise little nod. "That is precisely why you should *not* negotiate," she said. "That is why I want someone else to talk with those people in the library."

"You know it will be a black eye for Spottswood Parish if we have to call in help. I think my department is capable of dealing with this once the sun comes up and we can get a better look at the situation."

"Excuse me," Sorrel said, his pen poised on his notebook. "Could I have some clarification regarding these shootings and riots that Mrs. Ashenden mentioned?"

Omar felt sweat breaking out on his throat, on his forehead. "You know two people got killed when we fenced the camp," he said. "You know there was a riot when Dr. Patel and the Red Cross came to inspect the place. If anything else happened down there, Jedthus didn't tell me about it."

"Sheriff Paxton," Mrs. Ashenden said, "you've lost control of the situation. Will you call for assistance, or will you not?"

Omar drew himself up, and hitched his gun belt higher on his hips. "Mrs. Ashenden," he said. "You have no official standing in this parish. You can't give me orders. Now, why don't you go home and go to bed? You've been ill and should get your rest."

"I will speak to members of the parish council," she said.

"We have just had a major earthquake. I imagine they're very busy."

"I will use the nice satellite phones the Emergency Management people gave us."

Omar looked down at her. Exasperation and headache beat each other to a standstill in his skull.

"Just let me alone to deal with this situation, Mrs. Ashenden," he said. He reached out and took her arm. "I would appreciate it if you would leave and let me get on with my business."

Mrs. Ashenden seemed a little taken aback as Omar took her through the kitchen to the back door—perhaps none of her inferiors had ever laid hands on her this way. Omar dropped her arm, then held the screen door open for her to pass out of the house.

"Just a moment, Sheriff," Mrs. Ashenden said. "I have something here for you." She reached into her little clutch bag.

"Watch out for those killers, now," Omar said. "I don't want you to get shot." For a brief, hopeful moment he considered shooting the old lady himself—why not finish off as many of the people he hated as he could before vanishing over the bayou?—then concluded it wouldn't be wise. Not in front of the press. Not in front of the boys, who might well understand eradicating a bunch of niggers, but maybe not an old white lady.

But the press, now, he thought. Why not send Sorrel Ellen off to the library like he wanted? Not as a negotiator but as a hostage? Hell, they'd probably cut his head off.

Now that was a happy thought.

Omar reached out, took Mrs. Ashenden's elbow again. "Ma'am?" he said.

"Just a minute, Sheriff. It's a thing I brought for you specially." Her little bag didn't have much room for anything, but she seemed to be taking her time finding it.

A silver teaspoon? Omar wondered. Some porcelain knick-knack?

"Ah," she said brightly. "Here we go."

It was a gun, Omar saw in surprise. It was small and silver and had two barrels, both of which were very large.

And when it went off, it made a very large noise.

Dawn rose over the water, turned the wavelets pale. The bass boat picked up speed, headed downriver as if those aboard knew where they were going.

But they didn't. They were lost.

Bubba, the former bowman, thought they were in the Mississippi. Certainly the body of water in which they traveled was grand enough to be the great river. But the river had changed its course, he thought, and he wasn't sure where the Mississippi was in relation to anything else.

They should have seen Vicksburg by now. They had been making fairly good time, at least for a small boat. Bayous were usually still, slack water, but there had actually been a perceptible current in the bayou as they'd set out, rainwater pouring off the land with two or three knots of force. The current alone should have carried them to the Mississippi by morning.

But there was a lot of low-lying back country in Louisiana, with many bayous and horseshoe lakes and chutes that had once been part of the Mississippi system. Bubba was inclined to think that the Mississippi had swallowed these old channels again, at least temporarily, and that they'd traveled along these during the night. They may have bypassed Vicksburg entirely.

In that case, however, they should have crossed an interstate highway and a line of railroad tracks. They hadn't seen any such thing.

Though, if the highway and the railroad had been washed out over enough of its length, they might have passed through the gap at night without noticing.

Manon and Bubba debated this possibility as Manon headed downstream. The only map that either of them possessed was an AAA road atlas that one of the refugees had in his car, and the road map was singularly lacking in navigational data for inland waterways. Jason lay inert in his seat, turned to the port side, his body swaying slightly left and right as Manon turned to avoid debris. Since the river had broadened to its current magnitude the once-brisk current had grown sluggish, almost undetectable. The river was wide and gray and still, full of rubbish and timber. Sometimes whole rafts of trees moved downstream with their tangled roots uppermost, like floating islands overgrown by strange, bare, alien vegetation.

The water was so wide and still that it seemed almost a lake. It reminded Jason of something, but he couldn't remember what.

Jason had drowsed through the night, half-conscious of the movement of the water, the trees shivering in aftershocks, the slow grind of pain in his back. By morning he had stiffened to the point where he could barely move. His face hurt. His throat was swollen from his near-strangulation of two days ago, and he could only relieve the sharp pain in his trachea by tilting his head to the left. He could breathe only in short little pants, like a winded dog. He suspected he now bore a strong resemblance to the Hunchback of Notre Dame.

But Arlette was alive. There were cuts on her face, but she was otherwise unharmed. She sat on the foredeck opposite him, her legs dangling into the cockpit. In her hands she cradled her grandfather's watch, something she'd seen dangling across the chest of the red-haired deputy when he'd threatened her. Just seeing the watch had so overwhelmed her that she hadn't been able to say a word in answer to the deputy's questions.

Jason rested one hand on her bare knee. She smiled at him, that close-lipped Mona Lisa smile. When he looked at her, his pain faded beneath a warm surge of pleasure.

"I think we passed it," Bubba said. "I think Vicksburg is way the hell behind us."

He had replaced Manon at the controls of the boat. He had the AAA map of Louisiana propped in his lap, for all the world as if he was taking a car out for a Sunday outing.

He was a small, wizened man with skin parched and wrinkled as a raisin. He had a little mustache and knobby knuckles and narrow, peglike tobacco-stained teeth.

"What's the next town, then?" Manon asked.

"Natchez. Thirty, forty mile, I guess." His face broke into a grin. "Big ol' gambling boat down there. I won two hundred dollar there, one time."

"And if we turn around and head back to Vicksburg?" Manon asked.

"Same distance, maybe a little less. Best we go with the current, I reckon."

Jason couldn't work up much interest in the matter one way or another. He was just glad to be out of Spottswood Parish, glad to be on the river again. The river had become his home, his fate, the thing that nourished him. The longer he and Arlette stayed on the boat, the farther they could get from the forces that would separate them. If only it weren't for Nick—if only he knew that Nick was safe—he would happily follow the river forever.

But now the river was strange, limpid and stagnant and steel-gray in the morning sun. It reminded him of something, but he couldn't think what.

The boat swayed as Bubba steered clear of a raft of lumber. Gulls perched in the twisted roots.

And then Jason remembered where he'd seen a river like this before. "Oh, no," he said.

Manon looked at him in concern. "What is it, honey?"

Jason straightened, clenched his teeth against the pain. "We're in a, a reservoir," he said. "The river's all dammed up with crap. With—" He gasped in air, pointed at the raft of floating trees. "With that," he said. The pain in his throat was intense and he tilted his lead to the left. "Nick and I ran into something like this upstream," he said. "We don't want to get caught in that dam, and we don't want to be around when it breaks. You're going to see rapids like you've never imagined, with timber instead of rocks."

Bubba frowned. "Twelve year on the river," he said, "I never heard of nothing like that. Not on a river big as this one."

"You've never been in an earthquake this big before, either," Jason said.

"I don't know," Bubba said, and scratched his chin. "There ain't much current, that's for sure."

Jason looked up at Arlette. "Can you get my scope?" he said. "Look ahead and see if you can find anything ahead."

Arlette put Gros-Papa's watch in her pocket, then took the battered red Astroscan from one of the boat's compartments and set it on the foredeck. Bubba throttled the outboard down, the boat settling onto its bow wave until the bass boat was barely making headway. Arlette put her eye to the scope. "It's upside-down," she said.

"Just look at the horizon," Jason said. "Tell me what you see."

Arlette adjusted the scope the wrong way, overcorrected, then finally found the horizon. "The river bends around to the left, I can't see much," she said. "But what I can see is white. Like fog or something."

"Mist," Jason croaked. He gulped a shallow breath. "That's from water going over the falls."

Arlette nudged the scope, panning along the horizon. Then she gave a start. "There's a boat!" she cried. "A big boat right ahead of us!"

Bubba grinned, showing his yellow peg teeth. "Now that's the best news I heard in three weeks."

He pushed the throttle forward. Jason winced at a jolt of pain and turned again to hang over the port side of the cockpit. The bow planed upward, and Arlette put the cap on the telescope to keep spray from spattering the lens, then returned the Astroscan to the nearest of the boat's coolers. Delight danced in her eyes.

"It's over!" she cried. "It's over!"

Jason didn't know whether he was pleased by this prospect or not.

Debris clattered on the hull, then was left bouncing in the wake. Rafts of logs were overtaken and left astern. Bubba leaned out over the starboard side, frowned at what he saw ahead.

"That's not a boat," he said. "That's a barge." He reached a hand to the throttle to lower his speed, then hesitated. "Hey, they's people on board!" he said. "They must have lost their tow in that quake last night."

Jason straightened again, biting back the pain, and peered over the bows. A slab-walled barge was clearly visible downstream, broadside to the current. He could barely make out two people on board, both waving frantically.

"Well," Bubba said. "At least they can tell us where the hell we are."

He throttled down as the bass boat neared the barge. It was loaded with what looked like huge steel bottles, and mooring hawsers trailed fore and aft.

As the noise of the outboard lessened and the bow dropped into the water, Jason heard a rumbling sound ahead and looked to see the horizon ahead filled with white mist.

"Look!" Jason said, pointing, and he hissed with pain at his own abrupt gesture. "Mist from the falls!" he panted. "There's a dam ahead! We've got to get those people off the barge before it goes over the dam!"

Bubba looked startled. He maneuvered *Retired and Gone Fishin'* alongside the rust-streaked flank of the barge, looked up at the two hard-hatted men peering over the gunwale.

White men, Jason thought. The pale faces looked strange after his time in the camp.

"Get in, you fellas," Bubba said. "Before the barge goes into them rapids."

"We can't!" one of the men said. "You've got to tow us clear!"

Bubba made a scornful sound, spread both hands to indicate the bass boat. "This look like a towboat to you? We got a fifty-horse Johnson here."

"This barge is full of nuclear waste," the man answered. "If it goes over the falls, it'll poison the river for twenty years."

"You've got to tow us clear!" the other man said.

Bubba looked bewildered. "Ain't gonna happen, man! Look at this little boat! How many tons cargo you got there?"

"It doesn't matter!" the first man screamed. "You've got to tow us out of here!"

Nuclear waste, Jason thought. What he'd seen already on the river was bad enough, the rafts of dead birds, the terror of the harbor of Memphis and the gassed-out city of Helena, but this . . . *poison the river for twenty years.*

Jason looked at Bubba. "We need to try," he said.

"Yes," Arlette said. "There's not much current."

"Try," Bubba snorted. Then he shrugged. "Okay. We try." He looked up at the two crewmen. "Pass us a line," he said.

One of the crewmen ran to the bows, pulled the dripping mooring line from the river. Bubba nudged the throttle, steered the boat to where the crewmen waited. "Look at that!" Bubba said, gesturing at the six-inch-thick hawser. "What are we going to hitch that to?"

Jason wrenched his head around to look at the little mooring cleats placed fore and aft on the bass boat. There was no way the hawser could pass around them.

"Tie it to my seat!" he said. "I'll sit on the deck up front!"

"You'd just have your seat ripped out," Bubba said.

"We'll pass you a cable!" the crewman shouted.

He dangled a steel cable over the flat bows of the barge. Manon grabbed it, pulled, gave a surprised shout as the cable tried to rip the flesh from her hands. "Sorry!" the crewman said, removed his pair of leather gloves, and tossed them to Manon.

"There's no way," Bubba said. "Those little cleats will tear right off."

"Use *all* of them!" Jason said. "I've seen how you tie barges together!" He moved over into the little jumpseat between him and Bubba. "You lash the cable onto the cleats. I'll steer—I'm used to the boat."

Bubba gave Jason a dubious look, then jumped up and took the pair of gloves from Manon. The crewmen on the barge began feeding him cable. Jason wedged himself in behind the wheel of the bass boat. The seat and the side of the cockpit was in just the right position to put pressure on his wound, and a sudden sharp spasm made him draw in a shuddering breath.

He could hear the roaring of water ahead. He looked downstream and saw that more of the bend ahead had been opened as they'd come downstream. White mist rose between the trees.

Bubba lashed the cable around all six of the boat's cleats, the steel wire zigzagging over the casting platforms fore and aft of the cockpit. Manon and Arlette stepped clear as the cable passed beneath their feet. "I tell you one thing, man," Bubba said. "One of these cleats tears free, this wire is going to cut us in half." He looked at Jason. "All set, boy," he said.

Ignoring the flare of pain, Jason looked over his shoulder at the bows of the barge that loomed behind them, took a gasping breath. "You guys ready!" he said.

"Go! Go!" one of the men screamed.

"God," said Bubba. "I wish I had a smoke."

Jason shifted the boat out of neutral, nudged the throttle forward. *Retired and Gone Fishin'* began to move forward, then came to a sudden check as it reached the end of its tether. The engine took on a labored note as it began to feel the strain. Jason pushed the throttle forward, saw the cable tighten around the cleats. He was breathing in rapid pants, the oxygen fueling the adrenaline that snarled through his body. He could feel the boat vibrating at the end of the steel wire. He pushed the throttle forward again, slowly moving it as far forward as it would go.

The engine roared. The stern dug into the water, and the bow lifted, not because it was planing out of the water, but because the cable was holding the boat back. Jason turned the wheel, and somewhat to his surprise he found that he was swinging the bow of the barge upstream, toward safety.

He straightened the wheel and the full weight of the barge came onto the cable. The stern dug in and the racing engine began to labor. Pungent engine exhaust drifted over the boat, stung Jason's nostrils. He gasped for a breath of fresh air. Foam creamed aft of the boat, whipped to a froth by the racing propeller. Bubba, standing on the foredeck, began to dance a few nervous steps as he looked at the cable drawn taut over the deck.

Jason looked left and right, tried to judge his motion relative to the trees in the flood plain. "Are we moving?" he breathed. "Can you tell?"

Manon and Arlette peered at the cypress on the banks. Long minutes ticked by. The bass boat shivered and hummed as it strained at the end of its leash.

Manon turned to Jason, shook her head. "We're still going downstream," she said. "The current's beating us!"

The current was slow, but it was remorseless, still stronger than the little outboard trying to tow the huge barge.

"Okay, then," Jason said. "I'll go across the current, not into it." If he couldn't get the barge upstream, he would try to drag the barge into the flood plain and moor it to a cypress.

He turned the wheel. Relieved of the weight of the barge, the boat jittered over the water like a junebug on the end of a string. Jason heard shouts behind him from the bargemen, who clearly thought he was abandoning the job.

"Tell them what I'm doing," he said. He didn't think his lungs were up to more shouting.

Bubba bellowed at the bargemen through cupped hands. The boat shivered as weight came onto the cable again. The barge's bows swung around. The Johnson outboard took on a throatier roar. Jason aimed forty-five degrees off the current, to bring the barge in to a landing on the tree-filled point short of the bend.

Bubba peered downstream, the wrinkles around his eyes deepening. "I think you got less'n a mile 'fore we hit that bend," he said.

"You tell me," Jason gasped. "You tell me if this is working."

He could see the trees moving past the bow of the bass boat faster now, as he was no longer fighting straight into the current. If the trees were getting any larger, they were doing so very slowly.

The boat bucked and spat and juddered. "We're moving!" Arlette shouted with a triumphant grin. "We're getting there!"

Even over the sound of the screaming outboard Jason thought he heard a rushing sound, the water rolling over the falls. He looked to his right—working around his injuries involved a corkscrewing of his body that had him looking out from under his own right armpit—and he saw the trees on the point nearing. "Come on, come on," he muttered. He beat an urgent tattoo on the wheel with his palm. "Move move move." Then he stopped speaking, because it hurt too much.

Manon and Arlette were suddenly dancing their delight, their cries dimmed by the roaring that now filled the air. Jason saw a willow float cross his bows only fifty feet away, its dangling leaves trailing in the water. Jason looked under his armpit again and saw that he was right on the point, that a pair of trees were going to cut along the length of the cable between the barge and the bass boat. He turned the wheel, felt the cable slack slightly as he aimed the boat into the trees. There was a sudden lurch as the cable went around a willow, and Jason spun the wheel to the right. The propeller began to chew up willow leaves. Bark peeled in tight curls from the tree as it took the weight of the barge. Jason throttled back as he circled the tree, wrapping the taut cable around 270 degrees of stout trunk. The cable draped across two more trees. Through the trees on the point, Jason saw the barge fall wide of the point, saw it hang in the current with white water just a few hundred feet beyond its stern.

Yes! Jason punched a hand in the air, then winced with the pain. He leaned over the boat's wheel and panted for breath.

The roaring sound increased, and a dark shadow crossed

the sun. Jason's heart gave a lurch as he saw that the roaring he'd heard over the straining outboard had not been falls or rapids downstream, but a helicopter circling overhead.

The helicopter was losing altitude now, the dawn light edging its rotor blades with silver as it dropped toward them, safely upstream of the point and its foliage. The river water was chopped into a froth by the downdraft as the helicopter hovered with its skids just a few feet above the surface. Jason blinked and narrowed his eyes against the furious gusts of wind. The helicopter was modest in size and olive green in color. Jason could see through the canopy to a helmeted figure inside, someone talking into a microphone. With modest surprise Jason realized the figure was a woman.

And then the woman raised a hand in greeting, and her face broke into a spontaneous, devilish grin, a grin of shared joy and wild mischief. So unexpected was the smile that Jason found himself grinning back.

At that moment Jason looked up to see an additional four helicopters, big ones, thundering over the water toward them.

The U.S. Cavalry, he thought. *They've arrived.*

"People seem to think I'm some kind of Tennessee Williams character," said Mrs. LaGrande Shelburne Ashenden. "They think I spend my days languishing under a ceiling fan and dreaming about past glories. Well, *they* might have forgot that my family got where it is by knowing how to kill Indians and drive niggers, but *I* haven't."

General Jessica C. Frazetta gazed at Mrs. Ashenden with curiosity. What, she wondered, does a Southern gentlewoman of a certain age wear to a political assassination? A celadon chemise-cut summer linen dress. Straw summer hat with matching ribbon. Rolex with platinum-gold expansion band, tiny little earrings with freshwater pearls, sandals, and an Hermès tapestry clutch bag containing a very ladylike pearl-handled nickel-plated two-shot derringer.

Jessica was feeling decidedly outgunned, at least in the fashion sense. The fact that she could only see with one eye did nothing for her social confidence.

Mrs. Ashenden sat demurely in the straight-backed wooden chair in the coroner's office in the parish courthouse. Knees and ankles together, hands in her lap, as she had no doubt been taught in dancing school. Her careful affect was only slightly spoiled by the plaster arm cast that had just been applied by Dr. Patel. The derringer had been loaded with .357 magnum rounds, which on discharge had broken Mrs. Ashenden's wrist.

"The Paxtons were always trash, I'm afraid," Mrs. Ashenden said. "And they're not one of the older families, not really. They arrived just before the War." She sighed. "It's a pity about his wife. She's a Windridge, you know. She married beneath her in choosing a Paxton." She looked up at Jessica with bright birdlike eyes. "Do you think I should undertake her social rehabilitation? Perhaps I should invite her into my bridge club..." She looked uncertain as a thought struck her. "Oh dear, someone will have to tell poor Wilona about her husband's demise. I fear that task may fall to me." She looked at Jessica again. "Unless I am under arrest? I'm afraid I don't quite know my status."

Jessica didn't know, either. Ever since she'd flown into this situation, she'd been unable to decide whether she'd wandered into *Gone with the Wind* or one of the more macabre works of Edgar Allan Poe.

"If you can assure me," Jessica decided, "that you're not planning on shooting anyone else, then I suppose I can let you go home."

Mrs. Ashenden gave a little purse-lipped smile. "Oh, I don't imagine I'll need to shoot anyone else, dear. Sheriff Paxton was the sole remaining obstacle to a resolution of the crisis. The only one who was still dangerous." She rose, smoothed the straight lines of her dress. "I think now that Omar Paxton has gone where the woodbine twineth, you will find things much easier."

"I hope so, ma'am."

"I think you should just take all of those people *away*, you know, the refugees. In your helicopters, or whatever they are. I do not imagine they would be comfortable here, nor do I imagine the people in the parish would be comfortable with them present."

"I'll consider that," Jessica said.

Mrs. Ashenden made her way to the door, then paused. "Oh by the way," she said, "I hope I will get my gun back eventually? My husband gave it to me some years ago, so I could protect myself when he was away, and it has sentimental value."

"That may not be up to me, ma'am," Jessica said. "But I'll see what I can do."

Mrs. Ashenden gave a smile and passed out of the room, leaving behind the faint scent of roses. Jessica paused a moment, trying to collect her thoughts, then followed. In her helmet, BDUs, and heavy boots, she felt very unladylike as she followed in the wake of the Mistress of Clarendon.

And she knew she sure as hell didn't smell like roses.

Less than two hours ago, one of her big Sikorsky helicopters had simply sat in the water and, with the power of its six titanium-edged composite rotor blades, towed the barge of Poinsett Island waste up the river to a meeting with its towboat. Another helicopter had taken the people off the little bass boat and carried them to Vicksburg along with the boat itself, which had been lashed to the hull of the chopper. By the time they landed, the crew chief of the copter had called Jessica on the radio and told her that, according to his passengers, there were some serious developments in Spottswood Parish, and she had better talk to the people off the bass boat. One of whom, the crew chief added, had been shot.

Jessica had therefore abandoned the rescue of the barge, which seemed to be well in hand, and flown to Vicksburg to interview the boat's passengers. One of them, the white boy, was carried off by medics the second he landed, but the rest were able to give Jessica a coherent and horrifying picture of the situation in Spottswood Parish.

Prime Power, as usual, was a problem. The Ranger unit that had liberated Rails Bluff had returned that morning to rubble-sorting duties in Greater Memphis, the military police unit that had replaced them was fully occupied, and all of Jessica's other units were fully committed.

But the situation in Spottswood Parish demanded instant attention, so in the end Jessica flew in with everything she could scrape together: part of her headquarters staff, a few military police, and a platoon of engineers. They took off in four big Sikorsky helicopters so as to seem a more impressive force. By this point she was receiving distress calls from Spottswood Parish itself, from members of the parish council who had first called the Emergency Management people, then been shunted around the various departments of the federal bureaucracy until at last someone had thought to have them contact Jessica.

Landing at Clarendon, she'd been met by local dignitary—a little white-mustached fellow who introduced himself as a judge named Moseley—who had then taken her to the courthouse, where she'd met Mrs. Ashenden, who calmly announced she'd shot the sheriff dead with her derringer and settled the whole problem.

Jessica thought it smelled hinky. She'd been involved with Army politics long enough to know the scent of a coverup, and she had the feeling a whitewash was settling very solidly into place here, that blame had been preassigned and that certain people—who very conveniently were dead—were going to take the fall. But she didn't have enough force to simply take over the parish—not yet, anyway—and she didn't have enough properly trained personnel to launch an investigation. She decided that for the moment she'd settle for keeping all the locals from killing each other.

She called the field near Clarendon where the helicopters had put down, and she sent one of them to the refugee camp north of town, and told them to wait there and prevent any of the locals from disturbing whatever they found there.

Whatever happened, she could preserve the evidence.

She told the sheriff's department to stand down. She ordered the auxiliaries to go home. She replaced the deputies at the barricades around the Carnegie Library with her own people.

Which put her own soldiers in the middle, between the library and the locals, and this was something she did not like. She made sure more soldiers were on the way—she called the Old Man and asked him to send her a battalion of MPs ASAP—but that still left a lot of armed people in the Carnegie Library who could lose their patience and start shooting up everything in sight whenever they decided to do so. Somebody needed to talk to them.

And she, unfortunately, was the person on the spot.

According to the locals, the people in the library had been calling out that they'd wanted to negotiate since at least the middle of the night. That, at least, was hopeful. So she had a sheriff's department bullhorn delivered to her, and she shouted out from behind one of the neighboring buildings that someone from the Army was coming out to talk to them, and then she straightened her helmet and her shoulders and took a long breath and walked around the corner, into the sunlight, and into the sights of anyone in the library who cared to shoot her dead.

She marched down the sidewalk until she was opposite the front door of the library, made a precise military 90-degree turn, and crossed the street and onto the uneven concrete walk that led between live oak to the library door. The library loomed before her, clear in the right eye, a blur in the left. Jessica stopped halfway to the door, by the blackened remains of a burnt-out police car, and dropped into the at-ease position, feet balanced and apart, hands clasped behind her back. She cleared her throat. Her hammering pulse rang inside her helmet like a bell.

If the locals want a massacre, she thought, *this is where I'm shot dead. And if the people in the library want to make another point, they can shoot me, too.*

"Is there a Nick Ruford in the building?" she called.

She hoped that tension hadn't tautened her vocal cords to the point where she sounded like one of the Chipmunks.

There was a moment's pause, and then a voice answered, "I'm Nick Ruford."

"I'm Major General J. C. Frazetta, U.S. Army Corps of

Engineers. I am taking command in this parish as of now. I spoke to your wife and daughter a couple hours ago, and they want you to know that they're safe and well."

There was another pause. "Where are they?" asked Nick.

"They are at my headquarters in Vicksburg. They came down the Mississippi on a little boat, and encountered some of my units conducting a search-and-rescue mission."

When Nick next spoke there was a tremor in his voice, as if relief had almost sent him into a swoon. "And the other families?" he asked. "Where are they?"

"I don't know," Jessica said. "I have no reason to believe they are anything other than safe."

There was a buzz of voices from inside the library. Jessica waited a moment, then spoke again.

"Mr. Ruford, may I come inside? It will make things easier, I think."

There was more discussion. Jessica distinctly heard someone say, "We don't let Whitey in our fort!" But in the end the front door swung open, and Nick Ruford's voice came from the interior.

"Please come in, General."

"I'll take off my sidearm first," Jessica said. She took off her pistol belt, put it on the trunk of the burnt-out car, then walked into the library.

The tang of gunsmoke still hung in the still air. There were about fifteen men in the library, and two women, all armed. All were bigger than Jessica. Not all of them looked friendly.

"I'm Nick Ruford," one of the men said. He was in his mid-thirties, Jessica judged, with a week's growth of beard and a pistol on his hip. He stood somewhat behind the open door, and he limped to the door and pushed it shut.

Jessica's heart gave a leap. She had been hoping not to be shut in with these people.

Instead she looked at them. Tried to make eye contact with each in turn. Allowed herself a slight smile.

"Mr. Ruford's family has told me what's been taking place here. That's why I am placing this area under military control and calling in troops. The first units have already landed.

The local sheriff, who may have been responsible, was shot dead last night. His department has been taken off duty. I believe the crisis will shortly be over, and you will be reunited with your families."

She looked at them, saw wild hope mingled with scornful disbelief.

"I want national media here," Nick Ruford said. "I want the networks. I want CNN."

Well that *is smart,* Jessica thought. "I can arrange that," she said. "I have about fifty of those reporters camping out at my headquarters with nothing to do but bother my people, so I imagine we can send them here to bother you."

"I suppose you want us to surrender!" one man said. "I suppose you want us to put down our guns and walk straight into jail!"

Jessica thought about this for a moment. "No," she said. "No, I don't. I don't have enough people here to guarantee your safety. I think you're safest right as you are." She nodded at the belligerent man. "Eventually, when we can guarantee your safety and reunite you with your families, I hope you will put down your weapons. If what I have heard from Mr. Ruford's family is anything like the truth, I don't believe any of you will be charged. I will take you all out of Spottswood Parish on military aircraft, and I will take you to my headquarters. You will have your media coverage. And I will protect you—you have my word on it."

She still saw loathing on the man's face. Most of the others looked thoughtful. She looked at them all again, and as she did so a wild inspiration struck.

"And in fact," she said, "until I can move you to my headquarters, I propose to move my headquarters here. With your permission," she nodded toward Nick, "I hereby declare this building the headquarters of the Mississippi Valley Division, U.S. Army Corps of Engineers."

"No, sir," Jessica said, "I am *not* a hostage. These kind people let me move my headquarters into their building. I'm carrying on business as usual."

Indeed she was. She'd persuaded the Warriors to allow her a couple of unarmed communications techs, and she'd moved communications gear into the Carnegie Library, set up a satellite dish on the lawn, and had been in touch with her command for the last six hours, deploying her people in response to the last major quake.

"This is a very singular thing," said the President into Jessica's ear. "Are you certain you know what you're doing?"

"No, sir," Jessica said. "I'm not certain at all. I'm way the hell off the map, is where I am, and I know it."

The President seemed amused. "Well, Jessica," he said. "If you survive, you'll be a hero. I suggest that you try to live."

"I will do my very best to follow your advice, sir."

"I should mention that the Justice Department is expressing a considerable interest in what has occurred there in—is it Spottywood Parish?"

"Spottswood, sir."

"Yes. The Justice Department would like to handle all criminal investigations."

"I don't see that would be necessary," Jessica said. "I'm sure the Defense Department has all the necessary expertise."

"The Attorney General tells me that the FBI has the finest forensic investigators in the world."

"I believe that the Defense Department can match them, sir. After all, we have people that are regularly called to identify corpses found on old battlefields."

The President paused a moment. "Jessica," he said, "I suggest you concede this one with grace. After all, they won't be investigating *you* this time. You haven't shot anybody yet."

Jessica smiled. Her argument had been *pour l'honneur du pavillion*, as it were, strictly for the record. She was perfectly happy to hand the investigation over to Justice. *What if we bungled it?* she thought.

"I'll do as you advise, sir," she said.

"Very good. You call me if you need anything, now."

Jessica put the handset of her secure phone into its cradle. She looked up at Nick Ruford, who was sitting on the edge of the reference librarian's desk.

"That was my boss," she said. "He wanted to make sure you didn't have a gun pointed at my head."

"Well, that's good," Nick said. "I've had bosses who wouldn't have cared one way or another."

In the hours that had ticked by, Jessica had been able to make more deployments into Spottswood Parish. She'd put a guard at the broken Bayou Bridge to keep people from slipping out of the parish. Another guard went onto the Floodway. The guards were only of modest value, since people who knew the country could boat out elsewhere, but they would have to do until more personnel came along.

She wouldn't be able to accomplish much until the Rangers came from Memphis, which should happen late tonight or early tomorrow morning.

Her guard on the A.M.E. camp reported that the place seemed undisturbed. They'd chased buzzards and dogs off a number of corpses, but were otherwise keeping the place pristine until forensics people could show up. Whatever had happened there, no one had yet had the notion of cleaning it up.

By tomorrow, she figured she'd have Spottswood Parish under wraps.

She'd also sent out for MREs and fresh water. It was the best she could do without setting up a field kitchen in the Carnegie Library. Still, she noticed that some of the Warriors didn't eat a bite until she demonstrated the food's safety by eating some herself.

Another call came in, from one of her scout helicopters she'd sent out to look for refugees, one with a mandate to check Spottswood Parish on the far side of the bayou in order to look for the refugees who had fled from the A.M.E. camp.

She received the message, acknowledged, then stood behind her desk, raised her voice so all could hear. "Excuse me," she said. "I wanted to let you know that your families have been located. They are on the far side of the bayou, and apparently they are all safe. My pilot would like to know if he should attempt to make contact."

What she did, in the end, was order the chopper to land so

that she could put the Warriors and their families in direct radio contact with one another. She stood back from the radio and watched as the heavily armed guerrilla fighters laughed and sobbed along with their wives, husbands, children, and parents.

She felt tears sting her own eyes at the sight. She looked up at Nick Ruford, saw him watching the scene with the expression of a man just dragged by his hair from quicksand. "I really thought we were all going to die," he breathed.

"Nope." Jessica grinned. "I bet it's nice to have a life in front of you, isn't it?"

"Yes, ma'am." The words sounded heartfelt.

Jessica looked at him. "I served with a General Ruford once," she said. "He was my teacher at the War College. I don't suppose you're related?"

Nick absorbed this, then gave her a sly look. "Sun Tzu, right?" He laughed at her startled expression. "General Ruford was my father," he said.

"He was a good soldier."

Nick nodded. "I know."

"You look a lot like him."

And then, to Jessica's surprise, Nick turned away, and sobs began to shake his shoulders.

THIRTY-SEVEN

*The damage to stock, &c. was unknown. I heard of only two
dwelling houses, a granary, and smoke house, being sunk.
One of the dwelling houses was sunk twelve feet below the
surface of the earth; the other the top was even with the surface. The granary and smoke house were entirely out of sight;
we suppose sunk and the earth closed over them. The buildings through the country are much damaged. We heard of no
lives being lost, except seven Indians, who were shaken into
the Mississippi. —This we learned from one who escaped.*

Narrative of James Fletcher, Nashville, January 21

The President watched on television as Jessica Frazetta
and the people who had been occupying the Carnegie
Library in Shelburne City left the building, stepped into
school buses escorted by Humvees filled with Army
Rangers, and drove to the field near Clarendon where
helicopters waited. He watched as the helicopters rose
into the Louisiana sky, then descended onto grassy
Mississippi soil near Vicksburg. The President watched
as the refugees stumbled out of their doors of the Hueys
and ran across the downdraft-beaten grass to be reunited with the families. He watched the weeping, the
embraces, the celebration, the cries of joy.

He turned to Stan Burdett and his two principal
speechwriters. "You boys better write me a hell of a
speech," he said.

"Yes, Mr. President," one of the speechwriters mumbled.

They and the President sat on couches in the Oval
Office, and watched the news on a console television
carefully disguised as an antique piece of furniture.

"I want *drama*," the President said. He waved his hands

in the air. "I want *compassion*. I want a promise of *punishment for the guilty* along with *protection for the helpless*. I want to call for *reconciliation*. I want to appeal to the *angels of our better nature*. When I go to Mississippi, I want to deliver the best speech heard on this continent since Lincoln's Second Inaugural. I want this to go down in history as the Vicksburg Address."

"Yes, Mr. President."

"Now get busy."

"Sir."

The speechwriters left. The days in which a President scrawled out a speech on the back of an envelope and kept it for safekeeping in his hat were long gone.

Stan Burdett stared for a long moment at the scene on the television. "I can't believe this happened," he said.

"*I* believe it," the President said. He shrugged and reached for his cup of coffee. "What does it take to make evil come into the world?" he asked. "A can of beer and a cheap handgun. That's all. In this case, we had a psychopathic sheriff who was in a position to enforce his orders through martial law. He was a weak and malevolent man put into a position of power during a period in which the normal checks on his power ceased to exist. His actions don't surprise me in the least."

The President shook his head. "Where Paxton seems to have been naive is that he apparently thought he could do it without anyone finding out. That was absurd of him—we have a whole class of people in this country who do nothing but hunt out the things that people want to hide."

He shook his head. "You'd better have Bill Marcus contact Jessica Frazetta real soon," he said. "She showed good political instincts here. We need to get her on the campaign trail soon, and run on *our* ticket. Oh—look at this." He pointed at the television. "This guy's priceless."

The Grand Wizard had appeared on the television, gazing firmly at the camera through glinting spectacles. "Omar Paxton was a great American," he said. "He was a hero. Whatever he did, I'm sure it was for the safety of the good people of Spottswood Parish. But now the liberal media are blowing everything out of proportion and trying to make it seem like Omar was some kind of crazed killer! Well, who got killed, that's what I want to know. Omar Paxton got killed, and his deputies! They got massacred! Cut down in performance of their duty! The liberal media can say anything they want about the dead, I guess, 'cause the dead can't defend themselves against slander, but I know in my heart that Omar Paxton was right."

The news program switched to a commentator, one of the legion of pompous talking heads who provide instant analysis for the media. The President reached for his remote and switched off the set.

"How's that Grand Wizard for spin?" the President asked. "How's that for the new party line?"

"That's vile," Stan said. "That's beyond putrid."

"I bet the Klan gets a thousand recruits in the next week," the President said. He sipped his coffee. It had gone cold, and he put the cup down.

Stan looked at him. "People say I'*m* cynical," he said.

"Human evil is bottomless," the President said. "I suppose we can hope that the same can be said of good, but in my job I don't deal with good very often." He looked at Stan, and amusement tugged at his lips. "Do you think if I went to Purgatory Parish, or whatever the place is called, and made a speech eulogizing Omar Paxton and calling for race war, that I couldn't get a war started?"

Stan looked horrified. "Sir!" he said. "You can't be serious!"

"No point in it." The President shrugged. "The experiment's already been tried, in Bosnia and Rwanda." He looked at Stan again. "It wouldn't be hard, though. Plenty of people in rural areas would listen. Their way of life's been destroyed, and not just by the earthquake. Fifty years ago the U.S. government decided there were too many farmers on the land. Programs were put into place. Congress passed laws. And rural America was wiped out! The farmers—the backbone of the nation, we used to call them, salt of the earth, the yeoman that Thomas Jefferson hoped would guarantee the independence and virtue of the republic—they were all nudged off their own land. Now almost all American agriculture is controlled by a few companies, and folks who work on the land are tenant farmers plowing the land their fathers once owned.

"Why shouldn't they be angry?" the President asked. "Why shouldn't they look for someone to blame?" He pointed at the blank television screen. "Sheriff Paxton and that Reverend Dingdong Frankland there, *they*'re the only people helping the rural poor understand what's happened to them. Their answers are violent and insane and based on a delusional understanding of how the world works, but at least they *have* answers. The only answer the government has for those people is, 'Hey, you're redundant, you should have abandoned the land and gone to work in a factory years ago.' No wonder those people start joining apocalyptic cults. To them, the end of the world isn't a strange idea. *The Apocalypse already happened to them!* Their whole world was destroyed."

The President laughed. "And now those poor countrified bastards have been hit again. Agribusiness won't be hurt by the quakes, not for long—Congress will make sure that almost all the relief money will go to the big agricultural conglomerates, just the way they've done for fifty years—but all the small businesses, and the family farmers, and the small entrepreneurs will be kept living under canvas for months, and when they come out they'll find out that all their dreams will have been repossessed. Then the *next* generation of Franklands and Paxtons will tell them who to blame, and then we'll have a heavily armed rural proletariat—the backbone of the nation, we used to call them, salt of the earth—all lynching all the wrong people, the way they've always done."

The President fell silent. Stan looked at him for a long moment. The President shrugged. "Don't blame *me*, Stan," he said. "*I* didn't do it. It all happened practically before I was born."

"Yes, sir," Stan said.

The President looked at his friend. "It's the American way," he said. "We don't respect our fathers, we don't overthrow them, we don't bury them. We just *forget*. It's not like there was a hidden conspiracy to destroy rural America—it was all in the open. All the documents, all the policies, all the legislation . . . it was all public. People could have read all about it if they'd wanted. But they forgot. The earthquakes of 1811 weren't a secret, either—people could have read about them if they'd wanted to. But they didn't know the history. They forgot their fathers. That's what Americans do—we think about the present, and often about the future, but never about the past. Our fathers have always been dead to us. We just *forget*."

The President rose, put his hand on Stan's shoulder. "Our job is to help them. That's why I have to go to Vicksburg and make a speech that will help everyone put all this to bed . . . to help them forget. If no one remembers Omar Paxton in twenty years, then we'll have done our job."

He straightened, then walked to his chair behind Rutherford B. Hayes's desk. "Better get busy, Stan," he said. "And don't forget to have Marcus call General Jessica, get her political career started."

Stan rose slowly from the sofa, took a few steps, then hesitated. "I can't decide," he said.

The President took his seat behind the massive desk. "Decide what, Stan?" he said.

Stan looked at him blankly. "I can't decide if you're crazy or not," he said.

The President gazed at the papers in front of him. "I'm doing my job, Stan. And if I stop doing my job, I have lots of bright young folks like you to tell me."

Stan licked his lips. "Yes, Mr. President."

"It's much easier when you don't care. Really it is."

"Yes, sir."

"You should try it sometime."

Stan left the Oval Office in silence. The President frowned at his paperwork for a moment, and then his glance rose to the photograph of the First Lady that sat on a corner of the broad desk. A knife of grief suddenly twisted in his heart, a pain so pure and exquisite that it took his breath away. For a moment tears spilled down his face.

Then the moment passed, and all was tranquil again.

It was much better this way, the President thought as he wiped his face. Much, much better.

Jason could breathe again. This was the good news.

The bad news was that his journey was over. When he left the Army-run refugee camp near Vicksburg, it would be to join his family, his father in California or his aunt in New York State. He would return to a human environment that was in its essence intact, that nestled in comfortable dominion over Nature, a world that had not been destroyed and ravaged and remade, like the Mississippi Delta. Like himself.

The world to which he would be called seemed alien and strange, its comforts false, its reassurance suspect. It seemed to him that the life of the refugee was somehow more genuine than any other form of existence. It seemed to him now that, whether he knew it or not, he had *always* been a refugee, thrown like a chip into the Mississippi, carried by accident and destiny down its broad, brown expanse.

It seemed to him that everyone was a refugee, if they only knew it.

The deputy's bullet had broken three ribs and burrowed a long, erratic path along the large muscles of his back. Neither the bullet nor the broken ribs had punctured a lung—his breathlessness was a result of a wrecked rib cage and trauma, not internal hemorrhage. Once he'd had his ribs strapped he was able to breathe again—strange how a tight bandage permitted breath rather than restricted it. Drugs had eased the pain and swelling of his torn back muscles.

The presence of Arlette had healed him faster than any drug. The breath he drew from her lips was sweeter than any air he had known. With his ribs strapped, he could walk with Arlette about the encampment, along the lanes between the ruler-straight Army tents where refugees lived with their families.

Now that the journey was over, Arlette wore her birthday presents all the time. Diamonds glittered in her ears, in the little golden lily in the hollow of her throat. And in her pocket she carried her grandfather's watch.

Jason knew he had at most only a few days to enjoy his

time with Arlette before he was shipped out. The Mississippi had relinquished control of his life, but that did not mean he was free. It meant he was now controlled by adults, adults whose decrees, so far as he was concerned, were as arbitrary and implacable as those of Nature.

Bright green wings flashed overhead, and Jason looked up to see a parrot perch on a nearby awning. In the chaos of the earthquakes and evacuations, the parrot had been set free. It had been living in the vicinity of the refugee camp for as long as Jason had been there. Some of the refugees had tried to catch the bird, but thus far it had evaded them.

"What will you do now?" Jason asked. "You and your mom, I mean." His throat was still swollen, and he still needed to tilt his head to speak without pain.

"I don't know," Arlette said. "I don't think *she* knows, yet. The house in Toussaint is all right, so far as we can tell, but the country is still flooded, and will be flooded for weeks, and there isn't any way to get there unless we can use a helicopter." She touched the pocket where her Gros-Papa's watch rested. "And—well, it's not nice there right now."

Jason took her hand and squeezed it. "I wish we could stay together. Maybe I can talk to my dad, to Aunt Stacy, to *someone* . . ." He looked up. "Oh, my gosh," he said.

His father was walking toward him, striding down the lanes between tents. He wore khakis and a Dodgers cap and a button-down shirt with a sky-blue tie, which was his idea of casual dress. But Frank Adams wasn't alone: a whole mob trailed behind him, at least two television cameramen, a pair of skinny bearded men with microphones on long booms, a blond-helmeted reporter picking her way in high heels and short skirt past the refugees and their clutter.

Jason was stunned. He stood rooted to the spot while his father came close to him and threw his arms around him. "Careful!" Arlette yelped, wary of his broken ribs. But Frank didn't put much strength into his hug.

"Hello, son," Frank said. "Surprised to see me?"

Jason looked at the cameras. He could see the lenses focusing on him, zooming in for the closeup. "Who *are* these people?" he asked. Pain knifed through his throat, and he winced.

The blond reporter quickly explained that they were from a television news program—Jason recognized the name, a tabloid show so consistently sordid that his mother automatically shifted stations to avoid it—and they had flown his father into the camp on their helicopter so that he and Jason could be reunited.

Jason tilted his head to speak. "Great," Jason said.

The reporter asked him how he felt now that he and his father were together.

"Great," said Jason.

Jason saw out of the corner of his eye that the camera crew were jostling Arlette away, and he reached for her arm and pulled her closer.

"Dad," he said, "this is my girlfriend, Arlette."

Frank seemed a little taken aback—not because Arlette was black, Jason assumed, since a man married to a half-Chinese scarcely had any room to object—more likely Arlette's existence was a complication he'd never suspected. After a moment's hesitation, he shook Arlette's hand.

"Nice to meet you, Arlette," he said.

"Sir," said Arlette.

The reporter asked if Jason and Arlette had met in the camp.

"The camp in Rails Bluff," Jason said.

The reporter asked more questions, starting from Rails Bluff and going on from there. Jason answered the questions in as few words as possible. He had spoken to reporters before—the camp was infested with them—and this interview was much like the others. He had the impression that his answers didn't matter, that the reporter had decided in advance what his answers were going to be, and asked questions calculated to get the answers she wanted.

The reporter asked Jason if he thought of himself as a hero.

"No," he said.

Then the reporter asked Arlette if Jason was a hero.

"Yes," Arlette said, and a rocket of pleasure soared up Jason's spine.

The reporter asked Jason what he wanted to be when he grew up. "An astronomer," he said, which got a surprised look from Frank.

Jason didn't know whether he wanted to be an astronomer or not, not really. But he knew he still had a few issues with the cosmos, and thought maybe astronomy would help him think about them.

"Excuse me," Jason said. "But I've got to go to the infirmary. The doctors wanted to see me about my—" His hands made scratching motions near his waist. "About my broken ribs."

Jason made his escape to the infirmary tent, where he had a cot and where reporters weren't allowed. Frank and Arlette followed. Jason turned to his father.

"Why did you bring those people?" he demanded.

"I'm sorry, Jase," Frank said. "But it was the only way I could get here. The government isn't letting people fly into the earthquake zone, not unless they're aid workers. I would have had to fly into Meridian, then rent a four-by-four and try to get here on my own. And even then I might have run into roadblocks. But the tabloids have their own helicopters, and fly in whenever they want, so I thought—" He hesitated. "Well, I sold our reunion story for twenty thousand dollars, and that will help pay for your college."

Jason stared at his father. "I don't believe this," he said.

Frank looked at Arlette. "Honey," he said, "can you excuse us for a little while? It's nice to meet you, but I'd like to talk to my son."

Jason snagged Arlette's arm and kissed her good-bye before she made her dutiful exit. It was one of the last kisses he was likely to get, he figured.

He led his father to his own cot, and they sat down. The infirmary tent was large and smelled of canvas and antiseptic. It was light and airy, since the canvas sides were rolled up, but the mosquito netting was down and kept out the bugs. None of the people in the tent were hurt very seriously—the critically injured were kept elsewhere, in the field hospital. Half the cots in the tent were empty, because refugees were constantly being evacuated inland, where the water was safe and the quake damage much less severe.

"We'll be leaving on the helicopter before dinner," Frank said. "We'll fly to Houston, stay overnight, then get on a plane to Los Angeles."

Jason looked up at him. "I'm going to L.A., then? Not to Aunt Stacy?"

Frank sighed. "I guess you won *that* argument, Jase."

Sadness crept through Jason's thoughts. Once he had wanted nothing so much as to fly to Los Angeles. Now he wanted nothing so much as to stay.

"Can Arlette come with?" he asked. He knew perfectly well the question was hopeless, but he also knew this was a question that had to be asked.

"Jase," Frank said, "there's hardly enough room in our apartment for *you*."

"Yes," Jason said. "I know." A fragment of hope lodged in his heart. "Can I visit her later? Spend some of that money to fly out here, and—"

"We'll see," Frank said, in the tone that said, *See how I humor my child?*

"There's something else I need to tell you," Frank said. "This money from the tabloids—that could be just a beginning. Your story is getting out to the media now. There's some real interest. I've been talking to some of the intellectual property people at the firm, and they're very excited. We're thinking of contacting some literary agents and publishers, some people at the studios. You could be famous." He grinned and slapped his knees. "What do you think of that?"

Jason shrugged.

"All you'd have to do is cooperate," Frank said. "Just tell the writers, or whoever, exactly what happened. And they'll write it down, and it'll be a book or a movie."

"I can be famous," Jason said, "but I can't see my girlfriend."

"I said *we'll see*." Irritation was beginning to creep into Frank's voice. "The point is," he went on, "there is some real money here. It will go into trust for you, and pay for your education. This is a terrific break for you."

"Great," Jason said.

Frank looked at him severely. "I thought you'd be more excited," he said. "Don't you understand how colossal this is?"

"I've been shot," Jason said, "I've been beat up, and I've come hundreds of miles in a little boat with the whole world trying to kill me. I've fallen in love with a beautiful girl. Movies and books just aren't very exciting right now. I'm sorry."

Frank looked at him for a moment. Then his lips tightened. "It's that Nick Ruford's fault," he said. "He put you through this. I'm going to talk to some of the litigators at the firm. We'll sue him naked."

Jason looked at his father. "If you do that," he said. "I'm testifying for Nick."

"Don't be ridiculous," Frank said. "You don't know what you're talking about."

Jason rose from the bed. "I'm going to go say good-bye to my friends," he said. "I'll see you at the helicopter later." He reached under his cot, pulled out the Astroscan. "This is all I've got," he said. "Could you hold onto it for me?"

Frank looked at the battered red telescope in surprise. "What is it?" he said.

"It's the birthday present Una sent me," Jason said. "But don't worry," he added as Frank turned pale, "she signed your name."

"So," Jessica said as she looked, with her one good eye, at the message from Bill Marcus, the President's political consultant, "you think I should call him back?"

"That depends on whether you want to run for office," said Pat. He was reclined as far as possible in a chair by Jessica's bed, and he picked repeatedly at a mandolin as he twisted at the tuning pegs.

"*Do* I want to run for office?" Jessica asked.

"If you think," Pat said, "that I'm going to play folksy tunes at your rallies and otherwise behave like a buffoon, you can think again."

Jessica frowned and touched the bandage over her left eye. She'd had an operation that morning, a much more elaborate procedure than she'd undergone with the laser. Instead of cooking the interior of her eye with a laser, this time her eye had played host to a freezing probe that had chilled her eye tissue and, it was hoped, returned it to its normal position.

She was now at home in a semidarkened room. She had been told to lie with her head on two pillows and avoid straining at bowel movements for at least six months.

She planned to be back at her desk in the morning. Perhaps she would wear a dashing Moshe Dayan eye patch.

Army troops were firmly in control of Spottswood Parish. The place had also been flooded by Justice Department investigators, all now in the process of mortally offending the locals with their earnest Yankee tactlessness.

It was beginning to look as if those responsible for the Spottswood Parish massacres were truly dead. Even David Paxton, the sheriff's son, who according to some of the chronologies might have set off the whole thing. He had got across the bayou and was walking south, but he'd run into the main body of the A.M.E. evacuees, who had also crossed the bayou at night and were heading in the same direction. David had been shot dead on the spot, and there were about ten people who claimed the honor of killing him.

The person Jessica most wanted to talk to was the swamp hermit known as Cudjo. But that strange man hadn't been evacuated with the others: as the helicopters came in to carry the others away, Cudjo had faded back into the bayous and swamps that were his home. Perhaps he was just shy, but there was a story that a warrant was out for the man in another part of the state, and that he'd slipped away from the law. In any case, Jessica doubted that Spottswood Parish would ever see him again.

Jessica looked at Bill Marcus's message again, then sighed and held out the piece of paper to Pat.

"Dial it for me, will you, sweetie?"

"Yes, ma'am."

She looked at the ceiling and sighed. "I have but one eye to give for my country," she said.

Jason heard the sound of bells chiming "Claire de Lune," and he followed the sound to Arlette sitting cross-legged beneath an awning near the infirmary tent. Sorrow brushed her face as she held the watch in both hands and gazed down at it. He crouched down next to her, touched her arm.

"You okay?" he asked.

She closed the watch, gave him a sad little smile. "I miss my grandfather," she said.

"I know."

"How's your dad?"

"He's planning on becoming some kind of media tycoon," Jason said. She looked at him in surprise.

"He thinks he can make a lot of money off my story." Jason shook his head. "I always wondered what it would take to get him to pay attention to me. Now I know."

Arlette leaned forward, kissed his cheek. "I'm sorry," she said.

"All his plans depend on my cooperation, though," Jason said. "And if he wants me to cooperate, there are things I will want him to agree to." He looked at Arlette. "Things involving you, maybe." He rose from his crouch. "Let's go find Nick and your mom," Jason said. "I want to tell them good-bye."

Nick and Manon stood in the shade of some trees across from the Post Exchange, some of the few trees that had survived the quakes and Army Engineers bulldozers. In the helipad beyond, the engine of a Huey began to cough, then spit black smoke while drooping rotors began to turn.

"So," Nick said, "what do you think? I shouldn't have any trouble getting a job, not with so much reconstruction going on. Maybe lodging would be a problem, but I don't see it being any worse than here."

"I don't know," Manon said. "I don't know where I stand with everything gone."

"You're standing in the same place as me," Nick said. "I don't know if I have a single possession left. Even these clothes belong to someone else."

The Huey's engine roared. Blades flogged the air. Manon looked up at Nick. "Because there's nothing left?" she said.

"Is that a reason to live with someone? Really?"

"It makes the decision easier," Nick said. "I would think."

She came slowly into his arms. *Oh God,* he thought as he kissed her, *I hope this works.*

He suspected, however, that it would. A few days ago, he'd been resigned to his own death. Now, having survived all that the river and all that mad, sorrowful humanity could throw at him, he had the feeling his luck was in.

Starting from nothing, sometimes, could be a *good* thing.

Dust and wind buffeted them as the Huey flogged its way into the sky. They winced away from the blast, then began, hand in hand, to stroll back toward the camp.

Nick smiled as he saw another couple heading toward them. "Hey there," he said.

Arlette looked from one to the other, recognized in their eyes a mirror of the glow that was in her own. "Hey," she said softly. "What's going on?"

Nick let his arm slip around Manon's waist. "Your mother and I," he said, "we're, ah, going to try this family thing again." *What have we got to lose?* he thought dizzily.

A smile broke across Arlette's face. She threw herself into her parents' embrace. Nick hugged her and stroked her, warmth throbbing through his heart; and then looked up at Jason, saw him watching, standing a few feet away, a wistful, lost little smile on his lips.

"Congratulations," Jason said. He had to tilt his head to the left to say it.

"Thank you."

"My dad's come," Jason said. "We're flying out later today. I wanted to say good-bye."

Sadness whispered through Nick's veins. He left Manon and Arlette and walked to the boy, put his arm around Jason's shoulders.

"I'll miss you," he said. It was the truth, strange though that seemed.

Jason looked up, and desperate hope blazed across his face. "Can I come see you later?" he asked. "I'd like to come for a visit."

"I don't know where we'll be living," Nick said. "We may not have room." His words faltered at the look on Jason's face, at the blighted dreams and despair . . . "We'll try," Nick said. "If we can arrange it, we'll try to bring you out."

Over Jason's shoulder, Nick saw Manon flash him an exasperated look. Nick gave her an apologetic smile.

We're a family again, Nick thought at Manon, *you and me and Arlette. But Jason can't have that. We owe it to him to be kind. It could so easily have gone the other way.*

Hope flared again in Jason. "Thanks, Nick," he said. "I've given Arlette our phone number in Los Angeles. She can call and let me know where you're staying."

"Good," Nick said. "I hope we can talk soon."

Jason threw his arms around Nick, squeezed tight. Nick hugged him back, careful of his broken ribs. "You'll be okay," Nick said. "You *know* that, right? After what you've been through, adolescence in Los Angeles is going to be *easy.*"

"I guess," Jason said.

And then, as they stood in their embrace, the earth gave a sudden jolt. Thunderous booms crashed through the air. Nick and Jason stepped back, legs and arms both wide for balance, as the earth shivered, a series of sprawling, looping rolls that almost sent them tumbling like circus clowns.

And then it ceased. The southeast horizon boomed as the earthquake sped away. Nick stood on the green earth, his heart lurching crazily in his chest.

"Aftershock," Manon said, in the sudden, expectant silence.

Nick and Jason looked at each other, and Nick saw that they both understood the pitiless message sent in that moment by the violence of the earth. That the world was not done with them; that they were atremble always on the edge of the crevasse; and that in the end the world, this ancient and multifarious remnant of an exploded star would have its remorseless way.